John Harris was born in 1916. He authored the best-selling *The Sea Shall Not Have Them* and wrote under the pen names of Mark Hebden and Max Hennessy. He was a sailor, airman, journalist, travel courier, cartoonist and history teacher. During the Second World War he served with two air forces and two navies. After turning to full-time writing, Harris wrote adventure stories and created a sequence of crime novels around the quirky fictional character Chief Inspector Pel. A master of war and crime fiction, his enduring fictions are versatile and entertaining.

BY THE SAME AUTHOR

JOHN HARRIS

CHINA SEAS

REDWOOD
EDITIONS

China Seas
Published in 2003 by Redwood Editions
An imprint of Hinkler Books Pty Ltd
17–23 Redwood Drive
Dingley VIC 3172 Australia
www.hinklerbooks.com

REDWOOD
EDITIONS

Previously published by House of Stratus in 2001

© 1987, 2001 John Harris

The right of John Harris to be identified as the author of this work has been asserted.

All rights reserved. No part of this publication may be reproduced, stored in a retrieval system, or transmitted in any way or by any means, electronic, mechanical, photocopying, recording or otherwise, without the prior written permission of Hinkler Books Pty Ltd.

ISBN 1 7412 1117 4

Typesetting: McPherson's Printing Group, Maryborough, Vic, Australia
Printed and bound in Australia

This is a fictional work and all characters are drawn from the author's imagination. Any resemblance or similarities to persons either living or dead or are entirely coincidental.

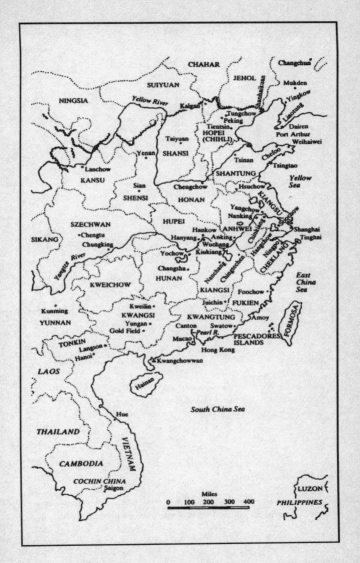

PART ONE

1900–1903

one

The siege was an ordeal that went on and on. There was no respite, and all the time in their ears were the high screeching yells of the fanatical Chinese. From time to time the screeching became frantic, so that the women closed their eyes and wept, and the tension rose in direct proportion to the number of casualties. Three weeks had passed by this time and there was no sign of relief. Had they been deserted? It was a thought none of them liked to entertain for long, and occasionally there were flashes of bitterness and temper, and then the huge, enormously thick walls surrounding them seemed larger, closer, more brooding, only the pink and yellow tiles of the buildings beyond indicating there was a world outside.

Willie Sarth lit a cigarette. There were plenty of them, which was as well because everybody smoked, even the women, which in 1900 was unusual. The reason was simple: Peking was never the sweetest smelling of cities, especially in summer, and now the problem of sewage disposal inside the besieged legations had become overwhelming. To make matters worse now that the rains had finished and the hot summer drought had set in, water was short and not everybody bothered to bath, even if they could, and tobacco smoke helped to turn aside the smell.

Drawing meditatively on the cigarette, Willie shifted his position. Stone was hard to the backside and the barricade where he crouched was not very spacious, so there was little room to stretch and he was a tall, well-built young man, dark-haired as any Chinese and handsome in a way that didn't seem quite English.

History he thought was being written in blood and suffering behind the Tartar Wall. It crossed his mind that that sentence was worthy of a better place than in the brain of an ordinary young man of nineteen with few prospects to begin with and, now, with the Boxer Rebellion, none at all beyond a very uncomfortable death. It should, he thought, have been written by a novelist or a newspaperman so that it could be read by others. He'd try to remember it, he decided, so it could be repeated later. He paused frowning. If there *was* a later, he thought.

He was sitting behind the sandbag barricade with other members of what was contemptuously called by the military the Carving Knife Brigade. They were mostly civilians or ex-soldiers who liked to tie knives to their rifles to make them equal with the regular soldiers who had bayonets, and they were not popular, because for the most part they were not skilled and half of them didn't know how to shoot. A few of them were missionaries, in fact, whose idea about refusing to do violence to others had rapidly withered under the changing circumstances. For a long time they had felt that the love they preached with the Gospel would deal with all their enemies, but, after a few hundred of them had been massacred, their views had taken a radical turn for the worse. And not surprisingly, either, Willie thought. Twice blest was he whose cause was just. Thrice blest was he who got his blow in fust. It didn't pay to stop and argue with a maddened Chinese peasant decked out in red Boxer ribbons who was advancing on you with a huge two-handed sword, honed to the sharpness of a razor. Willie had seen the damage they could do and preferred to shoot first and ask questions afterwards.

All the same –

He paused. The Chinese had a point when you thought about it, he had to concede. The European nations who had demanded – and received – trading rights in China had begun to carve up the country as they had carved up Africa years before and the Chinese had finally come alive to the fact.

He wiped the perspiration from his face with his sleeve. A lowering grey sky pressed down, the air still heavy from the recent rains, the oppressive summer heat adding to the sense of doom. It was in Peking, the capital city of China, situated in the northern provinces of that vast land, where the trouble had come to a head and the long-festering uprising had localised, bringing death to the yang kuei-tzu, the white-skinned, pale-eyed foreign devils the Chinese hated so much, the 'barbarians from outside' as they were scornfully called.

Willie had another go at his face with his sleeve, wiped his hands, which were slippery with sweat, on the butt of his ancient rifle, and peered ahead of him along the Tartar Wall. Hours sometimes passed without anyone actually seeing the enemy. Their presence was always known, however, because of the almost continuous stream of rifle fire, though no patrols were ever sent out to check where it came from, because the enemy occupied all the territory beyond the immediate walls. Fortunately, in China, city walls were built to last and, sitting behind the barricade of sandbags, Willie Sarth thanked God for it. The Tartar Wall where the barricade was situated – one of several designed to stop an attack – was wide enough for four carriages to be driven abreast along it at full speed, so there was little chance of the Chinese knocking holes in it, especially since they had few guns and none of them of any size; though, even at that, they were bigger and more numerous than anything the defenders possessed. The only real weapon the defenders could fire was a nine-pounder they had made themselves from the wheel-less barrel of a relic of the Anglo-French expedition of forty years before. And even that was inaccurate at any distance and was usually loaded only with old nails, scrap iron and nuts and bolts.

At the end of the Tartar Wall, where you could see into the Chinese City, there was a patrol of Russians, under a naval ensign from the Russian Legation called Zychov. He was a count or a baron or something, a tall handsome young man who spoke French, English and a little Chinese and wore a curling moustache which he was believed to wear in a bandage every night to enable it to keep its shape.

'If we've got to die,' he had once pointed out with a great show of gallantry, 'we might as well die looking our best.'

'It doesn't seem to matter how we look if we end up dead,' Willie had replied and Zychov had laughed.

'That's the difference between the way we've been brought up,' he said. 'No aristocrat would think of facing death looking as if he'd just been dragged out from under a hedge. Why do you think the French nobles wore wigs and powder to the guillotine?'

Willie shifted again, wondering what he was doing there. Certainly his older brother, Arthur, his legal guardian since the death of his parents in a pleasure boat accident on the Thames seven years before, had not agreed with his wish to head east in search of his fortune.

'You're barmy,' his brother had announced, and, sitting on the Tartar Wall in the besieged city of Peking, Willie decided he had been dead right.

But work as a clerk in the dark offices of Wainwright and Halliday's, exporters and importers, in the city of London, had long since grown dull when Ortho Bohenna had walked into the office. Bohenna, a Cornishman, who had gone to sea thirty years before as a deckhand, had jumped ship in China, and, setting up an office in Canton, within ten years was trading in tea, silk, cotton cloth, wool, metal, pepper, spices – and opium. Though people didn't speak out loud about it, every day in the City knew that the British held a virtual monopoly on the opium trade. And when the tax on tea had been lowered in 1890, it had required only a little astuteness to realise that the consumption of that beverage in Britain would increase a hundredfold. Bohenna had been quick to spot the change and, falling in with a schooner skipper whom he had persuaded to import Indian opium and export China tea, in no time at all he had made them both wealthy. The schooner skipper had eventually been lost at sea in one of the squalls which blew off the South China coast, and Willie had once heard George Wainwright, who ran Wainwright and Halliday's, say that he thought Bohenna had pushed him overboard to get his hands on his ship and avoid having to share the profits.

Certainly Bohenna's appearance and manner indicated that it might be possible. He was a big man, with a hard face brown as saddle leather that looked as if it had been hewn out of a tree. His manner was breezy and he waved aside all objections, so that George Wainwright and Arthur Halliday, neither of them prepossessing figures despite being a power in the import trade, gave way again and again to him and he practically dictated his own terms.

By 1898, however, he was an old man and talking of retiring, though he still couldn't bear to let the profits that were to be made in the East slip through his fingers.

'They say the boom's over,' he had said, sitting opposite Willie, his feet on Willie's desk as he waited for Wainwright and Halliday to finish dealing with the customer they had in their room. 'But don't you believe it, son. It's hardly started. There's a lot to be made around the China seas. It's not just the money either. You can do what you like out there. There's everything a youngster wants. Life. Adventure. Cheap booze. Sing-song girls.'

Willie hadn't been sure what sing-song girls were, but he had a shrewd suspicion that they didn't just sing songs and, as a seventeen-year-old virgin beginning to feel the restrictions of the late Victorian age, he itched to see something of this paradise Bohenna described.

'How do you go about it?' he had asked.

'Well,' Bohenna had said, waving his cigar, 'for one thing, you don't sit behind that desk there asking how to go about it. You get up and make your way to China.'

'How?'

'Sign on as a deckhand, and jump ship when you get there. That's what I did.'

So Willie did, too. It had taken some doing to screw up his courage. Five years of eight-to-six working, bread and dripping breakfasts at his brother's house in Balham, bread and cheese lunches, and sausage and potatoes for tea – with not much variation, except at weekends when there might be a rabbit, or at Christmas, when his brother Arthur's wife produced a goose – had left their mark. Life had consisted of work, church on Sunday and the Young Men's Christian Endeavour, or playing the piano for a social evening with a cup of tea and a bun during the week. Only once in his life had Willie broken away from it – when Bohenna had produced a bottle of grog and managed to get him half-drunk.

Brushing aside Wainwright's indignant protests, he had called a hansom to take Willie home, but it hadn't done him a lot of good in the office and somehow he had a feeling that his fall from grace would prevent him in the long run from ever reaching that cherished job of chief clerk, who, because of his eminent position, enjoyed a small office to himself. After Bohenna's final encouragement, however, it hadn't mattered much.

The argument at his brother's home had gone on for days. Arthur Sarth had not wished to see the money Willie contributed to the household finances disappear, but Willie had been adamant. He had looked up a ship, learned that there was a job going as a deck boy, and signed on.

Having taken the step, he had gone down to Brixton, where Edie Wise, with whom he was solemnly walking out in the evenings, lived with her parents, and made his announcement. She fell into his arms in floods of tears and swore she'd die without him.

'You can't! You can't!' she said.

'I've got to. I've already signed the ship's articles. Name of *Lizzie Hart*. Four-master. Mixed cargo.' He spoke with a certain amount of pride, feeling a terrible dog.

'It won't be that long,' he had pointed out. 'I'll be back in eighteen months. It's easy to make money out there.'

The idea of being married to money dried Edie's tears and she began to eye Willie with new interest. 'Will you be rich?' she asked.

'You should see some of 'em,' he said. 'They come into the office, smoking cigars and wearing hand-made shoes and shirts and all that. Rings on their fingers. Pearl tie pins. And their wives! You should see *them*.'

Somewhat mollified, she swore she'd wait for him, and their parting that evening was passionate enough for her to allow him, as they clung together in the front room of her parents' home in the semi-darkness, to unfasten the front of her blouse and place his hand on her breast. Willie felt a proper roué.

The following day he went to the docks, carrying a small brown paper parcel containing his belongings, and readied himself for his meeting with China. Unfortunately he had not examined the ship's articles very carefully and the *Lizzie* went to India.

It hadn't even been a very pleasant trip. They had run into a lot of bad weather, the first mate was a hard taskmaster and, being Johnny Newcome, Willie was treated as a skivvy by everybody else in the crew. It didn't take him long, however, to learn the art of withstanding bullies. He had offered to take on the first of them then and there on the deck and sensing that in addition to dealing out punishment he might also receive a little, his tormentor had backed off with a lot of loud threats that came to nothing. After that Willie was left alone.

Considering he was half-way to his destination, when the ship had left Bombay, Willie had not reported aboard and had watched her sail for home. After a week of starving and sleeping in the hut of a soft-hearted dock foreman, he had learned of a steam freighter going to Shanghai and found himself aboard. She was a profit-making, ill-designed, meanly-found vessel as obsolete as the gallows, but the galley boy had sliced open his hand and been rushed to hospital apparently bleeding to death, and Willie had found himself doing the job instead, living among the cockroaches in the glory hole and wistfully watching the deck crew as they went about their business, walking wide-legged on the deck, always a freer, more self-confident lot than the stewards. Especially when the chief cook went round the bend and started going for everybody with a knife. It was a good thing for Willie that the engineer finally clubbed him with a spanner as long as his arm as the ship staggered across the South China Sea with the wind on the beam and lockers bursting open and exploding their contents everywhere. Ending up as cook, Willie was quick to leave the ship in Shanghai.

The cargo, largely Indian cotton, had been put ashore, but there had been a great deal of quiet talk on the quayside between the ship's captain and the owner of a dry-goods warehouse ashore. Willie knew what was going on and, keeping his ears open, had heard the word 'opium'. When the ship returned to India, he had looked up Wainwright and Halliday's agent, and had learned that the ship was shortly due to return to the mouth of the Peiho River. A quiet discussion with one of the clerks, a yellow-faced young Yorkshireman called Hackett, had ended with him being trusted with a small package which he was told to hand over to a man called Howell whom he would meet in Tientsin.

Willie knew exactly what was in the packet and he was terrified. When he went ashore at Tientsin the package was in his shirt. Howell wasn't hard to find and he had handed over the money without argument.

'When are you coming again?' he asked.

Willie had hedged and said he wasn't sure and Howell said he'd always be glad to see him. 'Indian opium's better than Chinese,' he had said. 'Fetches a better price.'

When Howell had disappeared, Willie found a teahouse and sat for a long time staring into space. He had a feeling he was on to a good thing and even on the point of ending up with a lot of brass. More by luck than judgement, he had already made contact with the two ends of the opium trade and, as he well knew, it was opium that made money. Nevertheless, the thought disturbed him. He had been decently brought up, first by his parents and then by his elder brother, and, taught right from wrong, he knew that selling opium was reprehensible. His brother was an elder of his chapel who sometimes preached from the pulpit and he had once delivered a lecture on the evils of the trade, painting horrifying pictures of stupefied Chinese lying in stinking bunks in dens filled with scented smoke. Where he had got the information Willie couldn't imagine, because Willie's brother was a clerk like himself and certainly not a man who had seen the seamy side of life.

However, Mr Gladstone himself had condemned the trade and, according to what Willie had read in the newspapers, at the time of the Opium Wars had even announced that he could not be a party to exacting by blood opium compensation from the Chinese. Brought up as a good Liberal, what was said by Mr Gladstone, who after all had been Prime Minister and surely knew what he was talking about, had carried a lot of weight and Willie was not easy at the thought of entering the nefarious trade. But what else? Cotton? Silks? Tea? It seemed to call for a little investigation and he felt he couldn't do that at the mouth of the Peiho River. Born and brought up in London, he had always felt that city to be the centre of the world. And if London was the centre of the European world, surely the centre of the Chinese world was its capital, Peking. That, surely, was where he must go to make his fortune.

Clutching his rifle, waiting for the next screeching attack by the Chinese, Willie reflected that he had very nearly *not* made it. On his way to the station, he had been waylaid by a gang of men trying to make up the crew of a clipper heading for Australia and had come very forcibly to realise the meaning of the word 'Shanghai-ed'. By sheer chance a group of British sailors from a man-o'-war lying in the rivermouth had come past at the crucial moment and rescued him. Treating them all to a drink out of gratitude, he had headed as fast as he could for the railway station.

At that particular moment, he had thought anything would be better than Tientsin, but he was now beginning to realise that he had stepped out of the frying pan into the fire. He had expected one capital city to look like another and Peking to be like London. In fact, he had found himself stepping back into the Middle Ages.

Peking did not look at all like London. It was, in fact, a city composed of other cities. Within its bounds were the Tartar City and the Chinese City, whose northern wall, the Tartar Wall, served as the southern rim of the other city. And even the Tartar City was a city containing other cities because within its boundary was the Imperial City, the domain of the royal Manchu dynasty, and, within that, the Forbidden City, which contained the royal palace where lived the Dowager Empress Tzu-Hsi, the instigator of all his present troubles.

Because in the Orient all trades and crafts were concentrated together, there was the Street of the Tanners, the Street of the Goldsmiths, the Street of the Food Merchants. Foreigners were treated in a similar manner and all the foreign diplomats were housed within a single area, the Legation Quarter, where eleven legations were situated in a space roughly three-quarters of a mile square. Close by were the foreign merchants, the banks, the offices, shops, the Hotel Wagons-Lits and the European Club, together with the officials of the Post Office and Customs and a sprinkling of teachers from the university.

Willie had arrived, eager to start making his fortune and expecting to be welcomed with open arms. Instead he had found that the foreigners were not even of a single mind and, in fact, fell into two distinct divisions whose relations with each other were always strained. Half the foreigners in Peking were missionaries, working in churches, hospitals, orphanages and schools scattered about inside the Tartar Wall, and even they were divided by their work and their doctrines, their different beliefs bringing nothing but confusion to their would-be converts.

The other community of foreigners was entirely secular, at their head the Diplomatic Corps, which was insulated not only from the native population, to whom they paid little attention, but also from the traders, the bankers, the shopkeepers. It had been harder than Willie had imagined to find himself accepted. Finally, he had been taken in by an old man called Wishart, who ran a large trading emporium, importing goods from England and India and exporting goods from China, and he had found himself doing exactly the same job as he had in England, just one step higher than the Chinese clerks and with the added discomfort of having no home to go to and having to sleep at night in a small cubby hole in his office.

It had been with some surprise, nevertheless, that Willie had noticed the speed with which old Wishart had ushered him into his premises and given him his job. At first he had thought it was because old Wishart had a daughter, Emmeline, tall, a few years older than Willie, pale-faced like many of the Europeans in Peking and even from the first moment given to eyeing Willie boldly. She was a plump pretty blonde girl and she had noticed at once that, despite his extreme youth, he was a well-set-up young man with a straight nose, aggressive brown eyes and crisp dark hair. There was not even a suggestion of humility about him – rather the self-assertive cockiness all sailors acquired. I've learned about the sea, he seemed to say. What have you done? His head was held high, though she had no idea that that was largely caused by the fact that his collar was old and, under the starch, the edge was rough and was sawing a raw line under his ears. Watching her, he saw that she seemed to be appraising him and decided to tread warily because he had heard old

Bohenna's tales of the voracious Englishwomen of the East.

'Could you start at once?' Wishart asked as Willie outlined his experience with Wainwright and Halliday. 'You seem to know what to do.'

'I could start now if you want,' Willie said smartly.

'Well, we could do with you. The last clerk left a week ago. Suddenly. He wouldn't say why. I think he was scared of the political situation. Young men aren't what they used to be. The one before him left, too. Said he preferred to be near the coast. Can you use a gun?'

'A gun?' Willie's eyebrows rose. Was the old man taking him on to act as a guard for the premises in his spare time? Being a guard at night after being a clerk during the day wouldn't give him a lot of time to pursue his own ambitions and make that fortune he was after. 'What would I want a gun for?'

Wishart peered at him, a bent old man with fluffy grey hair, spectacles and a blue bulbous nose that indicated a fondness for the bottle.

'Never mind that. Can you use one? Have you ever fired one?'

It so happened that Willie had. He had an uncle with a farm in Kent, where he had been sent as a boy for holidays in the hopfields, and it was there that he had fallen in with the man who kept down rabbits and other vermin on the farms. He was given a farthing a tail, which he had to produce as evidence, and sold the carcasses to butchers at twopence a time while the skins went to a glove manufacturer in Tunbridge Wells who had discovered that young ladies liked muffs lined with rabbit fur for use in winter. Being also a poacher who helped himself to the pheasants of the local gentry, it was he who had taught Willie how to use a rifle.

'Shotguns is no use,' he had said. 'Spoil the fur, see, when you use 'em on rabbits, and make a mess of the flesh when you use 'em on pheasants. At least at the range I use 'em they do. I ain't no sportsman, waiting to get 'em on the wing, see. I nobble 'em when they're standing still, and for that rifles is the thing. If you 'it 'em in the 'ead, no damage is done, because no bugger wants to eat the 'ead, does 'e?'

He had taught Willie well and he answered old Wishart confidently. 'Yes,' he said. 'I can use a gun.'

'What sort?'

'Any sort, I reckon.'

'Right, lad.' Wishart beamed. 'I'll give you the equivalent of seven shillings a week and your keep and you can sleep in the shop.'

It was hardly the fortune Willie had had his eyes on, but it was a start. The fortune could come later when he'd got settled in.

The following day he had learned about the Boxers.

t w o

'To the average Chinese,' old Wishart had said, 'the rising of the Boxers was inevitable and just.'

The explanation came during Willie's second day in Wishart's employment. They had sent him to a Chinese tailor for a new suit of clothes to replace the grubby salt-stained garments he had worn when he had arrived, given him two shirts and several stiff collars from stock, and shown him his room. It was just big enough to turn round in and the bed was in a sort of box let into the wall, wasn't a lot deeper than a coffin, and was actually the bottom half of a deep cupboard where the ledgers were kept. It was stuffy at night And the bedclothes, which couldn't be tucked in at the back, invariably ended up on the floor.

The second evening, he was invited to dinner. The meal consisted of Chinese food with rice and there was wine, but, so that he shouldn't get ideas above his station, the crockery was the second best. As they finished their lychees and emptied their glasses, old Wishart leaned forward and let Willie know what he was in for.

'The Manchus,' he said, 'are a foreign dynasty and they prefer to live in the traditional ways. They prefer to be aloof from outsiders and aren't concerned that the world is on the move. They let foreign merchants in, and after the Opium Wars they lost the island of Hong Kong and Kowloon, and the ports of Canton, Amoy, Foochow, Ningpo and Shanghai were opened to foreign trade. That was what started it all, because other foreign powers decided they wanted a share. The Taiping Rebellion fifty years ago wasn't against us, it was largely against the dynasty, the pigtail which the Manchus forced people to wear, and the corrupt practices of the court and its officials.'

'It was about that time that Yehonala, the Empress Dowager, appeared,' Emmeline said, one eye on Willie. 'She was given to the Emperor Hsien-Feng as a concubine.'

'He didn't know what he was letting himself in for,' Wishart put in. 'Because not only was she beautiful, she was also too clever for her own good.'

'She knew how to give herself to the Emperor, though,' Emmeline said, a trace wistfully, and Willie's eyes switched to her. To his surprise she was watching him intently across the table and it dawned on him that she was identifying herself with the mythical Yehonala.

'She bore the Emperor a son,' Wishart went on, unaware of the sudden electrical current passing between the two young people, 'and her influence grew. With her help the Emperor defeated the Taipings. But Yehonala had made enemies and was soon in a power struggle against the mandarins and princes as the emperor fell ill and began to die.'

'She was a very clever woman,' Emmeline said, her eyes glowing as she stared at Willie. Emmeline was a great reader of romantic novels, as he'd already discovered, and her mind ran in romantic grooves. 'Gradually, power passed into her hands.'

'But she was still a Manchu,' Wishart joined in, 'and her attitude towards Europeans was a Manchu attitude.'

Aware of Emmeline's eyes on him all the time, Willie listened spellbound, conscious that what he was hearing was going to become part of his background. He still had big ideas of founding a fortune, but he was no fool and he was well aware that to make money there he would need to know all there was to know about China.

The Second China War, which had ended with Britain and France capturing the Taku Forts at the mouth of the Peiho, the taking of Peking and the razing of the Summer Palace, had, it seemed, brought France, Portugal, Russia, Britain and a whole lot of others to China, all grabbing for a foothold in the country. With their imports they began to destroy Chinese trade so that the peasants began to feel the barbarians had to be taught their place in the scheme of things, and new railways built by Europeans were torn up and telegraph wires were pulled down.

'They said they were disturbing the graves of their ancestors,' Emmeline explained solemnly. 'Ancestor worship's important and, as there are graves all over the shop in China, it was impossible to put down a bit of railway track or a length of telegraph wire without disturbing one.'

Wishart leaned forward. As he did so, he knocked over his empty wine glass. It fell with a clatter that made Willie, occupied with the new fear of the Boxers, jump in his chair.

'But the Europeans continued to hack out great chunks of territory and profit.' Wishart replaced the wine glass on its base with a thump. 'And eventually Japan, Italy and America joined in. That's about the time I arrived.'

'Yehonala was still in power,' Emmeline interrupted. 'She had been since the emperor died in 1861. Her son was declared emperor in 1872, but he died three years later, and when he was succeeded by a child, Tzu-Hsi – which was what Yehonala had started to call herself – became regent and the centre for all the objections to foreigners. And it was then that the Boxers were noticed.'

'Boxers?' Willie had never heard of the Boxers. They sounded like some sort of sports club, but he had an uneasy feeling that they weren't.

'The I Ho Ch'uan,' Wishart said.

'The Fists of Harmonious Righteousness,' Emmeline explained sharply. 'That's what they call themselves. A secret society.'

'There've always been secret societies in China,' Wishart went on. 'They're a way of life out here. But this one's different. They don't have any single leader. Just thousands of 'em. They came from nowhere like a lot of ghosts, but they aren't like the Taipings because they aren't against the dynasty.'

'But Boxers?' Willie said.

'A nickname some American gave them,' Emmeline said quickly 'The North China Daily News used the name and it stuck.'

'Who are they? I bet they're not Robin Hood and his merry men?'

'No. They're not against authority. Just against us. Foreigners, Christians.'

The thought seemed to worry Wishart and he reached behind him to a cupboard and fished out a bottle of Plymouth Gin. As he poured himself a stiff measure,

Willie noticed that the glass was grubby as if it were often used, and that Wishart didn't offer any to Emmeline or himself.

'The peasants – ' the old man stopped to take a good swallow from the glass ' – they think the Boxers have been sent from Heaven and are immortal. They go in for vivid costumes and a lot of ritualistic mumbo-jumbo, and they posture and use their arms. Perhaps that's why they're called Boxers.'

'What do they do?'

'Kill people.'

Willie began to wonder what he'd let himself in for. 'They don't like the missionaries,' Emmeline said. 'Or the Cross of Christ. And they believe they can't be killed. When one of them is, they simply say he's not a true believer.'

'Where did they come from?' Willie was beginning to grow nervous.

'Chiefly Shantung and Chihli,' Wishart said, emptying the glass and refilling it. 'Two bad harvests, a plague of locusts, and the flooding of the Yellow River were all blamed on us – foreigners – and they started to murder missionaries.'

'The missionaries ask for it,' Emmeline snapped. 'They isolate themselves in the provinces where they can't be protected and even build their churches with spires, which the Chinese think is bad for evil spirits. It's getting worse.'

'The outbreaks are coming more often,' Wishart agreed. 'There was a riot at Shashih, another in Chihli, more in Szechwan and Kwangsi, and more in Foochow, Yunnan, Paotingfu and Kienming.'

'Widespread murder and looting,' Emmeline added as if she were trying to chill Willie's blood.

'They've beaten up Americans and British,' Wishart ended. 'To say nothing of French and Japanese. There's a big confrontation building up.'

Willie swallowed. The Boxers were something he hadn't expected, something which didn't seem to fit into his plans to make a fortune.

'Where are they now?' he asked.

Emmeline sniffed. 'Here,' she said.

It had seemed to Willie to be a good idea to learn a little more about the mythical Boxers and in the next few days he had begun to make enquiries as he went about his business. But the people who mattered, the big businessmen and the diplomats, hadn't seemed worried and he had come to the conclusion that the Wisharts were panicking unnecessarily.

Yet half of North China beyond Peking seemed to be in a state of anarchy. It was because it was the first year of the new century, some said, but either way, when he looked into it he learned that bands of armed men were roaming the countryside and that somehow the Empress Dowager, together with the princes, mandarins and senior officials, was behind them. He began to wonder even if it would be possible within a short space of time to raise sufficient money to pay for a railway ticket back to the coast. It wasn't, he told himself, that he was afraid, but he couldn't see any point in getting killed at that stage in his career. They had just heard of a missionary not far away who had been chopped to pieces and he didn't really feel it would help his career if he ended up in small cubes of bloody flesh in a drainage ditch.

Very soon, the dry heat of summer would be over the North China plain and Peking would become a sweltering mass of noisome smells. Some of the diplomats had already sent their families to Weihaiwei or the Western Hills, where they sat out the high temperatures in converted Buddhist temples, but this year it was difficult, it seemed, and some of the European families had found everything so unsettled they had returned to the capital, accepting the heat and the chance of disease that went with it.

Then, when the Boxers, drawing nearer to Peking, had burned down the railway station at Fengtai, European and Japanese warships had moved to the mouth of the Peiho and Willie couldn't imagine why the diplomats, who were supposed to know everything, had failed to notice the danger. Even as they had been announcing that everything was quiet, villages were being razed and converts massacred and, as foreigners headed for the capital and safety, detachments of foreign soldiers had begun to appear in Peking to guard the official residents against attack. As more and more people came within their protection, it had finally been decided to request help from the ships at Taku.

Lying in his bunk-like bed, underneath the ledger cupboard in the office of Wishart and Co., Willie had stared at the underside of the oak slab above him, wondering what he had got himself into. The oak was scarred where it had been smoothed by the mattocks of Chinese workmen years before and gazing up at it, he wondered what it would be like to feel the edge of one of those huge, sharp blades biting into his flesh.

He had frightened himself to death with his enquiries. Old Wishart had shown him the columns of *The North China Daily News* and reports from friends in the interior, and Emmeline had produced scented letters from the daughters and wives of other businessmen, all of them full of fear. She had never seemed to be far away from Willie from the moment of his arrival and he had long since come to the conclusion that she had her eye on him.

His mind had roved over his problems. He didn't fancy the sound of the Boxers, especially now he'd learned something about them. He also didn't fancy what might happen if they arrived in Peking, but the shopkeepers and businessmen he met – and he pumped them all for information – seemed to think that, whatever the Chinese might do in the interior, they would never dare use violence in the capital.

Can't see it makes all that difference, he had thought. Inside or out. A dead man's a dead man.

And he had no wish to be a dead man. He had far too much to do. He had to make his fortune. He had to go back to Wainwright and Halliday as old Bohenna had, smoking a big cigar and able to say 'I told you so' to old Wainwright and his partner, Halliday, both of whom had warned him of the dangers of giving up a good job in exchange for a very dubious future. He had also – being well brought up, he hesitated to dwell on it – never been with a woman, and he not only didn't fancy ending his life a virgin but he also still cherished hopes of returning to claim Edie Wise as his bride.

'Trouble with me,' he said out loud to himself, 'I've been too well brought up.'

'So have I, Mr Sarth.'

The voice, close to his ear, startled him so much he sat up suddenly, banged his head on the underside of the oak block that formed the base of the ledger cupboard and almost knocked himself silly.

'Sweet suffering J!'

Dazed, half-blinded by pain, seeing little lights flashing all round him, he was aware of Emmeline kneeling beside him and warm fingers touching his head gently. He jerked away nervously.

'It's all right, Mr Sarth.' Emmeline's voice was soft and low. 'Just lie still.'

He heard the tap at the back of the shop running, then he felt rather than saw in the darkness that she was alongside him again, exuding a fragrance that came from Chinese perfumes, much more than she normally wore, even a warm body smell, and felt a cold cloth placed on his head.

'What are you doing here?' he asked.

'I came to see if you were all right.'

'Why shouldn't I be all right?'

'Well, sleeping under there can't be very comfortable.'

He jerked away again. It wasn't a good thing to be caught with the boss' daughter in his night clothes especially when – as he could see now – she was in her night clothes, too, a pink flowered kimono over a pink nightdress that showed a bare throat and a lot of pale flesh.

'It's all right, Mr Sarth.'

'It isn't all right,' he said warmly. 'What will your Pa say if he finds you here?'

'He won't,' she said with a firm assurance. 'He went for gin. He's worried and he always goes for the gin when worried. He never hears anything and I'm frightened.'

'So am I,' Willie said warmly. 'Especially now.'

'About the Boxers?'

'No. About you being here.'

'There's no need to be.'

'That's what you think,' Willie said. 'What are you doing anyway? This is no place for a girl.' He sniffed. 'It's not much of a place for a man, come to that.'

'Move over.'

'What?'

'Move over. I want to come in with you.'

'You can't!' Willie's voice rose in a bleat of protest.

She ignored it. 'Yes, I can. I'm scared. All I hear is Boxers, Boxers, Boxers. All day and every day. My father's scared, too. I think everybody's scared.'

'*I* am,' Willie agreed.

'I bet you're not.'

'You don't know me.'

'You'll be all right. I think you're a survivor. Somehow you'll be all right.'

'I will?'

'Yes. The other clerks weren't. They bolted.'

'Weren't *they* survivors?'

'No. I can tell. I can tell a brave man.'

'I'm not brave.'

'That's what you think. Move up.'

'No.'

'Don't be silly. I'm not going to bite you.'

It wasn't her biting him that Willie was afraid of. He moved over, nevertheless.

'There.' He felt her shuffle alongside him and felt the warmth of her body and her legs against his. 'I'm in. Pull the sheet up.'

'What will your Pa say if he catches you?'

'I don't care. I need more than a drunken old man to look after me.' She leaned against him and warm fingers slipped inside his night shirt and began to play on his chest.

'You're hairy, Willie.'

'Always have been.' The answer came with a touch of pride.

'Even down on your stomach, you're hairy.'

He moved uneasily and his hand closed over hers. 'Here, steady on!'

The fingers moved again and he jumped. There was a giggle. 'Willie, I think you fancy me.'

'What do you expect, coming in here in your nightie and nothing else?' A sudden suspicion struck Willie. 'You ever done this before?'

'Not often, Willie.'

'Is this why the last clerk left?'

'I didn't ask him.'

'What'll your Pa say?'

'Stop saying that. I don't care. I'm twenty-two and the warm weather makes me think things. I bet it does you, too.'

'Yes, it – stop doing that!'

'Why?'

'Well –' Willie became silent.

'I begin to think the Boxers are coming,' she went on. 'And then I wonder what we're all doing here. What if they came? We'd all be killed.'

It wasn't a prospect that appealed to Willie.

'And then where would we be? Dead.'

That didn't appeal much either. Willie wasn't used to being murdered and he didn't fancy being dead.

'So why not enjoy ourselves?'

'We might *not* be killed,' Willie suggested.

'No,' she agreed reasonably. 'We might not. But we'll probably be evacuated. And then my father will be without his business. I'll be without my friends and you'll be without a job.'

Willie frowned.

'So I think we ought to live while we can, don't you?'

Willie was all for living.

'Properly, I mean. Like a man and a woman.' There was a silence again as the soft fingers moved. 'Willie, you're big. I didn't think you'd be big like that.'

Willie felt a twinge of pride.

'Come on, Willie. Are you afraid?'

He had still hesitated, conscious that he was betraying a trust, then she took his hand and placed it on her breast. It was warm and soft and the nipple was stiff beneath his fingers.

'It's all right, Willie.' She leaned over and placed her lips on his. Her mouth opened and he felt her tongue. He had never been kissed like that before and he went hot all over. Even at that crucial moment he might still have retreated, but she had rolled on to her back and began pulling him on top of her. His night shirt was pushed up and he was aware of warm scented flesh beneath him and her thighs against his.

'Go on, Willie! It's all right! It really is.'

His common sense still held him back, but she was moving beneath him, her mouth against his, her fingers playing up and down his back. 'No,' he told himself, but the squirming shape beneath him was too much for him and a flame of desire shot through him that threatened to scorch him.

It was all he had hoped for, and more, but it was over much more quickly than he'd expected. Emmeline seemed satisfied, however, and curled up in his arms. Staring wide awake at the underside of the ledger cupboard, Willie was stricken with guilt.

'What'll your Pa say?' he murmured.

'I shan't tell him,' Emmeline said. 'And I advise you not to, as well.'

'I feel awful.'

'Why? Didn't you like it?'

'Yes. Of course, I did. But – I – I mean – doing *that* in his house.'

'Oh, forget it, Willie!' she said. 'It's done now and he'll never know. Was it the first time?'

'Yes. I bet it wasn't with you.'

'No, it wasn't. And I don't know what you're worrying about. If the Boxers come and kill us all – ' it was obvious she didn't expect such an event ' – then at least you can die feeling you've become a man.'

As she curled up and went to sleep against his chest, he decided that she had quite a point. Perhaps, he had thought, there was something to be said for the Boxers after all.

three

Willie cradled his rifle against his chest and leaned back against the stones of the Tartar Wall, his eyes distant, his thoughts busy.

After that first time, Emmeline hadn't bothered to come to the crammed space under the ledger cupboard where it was like making love in a coffin, but had told him how to reach her room and which treads on the stairs to avoid because they squeaked. Willie had felt he had grown older by several years within a month.

The tension had increased, but nothing had been done despite appeals by the French Vicar-Apostolic of Peking, who had warned that the Boxers' aim was to get rid not just of Christian converts but of *all* foreigners. Then the French engineer in charge of construction work at Paotingfu had decided that, even if the diplomats in Peking were satisfied, he wasn't, and, collecting boats, he had gathered a party of thirty-three people, including seven women and one child, armed them with rifles and revolvers and set off downriver. They had been attacked and had had to abandon the boats to struggle on foot to Tientsin, with four of their number dead and many more wounded, while a troop of Cossacks sent to rescue them had been almost annihilated.

More missionaries had appeared in Peking, abandoning their schools and churches and hospitals as they sought safety for their families, and finally, as it had become clear that the Empress Dowager was not only not prohibiting the Boxers but was actually encouraging them, the grandstand of the European racetrack just outside the city was set on fire. The destruction of this private European preserve had finally brought home the seriousness of the situation, and an appeal had been sent to the British admiral at Taku for a relief expedition.

Willie's eyes became empty. Ahead of him the shadows seemed to move, but he knew there was nothing in the darkness. Somewhere down below him Emmeline Wishart was sharing a room with friends. No news had come of the relief expedition and they had no knowledge of whether it had set off or not. North China by now had become an inferno and the crisis had lain like a miasma over Peking. The streets had become deserted as people had become afraid to leave their homes as word of new outrages, wanton murder and destruction of foreign property had seeped in.

They had still not been besieged, however, and Willie had crept regularly up to Emmeline's room. Once they had almost been caught when a band of Boxers had swarmed into the Tartar City, shouting war cries, looting shops and homes, and slashing at pedestrians with their razor-sharp swords. A trail of fired buildings had marked their path and that night, as the sky was lit by flames, the wind carrying the agonised cries of roasting Christian converts unlucky enough to be caught, old Wishart had wakened from his drunken sleep. As they had heard him pounding along the corridor, Emmeline had kicked Willie from the bed. 'Underneath,' she had snapped and he had rolled out of sight just as the door burst open.

'Father,' she had snapped at the wild-eyed old man in the doorway, his hair standing on end, clutching his night shirt about his knees. 'You don't burst into a lady's boudoir like this – not even your own daughter's!'

'They've set the East Cathedral on fire,' Wishart had said. 'They've also set fire to the South Cathedral.'

'Well, I can't do anything about it. Go back to bed, Father. Take the gin bottle with you. It'll help you to sleep.'

As the door had slammed, Willie, cowering under the bed, saw Emmeline's face appear upside down alongside his. 'It's all right,' she had whispered. 'He's gone.'

Sitting on the Tartar Wall, Willie's eyes grew distant as he remembered their lovemaking. It had been particularly passionate that night. He had never imagined for a moment Emmeline was in love with him and he was certainly not in love with her. But she was a hot-blooded young woman and Willie, young, uncertain, uneasy, afraid of being found out, more afraid still of being trapped into marriage had begun to look desperately about him for a means of escape.

In England, at a distance of thousands of miles from China, seeking a fortune, even *making a* fortune, hadn't seemed to include what he had become involved in. He had a mistress! He had read about men with mistresses, but had never imagined he would have one – certainly not at the age of nineteen. But Emmeline was voracious and – he had to admit it – skilled, and she never let him off the hook. Not even as the news grew worse.

Through it all, through all the lovemaking, the horizon had grown blacker. Chaos had spread and the Imperial

Chinese troops had watched impassively as the murder and looting continued. The commercial quarter of the city had been set on fire, the flames destroying the ancient Chien Men, the great central gate between the Tartar City and the Chinese City that was crowned by a five-hundred-foot tower.

Yet it still hadn't become war. Though it wasn't war, however, it had nevertheless been a strain. The servants had disappeared and old Wishart's business had come to a standstill. Hundreds more Christian converts had arrived in the city, unwanted by those already there because it had been felt that if there were to be a siege they would have to be fed.

Then on June 19 the whole thing had come to a head. While people were still trying to organise their departure from the city, the German Minister had been murdered in his sedan chair and all thoughts of leaving Peking had been dropped at once. As they got down at long last to preparing for battle, Methodist missions in the country had been evacuated overnight and people had streamed into the British compound, which was one of the few not dominated by the Tartar Wall. In it now were around a thousand people, plus ponies, mules and sheep. Carts containing furniture had jammed the streets and Chinese converts had swarmed about, unloading their belongings. One building had been assigned to the French, another to the Russians, a third to the Customs officials. Rooms were heaped with provisions or made into kitchens or communal dining rooms. One corner represented a bank, another was a military headquarters hung with maps. Other legations were crowded in the same way.

Old Wishart had been out trying to find out what was happening when the news had come to gather in the

British Legation. Emmeline had swept Willie to her room. 'He won't be back for some time,' she said. 'Come on!'

'What?' Willie had said, shocked. '*Now*?'

'I'm not going to die without knowing love,' she said dramatically.

'Dammit, you know love!'

'Well, again, then.'

'Jesus, Em, this is no time to go in for that sort of thing!'

'Any time's the time to go in for it.' She was already unbuttoning his shirt with one hand and with the other working at the hooks and eyes on her dress.

'Em!'

'Oh shut up, Willie! Don't be so cowardly.' She gave him a push and they fell across the bed together.

By the time old Wishart had appeared it was over and they were busy stuffing clothes into cases and collecting the food they had been hoarding against the emergency. Wishart slapped Willie's shoulder. 'Good boy,' he said. 'Thank God I can trust you to take care of my little girl when I'm away.'

Emmeline looked at Willie. 'Oh, Willie's taken care of me, father,' she said gravely. 'And I've taken care of Willie. We'll take care of each other all the time from now on for ever.'

That had been three weeks ago, Willie remembered as he sat in his little niche on the Tartar Wall. As they had gathered in the British compound there had been an air of unreality. Not only had the Chinese taken up arms against the might of the European powers but they had also violated diplomatic immunity and the Legations were now fighting for their lives. Some legations, situated on the edge of the diplomatic quarter, had even been

41

abandoned, the vacuums promptly filled by the Boxers. On the third day of the siege there had been an alarm when word had flown round that the Boxers had broken through and in the panic several units had abandoned their posts. Staring along the Tartar Wall at the group of Russians and the tall figure of their commander, Willie remembered that among those who had bolted had been the posturing Zychov and his men.

The alarm had brought to a head the need for an overall commander to run the various nationalities as a whole and the British Minister, Sir Claude MacDonald, had been voted into the job. He hadn't much to command, Willie decided – a mere twenty officers and less than four hundred men from eight different countries, all with their own ideas about defence – though there were also seventy-five former military men, now civilians, and the even more irregular Carving Knife Brigade to which Willie belonged.

'Formidable both to friend and foe,' he had murmured to Emmeline as he had met her.

She had looked at him longingly, but in the crowded conditions of the compound there was no possibility of her getting him in a corner, let alone a bedroom. He wasn't sorry. There was something ominous about that business she'd mentioned of looking after each other. 'We'll take care of each other all the time from now on for ever,' she'd said. He suspected she'd begun to think of marriage, and he felt he was too young to die.

He shifted his position, brooding on the siege. A fully fledged Boxer was a terrifying figure – like a demon in one of the pantomimes he'd seen back home. The fact that he was a peasant in fancy dress didn't mean a thing; he was still terrifying with his red ribbons, girdles, head bands, the banners he carried, the spears, the huge curved swords, and his cry of 'Sha! Sha!' Kill! Kill! It kept everyone on the wall jumpy and constantly looking over their shoulders.

There had always been a shortage of food and now everybody was on a diet of malodorous pony meat and rice. And, with summer replacing the damp, mosquito-filled monsoon weather, there had come an intense dry heat that left Peking sweltering.

Somewhere in the darkness beyond the Russians a patrol was scouting the walls. It was led by a Japanese called Yahitsu Shaiba, who was a clerk at the Japanese Legation and who had proved one of the heroes of the defence. He was a short, sturdy man with a mouthful of teeth like the headstones of a graveyard, but he was brave, intelligent, very active and surprisingly able for a civilian. Everybody liked him, even the Russians with whom he was always chattering and laughing. They pulled his leg, boasting of Russia's might, but he took it all with a wide smile, and once Willie had wondered if he were a spy.

It was fortunate there had been a few men like Shaiba because there was a grave shortage of ammunition and because everybody used different weapons, there was no common reserve. Until the old cannon had been built they had had only four pieces of light artillery, among them a British five-barrelled Nordenfelt which always jammed after four shots. However, there were wells in the compound, a store of wheat, rice and maize, and the racing ponies that had been left over from the spring meeting in May.

But children had begun to die, and the first alarm had been a fire, when the Boxers had sneaked into a corner of the British compound and put the torch to a cluster of native houses, so that a bucket chain had had to be formed, to come at once under fire from the rooftops of the Mongol Market, volley after volley coming through the smoke as they struggled to contain the blaze with soup tureens, jugs, pans, even chamber pots. From then on the smell of smoke seemed to be always in their nostrils.

In another attempt to carry the place, the Boxers had rained shells into the American and Russian sectors from a distance which could not be reached by the Legations' lighter weapons, so that trenches, roofed with beams and earth, had been dug and the women set to making sandbags of silks, satins, curtains, trouser legs, anything that would hold sand. Almost without exception they had burst in the torrential rains at the end of the month which had flooded the trenches and saturated them all. With lack of space, lack of information about the outside world and the smell of rotting corpses in the Chinese City, the place had rapidly become a slum.

'I've had to give up Mother's best curtains,' a pale-faced Emmeline had stared indignantly at Willie as they met in one of the communal eating rooms. 'She always wanted me to have them for my bottom drawer.'

'Why do you want a bottom drawer? You thinking of getting married?'

She eyed him sharply. 'You know I am,' she said.

'Who to?'

She had not replied, but he knew she meant him. He must have given her a great deal more satisfaction than the other clerks had managed and she had decided he would do. It wouldn't be a bad arrangement, he knew, because she was Wishart's only child and would inherit the business and, at least, it would be a step on the way to making his fortune. But – Willie paused – it hadn't been his intention to *marry* money. He'd wanted to *make* it. And though a fortune of sorts went with Emmeline and it would save a lot of trouble and give him a start, she didn't ring bells. He knew he wasn't in love with her. Getting into bed with her was one thing, sharing the rest of his life with her was another. She didn't laugh much, as if she had her sights on something and was concentrating, and Willie enjoyed laughing. And he had always felt that when you fell for a girl, lights flashed, stars danced and the spheres whirled in their courses. Or something. He expected crashing cymbals when he met the girl he wanted to marry. With Emmeline there was a lot of passion, but it was the wrong sort and it didn't generate a single tinkle.

The fighting had continued to be fierce, the Boxers always trying to advance along the top of the Tartar Wall to shoot down into the American Legation. Willie's corner on the Wall allowed him protection from a stone buttress. In front of him was a sangar of sandbags with a loophole. After a short spell as a stretcher bearer with a first-aid party, his prowess with a rifle had been discovered. Shooting at men was different from shooting at rabbits, but it hadn't taken him long to get the hang of it and overcome his qualms. His eye was good and his aim was steady. Moreover he was fast and, as one man after another had fallen before his rifle, he had been given the job of sniper, his job being to break up impending attacks before they could get going.

Living conditions were growing worse now that the heat had come. You could hear the pigs and dogs rooting after the corpses buried among the rubble that gave off such an appalling smell during the day when the temperatures shot up to 110 in the shade. The heat was making the children die more quickly and tempers shortened as those missionaries who were unable to bring themselves to handle a weapon felt it their duty to serenade the embattled fighting men with 'Marching Through Georgia' and 'Nearer, My God, To Thee'. They were already near enough to God, Willie considered, without being constantly reminded of the fact.

'There they go again.' The man next to Willie spoke as the choir below them began to tune up. He was an American called Frisbee, with a huge handlebar moustache. 'With their goddam singing.'

Willie nodded, his mind far away. Despite everything, at that moment he would have given a great deal to be in Emmeline's arms and in Emmeline's bed with her warm body against his, her full red lips on his mouth. The thought made him groan.

Frisbee's head turned. 'You all right, kid?'

'I'm all right.'

'Thought something had happened.' Frisbee frowned. 'They say an army's landed on the coast and started marching to relieve us.'

'I heard that too,' Willie said.

'Twenty-five thousand men.'

'Million. I heard.'

'You're joking.'

'Yes.'

'But they *have* landed. Americans, I heard.'

'No, British.'

'Americans.'

'British.'

'Americans!'

Willie felt better. He had forgotten Emmeline's arms, even forgotten the siege. 'Bloody British!'

'You're talking goddam rubbish!'

Willie grinned 'So are you. And you know you are.'

Frisbee grinned back. 'Yeah,' he agreed. 'Rubbish. There ain't no relief column. We're all going to die here.'

As they talked, they heard a flurry of footsteps and highpitched tones that made them reach for their rifles. Then they heard the password and recognised the voices of Yuhitsu Shaiba, the Japanese, and his returning patrol. As they stopped, a shot rang out and the bullet clinked against the wall above Willie's head to whine away into the dusk. Immediately they heard the harsh blare of trumpets and the shrill yelling that always preceded an attack, and, swinging round, they saw a horde of Chinese running towards them.

The first of the defenders to appear were the retreating Russians, who came hurtling along at full speed, dropping their equipment as they ran. In the lead was Count Zychov.

'Get behind the barricades!' The yell came from an American Marine sergeant who was manning a barricade just behind Willie. 'And hurry, goddamit!'

As the Russians clattered past, Willie and Frisbee snatched up their rifles and sidepacks and started to follow, almost falling over the Japanese as they scattered. Willie was scampering, just behind Shaiba, his eyes flicking over his shoulders as he ran for a glimpse of the terrifying curved two-handed swords, then Shaiba stumbled and Willie fell over him and went sprawling. Sitting up, he saw Shaiba clutching his leg, and, without thinking, he grabbed him by the collar and dragged him to his feet.

'Come on, you sonofabitch!' the American Marine sergeant was yelling. 'How the hell can I let fly with you in the way?'

Still struggling to help Shaiba, Willie heard him giving orders 'Load,' he yelled. 'When I give the word, rapid fire. Pick your targets. And don't miss.'

'For Christ's sake,' Willie screamed, terrified. 'You'll hit us!'

'Let me down,' Shaiba shouted. 'I'm prepared to die!'

'Don't be daft!'

'Down!' the American roared. 'Flat on your faces!'

For a second, Willie didn't understand what he meant. After all there seemed to be a couple of hundred screaming lunatics thundering down on him, but then it dawned on him what the sergeant was after and flinging Shaiba down, he sprawled on top of him. The volley almost shattered his eadrums.

For a moment, though he could feel no pain, he was convinced he was dead. Then he heard Shaiba moaning beneath him as he struggled to throw Willie aside.

'Another one!' the sergeant yelled and another volley screamed over their heads.

'Up you sonofabitch!' the sergeant roared. 'While we've stopped them!' Looking round, Willie saw that the Boxers had fallen back, struggling over the fallen bodies of their comrades, and, scrambling to his feet, he began to pull Shaiba after him. Jumping over the barricade, two American soldiers grabbed Shaiba's arms, and with Willie scuttling along behind, dragged him to safety.

The sergeant grinned. 'Nearly got your head blowed off there, son,' he said.

They didn't go back to their niche again that night and as they changed places with their relief an hour later and slipped down the ramps into the compound, a British major called Birkett was waiting for them.

'We need volunteers,' he said.

'I'm already a volunteer,' Willie said.

'It's not for here.'

'Where then?'

Birkett looked hard at Willie. He found it difficult dealing with civilian soldiers. They had little respect for army ranks, never called anyone 'sir' and considered that after three weeks of siege they knew as much about fighting as the army.

'Outside,' he said.

'Outside where?'

'Outside the city. Shantu. Shensi province.'

Willie looked at Frisbee. 'That's thirty miles away,' he said.

'No more than a day's good march,' Birkett pointed out.

'What's at Shantu? Have the relief column arrived? Do they want guiding in?'

'The relief column hasn't arrived,' Birkett said coldly. 'It probably never will. It's Gordon and Khartoum all over again, I expect those bloody idiots in the House of Commons are still arguing over the cost.'

'So what's it all about?'

'There are missionaries there, around two hundred. Mixed French, British and American. Catholics, Anglican, Presbyterian, Baptist, the lot.'

'And we're going to fetch 'em in?'

'Somebody's got to.' Birkett hated the arguing that always followed his orders. 'We can't let them be massacred.'

'It's a goddam wonder they ain't been massacred already,' Frisbee said.

'How many men are you intending to send?' Willie asked.

'Twenty.'

'You're talking out of the top of your head. They'd never make it.'

'They've got to.'

'We've got around a thousand people here to defend and we have around four hundred and seventy men to do it! Less, now. And you're talking of reducing 'em by another twenty to bring in a lot of half-baked Bible-thumpers who hadn't the sense to get to safety while they could. Why *didn't* they come in?'

'They –' Birkett hesitated then faced up to the fact ' – they felt their faith would protect them. God will provide. That sort of thing.'

'They deserve all they get,' Frisbee growled.

Birkett gave an irritated gesture. 'It can't be helped. We want volunteers. I submitted your names.'

'You call that volunteering?' Willie yelled furiously.

'Somebody's got to go. You will, won't you?'

'No,' Willie said.

'Dammit – !'

'Somebody once called me a survivor –' Willie's face went blank as he remembered Emmeline and the circumstances surrounding the event – 'and that's what I intend to be. A survivor.'

'Sir Claude MacDonald wants to see you before you go.'

'I'm not going.'

Birkett ignored his protests. It was as if Willie had never opened his mouth. 'We need the regular soldiers here,' he said. 'So we've picked the best of what's left. Most civilians can't hit a pig in a passage. You two can.'

'Who else is going?'

'Sanders. Ornini. De Faillat. A few British and Americans who've offered. All civilians, with an experienced officer to run the show. If you'll come with me, Sir Claude will see you now.'

Willie looked at Frisbee. 'Jesus Christ on a tightrope,' he said.

'You said it, bud,' Frisbee agreed. 'With knobs on.'

Sir Claude MacDonald was a tall man with sweeping moustaches, imbued with diplomatic calm. He had taken to his new job like a duck to water and had made a surprisingly good job of it. At that moment he seemed full of confidence and the certainty of victory. Willie hated him.

'You can get out by the Tartar Wall,' he said. 'There's a sewer goes out there with an iron grille. It can't be seen from the Chinese positions.'

Willie's hatred increased. It was typical of men like Sir Claude to order other men – among them Willie Sarth – to plough their way through a sewer full of shit to the rescue of a couple of hundred idiots who'd thought that prayer would stop the bullets and swords of the Boxers.

'Once out,' MacDonald continued, 'you'd better make your way first to the river. There'll be guides waiting for you.' His lips twitched. 'Besides, I imagine you'll probably want to wash a little. After that you can go straight across country to Shantu. We understand there are no Boxers on that side of the city so it should be pretty straightforward.'

Pretty straightforward! Willie's brows came down. As if anything was ever straightforward! He had thought making his fortune in China would be straightforward. But he had reckoned without Emmeline Wishart and the Boxers. Still – with a bit of luck the mythical relief column might just be genuine and would arrive while they were away and then he need never come back. He could sneak himself away somehow and, hiding among the troops, keep out of Emmeline's clutches.

'You are among our best men,' Sir Claude continued, 'and we depend on you. Good luck to you.'

As MacDonald disappeared Frisbee crossed himself, as if he didn't think much of his chances.

'Who's leading?' Willie asked nervously.

Major Birkett gestured. 'Count Zychov, the Russian.'

'Him!' Willie's voice rose to a yell of rage. 'He couldn't command a platoon of Chinese pedlars!'

Frisbee's face had gone red. 'I'll bet they think we'll not come back,' he snarled, 'and they're sending Zychov in command because he's the one goddam regular who can best be spared.'

Willie gave him a plaintive look. 'Perhaps,' he said, 'that's why they picked us, too.'

four

It was dark as they assembled in the fire-scarred streets near the Tartar Wall. They had to pass through a few of the dark areas of the Chinese city before they reached the safety of the countryside and none of them was looking forward to it.

Hefting his rifle, feeling the weight of the sidepack containing a few wretched rations he'd been given and the weight of a bandolier of ammunition, Willie waited in the shadows close to the American Methodist Mission. He didn't feel very brave. He had been to see Shaiba in the hospital and found him lying with his leg swathed in bandages but with his spirits high, his wide mouth filled to capacity with square white teeth.

'You saved my life, Mr Sarth,' he said.

'It was nothing.' Actually, Willie had decided, it was quite a lot, though at the time he had acted largely out of panic.

'I shall always be grateful,' Shaiba went on. 'One day perhaps, I'll be able to do something for you.'

Willie couldn't imagine what and, at that moment, crouching against the walls, thinking about the security of the hospital he wished he weren't leaving it behind. Zychov, the Russian officer, seemed nervous.

'I don't regard being shot at a sensible pastime,' he was complaining to Birkett.

Slung about with his map case, revolver, sidepack and binoculars, he looked like a dressed Christmas tree. Frisbee stood next to him, his face in shadow. He and Willie had become close in the fortnight or so since the siege had started. Danger and fear of death made for quick friends. Willie studied the American. He was a self-assured older man who had once fought Indians and Willie wondered what it would feel like if he were killed. It never occurred to him that Frisbee might be looking at him, wondering what it would be like if Willie were killed. I'd probably miss him, Willie thought, but he couldn't imagine being miserable for long.

'So,' Zychov stiffened. 'It is time we must go.'

A door opened and Willie saw light beyond, then they began to file through, their hands clutching their weapons so they wouldn't chink and give the game away. Alongside them the wall had scorch marks on it. Two men with pigtails were waiting for them and they spoke briefly with Zychov then led the way through the piled refuse in the deserted streets. Willie didn't like the look of them and felt sure they were intending to betray them.

There was a glow in the sky to the west where fires were burning, and occasionally they heard stray shots and cries, but the streets in their immediate vicinity seemed to be deserted, and only once did anyone pass them, a figure in the blue clothes of a coolie, his carrying pole in his hands.

Groping in the blackness, their hands on the stones, they pushed into the shadows, the dim bulk of the city faint against the sky, then they found themselves stumbling in and out of ditches and falling over broken masonry or charred beams. There was a smell of burning everywhere and the stink of death, and several times they heard rats squeaking among the rubble, their claws castanetting over the stones.

A tunnel opened before them like a black hole in the wall, and Zychov led the way into it. The smell immediately let them know they were in the sewer.

'Jesus Holy Christ,' Frisbee said.

Nostrils twitching at the odours, lungs aching, throats burning, chests raw as they tried to hold their breath, they pushed ahead to where they could see a faint light filtering through an iron-grilled gate that closed off the tunnel from the outside. It was half raised and Zychov signed to them to duck under it.

'Duck under it?' Frisbee said. 'Into the shit? You crazy?'

He began to yank at the gate. It refused to move, but he was able to smash the lock with his rifle butt. The rusty hinges screeched as they pulled at it, but they managed to open it enough to squeeze past. At the other end of the tunnel they gathered in a group, sickened by the stench and waiting for the rush of screaming men and the slash of swords. But there was no sound and Zychov consulted a compass.

They were in dark, deserted streets, the only light the yellow chinks from closed doors and shutters. Skirting stray houses and broken-down hovels, they scrambled over a cascade of broken stones where a store had once stood and headed down an alley, hardly daring to breathe.

The place was ominously quiet. An occasional stray shot still echoed over the houses, but every door and window was shuttered and barred. Splashing through stinking drains, holding his breath against the smell of ordure and years-old rotting rubbish, Willie found himself thinking again of Emmeline. It was funny how every time he was in difficulty or discomfort he thought of her. After all, he thought, whatever designs she had on him, her bed was a damn sight pleasanter than this and a whole lot safer, too.

Eventually they came to a wider road and down it they could see across the whole width of the Chinese City. Zychov turned right and they found themselves at a huge bronzestudded gate. Above them the city wall towered like a cliff in the darkness.

'The Hsia Kuo Men gate,' Frisbee whispered.

Willie had seen it several times before, when, in the early days after his arrival, fascinated by the quaintness of Chinese life, he had gone exploring.

There was a single sentry by the gate, which was standing ajar, so that a narrow sliver of light sky showed beyond. Zychov stopped dead and they all stumbled into one another as they came to a halt. The sentry had a rifle on his back and a huge sword in his hand.

'Somebody's got to take that guy,' Frisbee said grimly. 'But I'll need help. You comin', Willie.'

Willie swallowed. 'Do I have to?'

'Some guy's got to.'

'What do I do?'

'When he sees me, he'll turn. But we'll have a second while he hoists his sword or reaches for his gun. You jump on his back.'

'Think I can?'

'Bud, you got to.'

The two of them crept to within a yard or two of the sentry, then, as Frisbee straightened up, the sentry heard him. Swinging round, he shouted something – not a challenge or a warning, just a cry of alarm – and hefted his sword. As he lifted it, Willie grabbed his arm and heaved. The sword fell with a clatter and Frisbee swung his great fist. As the Chinese went limp in Willie's arms, Frisbee grabbed the sword and swung it. The sentry's face seemed to split open, and the legs twitched once then he was still.

'Oh, Christ!' Willie turned and brought up the remains of his last meal.

'Better him than you, kid,' Frisbee said.

The others appeared within seconds and they crowded through the gate into the open country. Outside the walls there were carts and waggons and the huge barrows the Chinese used, all waiting to be allowed in the following morning. Nearby, there were native huts and a few scrappy tent-like structures of canvas and rush matting and the faint glimmer of dying fires. Mules, donkeys and oxen, even camels, were tethered in the shadows, but there was no sign of human beings, and they slipped past unimpeded. Within minutes, they were staring back at the city walls and the glow in the sky where the fires still burned.

'I think we're safe,' Zychov said cheerfully.

Willie wasn't so sure.

By daylight they were five miles from the city walls and beginning to breathe normally again. The land was a chequerboard of fields, broken only by the distant ribbon of road that seemed to reach from one horizon to the other. China seemed to be totally devoid of landmarks, but, as the light increased, they saw small villages in the distance, surrounded by maize and sorghum fields and the inevitable rice paddies. There seemed to be no woods, no highways, only lakes and interwoven cart tracks spreading like the tentacles of an octopus from each village to connect it to those about it.

After a while two men on saddled horses approached them. They looked like ordinary peasants, but Zychov, who was growing more nervous with every mile they marched, ordered them to be captured and shot. The two men raised no objection when they were surrounded and only started yelling when they were placed against a wall facing a firing squad. Willie backed off hurriedly and kept out of the way.

'They're not Boxers,' he said to Frisbee. 'I reckon they were coming for help.'

The crash of the volley stopped the argument, and when Willie managed to turn round the firing squad were tossing the bodies over the wall. Zychov ordered the horses to be brought forward, and, as he and his sergeant climbed into the saddles, they moved forward again. There was a little muttering, because other people had also had their doubts about the guilt of the two men, but with Boxers everywhere, there was no point in taking chances.

Then Willie began to notice that Zychov kept getting well ahead of the main party and he glanced at Frisbee. 'What's he up to?' he asked.

'What *would* he be up to?'

Willie frowned. 'He's in a good position to bolt.'

After a matter of fifteen miles, with Willie's feet beginning to grow sore, they crested a small rise and dropped into a shallow valley which was full of woods.

'We'll halt here,' Zychov said.

They pushed among the trees and sat down to eat and rest. The Russian allowed them a short sleep, and it was warm enough to lie where they fell. At midday, they were awakened by the sound of voices, and peering from the woods, saw a column of men armed with swords, bows and arrows and ancient rifles moving past on the dusty road. Some of them were Kansu horsemen and they wore red trousers and jackets of every colour marked with black dragons and tied with red sashes. They had red ribbons round their heads and carried black banners with crimson characters on them like splashes of blood.

'Boxers,' Frisbee breathed.

'They said there weren't any round here,' Willie said bitterly.

'Well, hell, now there are.'

Watching the Boxers move on, the rescue party lay low until almost dark, then Zychov got them on their feet and they set off once more. Shantu came up at last, a small rural town whose smells were those of a great feudal village. Outside the gate was a row of hovels built of dried mud, so dilapidated they looked as though a good shove would lay the lot flat. The town walls, old, crenellated and twelve feet thick, were topped with weeds and nettles. Swinging right, they came to the Mission.

It was a straggle of buildings built round a central courtyard and, as they approached, they saw figures appearing. Then children began to run towards them, shouting with delight. As they reached the gate, eager hands reached out to greet them. The missionaries were mostly American Baptists, but there were a few Anglicans and a few French Catholics standing aloof, as though they disapproved of something that was not the True Church. Almost without exception, they were dressed in drab Chinese clothes, both the men and women wearing trousers, and their quarters seemed to match their clothes for cheerlessness. The few small rooms seemed for the most part to be only for sleeping and everybody lived in a huge communal room which, judging by the blackboard at one end, was used during the day as a school.

An old man with a thin white beard like a Chinese and wearing a conical straw hat greeted them. 'We're delighted to see you,' he said. 'Did you meet the messengers we sent?'

It was clear they had stood innocent men in front of the firing squad and they all avoided looking at him, all trying to shuffle off the feeling of guilt. The old man didn't ask questions and gestured to the door.

'You must come in and rest,' he offered.

'There is no time,' Zychov said. 'We must leave at once.'

The old man's eyebrows rose. 'But surely you'll take tea and something to eat? We haven't much, but we can provide a meal.'

'Quickly then. And while we eat you must prepare to leave.'

'We have the oxcarts ready packed.'

'No carts.' Zychov chopped a refusal with his hand. 'Too slow. Just what you carry on your backs.'

'But we have our books, the children's belongings. We can't leave them behind.'

Zychov paused, his eyes moving nervously, then he swung round to the men behind him. 'Form up' he said. 'We leave at once. They don't wish to be rescued.'

Willie's jaw dropped and he saw Frisbee was looking startled, too. He had always thought Zychov a perfect example of his country's decadent army. He wore scent with his little waxed moustache and liked to wear his short-peaked cap cocked heavily over one eye. His present determination seemed based on a desire to get back to the shelter of the Legations as quickly as possible.

'You can't go.' The old man's voice was a wail and Willie saw the faces behind him go blank.

'We go,' Zychov said. 'You have one half-hour and then we leave.'

A babble of voices rose and another old man in the soutane of a Catholic priest pushed forward and a fierce discussion started, the more practical among the missionaries obviously arguing for immediate evacuation, the older, more ardently religious arguing for remaining. For a moment Willie thought they were going to start fighting and wondered who would win. Then his eye caught the women and he began to study them with interest, wondering what sort of people could give up homes and everything a woman cherished to live in a place like this for the doubtful joy of teaching religion to the Chinese, who were largely indifferent anyway. For the most part they were a dreary lot, so that he began to wonder if they'd opted for the life they lived because they'd never been able to see a future for themselves elsewhere, then, among them, he spotted one face that seemed animated and attractive, small and heart-shaped, surrounded by straight black hair so that she looked almost Chinese.

He was still watching the girl when more people pushed forward to join the argument and eventually the first old man shrugged and turned to Zychov.

'We will go,' he said. 'But first you must give us time to cook food to take with us. There are children to consider. We need bread and meat.'

Zychov didn't budge from his decision. He looked more nervous than ever. 'Half an hour,' he said.

The old man threw up his hands. 'We will be ready,' he said.

The column seemed to cover a quarter of a mile of the road. Zychov led the way, with half a dozen men, then the refugees, first the Roman Catholics, then the Anglicans, then the Baptists – all of them making sure they kept a small space between their own group and the other denominations, as though they were afraid they might be defiled by coming into contact. On either side at intervals Zychov had placed men with rifles and the rear was brought up by Frisbee, Willie and four other men.

As they left, there was a lot of weeping by the Baptists, who seemed to feel they were suffering a great loss by abandoning the comfortless mission. Willie couldn't quite see why. In front of him was the group led by the old man with the thin beard, then a whole host of men and women dragging along wailing children. The rear and flanks were covered by young men, none of them, Willie had to admit, terribly strapping specimens. Half of them wore glasses and they looked half-starved, as if they had been sustained more by their beliefs than the food they'd eaten, and none of them was armed. Among them were a few women, all of them dressed in the ugly Chinese garments, all carrying bags on their backs containing their belongings, which, judging by the size of the bags, didn't amount to a great deal.

Trudging across the empty plain, trailing a cloud of yellow dust, they made their slow way north-east towards Peking. The plain remained empty and nobody from the distant villages took the trouble to investigate the exodus. Once a lone horseman, riding a skinny nag, appeared. As he passed the guides who had led them from Peking to

Shantu, he stopped and spoke to them. There was a hurried high-pitched jabbering.

'What are they saying?' Frisbee said.

'Asking what won the 2.30,' Willie suggested.

'They're asking,' a voice said, 'where we came from and where we're going.'

Willie turned and found himself facing the girl he'd noticed at the mission. She was small and slight, with a face which at that moment was streaked through the dust which lay on her skin with the smudge marks where she had tried to wipe away the sweat.

'You speak the lingo?' Frisbee asked.

'Yes.' The girl had a light musical voice and Willie found himself wondering what she'd look like with a clean skin, her hair done in a proper fashion, and dressed in pretty clothes. She smiled and it lit up the small pert face. 'I learned it. It's not much good trying to teach them Christianity when you can't speak their language. It's bad enough as it is. The missionary societies have given them five different names for God. They already had two before we came, then the Jesuits produced another, and the Protestants a fourth, and finally we found a fifth to win more converts than anyone else.' She seemed to think it all rather amusing and pathetic.

'Did it win 'em?' Willie asked.

Again the wide smile came. 'No,' she said bluntly.

Later that day, the horseman on the sorry nag passed them again, going the other way. Willie noticed that he waved to the guides, then he pushed on ahead, followed by the usual cloud of dust.

Towards dusk they reached the fringe of the stretch of wood where they had rested on the way from Peking. Zychov was still nervous about the long tail-back of the column, and he trotted up and down, urging everybody to close up. But it was impossible, because by this time the older men and women were growning tired and were lagging back, and the younger people were anxious to push ahead.

'Them woods is dark,' Frisbee said, staring about him. 'I don't like the look of 'em.'

Willie noticed that once again Zychov had widened the distance between himself and the rest of the column and his head was turning from left to right.

'He's worried,' Frisbee observed.

'He's probably looking for a chance to bolt,' Willie said.

'Perhaps that's why he had those two guys shot. So he could grab their ponies.'

The road was stony and walking was difficult, and as they approached the woods the girl who had talked to them about religion gave a little cry and stopped.

'Come on, Miss,' Frisbee said. 'Don't hang back.'

'I'll catch up,' she said. 'I've wrenched my ankle. It'll be all right in a moment.'

Frisbee frowned and set off again, chivvying on the laggards. It was hot and they had discarded some of their heavy clothing and were carrying it draped over their packs. Willie stopped, looking back. The girl was sitting at the side of the road near the trees rubbing her ankle. She looked small against the vast background of the countryside.

'Come on,' he urged.

'You go on.'

He frowned, nervous. 'I'll wait for you,' he said.

He stared about him uneasily. The approaching darkness made the woods look evil and threatening. The girl was still rubbing her ankle, and now had her shoe off, massaging her foot.

'Come on,' he snarled.

'I'm coming.'

As she spoke, a shot rang out, then another, then a whole fusillade. An old woman at the tail of the column fell on her face and Willie saw that the back of her shapeless garment was covered with blood.

As he swung round, wondering what was happening, he saw Boxers emerging from the trees. One moment the countryside was quiet then suddenly it was alive with them. They were on foot and many of them had rifles, but there were also gingals, huge two-man blunderbusses which fired from a wooden stand. Red ribbons fluttering in the warm breeze, they were advancing towards them in a ragged skirmishing line, as though attacking an armed column. Then, without warning, they dropped to their knees and raised their arms as if praying, before slowly climbing to their feet again and advancing once more. At their head was the man on the horse.

The column of refugees had closed in on itself, the women shrieking with terror, the men shouting orders and instructions. A high-pitched voice rose above the wailing and there was an unsteady rattle of fire. Kneeling, Willie fired off half a dozen shots and he saw several of the Boxers fall, then as he reached for more ammunition, the Boxers charged in a howling mob, brandishing their weapons.

As they did so, Willie saw Zychov put his heels into his pony's flanks and it broke into a gallop, racing across the plain away from the column.

'Come back, you rotten sod!' he yelled.

Zychov's sergeant, seeing his officer vanish, had swung round and begun to hurry back to the column. The Boxer on the horse had also kicked his horse into a gallop and was crossing Zychov's front. As they crashed into each other, Zychov's hand, holding a pistol, lifted. There was a flash and a puff of smoke and the Boxer went backwards over his horse's tail.

The sergeant was galloping at full speed towards the column now, but it was hopeless immediately because the column had broken in collision, so that the rescue party found themselves trying to defend a constantly shifting formation that was impossible to keep together. Many of the missionaries had panicked at once and the women began to snatch at the children. Several of them dropped to the badly aimed bullets from the Boxers and the charge came on, the battle cries mingling with the moans of the wounded, the screams of the women and the wailing of children. In no time it was bedlam. Women were running for the woods, but the Boxers had split up and were circling them, whirling their huge curved swords as they rounded them up like cattle. A woman with a child in her arms was caught by a huge Chinese stripped to the waist. The sword swung and Willie saw blood spurt. Zychov's sergeant had managed to gather a few of the refugees round him and was trying hopelessly to defend them with the dozen men of the vanguard, but they were overwhelmed and, horrified, Willie saw them go down under the rush, and the huge swords rising and falling.

By this time there was no longer any order in the column, and men, women and children were scattering in all directions, followed by groups of red-sashed men yelling their hatred. The old man who had first argued with them stumbled away, his hands in the air, fleeing from a man with a gun, but he ran straight into another Boxer and, as the huge sword whirled, the old man's hands leapt into the air from his arms.

Waiting for the girl, Willie had become separated from the rest of the column and it was obvious there was no hope of rejoining it. The Boxers were between them and were working their way through what was left of the missionaries.

Horrified, Willie looked round and found the girl standing there, as shocked as he was, petrified by what was happening, still holding her shoe in her hand.

A hundred yards away, Frisbee was working the bolt of his rifle furiously when he stopped dead, a look of surprise on his face. Willie watched, wondering what was wrong because he could see no wound, then suddenly blood gushed from Frisbee's mouth. He turned slowly, his eyes bewildered, and stared at Willie almost as if he could see him and were accusing him, then he crumpled slowly to the ground.

Suddenly there seemed to be no sign of anyone still on their feet, just groups of maddened Chinese screaming their hatred and hacking and stabbing in the dust. The missionaries all seemed to have been cut down, and among the lunging, screaming Chinese Willie could see the two guides who had led them from Peking. His opinion had been dead right.

Swinging round again, he saw the girl still standing there, and, without thinking, he grabbed her hand and dragged her towards the trees.

'My shoe!'

'Bugger your shoe!' he snapped.

Plunging into the undergrowth, gasping and shocked, he went on running until a root tripped him and flung him down. He was still holding the girl's hand and she went down on top of him. They lay together, dazed and winded, alongside a bush, trying to get their breath. Then, recovering his senses, Willie scrambled under the bush and dragged her after him.

'My shoe! My shoe!'

'For Christ's sake!'

Dragging her through the bush so that it tore at her clothes and scratched her face, he rose at the other side and plunged deeper into the trees. Starting to run again, indifferent to the twigs and branches that snatched and slapped at them, they pressed deeper into the wood until they finally realised it was dark and they were safe. In the distance they could hear the furious high screams of the Boxers, still hacking at the corpses of the refugees.

Stumbling through the trees, they fell into an unseen ditch and rolled together to the bottom, clutched in each other's arms. For a long time, they lay still, their breath rasping in their throats, then Willie became aware of the girl lifting her head. In the last of the light he saw that the dust on her face was runnelled with tears.

'They're all dead,' she whispered. 'I knew them all.'

'I knew a few of them,' Willie said, thinking of Frisbee.

'What shall we do?'

'Not much we can do except keep our heads down.'

'I'm frightened.'

'So am I.'

'I'm cold too.'

It had been hot all day so he assumed it was shock that had gripped her, and he put his arms round her and leaned back against the slope of the hollow, murmuring to her.

'It'll be all right,' he kept saying.

'It'll be all right.' It was only when he noticed her steady breathing that he realised she was fast asleep.

five

It was growing daylight when Willie woke. Almost at once, as he blinked himself back to consciousness, he became aware of a weight against him and a tightness around his waist. Then he realised the weight was the girl's and the tightness was because at some point during the night she had awakened and, terrified, had clutched at him for reassurance.

As he stirred, she opened her eyes. For a long time they stared at each other, neither of them sure what to say.

'Are we all right?' the girl asked eventually.

'I think so,' Willie said. 'At least we're alive and nobody's here.'

She was silent for a second then her eyes filled with tears. 'They're all dead,' she said again.

'*We're* not,' Willie said stoutly, trying to appear confident beyond his years.

'What are we going to do?'

Willie didn't know. He had never been thrust into such a situation before. Even in Peking he had taken orders from other people who knew more about things than he did.

'Will any of them be alive?' The girl asked.

'I don't know.'

'Perhaps we ought to see.'

Willie nodded. 'I'll go.'

'I'll come with you.'

'No!' Willie's voice was harsh. Having seen at close quarters in Peking what happened when a man was caught by the Boxers, he had no wish for her to see it too. He had no wish to see it himself for that matter, but he felt he ought to try. 'You stay here. I'll go.'

'Don't leave me!'

'I've got to go. Stay out of sight. Keep an eye on me. If anything happens make your way south.'

'Which way's south?'

He explained. 'I think it's safer going south. But keep away from the river and big towns.'

She didn't argue, but he could see she was trembling. Sighing, he picked up the rifle and headed for the road. Eventually she began to follow, moving just behind him until he reached the road, where he signalled her to remain hidden.

As he left the trees, he knew he was wasting, his time. He could see the road littered with bodies, with more bodies scattered about on either side. Nervously he stepped from the trees. He preferred to remain out of sight, but somehow he felt he must find out what had happened to Frisbee and the rest of his party because, if he ever got back to Peking, somebody would be bound to ask.

There were a lot of crows and kitehawks about, big ungainly birds lurching about among the bloodstained bodies. The first person he came across was the old woman who had first fallen, a long way back from the others. But now her head was missing.

As he moved towards them, the birds lumbered into the sky like drunken undertakers and when he thought of what they had been doing, his stomach lurched. Among the bodies were their pathetic belongings, a bag containing a little food, a sack containing pots and pans, the ugly garments they all wore. Then he found Frisbee still lying on his back, staring at the sky, his big moustache clotted with blood. Moving further, he found Zychov's sergeant surrounded by a few of his party, as if he'd rallied them for a last stand. They'd all been chopped and slashed, but the hatred seemed to have been chiefly reserved for the missionaries and the Chinese converts, whose bodies, even those of the children, had been hacked to pieces. His face drawn and white, his stomach heaving, he turned back, aware that he could do nothing and was unlikely to find anyone alive. What hatred the missionaries had engendered! How stupid they'd been, to assume that, because *they* believed in kindness and love, people who'd been pagans for centuries would accept them, too.

Reaching the trees again, he saw the girl rise up out of the bushes. She seemed to sense his nausea and horror and she moved towards him and took his arm, guiding him back into the trees. For a long time he sat on a fallen log, unable to speak, unable to absorb the shock of the massacre, then the girl's voice came to him.

'I'm sorry,' she said softly. 'I shouldn't have suggested it.'

'It's all right.' He held out his hand. 'I found your shoe.'

'Thank you.' She took the shoe and slipped it on. 'What are we going to do?'

Willie managed to rouse himself. 'We ought to move on,' he said. 'Go south. Away from Peking. In case they send anybody to find out if they left anybody alive.' He remembered Frisbee and the others, all braver men than he was, and the hacked bodies of men, women and children.

'Why in the name of God,' he burst out, 'didn't you come in before?'

She stared at him with large eyes full of tears. 'They didn't consult me. I just did what I was told.'

'What?'

'Teaching. Nursing. A bit of religion.'

'But staying there! Thirty miles from safety! You could all have got in if you'd started in time. Others did.'

'It was nothing to do with me,' she said. 'Besides, they kept waiting for others who were further out. They wanted to collect everybody and all move off together. By the time everybody came in it was too late.'

'It was bloody crazy!'

'It wasn't my fault! I told you.' She snapped the words at him, her face pink.

'You're *all* crazy!' The thoughts that had occurred to him as he had stared down at the hacked bodies swept over him. 'Thinking you could push your bloody silly religion down the throats of people who didn't want it.'

'Some did.'

'Not many.'

'No,' she agreed. 'Not many.'

'Then why did they do it?'

'Because they felt they had to.'

'Did *you*?'

'I heard the call.'

'Call?' Willie's laugh was slightly hysterical. 'A call to die! A fat lot of good it did you all.'

Unexpectedly, she swung her arm back and delivered a flat-handed swipe at him. It caught his cheek with tremendous force and jerked his head back. Blinking the tears from his eyes, he saw her staring at him, horrified, then her eyes filled with moisture and she crouched in front of him, sobbing.

'I'm sorry,' she wailed. 'I'm sorry! I'm sorry! I shouldn't have done that. Not after you saving my life and all. But you shouldn't have gone on at me.'

He didn't know how to excuse himself and she did it for him. 'It was seeing all those bodies,' she said. 'That's what did it. Oh, Lord Jesus, what shall we do?'

He knelt and put his arms round her, holding her close to him, allowing her to sob on his shoulder. Crooning encouragement, he stroked her hair until the sobs died. Then suddenly, abruptly, she sat up.

'It's no good staying here,' she said.

'No,' he agreed. 'It isn't.' He rose stiffly, like an old man, and held out his hand to pull her up. Standing alongside him, she stared at him.

'I'm sorry,' she said again.

'It's me who ought to be sorry,' he pointed out. 'I shouldn't have said those things.'

'It's understandable,' she admitted. 'A lot of people think those things. It seems silly to some people. It seemed silly sometimes even –' she stopped dead, touched his hand and gestured towards the road. 'I think we ought to go, don't you?'

Willie shuddered. 'Not that way,' he said. He couldn't bear the thought of seeing Frisbee and the old beheaded woman and the butchered children again. 'Let's go through the wood and see what happens on the other side.'

She nodded. 'Shouldn't we try to look like Chinese,' she said. 'You especially.'

What she said made sense. 'I'll go and find something,' he said.

Forcing himself back to the road, he picked up one of the all-embracing garments that were lying about. Putting it over his arm, he picked up two of the conical straw hats, then, steeling himself, he moved towards Zychov's sergeant and detached his revolver from the lanyard round his neck. It was a big Russian-made Nagant, similar to one he'd been using in Peking, and for a while he stared at the Russian words on the butt, then he loaded it with cartridges from the dead man's pouch and thrust it into his belt. Filling his pockets with the ammunition scattered during the brief fight, he was just about to turn away when he saw a map case that Zychov must have thrown aside. Dragging out the maps, he stuffed them in his shirt, pulled a pair of binoculars over the Russian sergeant's bloodied head and strung them round his own neck. It might help, he thought, to see other people before other people saw them.

He was pale and drawn when he returned to the girl, carrying over his back a sack containing his findings and a few scraps of food he'd discovered. She helped him into the long Chinese gown and watched him checking the things in the sack.

'Shouldn't we darken our faces?' he said.

'With what?'

'Mud.'

'There is no mud.'

'I can soon make some,' Willie said bluntly.

She turned away as he unbuttoned his trousers, then he stirred the dust with his foot and rubbed his hand into the dirt and spread it on his face. He saw her wince but she did the same. In their shabby, torn clothes, they might now just pass for Chinese peasants.

'Ready?'

She nodded and, as he set off, she automatically took up a position behind him, as if that were her proper place, her head down, meek again as she had been before their argument.

They were soon through the wood, and began to head across the rolling plain, trying to keep to the valleys for safety. Occasionally, they saw peasants, once a man riding a horse who gave them a fright, until they realised he was heading away from them. On another occasion, they passed a boy leading an ox and then a man pushing a single-wheeled barrow on which two young women were sitting.

Neither Willie nor the girl spoke much and all the time the girl kept behind Willie, which was where a Chinese woman would walk with a man. Fear kept them moving and it was only towards evening that Willie realised how tired he was. He stopped and looked back. The girl was still walking, but her head was down and she was weaving from side to side. As she drew level she stumbled and almost fell. Catching her, he helped her to the side of the road where he sat her down on a rock.

'I'm tired,' she excused herself. 'I'm sorry.'

'My fault,' Willie mumbled. 'Didn't realise. I think we ought to find somewhere to sleep.'

'Can we eat first?'

In his anxiety to put as much distance as he could between them and the horror on the road near Shantu, he had forgotten about food. He nodded and indicated a small hill, covered with trees.

'Up there.'

His legs were stiff with walking and the girl could barely move. He took her weight and helped her into the trees, then dragged from the sack a scrap of bread and cooked meat and handed it to her. Taking his own share he began to eat hurriedly. Neither of them spoke, but, as he finished his first mouthful, his eyes fell on the piece of meat he held in a dirty hand. It had been hastily cooked and was almost raw, and suddenly it reminded him of what he'd seen on the road. His stomach heaved and he had to jump up and move away to be sick. Returning, wiping his mouth, he apologised.

'I understand,' the girl said.

'I'll go to the stream,' he said. 'Douse my head. I'll feel better then.'

Among the things he had salvaged was a tin cup and, returning with it full of water, he handed it to the girl. 'Drink it,' he said. 'I'll fill it up again.'

'I don't need much,' she said. After a few sips, she handed the cup back to him and he realised she had deliberately refrained from drinking too much, so he wouldn't have to walk down the hill again.

The plain seemed totally empty so Willie searched the copse for a hollow out of the dry, dusty wind that was blowing. Throwing down the sack, he shuffled the things inside it until it made a pillow, then sat down with his back to it. The girl sat down alongside him. Without a word, Willie took her in his arms and lay back. She didn't argue and simply crept close to him, her hand on his chest, her head against his shoulder. She was asleep within minutes.

When Willie woke, the girl was staring at him. Her features were good, he realised, under the streaky mud on her cheeks. Her nose was small and her mouth full and well shaped with a short upper lip. Her hair was black and straight and her eyes were dark brown, and long-lashed. Thank God she wasn't blonde, like Emmeline, he thought.

She continued to stare at him, appraising him, taking in his features. For a moment she said nothing as she saw he was awake, then she lifted her eyes to his. 'I don't even know your name,' she said.

'It's Willie,' he said. 'William really, but my Ma came from Glasgow and up there a lot of Williams are Willies. It's not a name for a baby.' He gestured. 'It always seemed a bit soft to me.'

'No.' She cocked her head to one side, weighing the name, considering it. 'I like Willie. It's an honest name, a –' she paused ' – a comfortable name.'

It was the first time anyone had ever thought anything like that, so Willie didn't argue.

'It's Willie Sarth,' he said. 'Ordinary sort of name for an ordinary sort of cove.'

'You're not ordinary,' she said. 'We're only here because of you. What do you do?'

'I was a sailor.' It sounded more interesting than clerk, and just then he wished he were still a sailor because there were no Boxers at sea. 'What's your name?'

'Abigail,' she said. 'Abigail Caddy. Abigail's biblical. It means "Father's joy". I guess I was my father's joy. At least until he died, I was. He just fell down dead. His heart, I guess. My mother died soon afterwards.'

'I'm an orphan, too,' Willie said.

'That's curious, isn't it? Two of us.' She seemed to be recovering a little as they talked. 'What happened to you?'

'I went to live with my brother. He was seven years older.'

'Were you happy?'

Willie considered. He had never really thought about that aspect of his youth. 'I think I must have been,' he said. 'We argued a bit, but he looked after me. One day, when I've made some money, I'm going to make it up to him. Were *you* happy?'

It was her turn to consider. 'Not really,' she said after a little thought. 'When my father died, my mother worked to keep me, but then she died and I was sent to an aunt in Seattle. She was a praying Baptist and there wasn't much fun. Church a lot. That sort of thing.'

'Is that why you came out here?'

She eyed him steadily. 'I had a call,' she said. 'It seemed the thing to do.'

'Did you like it?'

Her eyes never wavered. 'I had a call,' she said again. 'I told you. When you get a call, you don't argue with it.'

'What's a call like? Like receiving a telegram. "Report to God. You're needed." '

She flushed crimson. 'Now, I guess, you're being insulting.'

'I'm sorry. I don't know much about these things. I didn't intend to hurt you. We've got a long way to go still so it would be barmy to quarrel. Besides, I wouldn't want to upset you.'

She paused, then, like all Americans, didn't stand on ceremony and started to use his first name instinctively and easily. 'How old are you, Willie?'

'Old enough.' He was sensitive about his age. 'How about you?'

She, too, ignored the question. 'Why did you come to China?'

'I came to make my fortune.' Willie frowned. 'But I reckon fortunes aren't that easy to make, judging by what's happening at the moment.'

She smiled again. 'I expect you will, eventually.'

'I hope so.'

'I guess we know all about each other now.' The girl started to collect her belongings. 'Perhaps we ought to make a move.'

Willie took her hand and pulled her to her feet. 'I reckon when we reach safety, we ought to celebrate.'

'How?'

'A couple of drinks.'

She frowned. 'I've never touched intoxicating liquor,' she said. 'I took a vow.'

'You could break it just this once. After all, it'll be something to celebrate if we get away with – ' Willie stopped, aware of dropping a brick ' – our lives,' he ended lamely.

six

Before long they lost all count of time and had no idea where they were. Zychov's map seemed to be useless, but the truth was that they didn't really know how to associate the knobs and hills with the markings on the paper.

Every night, without thinking, they crowded close together and slept like two children. During the day they trudged on, bartering anything they could for food when their rations ran out. On one occasion, Willie managed to catch a guinea fowl – more by accident than design because, as he chased the flock, one of them darted under his feet and he fell over it, and it was Abigail who snatched it up and twisted its neck. When she set it down and looked at Willie, it promptly staggered to its feet and she screamed with horror, so that Willie had finally to despatch it with a blow from a stick.

They plucked the carcass and disembowelled it, then entered a wood where they cooked it over a fire of twigs. It was half-raw, but they devoured it hungrily, feeling full for the first time since they had left Shantu. His face greasy, his clothes covered with feathers from the plucking, Willie looked at Abigail, who smiled back at him. Now that they were away from Shantu, away from fear, she had recovered her spirits. The dark rings had gone from below her eyes and she even seemed to be enjoying herself.

Willie grinned back at her and, leaning over, kissed her gently on the cheek. 'You've been smashing, Abigail,' he said.

'Most people call me Ab,' she pointed out quietly. She sat still for a long time, her eyes on the dying fire. 'I've never been kissed by a man before, Willie,' she said. 'Only my father and I don't remember that much. My uncle never kissed me. He considered kissing bad.'

'Didn't he ever kiss your aunt?'

'I don't think so. He once tried to touch me.'

'Where?'

She placed her fingers on her breast. 'Here. I was frightened. That night I thought I ought to leave, so I went to the Pastor, and he suggested I leave home for my own safety.'

'And you came here?'

'Yes.'

'That was the call?'

She blushed, frowned and looked angry, then she lifted her head and stared him straight in the face. 'Yes,' she said. 'I guess that was it.'

Willie was silent for a moment. 'I bet he kissed a few other people on the quiet,' he said eventually

'I guess he probably did,' she agreed quietly.

When the rain came it turned the road into a quagmire and saturated them. But it was warm and humid and, huddling close together at night, they were able to hold off the worst of the night's cold. Because there was nothing else to do after dark they talked.

'That fortune you're going to make, Willie,' Abigail said. 'How're you going to set about it?'

'Dunno,' Willie admitted. 'I don't think I really gave it much thought. I think I felt that all I had to do was arrive here and there it would be – waiting.' He described his first transaction with the opium and how he had decided he couldn't reconcile it with his conscience.

'I think that was wonderful of you, Willie,' she said admiringly.

Willie thought so, too, but he had to admit that the real reason he hadn't touched it again was because he had been scared of being found out.

'There must be a thousand ways of making money in China,' she went on thoughtfully.

'I suppose you're right. But it never occurred to me that to sell goods in England – or China, for that matter – you've first got to have money to buy 'em. I wonder how many of these great taipans who've made their fortunes out here were dishonest at the beginning.'

Three days later, with the rains gone and the sun turning the mud into dust once more, they saw the glint of the river ahead.

'It must be the Peiho,' Willie said. 'It can't be anything else.' They consulted the bloodstained map and decided he was right. Sitting down, Willie took out his binoculars and studied the distant water. His gaze roamed over the banks idly. He could see a string of junks and sampans moving slowly upriver. They meant nothing at all to him until, as the binoculars shifted, he realised he was looking at a string of mules. They appeared to be pack mules, all heavily laden, and there appeared to be hundreds of them.

He sat up abruptly. Mules in that quantity surely weren't Chinese!

He glanced at Abigail, who was watching him intently, her eyes on his face, then stared through the binoculars again. This time he noticed there was a sameness about the clothes of the men who were working the mules, and it dawned on him he was staring at men in uniform, tall men, taller than Chinese, and wearing khaki trousers and dark shirts and what looked like cowboy hats. They were soldiers!

'Ab,' he yelled. 'It's the army! It's the relief force! They're coming up to relieve Peking! There they are. Hundreds of them! Mules and carts and junks! All moving up together! Look!'

He handed her the binoculars and she stared through them. It was a long time before she spoke, then she turned and stared soberly at Willie.

'That's the American uniform, Willie. Those are American soldiers.'

'Ab, we're saved! We're saved.' He flung his arms round her and hugged her, his cheek against hers. It was some time before he noticed she was hugging him back. He held her at arm's length, and they stared at each other, shining-eyed, then clutched each other again and started to dance in a lumbering sort of waltz on the rough ground, until they tripped and fell, rolling in the grass. When Willie sat up, he found Abigail's face within an inch of his own, tears running down her cheeks, her hair over eyes that were bright with joy.

He kissed her ecstatically and she kissed him back, clumsily, so that their noses got in the way, two young people delighted with their salvation. As they drew apart, he kissed her again, hugging her, cheek against cheek once more, but then she pushed him away and he saw she was blushing furiously.

'That'll be enough of that,' she said firmly.

Slowly, faintly awkward with each other, they gathered up their belongings.

'They're south of us,' Willie announced, staring towards the river. 'If we go due west, we're bound to appear at the river just ahead of them. They'll look after us. Come on, Ab.'

They set off in a rush, almost in a run, but after they had covered about a mile they realised they were pushing themselves too hard. The breath was rasping in their throats and their chests and lungs ached.

'It's no good, Willie,' Abigail said. 'I can't keep up with you.'

Willie gasped. 'I can't keep up – with me – either.' He gathered his breath. 'We've got to be sensible. It'll take all day to get to the river, but, if I know anything about that lot, it'll take them longer than that to reach the same point. Let's make sure we get there 'stead of rushin' it.'

The heat was at its unbearable worst. Perspiration blinded them as they stumbled ahead, shimmering heat waves lending an unreal air to their struggle as their pace slowed.

'From a frantic scramble to a mad rush,' Willie said.

They hardly dared stop to get their breath in case they were too late, struggling into the valleys and out of the other side, one eye always on the sun, terrified they would be lost. The didn't stop until evening, by which time they were close to the river, just behind the rolling hills that edged it.

'We've got to eat, Willie,' Abigail pointed out. 'Nobody can go on without eating.'

'We haven't much left,' Willie said. 'It's nearly all gone.'

'Then we'd better enjoy what's left so we've strength to go on through tomorrow.'

They ate what they had and settled down for the night. As usual they started back-to-back to keep each other warm, but when they woke, they were clutched in each other's arms. Scrambling to their feet, they swallowed the last crust of stale bread, and dumped as much of their equipment as they could, retaining only the sergeant's revolver and binoculars. Then they set off again, their progress still frighteningly slow. The roads were little more than gorges cut over the years by hooves and wheels, and turned by a sudden unexpected rainstorm into a morass through which they had to drag their feet.

They reached the river the following morning, but its winding course was empty. There was no sign of the junks they had expected, none of the mules, the waggons, the guns, the marching men.

'We're too late,' Abigail wailed.

Even as the tears of frustration, disappointment and fear came, however, they saw the first junk nose its way round the hill that marked the bend of the river. It was awkward-looking and angular with its square slatted sail, and, following it, came another, then another. Then they saw the first of the mules plodding along the road that topped the bank. They stared in silence, then turned to each other, Abigail in tears, Willie speechless with joy, and put their arms round each other silently.

To their surprise, the troops turned out to be Russian, not American, and neither group could understand anything the other said. The Russians were startled to see two Europeans and they were bustled along to see an officer who spoke a little English but was able to extract from them little more than the knowledge that Willie had come from Peking, and that when he had left it days before it had still been holding out. They seemed to think he was a deserter, but Abigail indignantly set them right on that score, when an interpreter was found at last, with the story of the rescue from Shantu and the ensuing massacre on the road.

They were given food and tea in glasses, Russian fashion, and they began to learn a little of what was happening. The relief they had expected weeks before, overwhelmed by the numbers of Boxers they were facing and a shortage of ammunition, had got not much further than Tientsin when it had had to retreat and, to secure its rear, had been obliged to set up an attack to capture the Taku Forts at the mouth of the Peiho. After that, it had taken time to get a second relief force organised, but eventually, with troops rushed from Europe, a force of 20,000 men of eight nationalities had been mustered. It appeared that the Russians were in the van of the force and behind them came British, Americans, Japanese and French. The advance had turned into a race, in fact, as each nationality strove for the glory of being first to the rescue, and out of the four hundred pack animals that had started the march north only a few were left, as they broke legs, died or fell into gorges. The US 6th Cavalry had not been able even to start because their horses were unfit after the long sea voyage and only a handful of Cossacks and Bengal Lancers were available for scouting purposes, while, plagued by supply problems, the Italians, Austrians and Germans had had to return to Tientsin and the French had been reduced to nothing more than a few sailors.

Though falling over themselves in their attempt to be gallant in front of Abigail, the Russians still seemed unable to decide what to do with her. And when the interpreter was sent off to contact the Americans and the British they were left without anyone to translate.

They were not sorry when the column reached the town of Fansan, where the Russians suggested they should wait for the Americans or the British. At first sight it seemed a good idea, because Fansan seemed an imposing place which had fallen to the Russian vanguard without a shot being fired, but on closer acquaintance the city walls turned out to be crumbling and gaping with holes, and along the river side they were festooned with washing. More flapped under the arches of the great iron-studded gates.

The Chinese regarded them with curiosity but without enmity as they pushed between the bustling coolies and water carriers, and the women carrying chickens in wicker baskets. Camel trains and shaggy sore-backed mules moved among the pedestrians picking their way round the heaps of dirt, where babies and scavenging pigs wallowed together. Chinese men, slouching and slovenly, watched impassively as a bunch of lunatics and criminals, tied together by their pigtails, struggled past, followed by nomad horsemen clutching toffee apples as they jogged past old ivoried men with fans and black-garbed peasants carrying aged relatives on their shoulders. The smell was one of sweat, fatigue, cooking oil and rice wine.

The streets were steep and moved down to the river in a flight of enormous stone steps, where the women sat to pick the lice from their children's hair, and there were no wheeled vehicles, only sedan chairs carried by coolies with callouses on their shoulders as big as oranges. There were no foreign business premises, but no sign of hostility to Willie and Abigail as they looked for somewhere safe to spend the night.

Eventually in a cellar they found what looked like an eating house. It had spidery antique tables of black wood that had been worn and polished for centuries, and was full of girls, bright as butterflies and chirruping like a flock of gaily coloured birds. At the entrance was a middle-aged woman in black, a pair of European satin bloomers with frills worn over her trousers. She seemed surprised to see Abigail, but made no comment.

The waiter's fingernails were long and his hands none too clean, but he was cheerful and, though it looked like the contents of a paint box, the food was good and no one seemed to mind. Through the clatter of crockery, men moved in and out of back rooms, nodding courteously to the couple as they passed, then a small orchestra of horns, gongs and one-stringed fiddles started. A man approached Abigail and whispered something to her she didn't understand, so he went to the woman in the satin bloomers, who marched across to them and tried to explain that the man wanted to take her upstairs, and it finally dawned on Willie where they were.

'Ab,' he gasped. 'We're in a – a – well, you know.'

'A brothel?'

He was surprised she knew the word, but he nodded speechlessly. 'You know about these things?'

'Sure I do. We once had to rescue a girl from one. But this one's different.' She looked at Willie in bewilderment. 'Everybody seems happy.'

With gestures, a lot of shouting and a few blushes, they explained their mistake to the Madame, who burst out in a high-pitched giggle that sounded like a macaw's chattering. One of the girls joined her, asking what the joke was, then she started laughing, too. Then the others joined them, together with one or two of the men, until the whole restaurant was laughing. The Chinese had a puckish sense of fun and the laughter was infectious, rippling round the room. Even Abigail joined in. Then Madame clapped her hands and wine and samshui appeared and she insisted they drink.

Abigail looked at Willie. 'I've never drunk intoxicating liquor, Willie,' she said nervously. 'I told you. I took the oath.'

'It might he a good idea just this once to break it,' Willie said. 'They're in a good mood. It might be as well to keep 'em in it.'

She nodded, frowning, and, picking up her glass, drained it at a gulp. Shuddering, her eyes beginning to water, she put it down on the table.

'Not like that,' Willie warned. 'Sip it. Make it last a long time.'

Before they knew what had happened, the glass had been refilled and Madame was gesturing to them to drink again. Abigail looked at Willie uncertainly, then she took another sip. The orchestra was going like mad now, all clangs and whistles and whines, but everybody was still laughing, and one of the girls, her face enamelled chalk-white, her lips henna-red, began to sing. Willie kept looking for a chance to make an exit, but it was impossible, and everybody seemed to want to go on enjoying the joke. Every time they took a sip from their glasses, Madame filled them up again. One of the men began to dance with one of the girls and gestured that Willie and Abigail should do the same.

'I've never danced in my life,' Abigail said.

'Time you learned.' Beginning to feel the effects of the drink, Willie was all stern manliness. He pulled her to her feet and they tried to waltz. It wasn't easy in the crowded room, especially since the orchestra wasn't playing a waltz, but it was pleasant to have his arm round Abigail's slim waist. She was light on her feet and managed to follow him after a fashion, her eyes never leaving his face, her expression faintly puzzled and doubtful.

Eventually, as the drink flowed more and more, a noisy free-for-all started, everybody jostling each other, and touched by the drink, Willie finally brought the house down by trying to teach Madame how to do the military two-step, learned at the Balham Methodist Church social evenings. The gathering had become a celebration by this time, the Chinese totally indifferent to the nationality of the two visitors.

Abigail was weeping with laughter as Willie returned to her and she leaned heavily against him, choking over her mirth. The party seemed to go on forever until Willie, watching the dancers, became aware that Abigail's weight against him had become heavy and inert. He looked at her in alarm and it dawned on him she was asleep. He tried to rouse her, but it was impossible, and he realised that, unused to alcohol, she was drunk. He began to wonder what on earth he was doing to do with her. They had nowhere to go because, caught up in the hilarity, they had forgotten all about accommodation.

The Madame approached and spoke to him. He didn't fully understand, but he caught the drift of her words. She was sympathetic and seemed to be indicating the stairs. She gestured with her arms as if she were lifting something and it dawned on Willie that she was indicating he should carry the sleeping Abigail. Getting his arms round her, he staggered to his feet and followed her, surrounded by murmured sympathy from the girls and the watching men. Stumbling up a narrow winding stone staircase, he was shown into a room where there was a wide bed on which a grubby blanket was spread. Madame indicated it and he laid his burden down.

Refusing the money he offered, Madame indicated that she had enjoyed the evening and closed the door behind her. Staring down at the sleeping Abigail, Willie moved round the bed. It was constructed of timber with wide strips of leather, and was as hard as a board. He wondered what he should do. He could hardly leave Abigail alone in case someone entered and, thinking she was one of Madame's girls, tried to climb in with her. Yet he could hardly sleep with her. She would be shocked and horrified. He decided he'd sleep on the floor and began to drag off her worn shoes, but she made no sign that she was conscious of it, so he sat on the edge of the bed to drag off his own cracked boots, wondering how hard the floor would be. The matter was taken out of his hands. What he'd drunk was making him unsteady too, and he overbalanced with one boot still on and the other in his hand and flopped down alongside the sleeping girl. He was too tired and too drunk to be bothered to move, so he simply dropped the boot on the floor, turned on his side and closed his eyes.

Coming to consciousness, Willie was aware of grey daylight coming through a small window covered with wax paper. For a minute or so he had no idea where he was. The ceiling consisted of beams, and the whitewashed walls, where a couple of lizards clung, were covered with dirty fingermarks. Then he realised someone was on the bed with him, and turning, he saw Abigail alongside him, her face full of apprehension.

He sat up abruptly. She didn't move, lying stiffly, her hands across her chest.

'What happened?' he asked.

Then he remembered. 'Madame said we could sleep here,' he said. 'I was going to sleep on the floor, but I fell asleep here instead.' He indicated his foot still in his boot. 'I didn't even take my boots off.'

She was still lying rigidly, staring at him nervously.

'It's all right, Ab,' he reassured her. 'I didn't do anything. I promise. Nothing happened. I never laid a finger on you.'

'Why not?'

He stared at her, and she tried to explain. 'I thought something *always* happened. I thought that was why men slept with women.'

Willie's face cracked in a grin. 'It never crossed my mind,' he said.

'Are you sure?' she asked again.

'Quite sure. I wouldn't do that, Ab.'

'I thought men were lustful. "Watch and pray, that ye enter not into temptation...the flesh is weak." Matthew, 26, 41.'

'It isn't all like that,' Willie explained. 'Some men respect girls. I do.'

He thought briefly of Emmeline, but pushed her hurriedly out of his mind, consoling himself with the thought that all that had gone on between them had been Emmeline's doing, not his.

Abigail said nothing for a while then she sat up slowly, examining herself, as if she were checking that her clothing had not been disarranged. Then she passed the back of her hand across her forehead.

'I have a headache,' she said.

'I'm not surprised,' Willie admitted. 'The way you were knocking back that stuff.'

'Was I drunk?'

'A bit.'

'Did I do anything foolish?'

'Only fall asleep on me. I carried you up here.'

She said nothing for a long time, then she gave a little hiccupping giggle. 'It *was* funny, wasn't it, Willie?' she said, and he realised that probably never in her whole life, thanks to her upbringing, had she ever known the pleasure of genuine laughter.

'Yes it was,' he agreed. 'We laughed a lot. You laughed a lot.'

She frowned. 'I haven't ever laughed much, Willie.'

'Time you started.'

'My uncle considered it sinful to laugh.'

'Laughter's always worth a guinea a box. Having a good laugh's better than any medicine.'

She nodded, frowning as she did so. 'I must laugh more,' she said.

Willie grinned and put his arm round her shoulder. 'Leave it to me, Ab,' he said. 'I'll teach you.'

seven

British troops entered Fansan during the morning, with the Americans just behind. The day was hot, with shimmering heat waves hanging in the air, and in their heavy uniforms they were half-blinded by perspiration. They had fought a battle at Yangsun and another at Hosiwu before pushing on to Matou, Changchiawan and Fansan.

As Willie and Abigail ran forward to meet them, the officer in the lead held up his hand and the column behind, heads down, marching blindly, stumbled into each other before they came to a halt, cursing and panting in the heat.

The officer waited with is hand on his revolver as Willie moved forward, then he jerked it out and pointed. 'Stop,' he shouted. 'Halt there, Chinese!'

'Fat lot of good that would be if I *was* Chinese,' Willie snorted. 'I wouldn't have understood, would I?'

The revolver lowered. 'Who're you?'

'Willie Sarth. From Peking. This is Abigail Caddy.'

'Is she from Peking, too?'

'No, sir. She's from the Mission at Shantu. We set out to rescue 'em. We're all that's left. Just the two of us.'

'What about the rest?'

'Massacred.'

The officer seemed to have some difficulty believing Willie. 'Shantu's well north of here,' he said.

'We walked. Trying to escape. We saw the junks and came to meet you.'

Other officers had now joined the first, then a man with red tabs on his collar appeared, and in no time they were whipped to the rear and found themselves facing a tall old man with sagging cheeks and a drooping white moustache. Since he seemed to tell all the others what to do, Willie decided he was a general.

'How were they in Peking when you left?' he asked.

'Tired. They'll be more tired still now. We left over a week ago and we've been wandering around ever since.'

'Are they still fighting?'

'I don't know,' Willie admitted. 'There weren't a lot of 'em and there were a lot of Boxers.'

As they spoke, another senior officer in a different uniform, a man with a clipped moustache, glittering eyes and a jaw like the prow of a battleship, cantered up.

'What's holding us up?' he demanded.

The first man turned. 'Ah, General Chaffee,' he said. 'We have here someone who got out of Peking.'

'It's fallen?'

'He doesn't know.'

'We need to find out.'

'I suspect we do.'

The man with the white moustache indicated the iron-jawed officer. 'This is General Chaffee, leading the American contingent,' he explained. 'I'm General Gaselee leading the British contingent. The Russians are just ahead.'

'We bumped into them. They said you were coming.'

'We are indeed.' Gaselee turned to an officer alongside him. 'Frank, see these two young people are fed and then we'll talk.'

Later, full of food and clad in British army shirts, they sat in a tent as the relief force occupied Fansan. The day was being spent resting, regrouping and waiting for the riverborne supplies to catch up. With two reasonably easy victories under their belts, the relief troops were heady with visions of glory and loot. The abandoned compound of an American mission had been chosen as suitable to set up a market for the buying of local produce, but an American missionary, attached to the staff, objected bitterly.

'You'd do better, General, to have nothing to do with these savages,' he said. 'What you ought to do is make a gigantic bonfire of the place. It will teach the Chinese the lesson of their lives and the people in Peking will see the glow at night and know we're coming.'

Gaselee glanced at the American general alongside him. 'I think,' he said gently, 'that perhaps we should not. There are three hundred and fifty million people in China and we have no wish to antagonise them all.'

Rumours were rampant that Peking had succumbed and officers suggested that their approach would cause the death of the diplomats and civilians in Peking.

'That's always a possibility,' Gaselee agreed. 'But to the best of our knowledge, the defenders are still fighting and the patrols have reported no signs of organised resistance ahead of us.'

They picked Willie's brains about the approaches to the capital and the plan that was outlined was that each nation's troops should direct its assault at a different gate in the city walls and that they would bivouac three miles outside for the night before the massive co-ordinated assault took place. The plan's simplicity appealed, chiefly because no single detachment would get in another detachment's way, and there would be no nationalistic recriminations.

The following day was gloomy, a lowering grey sky pressing down, the air thick and oppressive in the enervating summer heat. From the direction of Peking they could hear the crash of rifle fire, rolling over the intervening distance like thunder, and they learned that the Boxers had launched a last furious attack, hoping to overwhelm the defenders in one crushing onslaught before the relief arrived.

Moving out in parallel routes towards the city through a downpour of luke-warm rain, each column headed for its predesignated gate, the British on the left with the Americans on their right, then the French, the Japanese and finally the Russians. Abigail was riding in one of the British waggons, a sergeant alongside her with orders to see that she was not troubled by the attentions of the troops tramping past, their eyes full of lust. Willie was up with the leading files in the not very sanguine hope that he might be able to lead them into the city.

Maintaining order soon became impossible. The rain had turned the fields into a quagmire and the soldiers slipped and fell in the thick mud and their rifles became clogged and jammed. The heat was appalling and all the time the irrigation ditches criss-crossing the line of march further disrupted the approach. Villages, pagodas, temples, all caused detours, and sunken roads scattered the troops even further. As the advance began to become disorganised, when the order to bivouac was given three miles from Peking everybody flung themselves down to regain their breath, their ears full of the distant rattle of musketry.

'The Chinese have got in,' someone said.

'They were always in,' Willie pointed out. 'It's a Chinese city.'

There was a deluge during the night, and Willie fought vainly to stay dry and obtain sleep. At midnight rifle fire started from the direction of the Tung Pien Men gate, the American target, and they learned that the Russians, advancing ahead of time, had found an opening and had become trapped between the inner and outer gates of the city walls in a courtyard constructed for that very purpose.

The attack signaled the beginning of the race to be first into the city. The French turned up in the wrong place, the Japanese relied on artillery, and the Americans scaled the wall with ladders and ropes near the Tung Pien Men gate. Humping a rifle once more and sweating and drenched in the rain, Willie was with the British as they pounded through the Hsia Kuo Men gate. At the other side, they came to a full stop, in the deserted streets of the Chinese city, south of the Tartar Wall, which cut them off effectively from the besieged Legations on the north side in the Tartar City.

As they clustered together, nervously staring about them, the officers, determined not to allow the impetus to slow and the initiative to be lost, urged them to push forward. They moved rapidly at first until the eerie silence that engulfed the place slowed them down, and they began to inch forward cautiously in the shadows, using doorways, walls and corners to protect them from an unexpected fusillade.

'It's a trap,' an officer alongside Willie said. 'Where the hell are the Boxers?'

As they turned the corner, they came in sight of the vast bulk of the Tartar Wall looming ahead of them. Three flags, American, British and Russian, hung lifeless in the still air.

'They're still holding out,' the officer said.

'No.' Another officer halted him as he began to move forward. 'Listen.'

The silence was deep and no sound came from the Legations.

'That can only mean one thing. They're all dead.'

Gaselee appeared, riding through the jostling men. 'What's holding us up?' he demanded.

'I think there's no hope of finding anyone alive, sir.'

'What about those flags?'

'A ruse, sir? To lead us on?'

Gaselee studied the flags. He was an old man and he looked tired, but he shook his head. 'There's no choice. We push on.'

There was a surge forward, but there was no means of climbing the walls, no sign of life on them, and no sign of an entrance. Willie pushed forward.

'General, sir. There's an opening over here where the canal comes through. Right next to the American Legation. At the other side, the road leads straight to the British Legation.'

'You sure, young man?'

'Yes, sir. I know it because that's the way we came out when we left for Shantu. It stinks a bit, sir, but – '

'Never mind, young man. Show us.'

His heart thumping, Willie led the way towards the seven-foot tunnel they had used for their exit. The smell alone directed them to the entrance and, as they halted again, a man appeared on the wall high above and began to signal with a pair of blue and white flags.

'What's he say?'

A signaller read the moving flags.

' "Come in by tunnel", sir.'

'Tell him we're already on our way.'

Indian troops, tall men in turbans, wrenched away the rotting iron grille and plunged forward. Above them they heard shouts and yells as Americans and Russians united in a charge to drive the Boxers from the Chien Men, and Sikhs, naked to the waist, their long hair flowing, their legs thick with slime, their faces gaunt with weariness, began to appear on the north side of the wall. As they swarmed out on to a set of tennis courts waving their rifles, they heard a low cheer and saw men coming towards them. There were a few last shots as the Chinese bolted and, rounding a corner looking for somewhere familiar, Willie found himself face to face with what must have been the last pocket of resistance. For a second, he found himself gazing at furious yellow faces surmounted by strips of red and realised he was staring straight into the blunderbuss muzzle of a gingal.

'Oh, Christ!' he yelled and dived over a low wall just as the huge gun went off. A rusty nail caught him in the behind and carried him the rest of the way, while the remainder of the charge of scrap iron, nails and bolts swept aside half a dozen Sikhs before the rest of the party plunged forward with their bayonets and wiped out the gun crew.

Lying on his face, his trousers wet with blood, tears of pain running down his cheeks, Willie listened to the noise die down until he could hear only the cries of joy at the relief. Then he heard a female voice that he recognised as that of Sir Claude MacDonald's wife, high pitched, sure of itself and confident.

'General Gaselee,' she was saying. 'How good of you to come!'

Someone started to yell, then there was a call for three cheers and the hysterical yelling started again. Willie was convinced he was drawing his last breaths and – what was more – was going to draw them alone and unnoticed. At the other side of the wall, he could hear men lifting the bodies of the Sikhs who had been killed in the last desperate discharge of the ancient gun and realised that, hidden as he was, nobody was aware he was there.

'Help,' he called out. 'I think I'm dying.'

Sitting up in bed in the hospital, much of it emptied of wounded now that, with the arrival of the Relief Force, other places had become available, Willie found himself staring at the face of Sir Claude MacDonald. Behind him was General Gaselee, with General Chaffee and other officers of various nationalities.

'You did well, my boy,' the Minister said. 'You'll be suitably rewarded.'

He listened with a grave face as Willie described the massacre near Shantu, then he leaned forward and placed an envelope in front of Willie. 'A small gift, my boy,' he announced. 'From Legation Funds. All the legations contributed, to say nothing of a few civilians.'

Willie stared at the packet, startled to realise he was considered a hero, then Gaselee motioned to an officer beside him, who stepped forward with a little canvas bag which he placed on the bed.

'Somethin' to be going on with,' he said, faintly embarrassed. 'Officers had a whip round, y'know. To show their appreciation. Everybody joined in. Americans, Russians, Japanese, British. Probably saved us a lot of casualties, findin' the sluice gate.'

Finally Lady MacDonald did the same – 'From the grateful ladies of the Legations,' she said.

Willie was about to protest that he hadn't found the gate but had had it pointed out to him as he'd left the city for Shantu, but before he could speak everybody turned away. Then he realised he ought to have reported Zychov for bolting, but by the time he remembered, the group was moving down the room to talk to other wounded men and he decided that, since Zychov wouldn't have survived, perhaps it didn't matter. He stared at the packets in front of him, a little dazed and wondering how much there was in them. When he counted it, he was startled at the amount.

He asked himself what had happened to Abigail, whom he had last seen riding on a baggage cart, and he began to realise he was missing her cheerful optimism.

By this time the streets of Peking were littered with the scarlet trappings of the fleeing Boxers, but there was still a little fighting going on to the north, where the siege at the North Cathedral still had to be raised. But the Imperial Court had fled, dressed as peasants, and were said to be wandering the countryside somewhere, wet, miserable and desperate for food. Peking was different, though, and some people, chiefly those who had kept themselves safe in the dug-outs during the siege, were already beginning to look back on their ordeal with some nostalgia. The Boxers had made themselves hated by foreigners and Chinese alike for their butchery, looting and rape, but with the end of the siege the foreign troops had proved to have even more voracious appetites. Shops and warehouses, even the Forbidden City, were not immune. The stories that filtered through to the hospital indicated that temples and audience rooms had been plundered and precious jewels had been stolen, while Chinese women of all ranks had been molested. Social rank had even seemed to increase the lust and whole families had committed suicide to expunge the shame.

When a victory parade was organised for all the Allied forces, some of the patients from the hospital were carried down to watch. To Willie's amazement, prominent among the Russians was Zychov.

'The Russians are going to give him a medal for his attempt to rescue the people from Shantu,' he was told.

'Rescue 'em?' Willie snorted. 'The bugger ran away!'

Nobody believed him and he watched with smouldering eyes as Zychov marched past at the head of a company of men, smart in his splendid naval dress uniform, his moustache waxed, his cap worn rakishly over one eye, his sword at the carry.

Scowling, Willie shifted uncomfortably on the litter. They had dug the old nails and bird shot from his backside and the pain was subsiding, though it was still difficult to move. It had dawned on him by now that for the first time in his life he had funds. It wasn't the fortune he had set out to find, but it was a step in the right direction.

He was still considering what to do with it, and wishing Abigail would appear so he could tell her about it, when he heard a voice at the end of the ward, imperious and important.

'Sarth's the name,' it was saying. 'William Sarth. He worked for my father and I want to see him.'

'Oh, Gawd,' he said out loud. 'Emmeline!'

She didn't seem to have suffered greatly during the siege and he knew that she hadn't got herself too involved with the fighting or the nursing – or even with the cooking and caring for those who did. He also knew that she had been gathering supplies round her for some time before the alarm had gone so that she'd had enough little titbits in the form of tinned, bottled or jellied foods to keep her going for a long time.

She was dressed in a smart blue dress and a wide flowered hat, and she swept down the ward towards him, brushing aside a volunteer nurse who tried to protest.

'Willie,' she said, arriving at his bedside.

He barely managed to meet her eyes. ''Lo,' he muttered.

'You might sit up when a lady appears.'

Willie glared. 'If you had a lot of old nails and pieces of scrap metal in you,' he said indignantly, '*you'd* be careful how you moved.'

She managed to look interested. 'Were you wounded?'

'Yes.'

'Where?'

'In the bum.'

'I meant where did it happen?'

'Near the tennis court. Last shot of the match I reckon. I was lucky. It killed five other fellers.'

She found a chair and sat down by the bed. 'They tell me you're going to get a decoration. For leading in the relieving forces.'

'I didn't lead 'em in. I just showed 'em the way, that's all.'

'It was brave.'

'No, it wasn't. I was surrounded by soldiers. Nothing brave about that.'

'All the same it will be nice to have a medal to show for it. I shall be coming to take you home.'

Willie made no comment and she went on without noticing his lack of enthusiasm. 'Father's home already,' she said. 'Tired, of course, but making more of it than he need. He wasn't hurt. He's thinking of letting us take over the business.'

'Us?'

'You and me.'

'Emmeline, I –'

'Just don't worry, Willie.' Emmeline's voice was as aggressively certain as ever. 'I'll handle everything. Just leave it to me. I'll be back tomorrow.'

When she'd gone, Willie lay staring at the wall, his mind busy. How was he going to get out of this one, he wondered. Until the siege, he had accepted Emmeline's forceful attentions because he was too inexperienced to do otherwise. But he hadn't enjoyed playing second fiddle, summoned to the presence like a – like a bloody bull to serve a cow, he thought savagely.

How the hell did he get out of it, though? Emmeline clearly had plans for him and he wondered if he could get a job with the British Legation. They obviously thought highly of him and there would be a lot of new jobs going now. The city had been carefully partitioned, different nations governing different zones, but the population of Peking had shrunk, thousands of people fleeing before the relieving force and a lot slow to return. He was still wondering what the future held when he heard Abigail's voice.

'Hello, Willie.'

In his eagerness to see her, he heaved himself round too quickly and yelped with pain as it tugged at his wounds.

'Oh, my God,' he whispered, sinking back, tears in his eyes.

'What is it, Willie? They said you were hurt. Is it serious?' Through the blur of tears he saw the concern in her eyes.

'No,' he managed. 'It's not serious. I was lucky. I missed most of it. All I got was a couple of rusty nails and a bit of bird shot in my bum.'

She stared, giggled, then stopped and composed her face. 'I'm sorry, Willie,' she said. 'I shouldn't have laughed.'

'No, you shouldn't,' he agreed. Then he managed a grin. 'But it's a barmy place to get shot, isn't it?'

'Will it take long to get better?'

'Few more days then I'll be able to sit properly. I can walk a bit already.'

'Willie, I was worried. You disappeared. I thought I'd never see you again.'

'Did it matter?'

'Of course it did. After all we went through.'

He stared at her small anxious face, wondering why he'd never noticed before how attractive she was.

'Ab,' he said, 'you're ever so pretty.'

She blushed. 'Am I?'

'Didn't you know?'

'I was always told it was sinful to think about yourself like that.'

'What happened to you?' he asked. 'Where are you living?'

'In the city. I've found a room with two Americans called Sumter.'

'Missionaries?'

'Sort of. They took me in when they learned I had nowhere to go. They said I could take you there, too. There's room.'

Alarm flooded over him at the memory of Emmeline. 'When, Ab?'

'As soon as you're better.'

'Let's go now.'

'You can't, Willie. You might start bleeding again.'

'You've done some nursing. You told me so. You can bandage me.'

She stared at him, shocked, then her face creased in a wide grin. 'Willie!'

'Somebody's got to. Nurses do it here. Why can't you do it there?'

'Well, I guess I could. But not yet, surely?'

'I've got to, Ab.'

'Why?'

'Because – because – ' Willie paused, then gave her the whole story. At least, not the *whole* story, but enough of it to let her know how Emmeline had her eye on him and wanted to take him back to run the business.

'I don't want to run the bloody business,' he said.

'What'll you do?'

'I've got some ideas.' He reached out for her hand. 'Ab, I've come by some money. They're going to give me a medal and they all had a whip round for me because they said that by leading them into the city, I'd saved a lot of

108

lives. Everybody was at it. You'd be surprised how much it comes to.'

'What are you going to do with it, Willie?'

'Use it to make my fortune, like I always planned.' He was suddenly alarmed. 'What about you? You're not going back to Shantu, are you?'

'I couldn't.' She shuddered.

'So what then? Missionary somewhere else?'

There was a long silence before she spoke. 'I think I've become a bit disillusioned with missionary work, Willie,' she said eventually. 'I think I had been for some time. Ever since the day I was talking to the converts about Jesus and one of them said "Who's he? He's nobody from here." ' She managed a little giggle. 'I think they thought he was a tax collector. I don't think they were very interested, anyway. I think *we* got more spiritual comfort out of it than they did.'

'Let's set up together then.'

'To do what?'

'I don't know. Anything. Business. Whatever you like. Open a teahouse.'

'You won't make a fortune at that.'

'There are a lot of people in this city who'd like a good cup of tea and some buns. First thing, though, you've got to get me out of here before Emmeline comes back.'

'*She's come back!*'

The voice, sharp and authoritative, made Willie's head jerk round. Emmeline, not Willie, had always made the running, but now she even seemed to be dictating everything he thought and did.

'I've got a sedan chair outside,' she announced.

Willie scowled. 'I can't sit down.'

'You'll manage, I'm sure. Father's waiting for you. I've got a proper contract drawn up. In two years he relinquishes the business – if he doesn't kill himself with gin first.' She turned to Abigail. 'Get him up, please, nurse. Where are his clothes?'

Abigail's small face set. 'I'm not the nurse,' she said.

'Then who are you and what are you doing sitting there?'

It seemed to be time for Willie to speak up. 'She's with me,' he said. 'We went all the way down from Shantu to Fansan together.'

Emmeline stared down her nose at Abigail, then she turned again to Willie. 'Ask for your clothes, Willie,' she commanded. 'We have better things to do than stand here chatting to some cheap little chit you've picked up.'

'Hey – !'

Willie was just about to protest when Abigail saved him the trouble. Just as she had with Willie, she swung her arm with all her strength and her hand connected with a whack against Emmeline's cheek. As Emmeline staggered back, her hat over one eye, a livid red mark on her cheek, she caught her heels against a stool, lost her balance and sat down heavily.

'Nine,' intoned one of the wounded Americans at the other side of the ward, 'ten, out. Boys, we got a new champion.'

For what seemed minutes, Emmeline sat staring at Abigail, her face suffused with fury. Abigail stood over her, her small fists clenched, as though she were prepared to go the requisite number of rounds if necessary. Then she turned away abruptly and, taking advantage of her indifference, Emmeline climbed to her feet, shoved her hat straight and stalked for the door.

'You as good with your left, Miss?' the American asked. 'That sure was the prettiest right hook I ever seen.'

Blushing furiously, Abigail turned to Willie. 'I'll get your clothes,' she said.

eight

The Sumters, the American couple who had loaned Abigail a room, had set up a small dispensary in the Chinese City. They were a quiet couple, dedicated to their work, and they asked no questions.

When Willie appeared, they supported him to his room and helped him to sit down, still without asking questions, then they provided tea and left them to it.

'I think,' Willie said, 'that we ought to get away from here before too long.'

Abigail's face was concerned. 'Because of – of her?'

'Yes.'

I saw her this morning, Willie. When I was out with Mrs Sumter. She was riding in a chair, looking very high and mighty. She was just stopping at their office. It's open again and they've got a clerk in there. Mrs Sumter says he's a deserter from the French army. She says they have to sleep under the counter or something. She's a wicked woman.'

'She is?' Willie was all innocence.

'Mrs Sumter said she's the reason why they could never keep their clerks. Did she –' Abigail's eyes were large. '– did she ever try – well, you know – with you.'

'Never!' Willie lied stoutly. 'But I hadn't been there long. Perhaps she hadn't got round to it. All the same – ' he frowned ' – she's not going to like being pushed about. They worked me to the bone.'

'She'll not find us here.'

'And we've got a little money to live on.'

Emmeline never turned up and at the end of the fortnight Willie was walking normally, itching to be using the money that had been given him to make that elusive fortune he was after. Not for one minute did it occur to either of them to go their separate ways.

'What about tea?' Abigail suggested. 'Everybody wants tea. You could sell China tea in England, buy other things in England, and sell them in India, then pick up Indian tea and sell it here.'

'It sounds pretty complicated,' Willie said. 'And bulky too. And we'd have to charter a ship for it, or part of a ship, and I haven't that much money.'

'Cotton? The Chinese like cotton cloth.'

'I don't know much about it, do you? I reckon I'd get diddled.'

Loath to commit too hurriedly the money Willie had been given, they discussed the making of his fortune day after day, moving about the narrow streets of the city, studying the shops in the hope of deciding on some useful commodity that was easy to import, cheap to buy and profitable to sell. But for the most part the ordinary Chinese didn't appear to have enough money for there to be any profit in selling anything to them and the wealthy Chinese who had sides with the Empress had fled into the hinterland with her, while the Europeans and those wealthy Chinese who had remained behind obviously weren't going to buy from an unknown like Willie.

He was beginning to grow depressed. For the first time in his life he had a little money and he didn't know what to do with it, and the longer they remained idle the less it became, because, though the Sumters didn't ask for it, they had to be paid for food and the roof over their heads.

Then, sitting in Willie's room, sharing the edge of the bed because there was nowhere else to sit, Abigail had an idea. Willie had flung himself back on the blankets and was staring at the ceiling with blank eyes, his mind a void, drifting and empty of ideas.

'Willie,' she said slowly. 'I went back once to Seattle. I was sick and, because I had some money of my own, they sent me home to get over it. I took a few things I'd bought here with me to show people. Little bits of jade and carved ivory I'd found. That sort of thing. My uncle said they were junk and threw them away, but I rescued them and, when I became short of money, I tried to sell them in a shop. They said the same. But when I went to San Francisco to catch the ship back, I tried again and *they* thought they were good. They gave me a lot of money for them. 'Least, I thought it was a lot, but it wasn't really, because the next day I went past the shop again and there they were in the window, being offered at three times the price I'd been given.'

'That was a rotten thing to do!'

'Perhaps. But it's business, Willie. Suppose you bought a lot of these things and took them to the States. Or to London. And offered them. You could, because they're not very big. Would people buy them?'

Willie stared at the ceiling. 'They might,' he agreed. 'They're going for oriental things a lot these days. Fans.

Japanese pictures. That sort of thing. Perhaps it's the beginning of a fashion. Where did you get 'em, Ab?'

'I bought them in Shantu. They're all over the place in Shensi province. They carve them all the time. They don't think much of them there, though, and I even had several given. When someone was ill and we nursed them that's how they tried to pay. We once went as far south as Sian, the capital. It's one of the cultural centres of this part of China. I found some more there and bought them for myself. There are a lot of them here in Peking, too. I've seen them. Loot. Picked up by soldiers after the relief.'

'Do you know anything about the stuff? Its value? That sort of thing? I don't.'

She thought for a moment. 'Yes. Not its value, of course. That's something we'd have to find out. But it seems to be very valuable if it's sold somewhere other than in China. And I was interested in it while I was here. I read it up a bit.'

'Would it cost much to buy this stuff?'

'They almost give it away. I don't think the Chinese know its value and money's more important to them. They live a pretty primitive life and the most important thing is feeding themselves. If we could give them money, I think they'd sell all right.'

Willie took her hands in his. 'Ab,' he said. 'I think you might have got something. We could take a few suitcases full of these things home. Pack 'em ourselves to save money. Perhaps even a crate or two. Take 'em to London or somewhere –'

'You could go to London and I could go to San Francisco. That way we'd find the best market.'

He looked at her, one arm round her slender waist. 'You ever been in business before, Ab?' he asked.

'My uncle kept a store. I had to help in it. I learned a bit about buying and selling.'

'And I learned a bit about book-keeping because I was an accounts clerk. Ab, I think we've got a business. But it would mean going back to Shantu.'

He wasn't very keen on such a journey. He'd met a Frenchman called Pierre Loti, who was a reporter for one of the French newspapers, who had told him of the horrors he'd seen committed by Allied troops in Tungchow, only twelve miles to the east of Peking, and the memory of the massacre near Shantu was still vivid in his mind.

'Not just me,' he went on. 'You, too. Because I don't know anything about these things or where to find 'em. You'd have to show me. Could you do that?'

She looked at him quickly, nervously. 'They – all those people – they wouldn't still be there, would they?'

'No, Ab. They'll all have been taken away and buried by now.'

'I don't think I –' she paused and her chin came up ' – yes, Willie, I guess I could force myself to go up there with you.'

'It'd be primitive.'

'There couldn't be anything more primitive than the mission.'

'We'd have to live in all sorts of places.'

'Do you want me to?'

He stared up at her and took her hand in his. 'Yes, Ab, I do.'

'Okay, then, I'll come.'

His hand caressed her fingers. 'Ab,' he said. 'You're beautiful.'

'Because I'll go to Shantu with you?'

'You're always beautiful. You've got nice eyes and a nice mouth. But I think most of it comes from inside.'

She blushed. 'You shouldn't say those things, Willie.'

Willie's other arm encircled her and he pulled her to him. For a second they stayed together, their faces only an inch or two apart, then his hand slipped underneath the army shirt she was still wearing. Above the cotton trousers he felt the warm skin in the hollow of her back, and the sudden quivering tension of her body.

She shuddered again, then suddenly she was murmuring soft endearments to him, her face hidden in the curve of his neck, her fingers digging into his muscles.

'Oh, Willie!'

At her cry, Willie's arm tightened round her, holding her to him until the shaking stopped. As she allowed herself to relax, he could hear her whispering and for a while he lay motionless, his arm round her quivering frame. Then, moving on the bed, he allowed her to slip down and lay alongside him, before reaching up and pulling the blanket over them both. As he reached for her, she caught at his hands, but not to put them away. As she pulled him to her she was mouthing little pleading sounds in his ear.

For a long time they lay still, in the silence of the darkening room, then Abigail gave a little giggle. 'I'm lost, Willie,' she whispered. 'I'm a lost woman.'

The sheet had slipped to the floor and Willie was far away. Their lovemaking had been clumsy because he was young and she was innocent and a little afraid. But there had been bells. There had definitely been bells. Emmeline had been older and experienced and more skilful, but there had never been bells. Not even a tiny tinkle.

'Willie – '

'What?' He realised she was addressing him. 'What is it, Ab?'

'I said I'm a lost woman.'

'No, you're not.' He smiled. 'Perhaps, in fact, you just found yourself.'

'But that's what they always said about it,' she went on in a quiet, troubled voice. There was a long pause. 'That you're lost when you do that. They warned us against it.'

'Who did?'

'In Sunday School. At church. The wages of sin is death, they kept saying. Romans, 6, 23. And that, they reckoned, was the worst sin of all. They said it was worse than that, in fact.' She paused. 'Is it always like this, Willie?'

He almost put his foot in it and, thinking of Emmeline, nearly said, yes, it was. But he caught himself in time. 'I suppose it is,' he said, injecting a great deal of thought into the comment as though he were extremely doubtful but still full of hope.

'Does it get better?'

Willie was more cautious this time. 'I reckon so,' he said. 'Experience and all that. Especially if you always do it with the same person.' He felt old and wise. 'Love and trust have got to come into it, I reckon.'

'Do you trust me, Willie?'

'I'd trust you with my last farthing.'

'What about love?'

He paused before he answered 'yes' and she looked quickly at him. 'Aren't you sure?'

He laughed. 'I'm sure,' he said. 'I was just considering it to make certain. It's an important question.'

'It sure is.'

'But I'm sure.'

She was silent for a moment. She was older than Willie and to him she was wise and womanly in a way Emmeline had never been. But, after the arid life she had lived at Shantu, she had felt she had known nothing of the outside world beyond the mission. Yet she guessed Willie was lonely and, for once, a bit lost, but at the mission she had begun to feel she would never know love and was conscious of a deep motherly feeling towards this young man into whose company she had fallen. She was glowing with life and, inspired by his warmth, when he had put his hand to her throat, she had caught it and put it to her bosom. Conscious of his kisses and the hands that tugged at her clothing she had pressed him to her.

'How old are you, Willie?' she asked.

'Twenty-four,' he lied.

'No, you're not. I saw it written on a paper on your bed in the hospital.'

He flushed, looking very young. 'Well, no,' he admitted. 'Not exactly.'

'You're a lot younger than I am, aren't you? It's not usual for a man to be younger than the woman. Would it matter?'

'Don't see why it should.'

'I'd need to feel loved, Willie. I wouldn't want a man just to use me.'

He put his arm round her and drew her close. The affection in the gesture was implicit and she was silent for a moment. Then she spoke slowly.

'It sure was nice,' she said. 'I guess you'll *have* to marry me now, to make me an honest woman.'

'I reckon we're already as much married as we'll ever be,' Willie said sagely.

'I guess we are. Do you *want* to marry me, Willie?'

'I'll marry you tomorrow if that's what you want.'

She gave another little giggle. 'I'm not sure it's worth it. My uncle and aunt never seemed to get much fun out of being married. And, as you say, we're as much married as we'll ever be. Besides, gettin' married costs money, doesn't it? Let's save it to buy more things from Shantu to sell in the States.'

'Okay. So now we're married.' Willie made a circle of his thumb and forefinger and, taking her left hand, shaped it round the second finger. 'With this ring I thee wed,' he said. 'How's that?'

'Say it all.'

'For richer, for poorer. In sickness in health. As long as we both shall live. Now you.'

'Okay. Forsaking all others, me only unto thee, so long as we both shall live.'

She sat up, her back curved as she bent over him, her small breasts warm against his chest, a wing of black hair across her face. She was silent for so long he sat up with her.

'What's the matter, Ab?' he asked.

'I've never seen a man without his clothes before.' She paused. 'Well, no, I guess that's not right. I've seen the coolies bathing in the river at the mission. But that's different. They always hid themselves as much as they could and, besides, they're not white like us. You're beautiful, too, Willie.'

'I am?'

'Yes. Strong. Able.' She suddenly seemed to realise she was naked, too, and covered her breasts, then she lowered her hands. 'I guess it doesn't matter now,' she said. 'Seeing each other without clothes. Not now we're married.'

Willie smiled. 'We ought to celebrate,' he suggested. 'You don't get married every day.'

She lay back and reached out to him her face suffused with pleasure.

'It's just as it says in the Good Book, Willie,' she said. 'Ecclesiastes. There's a time for every purpose under the heaven. A time to be born. A time to lie. A time to kill and a time to heal. A time to weep. A time to laugh, a time to embrace, a time to love.' She pulled him down to her. 'Oh, Willie,' she said. 'I'm not lonely any more. I'm so happy. I sure am happy and I can't think of a better way to celebrate getting married than in the way we're celebrating it already.'

She looked at him tenderly, aware of his straight nose, crisp dark hair and steady brown eyes. Even when he was bewildered and puzzled, uncertain of himself, he had a capable look, the look even, she thought delightedly, of a buccaneer, some modern John Paul Jones. Suddenly she felt incredibly fortunate. Her life had often been lonely and frustrating and, in the last few years, empty, so that she had begun to come to the conclusion that it would always be solitary. But here was this young man – good-looking by any standards – sweeping her away, wanting to share his life with her.

He grinned at her. 'We ought to tell the Sumters,' he said. 'Will they mind?'

'Not they.'

'Let's tell 'em then.'

As he made to move away, she was caught by a feeling of overpowering love and warmth towards him and wanted nothing more than to prove it to him.

Holding on to him, she pulled him closer. 'Later,' she said. 'Later.'

nine

The road to Shantu had been cleared, but the mission had been razed to the ground.

There was nothing left except a broken cart, a half-wild cat and the charred beams and timbers of what had once been buildings, resting on blackened stones. Her face bleak, Abigail stared about her, trying to pick out where the forge had been, where the cooking had been done, the quarters where she had slept and eaten, the house where the mission superintendent had lived with his family. The memory brought back the pictures of the massacre on the road to Peking and that night she shuddered in Willie's arms.

It had cost her more than Willie realised to go back, but the looting and murder the foreign troops had exacted on the Chinese as a means of working off their vengeance after the relief had cowed the countryside. The Empress had gone, the Boxers were scattered, and, because no one was prepared to show defiance, everything was quieter than they had ever expected. And while other Europeans, remembering the butchery in and around Peking, had preferred to remain within a safe distance of their own troops, Willie and Abigail, taking a chance, found they were first in the field by a long way, with Abigail's six years' experience of China and its dialects an added advantage.

The next morning, she put her fears behind her and behaved as if nothing had happened as they bartered for the little ivory figures she remembered – Taoist saints in rose, sandal and peach wood, Shishi lions and dogs, mandarin ducks and Senkyo mythological men, cosmetic boxes and red lacquer tables. They even found engraved Chinese swords, but Abigail steadfastly refused to handle them and it was left to Willie to do that part of the business. It surprised them how much was available, but, though Shantu was a small town of no great importance, in the past it had been the centre of business, wealth and some culture and it was possible to pick up articles easily in the narrow streets.

When they returned to Peking, the Allied troops were still arrogantly in occupation, but the looting was far from over. Unaware of its value, soldiers had destroyed priceless porcelain as they looked for treasure, and there was a story going the rounds about an American soldier holding up a fur coat. 'That's a fine sable coat,' his friend had said. 'There's a Chink inside it.' 'Okay. Give it a shake. He'll fall out.' It summed up the attitude. Anything was fair game.

At once they found there was a ready market for what they'd found. Officers due to go home wanted souvenirs to show their families and it wasn't difficult to arrange with the Sumters to allow them to use part of their premises to display what they'd acquired. It was always assumed that what they had to sell was loot and the questions were always the same.

'Where did you pick it up?' they were asked again and again.

'Shensi province.'

'Pinch it?'

'We bought it.'

'You mean you went *up there* and bought it?'

'Yes.' Willie preened himself a little. 'We know China, you see.'

'Well, old boy, rather you than me. I wouldn't trust myself with these treacherous yellow bastards for a bit of loot.'

In secret, Willie had felt much the same as they had set off for Shensi, but he still had the revolver he'd taken from Zychov's sergeant. It was a huge weapon and he always kept it handy, while Abigail carried in her pocket a small Italian weapon they had bought. She had been troubled at first at being away from Peking, but somehow seemed to find security in Willie's presence and was never afraid when he was near. She little knew how much comfort he drew from *her* presence.

The years she had spent in China and her knowledge of buying and selling had proved invaluable and they sold every one of the articles they brought back. And, as the news of what they were dealing in spread, they found other things being offered to them, even in Peking. Shifty-eyed soldiers – British, American, French, German and Russians – appeared on their doorstep offering small looted articles which they were anxious to exchange for money for drink.

During the relief, in the welter of vengeance that had taken place, with corpses still in the streets, brocade and porcelain had spilled out of the broken fronts of shops, and among the things that appeared were *objets d'art* of every kind, candlesticks of gold, porcelain vases, jade animals, enamels, stones, snuff boxes, gold coins, silks, carvings, lacquers, and miniatures which had lain undisturbed, watching the Manchu emperors pass, for hundreds of years. The pillaging and raping had gone on unabashed. One soldier offered a Louis XIV gold belt buckle, another gold ear-rings. There were gold vases, lacquered coffers, gold embroidery, jade imperial seals, necklaces, brooches, fur coats, and a long robe of Amur River sables, all going for the price of a drink or two.

By selling as fast as things were offered and using the money they gained, they were able to acquire most of what they were shown and the supply seemed endless, because everybody had helped themselves; the Russian general was said to have got away with ten trunks of valuables and gold and silver bars. Buying cheaply and selling quickly, they found their profit margin enormous, especially where there was some hint that what they offered had come from inside the Forbidden City. Despite the orders to respect it, some people, even some women, had got into the palace and brought out reports of what they had found, and one of the Empress' jewelled shoes was said to have already disappeared to Europe and was likely to be sold for thousands of pounds. It pushed up the prices still further and when they were asked, as they often were, if the articles had come from the Empress' palace, they said neither 'yes' nor 'no' because it seemed more honest. But it was always assumed that they had, and they didn't go out of their way to disillusion anyone.

By the time several weeks had passed, it began to seem possible to move further from Peking. The countryside was safe again, commerce was starting up and Allied soldiers were never far away.

'I reckon we ought to try towards Sian,' Willie suggested.

Abigail looked shocked. 'Willie, it's three hundred miles or more!'

'Nothing'll happen, Ab. After what's been going on here, nobody would dare lift a finger against us. We could pick up stuff worth a fortune.'

'I'd be scared.'

'With a gun? There's more to you than that.'

Sensing huge profits, in the end they hired a junk with a sound captain and recruited bodyguards they could trust and, putting them under the command of a young ex-soldier, sailed upriver towards Tung Kwan, buying everything in reach. Because they were dedicated, they were unafraid, and they didn't attempt to defraud the sellers, because, as Abigail said, they had to make a reputation, both as purchasers as well as vendors. Eventually they found people were actually bringing things for them to see.

It was while they were at Yang Chih, at the junction of the Wei and King rivers, that it dawned on them they were close to where the Imperial Court was supposed to have settled. Its power gone, it had left Peking in a caravan of carts unnoticed in the rain, the shabbily dressed occupants without luggage or spare clothes. They had headed south and west by a roundabout route, forced to drink rainwater because wells had been fouled by bodies, and food was scarce because the Boxers and the fleeing Imperial army had looted the villages.

Every little township Willie and Abigail passed through seemed to have news of them. The small caravan had grown rapidly, the reactionary officials who had managed to escape joining it because they couldn't imagine life away from the court. The rough food they had been obliged to eat at first had soon changed for the better and the Peking carts had been changed for sedan chairs and as, to their surprise, they realised that the foreign barbarians had no intention – as they would have had – of seeking vengeance on them, the court and its officials settled down and intrigue and corruption started again. They were finally believed to have discovered a refuge near the River Wei and the allied powers were still endeavouring to find them to get peace negotiations under way. Because there had been a war, there had to be a peace, and it had to be official.

'Sian,' Abigail said. 'That's where they are, I bet. It's the capital of the province and the old imperial capital of China.'

It seemed to be worth trying to get nearer, so they hired ponies and began to move through the mountains, eventually setting up a headquarters at Shinshi.

'What are you expecting, Willie?' Abigail asked.

'I don't know,' Willie admitted. 'But something.'

'What sort of something?'

'I dunno. But if the Imperial Court *is* at Sian and we're here in Shinshi, *something* ought to turn up.'

It turned up, in fact, at the end of a week when they had found themselves being offered a surprising number of unexpectedly valuable articles.

Among them were seals of state, incised in ivory, jade or gold, and other valuables, some of them large and heavy, with cinnabar in the form of vermilion paste used as pigment, some of them violet or purple to indicate mourning. With her six years' experience of China and all the reading she had done, Abigail recognised them at once.

'You know where these are coming from, don't you?' she said.

She held out a jade camel for him to look at. 'That's no village masterpiece, Willie. That was made somewhere in the south. So how did it get up here? It came from Peking and it belonged to someone who's left his treasure behind and is short of money.'

Two days later a caravan of ponies approached and a large stout Chinese, gesturing for Willie to approach, asked if he spoke Chinese.

Willie indicated Abigail, who was watching from a distance, and the Chinese frowned. Women in China were unconsidered chattels, but there seemed to be no way they could talk without an interpreter, and in the end he agreed to her presence. He wanted them to go to his house, he said, where certain gentlemen wished to speak to them.

That night, Willie looked at Abigail, who was studying him worriedly. 'Are we going, Willie?'

'I think we should.'

'Suppose it's a trap?'

'I don't think they'd set up a trap, old girl. Not now. I don't think they'd dare.'

'Why not? Nobody knows we're here. I don't like it.'

'I don't like it much myself,' Willie agreed. 'But we've got to go. If they're going to do for us, they can do for us here, and if they want to they will, whether we go or not. But if we do go, we might do well out of it. Let's give it a whirl.'

The house was twenty miles along the road to Sian and they covered the distance on the hired ponies. Abigail was still nervous, but Willie had a feeling that the fortune he was after might be concealed somewhere at the end of the journey.

Eventually at a village called Pangyan, situated on a crossroads that had been described to them, they were met by a man with a long gown and a black hat with the red button of a mandarin. He gestured to them to follow him and they were led through a round moon gate in a wall to a house furnished with some style, where the Chinese informed them they would be staying the night.

Abigail gave Willie a nervous look, but he nodded and the Chinese motioned them to follow him. Three sedan chairs, heavily carved and enamelled, with curtains of stained yellow silk, appeared, and, wilting in the heat, they set off through the village, here and there handed over the heads of the crowd, who were cleared by an officious-looking man shouting at the top of his voice for the way to be cleared. On the pavements, hawkers were offering food from portable stoves and shooing away the lean dogs that sniffed at their heels, barbers were shaving chins and heads, sellers of seed oils pushing past the vendors of fresh manure and the women buying hair ornaments and shoes with high cork soles. The air was full of story-tellers' singsong chants, the cries of children's puppet shows, and the chatter of bird lovers showing off their pet starlings and jays.

As they passed down a dirty rubbish-littered street, they could hear the thump of a wood carver's mallet and the clink of hammers on metal that sounded like the tinkle of Chinese music. The smell was of excreta, charcoal, camphorwood and lacquer, but Willie made a note to visit the place later for what it might contain.

The streets grew narrower until they were mere alleys roofed with matting, then suddenly they burst out of the village and were padding along a dusty lane between overhanging trees. Eventually they came to a white wall, with a circular moon gate. Beyond it was a courtyard full of doves but littered with rubbish. Soldiers in unmilitary uniforms lounged to their feet in a sagging line that bulged out as they leaned forward, bursting with curiosity to see who'd arrived. While they were still wondering what was going on, an official with a curved sword led them through another moon gate into a garden that was so different it could have been in a different part of China. There was a green lawn, a patch of feathery bamboo and, in a paved courtyard and overhung with willows, a pool that caught the jade light of the sky. The house consisted of a massive ironwood frame filled with latticework panels, with a roof of green tiles bristling with small creatures in coloured earthenware – dragons, phoenixes, unicorns and tortoises, all animals of Chinese celestial mythology.

In the courtyard was a pool of pink lotus, surrounded by dwarf trees, rockeries and shrubs in jars, with thrushes singing in cages among the wisteria. Inside, the house was an amazing mixture of all that was best in China and all that was worst in Europe. There were cabinets of lustrous lacquer, phoenixes of carved gu-wood, camphorwood chests encrusted with mother of pearl, lacquered dragon tables and settees in vermilion, olive green and canary. But, in addition, there were cheap cuckoo clocks, a vast ugly German statue of a woman in bronze, a mahogany commode, all standing among the rosewood whatnots and exquisite tomb figures, and the camels, horsemen and musicians of the Sung period. An ugly plush elephant was surrounded by exquisitely carved muff bottles in mauve, grey and orange jade; a clockwork dog stood among tortoiseshell and ivory and lanterns of translucent porcelain like lacework; electric lamps shone on Peking rugs worked with the Imperial Ming peony device, their reds, blues, oranges and violets unfaded by the years; and temple rugs of Mongolian camel wool in turquoise and biscuit hung alongside a gramophone with a cheap tin horn. The walls were covered with silken panels embroidered with black tortoises, vermilion phoenixes, azure dragons and white tigers, and with scrolls with elegant brushwork, maxims exquisitely worked by master calligraphers of the fifteenth century, and studies of flowers, blue tits and pheasants, all alongside lurid framed supplements from French magazines.

'It's here, Ab,' Willie breathed. 'It's all here.'

The man they had first met came forward to meet them, now carrying a gold-mounted cane and wearing a six-ribbed skull cap with the red button of authority. His grey silk gown was voluminous and on his feet he wore elastic-sided boots. Behind him came other men, all dressed in the same splendid fashion. Sticky drinks in small glasses and exquisitely contrived cakes that looked dangerous inside, were handed round, then dinner was announced by a cracked gong, and there was a great deal of fuss as they took their places at the table. Hot moist towels were handed round to wipe faces and Willie immediately remembered a story he had heard of how enemies were given smallpox by first passing the hot towel over the face of a sufferer, and he suddenly wondered if it were a trap as Abigail had suggested.

Then he noticed the Chinese were staring at Abigail with some displeasure and a small fat man with a wide mouth with teeth like a set of dominoes appeared at his side and jabbered at him for some time, indicating Abigail.

'He's saying I can't eat with you,' she said.

'Why not?'

'Because I'm a woman.'

'How the hell do we talk then? You're the one who speaks the lingo.'

When Abigail translated, the man with the teeth looked baffled then his wide smile appeared again.

'He says I can take my meal outside,' Abigail said, 'and we can talk through the open door.'

Willie tossed his towel down. 'Tell him you eat with me,' he said, 'or I don't eat at all.'

Abigail nervously translated and the man with the teeth explained to the others, who went into a huddle, muttering in low voices. Eventually the man with the teeth announced that a solution had been found. A group of singsong girls appeared, dressed in lace-fringed trousers, their faces enamelled and rouged, and began to chant amorous songs. Since there were now other women in the room, it appeared to have satisfied the susceptibilities of the Chinese and they headed for the table again.

It took a great deal of time to get seated because no one appeared to wish to sit down before a tall thin man wearing carpet slippers, who seemed to be the chief guest. His face was covered with tiny wrinkles and the ends of a wispy moustache hung well below his chin. He gestured with a hand with one long nail tipped with silver, to indicate he didn't wish to seat himself before his host and the other guests and there were several half-hearted tries and a lot of embarrassment and giggles before they all managed to sit simultaneously.

On the table were scores of little bowls containing dainties. Some sweet, some apparently pure mustard. One was orange, black and gelatinous, another had the smell of sulphuretted hydrogen. Served in blue-and-white porcelain bowls, they were so highly spiced as to be almost uneatable, but Abigail whispered that they were only offered out of politeness for their rarity or because they were aphrodisiacs, and it was usual to leave the larks' tongues, dormice in syrup and hundred-year-old eggs untouched.

There seemed to be dozens of courses, most of them consumed by the Chinese holding the bowl to the mouth and sucking loudly at what their chopsticks dug out. Noise seemed to be essential to show appreciation and, from time to time, Willie's neighbour offered him titbits from his own bowl. Hot rice wine and rose petal gin were served, then, as the real meal started, the singsong girls, who had been doing their act in a muted fashion, burst out at full blast.

The Chinese kept clearing their throats with a noise like a file rasping on an anvil and spitting what they brought up through the window, then the thin man at the head of the table opened his mouth to speak, closed it again, glared at the girls, then gestured at them, so that they faded away to a corner of the room, their volume reduced to a minimum. He began to speak, Abigail translated as he went.

'He's saying,' she pointed out to Willie, 'that the Imperial Court feels it's time to meet the powers in Peking and start peace negotiations, and that you should let it be known.'

Willie stared at her in alarm. 'Are they wanting me to be some sort of ambassador or something?'

'That's what it looks like.'

Abigail seemed remarkably calm and Willie gave her a worried look. 'Lor', Ab, I hadn't planned on going back just yet. We haven't got all we came for.'

Abigail took a different view. 'This could do us a power of good, Willie,' she whispered. 'We'd be the confidants of the Legations and the confidants of the Court as well. They want to return to Peking, and we'd be there to speak for them.'

It didn't take Willie long to catch on. 'It makes sense,' he agreed. 'Tell 'em we'll take their messages. We'll come back afterwards. And, when we do, they might tell us where to look. They might even provide escorts to make sure we're safe. What's he say?'

'He says they anticipate heavy demands for punishment and retribution and that the Empress has therefore banished certain princes for life. Others have been confined to their homes or demoted, while others have been imprisoned or sent to the frontier with hard labour. She's also prepared to have a few decapitated and buried without their heads.' Willie gave her a startled look. 'A great disgrace, because you can't look your ancestors in the face.'

The thin man was still droning on.

'They'll also order others to commit suicide and even provide the silk rope for them to strangle themselves. They offer to send men to Germany to apologise for the murder of the German Minister and to erect a monument on the spot where he was killed. All officials in cities where foreigners were ill-treated will be suspended or executed, according to the wishes of the people in Peking. They've also agreed to prohibit, on pain of death, membership of any foreign society.'

'Like the Boxers?'

'Like the Boxers. There are a lot of other things I didn't catch, but they think that it's as well to encourage the foreigners to indulge in commerce because it would he an effective check on their ambitions. It seems the USA has already requested the powers not to interfere with other nationals and to respect the integrity of China.' She gave a little laugh. 'He says it's a warning from a burglar to the rest of his gang not to deprive him of his share of the loot.'

'He's right, too,' Willie grinned. 'The Russians'll be watching the Japanese and the British, and the French'll be watching the Germans, and the Americans'll be watching the lot. Anybody who steps out of line will be accused at once.' His smile widened. 'They're not as stupid as Europeans think them, Ab. Did you understand it all?'

'It was difficult, but I think I got it right. They want us to take back a ready-made offer and ask for a meeting.'

'And us?'

'You're the go-between.'

'What about you?'

Abigail turned to the thin Chinese. For a while he ignored her as she spoke, then he nodded and spoke back to her. 'He agrees that I shall interpret.'

'Not a man?'

'He doesn't object to a man, but he wants me there. He says he trusts me. I think he feels he can push me around a bit if necessary.' Abigail smiled. 'But I quoted their own proverb at him – a man thinks he knows but a woman knows better. As all this comes from the Empress Dowager, it has a lot of meaning and he knows it.'

t e n

They were seen off in style. A large cast-iron urn in the garden filled with prayer paper and fireworks tied like blossom in bunches to trees were set alight. With several of the officials kneeling and touching their foreheads to the floor, they left surrounded by blue smoke, staccato crackling and sprays of golden sparks, riding in the same sedan chairs they arrived in and surrounded by horn-blowers and bannermen.

Still escorted by soldiers and bannermen, they picked up their ponies where they had left them and, returning to their headquarters, ordered everything to be packed up, and headed for Tung Kwan, where the junk was waiting. Moving downriver to Yuwei they unpacked everything from the hold, repacked it into carts, and headed for Peking.

The Sumters greeted them enthusiastically with the news that everything they had brought back from their last trip had been sold, and that people were asking for more.

'No time for that now,' Willie said. 'Other things to do.'

Bathing and dressing in their best clothes, they headed for the British Legation. A frozen-faced elderly official met them at the entrance and demanded their business.

'To see Sir Claude MacDonald.'

The official looked down his nose. With the relief, things had returned to normal and he intended having nothing to do with unofficial complaints. 'You had better submit your request in writing,' he said.

'I'm not requesting,' Willie pointed out. 'I'm insisting.'

The official smiled. 'You don't insist here, young man.'

'This time – old man! – I do. I have a request for Sir Claude from the Empress Tzu-Hsi.'

The official's face changed at once. 'I don't believe you,' he said softly.

'Try me and see. If I don't see Sir Claude, I'll go to Mr Conger at the American Legation. And then what'll happen to you when he sees what I've brought and it becomes known what you've turned away?'

The official became wary. 'What is it you've brought?' he asked.

'A request to reopen negotiations between us and the Imperial Court.'

'You know where it is?'

'We've talked to officials.'

'You'd better inform me.'

Willie began to grow angry. 'I'll inform Sir Claude and no one else and if you don't look bloody slippy you'll be in trouble.'

The official stared hard at him, still clearly not believing him, but the threat to his career was enough to stir him.

'Wait here. I'll see Sir Claude.'

Within minutes he was back. 'Sir Claude will see you,' he announced. 'Perhaps the lady would like to remain here.'

'Don't be damn silly, man,' Willie snapped. 'She's the one who knows what went on, not me. She's the one who speaks the lingo. She's the one who led the discussions.'

The official blenched, but soon afterwards they were being ushered through two large double doors to where Sir Claude MacDonald was standing by his desk.

'Mr Sarth,' he said, smiling and holding out his hand. 'I heard you'd gone into business. And this lady? Your wife?'

'Yes.' The lie came easily. 'And my partner. And at the moment we seem to have become sort of official messengers from the Imperial Court.'

MacDonald's eyebrows rose. 'You've found them?'

'They're in Sian.'

'So we heard.'

'We were working our way along the Wei when they contacted us. They've made offers.'

MacDonald studied them for a moment. 'Please go on,' he said. 'The Viceroy at Canton has arrived here for them, but so far we haven't seen him and we don't know what he has to say. Do you?'

'Yes. We met officials of the court. My wife was interpreter.'

'A woman?' MacDonald's eyebrows lifted again. 'That's unusual.'

'The Empress is a woman,' Abigail said gently. 'She's done okay.'

'There was nobody else who spoke the lingo,' Willie explained. 'We talked for an hour or more. I didn't understand it but my – er – wife – she did. She wrote it all down later.'

Abigail held up the notebook in which she had written up the Chinese offers before leaving Pangyan. 'I've also got a scroll here that I was asked to present. It's a copy of a decree they're going to issue. They've had enough of exile and want to return to Peking. We think the Empress Dowager had it written out.'

She offered the scroll and MacDonald asked her to read it.

' "Our Sacred Mother's advanced age," ' she intoned, ' "renders it necessary that we should take the greatest care of her health, so that she may attain to a peaceful longevity. She ardently wishes to return to her home in Peking and, all being willing, wishes to make the journey as soon as possible." There's a lot more of the same sort. It ends with the usual "Tremble and obey." '

'This is from the Emperor?' MacDonald asked.

'Given to us by Minister Na-Chang. He said he was representing Prince Ch'un.'

MacDonald was impressed. 'This seems to be most important,' he said. 'Will you kindly wait next door while I summon Mr Conger and the other ministers? You'll be given refreshments.'

Half an hour later they were summoned back into the office. This time, the American minister, round-faced and black-browed, was there with the French minister and the man who was running the German Legation since the murder of Baron Von Ketteler, as well as Generals Gaselee, Chaffee and Count Von Waldersee, the German who had arrived to command the Allied forces.

The American minister moved forward at once to shake Willie's hand and then Abigail's.

'Splendid, splendid,' he said. 'You young people have shortened the negotiations by months.'

There were congratulations all round, then a Chinese servant brought in champagne which was handed round before they got down to brass tacks.

'It's going to take some negotiating,' Conger said. 'We're not satisfied with their offers. Some of these people need more punishment than they're suggesting. And there's the matter of the forts at Taku. They've got to be levelled to make access to Peking certain. There also have to be amendments to the Treaties of Commerce and Navigation and a change at the Tsungli Yamen. It has too much power over Chinese foreign policy. They also make no mention of indemnities. My government considers two hundred million dollars would be agreeable.'

'Not enough by a long way,' MacDonald observed. 'Three hundred and fifty would be more realistic.'

'That's too much.'

Von Waldersee gestured. 'We should have pursued them with every man we've got when they fled,' he said.

'The United States would never agree to that,' Conger said.

Waldersee turned on him. 'It seems to me the United States wants nobody to get *anything* out of China. We should fix a hard sum. Something that would be difficult for them to raise.'

'We'll never get it.'

'Then we should take over some of their resources. Maritime Customs, part of the Internal Customs.'

The argument went on, with Willie and Abigail forgotten in the background. Eventually, they decided the discussion was nothing to do with them, and slipped out unnoticed. But they had barely sat down when an official appeared with a request for them to return at once.

Only MacDonald and the American and French ministers were there this time. MacDonald apologised for ignoring them.

'Would you be willing to return to Sian,' he asked, 'and inform your friends that we're prepared to talk? It's only fair to say you might not be so well received this time, because we can't agree on their offer and feel the dynasty should suffer greater punishment than it offers.'

Willie looked at Abigail. Through both their minds was running the thought that if they could persuade the Chinese to agree to their demands, they would be in a position to profit from both sides of the deal.

'We'll go,' Willie said.

Na-Chang seemed relieved to see them again. He rose as they appeared at the house at Pangyan and summoned servants with tea and the usual sticky buns. When they explained why they were there, he frowned.

'Prince Ch'un will object,' he said. 'The Empress Dowager will never agree to so much.'

'Tell him they haven't much choice,' Willie told Abigail. 'If they don't agree, they'll never be able to go back to Peking.'

It was agreed that they should return to Yang Chih and that Na-Chang should carry their message to Sian. Three days later they were summoned back to Pangyan with instructions that they were to be escorted to see Prince Ch'un at Sian. Willie looked quickly at Abigail and saw that her eyes were bright with excitement.

'We'll go,' he said.

Sian, the capital of Shensi province, on the River Weiho above its consequence with the Yellow River, was the old imperial capital and was considered the cradle of Chinese civilisation. It was a jumble of low buildings and pagodas, the walls high and buttressed so they could see only greentiled roofs as they approached.

Na-Chang seemed nervous and anxious to talk, almost as though he feared their mission might fail.

'The Empress Dowager knows what is going on,' he told Abigail. 'She always knows. People have plotted her downfall in the past, but there were never any secrets from her. Old Buddha is a vital and forceful woman. She is almost seventy, but she is still a force to be reckoned with.'

A troop of horn-blowers and bannermen was waiting for them outside the town and they were escorted with considerable ceremony through its narrow streets to a large pagoda near a stream fringed with willows. Prince Ch'un, the tall thin Chinese they had met at Na-Chang's house at Pangyan, was waiting for them. His expression didn't change and he made no indication that he had ever met them before.

Behind him there was a set of gauze curtains of some filmy material beyond which they could see a small figure sitting silently in a black and purple enveloping garment. Alongside it were two other small figures, dressed in red, but, though the faint warm breeze moved the curtains, they were unable to see beyond them, and could only guess that the watching, listening figures were the Empress Dowager's representatives, sitting in on the talks to be able to report back to her.

Rice wine was brought and handed round with a basket full of the usual sticky pink cakes. Na-Chang started to talk to Abigail and, as she told him what she had been instructed, he turned and spoke to the tall thin man. There was a lot of whispering and nodding and head shaking and once a furious whispered argument. At one point Na-Chang turned to Abigail to confirm what had been said and there was more head wagging before he turned once more, his hands inside his voluminous sleeves, and spoke again.

'Prince Ch'un,' Abigail murmured to Willie, 'isn't happy with the demands, but he thinks it might be possible to talk. The Empress is tired of exile.'

'They agree?'

'They want more talks, but they accept that their representatives should meet ours.'

As they turned away, the breeze, which had been moving the gauze curtains throughout the talking, banged a shutter and the curtains drifted sideways. Beyond them, for a brief second, they saw two women, their faces enamelled, and between them a tiny figure, whose long hands were folded on its lap, six-inch fingernails lying on its knees. Jade ear-rings dangled from small ears and an elaborate pearl necklace encircled its throat. The woman was looking straight at them as they turned away, a once-beautiful face with jet black eyes that were totally without expression.

Outside, Willie looked at Abigail as they climbed into their chairs.

'You know who that was?' he asked. 'It was the Empress Dowager herself. And that was what they call an audience curtain.'

A few days later a messenger brought the news to Pangyan that the court would accept most of the demands, but that there needed to be more talk on others, and once more they began the long journey back to Peking, for most of the way with an advance guard of trumpeters and bannermen to make everything official. This time they were received without delay and gave their message to a full council of Ministers from the Legations.

Because they were asked to hold themselves in readiness in case of the need to exchange more messages, they confined their activities for the time being to the area round Peking while talks were held. It made little difference. Their reputation was already made. More looted artefacts turned up at the Sumters' and it was clearly pointless to suffer from any conscience over them because it was impossible to decide where they had come from and the vendors certainly had no intention of informing them. Just as quietly and quickly, they were sold to officers returning to Europe.

It was early in the following year as she organised the display of the goods they had picked up, that Abigail was called to an elegant sedan chair which stood in the street outside. She recognised the man inside at once as one of NaChang's officials. He handed her a scroll of paper bound with red ribbon.

'My master sends this,' he said. 'The Empress Dowager insisted that a copy should be brought to you. She expressed great admiration for your courage as a woman.'

The scroll was a copy of a decree issued by the Emperor.

'Our Sacred Mother,' it announced, 'has decided after much consideration that it is time to return to Peking, where she hopes to live in peaceful longevity…' There was more in the same strain, saying that, since a long journey in the heat was undesirable, the route to Peking would be by way of Honan. 'We have fixed,' the decree ended, 'on the nineteenth day of the seventh moon to commence the journey.'

'She's coming back?' Abigail asked.

'All is agreed.'

Some time later, they watched with Na-Chang from a specially erected pavilion as the royal caravan left Sian, two thousand carts and baggage waggons containing silks, jade, furs and bullion, and escorted by cavalry and hundreds of mounted officials. Thousands of coloured flags, the imperial yellow predominating, fluttered in the autumn breezes, hundreds of mounted Manchu bannermen preceded the cortège, and mounted trumpeters with blaring horns cleared the roads ahead.

Several days later feasts and theatricals were held, and the Empress' birthday was celebrated with fireworks. In the centre of the procession was the Imperial party in yellow sedan chairs surrounded by courtiers and servants. This was no defeated ruler crawling back to beg mercy, but the return of someone who knew her own value and had only stayed away to let tempers cool.

The cortège had to cover a matter of seven hundred miles and progress was slow, because not only were the roads unpassable after the rains, but it was encumbered by its own baggage and the tributes to the Emperor and the Empress Dowager that had come in from the provinces. As it drew nearer Peking, the caravan assumed an almost triumphal aspect and Willie and Abigail watched the ladies of the court cross the Yellow River in a gilded barge specially constructed in the shape of a dragon, with garlands of flowers floating on the water around it as it moved. Imperial standards fluttered on the banks under the autumn sky, with choirs to intone litanies in a smell of burnt incense. The road had been levelled and made wider to make progress easier, and the peasants had turned out in hundreds to witness the passage.

Feeling that the Empress Dowager's presence would restore some order to the chaos that had reigned since the end of the siege, Peking had been preparing for the arrival for days and streets were cleared of rubbish and as many of the scars of the recent fighting as could be removed were erased. Guards of honour were drilled until they were dizzy with fatigue, uniforms were cleaned, brass and leather polished, moustaches waxed.

The last part of the journey was undertaken by rail, the first half from Chengting to Fengtai on a Belgian-operated section of the line, then from Fengtai to Peking on a Britishoperated section. The British terminus in Peking had been brought especially from Machiapu to a point inside the city where a pavilion had been constructed and furnished with thrones of gold lacquer, jars of *cloisonné* and vases of fine porcelain.

The special train was waiting at Paotingfu and, so concerned was the Empress that she should arrive at the very moment when her soothsayers and scribes had prophesied would be most portentous, she insisted on a railway official being brought to her presence to swear the driver would neither delay nor hurry unnecessarily and that the party should detrain outside the city and enter in the traditional way.

The train was exactly on time and, as it rolled in, a military band struck up a rousing march. European soldiers in full dress uniform snapped to attention to present arms with a clash of weapons. There was silence as a door opened and a Chinese official stepped out. Men stiffened and the silence increased, then a tiny figure in the favourite black and purple appeared, and Sir Claude MacDonald stepped forward, bowing low.

There was a hurried whispered conversation as the ministers crowded round the peacock figures of the Chinese court officials. Somebody set off at a trot down the platform and returned with the railway official who had been riding at the front of the train with a watch in his hand to make sure the promise to arrive on time was kept. He looked slightly dishevelled as he stopped in front of the Empress to receive her thanks, then she turned and, from a cushion held out to her, she produced a yellow sash with an enamelled and jewelled decoration on the end of it, which she handed to one of her officials to hand to the railwayman.

The entrance to the city was made in full panoply, heralded by yard-long trumpets blaring a tuneless call, then, under a canopy of fluttering banners, the Imperial Chariot, transported for speed on the train, rolled through the Yung Ting gate, up the broad thoroughfare of the Chinese City and through the Chien Men gate.

The road was lined with Imperial troops, who knelt with bowed heads as the cortège swept by – at full tilt because the higher the dignitary the greater had to be the speed. Foreign ministers had warned their nationals against showing themselves, but no one had paid any attention and most of them were on the wall above the Chien Men gate. A line of shops around the outer wall had been destroyed by fire during the siege and a tower gutted, but despite the strong wind that was lifting the yellow dust in clouds, hordes of people had gathered.

In a new dress sewn in a hurry by a Chinese seamstress and wearing a new hat sent up from Shanghai by steamer, Abigail stood in the official party alongside Willie, who was dressed in a new suit with a buttonhole, a high starched collar sawing at his ears. They had spotted Emmeline in the crowd as they moved to their places. She was accompanied by a young man of pale appearance in a grey suit with spats, and Willie wondered what duties he was performing for her.

First to appear were the Manchu bannermen on very little steeds like woolly bears, trotting up in fours wearing gorgeous brocaded robes. Next came a group of officials in gala robes, then the Imperial palanquins. At the wall, the chairs halted and the Emperor and Empress stepped down to burn incense and recite prayers in the tiny temple set into the wall. As the Empress Dowager appeared, she glanced up at the crowd lining the wall and, though the eunuchs tried to move her on, she remained there, supported as was customary for a great personage by two of her ladies holding her arms, then she lifted her head to gaze at the Europeans on the wall, closed her hands under her chin and made a series of little bows.

'I think,' Willie whispered, 'that we've just seen the beginning of a new policy.'

eleven

As Willie had predicted, their involvement with the Imperial Court was the turning point.

They were known – not only to the hoi-polloi in Peking but also in the Legations and to the Court officials. *The North China Daily News* made a point of mentioning their involvement in the talks and the *Illustrated London News* correspondent even produced an article with pen drawings of the Empress Dowager and of Willie and Abigail, all done from imagination.

A minor decoration had been suggested for Willie by Sir Claude MacDonald, and it duly arrived from England in a red leather box and was handed over without much ceremony at the Legation by the Minister. Not to be outdone, the Germans offered one also. But that wasn't the end. Willie was informed by the Minister that he would be one of a group attending the Imperial Palace, and to dress himself in a morning suit. Done up to the eyebrows in borrowed pearl waistcoat, black jacket and spats, he was convoyed with a whole group of Legation officials into the Imperial presence.

The Empress was small, but, despite her age, she had kept her figure. She had a fine broad forehead and delicate arched eyebrows over brilliant black eyes. Her hair appeared still to be jet black, but Willie noticed that she wore a tight-fitting black satin cap so that it was difficult to tell where the cap finished and the hair started. She had used no paint on her face or lips since she had been widowed and her skin was smooth and unblemished.

She was dressed in embroidered garments which combined silk threads of different hues to outline the image of a dragon. Because of the gold in it, the robe seemed to be surrounded by a halo of violet rays, and, as she moved, the alternating blue and green thread had the effect of changing colours. Over it was a flowing coat of gold net over gold leaf, and a long tassel of eight strings of large pearls hung to her right shoulder from the wing of a headdress decorated with the tiny feathers from a kingfisher's breast. She wore a cape of pearls, while the hem of her skirt was also fringed with hanging threads of pearls. In her hand she held a snuffbox which he realised was an enormous hollowed-out pearl.

'God,' he thought. 'She must clank when she sits down.'

One after the other, officials bowed before the old lady until it was Willie's turn. As he moved forward, MacDonald whispered to him.

'Bend your head,' he said. 'She's not very tall.'

'Order of the Double Dragon,' Willie announced to Abigail on his return. 'For initiating the first peace talks.'

The Empress wasn't slow to realise the success of her reception for the foreign devils and eventually women were also invited to the Imperial Palace. As the old lady set out to captivate them, the not very sophisticated women from the Legations succumbed completely to her charm. She was a good actress and it wasn't difficult. First of all there was the thrill of entering forbidden precincts, where, expecting hostility or deviousness, they were agreeably surprised to be greeted by a beautifully dressed old lady with shrewd eyes, a gracious manner and winning smile.

Shown through the palace pavilions with blaring trumpets and clashing cymbals, they moved between ranks of eunuchs in embroidered robes, gazed on lotus-covered lakes and heard the sound of muffled temple bells. Drinking it in ecstatically, they forgot their hatred, and swelled with pride at the honour that had been bestowed on them. But never at any time was there ever any getting away from the fact that Abigail had been the first, that she had gone alone, and that unlike the others, she, too, had returned wearing the yellow sash of the Order of the Double Dragon and the gift of a magnificent jade bowl.

'She said I was as brave and intelligent as all women should be,' she told Willie. 'She hoped I was her friend and held out her hand for me to touch.'

Once more they were news and the subject of gossip. A few high-nosed women still regarded Abigail with contempt, but now it was tinged with envy, and there were plenty more who were friendly, and curious enough to want to know what had been said to her by the Empress.

Invitations arrived, occasionally from the Legations, and they felt confident enough to accept those they wished to and resist those they didn't. Privileged as they were, items of great value found their way into their hands – lacquered netsuke ware, inros, kinchakus, kagis, miniature temples, animals and warriors in ivory, boxwood toys, porcelain, urns, early dynasty horses, flowered vases, carpets from the north showing the cloud bands of eternity and flying butterflies signifying happiness. Some of it, they knew, had come from the privileged homes of important Chinese officials and was in great demand. Because they were believed quite wrongly to have the ear of the old Empress and were believed to be experts, they had to be quick to learn. Occasionally they made mistakes, but they preferred to let things go rather than commit themselves to something that could be totally wrong and destroy the reputation they were building up, and by the end of the year they felt they had collected enough to take it to Europe and the States.

Many of their friends, nervous after the siege, had left Peking, but the Japanese, Yuhitsu Shaiba, still limping a little from his wound, was still there, still friendly, still drinking with the Russians, always invited to their parties because he had the capacity they liked to hold his drink. He seemed to be at all the receptions they attended, always with the Russians, always smiling and doing little talking, just nodding his head, his face impassive behind his smile, taking everything in.

As the memory of the siege receded, Shaiba told them he had been ordered to Shanghai. 'Business,' he said. 'Shanghai is the coming place. Before long it will be as important to the East as London is to Europe and New York to the Americas.'

They travelled with him to the river mouth, where they took a coastal vessel to Shanghai. There they separated Abigail for San Francisco, Willie for London. They put up for the night at a hotel, uncertain what the future held. It was Abigail's intention to see her aunt and uncle because she felt it her duty, but, like Willie, her main aim was to discover what interest there might be in what they had to offer.

'Go to the newspapers,' Willie advised. 'Tell them what happened. Tell them about the siege and the Empress. Show them your medal. When you put the things on display they'll fall over themselves to get at 'em.'

'What will you do, Willie?'

Willie paused. Somewhere in London there was a girl called Edie Wise, whom he'd once promised to marry. But three years had passed since then and he couldn't imagine her still waiting for him.

As they prepared for bed, Abigail clutched him. 'I'm scared, Willie,' she said.

'What of? That uncle of yours?'

'He'll try to keep me to home.'

'Tell him you're married.'

'I'm not.'

Willie gestured. 'He's not to know and you don't have to produce a certificate.'

'You don't know him. He'll want proof.'

'Ab,' Willie urged, trying to instil his own confidence into her. 'You walked out on him once. You can walk out on him again. You've got money in your purse and money in the bank. You're not beholden to him any more. You don't have to take orders from anyone.'

'Not even you?'

'Not even me. Well –' Willie grinned at her as she slipped out of her dress ' – a bit from me.'

He put his arms round her, his hand moving on the bare flesh above her slip.

'It takes off,' she said quietly. Her eyes were on his, her face pale as marble.

He slipped the straps from her shoulders and allowed the slip to fall at her feet. Her fingers were undoing the buttons of his shirt.

'Willie, is it wrong that we aren't married? I feel married. Suppose somebody produces proof that we're not? Even the Sumters think we're married. I told them we got married up in Shantu before we left. I feel awful lying to them.'

'We'll get married when you come back. I'll be waiting for you. At the moment we're short of time. We both leave tomorrow and the night's growing old.'

Sitting on the side of the bed the following morning, wrapped in a sheet, Abigail was aware of fear. She had still not quite thrown off her background, and the indoctrination she had received at the Mission had sunk deep within her, so that she still felt guilt. She was about to be separated from Willie for the first time since they'd met and she was afraid of what might happen without him. Though she was older, her life as an adult had been very sheltered, while Willie, living and working close to London Docks, seemed to know his way about how everybody would react, the value of everything.

She didn't entirely believe in his innocence because she'd heard rumours about Emmeline and her clerks, but he'd shown no interest in anyone else in the time she'd been with him so she'd accepted that his eyes weren't wandering elsewhere. But, because of her period with the Baptist Mission, she didn't really trust men either. Her uncle had often tried to get her in dark corners and she knew that at least one of the missionaries at Shantu had had a child by a Chinese girl. Though he had been elaborately forgiven after a ceremony of public remorse and penitence, it hadn't excused the fact and she had a suspicion that all men were the same.

Willie's eyes opened and he looked up at her. 'What are you thinking?' he asked.

She smiled, pretending there was no worry. 'About the States,' she said. 'I wonder what it looks like, what they're up to?'

'Never mind the States,' he advised. 'Keep your eyes open for American men and what *they're* up to. You're pretty enough to make a few eyes click in their sockets.'

He reached out for her and, in the heat of the early sunshine, they made love, more passionately because they were about to be separated. During the morning, Willie called a rickshaw and drove with her to the launch which was to take her to the ship lying in the Whangpoo waiting to leave, her luggage and all they had to sell in the States already in her hold.

'You'll probably be back first,' he said. 'You've only to go across the Pacific. I've got to go all the way round China, India, up the Red Sea and through the Mediterranean. But I'm doing it the way the nobs do it – port out, starboard home. P.O.S.H. Posh.'

'I'll be scared you'll not come back.'

Willie looked at her disbelievingly. 'Get away!' he said. 'You'd never think that.'

All the same, he decided, as he saw her into the cutter that was to take her out to the ship, the fact that they might not see each other again was something that was nagging in a small fear at the back of his own mind, and he returned to the hotel, ordered himself a large stengah and sat back to drink it until it was time to leave.

London seemed full of fog, smoke and driving rain and, although it was supposed to be spring, Willie was wearing a muffler and overcoat and a heavy tweed cap.

His first call, since it was handy, was at the office of Wainwright and Halliday's. A new young clerk showed him to a chair and it was Halliday, pale plump and spectacled who received him.

'Willie Sarth,' he said cheerfully. 'Fancy you turning up. Looking for your old job back?'

'Not likely,' Willie said. 'I'm in business on my own now.'

'And doing well at it by the look of you. There was a story about you in the *Illustrated London News*. Said you'd been given a decoration by the Empress of China.'

'That's right.' Willie looked about him. 'Where's Mr Wainwright?'

'Dead.' Halliday said cheerfully. 'I'm running the place now. On my own. Heart it was. Six months ago.'

'Good Lord. What about old Bohenna?'

'He's dead, too. Shot himself. Went bust. Over-extended. Typical of that sort. Spent too much. Show-off and all that. Suddenly he found he'd spent more than he was earning and couldn't pay his debts. Wife and three kids, too.'

It was a chastened Willie who left the office. Show-off, he thought. Over-extended. Went bust. Typical of that sort. He had just bought an expensive overcoat, cap and shoes. He decided that for the time being, it would be enough.

Before going to his brother's, he took a cab down to Brixton and made a few enquiries about Edie Wise at the pub at the end of the street. Neither of them had ever been letter writers and, after the first two or three sweated missives, their correspondence had dried up. He needn't have worried, however.

'She's married,' he was told. 'Must have been a year ago. Had to. In the family way.'

She hadn't waited very long, Willie thought bitterly.

Taking another cab, he arrived at his brother's house just as he arrived home from work. Willie was still staring at the street, wondering why it looked so much more crowded and narrower than it had, though he was used to narrower, far more crowded Chinese streets, when a hand dropped on his shoulder.

His brother didn't look much different but he was still a clerk and seemed overworked and tired. But he and his wife made Willie welcome and gave him a meal, and Willie produced a bottle of whisky, something they never normally tasted, so they all became a little tipsy. Before he left, he slipped a handful of fivers into his brother's pocket and refused to let him see how much until he'd gone.

'For old time's sake,' he said. 'It might be a while before I see you again.'

His brother's eyebrows rose. 'You mean *you're going back*? To China?'

'Why not?'

'But this is where you live! This is home.'

'Not now,' Willie said firmly. 'Not any more.'

He had often heard old China hands say how much they itched to see England again and, having seen it, how much they itched to get back to the East. Suddenly he knew what they meant.

The following day he went to Bond Street with a suitcase and dived into a fine arts shop with the gilt sign, Brassard, over the door. A blond man in a velvet jacket with a bright orange cravat in a soft collar met him.

'Nothing today, thank you,' he said at once.

'Don't talk so bloody silly,' Willie snapped.

The man's eyes travelled over Willie's new suit and it occurred to Willie that it might be a good idea next time, instead of buying his suit off the peg in a store as he had done, to go to a decent tailor. 'You haven't seen what I've got,' he pointed out.

'I can guess,' the man said.

Willie snorted. 'You'd guess wrong,' he said, opening the suitcase.

Immediately, the man's tone changed. 'Where did you get these?' he asked suspiciously.

'I didn't pinch 'em.'

The man eyed him dubiously and disappeared to the back of the shop. Shortly afterwards he returned with a young woman, who began to make her way to the shop door.

'If you're sending her for a policeman,' Willie said sharply, 'you'd better think again. I'm not a bloody burglar and if a bobby turns up here I'll sue you for everything you possess.'

He had no idea how to go about suing anyone and even suspected that, if he tried it, he would lose, but the man hesitated and signalled to the girl to wait. As she did so, Willie produced the copy of the *Illustrated London News* which had featured himself and Abigail. 'That's who I am,' he said. 'I have the ear of the Empress Dowager, and my business is Chinese crafts. You can either buy 'em or not. Just say. If *you* don't want 'em, I'll take 'em elsewhere.'

The man swallowed. 'I think you'd better come into the office.'

He gestured at the girl. 'That's all right, Doris. You can forget it.'

'I'm Julian Brassard,' he said as he ushered Willie into his private department. 'I run the business for my father.'

'You *were* sending for a bobby, weren't you?' Willie said as he sat down to a cup of tea in fine bone china cups.

A frown crossed Brassard's pale, fleshy face and he went pink. 'Yes, I was,' he admitted. 'I'm sorry. But so much of it goes on.'

'Not with me. I'm straight.' Willie reopened the suitcase and saw Brassard's eyes widen again. 'What about that lot then?'

Brassard's expression went back to a professional blank. 'They're not bad,' he said. 'But you look a bit young to be an expert.'

'I'm not an expert. Just growing into one. My partner found these things. She's the one who knows about them.'

Brassard began to pick up the articles one by one, eyeing them, studying them cautiously before putting them down on a nearby table with great care.

'Not bad,' he said again.

'They're better than not bad,' Willie observed. 'Or you wouldn't handle 'em like eggshells. How much are you willing to offer?'

Brassard shrugged. 'Hundred pounds the lot.'

Willie grinned. 'Don't talk daft,' he said. 'You'll sell 'em for a lot more than that. I've been having a look round. Give me a good price for them and I'll see you get more.'

'You've got more?'

'Plenty.'

'Here? In England?'

'Some stored away. And more where they came from.'

Brassard hesitated. 'Well, I can only guess at the real value – '

'Don't kid me,' Willie said.

Brassard swallowed. 'Very well then,' he agreed. 'Five hundred.' It came so easily, Willie decided to try harder and eventually he pushed the price up to seven hundred and fifty. Even at that Brassard seemed pleased.

'When can I see the other things?' he asked. 'I thought we might put on a bit of an exhibition. That way we'll get better prices.'

'I can fix it,' Willie said.

'When will you be in England again?'

Willie wasn't so sure he wanted to be in England again. Apart from the money, it hadn't come up to expectations. 'It might not be for some time,' he said. 'So I'll want an agent. Somebody who'll sell the stuff. Top prices.'

'Perhaps I could be of help. Find one for you.'

'He'd have to be honest.'

'I'm honest.'

Willie eyed him. 'You tried to do me down just now!'

'That's business.'

'So's this. It would be on commission. A good one, though. Even if you decided to buy 'em yourself. And I'd want it all doing proper. I'd want everything itemising. Profit, costs and commission, all down on paper. And clear, too. I'd know how to study it. I used to be an accounts clerk here in London.'

By the time Willie left, he had a British agent for what he had to offer and a certainty that he could get rid of the other things he'd brought with him. It made him itch to get back to China and collect more.

The Whangpoo, where the ship dropped anchor, was a greylooking river twelve miles up the Yangtze, teeming with life and with sampans moving like clouds of brown beetles round the tugs and vessels anchored in midstream. Steamers, black and red funnelled, drifted past, sirens roaring at the sampans that manoeuvred dangerously across the fairway, and at the junks with poops and prows like Elizabethan caravels, huge painted eyes on the bows, as they swung awkwardly on the whirling tide.

As the bridge telegraph rang to stop engines, the sun began to turn the river into liquid gold. The seething number of boats indicated the crowded life ashore, a shadowy junk sliding past against the sun, its patched brown sail webbed like a bat's wing. Over the water came the steady chanting of the crew heaving at the huge stern oar, and with it a smell, of rotten fish that was both pungent and nauseating.

Willie breathed deeply. It was exciting and turbulent and he had known he was approaching the Yangtze miles before he had spotted land because the water had become yellow and oozy with the silt that flowed down from upcountry and emptied itself into the thirty-mile-wide river mouth. Because he had money in his pocket, he had enjoyed the voyage, seeing for the first time places like Colombo, Penang and Singapore, where the sun sank in a glory of crimson, purple and gold, to begin the deep Malay night.

He was proud of himself and flush with money, and he was well aware that people were asking who he was. Feeling it was important to be noticed, he had travelled first class and his dark looks, new suits and the silver-topped cane and boater he had acquired had attracted attention at once. There had even been a quick shipboard romance with the daughter of a wealthy Singapore businessman who had chased him round the ship until she got her claws on him. She had even got him into her cabin, but he had not let it come to anything and had left her spitting obscenities at his back, startled at the words a well-bred young lady knew.

As the ship worked alongside next day, he stared across the water to the line of the bund, and saw that Shanghai was growing fast, a strange mixture of East, West and America, with here and there new electric signs, glaring advertisements and big hotels. Mule-pulled trams ground round ever corner, edging past the pony carts and rickshaws, and there were already people of all nationalities there, British, French, Japanese, Croats, Balkan Slavs and Russian anarchists who had fled from the secret police of the Tsar's autocratic empire to the north.

Hawking and spitting as they moved, blue-clad coolies swarmed along the shore, trudging backwards and forwards across the moored junks that made a heaving catamaran, selling food, hoisting bales, pulling carts or pushing barrows with huge single wheels that screeched like chalk dragged across a slate. The noise was staggering, the honking of launches and the roaring of klaxons dulled by the high yelling of the Chinese labourers, brassware sellers, sweet vendors, goldfish hawkers, cooked-noodle merchants and recipe designers, as they struggled for right of way among the rickshaw boys, chair carriers and wheelbarrow porters.

A gang of coolies were unloading sacks of rice from Rangoon from a steamer, the sun glowing like a golden orange through the hanging cloud of dust they stirred up. From the coolies, their ribs showing like bony fans as they laboured, came a song like the humming of a swarm of bees, a few notes that rose and fell, never stopping as the men jogged up and down the gangplank under their loads. Beyond them, the whole line of the shore heaved with humanity, a blue and brown ants' nest of people shoving and pushing in a constant struggle to find space to work, to live, to raise a family, to eat, to sleep, to breathe, even to die.

The ship north from Shanghai was an old steamer with a funnel like a cigarette that poured soot over the huddled Chinese who travelled on the deck, eating and sleeping there, preparing their own food on little charcoal stoves, squatting patiently among the deck cargo, apparently indifferent to what happened. The first class area was better but still shabby and well worn, and the officers wore revolvers as a protection against the pirates who from time to time appeared in fast boats from the cheeks or inlets along the shore.

They liked to pounce on becalmed sailing ships, appearing in swift sail-and-oar prahus, driving in on all sides, so that even a ship with guns couldn't stop them. Showering their victim with stink balls to blind the crew with smoke and fumes, they swarmed over the sides, shooting, stabbing and totally merciless. Steamers were more difficult to tackle, but occasionally, when they broke down and had to make repairs, even they became victims.

This time it wasn't pirates but an unexpected gale opposite the old mouth of the Hwang, lumpy head seas that set the ship shuddering under the blows, and sent water pouring over the bulwark to wash out the galley and smash plates and bottles. It piled junks and sampans ashore and left a mat of drowned Chinese floating in the shallows. It didn't worry Willie, who was a good sailor, and as the wind dropped, he enjoyed the voyage past

Tsingtao, the promontory of Shantung and Weihaiwei, to Tientsin, from where he could take a train to Peking. He was longing for Abigail. Would she be there? There were no real ties between them and if she had used her brains as he had – and he felt sure she would have done – she would have as much money in her possession or nestling in the bank making interest as he had. But there was really nothing to bring her back. She had been disillusioned with China and, despite her enthusiasm for what they were doing, she might well have decided to stay where she belonged in America.

He swallowed quickly, his eyes bright with anticipation but a worried frown between his eyes. Dozens of people, both Chinese and European, were waiting for the ship. As he searched among them, his heart sank because there was no sign of Abigail's blue coat. Coming from the Mission, she had never possessed much but Chinese garments, cotton for the heat, quilted for the winter, and almost the first thing he had done for her as she had thrown in her lot with him was to buy her two or three European dresses and the blue coat in Peking. They had thought it smart, but he realised now it was no smarter than the suit he'd had made by a Chinese tailor who had worked overnight to deliver it the following day, so he could appear presentable in front of the people who bought what they had to sell.

Then he saw a woman in a long pink coat over a cream dress, and a wide straw hat with cherries and a feather on it that was pinned to her hair with hatpins decorated with butterflies. She was jumping up and down excitedly and waving a parasol.

His heart missed a beat as he realised it was Abigail, and as he stepped on the quay from the gangplank she fell into his arms.

'Oh, Lor', Ab,' he said with heartfelt thankfulness and relief. 'I'm so glad to see you.'

'And I'm glad to see you!'

'New coat,' he pointed out between kisses. 'You look smart.'

'Bought it in New York,' she said. 'People stared at me in the blue one. It was so out of fashion.' She ran her hand down the garment, enjoying the feel of the material. 'Right up to date. Even the brocade on the front. I thought I ought to look the part.'

'Me, too,' Willie admitted. 'Good for business. Put it down to expenses.' He grinned at her, surprised how pleased he was to see her, how excited by the feel of her alongside. 'We need a hotel.'

'We could catch the train straightaway.'

'We need a hotel first. Good meal. I did all right.'

'Me, too.'

'We need to celebrate then. And we need a bed.'

'Are you tired?'

'No.' He grinned.

She smiled back at him. 'We'll have to be careful now, Willie,' she said.

'Why?'

'I'm going to have a baby. That's why I was so glad to see you back. And we ought to get married, too, if you want your son and heir to be legitimate.'

'I was surprised by the enthusiasm,' Willie said as they sat on the edge of the bed drinking warm champagne with a lump of ice for a cooler. 'We can sell more, lots more. I fixed up an agent in London to handle things. Chap called Julian Brassard. He's honest all right. Bit of a flower but he's straight. How did you do?'

'The same. People in San Francisco went crazy for what I had. I went first to someone I knew from the Bible Society – the people who paid for me to go to China. They didn't think much of what I showed them. Said they were pagan. But then I decided to try one of the big antique stores. They didn't argue. They took everything I offered. Then I thought perhaps San Francisco was too close to China and that bits and pieces must always find their way there across the Pacific, because it's the nearest point in the States. So I took a train to New York. Took days, Willie. But they fell over themselves. It was worth every cent I paid for the ticket. I sold everything.'

'How much?'

'You'd be surprised. I was. I have the accounts in my case for you to see.'

He grinned, delighted with their success. 'Ab,' he said, 'we ought to go to Sian again. There must be tons of stuff there. We can keep going on it for ever.'

'Perhaps not forever, Willie.' Her face clouded. 'In the States things go in fashions and we ought not to put all our money into it in case the prices fall. We should try other things.'

It made sense.

'Such as what?' Willie asked.

'Silk. Things like that. Shantung silk's very popular.'

'All right. Let's do that. I thought also we might do a bit of importing to pay for the exports, so I brought back a few candles and bales of Lancashire cotton, a few tin foods, and dishes and pots that I picked up in Birmingham from a firm that went bust, and a few

Sheffield knives and machetes. Crude things, just a blade and a wooden handle. But they're solid. They sell in Africa. Perhaps they'll sell here.'

His excitement caught her and she laughed. 'We can get things from the States, too, Willie. It's the best place in the world for mass-produced goods. We could make a fortune. *I* brought a few things back, too.'

'Peking's not a good centre, though,' he warned. 'Too far inland. Too many transport costs. Too expensive. Too much under the eyes of everybody. But the Chinese have had to grant more concessions and there'll be more treaty ports along the Yangtze now, where we can set up and expect help. Chinese merchants'll come to us. What about going to Yangpo? It's in Hupeh, just before you get to Hankow and if we get in first we could get the best position.'

Abigail's eyes were eager. 'There's a Scottish Presbyterian pastor I know who went to Yangpo,' she said. 'He could marry us. It'd be nice to have someone we know.'

Convinced that, after the Boxers, the Chinese had got their hatred for the foreign devils out of their system, they returned to Shanghai by the next ferry and started upriver the following day in a brand-new red-funnelled three-decked ship called the *Fan Ling*. Someone had already realised that quick travel was going to become essential and that travellers would demand more comfort than they received aboard the passenger junks, and had started a new service, aiming eventually to provide one ship upriver every day. In the hold were crates of pots and pans, machetes and candles.

The channel was marked by buoys and the shore on either side was lost in a heat haze that made the land quiver and dance. Later, the haze began to lift and it was possible to see ditches and landscapes like the ancient Chinese paintings they sold. What had seemed like blank terraces of earth came alive and the land seethed with cotton-clad ants. Every now and then, roofs lifted over the banks, some of tiles, others of tattered rush matting, but all with curving eaves; then, as the banks fell away again, they looked into paddy fields where women were transplanting the green shoots.

Strings of mules and horses headed along the banks, ears and tails flicking at the flies, then a wheelbarrow loaded with giggling girls holding sunshades. A canvas sheet had even been spread above it like a sail and the coolie pushing it was being driven along in giant strides. Then, as the ship's wash swilled through the open door of a hut, a woman hurtled out, with the swarm of pigs and dogs that shared it, to scream curses at them.

Eventually, the river became a cinnamon ribbon fringed with reeds, its rocks and banks hidden under swirling waters, and the heat became enervating. As they fought to keep cool, the people on the foredeck among the cargo rigged up shelters to provide shade. Mosquitoes were everywhere and that night they were savaged by them. But this was a part of China they had never seen before and they were too excited by their prospects to care. The shore was a dark enchanted shadow, backed by the shapes of the hills and pinpricked with yellow lights.

By the following morning, they were among tree-clad mountains, blue in the mist, and small hills sloping down to the river, where the banks were topped by ancient fortifications or crumbling temples. Junks, a huge raft of floating logs filled with people, dogs and huts and steered by sea anchors, passed them. Great flocks of ducks filled the sky as they passed through a series of lakes, then, round the bend, they saw Yangpo. A Union Jack flew from a flagstaff and huts were spread along the banks near the town walls. As they swung round to go alongside, they passed a sunken river boat lying on its side, the water sluicing in and out of its ports.

'Someone moved a buoy a few nights back,' the mate of the *Fan Ling* told them. 'She was holed and turned on her side. Because of the heat, all the ports were open and everybody was drowned.'

'Who'd shift a buoy like that?' Willie asked.

'They're always at it.' The mate shrugged. 'Bandits. Revolutionaries. This time it was a feller called Fu Su-Lee. General Fu Su-Lee. He was one of the Empress' generals and when the Boxers disappeared he found he was left with an army and no one to fight. Then it occurred to him that, because he had soldiers, he was running the show here, not the government in Peking. So he bought arms with the money he gets from the merchants for not burning their houses down and used it to buy guns and ammunition.'

'Sounds a nice chap. Has it spoiled business?'

'Oh, no! Business is thriving. They never touch Europeans. They've already built a club. Always comes first, a club and a bit of a park, so you can have a walk or a drink without the Chinks butting in. They've built godowns and even one or two houses. Chinese style, of course, but they'll do until they really get established. You thinking of setting up here?'

'Might be. Any space going begging?'

'There's a Portuguese chap called Luis Da Braga who's got half a warehouse spare. Third one along from the landing stage upriver. Red doors.'

That afternoon, before they had even properly established themselves in the only hotel in Yangpo, a two-storey wooden building with a tin roof that was still only half-built, they went to see Da Braga, a young sallow-faced Goanese only recently out from India, who was busy exporting wood oil.

He was friendly, fat, easy-going and quick to smile. 'Sure,' he said, producing a bottle. 'You have one half of the warehouse. I have the other. We do business.'

He promised to store their crates of goods and look after them when they were away, and told them where to find the pastor Abigail knew. The pastor was a slight, grey-haired man called McEwan in grubby white trousers, sandals and an alpaca jacket, a battered straw hat on his head. He said a prayer for them and told them to come back the following afternoon.

They turned up in their best clothes, both a little nervous but confident it would work. Luis Da Braga appeared to give the bride away and the mate from the *Fan Ling* agreeing to be best man, and they stood solemnly in front of Pastor McEwan as he intoned the marriage service over them. When he'd finished, Willie solemnly kissed Abigail on the cheek.

'It's all right after this,' he whispered. 'We can do it legitimately now.'

Her giggle brought a frown from McEwan, then he reached forward to congratulate them and lead them away to sign the register. As he did so, the mate's head cocked and they heard a high-pitched whistle that seemed to hang in the air over them.

'What's that?' Abigail asked, then the mate grabbed the lot of them and pushed them up against the wall just as a tremendous explosion brought the windows in on them in a shower of glass.

'Christ!' Willie roared indignantly. 'What's that?'

The mate brushed the glass off of his uniform. 'It'll be General Fu,' he said. 'He'll be coming back into the town. I hope you've got money for squeeze.'

'Squeeze?'

Da Braga explained. 'He demands taxes from everybody intending to trade here.'

'I thought this was a treaty port and nothing to do with the Chinese.'

'It is, but he has soldiers. It doesn't pay to argue.'

That afternoon, after a little sporadic shelling, General Fu's troops marched into Yangpo. They were a sorry-looking lot strung about with pots and pans and teapots. One or two of them had dead chickens hanging from their belts, one even a dead dog. One dragged a girl along with a rope round her neck. Still in their best clothes and wondering what had hit them, Willie and Abigail stared at the straggle of grubby soldiers as they stumbled past.

'I reckon,' Willie said, 'that it might be as well to postpone setting up here for a year or two. This idea of considering you, not the government, have the power because you've got the soldiers is one that could grow.'

PART TWO

1904–1913

one

Willie's prophecy proved wrong. The Yangtze had always been an area of unrest, and the government in Peking, seeing the danger as quickly as Willie had, ordered troops there at once. They never managed to bring General Fu to battle because, whenever their troops appeared, Fu disappeared, and in the end his reign of terror was ended by the simple Chinese method of poison. A government agent was infiltrated into his yamen to doctor his tea. The agent was discovered and beheaded, but Fu was dead and, since his officers could not produce anyone of a similar stature, they lost control, his army melted away, and there was a degree of peace along the river, so that, to their surprise, the Sarths managed after all to start their business.

Concessions had been granted to European powers along the Yangtze and already they were busy setting up their consulates, and their businessmen and merchants were building their godowns and offices along the bund. Da Braga stuck by his agreement and, sharing his warehouse, the Sarths found themselves in a new venture hundreds of miles from Peking where they had originally started. Because it needed his presence occasionally, from time to time Willie had to leave Abigail in the care of the

Sumters, but, by this time they had an established home with an ayah to look after the baby, a son who was christened Edward Caddy Sarth. To their surprise, the child's birth did not go unnoticed and a small jade elephant arrived, brought by a man in a yellow chair. They had known immediately who had sent it.

'We could get a fortune for it,' Willie said.

Abigail's eyes blazed. 'We don't sell that!' she snapped. 'It belongs to Teddy. It'll always be his, and eventually his children's and his children's children. You're looking at a little piece of history.'

There was also a gift for Abigail, a picnic set of drawers only ten inches high in vermilion lacquer, the trays carved with birds of felicity and bats of happiness, the top with lotus flowers in cream, red and purple surrounded by green leaves floating on blue water.

'Willie,' Abigail gasped. 'It's real Tiao Ch'i. There's a lot of fake stuff about, wood carvings lacquered over, but this is real, a quarter of an inch of solid lacquer on top, applied in coats and polished on a whetstone. A man's whole working life has probably gone into that.'

Because of its unique position at the mouth of the Yangtze, the river that ran through half the provinces of China, it seemed to Willie that they ought to have an office in Shanghai. The place had always been an important centre and, once the British had been granted the right to trade there, the swamp and mud between Soochow Creek and the walled Chinese town had begun to grow into a city. The French and Americans had followed and eventually the original tract of land had grown into a Western oasis.

In winter there were sleet and snow and fogs that drifted in from the sea to chill you to the marrow. In the summer there was an oppressive heat that lay like a blanket over the place, with steamy sunshine and dripping humidity which nothing could ever drive away. But the bund was already growing into a commercial centre with banks, clubs and offices, a place of business houses and godowns, its pavements thronged with pedestrians, businessmen, hawkers, silk sellers, professional letter writers, shoeshine boys and beggars. Along the Bund, every vehicle that had ever been invented moved – sedan chairs, palanquins, ancient carts, rickshaws, horse-drawn trams, even an occasional noisy motor car, all moving alongside the river where the ships arrived with their cargoes. Vessels of every shape and size covered the water like a heaving mat – sampans, tramp steamers, lighters and junks, their sterns like castles, carrying silks, muslins, tea, peanuts, wood, vegetable oils, ironware, glass, paper and ivory.

There were already wealthy men in Shanghai and Willie, startled at the way his bank balance had grown, was beginning to have ambitions to be part of them. Above all, Shanghai was the doorway to the winding, meandering Yangtze and all the concession ports upstream where business was to be done. Chinese-owned factories were often nothing more than derelict sheds or houses where the Chinese labourers worked round the clock, grateful for the meagre wages they received and a daily ration of rice, cabbage and fish and somewhere to sleep. Most of them almost starved, though a few made fortunes by working with the European companies that were being set up. And what was best of all, over all the misery and the affluence there was a policy that nobody asked questions.

Sarth's was a small firm, not to be compared with the great hongs that existed, and at first they operated from a small room which eventually became two rooms, and before long a whole building. Life was exciting and full of incident, but eventually it had to be faced that money was coming in excitingly fast and Willie could not be in two places at once, so that he needed someone to run the Shanghai end of his business when he wasn't there.

It took him forty-eight hours to find a plump Chinese by the name of Lun Foo, who agreed to act as his agent. Not employed by Willie but working for him, Lun Foo was responsible for seeing that goods were shipped or unloaded and despatched to distant cities or across the seas to Europe. The opportunities for such men were dazzling and as soon as it had become known that Willie was seeking such a person he had been besieged by a dozen of them, all offering their services. Lun Foo had seemed the best of the lot, though Willie guessed he was as rapacious as all the others and that the coolies he employed would be on a starvation wage. But that was the way things were done in China and, since he would never be able to change it, he accepted it without question. He had *objets d'art* to leave China for Europe as well as Shantung silk, wood oil, tea, and peanuts, and the usual cargoes of cheap tinware, cutlery, tools and cotton to bring in. He was more than satisfied.

But then he saw Lun Foo with a man called Yip Hsao-Li, a small slender man who liked to consider himself westernised and wore European suits, but who had a reputation that seemed more than a little unsavoury and contacts with the criminal secret societies that worked the back streets of the city. He was a cheerful enough villain, always smiling, and he had no qualms about approaching Willie to do business.

'Perhaps you would like to work with me, Mr Sarth,' he suggested.

Guessing Lun Foo had put him up to it, Willie immediately began to wonder if he was as honest as he'd thought, because Yip was in the same line of business as himself and he had heard he also dealt in opium and even in girls. When he discovered he was Lun Foo's brother-in-law, he even began to wonder if Lun Foo were not only open to bribes but had actually been placed in Willie's path to provide information for Yip.

There was nothing he could prove, but he was well aware by now that that was the way China functioned. Every houseboy had a makee-learn apprentice, and the makee-learn apprentice sometimes had a smaller and younger assistant to do the jobs the makee-learn boy didn't like. Even the British gunboats that kept order upriver had Chinese civilians aboard to do the scrubbing, wash the decks, serve the meals and polish the brass, and they too had their makee-learns, so that there were almost as many unofficial Chinese aboard as sailors, all living in the tiller flat because there was nowhere else for them to sleep. It was the same in the home and one man Willie knew, going to his basement unexpectedly to look for a suitcase, found it inhabited by a dozen of his houseboys' relations. Influence was ubiquitous and 'squeeze' entered everything; it applied to the pencils in the office, the salt in the kitchen, the aspirin from the chemists, the houseboy who wouldn't let the tailor in without receiving his cash. Even the coolie who emptied the night soil buckets to sell as fertiliser, had to pay for the privilege. Everybody wanted a cut.

To protect himself, Willie employed a seventeen-year-old boy called George Kee, whose Chinese father had married a Frenchwoman. He had been educated at an English school, was good-looking, good-natured, reliable and apparently honest. In addition to English, he spoke excellent French and Shanghainese and Willie quickly promoted him over the other clerks with their Chinese mannerisms and pidgin English until he ran the office alone and with considerable efficiency.

'One thing more,' Willie said after six months of watching him work. 'In addition to being chief clerk, you're also my personal assistant with a salary to go with it. You'll know what I'm up to, but there'll be no title, so don't start using one. I want it to remain just between you and me. When I'm not here I want you to keep an eye on things – especially on old Lun Foo. I rely on your discretion. Got it?'

Kee smiled. 'Yes, sir. I've got it.'

When he returned to Peking, Willie found Abigail holding court to a dozen women, most of whom he knew to be the wives of Legation officials, wealthy businessmen or bankers. He did his duty, passing the time of day, pretending to be interested, listening to their gossip, then, as they sent for their chairs and departed, he found Abigail kicking off her shoes and stretching out on a *chaise-longue* in the salon.

'What's all this?' he demanded. 'How come you're so popular all of a sudden?'

Abigail smiled the small secret smile she kept for the occasions when she knew she was one up on him.

'The Empress,' she said. 'I was invited to the Forbidden City for another visit with her.'

'You were?' Willie's eyes bulged. 'What did you do?'

180

'We drank tea, and talked about children.'

Calmly, indifferently, as though it were an everyday occurrence, she gave Willie the details, the yellow chair which had come for her, the horn-blowers and bannermen who had preceded her, the audience chamber with the Empress sitting as they chatted behind the gauze curtain that was part of court protocol.

'What was she like?'

'Sharp. She's a wicked old woman. She gave me a photograph of herself.'

She produced a picture of the Empress in all her robes, surrounded by five of the ladies of her court. 'The one on the right's the Empress Lung Yu,' Abigail said. 'She's young and very pretty and she's the wife of the Emperor, though it's obvious that neither she nor he counts for much. It's Old Buddha makes the decisions.'

Willie gestured about him. A forgotten pair of gloves lay on a table, a small prayer book brought as a gift, a few personal cards, all from Legation wives.

'What about all these?' he said.

'They invited themselves. They wanted to know what she had to say.'

'It's not long since they were terrified that she wanted to have their throats cut.'

Abigail giggled. 'It's the atmosphere of depravity and murder that fascinates them,' she said. 'A few have been to palace receptions but none of them have had tea with Old Buddha on their own. They feel a new leaf's been turned.'

'Has it?'

Abigail smiled. 'No. But the Court's worried. There's an anti-dynasty movement about.'

Willie was still staring about him, at the empty tea cups, a misplaced fan, the photograph, the empty plates that had contained cakes and biscuits. 'Some of that lot couldn't stand us a year or so ago,' he said.

'It's different now. How did your trip go?'

'Everything's fixed.' Willie gave her a slightly bewildered look. 'Ab, we're making money. Hand over fist. Don't you think we ought to forget these antiques, these Chinese artefacts and things? There's a lot more money in imports and exports. China's a big country and they need things. They sell cheaply because they produce things with coolie labour on a starvation wage which we can sell at high prices in England. We're wasting our time with these other things. We should drop 'em.'

'No, Willie.'

'They're small fiddly things. Not simple enough. Not so much profit as straightforward goods.'

She still resisted. 'People regard us as experts now,' she said. 'They even come to me for advice. We should keep it that way. Something may go wrong.'

He saw there was sense in what she said. Like his wife, Willie was far from slow to learn and, while other Europeans around him basked in the calm that had followed the Boxer Rising, he had noticed that new feelings were afoot and there were malcontents anxious for a change from the dictatorial decrees of the Imperial Court. Dangerous, even lethal, ideas were being discussed openly and disseminated by the Chinese periodicals which were being smuggled across the continent by travellers and circulated hand to hand.

'There's talk of "Ko-Ming",' Abigail pointed out. 'Originally it meant the transition from one dynasty to another, from one ruler to the next. But it's now being freely translated and used in a different sense altogether. It now means revolution.'

It was then that Willie realised that the expression, which he'd heard but not fully understood, was being applied chiefly to the activities of a man whose name was being heard more and more often, a Cantonese Protestant by the name of Sun Yat-Sen, who had studied in the United States and Hong Kong and had practised medicine in Macao. He believed in China for the Chinese and his followers were multiplying. Once he had come within an ace of being executed and his prestige among the Cantonese was enormous.

The business at Yangpo began to flourish at once. Da Braga was an honest man. Plump, olive-skinned and with a nervous smile, he had appeared in China not long before Willie and still seemed uncertain whether he belonged there or not. He was a shrewd businessman though, and was always ready to welcome Willie with a brandy bottle on his desk. Other firms began to notice Yangpo, among them a French firm and an American firm called Wissermann's, then, to Willie's surprise, another godown appeared just along the Bund with the name Wishart above the door. It was obvious that others beside himself had noticed the possibilities of making money in the concession ports and a few enquiries revealed that old Wishart was dead and that it was Emmeline who was now running the show. He'd heard some time before that she was married – to the latest of a string of clerks and one this time, he heard, whose skills belonged to the bedroom rather than the counting house and was giving her trouble from time to time.

Business continued to increase, but what Abigail had advocated began to seem sound sense, because not only did small artefacts find their way from the Court to her for her appraisal, but she was also now being sought out by European collectors, some of whom appeared from London or New York seeking her advice.

Things were changing, though. The Russians had taken advantage of the Boxer Rising to occupy Manchuria and now threatened to move into China proper, and, as Abigail had said, immediately all the other burglars who were living off China, seeing their own interests in danger, sprang to the defence of their victim. British and German soldiers advanced northward, the British Yangtze naval squadron sailed to Taku and Japan sent troops to Korea. Faced with such strong opposition, the Russians stayed north of the Great Wall, but the threat still remained and, fearful of her interests in India, to everyone's surprise, Britain engineered an alliance with the Japanese that was clearly aimed at keeping Russia quiet, both sides offering to remain neutral if the other should find herself at war with Russia. The tension built, and for Willie the result was surprising.

There was rioting at Yangpo, but it was not political and not the doing of Sun Yat-Sen. Chiefly it was frustration by the Chinese who felt that their country was being snatched from under their feet. There had been tension for some time as students from downriver roamed the streets shouting slogans, against the dynasty for giving their country away against the foreigners who were taking it, and the trigger was a Russian merchant, a man with a title who had doubtless been in the habit of flogging his serfs back in Russia. He whipped a Chinese servant in a fit of drunken rage and within an hour there was a mob at his door and the windows of his house were smashed. The

Russian was smuggled to the river and aboard a British gunboat, but for several hours the mob rampaged up and down the bund beating up any Chinese who dealt with the foreigners, even the rickshaw boys who pulled them in their wheeled chairs. The place was not yet organised to combat the disorder and there were not enough Sikh policemen, while the Chinese troops simply disappeared and were probably even helping as the night erupted into flames and darkness. A warehouse was set on fire and the Russian's car, a Hispano Suiza, one of the first petrol-driven vehicles to appear outside Shanghai, was turned over and set on fire.

Listening behind the barred doors of the warehouse because it was impossible to get to the hotel, Willie began to ask himself if he'd been wise. He had even planned for Abigail to accompany him to Yangpo, but fortunately she had put him off.

'I can't,' she announced. 'I'm pregnant again.'

'Again?'

'What do you expect, the way you chase me round the bedroom?'

Willie had always thought the business of having a family consisted of one child after a decent interval and then, after a long gap to get used to the idea, perhaps another.

'At least it's legitimate,' Abigail had said, and it was true that it had required the handing over of a sum of money in Yangpo to produce a marriage certificate to show they had been married there, nine months and ten days before the birth of Edward Caddy Sarth, instead of the seven months and two days which was the actual figure. Willie had held up his hands placatingly. 'All right,' he had said. 'It's all right, Ab. I understand. It's fine with me. I'll go on my own.'

Now he was wondering why he'd come at all.

By morning, the noise had died down and there was only a shamefaced guilt about the place. Charred walls and blackened timbers rose out of the smouldering debris. The Russian, well guarded now by policemen and personal bodyguards, was studying the burnt-out wreck of his motor car, and a few coolies, mouths agape, were staring at the damage that had been done. Others, scowling and sullen and without doubt the guilty ones, watched from corners.

Abigail had been dead right not to let Willie give up the antiques business. That could safely be conducted through agents and now that they had made their contacts, the *objets d'art*, the carpets, the paintings, the manuscripts, the jade, the ivory figures, came in on their own. They would be living on a knife-edge for a long time, he suspected, and business that involved goods such as coal, tea and metalware might easily have to be abandoned at any time in the event of a major upheaval, simply because of their weight, whereas Abigail's treasures could almost be carried in their pockets.

A small procession came past – soldiers, a few Chinese peasants and a couple of students with their hands tied, a wooden collar on their necks. With them was a bare-chested man with a red hat and sash. Across his shoulders he carried a huge curved sword with a red tassel on the handle.

'Prisoners,' Da Braga said. 'Caught during the riot.'

'What'll happen to 'em?' Willie asked.

The Goanese shrugged and helped himself from the brandy bottle. 'They'll execute them,' he said. 'This afternoon.'

Willie nodded. There would be no trial. Merely an accusation, a pointing finger, and then the nerve-wracking wait for death.

'I'm going to the hotel,' he said. 'To shave and clean up.'

Yangpo's smells were those of a feudal village. Its walls were twelve feet thick and crowned with weeds and along their base on the river banks was all the town's refuse, dumped there to await the spring flooding of the river to carry it away. The streets were full of what had once been elaborately carved latticework, now decrepit with disrepair, and the crowding people surged round deep holes in the pavement where stone locks had been stolen to make bases for household stoves.

The hotel was drab, with a picture of Edward VII over the desk to show how Westernised it was, but the roofs were of corrugated iron and chickens scratched in the entrance for the scraps thrown from the dining room. Willie was in his room wiping his face when there was a knock on the door. Still without the stiff collar that gave him respectability with the Europeans and face with the Chinese, he opened it, expecting it to be Da Braga. Instead it was a woman. She was in full fig, in what looked like her best dress, a brocaded coat, and a flowered hat, a fox fur round her neck against the cold, her hands in a fur muff.

Willie stared, wiped his face, and stared again.

'Emmeline,' he said. 'Emmeline Wishart.'

'Emmeline Gummer now,' she corrected him. 'I married Russell Gummer a year ago.'

Willie tossed aside the towel and reached for his collar and tie. 'You'd better come in. It's a good job it's Yangpo and not Golders Green, or the neighbours would start talking.'

She sniffed and he probed. 'Gummer?' he asked. 'Clerk, was he?'

'Yes.'

'What happened to the thin pale one with specs?'

Emmeline shrugged. 'He was no man.'

'And Russell is?'

She didn't answer.

'Why didn't you bring him with you? Or do you leave him to look after the office in Peking or Shanghai?'

'He's here. In Yangpo.'

'Then what's he doing allowing his lady wife to visit gentlemen in their hotel rooms?'

'Because he's somewhere in the Chinese quarter of the town.'

'What?' Willie turned quickly. Despite his experience, Willie wouldn't have chanced going into the Chinese quarter just then. 'After business, was he?'

Emmeline's face grew stiff. 'No,' she snapped. 'He was after a woman.'

Willie's hands, working at his tie, slowed and came to a stop. 'A Chinese woman?'

Emmeline frowned. 'Can I sit down?'

'If it helps. What happened?'

Emmeline seated herself on the edge of a chair and took out a handkerchief to dab her nose and eyes. He knew she wasn't crying, because she was too tough for that. 'I shouldn't have left him here,' she said slowly. 'We set up the business here and had a compradore to look after things while we went to Shanghai. But he said someone ought to be here more often and there was such a lot to do in Shanghai. Things are just beginning to get going, Willie.'

'You don't have to tell me.'

'I stayed in Shanghai and sent him up. He was alone too long.'

Willie finished tying his tie, slipped into his jacket and began buttoning it. He knew what she was saying. Men in hot countries got strange ideas, and he thanked God he had someone as attractive and intelligent as Abigail.

'Virile sort, was he?'

Emmeline was silent for a second, then she stamped her foot. 'He couldn't keep away from women,' she snapped.

'Bit different from the chap with specs. *He* looked as if anything like that would have given him curvature of the spine.'

Emmeline drew a deep breath. 'He's a big man,' she said. 'Dark. Strong. He'd been a sailor.'

'Like me.'

Emmeline frowned. 'He didn't have your sense, Willie.'

'He couldn't have had. He didn't get away.'

Her head came up. 'That's not funny,' she snapped.

'No,' he agreed. 'It ain't.'

'He was always after girls. Whenever he'd had a few drinks. I knew about it.'

'Warn him?'

'I tried to. But I was afraid he'd up and leave me. I needed him.'

'Good in the counting house, was he?'

'Not very. But he was able and he could handle the Chinese. They were frightened to death of him. I arrived here two days ago and there was no sign of him. The Chinese clerk said he was out on business. But he didn't come back. He didn't come back to the house at night either. I have a house, a new one, along Concession Street. I expect you have, too.'

'Not yet,' Willie said. 'Sleep here or in a camp bed in the godown. Other things to pay for first.'

She drew another deep breath. 'When he didn't turn up the next day, I made enquiries. I found out he has a Chinese girl in Flowering Almond Street in the old town. I expect he's still there.'

Willie eyed her warily. 'So where do I come into all this?' he asked.

'I want you to fetch him back.'

There was a long silence as Willie digested her words. The Chinese quarter was no place to go just at that moment with tension still high and the hatred for foreigners unmuted.

'I can't go down there,' he said.

'Can't you get a few men together? Decent men. White men. A few policemen.'

'It would start the rioting all over again.'

'I need him, Willie.'

'In bed or for the counting house?'

She was silent for a second and he knew that neither was half so important as her own respectability. In the gossipy atmosphere of European women Peccadilloes soon surfaced alone in a foreign country with too many servants and not enough to do. It had always been different with Abigail, because she was always in demand for her knowledge of Chinese artifacts. In fact – the

190

thought suddenly occurred to him – some of the smooth bastards from the Legations who came for her advice might well be more interested in Abigail than the artifacts, and he decided he'd better keep his eyes open – not for Abigail, but for the smooth bastards.

'I can't do it, Em,' he said.

'Willie, you must!'

'Em, I won't even know where Flowering Almond Street is.'

'The servant does. He took him there. He'll lead the way.'

Willie had a feeling he was already neck-deep in trouble, but he couldn't quite see how he could back out. Emmeline was one of the few European women in Yangpo and he was one of the few white men. And, as he'd already told her, mustering a small army to make the rescue wasn't the answer. There'd be more rioting and probably more deaths.

'How far in is it?'

'Not far, the servant said.'

'Is this woman a – a – is she a professional, Em?'

'No. The servant says she's the daughter of a compradore who worked for the French. He got to know her somehow by just going about his business. The servant says he doesn't pay her. He just gives her gifts. Rolls of silk. Things like that. I imagine she's probably quite a decent girl – or was till he got hold of her. It's Russell who needs watching. Will you fetch him out?'

Willie frowned. 'You're better off without him, Emmeline.'

'No. I need him.'

He wondered why. He knew Emmeline's appetites only too well and perhaps Russell Gummer was the one man who could satisfy them.

'All right,' he agreed. 'I'll go. Tonight. After dark. Tell your servant to report to my warehouse, I'll be in the office there, waiting for him.'

two

'Willie, you are mad!'

Da Braga stood by the door of the office watching Willie, unable to understand why he was willing to risk his neck in what seemed a wildcat rescue. He, Da Braga, would never have taken such a risk. But, he had to admit, there was something about Willie that was different from other men. He was quick-witted, intelligent and brave, always willing to take a chance for business, never able to miss an opportunity, a merchant adventurer out of his time, willing to go into the vast interior of China in a way few others did.

'I've *got* to go, Luis.'

It was a matter of honour in a way, because Willie was often assailed by the thought that he had treated Emmeline badly. He hadn't, he knew, almost the other way round, but it was something that would probably never go away.

'Are you expecting rewards from this woman?' This was the only reason Da Braga could think of, because Willie wasn't in need of money and Emmeline was still good looking. 'What will she give you in return?'

'Business.' Even this wasn't true because Wishart's had never pushed trade towards Sarth's and he didn't think they ever would, but he had to make some excuse.

'Are you sure?' Da Braga asked.

'I'll make sure.'

'Is that all?'

'It'll do.'

They were still talking when the scratching came at the door. The servant Emmeline had sent was a small man with a twisted back, a grey wisp of beard and a pigtail. Willie stared at him, wondering if he could be trusted. If he disappeared into the maze of streets in the Chinese City, it wouldn't be difficult to betray him. Did the old man have strong feelings against the Europeans like the students? Did he resent the way they had taken over his country?

Willie drew a deep breath and pushed a cigarette at the Chinese who bobbed his head, grinned and lit up, puffing quickly and filling the office with smoke. Taking off his jacket, Willie slipped into a blue coolie's smock and picked up a wide-brimmed woven hat. Shoving the heavy Russian revolver he carried with him into his belt, he gestured at the Chinese.

'Right,' he said. 'Let's go.'

The Chinese bobbed his head again and tossed his cigarette through the door. 'Can do, Master,' he said. 'We makee quick, I think.'

It was bitterly cold, the night brilliant with frost, and they moved along the bund, their heads down so that the flaring torches stuck into the walls would not catch their faces. Yangpo was a strange place. In the spring there was a yellowgreen mist of new leaves along the banks with patches of pink and white flowers whose perfume sometimes even overlaid the smell of the winter's rubbish, but in the autumn it could be chill and damp and in the winter there were dull skies and misty rain, with the mountains behind black against the steely sky, and the river shrunken to grey channels between the sandbars.

As they moved among the piled refuse, a thin stream of coolies moved past them, one of them carrying two severed heads on a pole, and eventually, by the execution ground, they came on a huddle of wailing women crouched over a group of bodies, engaged in the grisly task of sewing more heads to headless trunks.

'Cannot meet ancestors without heads,' the old man said gravely. 'Very bad loss. Lose face.' He gave a sudden giggle as if he'd appreciated his unintentional joke.

Nearby, a group of coolies waited with coffins, but nobody had eyes for the two figures shuffling past. The executions had taken place that afternoon, the dead men lined up in a row on the edge of the river by the Chinese soldiers to be examined by the headsman. Willie had watched it all through the window of Da Braga's office. Eventually, the men had been led to a line of white stones by the road and made to kneel, then, one by one, a soldier had reached over them from the front, grasping the pigtail to drag the head down and forward. As the executioner had leapt forward with a shout and the huge shining blade had come down, the snick had been audible even in Da Braga's office, the severed heads rolling across the road.

Now and again, they passed a huddled figure, asleep or dead – it was hard to tell which, and nobody cared much – sometimes a coolie with his carrying pole still on his shoulder. They entered the city through the great studded gate in the river wall and, groping their way by the faint

195

light of hanging lanterns, the dim bulk of the city black against the sky, they stumbled in and out of crooked streets.

They could hear the remnants of the mob baying a few streets away, a few high-pitched shouts and once the crash of glass. Willie's eyes were everywhere, on the look out for treachery. He still didn't trust the old man, but so far he had given no indication of hostility. Several times he heard rats squeaking and once several of them ran across his feet. The place was ominously quiet, with every door and window shuttered and barred after the rioting. There were puddles filmed with ice and the smell of drains, ordure and rotting rubbish.

The Chinese turned into a street that was wider than the rest and gestured ahead. 'Master come,' he said. 'The Street of Flowering Almond.'

He stopped at a plank door and began to scratch at it. It was opened almost at once by a young man in a quilted coat. Behind him was a girl, small and pretty, her jetty hair done in wings on either side of her face.

'You come for Mastah Gummer?' the young man said.

Willie nodded and, as the door opened wider, they pushed inside.

'Where is he?'

The Chinese gestured towards a plank door. Gummer was in the room beyond, sprawled on a string bed, stark naked, his mouth wide open, his eyes closed, stinking of whisky. Willie stared at him furiously.

How in the name of God, he thought, was he going to get such a man to safety? Gummer was strong, muscled and powerful, his big dark-skinned body covered with black hair. No wonder he had suited Emmeline. No wonder she wanted him back.

'I shall need help,' he said. 'You have brothers?'

The Chinese nodded.

'Fetch them.'

The Chinese shook his head. 'No come.' He was obviously terrified.

'This is your sister?'

'My sister, Mastah.'

'If he's found here, it'll be death for her. You too. The students will kill you. Fetch brothers. Plenty money. I give.' He showed the money in his hand. 'For Chinaman. For helpee.'

The Chinese stared at Gummer's big body in terror, unable to see how he could be smuggled away.

'Coffin,' Willie said. 'Buy coffin. Plenty coffin on bund. Bring here. Understand? Old uncle dies. Must be buried. Got it?'

The Chinese nodded.

'Right. Chop chop. Quick. Go.'

As the Chinese disappeared, the door closing softly behind him, Willie stared at Gummer, hating him for the trouble he was causing him. The girl, standing in a corner, her arms round herself, hugging herself as if she were cold, watched him, her eyes fearful.

'You love?'

She shook her head and gestured with her fingers to indicate that the affair between them had been one of money only. For a moment, Willie sympathised with Gummer because the girl was delicate-looking, frail, gentle and very feminine. Perhaps she supplied what Emmeline failed to supply. From his own experience, he knew Emmeline was a domineering lover, and perhaps Gummer had decided that what he got from her wasn't

197

worth the security of being her husband with a business behind him.

Eventually, the young Chinese returned. There were four men with him and they were carrying a coffin.

'Tell Chinamen uncle die,' he said.

'Good. Shovel him in.'

Holes were bored in the coffin lid and it was unscrewed and Gummer stuffed inside, wrapped in a blanket, his clothes packed around him. It was Willie who crossed his hands on his chest.

'Screw him down,' he said.

It wasn't going to be easy because, if Gummer recovered his senses he'd wonder where he was and it wouldn't do to be found carrying a coffin with the body inside pounding on the lid to be let out. At least Gummer wouldn't suffocate.

'Right. Let's go.'

Money was distributed and they made ready to leave. Hoisting the coffin up was difficult because Gummer was heavy, but they got it on their shoulders and began to march solemnly down the narrow street. A coolie coming towards them flattened against the wall and bent his head in respect for the dead as they passed. Returning to the bund, they arrived at the place of execution just as the women finished their grisly task and began to stuff the bodies into the coffins the coolie's had brought. Solemnly, they waited in the shadows until they could join the little procession and move off after them. A few coolies and students watched silently.

The last of the unrest was dying away. Hardly daring to breathe at the front of the coffin, Willie pushed stolidly ahead. Behind him the Chinese muttered, terrified of being found out. At one point, above the yelling in the town, he thought he could hear muffled thumps and scratches near his ear and wondered if Gummer had recovered consciousness and was trying to fight his way out. Praying he wouldn't start yelling, he continued to plod forward and eventually the imagined bumps and shuffles died away and he decided he'd gone to sleep again.

At the end of the bund, while the little procession went one way, Willie's group went the other. Nobody seemed to notice and they passed on towards the European quarter. As they reached it, a Sikh policeman stepped forward, his hand raised.

'Get out of the way, you fool,' Willie snarled at him.

'You cannot come here, Chinaman.'

'Yes, I can, you bloody idiot,' Willie snapped. 'This is a rescue. There's a white man in here. I've fetched him out of the Chinese City. If we don't get him somewhere safe and open him up, he'll suffocate.'

The Sikh was obdurate and, desperate, Willie wrenched off his hat and stared at him. 'I'm Sarth,' he said. 'William Sarth. That's my godown there. Let me past.'

The policeman was finally convinced and they covered the last few hundred yards in a hurried shuffle. Da Braga was waiting as they appeared, and he opened the wide door so that they entered almost at a run. Panting, their breath hanging in little steamy puffs on the cold air, they put the coffin on a pile of crates and Willie sent the hat skimming out of sight.

'Screwdriver, Luis.'

As they lifted the lid, the stench rocked them back. Gummer had obviously recovered consciousness and been sick.

'Get him out.'

They lifted the fouled naked shape out and laid it on the crates. 'Fetch a bucket of water.'

Disgusted with Gummer, hating the trouble he had caused, Willie was not in the mood to be gentle. Taking the bucket from Da Braga, he sloshed it over the naked body, fully expecting Gummer to sit up spluttering, swearing and offering to knock somebody's head off. He didn't move.

'Willie –' Da Braga's eyes widened. ' – I think –'

Willie stared at him, then at the Chinese standing round him, their mouths open. Then he grabbed for Gummer's wrist and felt it. There was no pulse.

'Willie,' Da Braga muttered, 'he is dead.'

'He was alive when we shoved him in,' Willie said.

'He is not alive now.' Da Braga put his hand out to feel for a pulse in Gummer's neck. He turned to Willie and shook his head.

'He couldn't have suffocated in that time,' Willie said. 'There were plenty of breathing holes.'

Da Braga leaned forward and, forcing open Gummer's mouth, put his finger in and hooked out a set of false teeth.

'He didn't suffocate, Willie,' he said. 'He was sick and he choked on vomit and his own false teeth.'

Because of the heat, they buried Gummer the same afternoon, in the same coffin in which he had been rescued from Flowering Almond Street.

They carried the body in a horse-drawn cart to a small strip of ground at the back of a mission church near the Chinese cemetery, run by Pastor McEwan, the man who had married Willie and Abigail. He wanted to know what denomination Gummer belonged to, arguing that he couldn't be buried by him if he were not a Presbyterian. His shock of grey hair made him look fanatic and a little mad.

'How did he die?' he demanded.

'He was drunk.'

'Then there's no place for him here!'

'Don't talk bloody silly,' Willie snapped. 'He's a European and he has to be buried. What do you suggest we do? Stick him on the bund and let him fade away?'

In the end McEwan agreed on a modified service. Emmeline seemed indifferent and Willie even suspected that she was probably glad to be rid of her troublesome husband. There were plenty of other men who could fill her bed or occupy her counting house.

McEwan was waiting for them by the church, which was built in a style that was half Glasgow-Presbyterian and half Chinese. The graves behind carried a similar mixture of names, varying from that of the Rev. Archibald Munro, who had died in 1894, to that of Lee Chen-Si, a child who had been knocked down by a horse.

They had to wait until he had conducted the service for one of his converts and had to stand in the cold while the family sang a hymn and recited the Lord's prayer.

> 'Arthur, which art in Heaven,
>   Harold be thy name,
>   Thy kin done come,
>   Thee Willie Dunn...'

Listening, Willie wondered how much it meant to them.

In the Chinese part of the cemetery with its strange cupola-like headstones, they could see paper streamers fluttering in the wind on the burial mounds to keep away evil spirits. A student, the son of a wealthy merchant, who had been killed in the rioting, was being buried there and a vast procession was snaking in from the road, with lanterns, gongs and a band discordantly playing 'Colonel Bogey'. There were dragon kites, bouquets of flowers, models of favourite pets, a solemn portrait of the dead boy and a notice announcing his virtues printed on it in Chinese characters in gilt paint.

Paid mourners in grubby white clothes, moving in traditional attitudes of grief, were clearing their throats and spitting ready to give tongue as they edged to the grave, followed by musicians blowing throaty sighs from instruments like hand pumps. Pigeons with reeds in bamboo tubes attached to their backs were released in a cloud of drifting feathers to add the wailing sounds of the lutes to the din. Solemn Taoist monks, in mitre hats and carrying horse-hair fly swats and prayer scrolls, brought money, lacquer boxes, songbirds and effigies of dragons to accompany the dead boy to paradise.

Pastor McEwan stared coldly at them as they moved among the burial mounds with their yellowing skeletons in rotting coffins where the rain had washed away the soil, and refused to proceed until the noise had died down. 'Pagan music,' he said. 'I can't bury a Christian soul with that going on.'

Eventually the gonging, blaring and wailing died and, as the Chinese peasant spectators turned round, their heads along the dividing wall like coconuts at a fairground shy, he sniffed and proceeded with the service.

'For as much as it hath pleased Almighty God and His great mercy...' The high-pitched voice, scraping at the nerves, seemed totally lacking in emotion. Stiff in his best suit with his high starched collar, Willie stood alongside a silent Emmeline, who was dressed in a black alpaca coat run up in a couple of hours by a Chinese tailor and worn over a grey dress. He was wondering if Gummer had ever been to church; if he believed; if, in fact, the ceremony really mattered any more to him than the one for the converts.

He had not been back to the hotel long when he was called to the door of his room. The old Chinese who had led him into the city was waiting there for him with the reception clerk. He held an envelope and a large wrapped parcel.

'Missee send this for Mastah,' he announced.

Willie nodded and tipped him, wondering what Emmeline was up to.

The envelope contained money and a note saying it was to repay what he had handed over to bribe the Chinese. The wrapped object was a lacquered bowl which he recognised at once as Ming.

He sat with it in his hands, staring at it, knowing it was worth a small fortune. The note with it said simply, 'In gratitude. Always my love. Emmeline.'

He jumped up at once, guessing what she was up to. Having got rid of Gummer, she was taking advantage of the absence of Abigail to get her claws in him again.

Rewrapping the bowl, he marched out of the hotel, called a rickshaw and had himself driven to Emmeline's new house. As the rickshaw stopped in front, he saw a curtain move upstairs and knew she was waiting for him.

The servant who let him in bent low in a kow-tow. 'Missee upstairs. Massah follow.'

Stamping upstairs behind the Chinese, Willie found himself let into a bright sunny room furnished with a carpet from North China in blue, white and pink. Since getting her hands on her father's money, Emmeline had never stinted herself and there was a *chaise-longue*, an armchair and a dressing table. The curtains were of gauze and moved slightly in the breeze. Through the door, Willie could see into the bedroom, where there was a huge bed, with a canopy where the big mosquito net was furled.

Emmeline appeared almost at once. She was in white lace, with a flowing kimono-like garment over her shoulders, and her pale face was touched with colour. He guessed she had taken trouble with her appearance.

He got down to brass tacks at once and placed the Ming bowl on the dressing table among the flowers. 'That thing's worth a fortune, Emmeline,' he said.

'I know. I couldn't think how to repay you for what you did.'

'I didn't do much. Your husband died.'

'It wasn't your fault.'

'It might have been. Though, at the time, I couldn't think of any other way of doing it. Perhaps we ought to have brought him out face-down. But then he'd probably have died of suffocation.'

'You did what you had to. You were wonderful, Willie. I'll be eternally grateful.'

'I still can't accept that thing.'

'I must reward you for what you did.'

'*Tried to do*. I didn't succeed. You can put business my way instead.'

'Of course. We're old friends, Willie. I can always do that. In fact – ' she hesitated, ' – there's something you can have straight away. There's a collier, the *Lady Roberts*, full of best Welsh coal, at Port Arthur. He – ' the contempt she felt for Gummer showed in the word ' – he sent it. I bought it for the naval squadron at Shanghai, but, with the trouble growing between the Russians and the Japanese, he thought he could get more for it up there. But the Russians wouldn't touch it. They bring their own, they said, on the railway from as far away as St Petersburg. Make me a reasonable offer, Willie, and it's yours. All you have to do is collect it.'

'Port Arthur's no place to visit just now,' Willie pointed out. 'Not with the trouble between the Russians and the Japanese boiling up.'

'You can have it cheaply, Willie. I'll be glad to get it off my hands. Obviously now that *he's* dead, I've got to give all my attention to Wishart's and I've got to make sure he hasn't done anything else stupid. Give me a cheque now and it's yours.'

'You don't buy ships and cargoes like that,' he protested. 'You need papers.'

'I've got them, Willie. They're all here. He brought them with him. Proud as can be of what he'd done.' She snorted. 'He was useless! You'd make a profit if you got it down to Shanghai for the Navy.'

'If fighting starts, I might not.'

'I talked to the consul before I came up here. He assured me fighting won't start before the spring. Wars never start before the spring, he said. He said I had plenty of time. But now I haven't. I'm needed here, and then down in Shanghai. For all I know, he's bankrupted Wishart's.'

Willie paused, he liked the sea and was fascinated by ships. He always had been. Even at Wainwright and Halliday's he had always spent more time than he ought in London Docks, trying to catch the whiff of the river, inhaling the smell of rope and tar and tallow. He'd always fancied being a shipping magnate and, while owning one ship hardly put him in that category, at least it was a start. But he still couldn't believe she was offering him such a bargain. It was unlike Emmeline and he found it hard to understand.

'How much do you want for her?'

'Morgan's sold five steamers earlier in the year, 30,000 tons altogether, at cost price, subject to annual depreciation at five per cent for every year in service, making a total price of £200,000, with another £200,000 for good will and trade. You could have the *Lady Roberts* for eight thousand all in, coal and good will included. Just the thing for operating out here, Willie.'

The figure she suggested was not high, but it would use every bit of his spare capital. It was also important, it was clear, to get up to Port Arthur and take the ship over at once before the trouble that had been threatening between Japan and Russia broke, or he'd find himself in trouble with the amount of capital it tied up.

He weighed up the pros and cons for a while, not certain that he wasn't making a fool of himself. But the appeal of being in shipping was great and he found it hard to resist. His mind was racing, as he did quick sums in his head while trying to present Emmeline with an unperturbed front.

'I'll take her,' he said. 'When do you want your money?'

'Now,' she said. 'I'm in need of it.'

'Not doing so well?' he asked, alert for rumours of a fading business. Fading businesses meant cheap goods for sale and he was not one to miss an opportunity.

Emmeline gave him a sideways look. 'You mind your own business,' she said.

'My cheque good enough?'

'I'll cash it straightaway. If it comes back at me, the sale's cancelled.'

'It won't come back,' Willie said. 'There's enough to cover it.'

Only just, though, he realised.

The following day as he climbed from his bed, a vivid streamer of sun swept the sky, then it deepened to red and another streamer ended in the flaring flashpoint of the sun as it raced up in a blinding glare from the river. It looked a good omen.

He had spent half the night doing sums and had come to the conclusion that he could just manage the sale that had been proposed, so long as he got up to Port Arthur at once to claim the ship before the Russians or the Japanese did. Emmeline gave him the papers and he insisted on studying them carefully before he handed over the cheque. They seemed straightforward. Two thousand tons dead weight, modern triple expansion engine and apparently sound. He'd heard that P & O had bought up a line recently to act as feeders for their European trade, so perhaps they might like to use his ship to feed their China Seas trade. Based at Shanghai, he could move between the East Indies, India, Indo-China, Japan, the Philippines, even down the Pacific to Australia and New Zealand. He had been exporting and importing long enough already to know the possibilities.

'I'm grateful, Willie,' Emmeline said as he handed over the cheque.

She was standing in front of him, close enough for him to smell the perfume she was wearing, the lace over her bosom brushing his jacket. She paused. 'It's such a pity we parted all that time ago, Willie.'

Willie frowned. 'Lay off, Emmeline. We're doing business not hopping into bed.'

'We were lovers once.'

'Emmeline, I've got a kid and another on the way.'

She gave a romantic sigh. 'To think it might have been mine, Willie.'

'Emmeline, cut it out! I'm off.'

She put a hand on his arm and, as he swung back to her, she pushed close against him. 'I've always loved you, Willie. I've never forgotten what we were to each other.'

'You didn't give a damn!' he snapped. 'You just wanted me in your bed!'

Her voice dropped a couple of octaves. 'You were very good in bed, Willie.'

He began to grow angry. 'Christ, Em, we've only just stuck Gummer under the sod.'

'He was never any good. It was the greatest mistake of my life marrying him. He wasn't a gentleman like you, Willie.'

Gentleman, Willie thought. That was something he'd never claimed for himself, though, judging by some of the white men making fortunes out of China, he supposed he'd as much right to the title as any of them.

'Don't go, Willie.'

'I have to.'

'Stay and have tea. Have a drink.'

'Emmeline, for Christ's sake – !'

She had her arms round him now, her large firm bosom resting against his chest. He felt the *chaise-longue* behind his knees and collapsed on to it, Emmeline on top of him. Her fingers were already trying to unfasten buttons.

'Jesus Christ on a tightrope!'

With a heave, he jerked himself free and she landed with a bump on the floor, knocking over a table and a vase of flowers. She glared up at him, her bosom heaving. She had undone the buttons of her blouse and he had a bird's-eye view of a pair of splendid breasts.

'It's all right, Willie. It's all right. I want to. I want you to.'

'Well, I don't!'

As he headed for the door, she scrambled to her feet and stood with her back to it. 'I'm yours, Willie!'

'Don't be so bloody melodramatic!'

'Take me!'

He wrenched her out of the way, spinning her round so that she lost her balance and fell on to the *chaise-longue*.

'For Christ's sake, Emmeline,' he snarled. 'Grow up! I'm a married man and you've just become a widow.'

As he slammed the door behind him she was just reaching for the overturned vase and he heard it crash against the other side of the panelling. As he clattered down the stairs, the Chinese manservant was waiting at the bottom, a look of bewilderment on his face. As Willie shot through the front door, he heard Emmeline scream. It was a scream of rage and frustration and she was still screaming as he told the rickshaw coolie to take him back to his office.

three

By the time Willie reached Shanghai and booked his passage north in the coaster *Shu Chi*, he had been warned more than once that the deteriorating relations between Japan and Russia might make things difficult. There was even talk now of war, and any ship heading for Taku and the railway to Peking would have to round the Shantung promontory and pass through the narrows between Chefoo and the Russianheld Port Arthur. If fighting occurred, it would inevitably be there. It seemed he needed to hurry.

By this time he was beginning to suspect that Emmeline had cheated him. She must have known of the increasingly strained relations between Japan and Russia and was guessing that her ship, the *Lady Roberts*, would be holed up in Port Arthur by a Japanese fleet, or that the Russians, cut off from their supplies, might commandeer her. He even began to wonder if she'd offered him the coal at a giveaway price to get him into her bed. The price had been so low she'd almost been throwing it at him.

It was going to be a bloody funny war, he decided, fought between Japan and Russia on neutral Chinese territory, and it looked as if it might start at any moment because the news was that the Japanese were already threatening Chemulpo in Korea. Coasters were still running north, however, and according to the booking clerk at the shipping office, if Willie was prepared to take a chance on being caught in a naval battle, which was more than likely because the Russians had a fleet at Port Arthur and the Japanese had a fleet prowling round the Yellow Sea, then he could be carried. The clerk smiled. Would Mr Sarth care to take a chance? Mr Sarth would? Fine!

Calling at his office, Willie informed Lun Foo and George Kee what was in the wind, told Lun he trusted him, winked quietly at Kee to indicate that he didn't, arranged for a telegram to be sent to Abigail to tell her what he was up to, and headed for the docks.

There was a heavy mist as he boarded the *Shu Chi* and as he reached the deck he was surprised to see Yuhitsu Shaiba, the man whose life he'd saved at Peking, waiting on deck, half-submerged in a heavy grey coat.

'Yuhitsu! Are you travelling too?'

Shaiba smiled. 'I am going home to Japan,' he said. 'But first I must go to Tientsin. This is a bad time, Mr Sarth, with the trouble with Russia. It was my intention to go via Vladivostok, but I have received a message from Tokyo which warns me that the war might start, so when we reach Tientsin I shall take passage on a British ship.'

The ship left in the afternoon, and they were just south of the German-occupied port of Tsingtao when a German gunboat appeared on the port quarter. As it rushed past them, a shallow-draught vessel with a high bridge, a tall stack and a small popgun on the bow, a light began to wink.

' "War is likely between Japan and Russia",' Willie heard the mate reading out. ' "Do not put into Port Arthur." '

There was a discussion on the bridge, then the first class passengers were requested to assemble in the saloon, where the captain dispensed the news and informed them he would be unable to put into the Russian port.

'I hope no one has business there.'

'I have,' Willie said at once. 'Several thousand pounds' worth of coal and a collier that's worth saving. I've got to get in there.'

'There's a danger fighting might start.'

'It won't concern me.'

There were two other businessmen, an American and a German, who also had business in the Russian port, and it was agreed that, provided there was no activity in the area, the *Shu Chi* would go as close to Port Arthur as she dared and summon a junk to take them in.

'After that, it's your own affair,' the captain said.

Four hours later, with Weihaiwei, the Royal Naval base, on their port side and the wind coming like a knife from the north, they rounded the islands east of Chefoo. Edging further northwards, they spotted a destroyer flying the rising sun flag of Japan, but there was no other activity and it was decided to go ahead.

'He's just scouting around,' Willie said nervously, remembering Shaiba's warning.

With the northern shore just visible as a purple line in the distance, they stopped a junk and, as it came alongside, Willie and the other two men stepped aboard and started to offer bribes. With wide grins, nods and gestures, the Chinese captain agreed to take the three men north and land them as near as he could to Port Arthur.

'No Port Arthur, Mastah,' he said. 'Plenty trouble there. Foreign devil go chop-chop China many time. Now foreign devil go chop-chop foreign devil too. Mebbe good for China.'

As their luggage was brought on deck and they prepared to board the junk, Shaiba, who had been watching everything that was happening with an intense look of concentration on his face, touched Willie's arm and drew him on one side.

'I think you should not go, Mr Sarth,' he whispered.

'Why not? I've got business in there. A collier full of coal.'

'You might be wiser to leave it there and continue your journey.'

Willie eyed the Japanese shrewdly. 'Why?'

'I think there will be problems.'

Willie still found it hard to believe. 'Surely Japan won't be mad enough to go to war with Russia? The Tsar's got a colossal army and a large fleet at Port Arthur.'

Shaiba smiled. 'Neither of them very efficient, I suspect.'

'They can soon get reinforcements. Along the Trans-Siberian Railway.'

'That also I doubt, Mr Sarth. You can't carry a ship on a railway truck and the rest of their navy is in the Baltic, and that's half-way round the world. As for reinforcements – well, I know even if you don't, that the Trans-Siberian Railway isn't yet complete. There is a gap in it at Lake Baikal near Irkutsk and everything has to be unloaded and transferred to lake steamers, then reloaded at the other side for the rest of the journey to Port Arthur.'

The rumours that Shaiba was a Japanese agent came back to Willie's mind. 'Look here, Yuhitsu, old son, do you know something I ought to know?'

Shaiba held up his hand in protest. 'I can't tell you, Mr Sarth, but I would advise you, if you insist on going in, to be ready to leave before the night of February 8th.'

'Why?' Willie drew the Japanese along the deck away from the other passengers. 'What is it you know, Yuhitsu? Is that when Japan intends to declare war or something?'

'I cannot tell you, Mister Sarth. I am just warning you.'

'Because you know something?'

'I know things.'

'How?'

'Because it is my job to know things.'

So Shaiba *was* some sort of spy. He had always been talking about Russian naval strength and listening to the Russian officers in Peking. He obviously knew something of importance.

'Come on, Yuhitsu,' he urged. 'Give it to me.'

'That I cannot do, Mr Sarth,' Shaiba said. 'It would be more than my career's worth.'

'Career? What as? A legation clerk?'

Shaiba stiffened. 'I am not just a legation clerk, Mr Sarth,' he said. 'I am an attaché, though that is not generally known. I am an officer in the Japanese Imperial Navy.'

Willie stared at the Japanese. So the stories had been right, and he began to see why Shaiba had always found the Russians so interesting. Doubtless, he had all the time been filing away everything they said, all the secrets, all the little indiscretions they let slip, in a series of little niches in his mind.

'Still?' he asked.

'Still. I have the rank of captain. I should not be telling you this, of course, but without doubt you saved my life and I must discharge my debt. Be careful. Especially on the night of February 8th. After that Port Arthur will be cut off from the world.'

As he walked away along the deck, Willie stared after him, then, aware of the other two businessmen shouting to him to hurry, with a shrug he cocked a leg over the rail of the *Shu Chi* and dropped to the deck of the junk.

The *Shu Chi*'s telegraphs clanged, the water at her stern churned brown and frothy and she began to draw away. The junk's captain began to shout in a high-pitched voice and the slatted sail clattered up the mast and the water alongside began to move as she swung north.

For a long time they headed landwards without seeing any other traffic, then the hills of the Liaotung Peninsula came in sight, and finally the white buildings of the Russian naval base.

'No sign of the Japanese there,' the American businessman pointed out cheerfully, his head down in the fur collar of his coat. 'And look at the Russkies. They're obviously not expecting trouble.'

Certainly, there was no indication of warlike intent. The Russian warships, battleships and cruisers were anchored outside the harbour.

'That's to stop the Japanese getting in,' the American went on. 'They could never do it with that lot in the way.'

Staring at the silent shapes of the ironclads with their tall stacks, Willie could see guns and boats moving between them manned by uniformed men. He drew a deep breath. Emmeline's coal was as good as his.

But, as they drew nearer and the buildings ashore became plainer, a steam harbour launch came hurtling from behind the anchored war ships. Drawing alongside, it ordered the junk to stop. The slatted sail clattered down and a Russian naval officer, smart in a blue uniform with aiguillettes and shoulder epaulettes like planks, climbed aboard. He began to speak in French, but eventually switched to a halting English.

'No traffic,' he said, pointing to the shore. 'No is possible.'

'We have business,' Willie said, raising his voice because it always seemed easier to get a meaning across to foreigners by shouting at them.

The Russian shook his head. 'No possible. Must go to Tientsin.'

There was a lot of arguing in three or four languages, but the Russian got his point across by pointing out the small gun on the launch's bows, and the Chinese captain decided he was taking no chances. As the sail rose again, he turned the nose of the junk westwards.

'I take mastahs Chanchow,' he announced. 'That way more better.'

There was nothing they could do about it, but Willie was determined not to be beaten. Emmeline's collier and its cargo drew him like a magnet. He was a shipping tycoon now and he was going to remain one. Neither the Russians nor the Japanese were going to stop him.

Chanchow was a small fishing harbour, at that moment packed with junks and small sailing vessels because of the Russian closure of Port Arthur, but the Chinese were always quick to adapt and there were horses to be hired and a guide to lead them along the coast to the port. The horses, in fact, were ponies, small and shaggy and with a dreadful boneshaking trot. The travellers had to spend the night in a village inn, stretched out on wooden beds in a freezing room, scratching at the fleas that infested the mattresses. The next morning they set off again. As the roofs of Port Arthur came in sight, they found the road barricaded, and a Russian sentry, a blank-faced youth with a long bayonet, stepped in front of them and ordered them back. From the officer in command of the outpost they learned that the road was barred to everybody because of the tension, but the Chinese guide was equal to the occasion. He led them back down the road until they were out of sight, then turned off among the gullies and valleys, and led them by a roundabout route to a point north of the city.

Eventually he stopped. 'Mastahs walk now,' he said and they were obliged to continue the journey on foot.

It didn't seem to have occurred to the Russians that a barricade across a road could be by-passed, and nobody stopped them. Dusty, footsore and hungry, they finally arrived in the northern outskirts of the port, where they were able to hire a carriage which took them to the centre. It was bitterly cold, with the wind bringing flurries of snow as they arrived. It was also dark, but the place showed no sign of any preparations for war. The port facilities had been electrified and the sky blazed with light among the storehouses near the naval base. The first thing that was needed was food and, while the German and the American went in search of a hotel, Willie was satisfied with a dockside restaurant. It was full of merchant navy officers, with a few senior petty officers from the Russian navy. Drink was flowing freely among the noise and the smoke and, somewhere at the back, half-hidden by the diners, a man was playing a balalaika.

Finishing his food, Willie went in search of the *Lady Roberts*. She was moored alongside a wooden jetty, dirty and pocked with rust. She had a flat overhang stern and a stack like a long Russian cigarette.

'Oh, Lor',' he muttered.

The *Lady Roberts* looked as if she hadn't been painted in years. She was a deep-draught vessel and looked the last word in decrepitude and decay. Then he brightened up. The shipping contract he had obtained from Emmeline showed she had holds full of good Welsh coal which would bring him money if he could get it to Shanghai, where the navy controller wouldn't argue so long as he could show its quality.

The captain was a ginger-whiskered Geordie called Hankinson and, after searching among narrow alleyways all painted a uniform drab brown, Willie found him in his cabin with the engineer, who seemed to match him for ill looks, sourness and general shabbiness. They were both wearing overcoats, caps, gloves and scarves and were playing draughts and drinking tea laced with rum. Neither of them looked as though he had much to recommend him beyond a bad temper.

Hankinson was on his feet at once as Willie burst in. 'Who the hell are you?' he demanded.

'I'm William Sarth,' Willie said. 'I'm the owner of this ship.'

Hankinson's brows came down. 'This ship's owned by Wishart and Co.'

'Not any more. I bought her.'

Hankinson's glare hardened. 'Well,' he said, 'I hope you're a bloody sight better than Wishart's at paying. And since you're here, what the hell am I waiting for? My orders were to bring the coal, but I've been here a month now and nobody wants it.'

'*I* want it,' Willie said. 'I've paid for it and it's mine.'

'Right,' Hankinson said. 'How about our wages then?'

'What wages? The crew gets paid off when the voyage ends.'

'Crew, yes. Not me.' Hankinson gestured at the engineer. 'Not him. We draw salaries and we haven't been paid.'

Willie swallowed, aware once more that he probably ought to have been more careful. 'You will be,' he said. 'As soon as we get to Shanghai.'

'Right,' Hankinson clearly hadn't finished yet. 'What about the insurance?'

'What about it?'

'You paid it?'

'Should I have?'

'That bastard, Gummer, shoulda paid it before we left Hong Kong,' Hankinson said. 'I reckon he peed it up against a lavatory wall.'

'How much is it?' Willie asked.

The sum staggered him and again he realised he had been a little too precipitate in his desire to become a shipping magnate.

'We wouldn'ta got away with it in Newcastle nor anywhere at home,' Hankinson went on, growling away in a surly monotone. 'Out here it's a bit different. But, matey, you lose this ship and you're in bad trouble.'

'We shan't lose it,' Willie said, with more confidence than he felt. 'We're leaving, and when we get to a British port I'll sort everything out. Wages. Salaries. Insurance. The lot. I want you out of here as soon as possible and on your way.'

But when they went ashore he discovered it wasn't as easy as he'd expected. At the harbourmaster's office they learned that, because of the impending conflict, the harbourmaster's duties had been taken over by an officer at naval headquarters. Hankinson's attitude was one of rudeness to everybody and his method of getting anything to be as unpleasant as possible. In the end Willie told him he'd manage on his own.

Finding his way to the naval headquarters, he was shown into a splendid office where a man was staring through the window with a telescope towards the sea. Something about him seemed familiar and as he turned Willie found himself staring at Count Zychov.

'You!' he breathed. 'You!'

Zychov clearly didn't recognise Willie with the big fashionable moustache he had grown. His own moustache was still splendidly curled and Willie wondered if he still bandaged it at night.

'I don't know you,' he said.

'No,' Willie said. 'I expect you've forgotten Shantu. But I haven't.'

The reminder obviously struck home and Zychov's eye's narrowed. 'Who are you?'

'In addition to you and one woman, the only survivor of the expedition to bring in the missionaries to Peking. I watched you bolt.'

Zychov was clearly shaken and for a while he said nothing, but then he began to recover.

'I've never been to Shantu,' he said. 'Where is it?'

'China. Shensi province. South-west of Peking.'

'I was never in Peking.'

'You were not only in Peking, you took a party to Shantu and ran away when we were attacked by Boxers.'

It was the wrong approach, as bad for getting things done as Hankinson's rudeness, and they were on the wrong foot at once. Zychov continued to insist he had never been to Peking, still less Shantu, and within seconds the chances of getting the *Lady Roberts* away had evaporated completely. The demand for clearance was refused peremptorily.

'Nothing leaves Port Arthur,' Zychov said. 'We expect war to be declared before the spring.'

Swallowing his anger and his pride, Willie began to plead as he saw his chances of becoming a shipping magnate disappearing with his bank balance. If he didn't get the *Lady Roberts* clear, he stood to have practically all his capital tied up for the duration of the war and, if by chance the *Lady Roberts* was sunk either by the Russians or the Japanese, it would disappear entirely because of Gummer's failure to insure her.

'Once we've got steam up,' he insisted, 'my ship can be clear of the harbour in half an hour. I'm a British citizen and the *Lady Roberts* is a British ship. We don't want to interfere with your war. We just want to get to Shanghai.'

Zychov sniffed, an aristocratic sniff that intimated his disdain. 'You should have thought of that,' he said, 'when your country made its alliance with the toothy little men from across the Yellow Sea. Russia is being challenged by the precocious nationalism of a state that's barely fifty years old. Port Arthur will never be allowed to fall. It's Russia's most northerly ice-free port on the mainland of Asia.'

'It was Japan's once,' Willie said.

'And Russian pressure forced her out. Our conception of the balance of power in the east does not countenance the upsetting influence of this youthful country. We're not deaf to the aggressive sounds from across the Yellow Sea. Manchuria and Korea are rich in natural resources and it's intolerable that any country but Russia should be allowed to develop them.'

Outside the office, Willie stared about him furiously. Emmeline had put it across him! She had known all the time she was selling him a ship with a cargo of coal he couldn't use, that no salaries had been paid and no insurance taken out.

'Lor',' he said, shocked at his own stupidity.

Heading back to the *Lady Roberts*, he found Hankinson and the engineer again busy with the draughts.

'Look,' he said, 'how soon can we sail if I can get permission?'

'Right off if we had steam up.'

'Well, I'm not going to sit on my backside here for the duration of the war.'

'You'll be lucky, sonny,' Hankinson said. 'We've just heard that the Japanese withdrew their Minister from St Petersburg two days ago. They're going to fight.'

'I don't give a bugger if they are,' Willie snorted. 'And don't call me "Sonny".'

Returning to the hotel where he had booked a room, Willie was just frowning at his drink in a lounge surrounded by palm trees and ferns when he realised he was wasting money that he might well need in the near future. Swallowing his drink, he headed for his room, collected his luggage and booked out.

When he appeared on the deck of the *Lady Roberts*, Hankinson stared at him as if he were some sort of burglar.

'What's all this then?' he demanded.

'I want a room.'

'You mean a cabin.'

'All right – a cabin. With a bed –'

'Bunk.'

' – and a wall –'

'Bulkhead.'

Willie lost his temper. 'All right,' he roared. 'A bloody cabin, with a bloody bunk and a bloody bulkhead where I can hang my hat and coat!'

'We ain't got one.'

'Then you'd better find one!'

'I'm not in the hotel business, matey.'

'Then you'd better start.'

Hankinson glanced at the engineer, deciding that the new owner had more about him than was obvious on the surface. 'You'd better have the mate's,' he said.

'What about the mate?'

'He won't want it no more. He got his throat cut in Singapore. He went after a woman when we put in for water on the way here.'

Dumping his luggage, Willie immediately went ashore again to see what could be done. It was obviously pointless trying to see Zychov, who quite clearly knew who he was, so he decided to try someone else, if possible of higher rank.

But the Russians believed in a policy of strict working hours, and by this time, despite the imminence of war, all the offices were shut and there was no alternative but to wait. The following day, he tried again, but now no one even had time to see him. Japanese torpedo boat destroyers had been seen off Chemulpo and the Russians were worried.

Highly indignant because war hadn't been declared, they had no time for Willie's problems, only for their own concerns. The activity in the harbour increased and picket boats and harbour launches buzzed across the water like beetles, chugging away in clouds of steam as they went round the fleet. Ponderously, slowly, the great iron ships began to move.

Furious because he was now as much trapped in the Russian base as the ship and the cargo he had come to collect, Willie tried to hang on to his temper but, in the end, he was physically thrown out of naval headquarters. Hankinson picked him up. 'I'm still waiting, sonny,' he jeered.

Willie glared at him. 'I've told you,' he snarled. 'Don't call me "sonny". Just be ready. Have you got steam up?'

Hankinson gave him the pitying look of a sailor for a shore-sider trying to understand ships. 'Son,' he said. 'We coulda been ready for days. With steam up. But that woulda meant burning coal, and that woulda meant using our bloody cargo because the bunkers aren't so bloody full as they was. January's gone and it's gettin' colder. You've been here now a week yourself and nothin's happened. I'm still waitin'. Just you give me a date and a time and I'll be ready.'

Willie glared about him. The Russians had moved their heavy armoured cruisers, light cruisers, destroyers and torpedo boats into three lines, anchored fore and aft at the entrance to the harbour as if they were being used as a boom, the heavy ships on the inside line, the cruisers on the outside lines, with the torpedo boats near the Tiger Peninsula, which formed one side of the harbour. Nothing could get in, but also nothing could get out.

He stared at the ships angrily. They were ram-bowed and painted white and yellow, big and ungainly and somehow with a look of inefficiency about them. He loathed them for it. Once he had seen the Russian admiral, a stout bearded man with the round bland face of a child, wearing epaulettes, sashes and medals. How ready were they, he wondered, and how ready the Japanese?

The Russians were convinced the Japanese were weak and unwilling to fight and that their threats were nothing but bluff. But Willie had heard that the Japanese consul at Chefoo had chartered the British steamer *Foo Chow* to pick up all Japanese citizens from Port Arthur and Dalny. That seemed to be significant, but the point was that the Japanese fleet was still at Sasebo and so far had shown no signs of moving.

Then he remembered what Shaiba had told him, and his heart suddenly thumped. He'd forgotten all about Shaiba in the difficulties he had been having trying to get the *Lady Roberts* moving. 'What's the date?' he asked Hankinson.

'Second o' February. Why?'

'Never mind why.' Willie stared again with hatred at the lines of Russian warships. 'How long will it take you to get steam up?'

'Three – four hours. Why?'

'What about your crew?'

'Ashore. You can't keep 'em aboard. I expect they're after the booze and women like all sailors.'

'Get 'em aboard.'

'Are we leaving?'

'We are if I've anything to do with it.' Willie stared again at the Russian ships. He had no idea what Shaiba had been trying to convey to him, but Sasebo was only a day or two's steaming away and he suspected that the Japanese were up to something, and if anybody came up over the horizon and started firing at the Russians, any overs, any ranging shots that weren't exactly on the mark, could well land on the *Lady Roberts*. 'We're shifting our berth.'

'Why?'

'God's green footstool! Don't you know any other bloody word?'

'Well, I want to know,' Hankinson argued stubbornly. 'Shiftin' me berth for no reason at all costs money and it makes me look a fool.'

'If anybody tells you you're a fool – ' Willie was tempted to be the first ' – just refer 'em to me. We're shifting the ship to the west of the harbour. As far as we can get.'

Hankinson's mouth framed the word 'Why?' but he changed his mind and stalked away.

That afternoon, Willie went back on board the *Lady Roberts*. The crew were lounging about the foredeck, near the entrance to the forecastle, shabby, grubby-looking and hung over. They eyed Willie sourly as he climbed to Hankinson's cabin through the depressing brown-painted alleyways. There seemed to be not an atom of cheer about the ship and he decided that as soon as he'd sold the cargo he'd invest in a different one, with a young captain, and sell the *Lady Roberts*, together with Hankinson and all his crew.

Hankinson was playing draughts with the engineer as usual. As Willie entered, he turned round indifferently.

'You got steam up?' Willie asked.

'Aye,' the engineer said grudgingly. 'As instructed. Burning coal. Wasting coal. We've had to start shifting some of the cargo, we're so short.'

'We may have to move in a hurry. There's trouble coming.'

'What sort of trouble?'

'Japanese trouble.'

'You're talking through your hat, sonny.'

'No, I'm not.' By this time Willie was more convinced than ever that Shaiba had known something and had been warning him to he prepared. He swung round to Hankinson. 'Have you fixed the new berth?'

'Yes. There's a tug standing by.'

'Get him alongside.'

'It'll cost you money.'

'I'll worry about that. What about your crew?'

'All aboard except three.'

'Why not those three?'

'Because they're all bigger than me. I don't argue with 'em.'

'Where will they be?'

'*Bucket of Blood*. It's a bar. They call it that because there's always fights. Brothel's upstairs.'

'I'll get 'em.'

'They'll eat you.'

'I'll worry about that, too. Get your ship moving.'

Climbing ashore again, the big Russian revolver stuffed into his belt and held in place by his tightly buttoned jacket, Willie set out for the *Bucket of Blood*.

It was a seedy bar with a Russian name in Cyrillic lettering, full of smoke, women and sailors. Most of the men were Russians, but there were a few Frenchmen, Chinese and Scandinavians from ships in the harbour.

Giving the names of the men he wanted to the woman who met him, she told him they were all together upstairs, drinking. As he moved to the stairs, he was stopped by a sleazy girl. Others plucked at his sleeve, but, his face grim, he marched through them without seeing them. The three men from the *Lady Roberts* were sitting with three women round a table on which there was a large bottle of vodka. They looked up without interest as Willie appeared.

'On your feet,' he said. 'We're going back to the ship. I've got a cab outside. We can all get in.'

One of the men rose. He seemed enormous and appeared to tower over Willie. 'Listen, son,' he said. 'That ship ain't moving. She's grown roots.'

The others laughed, and Willie swallowed nervously.

'She's changing her berth now,' he said. 'She's leaving tonight, tomorrow or the day after.'

'Run off, sonny. You're interrupting the drinkin'.'

'We're going back to the ship. All of us.'

'Bugger off. Before I land you one.'

Unbuttoning his jacket Willie introduced the revolver and cocked it. The click was loud in the stillness. 'Get going,' he said.

The sailor stared at the weapon. 'It's not loaded,' he jeered. 'You wouldn't dare.'

As he reached out to take the weapon, Willie pulled the trigger. The roar seemed to fill the room and as the vodka bottle exploded into splinters of glass, there were shouts from below and screams from the women in the bar. In the drifting wisp of smoke the three men climbed to their feet.

'Lead the way,' Willie said.

As they moved down the stairs and through the bar, there were catcalls at the men and screamed curses at Willie. He gestured with the revolver and everyone became silent. Outside, the three men climbed into the carriage Willie had waiting.

The big sailor glared. 'You made me look a sodden fool,' he growled 'I'll get you for this.'

'Shut up, Archie,' one of the other two said. 'The kid says he's goin' to get us outa here. Let's give him a chance. I'm sick of this bloody place and we're not bein' paid. You payin' us, kid?'

'I'll guarantee your wages if you get the *Lady Roberts* to Shanghai.'

'The Russians won't let us out.'

'Leave me to worry about that. It might take a day or two, but we've got to be ready.'

The three men quietened down and Hankinson stared with surprise as they appeared alongside the ship where she lay in her new berth. Willie followed the men aboard and climbed to the bridge to stare towards the sea. The *Lady Roberts* was now laying beyond the end of the line of Russian ships.

'It'll do,' he said.

four

'If I'm to run a shipping line,' Willie said. 'I'll need to know something about it, won't I?'

Hankinson stared at him, distrustful of but at the same time impressed by this tall dark-haired young man who seemed to know exactly what he was doing. 'I reckon so,' he said.

'So how do I go about it? Can I get a mate's certificate?'

Hankinson looked at him pityingly. 'To get a certificate of any kind you got to do four years at sea.'

'Right,' Willie said. 'Then sign me on now. I've done some time already and it'll all count. What about the studying? Where do I get the books?'

Hankinson found himself being swept along. 'I got some,' he admitted. 'And there's some in the mate's cabin he won't want no more.' He took them down and held them out. 'Here you are. *Knots and Splices*, *Norie's Navigation*, *The Africa Pilot*, *Mother Shipton's Dream Book* and *How to Tell Fortunes*.' He grinned. 'They won't help you a lot.' He stared at Willie, puzzled. 'What's so bloody exciting about ships?' he said. 'The tide goes out, the tide comes in, you see an old hat floating past and know it's changed. I've never found ships all that hair-raising.'

'Never?'

'Well –' Hankinson hesitated – 'I suppose there was a time once.'

By this time, Willie was growing desperate for ready cash. The trip north, with the bribe to the junkmaster and the guide from Chanchow, the hire of ponies, the hire of the tug that had hauled the *Lady Roberts* across the harbour, had drained him of it and there was still some time to go. Then he realised he could earn enough to keep himself in food and drink by playing the piano in the bar he frequented, and began to feel he might hang on until the 8th, when, surely to God, something would happen.

February 6th came and went. Then the 7th and nothing happened. The Russians were in a ferment of excitement and anger over the possibility of attack, but it didn't seem to stir them from their sloth.

Every day Willie rose aboard ship, shaved, dressed and ate a drab crew's breakfast of burgoo, wondering if he'd guessed wrong. Perhaps Shaiba had known nothing and had just been showing off. On the other hand, Port Arthur was full of Chinese coolies, servants and labourers – some of them probably disguised Japanese – and the Japanese probably new everything that was going on.

During the day he went into the town, which was situated at the end of a large bay enclosed by two headlands coming together to form a long, narrow entrance. The Russian ships were still in three lines outside the harbour, with the destroyers and auxiliary vessels inside. Some of the bigger ships seemed to be engaged in coaling, but a lot of men were on shore leave, so that the cafés were full and there were crowds at a visiting circus which had pitched its tents on a stretch of open land near the centre of the town. Realising he was getting nowhere, he returned to the *Lady Roberts*, determined to do something about her, because he felt that if trouble started it would be as well to have her easily identifiable.

'I want the ship's carpenter to build two big signboards,' he said. 'One for either side of the bridge. I want 'em painted and slung over the side so they can easily be seen. Then I want the ship's engineer to arrange for clusters of lights to be hung over 'em – electric lights – '

'It can't be done!' the engineer growled.

'It can. Do it. I want 'em slung so they illuminate the boards. I want 'em to be seen. I also want boards slung over with the ship's name on 'em.'

'What about the other boards?' Hankinson asked. 'What colour do we paint 'em? Red and green for port and starboard?'

'I want 'em painting with the Union Jack,' Willie said. 'And quick. It doesn't have to be a perfect job. Just the right amount of red, white and blue in the right places.'

'Red we got. For the port light reflector. White we got. We mix it with black to make grey. Blue we ain't got. What would we want blue for aboard a tub like this? We don't have ladies' boodwars.'

'Fix it how you like,' Willie said. 'I'll get the blue ashore. When I come back I want a start made. Put everybody on it. It's important.'

When he returned, the carpenter and four men were hammering together a huge square of wood from planks and drilling holes in it for the ropes which would hold it over the side. The engineer was fixing cables for the lights.

'Blue,' Willie said, dropping the two cans of paint at Hankinson's feet. 'Bit light for the Union Jack, but it'll do. Add a bit of black. If there's any left, you can paint your cabin with it. It needs it.'

When February 8th came, Willie rose again, shaved, dressed and ate his breakfast, tense with nervous excitement. Nothing had happened. He had been half-expecting some sort of panic declaration of war, but nothing had happened.

The painting had been finished and the two huge boards were propped against the centre castle drying, with two more boards bearing the ship's name.

'Have 'em slung in place,' he said. 'Where they can be seen.'

'They're not dry yet,' Hankinson pointed out.

'A smudge or two won't matter. Get 'em up.'

Hankinson stared at Willie curiously, but he didn't argue. As Willie turned away the big sailor called Archie, who had threatened him at the *Bucket of Blood*, stopped him.

'We leavin', kid?' he asked.

'I hope so.'

'When.'

'It depends.'

During the day, still nothing happened and Willie began to grow nervous. If nothing happened at all, he'd look a fine old fool. Then he decided that if anything was going to happen it would happen at night.

Towards the end of the afternoon, a message arrived from the harbourmaster's office that the ship was to return to its former berth.

'Ignore it,' Willie said.

Hankinson was indignant. 'Sonny,' he said. 'In Russia, you don't ignore anything or they stick you in jug.'

'They won't stick us in jug,' Willie said, though he was far from certain that he was right. 'We're British citizens. And don't call me "sonny".'

Two hours later another message arrived. 'Lieutenant-Commander Count Zychov requests that the ship moves at once,' the officer who brought it said.

The old hatred bubbled up again immediately. Certain that Zychov was being deliberately obstructive, Willie shook his head. 'Tell him we can't,' he said. 'We haven't got steam up.'

Hankinson looked round sharply. 'But –'

'We'll get steam up during the night,' Willie went on quickly, ignoring him. 'And move first thing in the morning. It's almost dark now and moving in the dark we run the risk of collision.'

The messenger, who was an army man, was uncertain how ships operated and he let it go. Willie watched him head down the gangway. He knew he was gambling heavily. It was the 8th now and he was expecting something to happen. If it didn't, he'd probably end in jug after all – if the crew hadn't beaten him up first.

He ate a dreary evening meal in the bar as dusk was falling, then, hiring a cab, had himself driven out of the town. There was a considerable amount of activity around naval headquarters and he learned that the Japanese had put troops ashore at Chemulpo, and, after a skirmish between Cossacks and Japanese, two Russian warships and a merchant ship had been scuttled by their crews. The Russian officer who gave him the news was indignant and excited because war hadn't been declared, but the excitement didn't seem to have affected the rest of the fleet and Willie watched a boatload of officers and women heading for a party on the flagship and, as he passed the docks, he saw that a fourmasted barque had moved into the berth the *Lady Roberts* had occupied and was in the process of unloading sacks of flour. The Russians appeared to be stocking up.

Getting the cab driver to take him to the shore, he stood alone, staring out to sea, his worries driving in on him. The wind was icy as he stared across the harbour towards the Tiger Peninsula, the neck of land which formed the western arm of the harbour. Behind him he could see the lights of the town twinkling against the black loom of the hills. His head down in the collar of his coat, feeling the wind penetrating his clothes with ease, he wondered what Abigail was doing. He had hoped to send her a telegraphed message from Port Arthur, but the Russians were allowing no messages to leave the place so he could only hope she wasn't too worried.

The moon had not yet risen and from the town he could hear faint snatches of music on the breeze. The Russian warships stood out plainly, every porthole brilliantly lit, the glow of the lights from the town picking out the colours of the ships' paint. Behind him he knew the fortress guns were unmanned and even still in their winter coating of protective grease, because he had walked near them and chatted to a solitary bored sentry. The most powerful on Electric Hill had even had their recoil cylinders drained, and the gun crews were finding what amusement they could in the cafés and bars of the bleak little town. The only defences were a few light guns aboard the ships and he'd heard that even the torpedo nets had not been rigged.

As it grew dark he watched two destroyers, their lights glowing, leave their anchorage among the rest of their class, and move to sea past the three lines of heavy ships. Everybody knew what they were up to because you could hear it in every café and restaurant in Port Arthur. The Russian officers were always quick to boast what was happening, and he knew the destroyer commanders' orders were to search the sea in an area twenty miles outside the harbour before returning to report.

The big cruiser, *Pallada*, acting as duty ship for the night, was laying her searchlights on the horizon and he was still standing there as the moon began to rise, staring at the calm, silvery sea. Behind him on the muddy road that led into the town, the cab driver shivered inside the cab as he waited.

Wracking his brains for an explanation of Shaiba's words, Willie's fury consumed him. He had become a shipowner, had gone into shipping, with the chance of becoming a magnate in the near future – Willie was always an optimist – and here he was, unable to do anything about it. He kicked savagely at a stone and peered again out to sea, where a black sword blade of cloud lay across the pale sky.

Hearing the faint ting-ting of a ship's telegraphs he wondered where it came from. Then he realised it was coming on the wind from the sea. Trying to catch sight of the approaching vessel, he hoped it would have more luck getting in than he was having getting the *Lady Roberts* out. Then he caught a faint wink of light on the horizon, then another some distance away from the first, and gradually he realised he could see several lights and they were all in line. Puzzled, he stared again and faintly, very faintly, because he had kept his eyes averted from the shore lights, he realised he was looking at a line of ships, dark against the sky.

From among the line of ships a signal light began to flash again and again. For a long time the harbour didn't answer and he could imagine Zychov sitting with his feet up over a glass of vodka, probably even with a woman on his lap. Eventually a light began to wink from the harbour and was answered from the sea. Again the harbour light flashed a reply then went out. At sea all became darkness.

Willie stared. Who the hell was trying to get in? The British naval squadron from Shangai? Ships from Weihaiwei? Germans? French? Then a half-formed idea leapt to his mind. The Japanese, for God's sake! It couldn't be! War still hadn't been declared, and the Russian fleet was outside the harbour, their admiral obviously unworried, while the ships on the horizon had presumably satisfactorily identified themselves, because the Russians appeared to be ignoring them. But it could *only* be the Japanese! But what was their fleet doing out there? It didn't make sense.

Then suddenly it dawned on him what Shaiba had been trying to tell him. The ships on the horizon *were* Japanese, and they had arrived to attack the Russians without declaring war! Tossing aside the cigar he had been smoking, he began to run.

The first explosion came as he reached the side of the *Lady Roberts*. The two Russian destroyers he had seen heading out to sea had just returned, coming into the harbour at speed, a light flashing from the bridge of the leading vessel towards the flagship. An answering light, hesitant and uncertain, came from the flagship, then, even before she had stopped, the leading destroyer dropped a boat and it was just crossing towards the flagship when there was a crash and a sheet of flame rose from the side of the duty cruiser, *Pallada*. Swinging round, he saw a column of water lifting into the air like an icy stalagmite. Almost immediately there were two more explosions.

As he clattered to the *Lady Roberts*' deck, the crew came out from the forecastle alleyway and Captain Hankinson appeared on the bridge, clad in a pair of woollen combinations.

'What the hell's goin' on?'

Willie looked up at him. 'You still got steam up?' he yelled.

'Sure.'

'You might need it.'

'What's happening?'

'I think the war's started.'

When daylight came the city was overhung by a pall of smoke from burning ships. Two of the Russians' best battleships, the *Retzivan* and the *Tzarevich*, had been crippled, the *Retzivan* with a two-hundred-foot hole blown in her port side, the *Tzarevich* torpedoed in the stern, her bulkheads shattered, while the *Pallada*'s coal bunkers were on fire and still burning furiously. All three ships had got under way in an attempt to reach shallow water, but the *Pallada* had grounded near the lighthouse on the west of the harbour entrance, while the *Retzivan* and the *Tzarevich* had come to grief in the narrow gullet of the harbour, almost blocking the entrance. The Russians had achieved nothing and their guns and small arms had gone on firing long after the Japanese had vanished.

238

The crippled ships lay canting over, their masts askew, flames still belching smoke from their decks, around them a mat of smaller vessels taking off the wounded and bringing shore gangs to make repairs. The city streets were swarming with officers in carriages and streams of ambulances and carts carrying away the dead and wounded from the quayside.

Willie stared at the scene with Hankinson's telescope. The fight had been over in an hour or so. They had waited all night for a chance to escape, but none had presented itself and he could hear muttering again on the foredeck. The Russians appeared to have done nothing in the way of retaliation beyond sending the cruiser *Novik* to find the Japanese fleet, but the ship had returned at first light to report that they were nowhere to be seen.

The docks were full of rumours and, going into the city to find out what he could, Willie learned everything he needed in the bar where he took his meals. Through Hankinson's telescope he had seen marching men and officers on horseback, and later in the morning had learned that the Russian shore guns had not fired because their ammunition had been stored underground for safety. There had been a lot of noisy talk of vengeance from the Russians, but nothing was being done and he learned that the Russian admiral had called a conference ashore of senior officers to discuss what to do.

As he left the café, there was still a lot of shouting and he saw the Russian cruiser *Boyarin*, which had left earlier, returning, flying a flag signal which an obliging Russian sailor interpreted for them. 'Enemy in sight in force,' he said.

Expecting an immediate reaction, he was surprised when nothing happened. There was no sign of the senior officers returning from the conference ashore, no movement in the harbour beyond the small vessels and repair ships alongside the ironclads wounded in the previous night's attack.

Then he saw one of the Russian vessels begin to move and heard cheering. Bugles sounded and the high ting-ting of ships' telegraphs came across the water. Tremendous activity broke out on the bows of other ships as they prepared to up-anchor and sail.

'They're going out to meet the Japs,' Hankinson said.

'Right,' Willie said. 'Let's be ready to follow 'em.'

There was a sudden flurry of action ashore and an admiral's barge began to head from the quayside. Finding a cab, Willie had himself driven to the point where he had watched the start of the action the night before. Almost immediately, he realised he was having a grandstand view of the second stage of the battle. The Japanese were just coming into view again, more ships than he'd seen the night before, about six miles away and moving on a westerly course across the mouth of the harbour. Once again, he headed for the cab at full speed.

The crew of the *Lady Roberts* were all on deck as he arrived and, as the first shell screamed towards the town, everybody dived for shelter. Hankinson disappeared from the bridge into the wheelhouse and Willie heard the clink of the ring in the doorhandle as it slammed to behind him. The range was too high and the shell crashed down alongside the town quay beyond the Russian ships, falling on the wooden jetty where the *Lady Roberts* had been moored. Lifting his head, Willie saw that the masts of the barque that had taken her berth had been flung askew. Yards were a-cock-bill, ropes swung loose and torn sails were still flapping in the gusty air created by the blast. The deck hut where the cooking was done had disappeared in a flurry of flying planks and the deck was on fire where the stove had been flung. A dozen heads bobbed up on the *Lady Roberts*, looking towards Willie, every man aware that if they hadn't changed berth they would have been on the receiving end of the missile.

Another shell came screaming over the Russian fleet and hit one of the buildings behind the burning four-master and the whole front slid into the street in an avalanche of bricks, timber, slates and glass. The next salvo was more accurate and dropped among the Russian warships. They had steam up and were getting ready to weigh anchor, but, despite the men running about on their forecastle heads they made no attempt to go out to engage the Japanese or move beyond the protective fire of the shore batteries, merely tamely returning shells from where they lay, their four- and five-inch guns no match for the six-inchers of the Japanese. Only the Russian ship, the *Novik*, made an attempt to dash out of the roadway, but, as fire from Japanese guns was directed towards her, she swung away and ran for safety.

Pieces of the Russian ships were flying into the air in all directions and the whole line seemed to be enveloped in smoke. The Japanese continued firing as they crossed the mouth of the harbour until they neared Laotieh Point, where they broke off the action and turned south. The firing had started just after noon, and forty minutes later it was all over and the Japanese fleet was disappearing over the horizon. The Russian ships continued firing for a little longer, but it was largely for show, because they were hitting nothing and, one after the other, their guns became silent.

In the disturbed water outside the harbour, they were lying at all angles, making no attempt to head for the open sea. All they had managed to do was get in each other's line of fire. As far as it was possible to see, not one of the Japanese vessels had been lost.

There was a long silence as the guns stopped, as if everybody was holding his breath. Hankinson turned to Willie.

'You knew the little buggers was coming,' he accused.

Ashore, they could see what seemed to be a panic building up. Men were hurrying in all directions and here and there, where overs had landed in the town, houses were burning. In the silence aboard the *Lady Roberts* they could hear the wails of civilians and anguished cries from the Russian ships. Three of their larger vessels were still aground, seriously damaged from the night raid, and now four other heavy cruisers had been hit and were sending up clouds of smoke and steam.

'It looks to me,' Hankinson said, 'as if somebody very different's going to be running the show round here before long. Them little yellow buggers know how to fight.' He turned to Willie. 'Are we leaving?' he asked.

'Yes.'

'When?'

The Russian light cruiser *Novik* had pulled out of position in an attempt to get out of the murderous fire and Willie noticed it had left a gap on the western side of the entrance through which a ship might slip. 'Now,' he said.

'You must be bloody barmy!'

Willie pointed to the harbour entrance, where the casualties of the previous day's fighting lay, partly blocking the entrance. 'If we don't get out now,' he said 'we'll never get out. The Japanese are bound to try to block up the entrance before long. Let's get going.'

Hankinson stared at him for a moment, then swung away. As he began to shout, the black gang disappeared through the engine room hatch and the deck crew leapt to ropes and wires. Drumming up three or four scared Russian dockworkers to let go the shore lines, the *Lady Roberts'* winches began to clank. There was no tug available, so Hankinson went back on the spring until the bow edged outwards. When there was room to move, the dockworkers cast off the wire rope and the winches clanked as it was hauled in. As the ship's nose pointed to the harbour entrance, Hankinson shouted orders at the helmsman to correct the swing.

'Lights,' Willie said. 'It gets dark early up here.'

The clusters over the painted boards came on, illuminating the large Union Jacks which had been slung from the bridge.

'Let's have all the British flags we've got run up,' Willie suggested.

The *Lady Roberts* didn't run too much in the way of bunting, but they managed to hoist a Union Jack on the signal halyard and a red duster from the stern and, picking up speed, the ship nosed out close to the Tiger Peninsula. A man running along the shore shouted and a rifle was fired at them, but within minutes they were clear of the harbour and, with a bone between her teeth, the *Lady Roberts* began to head south. At the end of the line of Russian ships, the *Novik* was now listing badly. Smoke was pouring from a hole in the deck of the towering ironclad as the *Lady Roberts* slipped past, her bridge almost scraping the turrets built on the Russian ship's side. The Russian sailors were too busy to show any interest and the northern winter day soon became dark.

'We made it!' Hankinson sounded surprised.

A cheer went up from the deck and there was a lot of laughter. Then as it died and as the night deepened, a searchlight sprang up in front of them, the icy white beam turning the wave tops to silver and making the spray look like showers of diamonds. A black-painted torpedo boat destroyer emerged out of the darkness and they saw it carried the red and white rising sun flag at the masthead. A gun cracked and a shell landed in the water just ahead of them. As Hankinson rang down for slow, the Japanese vessel came alongside and one of the officers on her bridge began to shout through a megaphone.

'What ship?' he yelled.

'*Lady Roberts*,' Willie roared back. 'Registered at Newcastle, England.'

'Stop your engines.'

As the *Lady Roberts* lost way and came to a stop, wallowing in the black water, the Japanese vessel manoeuvred alongside, and the Japanese officer, accompanied now by a party of sailors, appeared on the deck. He was all smiles and politeness, but he was armed to the teeth and the sailors all carried rifles. Placing one man at the engine room hatch, two others on the foredeck watching the grouped crewmen near the forecastle alleyway, and a third at the foot of the bridge ladder, the Japanese officer climbed to the bridge, accompanied by the last two of his men. He spoke good English.

'Don't you realise there has been a battle?' he said. 'War has started between Japan and Russia.'

Willie grinned. 'So I've noticed.'

'Then why do you try to sail through the middle of it?'

'Not through the middle. Round the side.'

'This is no time to put to sea.'

'One of your officers, Yuhitsu Shaiba, told me it would be. He was with me at Peking four years ago.'

The Japanese smiled. 'Captain Shaiba is very much respected in the Imperial Navy,' he said.

He ought to be, Willie thought. He had probably contributed considerably to what was clearly an overwhelming victory that was going to alter the balance of power in the East for many years to come.

'You are a friend of Captain Shaiba's?'

'For a long time.'

'Captain Shaiba is with Admiral Togo on his flagship at this moment. He was picked up from Taku by a Japanese destroyer several days ago.'

Doubtless full of valuable information, Willie decided. He pushed his advantage. 'In case you hadn't heard,' he pointed out, 'my country formed an alliance with your country in 1902. It recognised the independence of China and Korea and said that in the event of any step by a third power prejudicial to the interest of one of the contracting parties the other would act in concert. In other words, it would maintain a benevolent neutrality and would itself go to war if a fourth country entered on the opposite side.'

The Japanese smiled. 'No one else will enter *this* war,' he said. 'Not now. Russia has already lost it. I must search your ship, however, in case there are Russians aboard or in case you are carrying materials of war.'

They waited as the Japanese officer prowled round the ship. As he reappeared, smiling, he waved. 'You may leave,' he said. 'And good luck go with you.'

As they watched the Japanese vessel pull away, Hankinson turned to Willie.

'Well, you clever young bugger,' he said. 'You did it.'

Willie grinned. 'I think,' he said, 'that we ought to celebrate. Isn't there some such thing as splicing the mainbrace?'

'That's the Royal Navy,' Hankinson said. 'We don't go in for them things in the Merchant Navy.'

'But you carry rum?'

'Course we do.'

'Right, then. Break it out. Let's see that everybody has a drink.'

As they moved southwards, over the throb of the old ship's engines and the swish of the sea alongside, an accordion and the big seaman called Archie began to dance a hornpipe on the foredeck.

'Now you've done it,' Hankinson said gloomily. 'I shall never be able to control the sods again.'

five

'Willie!' Abigail clutched her husband to her. 'I've been worried sick. Where've you been?'

Willie grinned. 'I've been getting into shipping,' he said.

He explained what had happened. 'The place is blockaded,' he said. 'And it's bound to fall eventually. We got away just in time. I've got a new line, Ab, not rooted to the ground any more. I've already started swotting for a mate's certificate.'

'To go to sea?'

'No. So I'll know what's going on. So I won't get cheated.'

'Where will you operate?'

'Here. Off the China coast. The China Seas. There's room for us. We'll be working the East and South China seas, the Yellow Sea, the Sea of Japan. Hong Kong. Hanoi. Nagasaki. Tokyo. Down to Singapore, Java and the Philippines.'

'Can you find cargoes?'

'You bet I can!' Willie was by no means certain, but he was sure of his own energy.

'Do you know anything about it?'

He had no doubts. He had dealt with lists of suppliers even in London, knew all about bills of lading, reports of loading, transactions, points of origin, destinations, volumes, weights, costs, multiple contract shipments. He sat back to describe his plans for the future. 'We ought to move to Shanghai,' he said. 'That's the coming place. Peking's a backwater. Shanghai's where the commerce is, where all the up and coming people are. Better for the children. They're opening European schools where there'll be other kids to play with. Besides, Peking's not safe.'

'Why not?'

'Ab, you must know it as well as I do, perhaps better. China's changing. It's shifting. It resents people like me and you because we've been living off her for years without giving much back.'

'We give employment to Chinese. A lot of Chinese now.'

'That's not the reason we stay. We pay no taxes and we're making a lot of money. That's the reason. Back home you have to be society to be noticed. Here you just have to have money. Shanghai's the most important city in the East and that's where we ought to be.'

'I'll miss my friends.'

'You'll make more. And you'll be safer. If trouble comes – and it might because there are people in China now saying that the Manchus have to go – ' Willie paused, '– if trouble came, we'd be too far from the coast in Peking. In Shanghai all we'd have to do would be to step on a British ship.'

'And leave everything behind?'

Willie grinned. 'Not everything,' he said. 'I arranged for a lot of our capital to go to England. It's safe in banks

248

there. That's where a proportion of everything we make here should go from now on. Then, if trouble comes, we head for Southampton or Liverpool and start again with what we've stacked away. We're in business in Yangpo and we operate up and down the river. The ferries are good now. You travel in comfort and there are gunboats so that if anything goes wrong you've always got the British Navy to look after you. We'll build a house at Yangpo – '

'I thought we were going to build it in Shanghai.'

'Why not one in both places? All the best people have a country retreat. When it's too hot in Shanghai we'll go up to Yangpo. When it's too cold in Yangpo we'll come down to the coast. What could be better?'

Abigail considered there were a lot of things which could be better, but she didn't voice her thoughts. 'But we don't give up the trade in Chinese artifacts?'

'That's your business.' Willie's gesture was expansive. 'You handle it. I'll look after the import-export business and the shipping.'

'Shipping?'

'I've got two now,' Willie said proudly. '*Kum Kum Kiuw*. Five-hundred-ton coaster. I bought her in Shanghai when I got back. Company that had gone bust. I've just started the Sarth Line.'

What Willie had suggested began to seem possible more quickly than he had anticipated. Moving with all their belongings to Shanghai, they set up house near the Bubbling Well Road among the new houses of other rising businessmen, and the office on the bund became the most important of their centres. It was not alone. There were plenty of others – Jardine Matheson's, Sassoon's,

Butterfield and Swire's, Mason and Marchant's, even Wishart and Co., because Emmeline, married now to another of her office managers, had quickly followed them, almost as if she had been watching which way the wind blew and was using Sarth's as the indicator.

With Abigail in Shanghai looking after the children and developing the new house there to her taste, Willie started building the house in Yangpo. Most of the materials were local, but all the timber and glass had to come upriver by junk. Already Yangpo was developing as fast as its trade, and there was even a social life of a kind, mostly a deadly round of drinking and dinner parties, which fluctuated with the ebb and flow of the foreign community in response to the approach or retreat of danger. Danger was something that was never far away because, although General Fu had gone, there were others looking round for the opportunities in the vacuum he had caused.

In the north, the Japanese were consolidating their gains in Korea and Manchuria and making sure that everybody noticed how powerful they had become. The Russians had lost not only their Port Arthur squadron but a fleet sent out from the Baltic to sail half-way round the world to suffer a shattering defeat at Tsushima. Despite the sneers and contempt with which the Japanese had been held, they had firmly established themselves as a power in the Far East.

Willie was too busy to be concerned, however. He had already dismissed the war from his mind and was occupied in developing the business at Yangpo. There was iron, silver, lead, zinc, antimony and limestone nearby and, eager to see it moved, Willie had bought another ship, a 1,500-tonner, the *Winifred Whitehead*, to move it to where it was needed – India, Australia and the Dutch East Indies.

'I got her cheap,' he explained to Abigail. 'Chap who wanted to concentrate ashore.'

'You seem to have a gift for picking up old ships,' Abigail commented.

'Well, we'll never be mail steamers,' Willie admitted. 'But she's not that old and she can get all the way up to Yangpo. There's a growing profitability in the China Seas trade.'

Abigail smiled indulgently. 'You sound like Samuel Cunard,' she said.

Willie grinned, well aware that his new enthusiasm had got a firm grip on him. 'Tramp ships take fifteen per cent of world trade Ab, and here they're important because the coastal railway services are non-existent. Reliability's important and people'll pay well for it. That's what I'm aiming at, that and having my ships in the right place at the right time, because seasons affect freight rates.' He looked faintly shame-faced. 'I've even got my eye on another coaster, the *Shamara*, *a* fishing boat, for dodging between the islands. Seventy feet long with a hell of a range and a new engine.'

Abigail gave him a worried look. 'You're not getting in too deeply, are you?'

Willie grinned 'Not me. Ab, old love, this is the time to expand. There's money to be made and we're neck-deep in it already.'

There was no wall dividing the British Concession from the Chinese City at Yangpo, only a road that was never crossed. On one side were the smelly, narrow Chinese streets, teeming with people, colour, life and a reckless sprawling vitality, on the other British-paid police, sanitation, traffic regulations, an esplanade where you could see women with wide-brimmed hats strolling among the azaleas, a small girl with a hoop, a boy with a whip and top, and all the dignified stodginess of a British crown colony with stiff collars, walking sticks and raised hats. On one side you spat as you pleased. On the other you were liable to a fine.

Willie loved it. He liked the gentle Luis Da Braga and enjoyed talking business with him over his brandy bottle, arguing with the compradores and listening to the high-pitched chatter of the coolies with their sense of fun and infectious laughter. There was nothing they liked better than to see the high and mighty in a position of indignity – a fat Chinese businessman slipping on a dog's turd, a self-important white woman with her hat knocked sideways. He was still young, and he knew the women eyed him because he was still slim, didn't drink much and wasn't one to sit over heavy meals on hot evenings as most men did, and he enjoyed it. In Shanghai, he and Abigail had become part of the city's society, always in demand, two attractive young people among a group of business taipans with their plump dull wives. Occasionally, he went to Peking either on his own to do business, which was still to be found there, or with Abigail when she was collecting Chinese treasures for sale in London, Paris or New York.

Brassard had been as good as his word and was working honestly with them, but occasionally it meant visiting England, taking in India on the way because there were more treasures to be picked up there, and then on to America or France before, faintly outlandish with their tanned skins among all the British-based parents, ending up looking at prep schools and public schools for their children, who, like the children of most businessmen abroad, would have to come home for their education. Travelling was easy now, however, because they always travelled first class and people no longer looked down their noses at them.

Then the Emperor died unexpectedly. Willie and Abigail were in Peking at the time, clearing up the last details of their move to Shanghai.

The Emperor meant little because he had always been a pawn in the hands of the Empress Dowager, but to everyone's surprise the following day the Empress Dowager died too. She had not been well for some time and, as she took to her bed, in typical fashion she prepared for her death with orders to everyone who mattered and a valedictory address to the Chinese people.

The funeral was magnificent, the red robes of the bearers contrasting with the yellow robes of the priests, the rich silver and gold embroidery bringing the appropriate colours of sunset. Missions from all over Asia arrived to pay homage as the corpse was carried to the Tung-Ling, the Eastern Tombs, and as the procession left the city the bier was preceded by one of the old woman's favourites, carrying her pet dog, a yellow and white Pekingese.

The corpse lay on a mattress embroidered with pearls and swathed in a coverlet of more pearls and a lace sheet with 'Buddha' outlined in still more pearls. It was dressed in jade ornaments and ceremonial clothes of gold thread, ropes of pearls encircled it and there were pearl images in the dead woman's arms. Gold, jade and carved Buddas were placed in the tomb with her, with jade models of fruit and lotus roots and hundreds more scattered pearls and other jewels.

'Worth looting,' Willie said dryly.

Almost immediately, they became aware of China's problems again because a strong man had arisen by the name of Yuan Shih-K'Ai. He had held a variety of positions, at one moment in power, the next in disgrace. At that moment he was exiled far from the seat of government as Viceroy of the Metropolitan Province. But, as the Sarths' home in Yangpo grew and Da Braga's wooden hut became a brick godown four times the size, as Edward Sarth disappeared to a prep school in England, accompanied by his mother, who was in a late state of pregnancy with a third child, Yuan was dismissed.

'There'll be trouble,' Da Braga said at once.

'For us?'

'For everybody with interests in China.'

'There are a lot of us.'

Da Braga nodded. 'When the Japanese started to invest capital to start Japanese-controlled industries in China, everybody followed suit.'

'So did we. We have cotton mills in Shanghai besides what we have up here. So have Wishart's. And Mason and Marchant's and Wissermann's. We're not the only ones either. We've all got places along the Yangtze, and we've all put money into the railways to make sure we can get to them.'

'Perhaps it will turn out to be a mistake. Railways have a habit of disturbing ancestors. The Chinese might object. Especially if Yuan decides he has the power to overthrow the dynasty.'

'Think he'll try?'

'I suspect it's more than likely.'

To Willie, Da Braga seemed to be making too much of the danger, but his worries seemed based on sound fears when, unexpectedly, riots started against the dynasty. In Sian, where the name of the Manchus had become execrated for their cruelty, corruption and reaction, hundreds of them and their followers were butchered by the angry population. Immediately, waves of nervousness swept through the European communities up and down the river. Then, in Szechwan, the provincial governor was replaced by a stronger man whose attempts at repressing the rising tide of hatred for the dynasty only made things worse, and at Wuchang, opposite Hankow on the Yangtze and close to Yangpo, where the fighting between the dissidents and the government troops had been ferocious, the garrison was instructed to put down the disturbance with the utmost severity.

Once again the European community at Yangpo began to grow anxious. Meetings were called to decide what to do, but nothing came of them because there were too many nationalities and too many different interests. It seemed to Willie that, under the circumstances, it was best that he should be in Yangpo, and he was just going through Da Braga's books, pretending to be interested but always with one ear on the sounds of dissension outside, when the Portuguese arrived. Da Braga was excited enough to leave the engine of his car running outside as he appeared in the doorway.

'There was an explosion in a house in the Russian Concession at Hankow,' he said. 'They found guns and ammunition and the names of members of a revolutionary plot, most of them officers of the garrison. There was only one thing they could do. They took the bit between their teeth and the governor fled. Wuchang's in their hands now and they've also occupied Hankow and Hanyang across the river, and declared their independence of Peking. The Regent's called on Yuan Shih-K'Ai for help.'

Immediately news came of similar uprisings across the whole country so that, within days almost, there were military governments in almost every province south of the Great Wall, most of them started by junior officers who had recruited senior officers to head their movement. With the Manchu army in disarray, the Regent – who was ruling the country because the Empress Dowager's nominee as Emperor was only a boy of six – called the strong man, Yuan, from his exile and instructed him to set the Chinese house in order. Almost immediately, he emerged as Prime Minister.

'Well,' Willie said, raising his glass to Da Braga, 'perhaps he's the one feller who's strong enough to restore peace. I hear the old revolutionary Sun Yat-Sen's arrived in Shanghai to become temporary president of a republic until they can organise things for Yuan to take office. I think the Manchus are finished.'

He was right, and the days of the Manchus were numbered. Within weeks they were gone and the Socialists and the followers of Sun Yat-Sen were forcibly cutting off the pigtails that the Manchus had forced people to wear. It was an indication of the way the future was shaping and, as Jardine Matheson's led the way in moving their capital away, everybody started using British banks instead of The Bank of China, because they feared some undefined upheaval which could affect their funds.

Sitting in the office in Yangpo, Willie read *The North China Daily News*' view of the situation to Da Braga. ' "History",' he read, ' "has witnessed few such revolutions and perhaps none of equal magnitude which has been carried out with so little bloodshed." '

Da Braga was not so sure of the situation. 'Some of us,' he said, 'are inclined to doubt whether a form of government alien to oriental traditions can suddenly be substituted for a monarchy. Especially in a nation ruled ever since the sun first rose by kings who've been regarded as semi-divine.'

Willie nodded thoughtfully. 'You might be more right than the *Daily News*,' he agreed.

By the time Abigail, after a visit to her old haunts in the States, returned, complete with a daughter born in a San Francisco nursing home, Willie had found new areas to conquer. He had been looking around for some time before it dawned on him that there was Russian territory not far to the north that was wide open to commerce.

He was already involved in cargoes of zinc, tungsten, maize, castor oil, aniseed, silk and mother of pearl from Indo-China, doing the trips himself to build up the years of sea time he needed for a mate's certificate, slipping into Haiphong where bougainvillaea draped the houses with magenta swathes and the gardens glowed with yellow and orange canna lilies, to Malaya for shellac and soya beans, to Hong Kong for British cement for Saigon. He was itching to expand further.

He had even tried Japan because, since their victory over the Russians, the Japanese had become suprisingly popular in Europe and prints of their victories were on sale everywhere, and a fashion had started in London for fans, butterflies, geisha girls and netsuke jewellery. Shaiba had greeted him warmly, and laughed at his adventures on the night of the attack on Port Arthur. But there was little business to be done. Looking far into the future, the

Japanese preferred to keep their trade largely to themselves and it was obvious that in their view if anyone was going to run the East it was not going to be Europeans but Orientals. They already had a foothold in China, not only along the Yangtze, but along the coast, and now, after the Russo-Japanese war, in Manchuria.

Realising, therefore, that Japan was not going to provide much business, he decided to try Vladivostok. After all, you didn't have to go to Moscow to buy Russian goods. Vladivostok was already in constant close touch with Shanghai, and was well known as a link in the opium trade, and the Shanghai customs always gave special attention to ships whose cargo manifests showed Vladivostok as their origin or destination. Officials didn't hesitate to hold up a cargo if they felt like it, but, if they were in a hurry or dishonest, it was always possible to bamboozle them. The Upper Section Wharves in Shanghai were the dirtiest, smelliest and most dangerous of the whole waterfront, embracing the cobbled bund of the French Concession and the more sinister bund of the old walled city, and there small steamers, changing berths at night, could easily leave the Customs men baffled by what appeared to be a change in identity.

Buying a Russian grammar, Willie set out to learn a few useful words and phrases. His education had been limited to a few years at a poverty-stricken church school which had taut him little more than the three Rs, but he was quick to learn and was always busy acquiring knowledge and, a good linguist and based in a place where he could hear every language under the sun without walking from his office, he had already picked up a smattering of Japanese and French and a lot of Chinese. It had surprised him to find how good he was and, with his master's certificate within sight as soon as he had completed the necessary number of years on the bridge of his own ships, he took to Russian like a duck to water.

Vladivostok was at the end of the Trans-Siberian Railway and was said to be an outlandish place on the edge of nowhere, short of the things he had to sell such as Hong Kong kettles, pans, axes, crockery, cotton, leather and rubber goods, cigarettes, matches, shirts, tins of enamel and varnish, footwear, rattan chairs and rolls of printed cotton. *Some* of it ought to sell, he felt. Perhaps all of it, and there were always agents to drum up trade.

George Kee had suggested a firm called A N Kourganov. 'They do business with Tientsin,' he pointed out. 'I've known of them for some time.'

Willie slapped his shoulder. 'Well done, George. Why didn't Lun Foo suggest this? He's been in the game longer than you?'

Kee smiled modestly. 'Perhaps he is not very clever, sir. Perhaps he doesn't listen enough. Perhaps he spends too much time eating and drinking.'

'Who with?'

'Wang Li-Jen.'

'Isn't he the agent for Wishart's?'

'Also Hamming's, Mason and Marchant's and James MacConachie, sir.'

'None of 'em very big. Or very sound either.'

'He also dines with his brother-in-law, Yip Hsao-Li.'

Willie frowned. The ubiquitous Yip seemed to be involved in everything without doing any work. He still liked to look European, always preferred suits to Chinese robes and, so Willie had heard, was even learning to dance Western dances. A collector of *objets d'art*, he had more than once visited Abigail in search of porcelain.

Because the European taipans were indifferent to her jade, embroideries, Sinkiang silver and porcelain, regarding them as 'Chink stuff', she had not neglected the wealthy Chinese, and Yip was a good customer.

Willie didn't trust him, nevertheless. 'He's in with the secret societies,' he said and Kee nodded.

'He is indeed, sir.'

'According to my information, George, that import-export business of his is a façade and he's not much better than a gangster himself. Why does he go down to Hong Kong so much, too? He doesn't do business there? I've heard he also visits Swatow and Amoy. What's his interest *there*? Keep your ears open, boy.'

Situated in Peter the Great's Bay on the western shore of the Sea of Japan, Vladivostok seemed to smell entirely of damp wool, damp leather and damp fur, and at night a skin of ice settled on the buildings, sidewalks and streets, muffling sound, diffusing the street lamps and blurring the anchor lights of the ships in the bay. From the moment Willie stepped ashore the place seemed to be covered in a cold drizzle which was neither rain nor snow but something in between. Newspapers became sodden. Droplets clung to moustaches and beards and even the church bells seemed heavy with the damp.

It had been an uneasy journey north, because lately the East China Sea had become infested with a new plague of pirates. They came from among the hundreds of islands along the coasts and to the south of Korea, and were said to have a base at Bias Bay, north of Hong Kong, where the deep water ended well out, so that warships couldn't follow their flat-bottomed sampans and junks. It was a bleak uninhabited area, but it gave access to a thickly populated countryside where they could disappear if they were pursued.

They liked to attack ships for the opium they carried, sometimes trying to bribe the compradores who acted as pursers and were always the first men they sought out after an attack because they carried the keys to the ship's safe. Recently, they had even started preying on ships crossing the Yellow Sea or heading for the Sea of Japan. There had even been women pirates, moving out by canoe to moored ships to entice the sailors with their oiled yellow bodies until it was time to draw their knives and take over the ship, but now the pirates were changing their tactics and even using small steamers and, after an attack on a 1,000-ton coaster out of Hong Kong, Willie had given orders that his ships were at all times to have their hoses connected to the boilers, and an attempt on the *Kum Kum Kiuw* off the Pescadores had been met with scalding steam.

Now, however, somebody was putting money into the game and organising the pirates so that, instead of out-and-out attacks and boarding, they were showing cunning and were infiltrating the passenger lists. No coastal captain ever felt safe and, taking the extra precaution of hiring Sikhs who had retired from Indian Army regiments, Willie placed them aboard as guards, a lead that was quickly followed by other lines.

But this time nothing happened and, with nothing worse than a gale that sent spindrift and showers of icy sleet across the deck, the *Winifred Whitehead* reached Vladivostok safely, with Willie signed on officially for the trip as a mate to give him sea time.

Vladivostok turned out to be a drab-looking place with a badly organised waterfront, something which didn't surprise Willie much, because, like most people in Shanghai, he had come to assume that everything about Tsarist Russia was ill-organised.

Even the commerce of the port seemed to move at only half-speed, because of the 5,000 miles which lay between Vladivostok and Moscow. Despite the Trans-Siberian Railway, little in the way of drive seemed to emanate from the Russian capital, but there were engineering works, fishing and whaling industries, iron ore from the Urals and timber from Siberia. There was by no means as much as he'd expected, however, and the place depressed him with its flat-faced Russian workers, Chinese and Koreans. It had a pronounced international character, however, with people of all nations there and, within forty-eight hours, he found himself approached to do business by a Frenchman, a Russian and an American, none of whom he trusted. There were department stores after a fashion, and one hotel, the Aleksandr, which seemed suitable for a man of his financial stature.

The firm of A N Kourganov occupied a set of offices near the docks and it was snowing as Willie climbed from the cab which carried him there. Much of the trade from Vladivostok was with merchants to the south, even with Japan across the China Sea, and the clerks had obviously been picked for their ability to communicate with customers in their own language. It was something Willie heartily approved of.

When he asked for A N Kourganov in person he was led down a corridor and shown into a large office packed with files. Behind a desk stacked with piles of invoices was a woman. She wore pince-nez spectacles, but as he entered she removed them. As she smiled at him, he was startled by the striking topaz eyes and thick brown hair touched with reddish lights. As she rose to greet him, he saw she was dressed in severe fashion in a dark skirt with a high-necked blouse, a cameo brooch at her throat.

'I'm looking for A N Kourganov,' he said.

She smiled again. 'I am A N Kourganov,' she said in excellent English. She gave him a tinkling laugh at his expression. 'Oh, it's quite true,' she said. 'I am the firm. In fact, I am Nadya Alexsandrovna Kourganova and perhaps that should be the firm's name, but I don't use it because the idea of a woman running a business tends to put men off. Does it put you off, Mr Sarth?'

'No,' Willie was still recovering. 'No. Not at all. Business is business. I don't mind. How did you come to set it up?'

'I didn't,' she said. 'A N Kourganov was Aleksandr Nicolaievich Kourganov, my father. When he died I took over.' She paused, looking at him quizzically. 'But I suspect, Mr Sarth, that you didn't come here to discuss my background.'

Willie, who was still a bit bemused, not only at finding himself dealing with a woman but also by her beauty, jumped. 'No,' he agreed. 'I didn't. I've got a load of things you might like. Tin kettles, pans, axes, crockery, cotton, leather and rubber goods, cigarettes, matches, shirts, enamel, varnish, footwear, rattan chairs, printed cotton. Are you interested? I thought that Vladivostok, being a long way from Moscow, might be able to use some of them.'

She smiled. 'We lack many of the things European Russians enjoy.'

She looked round to find a chair for him to sit on, but they all seemed to be stacked with files. She looked at him helplessly and he wasn't slow to react.

'Look,' he said. 'If we're going to do business, let's do it in comfort. Let's have lunch together somewhere. I suppose there is somewhere?'

'There is the Hotel Novgorod. It's the best Vladivostok can offer.'

'I have other business to attend to. Timber and coal. I don't want my ship to return in ballast, because an empty ship loses money, so I'll attend to that first and come back here at midday. Will that suit you?'

The smile came again. 'Excellently, Mr Sarth.'

The timber was good, but the coal turned out to be poor quality, though Willie knew he could sell it in the Dutch East Indies. He arranged for it to be delivered at the docks and loaded, and for the timber to travel as deck cargo, then returned with a cab to the offices of A N Kourganov prompt at midday.

He was curiously excited. Nadya Alexsandrovna Kourganova was a beautiful woman with a lot of charm. Quite different from Abigail, who was pretty, full of humour, but often grave and solemn as she became absorbed in something, Nadya Alexsandrovna was vivacious but given to brooding a little, a fact he put down to her Russian temperament. With her slender figure, her beautiful eyes and the mass of thick reddish brown hair, she stood out like a searchlight among the shorter, squatter people of Vladivostok with their wide mouths, darker skins and their Mongol cast of countenance.

She appeared at once. It had turned colder and she wore a fur coat with a hood that framed her face and caught the flurries of snow in little melting droplets like jewels round her face. The Novgorod was large and opulent but old-fashioned and outlandish, and the dining room was indifferent. Nadya Alexsandrovna apologised.

'Vladivostok is not Moscow,' she said.

The dining room contained more than its fair share of uniformed officers – most of them old and stout, as if they'd been sent to Vladivostok to get them out of the way – and of hard-eyed young businessmen, some of them in loud clothes with high, stiff collars and spats. A small orchestra was playing a selection of music on a rostrum, sweet, melodious and totally innocuous. It made sitting opposite a very attractive woman very pleasant.

She had taken the trouble to go home and change her dress and now wore a simple lavender gown and matching hat that set off her eyes. He was intrigued by how she came to be in Vladivostok. Somehow she didn't seem to fit.

'Were you born here?' he asked.

'No. In St Petersburg.'

'So how did you learn to speak such good English?'

She looked at him with her enormous eyes. One delicate hand lay on the table close to his. She had attended a girls' school in England as a child, and then the Smolnia, the leading Russian girls' establishment in St Petersburg. 'Most girls went to Paris,' she explained, 'because French is a second language for wealthy Russians and all our diplomats speak it, because, of course, no one outside Russia speaks our own barbaric tongue. My father, who was always different, chose England.'

'Then how did you come to turn up here?'

She paused for a moment, staring at her hands, then her eyes lifted to Willie's. 'My father was a baron,' she said.

'Which makes you a baroness?'

She inclined her head. 'That doesn't matter much here in Vladivostok. My father was also wealthy, but it isn't done for someone in society in Russia to go into business. But he enjoyed it and, when I tried it, I found I did, too. I insisted on helping him.' She shrugged. 'But my mother didn't approve and my sisters objected because their husbands said it lowered their standing in society.'

He guessed he had heard only half the story. 'But here?' he asked. 'Why here? You can do business as easily in St Petersburg.'

She stared at her hands again. 'My father was not very good at holding his tongue,' she admitted. 'He didn't approve of the Tsar and his methods of governing and what he had to say about them made him *persona non grata* in St Petersburg.'

'He had to leave?'

'Being a baron, of course, he could hardly be imprisoned. But he was advised to disappear to the provinces, to go away from St Petersburg. This was the farthest he could get. I came with him to look after him because I was sick of St Petersburg society. It's as simple as that.'

Willie eyed her. 'It couldn't have been all that simple. Wasn't there any man who wanted to stop you?'

She smiled gently at him. 'None I found wanted to stop me.'

There was something he felt he needed to know about her. 'Are you married?' he asked.

'Yes.'

'Is your husband in the firm?'

'I don't know where my husband is. He moves about a lot. I haven't seen him for a long time.'

'Left you, did he?'

'He found another woman within months – if he'd ever given her up – and left me after two years. There was no point in *not* coming here to join my father.'

He found he needed to talk about Abigail, feeling conscious of a vague guilt that he should be enjoying himself.

'My wife's in business, too,' he said. 'Antiques. Chinese *objets d'art*. Lacquer. Ivory. Carpets. Sandalwood. That sort of thing. She's an expert.'

Nadya Alexsandrovna gestured. 'I can find her things to sell,' she said.

Lunchtime seemed to drift far into the afternoon and when they parted they were on terms of close friendship and Christian names. It was all the more surprising, therefore, when a note was delivered to Willie as he sat at breakfast the following morning.

'Mr Sarth. I would like to see you at my office,' it said. 'A N Kourganova.'

A N Kourganova? When the previous day they had been William and Nadya. Finishing his coffee, Willie tossed down his napkin and headed for the hall. When he was shown into her office, she stood up at once and this time there were no smiles.

'I wished to see you, Mr Sarth.'

'It was William yesterday. And you were Nadya.'

'This is business.'

'Something wrong?'

'The footwear you produced, Mr Sarth. It is all left foot. Your matches don't strike, your tin kettles leak and your cotton print rolls have flaws in them.'

Willie's jaw dropped. 'They can't have!'

'I've inspected them. Did you?'

'No. I bought them in good faith from the same place I always buy them. I've sold them in Japan, Burma, Singapore – '

'Perhaps they are not as particular as we are.'

'They'd soon let me know if they'd noticed anything wrong. They'd probably cut my throat. Can I see these things?'

'They are in my warehouse.'

'Show them to me.'

She wasn't very willing, but she agreed and they rode in silence in a cab to the warehouse on the docks where Willie's crates had been delivered. They had all been opened and their contents scattered around. Willie picked up one of the men's shoes, stared at it, then began to paw among them. As she had said, they were all shoddy and most of them were left foot.

'Is it all like this?' he demanded.

'Not all. But several crates have been opened. My foreman sent for me to show me.'

'What about the leather and rubber?'

'All right. So are your cigarettes and chairs and the shirts and the enamel and varnish. We've found nothing wrong with those.'

Willie had picked up a bright tin kettle. There were marks of rust on it and someone had filled it with water which was dripping steadily to the floor. Watched by Nadya Alexsandrovna and her clerk, he examined the cotton print rolls and tried the matches. The cotton had flaws in it and the matches showed signs of having been in water. The labels were stained and the match-heads were soft, damaged in a leaky warehouse during one of Hong Kong's downpours.

'This isn't my stuff,' he growled.

'You sent it, Mr Sarth.' Nadya Alexsandrovna's voice was stiff and distrustful. 'I have also found opium. We don't deal with opium.'

His eyes jerked up to hers. 'Neither do I,' he snapped back. 'There's something funny going on. Let me see the crates.'

He moved the crates around, carefully studying them. They had been used many times and directions on them had been painted over more than once. Then faintly, beneath the Chinese characters stamped on them, he came across the name 'Wishart'.

He straightened up, his eyes angry. Emmeline! Was she behind this?

He looked at Nadya Alexsandrovna. 'I've been swindled,' he said. 'I'll take all this back. I know where it came from. Have it all packed up. I'll refund every bit of the cost. I'm not dishonest. I've spent too many years proving the opposite. I want to do business with you. I'd like to remain not only a business associate but the friend I thought I was yesterday. Will you agree?'

She studied him gravely for a while then suddenly she smiled. It transformed her face.

'I will agree, William,' she said and his heart warmed as she used his name. 'Now let us go to my house where we will celebrate the trust with champagne from the Crimea.'

She had a house on the Marizliyevskaya, an avenue that ran along the coast. Along the front was a vast veranda. 'My father wanted a veranda,' she explained. 'We had a veranda on the house we had at Yalta. But in Yalta you can eat on the veranda in the evening. Here, you need a fur coat most of the time.'

They ate in a small pink dining room where the walls were covered with pictures. 'Kourganovs?' Willie asked.

She nodded. 'And Anikins, which was my mother's family. Together with a few Gorkachovs, which was my grandmother's family. We go back a long way. Does your family?'

'As far as my Pa,' Willie said frankly. 'Beyond that, we don't know much.' He glanced again at the portraits. 'None of your husband?'

She opened a drawer and took out a small folding picture frame. 'Just one,' she said. 'I keep it to remind me that he was handsome and charming and that perhaps I wasn't such a fool as I've often thought since.'

She held out the folder to him and, as he took it, he almost dropped it. The picture was that of Count Zychov.

'Him?' he said.

She eyed him. 'You've met him?'

He described what had happened near Shantu and the difficulties that had been made for him at Port Arthur.

'That sounds like him,' she admitted.

'But his name's Zychov.'

'My proper name is Nadya Alexsandrovna Zychova. Kourganov is my father's name. I dropped my husband's name when I realised he was never coming back to me.'

It was startling to discover how small a world it was, how someone who had entered his life thirteen years before had still not left it. He wanted to know more about Zychov, but she clearly had no wish to talk about him and changed the subject quickly. She had collected a few things for him to take back to Abigail – a cameo scent bottle, a Swiss snuff box, a Statdler vase, some Venetian glass, which he knew would sell like hot cakes in London. There were also one or two items by Fabergé, which he

271

had long since learned were much sought after – a minute
gold automaton sedan chair containing a figure of
Catherine the Great with a jewelled crown borne by
turbaned servants, an egg picked out with diamonds,
thimbles, penholders, a kiwi, an elephant, a frog. He
picked up the sedan chair, knowing very well that Abigail
would swoon over it.

'This is worth a lot of money,' he said.

'Yes,' she agreed. 'It is.'

'Yours?'

'No. Someone I know.'

'Why didn't *you* buy it?'

'My interest is not in these things. Though –' she
paused ' – there may come a time when it will be.'

'I can't pay you for them. Not now. Not immediately.'

'I don't expect you to.'

'You trust me to take them away?'

'I know you'll send me the money.'

'Of course I will. My wife will sell these easily. Where
did they come from?'

'In Russia there are always people who live beyond
their means. It's a Russian habit. Then they have to sell
the family treasures. Many of them come to Vladivostok
to avoid their debts and I know their problems because I
belonged to their class. Knowing my contacts outside
Russia, they approach me. You could say I'm acting as
their agent. I sell for them and I suspect that in your wife
I've found a splendid outlet. I can send you whatever I
pick up. But of course they're too valuable to send by
casual arrangement.'

'There's no need. My ships will be coming here
regularly now.'

'You're a shipowner, too?'

'Yes,' Willie said proudly. Then he grinned. 'Three. Soon four. All little ones.'

She laughed with him and gestured with the Fabergé egg. 'There'll be more of these before long,' she said.

'What do you mean?'

'Can't you feel it coming?'

'What?'

'Isn't it clear to you what's happening?'

'Not in Shanghai, it isn't.'

'Russia's tired of the monarchy. It wants a change. It wants to run its own affairs. There are constant plots. It will get rid of Tsar Nicholas before long. And when that happens and people flee from St Petersburg, some will certainly come to Vladivostok.'

'You're certain of this, aren't you?'

'Very certain.'

'Are you sure it won't affect Nadya Alexsandrovna Kourganova.'

'Of course it will.'

'Doesn't it worry you?'

She laughed. 'Being part of the aristocracy has never done much for me – except bore me.'

'Revolutions can be dangerous.'

'I shall be all right. My father's dead now and my sisters are in the south. Me – ' she shrugged ' – they won't touch me. My father spoke too often against the Tsar and was exiled for his words. And, in effect, I went with him. It will stand me in good stead when the time comes to be judged.'

The talk of revolution worried Willie. He'd seen enough of that sort of thing in China.

'Are you on the side of the revolutionaries?' he asked.

'I'm on the side of whoever wins,' she smiled.

'If you ever need me, contact me. I might be able to help.'

She gave him a gentle smile. 'What a pity you are already married, William Sarth,' she said quietly. 'I could almost feel you are the man I've been looking for. In other circumstances I might have asked you to stay. I might even have attempted to seduce you. But I think I would have been unsuccessful.'

He nodded gravely. 'Yes. I think you would.'

'You love your wife?'

'Yes.'

'I'm glad. We shall just be good friends.'

Abigail crowed over the treasures he had brought back with him.

'Willie,' she said, 'they're worth a fortune! What did you pay for them?'

'Nothing. She let me bring them without paying.'

Abigail frowned. 'Then, if she trusts us, we must give her a good price. What's she like, Willie?'

'Beautiful, Ab. Very beautiful. And you'll never guess who she's married to. That bloody Russian, Zychov! The cowardly sod who left us in the lurch at Shantu and tried to stop me getting the *Lady Roberts* away from Port Arthur.'

She didn't seem as impressed by the discovery as he'd expected and seemed more concerned with the woman who had been Zychov's wife. 'Are you attracted to her, Willie?'

'Who wouldn't be? You would be too, Ab. Next time I come to Vladivostok, why don't you come with me and meet her?'

She gave him a thoughtful look. 'Perhaps I will,' she agreed.

She had news for him, too. China was going through another of its revolutionary throes. A series of assassinations had removed everybody opposed to Yuan Shih-K'Ai and when the revolutionary, Sun Yat-Sen, had decided it was safer to bolt back to Japan, Yuan had dissolved the Kuomintang, the Nationalist party Sun had formed.

'It'll be the usual chaos,' Willie said. 'They can't even agree which is to be the capital, Peking or Nanking. They've been fighting over it for years. Who's for him?'

'It's more a case of who's against him. General Chang, for one.'

Willie frowned. Whether as emperor or as president, Yuan in control might well be useful, because China had always been an unwholesome stew of nationalities, hostilities, ambitions and quarrelling commerce, and a strong hand on the wheel might make it more stable. As for Chang, the whole of China had heard of him for his cruelties and power and, sitting in Kiangsu province, smack across the land trading routes and beyond the reach of Peking and anything Yuan chose to send against him, such a warlord was always important to people like Willie Sarth.

'Chang was a follower of the Manchus, of course,' Abigail went on. 'He'd support anyone who had a hand in deposing them.'

'God help China if Chang gets control,' Willie said. 'When he got into Nanking in September he lost control of his men. They commandeered all the rickshaws to cart away the loot, and what they did to the women and girls was appalling. They were pulling them out of the river for days afterwards.'

Photographs of Edward had turned up from England, blurred and out of focus but showing him smiling and happy, while ill-spelled letters told them of his best friend, son of a captain in the Royal Navy, and of his wish to become a sailor when he left school.

'Isn't it dangerous, Willie?' Abigail asked.

'Shouldn't think so,' Willie said. 'The Royal Navy's the biggest in the world.'

'What about the German Navy? The papers say they're building like they're crazy.'

'They'll never be bigger than the British Navy.' Willie had all the in-built British admiration of the senior service and the same faith in its powers. Hadn't the British Navy brought peace all round the world? 'He'll be all right. He might end up an admiral. What about that then? An admiral in the family.' He gestured at his second son, Thomas, who sat with his nose in a book. 'What about you, lad? What do you want to become?'

'Chinese.'

'Chinese?' Willie roared with laughter. 'Why Chinese?'

'Because we live in China. I'll be a white Chinese.'

'You don't speak Chinese.'

'I'll learn.'

'What about your little sister, Polly? What do you think she'll do?'

'Grow up and get married.'

'Nothing else?'

'That's what girls do, isn't it?'

Willie looked at Abigail. 'Some of them do more than that, son. Whatever she does, though, you see you look after Polly. Remember, family first, second and all the way.'

He looked up to see that Abigail was frowning.

'I'm glad our children are young, Willie,' she said.

'Why?'

She gestured at the sheets of *The North China Daily News* scattered about the floor. The headlines were about China, but the leaders were showing concern for events in Europe. Quite clearly, they didn't feel they would affect China, but were important enough not to be ignored.

'The German Kaiser's talking big again,' she said. 'They seem to think there's going to be a war.'

Willie was reminded of the cargo of leaking kettles, flameless matches, flawed cotton, and left-foot shoes he had brought back from Vladivostok. He slapped his knees. 'Yes, by God,' he said. 'There is. Here. In Shanghai.'

As Willie entered his office the following day the clerks bent their heads to their ledgers. He was not often in a temper, but when he was it was best to keep out of his way.

'Kee!' The shout made them all jump and tuck their heads even lower.

As Kee appeared, Willie slapped down the invoices for the faulty goods in front of him.

'Dud, George,' he said. 'The crates had the Wishart name on them. Someone had tried to blank it out, but it was visible. Who's doing it? Do you know?'

'Yes, Mr Sarth. I know.'

'It's not you, is it?'

'No, it's not me?'

'One of the other clerks?'

'I think not.'

'Lun Foo?'

Kee was silent and Willie glared at him. 'I pay you to keep an eye on things. Spit it out.'

Kee shrugged. 'Yes, Mr Sarth. It's Lun Foo.'

'How long have you known?'

'Not long.'

'Why didn't you tell me?'

'I wasn't certain. Now I am. You've just made me certain. He's been taking bribes. He lives beyond his income. He's in debt. He's in touch all the time with Wishart's man, Wang Li-Jen.'

Willie sat staring at his desk for a while, then he stood up and gestured. 'You know where I keep my revolver, George?'

'Yes, sir. In the desk, there.'

'Hand it to me.'

'Sir – ' Kee's eyes became alarmed. ' – You're not going to – '

'Shoot myself?' Willie grinned, a quick grin that vanished at once. 'Not bloody likely, lad.'

Kee placed the big weapon in his hand and he stuffed it into his trouser top and let his jacket fall over it. Then he looked at it again.

'Better make sure I've got it on safe,' he said, 'or I might shoot myself in the balls.'

Kee gave him a nervous grin.

'Right, George, let's have Lun in. And stick around.'

Lun Foo appeared, smiling. Kee shut the door behind him and took up a position in the corner of the room.

'Sit down,' Willie snapped.

As Lun Foo sat, Willie slapped the invoices in front of him.

'Dud,' he snapped. 'Kettles that leak. Left-hand footwear. Faulty cotton. Matches that have been soaked. Where did they come from, Lun? They're not mine. There was also a consignment of opium. That wasn't mine either, because I've never touched the stuff. Where did that come from?'

Lun put on a big show of innocence. 'I cannot tell, Master. This very bad. Somebody cheat.'

'You?'

Lun rocked back as the word was spat at him. He recovered quickly. 'Not me, Master. Perhaps Kee.'

'I don't believe it. Why were the crates marked "Wishart"?'

'Perhaps he had dealings with their chief clerk, Master. He is a Korean called Kwok. He is not to be trusted.'

'Neither are you. Come on, Lun. Let's have it. Did you do this on your own?'

'I have no responsibility for it, Master.'

Willie crossed to the compradore and stood alongside him. Dragging the revolver from his belt, he stuck the muzzle in Lun's ear. 'Let's have the truth.'

'I tell the truth, Master!' Lun's voice rose to a shriek.

Willie's thumb heaved back on the hammer. The click was clear.

'I tell truth, Master!'

'All I have to do now is pull the trigger.'

'I tell, Master, I tell.' His eyes wide, Lun pushed Willie aside and dropped on his knees. 'I fix it with Kwok.'

'Opium, too.'

'Yes, Master!'

'Why?'

'I owe much money, Master.'

'Who to? Yip Hsao-Li?'

'Yes, Master!'

'So why did Kwok pick on me? Why did Wishart's push their goods in with mine? Why not someone else? Did someone put Kwok up to it?'

'I think so, Master.'

'Who? Missee Wishart? Or was it Yip?'

'Missee Wishart, Master. Kwok tell me so. He say she tell him.'

'George!' Willie turned round to the young man behind him. 'Give him his salary up to date. Then see him off the premises.'

As Lun Foo vanished, Willie laid the revolver on the desk and drew a deep breath. His heart was thumping. So Emmeline hadn't forgiven him, was never likely to forgive him! He found he was shaking with rage.

The door opened and Kee returned. Willie lifted his head, recovering his control. 'You're pretty smart, George,' he said. 'Could you run this place?'

Kee smiled. 'I have studied how things are done.'

'You could be very useful to me, speaking Chinese, English and French. I have to go away a lot. I need someone I can trust. Could you do Lun's job?'

'Of course, sir.'

'You're not very old.'

'I'm old enough.'

Willie considered for a moment, remembering he hadn't been much older when he'd started the business, then he slapped the boy's shoulder. 'You've got the job, George,' he said. 'With the appropriate salary. If you're ever short of money, don't try to make it out of me. Tell me. Ask me for it. I'll try to give it to you either as salary, a loan or an outright gift. But tell me. For Christ's sake, tell me. I want someone I can trust. Now I'm going to see Wishart's.'

Emmeline was not in her office when Willie arrived and the place was being run by her latest husband, a smooth, narrow-faced man called Henry Moberley, who wore a large moustache that made him look like a ferret peering through a hedge. Where in Christ's name did Emmeline pick 'em, Willie wondered. They all seemed the same – too small, too big, too smooth.

'Where's the Missis?' Willie snapped.

'Come in, Sarth,' Moberley said. 'Sit down. Fancy a drop of Squareface.'

'Bugger the Squareface,' Willie said, shoving aside the gin bottle that was held out to him. 'Where's Emmeline?'

'She didn't come today. We're having people in for dinner.'

Without a further word, Willie turned on his heel and left Moberley staring after him. When he arrived at Emmeline's home, a fanciful affair near his own close to the Bubbling Well Road, he didn't wait to be announced but pushed past the Chinese servant and went looking for her. She was just putting down the telephone and he guessed Moberley had been sending a warning.

Her face changed as she saw him in the doorway. 'Willie Sarth,' she said.

She hadn't grown any smaller. She was still a handsome woman – if you liked them big – but there was a tight line about her mouth now.

Willie slapped the invoices for the faulty goods down in front of her. 'Yours, I think, Emmeline,' he said. 'I'm having them delivered at your warehouse today and I'll expect a cheque for their value by hand – today! If it doesn't come, I'll inform everybody in Shanghai, including the police and a few of your friends. There was also opium.'

'I don't touch opium.'

'Your compradore does. He arranged for it to be included with your lousy goods. It's up to you what you do with him, but in future keep your rotten goods out of my affairs.'

'My goods aren't in your affairs!'

'They were shipped in among my last consignment to A N Kourganov of Vladivostok.'

'I don't know A N Kourganov. I've never been to Vladivostok and never done business with them.'

'I'm not surprised. She wouldn't touch your stuff with a barge pole.'

'She?' Emmeline's eyebrows rose, and she gave him a sly smile. 'Is she pretty, Willie? I bet she is. You always had an eye for a pretty face.'

'For Christ's sake!' Willie's explosion of anger was caused as much by the fact that Emmeline had touched on a raw spot as it was by the sneer on her face. He knew he had been attracted to Nadya Kourganova and it was nagging guiltily at him. 'I'm doing business with them, not chasing her round the bedroom. They're not all like you, Emmeline.'

She glared at him. 'I didn't send the goods!'

'Lun Foo says you did. He told me everything. It was arranged between him and your man – with your consent. What are you up to, Emmeline? Wanting to ruin me?'

She didn't deny it. She simply stared at him for a long time, then she spat her hatred out. 'I'll break you, Willie Sarth!'

'Not this way, you won't!' he snapped back. 'The only people you'll break will be Wishart's. I'll keep my mouth shut about it this time, but if I hear of anything more like it, it'll go round Shanghai like a forest fire.'

'I'll break you,' she spat again.

'Keep your threats, Emmeline. They don't interest me.'

'I'll break you. I will.'

'You're not powerful enough.'

'There are ways. There will be ways. Have no doubt about it, Willie Sarth. I shan't forget.'

As Willie climbed back into the cab that had brought him, he was shivering again with suppressed anger. Emmeline in a fury wasn't a pleasant sight to see.

PART THREE

1914–1920

one

The Sarth Line delighted Willie. Having tasted the sea, he had never really settled on land again and he had to keep reminding himself that running a shipping line meant office work, attention to reports, railway timetables, weather forecasts, costs, dates of arrivals, cancellations, contracts, and watching the shipping news for the position of his ships.

It was hard to keep away from his vessels and he came to know the forecastles as well as any of his officers, the bunches of vegetables and bits of dried fish and herbs the Chinese crews hung from the bulkheads, the joss sticks burning in a tin of sand – and always the smell of opium. Knowing his crews used it, perhaps even smuggled it, he always watched for it, eyeing his men as they mustered for signing on or paying, their belongings wrapped in Macassar mats of variegated straw, boxes with elaborate locks, or simple plaited baskets, but all wearing the elastic-sided boots that gave them 'face' and carrying the umbrellas they loved to buy and the cages of canaries with which they filled the ship. They bought them wherever they could get them – even the white officers, so that the mate had one and the Chief Engineer had two – and brought them out on deck whenever the weather was good so that they sang against each other in a shrill chorus all day in the sunshine.

He enjoyed the throb and creak that came like heartbeats as the ship got under way and loved to buy for his sons things like shark's spine walking sticks or swordfish snouts, which Abigail promptly consigned to the boxroom. But he was a simple man with a shrewd mind for business and nothing gave him greater pleasure than watching the evening sun go down from the bridge of one of his ships, an immense red molten globe just above the horizon, listening almost for the sizzle as it slipped into the blood-red sea, and watching when it was half-sunk for the leaping dolphin that was invariably silhouetted against the fiery disc. He loved to visit the engine rooms and watch the silent greasers, oilcans in hand at the bottom of breakneck ladders, oiling, oiling, always oiling; to watch the coaling in Java where they erected staircases of bamboo scaffolding, the grimy coolies – some of them semi-nude women with babies on their backs – tipping their baskets into the bunkers among the dust and the constant din of yelling; or listen to the Chinese seamen as they left port, banging gongs and yelling to drive away the devils that might otherwise accompany the ship on her voyage.

Absorbed in his business, he barely noticed the fact that war in Europe had crept up on them. As it happened, the assassination of the Austrian Archduke Franz Ferdinand at Sarajevo in 1914 didn't cause much stir at all in the countries surrounding the China Seas. Assassination was an occupational hazard for middle-European princes, and it could hardly affect life a great deal in Shanghai. The place continued as normal, with tennis parties, drinks and business, and the news that

Germany and France were mobilising came as a shock. Even when Britain joined in with Russia against Germany and Austro-Hungary, things didn't appear to change much.

Willie's attitude was one of indifference. 'They'll need a big gun to land shells on Shanghai,' he said. 'It won't affect us here.'

Within a week he learned that it would, because news arrived that the *City of Winchester*, a 6,000-ton freighter carrying cheap Indian coal and tea from Ceylon towards Aden, had been stopped and sunk by a raiding German cruiser. Immediately, it made him realise that being a shipping magnate wasn't all he'd expected, because by now he had six ships, all small, all old, all crewed by Chinese and – Christ, he thought – all over the shop. He called for his car – automobiles were beginning to replace rickshaws in large numbers now – and headed at once for his office. As the Chinese chauffeur, taught to drive by Willie himself, opened the door, he bolted inside and yelled for Kee.

'*City of Winchester*,' he said as he appeared. 'Heard about her, George?'

'Yes, sir,' Kee said. 'Everybody's heard by now.'

'What sunk her?'

'German cruiser, sir. Identified as the *Königsberg*. Three thousand six hundred tons.'

'How do you know?'

'I've been in touch with the Navy, sir.'

'Good lad.' Willie frowned. 'She's not very big, is she? The Navy'll soon finish her off.'

Kee pulled a face. 'The Navy isn't so sure, sir. All they have in the area are three cruisers, *Hyacinth*, *Astrea* and *Pegasus*.'

JOHN HARRIS

'That ought to be enough, for God's sake!'

'I hope so, sir.' Kee shrugged. '*Hyacinth* and *Astrea* are bigger than the *Königsberg*, it's true, but they're all old. *Hyacinth*'s sixteen years old and she's never done more than twenty knots. *Astrea*'s twenty-one and *Pegasus* seventeen.'

'You're a bloody pessimist, George. I must say.'

Kee smiled. 'I face facts, sir. The Navy isn't optimistic. The *Königsberg*'s only nine years old, they say, and carries ten modern four-inch guns and two torpedo tubes and can do twenty-four knots. The whole Indian Ocean's her hunting ground and she could threaten the shipping lanes to Australia, Singapore, Java, Calcutta, Bombay, Colombo, Hong Kong, Shanghai, Mauritius and every other British port of call in the East.'

'All our trade routes in fact.' Kee's pessimism suddenly caught hold of Willie and he swung round. 'Where are my ships?'

As Kee searched the ledgers, he looked at the photographs of his ships hanging on the wall. None of them were new by any means, but they made a profit.

'*Lady Roberts*,' Kee said. 'Karachi to Aden with Indian coal.'

'She's right on the spot,' Willie said at once. 'She'll get done sure as eggs is eggs.'

Kee shrugged. '*Atherfield Hall*,' he went on. 'She must be in the Bay of Bengal somewhere. She reported leaving Calcutta for Hong Kong.'

'She's all right. Well out of the way.'

'*Dahinda*. Somewhere between Singapore and Rangoon.'

'She's safe, too.' Willie stared at the chart on the wall. The small *Shamara* and the *Kum Kum Kiuw* were both

290

close to Hong Kong in the South China Sea. Which left only the *Winifred Whitehead*, his pride and joy. 'What about the *Winifred*?' he asked.

'Dar es Salaam, sir.'

'Well, thank God, she's out of the way, too,' Willie said. 'That's all right.'

He was pleased the *Winifred* was safe. She had been only four years old when he'd bought her soon after having the *Lady Roberts* wished on him by Emmeline. It was sad for the crew of the *Lady Roberts*, but he felt if he had to lose any of his ships he would rather it were the *Lady Roberts* than any of the others. She was really past her best; the fact that she'd been named after the wife of Lord Roberts of Kandahar, who'd been made a baron in the last century, pretty well established how old she was.

He headed for the Shanghai Club and made for the bar.

'Celebrating, Sarth?' The speaker was a middle-aged taipan called Gerald Honeyford, who ran Mason and Marchant's, one of the big Shanghai hongs with offices along the bund. He was a product of one of the big public schools in England and was always condescending and always correct, though that didn't stop him escaping from a boring wife to enjoy the favours of a Chinese girl he kept. Everybody knew about it but tactfully ignored it.

'Don't often see you in here, Sarth,' he said.

Willie shrugged.

'Heard about the *City of Winchester*? First blood to the Germans, what? Sunk by the cruiser, *Königsberg*.'

'So I heard.'

'Based on German East Africa. Probably originally part of the German East Asia squadron from Tsingtao.'

'Is that what they say?' Willie asked.

'We'll soon root them out of Tsingtao.' Honeyford smiled confidently. '*And* East Africa for that matter. They're completely cut off. They won't be able to get coal. They couldn't even take coal from the *City of Winchester*, I hear, because it was cheap Indian muck that would clog their boilers and wreck their power plant. Have you got anything up near Aden?'

'One old ship,' Willie admitted.

'You'll lose her.'

Willie tried to appear nonchalant. He was one of the youngest members of the Club and far from the wealthiest, and well-established people like Honeyford looked down on him as an upstart – although an upstart to be reckoned with because he moved fast and didn't believe in the old casual, languid Far Eastern habits. He knew they talked about him behind his back, so that he had always to appear more confident than he sometimes was.

'She's insured,' he said. 'There'll be compensation. It won't worry me much.'

'What about the rest of your fleet?' There was a faint contempt in Honeyford's voice because Willie's 'fleet' was a joke among the wealthier members of the club.

'They're safe,' Willie said. 'Well out of the way.'

Unfortunately, he was calculating time and distances on the speed of the *Lady Roberts* and wasn't allowing for the speed of a nine-year-old cruiser, and within a week he discovered that the *Winifred Whitehead* had disappeared off the face of the earth. Kee immediately got in touch with his contact in the Navy, but nothing was known, and it wasn't until August had passed into September that they learned that the *Winifred Whitehead* had been caught by the *Königsberg* north of Mombasa as she was running for shelter and she had been sunk with all her coal. The news had been late arriving because the crew had been put into boats and it had taken them some time to reach Mombasa, while the Navy was a little preoccupied, because a few days later the raider had caught the old British cruiser *Pegasus* in harbour at Zanzibar and blown her to pieces.

Willie was furious that it had to be the *Winifred Whitehead*. Why couldn't it have been the bloody *Lady Roberts*, he wondered. Nobody would have missed her.

It was Abigail who brought him down to earth. 'What about Edward?' she asked.

'What about Edward?'

'He's a naval cadet now.'

'They don't send cadets to sea,' Willie said. 'They've too much to learn.'

But then they heard that three naval vessels, the *Aboukir*, *Hogue* and *Cressy*, had all been sunk in a matter of an hour by one submarine off the Dutch coast. The fact that the ships were all old and almost toothless was some consolation, but they also learned that a great many naval cadets from Dartmouth had been sent to sea in them and that many were lost. Willie stared at Abigail, shocked.

'They'll never send Edward,' he said. 'He's too young.'

'He won't be if the war goes on and on.'

'It couldn't last that long!'

'Our civil war in the States did.'

It was a horrifying thought that they suddenly had to learn to live with, and the danger had also arrived on their own doorstep in the Far East because Japan had also declared war on Germany.

By this time it had become obvious that, despite what they'd thought, Shanghai *was* in the war and as the first news of the appalling casualties in France appeared with the first losses at sea, young men began to disappear homewards to join the army. Suddenly, familiar faces were no longer there as their owners took themselves discreetly off to the shipping offices to buy tickets for Europe, unable to stay any longer out of the conflict, and the City's ruling body, made up of senior taipans caught by a whiff of patriotism, made the suggestion that the residents should raise some sort of territorial force in the event of a landing being attempted.

'Who by?' Willie asked. 'The Germans? All this way from home? The Austrians? They haven't got a navy worth talking about. Turkey? They couldn't knock the skin off a rice pudding with *their* fleet. Some of the other places the Germans expect to come in on their side, like Bulgaria? They're only tiddlers.'

Despite Willie's scorn, a form of militia was raised which gave many people the pleasure of putting on a uniform without risking their necks, and George Kee represented Sarth's by joining it. Willie considered it for some time, but it came to nothing because he was suddenly called to Naval Headquarters.

As he left the office, Kee was talking business with Yip Hsao-Li. Despite left-footed boots and poor-quality cotton in Vladivostok, they had never been able to pin anything on him and he was still very much in evidence, still a customer of Abigail's, still full of smiles, still claiming Willie as a friend.

He never seemed to do much work and the trade he brought to Sarth's was infinitesimal. In fact, nobody knew for sure what he did. His trips to Amoy and Swatow were common knowledge, but still nobody knew why he took them, and it was assumed that from there he moved on to

Hong Kong where his brother-in-law, Lun Foo, Willie's former agent, had moved after his attempt to defraud Sarth's. Willie was certain he was in touch with the Green and Red Dragon secret societies which operated in Shanghai, that he was manipulated by the gangsters, and that his trips south covered some nefarious project no one knew about.

Still thinking about Yip, Willie was escorted to the office of the admiral, a brisk no-nonsense type he had met at a garden party, a short square figure with a face that was yellow with too many years in the East. Alongside him was a tall, languid individual who reminded Willie vaguely of Sir Claude MacDonald from all those years ago at the siege of Peking.

'This is Arthur Mallinson, Willie,' the Admiral said. 'Foreign office. He has something to ask you. I think you might be interested.'

Mallinson, who had a curiously high-pitched voice and appeared to be speaking from the back of his throat, took up the story.

'We're worried about the Japanese,' he said. 'Their Foreign Minister says that Japan has no desire or inclination to become involved in the European conflict, but that she believes she must be faithful to the alliance with Great Britain and ensure permanent peace in the East by protecting the special interests of the allied powers.'

'That's a lot of bunkum,' Willie said bluntly. 'What she's got her eye on is territory.'

Mallinson smiled suddenly. It transformed his face. 'That's what we think, too, Mr Sarth.'

The admiral smiled also and produced a bottle of Plymouth gin, known to everybody in the East as Jossman from the picture of the monk on the label. With glasses in their hands, they got down to business.

'They landed in Shantung fifteen years ago,' Willie said, 'but they got pushed out by the Germans. I bet they're after reversing it.'

Mallinson gestured. 'Do go on, Mr Sarth. It's a pleasure to listen to someone with an opinion.'

Willie grinned. 'Japan's only got limited access to Chinese raw material,' he said. 'And that's in the southern portion of Manchuria. The war in Europe's changed things to her advantage.'

'How do you come to that view, Mr Sarth?'

'Business dealings. Knowing Japanese. Listening to 'em talk.'

'What are your plans, Mr Sarth? Quite a few men as old as you have gone home to join the army. Is that your intention?'

Willie paused. He and Abigail had discussed it at some length. To Willie it seemed cowardly not to go home when Britain was in danger, but Abigail had taken the view that he could be of more use in Shanghai. 'It's crossed my mind,' he said.

Mallinson took a sip from his glass. 'I think you could be of greater value here,' he suggested.

Willie's eyebrows lifted. He had accepted Abigail's view that trade was essential and that he was part of it, but he couldn't imagine what use he could be to Mallinson.

Mallinson gestured. 'I believe you're acquainted with a gentleman by the name of Yuhitsu Shaiba.'

Willie nodded. 'He did me a good turn at the time of Port Arthur. Said I saved his life in Peking. He probably saved mine in return. I might have gone bust otherwise.'

'How well do you know him?'

'We were good friends.'

'Would you care to see him again?'

'Shaiba? How do you work that out? He's a captain in their navy.'

Mallinson stirred. 'Admiral now,' he said. 'In charge of naval building and repair at Nagasaki.'

'Is he?' Willie nodded approvingly. 'What have you got in mind?'

'I suggest a business trip to Japan –'

'I have no business in Japan. I tried. I couldn't get in. They keep too firm a grip on it.'

'You could try again. Perhaps you could suggest that England, which, of course, must export to pay for the war, has things to sell. Perhaps even suggest that, since Japan's also now in the war, *they* also might need to export to pay for their part in the conflict.'

Willie cocked an eyebrow. 'There are a lot of people in Shanghai more important than me.'

'Important, perhaps. But, so I understand, not as brisk, not as willing to take risks, and certainly not as young.' Mallinson smiled. 'While there, perhaps you could suggest a meeting with your old friend, Admiral Shaiba, and get him to talk. We'd be interested to know if their intentions are as you suggest.'

'Well –' Willie hesitated ' – I think he'd see me.'

The admiral beamed. 'Shall we have another gin?' he suggested.

'Special envoy,' Willie announced to his wife when he returned home. 'Better get my best suit out, Ab.'

Abigail smiled. 'I can't believe it, Willie. You!'

Willie grinned at her. 'Neither can I,' he admitted. 'But there it is. Laid on the mat for us to look at. After only a few weeks of war, too! It must be what we did at Peking. I'm taking George Kee with me, so *you'll* have to keep a watch on the business. Luis Da Braga can take care of the Yangpo end and everything else ought to function all right if you just keep one eye on it.'

'I'll do more than that, Willie. I'll keep both eyes on it. I know what goes on. I'll be in the office several hours a day.'

'With one eye firmly in Yip Hsao-Li,' Willie advised.

'That, too.' Abigail smiled and kissed him. 'I'm very proud of you, husband.'

It had been decided that Willie should make the voyage by passenger steamer, so he used his own ship, the *Atherfield Hall*, and there was a nervous crossing of the East China Sea with the passengers splitting into three watches to assist the crew in keeping a sharp look-out to the north, from where German raiders might well come. The German base at Tsingtao was still a threat. Admiral von Spee's fleet still had its headquarters there and at that moment was believed to be somewhere in Chinese waters, while one of his ships, the cruiser *Emden*, had been detached and was already creating havoc among merchant ships from the Indian Ocean to the Pacific.

As they dropped anchor at Nagasaki on the island of Kyushu, a steam launch flying the rising sun flag and with a large 'H' painted on its funnel appeared alongside. It was the harbour health officer's boat and out of it climbed no fewer than eleven Japanese doctors in gold-braided uniform, all looking like railway guards. The crew were lined up for inspection, Europeans to starboard, Chinese to port, and the senior medical officer gravely counted everybody to make sure they were all present, while his colleagues moved round, felt pulses, looked at tongues and prodded the Chinese in the groin to see if they had the plague. It was all very grave, and farcical when the engineer on duty was found to be missing. The ship's papers were examined, the engineer found, then, satisfied and with deep bows, the Japanese climbed back into their launch and disappeared.

'I dare bet half those fellers weren't doctors at all,' Willie said. 'They were naval men spying on foreign shipping.'

Shaiba's office was on the western shore of the enormous harbour. Willie had been there before and he stared keenly about him at the long bay with its crowded shipping and the hills around broken into deep ridges and long valleys terraced for cultivation. As soon as he and Kee had found a hotel, he sent a card to Shaiba's office with a note requesting a meeting, and sat back to wait. Within twenty-four hours, it was answered with a request for him to wait at the hotel, where a naval vehicle would collect him.

Shaiba hadn't changed much. The stiff black hair had thinned and Willie could see his bald brown pate shining through. Saké was brought in by a naval steward and they sat on opposite sides of Shaiba's desk beaming at each other.

'Admiral now,' Willie said.

Shaiba laughed. 'And you, I hear, are a business tycoon.'

'Only a little one. How did you hear?'

'I keep my ear close to the ground,' Shaiba admitted. 'I still know what goes on in Shanghai.'

'Why do you keep your ear to the ground?' Willie asked.

'Interest. What brings you to Nagasaki?'

'Business. England needs to sell to pay for the war. Doesn't Japan?'

'Of course. But why did you *really* come?'

For a moment, Willie floundered. It was obvious that Shaiba suspected something.

'No other reason,' he said.

'Come, Willie – ' Shaiba was still smiling ' – I don't believe it. You want to know what we're up to, don't you? Your country suspects us of deviousness over Shantung and Kiaochow, doesn't it?'

'No, it's not that at all.'

Shaiba's smile became a grin. 'You must come clean, as the Americans say. If that's what you want, I'll tell you. We are not hiding what we are aiming at.'

It seemed pointless to dissimulate any further, and Willie gestured. 'All right,' he said. 'What *are* you aiming at? There's a lot of worry.'

Shaiba smiled again. 'We have declared war on your side. How much worse if we'd come in on the Germans' side.'

'What are you after, Yuhitsu?'

Shaiba rested his elbows on his desk. 'I'll come clean,' he said. 'It's clear that England and France have too much on their hands at home to concern themselves with this part of the world, and the United States is concerned only with staying out of the struggle. They wish to neutralise the Far East because they themselves have all they want from it, but we disagree with that attitude, and our alliance with Britain gives us an excellent excuse for intervention of a particularly satisfying kind. More saké?'

They drank and Shaiba continued. 'The Shantung Peninsula has long since beckoned our generals. It was there we brought China to her knees in the war of 1898. But we let our grasp slip and it was the German Kaiser who entrenched himself there with leases at Tsingtao and Kiaochow and grabbed the railways and mineral rights. We have decided that now is the time to take them back. We sent the Germans an ultimatum requiring their surrender and when it was ignored we declared war. The Chinese Government in Peking has attempted to limit the scope of the hostilities by designating a certain specified area in the region as a battle zone.' Shaiba laughed. 'Typical Chinese naivety. Who ever fought a war within a limited area? "Let us go into this field, sir, and knock each other's heads in with clubs. Being careful, of course, not to damage the crops in the field next door." War isn't like that. It is our intention to regain Tsingtao and Kiaochow and, what is more, to ask aid from your country to see that the German leased territories are freed and ultimately returned to China.'

'China?'

'We wish to protect China's interest.'

Willie didn't believe him and his face showed it.

'That is what we say,' Shaiba insisted.

'Is it what you mean?'

Shaiba didn't answer and Willie tried a new tack. 'Will you pull it off?'

'With your country's assistance, of course.'

'And then?'

Shaiba shrugged. 'We had better have another drink,' he said.

Shaiba had been honest, but Willie had a feeling his honesty wasn't total. It wasn't difficult to prove it, though, because the Japanese could see a wider future opening up for them, and the businessmen he talked to were in a state of euphoria about the war and the opportunities it offered their country. Nevertheless, he managed also to exchange enough ideas about imports and exports to satisfy them and at the same time do enough business for himself to provide some sort of excuse for his visit. He had a feeling he was being watched all the time, however, so he tried to be as open as he could, talking frankly about British fears and asking point-blank questions about Japanese intervention. He was rarely disappointed.

By the time he returned to Shanghai the request from the Japanese for British assistance in the investment of Tsingtao and the attack on Shantung and Kiaochow which Shaiba had mentioned had already been made and troops were being readied in India.

Mallinson turned up in Willie's office, as languid as ever.

'All this about protecting Chinese interests,' he said. 'I don't believe them, do you?'

'No,' Willie agreed. 'I don't.'

'They won't pay the slightest regard to China. What are they after?'

'I think,' Willie said carefully, 'that they'll occupy the railway between Kiaochow and Tsinan and grab the mining regions nearby. After that, I think they'll expect to obtain all the rights the Germans had in Shantung and a few more besides. They'll want the lease of Port Arthur and Dairen, and they'll flood the place with their nationals and start grabbing land and minerals throughout South Manchuria as far as Mongolia. They'll also grab any big industrial concerns they fancy – or at least make 'em Sino-Japanese operations with the Japanese in control, of course – and they'll demand that China doesn't lease coastal areas, harbours or islands to anyone but them. Removing the Germans will aid the Allies because it clears the threat to our eastern seaboard trade, but, of course, it will immediately raise another.'

Mallinson blinked and smiled. 'I think, Mr Sarth, you're in the wrong job. I could use someone like you. That's quite a lot. How did you find it all out?'

'They make no bones about it. The businessmen know what the army and navy are planning and the army and navy know what business and industry want. Before you know where you are, they'll be demanding a hand in the government of a lot of places where we don't want 'em and expect to supply the Chinese army with weapons and military advisers.'

'Any more?'

Willie grinned. 'You don't believe me, do you?' he said. 'But I've heard this from people in touch with what's going on. They'll demand the option on the construction of railways and the development of mines and harbours.'

Mallinson sighed. 'I believe you, Mr Sarth. It sounds a lot, but the Japanese are a greedy people and they're determined to have a place in the sun. As a matter of fact, I gather some hint of all this has already been passed to Peking. I think we shall have to ask questions – officially, this time, because I suspect we shall have to stop them. They're getting too big for their boots.'

Willie frowned. 'I don't think they've even started yet,' he said.

two

Though war was raging throughout the whole of Europe and across every stretch of sea on the surface of the earth, as Willie had prophesied, Shanghai remained in the background. This didn't mean that Shanghai remained passive and indifferent, but events in China itself were holding all their attention. When Yuan Shih-K'Ai announced his intention of taking over the Chinese throne and forming a new dynasty, it was obvious that such a step depended on the support of his generals, but it was also clear that those generals were having second thoughts.

Willie summed it up to Da Braga over the brandy bottle. 'It's dawned on them that they've got the soldiers and the guns,' he pointed out. 'And, therefore, they, not Yuan, hold the power.'

Yuan disappeared from the scene, leaving it entirely to the commanders of his armies, and, as they grasped the opportunity with both hands, the country outside Shanghai began to drift into chaos. Within weeks, it was obvious that the warlords were exploiting the peasantry. Taxes were being demanded for years into the future, paper money was printed which immediately became valueless as the warlord who printed it was removed, by agreement or bribe, or by defeat, which was rare because, for the most part, the generals fought with silver bullets – money. China had suddenly become the sport of the military and, though there were authorities both in Peking and in the south, both assuming the name of government, both were really controlled by their own generals, and the generals backed or betrayed for money whichever government they represented. Organising the opium trade, they sold positions and filled their own pockets until they could finally retire to Japan or Singapore with immense fortunes. With the peasants oppressed and the soldiers more like bandits, the whole of China had become a battlefield.

The first indication of what was happening came when Da Braga telegraphed for instructions from Yangpo. A general by the name of Li Chi-Sao was controlling the area around the town and, while he was hesitating to demand taxes from the Europeans, who had gunboats and powerful backing, he was at least expecting squeeze – bribes to prevent him causing trouble.

Behind its carved lions, the Shanghai Club, many of whose members had interests along the Yangtze, was loud in its protests of indignation. Willie listened without saying anything, because it had occurred to him that what was being said in Shanghai, all the defiance and threats, meant little in the upper reaches of the river. Even the gunboats' authority extended only to the river banks, yet business interests always passed beyond that point to the interior.

'Pay up,' he telegraphed to Da Braga.

It was obvious he was setting a precedent and Gerald Honeyford of Mason and Marchant's was quick to complain, but he soon noticed that other businessmen

305

were doing the same thing and that Mason and Marchant's were quick to follow.

Because their hold on power was precarious, the warlords were not interested in long-term investment and looked first and foremost for quick profits, and for security to their troops. None of them had much skill, but, judging the value of their armies by their size, they press-ganged the wretched peasants, dressed them in ugly cotton uniforms, gave them ancient weapons and, making no attempt to drill them, counted on their numbers to frighten off their rivals. By the middle of 1915 there were almost a million men in some sort of uniform and, as they made alliances between themselves, huge, ungainly and totally unskilled armies began to march and countermarch across the countryside. When Da Braga telegraphed that General Li had concluded a deal with his rival, General Ching So-Fan, from the other side of the river, who apparently had more soldiers, Willie didn't hesitate.

'Transfer squeeze,' he telegraphed.

1917 entered in a curious mood of apathy. Shanghai still much affected, apart from the photographs that appeared in the newspapers of men who had gone home and been killed in the Somme offensive. But the tragedy in France was beginning to reach out to them at last and there was a mood of sullen obstinacy, a feeling of being resigned to the war, of hating it, of seeing no end to it, of wishing to God they could get the thing over and return to normality.

It was obvious by this time that the war they had expected to end in months was going to last for years. The Shanghai Militia wore uniform, looked important and drilled with the old Japanese rifles that had been acquired through Willie's good offices via Shaiba, but Willie refused to have anything to do with them, preferring to sit in his office and listen to George Kee's descriptions of their muddled manoeuvres. Even the old *Lady Roberts* had acquired a 4-inch gun on her stern.

'We've got a warship in the family,' Willie said.

As Shaiba had prophesied, Japan had gone into Shantung and Kiaochow, somewhat startled at the objections to their plans from Britain, France, Russia and the United States, and the inevitable wave of anti-Japanese feeling swept across Shanghai. It failed to stop China having to accept many of the demands that Willie had prophesied would be put. But while they held their own on the shores of the China Seas, to the north Russia was in sore travail. One offensive after another had failed dismally, largely because of inept general-ship and a lack of weapons. On his last visit to Vladivostok Willie had been conscious of a growing feeling of hatred for Tsar Nicholas' form of government and when Mallinson reappeared, requesting him to deliver rifles to Vladivostok, he was indignant.

'You're wasting your time,' he said. 'Nobody's fighting anyone in Vladivostok. Why do they want guns?'

'They can be transported to the front,' Mallinson argued. 'There's the Trans-Siberian Railway.'

'Nearly six thousand miles of it,' Willie pointed out. 'And mostly single track. Have you ever travelled on it?'

'No.'

'I have. Not far, thank God. It would take months to get those weapons to the front.'

Mallinson frowned. 'I have to admit,' he said, 'that that was my view, but the deal's been forced on me. However, we've had requests from Russia that someone should visit them to offer advice and deal with questions of military co-operation and supply. Lord Kitchener was on his way, as you know, when his ship was torpedoed and he was drowned. Now I think you should go to Vladivostok, deliver the rifles yourself and let us know what the feeling is there.'

'I'm nothing but an unpaid ambassador,' Willie complained as he started to pack his bags again. 'When they've nobody spare they send me and, what's more, they expect me to pay for the trip myself with a bit of business.'

Abigail laughed. 'All the same, Willie,' she said, 'it's an honour, isn't it? There are a few people I know who'd love to be asked. I met Mrs Honeyford yesterday and she's green with envy because it wasn't *her* husband who was asked. Will you see your friend Nadya again?'

'Your friend, too, Ab, I hope. Yes, I shall. That's the idea. I'm on business. And she wants more of our goods, and we want more of hers. Besides, she'll probably have things for you.'

Abigail gave him a shrewd look, but made no comment. Her business had fallen by the wayside a little with the war and the demands of family and home, but she still did well at it and was always in demand as an expert. In addition, poised, confident and elegant now, she was always available to give a hand with Willie's affairs because responsible Europeans in Shanghai, who were not already occupied, were growing harder to find since so many had paid their passages home to get into the European war.

So Willie went to Vladivostok. He took with him the old Russian revolver he had had ever since Peking. He had often thought of changing it but never had, and it was big enough to frighten off the pirates operating in the Yellow Sea. Only recently, one of his ships, the newly acquired *Shamarah*, had been called by a signal to a small Chinese coaster apparently wallowing in distress close to the coast of Shantu, only to discover it was an ambush. Fortunately, the trap had been sprung too soon and the captain of the *Shamarah*, a Shanghai Chinese, had managed to swing away and pile on steam before he could be stopped.

Vladivostok seemed much the same as before, dull, grey drizzly, with frosts at night that left ice everywhere the drizzle had touched, and the same smell of wet wool, leather and fur, the same muddy streets, the same leaden sea.

The character of the place had changed. The onion-shaped domes were still there – the churches, the shabby façades, the muddy streets – but now the town was full of old penniless refugees and indescribable beggars from European Russia. It was a hotbed of crime. Inflation had hit the place and on every street were Jewish moneylenders in shabby frock coats. There were Russian soldiers, a few British soldiers, hundreds on hundreds of Czechs, who had opted in 1914 to fight for Russia to free their country from Austrian domination; Levantines; Mongol horsemen in fur caps on shaggy ponies; Balkan adventurers; even a few German and Austrian prisoners of war. There was also a significant number of Russian officers, most of them members of the aristocracy, still arrogant, still haughty, but now with a hint of nervousness beginning to show through their demeanour. According to the captain of the *Shamarah*, the overcrowding had brought every disease imaginable.

Willie delivered his rifles to a Russian colonel, who appeared to regard them with some disdain, and decided the best way to get the feel of the place was to call at once on Nadya Alexsandrovna Kourganova.

She greeted him delightedly and immediately told her clerks she was going home. In the house on the Marizliyevskaya overlooking the sea, she took his hands in hers and gazed at him with sparkling eyes.

'Oh, Willie Sarth,' she said. 'I didn't expect you.'

'Always turn up,' Willie smiled. 'Like a bad penny.'

'You must stay for a meal. We shall manage.'

Willie's ears cocked. 'Are things bad, Nadya?'

'Yes, they are,' she admitted. 'And they're getting worse all the time.'

Food was short and it was known there had been riots in St Petersburg – now known by the Russian name of Petrograd – where, for a change, Cossacks had refused to fire on the rioters. There was immense dissatisfaction with the Tsar for taking over the position of Commander-in-Chief, because everyone – even the most fervent royalists – knew he was a weak character with no knowledge of strategy, tactics or logistics.

'All the muddle of the last two years is being blamed on him,' Nadya Alexsandrovna said. 'There's talk that he'll be asked to abdicate.'

'Will that mean Russia will go out of the war?'

'Oh, no!' A flicker of worry crossed her face. 'But discipline in the army's broken down, I'm told, and there's a lot of talk about the French Revolution.' She shrugged. 'Still, *that* changed France from a decadent monarchy to a military power.'

'It also directed its energies against Britain,' Willie pointed out.

'Oh, William, why are things so difficult?'

'Are they for you?'

'Money becomes valueless. What is the hotel like? They tell me the servants have become sullen and unwilling to help.'

'I haven't been there yet,' Willie admitted. 'I went straight to your office.'

She turned a radiant face to him. 'You must stay the night,' she said. 'It's a huge place and there are only the servants and myself.'

A small warning bell rang in his mind, but he put it aside.

'If there's a revolution, are your servants reliable?'

'I doubt it. But so far there is no revolution and Moscow, where it will undoubtedly start, is a long way away.'

They ate alone, Willie talking all the time about the political situation, Nadya about new *objets d'art* she had found for Abigail. She laid the valuables out for him, exquisite things mostly, that sparkled and shone.

'Do you notice anything about them?' she asked.

He looked at her, puzzled.

'All small,' she said. 'All things that will go into the pocket. A lot of them are turning up. It's clear what's happening. People are leaving Moscow and Petrograd. They can't go west because of the war and the trenches so they are taking the train here. They're afraid of what's happening. They're leaving their houses and they're packing their cases and trunks not with clothes but with things they can sell. I see them every day – in the restaurants and cafés. People with distant looks on their faces because they're staring into the distance, seeing things they don't understand.'

311

'What things?'

'Chiefly the end. A different way of life. You can see them asking themselves if they'll be able to survive because, if the revolution comes, they'll lose everything and they're afraid they'll not be able to live without it.'

She was in a curious mood, solemn, brooding, almost mystic, almost as though she could see into the future.

'Why don't you leave?' Willie asked. 'Set up again in Shanghai? We could help you.'

She smiled and laid her hand on his. 'My place is here.'

'What if the revolution comes?'

'I'll be safe.'

'Whose side would you be on?'

'I've learned not to take sides. Not to give favours. Not to expect anything. They can't object to me if I have no politics. And if they don't object to me, I shall be able to carry on business. I'm told they even favour equality for women. Women soldiers. Women politicians. Women in business also, I expect.' She gave a little laugh, but it was nervous and brittle as if she were afraid suddenly. 'I may marry one of their commissars.'

'Not talking like that, you won't.'

'No. I won't.' She leaned against him weakly and he knew her fear was of him, not of any revolution. As he put his arm round her, she turned her face to his, still nervous of him. He kissed her and, without even thinking, she kissed him back. But then she drew her head away sharply.

'Nadya!'

As his arms tightened about her, she didn't move, shivering a little as his hands touched her, moving lightly over her body. There was a warm animal fragrance about her and a curious oriental opulence that caught at his senses. Abruptly, with a little gasp, she turned in his arms to face him.

'Oh, William,' she whispered, 'why are you so much married?'

He knew that he had gone too far and ought to have drawn away, but there was a forthright sexuality about her now she had managed to hide until then, and it drew him on. As he tried to kiss her again, once more she turned her head away.

'Let me stay,' he urged.

'No.'

'I want to.'

He pressed his lips against her cheek and she gave a little gasp and turned her face to his.

'Oh, William!'

Her body was against his and he felt his blood pounding. 'Let me stay,' he said again.

Eventually, her head turning, struggling vainly to refuse him, she went limp in his arms, her face buried in the curve of his neck.

'Please, William,' she whispered. 'Be kind. I'm lonely. And I'm afraid. But yes. Yes, yes, yes! Please don't go away from me tonight.'

Mallinson was pleased with Willie's report and said so in a long congratulatory letter. But Willie was indifferent. He was suffering from a raging guilt at what had happened. He knew it was his fault and he was ashamed of himself, yet somehow he felt he had not done the wrong thing. But the thought that he had betrayed Abigail nagged at his conscience. His wife was faithful, God-fearing, law-abiding and good. She never asked him questions, was never suspicious, never devious. Above all, she was his wife and the mother of his children, and he had cheated her.

What Mallinson felt meant nothing to him and he tried to absorb himself in work. Luis Da Braga in Yangpo was wailing that General Chang had been replaced by yet another new general, Ho K'Ai-Kok, and he handed a telegram over to George Kee to send. It was longer than the first one. 'Transfer squeeze,' he said. 'Am joining you.'

This time Abigail insisted on going too, and he didn't question her decision because somehow it salved his uneasy conscience. She had said nothing and, though she had showed delight at the small treasures he had brought back and the promise of more to come, he guessed she had her suspicions.

'Will it be safe, Willie?' she asked.

'Soon make it safe,' he grinned and, borrowing the brush and ink with which Thomas tried to write Chinese characters, produced a note in the manner of an Imperial edict for her to carry. '*This woman is the favourite niece of Woodrow Wilson, supreme warlord of the United States. For every finger that touches her, one thousand heads will roll. Tremble and obey.*' He stamped it with every stamp he possessed and attached red ribbon from her workbox to it with sealing wax, which he marked with a crest from the back of an old teaspoon.

'If they ask for your passport, give them a visiting card,' he said. 'I've got away with it more than once. They never argue.'

She laughed. 'What about the children?'

'They have an amah to look after them and a house full of servants, and George Kee's wife will keep an eye on things.'

When they arrived in Yangpo there was little sign of trouble, though the German concession was beginning to look neglected and many of the stiff sentries who had always been on show had disappeared, probably dead in Flanders. In spite of the occasional groups of Ho soldiers wandering along the bund, shabby, ill-clothed and always ready to bully the Chinese, there appeared to be little military movement in the area and no hostility towards the foreigners. General Ho, Da Braga said, was established with his yamen to the north of the city, surrounded by officers, cars, women and eunuchs, counting the money he had raked in and fumbling half-heartedly towards the south of the river. Of the previous incumbent of the area, there was no sign.

'Gone to Hong Kong,' Da Braga said. 'Took the ferry downstream, with a few of his women and a chestful of gold. He's all right.'

There had been one or two sporadic outbreaks of shouting along the bund and the matshed roofing of the market place had been set on fire.

'Quite a spectacle,' Da Braga said dryly. 'Ho's soldiers in brass firemen's helmets marching to the blaze, swinging their arms and singing to a military band trying to play *Ta-ra-ra-boom-de-ay*. They didn't put out the fire.'

One of Ho's soldiers had been murdered by an infuriated coolie sick of his bullying, who had promptly been shot dead by a sergeant, so that the incident immediately drew an angry crowd that had rampaged round the city centre for two hours. The Sarth house was untouched, however, like those of their neighbours, but Abigail stared about her and at the bowing Chinese servants with a manner that was distinctly uneasy.

'I'm nervous, Willie,' she said.

'Nothing can happen,' he encouraged her, but in his heart he knew her instincts were strong and that she was rarely wrong. Something was happening to China. There was no longer any law and order because there was no government powerful enough to enforce it, and he had a feeling that eventually someone would rise who *would* be powerful enough to draw all the dissident generals together to throw out foreigners like himself.

The following morning they heard a group of Chinese merchants had been executed on the bund for objecting to the worthless banknotes printed by General Ho, and wailing women were at that moment retrieving their bodies.

'Trouble,' Da Braga said laconically.

They all looked quickly at him. Apart from a far-from-unusual riot and a far-from-unusual series of executions, nothing seemed to have changed. There were always riots and always executions, but there was an undoubted atmosphere of ill-omen about the city so that they felt they ought to make preparations for what was coming. But what *was* coming? Though they could feel in their bones that *something* was coming, neither Willie nor Abigail knew what.

The year ended in a sort of frustration which reached out all the way from London to Shanghai. Unaffected personally by the war, they could still sense the despair in Europe that the slaughter in France seemed to be getting nowhere, and they returned to Shanghai tired and faintly dispirited, beset by worries they had never expected when things had gone so well for them. In addition, Willie was unable to put Nadya Alexsandrovna from his mind and was always guiltily feeling that Abigail was watching him. The time he had spent in Vladivostok had been encompassed in a hectic few days. Nadya Alexsandrovna had not gone near her office and Willie's business had suffered, and the guilt made him wretched as he thought of the faithful Abigail praising the things he had brought back with him, even while she suspected that something had happened.

His spirits were low and the guilt refused to go away, and when one morning, as he appeared in his office and George Kee followed him in, he was immediately alert for disaster.

Kee didn't normally enter his office without being asked, but this time his face was grave and Willie began at once to search his conscience and set up half-formed excuses in case it involved Russia.

As it happened it did, but not in the way he expected.

'The Tsar's abdicated,' Kee said.

'What!' Willie's head jerked up. 'When?'

'Two days ago. He was returning to Petrograd from his headquarters and the railwaymen stopped the train. He was dragged back to headquarters and advised to go. The Russian monarchy's ended.'

three

For a long time, Willie sat motionless at his desk, staring at his hands, hardly hearing what Kee was saying and guiltily aware that his thoughts had turned immediately to Nadya Alexsandrovna.

He forced himself to show some interest. 'Can't say I'm surprised,' he said. 'How did it happen?'

'It started with strikes, it seems,' Kee said. 'Petrograd was paralysed. No transport, gas, water or electricity. All shops closed, no newspapers. A street demonstration turned into a riot and then into a revolution.'

'Who's running the show?'

'A council of workers' and soldiers' deputies.'

'Is it happening anywhere else?'

'There are reports of burnings and murder all over Russia.'

Jesus Christ on a tightrope, Willie said under his breath. And here I am in Shanghai where I can do nothing to help. What Nadya had prophesied had come to pass. Everything she had said would happen, had happened.

'Go on, George. What about the Tsar?'

'Virtual prisoner, they say.'

'And the war? Are they out?'

'They expect to pursue the war with greater vigour.'

'That's what they said in Vladivostok, George. I don't believe it.'

'Neither do I, sir. By the way, I heard this morning that we've lost the *Atherfield Hall*. Torpedoed in the Indian Ocean.'

Willie sighed. The war had hit the Sarth Line hard. The *Dahinda* had been commandeered to supply troops at Gallipoli – just round the corner, the Navy said, from India – and, returning to Bombay after disembarking a battalion of soldiers, had distinguished herself when torpedoed. One propeller smashed, the other's shaft bent, her gun supports destroyed, the 4-incher on the steering house split, her main steam pipe broken, her aerials brought down, the watertight bulkhead between the shaft tunnel and the engine room buckled, she had still made it to port under tow. Heroism didn't help a lot, however, because she was now in dry dock being repaired and, with the loss of the *Winifred Whitehead* in the first hours of the war and now the *Atherfield Hall*, the Sarth Line at the moment consisted of four ships, the everlasting and indestructible *Lady Roberts*, a newly acquired 2,000-tonner called the *Chinta*, and the two small coasters, *Shamara* and *Kum Kum Kiuw*. There had been another one for a while, the *Shu Ting*, acquired early in 1915 from the fleet of a man who had sold everything to go to England to join the army, but she had been sunk near Cape Town by a German raider and the previous owner had been killed in his first battle on the Somme. The bloody war, Willie decided, was intruding into all their lives.

Photographs continued to appear from England, where Edward, now growing tall, was at Dartmouth Naval College and planting vegetables in the grounds with other boys in his spare time to help feed an embattled country struggling against the ravages of the U-boats. At least, Willie thought, his family was safe. Edward was in England, but well away from the bombing German Gothas, Thomas was still in Shanghai at school, absorbed in Chinese customs and beginning to speak Chinese like a native. His daughter, Polly, was growing fast, and he still had Abigail alongside him.

He forced himself to come back to earth. 'We'll need to know what's happening in Vladivostok,' he said. 'Try to find out, George.'

He was itching to go and see for himself, but there was too much to do. The news from Russia had thrown Shanghai into uproar. Many of Willie's competitors had had a lot of business there, and they were running about like mad ants trying to sort something from the confusion.

For a long time he was occupied with reports and transaction dates and with checking what was happening, thankful to learn that Kee, who had been carefully watching his interests, had not despatched anything to Russia for some time. But he was restless. Other businessmen were taking ships north round the Korean Peninsula to attend to their interests in Russia through the only available opening, Vladivostok, and they brought back reports of total chaos, of the spread of the revolutionary feeling even to Vladivostok, the outermost point of the Russian empire. Some cargoes sent north had vanished *en route* altogether and corruption was rife. Vladivostok, they said, was becoming packed with refugees.

'There's some dissatisfaction with the present revolutionary government,' Emmeline's husband, Henry Moberley, was saying loudly in the Club. 'Chap called

Kerensky. They say he favours the Tsar too much and that his Soviet of Workers' Deputies is in the hands of the same old gang. But it seems there's a new chap now, called Lenin, the Germans slipped in to stir things up and force Russia out of the war. It's going to get a lot nastier than it is at the moment.'

For six months, Willie forced himself to keep his restless feet still because the Chinese were taking the liveliest interest in what was happening to their northern neighbour, whose position was very similar to their own. Both countries were large and backward compared with the industrialised nations of Western Europe and both had endured humiliation at the hands of the Japanese, so that, anxious to put their own house in order, they watched with concern what the new rulers of Russia were doing.

He could see the problems.

China had declared war against Germany by this time, but no one imagined she could contribute much beyond labourers to work with the allied armies or that it meant much beyond protecting themselves against the voracious Japanese. Besides, China was still ravaged by her own internal politics. Small revolutions constantly arose in one part or another of the vast countryside and were put down with horrific cruelty, the details of which always drifted down to Shanghai. Twice more the warlord controlling the area round Yangpo changed, and twice more Willie had to transfer the squeeze that was paid to prevent trouble.

Yangpo was changing fast. The road that divided the concessions from the old Chinese City still remained, sanitary and stodgily European on one side, insanitary, smelly and uproariously Chinese on the other. More buildings were rising, round grey tanks of the oil companies had sprung up and there was a succession of new tall buildings along the bund. The Hong Kong and Shanghai Bank had pushed up an imposing office block of shining white stone with marble facings round a massive wrought-iron door, and Sarth's, Wishart's, Mason and Marchant's and Wissermann's had been joined by one or two others.

Union Jacks, tricolours and Stars and Stripes flew from the flag staffs as a protection from the warlords, but there were pleasant houses and gardens and well-paved roads now in a well-lit stretch of the bund, complete with a European club and tennis courts. The British Concession was the senior concession and therefore on the right of the other concessions which stretched in a narrow strip for three miles downriver, so that you could visit five countries in a hired rickshaw for a few pence, running over smooth British roads, between towering British buildings and solid British credit. The French concession, guarded by tiny Annamite soldiers, was not as tidy, but the trees, if not so well cared for, were shady and, though the buildings were not so pretentious, they were in brighter colours and the smells of cooking and coffee were better. The Russian, German and Japanese concessions similarly reflected their countries, the Russian with a barbaric magnificence and rich ornamentation, as if the Russian aristocracy were still in residence, the German concession autocratic and bombastic-looking. The Japanese streets were similar to the Chinese but more tawdry and gimcrack, with a huge yellow barracks for the soldiers, whose officers trailed long sabres between tiny serious traffic policemen quick to whack any stray wandering Chinese across the shoulders – not cheerfully and in friendly fashion like the Sikhs, but as if to impress them with who was master. They loved to show their authority, and small stiff-faced men enjoyed halting rickshaws and taking names, a habit which was countered by the British by giving false Irish, Scots or Welsh names containing hardly any vowels and enough consonants to baffle any nationality in the habit of using a different alphabet. It was like living in half a dozen countries all at once.

Down by the river it was different. It was there that the godowns and working offices existed, and cheap bars had been opened for sailors, offering girls and cheap booze. Concession wives never went there, only their husbands, but for the most part even they left it to their agents and compradores, and preferred to remain in the fan-cooled offices further along the bund.

The news that a second revolution in Russia had over-turned the first and that affairs had taken a more bitter turn made it impossible to sit still. George Kee found himself despatching telegrams from the office to A N Kourganov in Vladivostok, outwardly concerning business but in fact trying to encourage replies that would produce reassurance. From time to time little packages arrived for Abigail, brought always by the hand of some businessman or ship's captain returning from the Russian port. Business had not stopped, but it was changing and, nowadays, as the ships came in, there were refugees aboard as well as cargoes. The new revolution had taken Russia out of the war and the new bitterness against the aristocracy that had lost it was driving the first terrified people to safety. The refugees were mostly members of the nobility and wealthy merchants who had suddenly found themselves dispossessed. None of them seemed to lack for comfort or money, however, because they had made sure that they had got away in good time – and with most of their possessions – but they were loud in their complaints and brought Shanghai up to date with what was happening.

It seemed that, with the end of the war, anti-revolutionary armies – often composed of ex-officers and loyal troops – had sprung up in various parts of Russia determined to wrest back control of the country from its Bolshevik rulers. There were armies in Murmansk and Archangel in the north, another in the south hoping to move north from the Crimea, and yet another being raised in Vladivostok to drive along the Trans-Siberian Railway. The volunteers who were being raised were hoping for help from Britain and France and were disgusted that it had not arrived. Then, with the cold, dirty waters of the river ruffled by the wind under the long arms of the cranes and the seagulls hanging in the air above the junks and lighters gathered round the anchored ships, a stern-faced Russian admiral called Kolchak arrived in Shanghai from a post he'd held in Japan, to bring order to the advance from Vladivostok. The Czechs, whose original few volunteers for the Russians in 1914 to bring down their Austrian oppressors, had now grown to an army corps, held the Trans-Siberian railway line, and he was intending to incorporate them into the army he was raising and take advantage of their control of transport.

Willie watched quietly as government officials, national representatives and a few important taipans tried to meet the Russian admiral. Among them was Gerald Honeyford, but, like the rest, he failed to obtain either friendliness or information.

'*I* could tell 'em what he intends, George,' he said to Kee. 'There are dumps of war material in Vladivostok. Provided by the Allies to help the Russians fight Germany. It's his intention to take 'em over.'

'And then what?' Kee asked.

'Advance on Moscow, rout the revolutionaries, restore the monarchy, and bring Russia back to her place among the powers of Europe – with himself running the show.'

Kee looked doubtful and Willie smiled. 'That's how I feel about it, too, George,' he said. 'But either way there'll be fighting. We've offered to send troops and so have the French, the Japanese and the Americans. It looks as though the war's about to start all over again at the other end of Russia and with a different enemy.'

It was more than he could do to remain indifferent. There was business in Vladivostok and he personally had contributed to the piles of supplies with Hong Kong- and Shanghai- made army pattern packs, kitbags, water bottles and harness. With British factories working at full blast to supply the troops in Europe, the War Office had handed contracts anywhere they could and Willie was anxious to know that his goods had arrived.

There was also the need to know what had happened to Nadya Alexsandrovna. He was a sailor as well as a businessman and sailors were always sentimental as far as women were concerned, but for some time there had been no reply to his telegrams and he had a feeling she was in trouble. Somehow, he sensed he was receiving signals by some sort of telepathy, and was so convinced, in fact, he made up his mind to go and see. He made his announcement to Abigail that evening as they finished dinner.

'I'm going to Vladivostok,' he announced. 'There are things there that have gone missing, and a lot of money's involved.'

Abigail studied him gravely. 'I thought we got everything to safety.'

'So did I,' Willie lied. 'But there's more than we expected. That bloody rogue, Lun Foo, worked hard at it and I notice his damned brother-in-law, Yip Hsao-Li, seems richer every time I see him. He doesn't do it by working at it either, and we know it isn't opium, so it might well be my property. I've got to go up there to find out what happened to it.'

'Can't George Kee go?' Abigail asked. 'He's very intelligent.'

'Too young.' Willie turned away, unable to face her with his lies. 'I've got to go myself.'

'And me?'

'You're in charge, Ab. As you always are when I'm away.'

For the first time ever, there was a protest. 'I got the impression that George could handle everything.'

'He can, but he needs your experience. Besides, what about the children?'

'As you said not very long ago, the house is full of servants and they're old enough now to look after themselves.'

'I'd rather you were in charge.'

Abigail's eyes were grave and her expression blank. 'See if you can bring more of your little "treasures" back from your friend,' she said quietly.

Other Shanghai businessmen were going north, too, and the fact that he was intending to go to Vladivostok was no secret.

'Vladivostok, Sarth, I hear?' Henry Moberley, Emmeline's husband, asked as they stood alongside each other at the bar of the Club.

Willie answered neither yes nor no, merely smiling over his glass.

'Things are happening up there,' Moberley said. 'This feller Kolchak's set to move along the Trans-Siberian Railway already. They say he's going to rescue the Tsar.'

'Good luck to him,' Willie said.

He didn't like Moberley and he'd heard that Wishart's were in difficulties again. Moberley liked spending too much and Emmeline had begun to lose interest in him.

'Hear they're doing all right in the south, too,' Moberley went on. 'Pushing the old Reds back. If they can get that lot from Murmansk to push at the same time, they'll all arrive outside Moscow together and that'll be that.'

'They couldn't do it,' Willie said flatly. 'The Russians aren't made that way.'

As usual, he planned to travel on his own ship, this time a newly acquired former Japanese ship called the *Shinonome*. She was old but just what he wanted for the job and, concerned with business punctuality, he had had the engines overhauled and had converted her to carry passengers.

The early sun was touching the tips of the ships' masts in the river when he turned up on the quayside to go aboard. He was surprised to find Moberley just ahead of him. Like everyone in Shanghai, Willie knew everybody else's business and he hadn't heard of Wishart's doing much trade in Russia.

'Travelling together, old boy,' Moberley said.

Most businessmen liked to cling together on their journeys, but Willie had never joined their drinking sessions *en route*, preferring to remain alone and keep his own counsel. He gave Moberley an icy look. 'I'm travelling with me,' he said shortly. 'You can travel with whom you like.'

Vladivostok had changed again. The cobbled streets beneath the onion-shaped domes of its churches were full now of penniless refugees who had fled from western Russia as the revolution had started. They had found themselves stranded without funds, because the White Army was printing its own roubles and there was a lot of speculation in currency going on.

There were also a lot of Russians wearing new uniforms, their officers with epaulettes like boards on their shoulders, but the streets below the flat-fronted Gothic façades contained a whole new lot of nationalities, all, like Willie, trying to establish a new base for themselves either in trade or merely to live – Chinese and Levantine merchants; Cossacks in fur caps; women on the make; Jews; mercenaries of all nationalities; enemy prisoners of war now freed by the revolution and waiting to go home. In addition there were enormous numbers of the old Russian aristocracy, such as had been passing through Shanghai in steadily increasing numbers, on their way to Constantinople, Prinkipo, Rome, Paris, and all stations beyond as far as the United States. They were still arrogant despite the disasters that had struck them, but, unlike those who had reached Shanghai, some of the unluckier ones among the latest batch were living in tiny cluttered rooms smelling of the creosote with which they tried to discourage the lice that swarmed everywhere.

Because of the overcrowding, smallpox was chasing diphtheria and typhus was chasing cholera.

Terrified of a spread of Bolshevism to their own countries, the allied governments had finally stepped in to back Kolchak and there were uniforms from Britain, America, Japan, France, Italy, China, Poland, Romania and Czechoslovakia on the streets and rumours of more to come because a miracle had happened. The Bolshevik forces were being driven back in the south, the troops from Murmansk and Archangel were also on the move, and Kolchak's army was driving slowly along the poorly defended Trans-Siberian Railway.

Guns, horses and crates of arms were being landed, but Willie didn't bother to check whether his own consignment had arrived safely but headed immediately for Nadya Alexsandrovna's office. She rose as he entered, her face grave at first, as though she had decided she must show no emotion, but before he had been in her presence a minute, her pretence had disappeared and she was in his arms.

To his surprise, she was in no need of help. He had thought they were so close mentally that they had been able to communicate through the air waves and that she had been appealing for his assistance, but she seemed well and safe and the business not only seemed to be doing well but was actually thriving under the new impetus given to it by Vladivostok becoming one of the centres of an anti-Bolshevik push.

She made no further pretence of doing any work and, turning her affairs over to her clerks, they headed for her house by the sea. There was no talk about a hotel and she showed him at once to a room alongside her own, excited and overjoyed by his presence and unable to take her eyes off him. 'Oh, William,' she said. 'It's been so long.'

'Too long,' he agreed gruffly, his happiness at being with her marred by his sense of treachery to Abigail.

They dined together in the town that evening. Restaurants were still open, though nobody seemed to know what to charge because White roubles were conflicting with Red roubles and nobody was certain what either was worth. A band in a corner played *Stenka Razin*, a Russian ballad that seemed to have caught the interest of the foreign contingents, and they held hands across the table, Nadya's eyes shining, Willie uncertain and nervous.

A soldier stood up and in a clear voice began to sing, his glass in his hand. When he finished, he shouted 'Na Moskvu,' 'On to Moscow', and threw his glass at the wall, and the whole restaurant burst into frantic cheering. With some doubt, Willie eyed the people around him, all of them flushed with enthusiasm and pink-faced with pleasure. Somehow, they didn't look like winners.

'It will be marvellous when Moscow is free again,' Nadya said.

Willie looked at her quickly. 'You'd like to go back there?' he asked.

She looked at him frankly. 'Oh, yes,' she said. 'Yes, yes, yes! It's been so long. And now there is no Tsar.'

'This lot want to restore him. They want to rescue him.'

She smiled. 'Russia will never accept him. The Romanov autocracy is finished. We will accept nothing but a constitutional monarch as England has.'

'Suppose,' he said quietly, 'that it goes wrong?'

'It can't.'

'Nadya, it can. It can. What then?'

She smiled and squeezed his hand. 'I shall still be here. I have not made a move in any direction yet. No one knows what I think. For generations in Russia it has not been wise to let people know what you think. I shall still be in business, waiting to trade with Sarth's, waiting for my William to come and sign the contracts.'

They went back to her house and there was no pretence about them sleeping separately. They made love gently but passionately. Afterwards she lay with her head on his chest.

'They say Russian girls are trying to marry British and French and American soldiers,' she said. 'Because they think that when they leave they'll be able to go with them. I am not taking out an insurance for my future.'

'No.' Willie grinned. 'Just signing contracts with Willie Sarth.'

She laughed, confident of the future, not only of the Kolchak adventure but of Allied support and of Willie's continued interest.

'I miss you,' she admitted. 'Dreadfully. But there is always the sweet and bitter relief of being able to cry and the knowledge that loving is enough. But to keep it alive, you have to remember – and always with a most painful tenderness. I can manage, my William, so long as you come from time to time.'

The days shot past. Two days after Willie's arrival a ship anchored in the bay and, as she was warped alongside and the gangways were thrown down, men in British khaki scrambled to the quayside. Willie recognised their badges as those of the Middlesex Regiment and they seemed to bring a faint taste of home, so he found himself cheering with the rest of the spectators. Nadya was clinging to his arm and as the last man stepped ashore, she kissed him.

'Help for poor Russia,' she said.

'They will achieve nothing,' a voice behind them said and Willie turned to find himself looking at a policeman who was watching the disembarkment with a sour expression. He was a big man with a flat face, a pale skin and Mongol eyes.

'Russia can manage her affairs without the interference of foreigners,' he growled.

'You sympathise with the Bolsheviks?' Willie asked.

'I'm no Monarchist.'

Willie smiled, determined to avoid trouble, then, as they turned away, he realised that standing just behind him, wearing a black overcoat and fur hat in the increasing cold was Henry Moberley. He gave Willie a knowing smile and raised his hat as they passed.

The following day Willie saw Moberley again, eating in the same restaurant, and he suddenly began to wonder if he were being watched. Why otherwise had Moberley come to Vladivostok? Wishart's had no business there. Was Emmeline up to something?

The same policeman was on duty on the docks as Willie left.

'Running away?' he asked with a sour grin.

'I'm coming back,' Willie said.

'Mind you don't get a bullet in the back, Tovarich.'

'Yours?' The man's manner irritated.

'It could be.'

Nadya clung to him as they pushed through the sightseers, trying to hold back the tears. As he went up the gangway and turned to wave to her, she made the sign of the Cross to him. As he climbed to the deck, Moberley was leaning on the rail, watching.

'Hello there, Sarth,' he said. 'Had a good trip?'

As the ship docked in Shanghai the news came that the war in Europe was over. Immediately, the Navy started firing maroons and Very lights and the Chinese started setting off firecrackers. The streets filled with both Europeans and Chinese and it was hard for Willie's taxi to fight its way through the crowd.

Abigail was waiting for him, breathless with pleasure. In her hand she held Edward's last letter, dated October and stating that he was now a midshipman in the cruiser *Cardiff*, at Scapa Flow and waiting for a last crack at the German High Seas Fleet.

'But it's over, Willie,' she said, her face pink with happiness. 'He'll not be in danger any longer.'

'I guarantee *he* won't be thinking that way,' Willie said dryly. 'I bet he's disappointed he hasn't had a chance to show what he's made of.'

It was hard to fit into a routine again. Vladivostok had unsettled him and he suddenly wasn't sure what he wanted. His business was thriving. There was money in the bank. His son was safe from the dangers of war. His children were growing up, his daughter now entering her teens, Thomas already curiously Chinese in his outlook as he absorbed the Chinese languages and dialects and the Chinese customs. But Willie was restless.

Was it age? They said that men got the itch after several years of marriage. But he didn't want any itch. He loved Abigail and trusted her, and he enjoyed having her around. Yet he could never quite throw off Nadya Alexsandrovna. Angry with himself, he tried to make sense of it all. Did he want *both* of them? All that talk he heard regularly at the Club about man being a polygamous animal – it was one of the regular clichés that pompous asses like Gerald Honeyford were always trotting out – was a lot of rot. Yet was it?

Henry Moberley had never mentioned Vladivostok to him again and when they met at the Club he merely nodded and passed the time of day. But Willie was under no delusions that he had failed to notice Nadya and how she had clung to Willie's arm and kissed him goodbye. What was he up to? What was he waiting for?

Wishart's, he heard, was sinking and he gave them only another few years before someone offered to buy them out. He wouldn't have minded buying what was left of the firm himself, but he knew Emmeline would never sell to him and, anyway, he wasn't sure there would be much left beyond the buildings.

Leaving the office, for the first time in his life he found he didn't want to go home. Instead, he went to the wharves, where one of his ships was washing deep tanks where coal had been carried, so she could take on a cargo of copra, sugar, spices, tobacco and gum for Java. He itched to go with her. He enjoyed Java, with its bumboats of turbaned, saronged Malays – barbers, tailors, dhoby men, cigar sellers, bootmakers, fruit hawkers and money changers. The scarlet mouths of the betel chewers gave the place a barbaric look and he always brought things back – battak, carvings, a decorative kris, all of which, as usual, Abigail immediately consigned to the spare room.

When he finally arrived home, she was in the garden toying with a trowel. The garden had always been one of her delights and she spent a lot of her time there. When she saw him, she straightened up. 'Jossman?' she asked, and returned to the house to mix him a gin. She seemed quiet and uncertain and he was nervous. They had been talking for some time before she came into the open.

'Willie,' she said slowly. 'Emmeline Wishart came to see me.'

His heart thumped inside his chest and he tried to make light of something he knew was not going to be light.

'Wanting us to buy her out, was she?' he asked. 'I wouldn't have thought she'd ever have offered to us.'

'Willie, it wasn't about selling,' Abigail said.

'It wasn't?'

'No. Her husband saw you in Vladivostok.'

Willie swallowed his drink and bent over the bottle to mix himself another one so she wouldn't see his face.

'That's right,' he said. 'I saw him on the ship. Can't stand the damn man.'

'She tried to tell me that it wasn't all business you were up to while you were there,' Abigail said quietly.

'What? What did she try to tell you?'

'She said he saw you with your friend, Nadya Kourganova – '

'*Our* friend, Abigail,' Willie said quickly. 'It's you she sends things to.'

'Yes, Willie.' Abigail's face was solemn and there was no hint of amusement. 'Emmeline said he told her that you stayed at her home.'

'He did?' Willie's heart went cold. Here it came. The denouncement. The scene. The threats. Divorce? Oh, God, no, not that! He drew a deep breath, trying to speak. But the words stuck in his throat. 'What did you say?' he managed at last.

'I told her not to talk nonsense.'

'Oh!'

'She was very insistent, though.' Abigail's voice was gentle but very steady. 'I said you often stayed with clients when business was involved. I said that I did a lot of business with Kourganov's also and that you were doubtless looking after my interests.'

Willie held his breath. 'What happened?' he asked.

'She continued to insist, but I just laughed at her. I think she went away disappointed.'

She put down her glass, crossed to him and kissed him on the cheek. 'And now I'd better get back to the garden,' she said. 'There's a lot to do.'

She left him standing alone as she disappeared through the French windows. For a moment he hardly dared breathe. Did she know? Was it a warning she was giving him, uttered in Abigail's own special way, quietly, without hysteria, knowing everything and offering him another chance.

It was a long time before he dared move.

four

Shanghai had done well out of the war. It had not been much touched and its taipans had kept the flag flying by using their profits to lay the foundations for huge new businesses.

The city was expanding rapidly now, making money fast, indifferent to what the future might bring, ruled not by a governor-general from England but by the very businessmen who had created it and were not anxious to introduce any rules that would handicap their efforts to make money. It had a magnificent geographical position because it not only had access to the China Seas and all the countries around it but also to the hinterland of China via the Yangtze, to which it was completely bound, a river which cut its way through mountain and plain, from snow to desert, through the gorges of Szechwan and rocky Chungking, before finally flowing through a rich fertile plain dotted with farms, towns and cities to the sea. It was the most prosperous area in Asia.

It was an extraordinary city, stiff-collared Europeans selling to Chinese merchants in flowered silk gowns and black skull caps who sat at their doors shielding their eyes from the sun with a fan. It was a city of contrasts in which nothing was done in moderation. It was already rich and had the biggest houses, offices and commercial establishments in the East. But the corpses of starved Chinese were regularly picked up in its wide streets and the narrow alleys of the poor ran within a stone's throw, while penniless prostitutes and Chinese courtesans living like princesses existed cheek-by-jowl with self-important European housewives.

No one could call it beautiful, but it was alive, the bund the centre, the heart with the great trading houses, among which suddenly Sarth's was beginning to be noticed. It was an area of offices and godowns, and pavements crowded with messengers, businessmen, clerks, hawkers offering cold drinks or cooking meals on their portable stoves to bring the spicy smells of food from every province of China. There were people selling silk; professional letter-writers with their tiny desks, ink and brushes, dashing off decorated ideographs on crinkly paper for lovesick youths; shoeshine boys; coolies gambling away their wages; story-tellers, beating a little song at the end of every sing-song line, their heroes' fortunes obvious in the face of the listeners. Though there was the constant sound of money changing hands and enormous deals taking place, they were still incredibly on the edge of the Middle Ages, with beggars of every category – blind, diseased, legless on little platforms. Among them plodded the indifferent coolies with their carrying poles that raised huge callouses on their shoulders calling out a warning to the people ahead. Electric tramcars had arrived now, grinding round corners, usually towing a trailer in which the poor, separated from the prosperous, carried their chickens and pigs and vegetables. Motor cars, appearing in large numbers now, pushed their way among the older traditional wheelbarrows, pedicabs and rickshaws, while round the jetties that projected into the river swarmed every kind of vessel imaginable, from sampans and junks to three-tiered ferries, great steamers heading hundreds of miles inland up the Yangtze, huge naval vessels and the flat-iron-shaped gunboats which kept order round the foreign concessions upstream.

To its European inhabitants, Shanghai was considered unique. It was never quite sure what nationality it was supposed to be, because it celebrated Empire Day, St George's Day, St Andrew's Day, St David's Day, the Fourth of July, Bastille Day, Washington's birthday, Garibaldi, Burns Night and Hallowe'en; there was every kind of currency from Mexican silver dollars to Maria Theresas; with every adventurer in the world there to spend them and every man with a nose for business anxious to make a fortune. You arrived in Shanghai either to make money or to dodge something you dreaded. That was enough, and nobody asked questions because it didn't pay. There were too many nefarious undertakings going on in the place, which was not only the centre of all missionary work in the Far East but also the centre of the drug trade. At night, the place reeked of the smell of opium and the perfume of the sing-song girls and the women who haunted the street corners. In addition, it was the known centre of piracy and now, with the passing of the Volstead Act in the United States banning all alcohol, it had, like Canada, immediately become a source of illegal booze, which made its way in fast ships across the Pacific.

It had never been a quiet place and there was always violence on its streets – to Shanghailanders, Hong Kong was considered tame – but to Willie Sarth, despite its faults it had become home. The Sarth fleet had been made up in numbers as the ships of former enemies, taken as reparations for the war, became available. Two former Turkish ships, the *Sivrihisar* and the *Yuzbasi Hika*, neither very salubrious but both in good mechanical condition, had been acquired and, with the *Dahinda*, her near-mortal wounds repaired, back in service, the fleet now stood at eight ships, while, under the intelligent guiding hand of George Kee, Sarth's trading had increased its business enormously. Setting the company's store room beneath its office, Kee had made it possible to superintend everything easily, from the invoices and the contracts to the loading of the ships with the produce of the Yangtze basin. Coolies merely had to cross the road, picking their way to the water's edge between the thronging cars, carts and the ancient buffalo waggons, laden with sacks, cotton bales, hides, silk, tea, peanuts, sesame seed and wood oil for the manufacture of paint.

Hotels for the businessmen from Europe had sprung up, but all the time there was always that special smell known to the old-timers as the Bouquet d'Orient, the smell of the foo-foo boats that carried away what was delicately known as 'night soil', the smell of refuse, of drains emptying into the muddy water of Soochow Creek, of spices and Chinese cooking. A cathedral had sprung up with all the adjoining ecclesiastical buildings, where Anglican officials pushed past hawking, spitting Chinese, and the homeless huddled together in groups at night to keep warm.

Only half a mile away lay the old Chinese city, a labyrinth of narrow potholed streets with horrifying slums and open drains peopled by blue-clad coolies and grave-looking merchants in the traditional silk gowns;

artisans working in open shops at ivory, jade, brass or gold; coffin makers; cross-legged tailors; bold-faced girls aware of their value; a barber shaving a customer in the street with a triangular razor that looked like a paint scraper, cleaning ears, eyelids, nostrils, and working arms, necks and spines like an osteopath. Among the floating red and yellow banners that announced the owner's trade, every street was festooned with laundry, the vividness of the colours incongruous against the smell of the sewers.

Brand new houses, bought from the profits of the war, were springing up in the area near the Bubbling Well Road and the Avenue Joffre, each one with its huge American automobile. To serve the people who lived there, new European shops had opened and in the hotels had arrived a new phenomenon, tea dances at which Willie's old enemy, Yip Hsao-Li, regularly appeared with twinkling patent leather feet. He still seemed to make money. Opium, Willie wondered. Could it be opium? Girls? There was always a traffic in girls in Shanghai from the day when they were given away as babies. It couldn't be gold because prices had fallen a lot since the war and there was little to be gained. He often wished he knew what Yip dealt with so that, if it were honest, he could deal in it himself. But Yip never seemed to think of anything but dancing. With his slim, slight figure, he was good at it, twirling his partners in the waltz, the foxtrot, and the veleta, which he particularly enjoyed. They were never professional dancers and it was said that they were always selected from the numerous concubines he supported.

Europe seemed a whole world away and the ecstatic letter from Edward describing the surrender of the German fleet at Scapa Flow made it seem even farther.

Since the early days when German raiders had operated in eastern waters there had never been any threat, and to be in touch with someone who had actually seen them was exciting. Edward's ship, the *Cardiff*, had been among those which had escorted the German High Seas Fleet to its humiliating surrender. 'We rigged a kite balloon,' he wrote, 'with a fellow in a basket watching for any sign of treachery. I saw them all come in. *Hindenberg*, *Derfflinger*, *Seydlitz*, *Moltke*, *Von der Tann*. It made up a little for not getting into the fighting.'

He now wore two medal ribbons, he said, but modestly pointed out that they meant nothing except that he had served in the war – just – and that everybody in uniform had received them. He had noticed the sullenness of the German crews and how they had insulted and ignored their officers, and was concerned with the effects of Communism which had spread from Russia, where it had been fostered by Germany to take Russia out of the war, to destroy Germany itself and continue westwards to become the threat which had led the Allies to intervene in the civil war in Russia.

The papers were full of the intervention in the north. The White armies had been advancing steadily for some time now and there had even been hope that the Tsar and his family, imprisoned near Irkutsk, would be rescued. But then had come the news that they had all been murdered and the advancing troops had found only the pathetic remnants of their life in Ekaterinburg. No bodies had been found, just a few fragments of bone and clothing and the body of the Tsaritsa's dog, nothing more.

The advance had continued and it had begun to seem that the dream of three armies, one from Murmansk, one from South Russia and one from Siberia, reaching Moscow together was actually going to come true. But the old Russian inability to plan, together with the vastness of the country and the lack of communication which made it difficult to co-ordinate attacks, began to work, and the advances were finally coming to a halt, still well short of Moscow and of each other's outposts. The fear of a return of the Romanovs in some form or other had been one of the greatest drawbacks to success. No one wanted the old days of privilege, and the Bolshevik leaders had obtained too solid a grip on the country.

The talk of Communism worried Willie because it was noticeable that the Chinese were taking a keen interest in what was happening, and Chinese intellectuals were intrigued by the way the Russians were putting their house in order. When they noticed that those powers whose greed and ambition had destroyed China were intervening in the civil war, their interest in the Russians warmed even to friendliness, and Willie could see that, if the intervention failed and the Bolsheviks remained in power, the friendliness could even turn to enthusiastic admiration.

There was talk of treachery among the Chinese delegates to the peace conference at Versailles. Japanese interference was suspected and a spontaneous rising started in Peking. Trying to consolidate his business after the wild trading of the war years, Willie was tired and more worried about what was happening in Russia than he could accept. Desperately uncertain of himself, he decided to put the East behind himself for a while to try to see things from a distance and, fulfilling a promise to Abigail made before the war but never fulfilled because of the difficulties of travel, he took his family to England for a holiday.

'We've earned it,' he said. 'Fighting the war the way we have for four years.'

It was meant as a joke because Shanghai had never suffered. A few men had disappeared, an occasional ship had limped in after a skirmish, a few businessmen had given up their time – but not much of it – to form the Militia but had never been called to do much more than down a few drinks. But, with Germany gone, her concessions upriver had been snatched up by the voracious Japanese, and the pavements there were echoing now not to the thump of jackboots but the clop-clop of sandals. The German eagles had lost their paint as if they had moulted and in the Russian concessions the decay was even more obvious because Moscow was uninterested and the only Russians there now were dreaming, shabby and short of money.

Summer was at its height when they reached London and the madness that had erupted at the armistice had died. Church bells no longer burst into excited peals, steamers no longer gave joyful toots as they passed each other and the roaring trade in the pubs had subsided with the dancing in the streets. Returning soldiers were finding work harder to obtain than they'd expected and disillusionment was setting in. The free drinks and free kisses had finished and bus conductors who had once let wounded soldiers travel for nothing were now demanding fares. Even that most wonderful prize of all – the awareness of having survived – was finally beginning to fade.

Nevertheless, there were still a lot of foreigners in London's streets and a lot of hollow-eyed youngsters

determined to snatch back a few of the years they had lost
in the fighting. Ideals had vanished in a feeling that all the
best jobs had been grabbed by men who had managed to
dodge the column, while the 'flu epidemic that had
gripped the world had killed with ease men who'd
managed to stay alive through the four years of slaughter.

The station was full of uniforms, a few heading for
demobilisation, a few, bent under their equipment,
returning from leave, and still a large quota of women in
mourning who flashed crucified looks at those on the arm
of a man.

To their surprise, Edward was waiting for them, smart
in his uniform, the white midshipman's patches bright at
his throat. He looked fit and well and was tall enough to
be a man. He was full of what he had seen, and delighted
to be among his family again.

They visited the museums, the parks, the theatres,
watched the changing of the Guard, voyaged up the
Thames, visited Hampton Court, all things that delighted
Willie as much as Abigail, because in his threadbare youth
he had never had the time or the money for them. In his
splendid premises in Bond Street, Julian Brassard was
delighted to see them and insisted on taking them to lunch
among the Second Empire gilt and red velvet of the Café
Royal. He had done well out of the things Abigail had
sent him, but he had been a good agent, honest and
straightforward. He had grown fat and more effeminate
than ever, but he had never let them down and was
grateful for what they had done for him.

'You've come a long way, William,' he said, 'from the
days when we first met.'

'When you thought I'd pinched what I had to offer and
wanted to send for a copper.'

Brassard's laugh was embarrassed and the comment started a train of thought in Willie's mind. For years he'd not been in touch with his brother and he had a sudden guilty feeling that he ought to have sent a few small contributions to the family which had looked after him on his parents' deaths.

Sending Abigail on a spending spree round the shops, he set off to find Arthur Sarth. But he was too late. His brother had died in the 'flu epidemic and, awkwardly, embarrassed, feeling he ought to have tried before, at least to have sent money to help someone who had been neither as clever nor as lucky as he had, he left a large cheque with his brother's widow.

'It'll help a bit,' he mumbled as he left.

Wainwright and Halliday's seemed to have disappeared entirely and the premises were now occupied by a different firm altogether. Curiously it seemed to be the trigger that made Willie itch to move on. He'd suddenly had enough of London and was anxious to return to Shanghai. He hadn't realised just how much his roots were there, and it was decided that the family, less Edward, who had returned to his ship, should cross the Atlantic in the *Berengaria*, visit New York and the agent who handled Abigail's antiques, see a few of the museums, then take the train across to the West Coast and finally return to Shanghai via the Pacific to complete a round-the-world trip.

Two nights before they had planned to leave, they went to the theatre and, as they crossed the foyer, Willie was surprised to find himself rubbing shoulders with Mallinson. He was in London now, still languid but now holding a more responsible position in the Foreign Office, and with a knighthood for services rendered during the war. He chatted amiably with Willie's family, but, as they turned to head for their seats, he touched Willie's arm and drew him to one side.

'Glad I met you, William,' he said. 'I see from the financial columns that Sarth's are inching up among the big ones.'

'Not all that far,' Willie said modestly. 'I've got better things to do than spend all my time just making money.'

'Glad to hear it.' Mallinson smiled. 'Because, as it happens, you're just the man I want to see. How about meeting me in the bar during the interval?'

It wasn't difficult to slip away and, as Willie entered the crowded bar, Mallinson pushed a large scotch into his hand. 'When are you due to go back?' he asked.

'End of the week. Via the States and the Pacific.'

Mallinson stared at his drink. 'Take around six weeks,' he said. 'More, shouldn't wonder.'

'I reckon so.'

'You could do it more quickly if you went via the Mediterranean and Suez.'

'Suppose I could.' Willie looked sharply at the Foreign Office man. 'Something's on your mind, Arthur? What is it?'

'Russia,' Mallinson said. 'What have you heard?'

'I've had a few dark reports.'

'So have I. Things aren't going as well as they should. This intervention thing was Churchill's idea. He made a mess of the Dardanelles and it looks to me as though he's probably made a mess of this one, too. A few British soldiers and fliers in a place as big as Russia aren't going to make all that much difference. What do you make of this feller, Kolchak?'

'Too full of himself.'

'That's what we think. He's started calling himself the Supreme Ruler and says he's taken command of all the forces of the land and sea of Russia. That's nonsense, of course. He has nothing to do with the troops in Murmansk, Estonia and South Russia. He's not even in contact with them, in fact, because he's too far away. But we keep getting reports from the British Military Mission that Red morale is deteriorating and that this winter their army will melt away. Any comments?'

'Yes. It's moonshine. At the first reverse, that's exactly what'll happen to Kolchak. He'll go into reverse.'

'We can't get proof of it,' Mallinson said thoughtfully. 'You know the army. They're permanent optimists. Look at the Somme. The Big Push that was to take us to Berlin. It got nowhere. Passchendaele and Cambrai. The same. It was only when we put our armies under the command of a Frenchman, Foch, that we began to get anywhere.'

The bell rang for the end of the interval and Mallinson downed the remains of his drink. 'Come and see me at the office tomorrow, William,' he suggested. 'I'd like to hear more of your opinions. I'll leave a message to have you shown in straightaway. Can you do it?'

Willie could. What was more, he wanted to. He was a man with a lot of energy and he was itching to be active. He had grown tired of visiting the sights and the theatres, and eating and drinking in hotels. Even the people around him didn't appeal to him. After the vibrant life of Shanghai, where everyone they knew was a driving force – sometimes even not too honest a driving force – London society seemed feeble, stupid and boring.

Abigail raised no objections, because she'd met Mallinson several times, and she took the children off to Kew Gardens to leave the morning free.

Mallinson rose as Willie entered, and indicated an overstuffed chair that seemed to envelop him. Coffee appeared at once.

'Go on, William,' he said. 'What else can you tell me?'

'If I were you,' Willie suggested, 'I'd tell the army to make sure their rear's well covered and they can back off. The whole of the Trans-Siberian Railway's in the hands of the Czechs and I hear they don't like Kolchak.'

'Tell me about the Czechs. They went to Russia to free their country from Austria. Well, it looks as if they've managed it, because Austria's finished.'

'The Czechs in Russia aren't,' Willie pointed out. 'When Russia collapsed they set off back across Siberia to fight in France, but they didn't hand in their weapons, because they were afraid of the Bolsheviks, and when they were attacked they seized every important town on the railway as far as Irkutsk and Vladivostok. That's what started the civil war. When it was seen that they'd beaten the Bolsheviks, everbody else thought they could, too. They won't though, Arthur.'

'That your considered opinion?'

'The Russians want to settle their own destiny, even if it's the wrong one. They don't want a government imposed on 'em by foreign troops. Besides,' Willie frowned, 'most of the White army regiments are led by officers who're largely useless, and the troops are unwilling conscripts who'll shoot them in the back if they get a chance.'

'The British government gave the Omsk government a loan of ten million quid, William. It's on one of Kolchak's trains somewhere near Omsk and we've just heard it's due to be despatched eastwards. They wouldn't do that if there was any chance of holding Omsk.' Mallinson frowned. 'The London banks are growing worried about it.'

'Shanghai bankers wouldn't have lent it.'

Mallinson frowned. 'When did you say you were returning?'

'I'll be back in Shanghai in six weeks.'

'Cut it short, William!'

Willie sat up and Mallinson leaned forward.

'We've had another report this morning that Kolchak's still advancing and that his troops are across the Tobol River and expect to be in Moscow before the year's out.'

'He's a hell of a long way from his base,' Willie observed.

'That's my view. We want to know the truth.'

'Meaning what?'

'I'd like you to go up to Vladivostok and get along that railway and find out just what *is* happening.'

Willie was suitably but not very convincingly indignant. 'You know what you're asking? I'm on holiday with my wife. The first holiday west of Suez since 1900.'

'We need someone like you, William. Someone the military won't suspect of spying on them.'

'I can't do it.'

'I think you can, William.'

Willie frowned. He wasn't looking forward to another six weeks of doing nothing, particularly as dark reports from George Kee were being passed on to him by Brassard. There had been a series of strikes and more than one riot at Hangkow, Yangpo and the treaty ports up the Yangtze. The increasing chaos created by the warlords was affecting business. In addition, he had plenty of reasons for wishing to return to Vladivostok, though he knew he daren't broach the subject to Abigail. She had never again mentioned Emmeline's accusation and he knew he would never know how much she knew.

Then, suddenly an idea occurred to him. 'I'll go,' he said. 'But I'll need to have someone with me.'

Mallinson shrugged. 'We shan't object to that. Who do you suggest?'

'My London agent. Chap called Brassard.'

Mallinson studied Willie for a moment. He'd heard of Willie's association with Nadya Alexsandrovna Kourganova, because there wasn't a lot that Mallinson missed, and he guessed that Brassard was some sort of alibi.

'Very well,' he said. 'That can be arranged. When will you be ready?'

Willie looked startled. 'You rushing me?'

Mallinson smiled. 'It's a rush job,' he said.

Abigail showed no sign of resentment when Willie put forward the bones of Mallinson's scheme to her. She had a suspicion there was more to it than he said because by this time she knew her Willie well. The old complaints she'd heard so often from men trying to make a pass at her – and they often did – 'My wife doesn't understand me' – carried no weight with her because she had long since come to the conclusion that nobody understood a husband more than his wife.

Willie wasn't reckless, she knew, and always had his feet firmly on the earth, and she believed that after his fashion he was faithful. But she had long suspected his trips to Vladivostok. Since, however, he always showed to her, Abigail, every sign of affection and no indication that he wanted to be rid of her, she was satisfied. Willie was old-fashioned in a way, the sort of merchant-adventurer that had gone out of fashion with the turn of the century, and, knowing she could never curb him, indeed, that trying to curb him would destroy both him and their relationship, she was content in her quiet way to accept his occasional disappearances. He had always come back and in her heart she knew he always would, and for Abigail, intelligent, honest, loyal, understanding and selfless – her thoughts, despite the business she had built up, the money she had in the bank, only for her husband and children – was content to leave it at that.

She knew with certainty, however, that he was up to something – perhaps some undercover work for Mallinson such as he had undertaken before – if only from his noisy protestations that he didn't wish to leave her and his wish that she should in no way feel inhibited.

'It's another government job,' he explained. 'Foreign Office. Practically an order. I'm to take Brassard with me to make it look like business. I've to travel along the railway as far as I can get, which will probably be Omsk.'

'It sounds as though it could be difficult,' Abigail said quietly. 'Especially with winter coming on.'

She agreed to take up the arrangements Willie had made and continue to America as planned, then proceed to the West Coast and return via the Pacific. Brassard's reaction to the proposed trip was one of fear and excitement at the same time. He was very much a Londoner and very much a city dweller whom even Hyde Park terrified with the width of its open spaces. But he couldn't resist the idea of a trip to China and Russia.

'I can put you in touch with trade,' Willie promised. 'Make arrangements with your bank to have money available.'

'Is your wife going?' Brassard asked.

'My wife'll be on her way to America,' Willie said shortly.

When he telephoned Mallinson to say he was ready and only needed to acquire the tickets to leave within forty-eight hours, Mallinson cut him short. 'Be at Portsmouth naval dockyard tomorrow at six p.m.,' he said.

'Liners don't run from the naval dockyard.'

'You're not travelling by liner.'

Puzzled, Willie said goodbye to Abigail the following morning. 'Spend what you like,' he said. 'Enjoy yourself.' There was a feeling of guilt behind his words because she had accepted the fact that he was going to Omsk via Vladivostok without comment.

The following day, Willie and Brassard travelled from Victoria to Portsmouth, Brassard already in a twitter of nerves. At the dock gates, they found they were expected.

'One moment, gentlemen,' the petty officer on duty said. 'Someone will be along for you. They're expecting you.'

Within a minute or two, a young lieutenant appeared with two bluejackets pushing a trolley. 'This way, gentlemen,' he said.

The luggage was loaded and they followed the officer across a wide stretch of asphalt and round the back of a large shed to the water's edge. In front of them was the grey shape of a warship.

Willie stopped. 'What's this?' he asked.

'Light cruiser, *Endeavour*, sir.'

'You mean we're travelling in a cruiser?'

'Those are our orders, sir. We're due for the Far East Squadron at Shanghai and we've been told to give you passage. It shouldn't take long because we're needed there in a hurry.'

Brassard was thrilled to be travelling in a warship and as he minced up the gangway the sailors eyed each other with grins. They had been given two cabins, both minute, and were hardly installed when they heard bosun's whistles shrilling and the sound of running feet. Soon afterwards, they heard the clank of winches and the quayside began to move past their portholes.

'We're off,' Brassard said.

And in a bloody hurry, too, Willie thought. Somebody was growing anxious, and it wasn't only Willie Sarth.

They took drinks in the wardroom and were invited to meet the captain, a tall, languid, fair-haired man with a row of medals like a sunburst on his chest. He was politely interested to learn that Willie's son was in the Navy, was clearly not very impressed by Brassard, but was certainly impressed by the importance of someone who had to be rushed to the Far East in a naval vessel.

The ship headed down-Channel at speed, running at once, as she rounded the point at Finisterre, into a Biscay gale. She barely reduced speed and the crashings and clatterings and the pounding decks reduced Brassard almost to tears and to wishing he had never left London. However, he cheered up as they sped through the Mediterranean, and finally recovered his excitement as he saw Egypt. But they didn't go ashore and all they saw of the Middle East apart from the top of a mosque as they passed through the Suez Canal, was from a distance. In the Red Sea, Brassard began to complain about the heat and continued from then on as they refuelled in Aden until they reached Shanghai. The captain of *Endeavour* seemed glad to be shot of them both, and they were dumped with all their luggage on the quayside, where a car, summoned by the naval dockyard, met them. George Kee, informed by telegraph, had the tickets for the trip northwards, together with a pile of invoices and bills of lading for Willie to inspect, then they were driven to the river again, where they climbed aboard the coastal steamer.

Brassard gave Willie a reproachful look as the ship cast off and swung towards the open sea.

'All this way,' he bleated. 'Egypt, India and now China, and I've seen nothing.'

Willie gave him a grim smile. 'You can take your time going back,' he said. 'I'll stand any extra expenses and you'll have plenty of chance to get to know Russia.'

Vladivostok was more crowded than ever, with Allied uniforms and flags everywhere. The best hotels had all been taken over, but by bribery Willie managed to find a room at the Alexsandr. It had a small salon which seemed suitable for doing business. 'Yours,' he said to Brassard.

'What about you?'

'I have somewhere to go. I'll send you an interpreter to help you and you'll find things are going cheap because there are a lot of refugees who've escaped only with what they could stuff in their pockets. They're desperate for money so don't do 'em down. I'll arrange for people to see you in your room.'

'You have an agent here?'

Willie avoided Brassard's eyes. 'Not exactly an agent,' he said.

five

Nadya Alexsandrovna was overjoyed to see Willie. She looked more beautiful than ever, but she had become thinner and looked a little tired and strained.

Vladivostok had changed, too. Never one of the most beautiful of cities, it was now grey with filth and degradation and swarming with people fleeing from the revolution. They lived in hovels or old railway trucks, the women determined, the men largely self-pitying. Americans, French and British ships were still bringing in war material and it didn't take Willie more than an hour or two to realise that the European powers had got the whole thing wrong. What they were trying to do was no more than a pinprick on the vast acres of Russia, and the recruits who were being brought in were the dregs of Siberia, without boots or hats, their belongings carried in a single small bundle.

Nadya Alexsandrovna made no bones about the situation. 'The Bolsheviki are advancing,' she said at once. 'Their direction of the fighting is much superior to the Whites' and their troops have conviction. Ours have none. They are averaging an advance of twenty-six miles every twenty-four hours.'

'Where's Kolchak?'

'It's not certain, but his government departments are supposed to be moving from Omsk to Irkutsk.' She took Willie's hands in hers. 'Oh, William, I can't believe that you're here again!'

She was clearly labouring under some stress and he insisted on knowing what was worrying her. At first she wouldn't tell him and he assumed it was the problems of the revolution affecting her business, but she claimed that trade was still good.

'What then?'

Still she hesitated then, suddenly, as if she needed to get it off her chest, she blurted out the truth.

'My husband was here,' she said.

It was like a blow in the stomach. 'Here!' Willie said. 'In Vladivostok?'

'He escaped to the Crimea when the revolution started, but he was sent here as part of a mission from General Denikin to co-ordinate the southern advance with General Kolchak.'

'More likely, to escape having to fight,' Willie said. In his mind even now after all the intervening years was the sight of a white-tunicked figure on a Chinese pony spurring away from the column of wretched missionaries he had left to be butchered by the Boxers.

There were tears in Nadya's eyes. 'Probably that,' she agreed. 'It would be like him.'

'Where is he now?'

'He was assigned to Kolchak's headquarters.'

'Then the rumours must be wrong and Kolchak *must* be succeeding. That twister would never be there if he weren't. He has no claim on you, Nadya. You divorced him.'

'He says I didn't.'

Willie grabbed her arm. 'Did you or didn't you?'

Her eyes filled with tears. 'I don't know,' she said. 'There were papers, but now he says they aren't genuine.'

'What did he want?'

'Money.'

'Did you give him any?'

'Yes. To get rid of him. He was smiling all over his hateful face. He promised he wouldn't come back.'

'He'd better not while I'm here,' Willie said grimly.

It was already October, but there was no sign of the colder weather and the rivers hadn't yet frozen, which meant, as Willie well knew, that if Omsk had to be abandoned, since Kolchak wouldn't be able to drag his guns across the ice, everything, guns, transport and heavy equipment, would all have to be abandoned. It was clear the Whites were intending to defend the place at all costs, even against the advice of the experts.

'I have to go there, Nadya,' he said, and immediately, from the look in her eyes, he knew that his guess that things were in a bad state was right.

'It's dangerous,' she said. 'Kolchak believes Omsk is a symbol and must be defended to the end. He talks of dying in the streets with his loyal followers.'

She promised to turn all her contacts among the refugees now arriving in Vladivostok in huge numbers towards Brassard at the Alexsandr. Brassard was beside himself already with the articles that were turning up, because the place was full of people who had arrived by road and rail, exhausted, hungry, and terrified by the excesses of the Bolsheviks. Trapped Tsarist officers were being stripped to their underwear and lined up against barns and shot by machine guns, their hated epaulettes nailed to their shoulders. Terrified women with children to feed were only too willing to sell the treasures with which they had escaped. Many of them had lost touch with their families and pathetic notices were displayed on the station platform. '*Piotr. We are moving south to Harbin. Join us there. Ilya.*' '*Mother. Please bring the children. Rudolf has gone to China as arranged. Join him at once. Natasha.*'

It wasn't difficult for Willie to obtain a seat in a train going west because by this time only the trains going east were of interest to the refugees. But he was regarded with some suspicion by the policeman on the gate. It was his old friend from the docks.

'Ah, my friend, the Anglichani,' he said. 'On your journeys again, I see. What is it this time? Spying for the Imperialists? Let's see your papers.' He studied Willie's passport then looked up over it. 'Why would you be wanting to go to Omsk, my friend? Most people are wanting to get away from Omsk.'

'I have a trainload of coal there,' Willie lied. 'I don't want to lose it.'

The policeman grinned. 'You'll have to hurry, Anglichani, because the Bolsheviki are coming on fast.'

'You sound delighted.'

'Perhaps I am. Vladimir Ilyich Mozhevsky has no love for the White armies.'

'But not enough for the Bolsheviki to go and fight with them?'

The policeman glared. 'Watch your tongue, Anglichani! I'll be looking out for you.'

The train was packed with soldiers, most of them none too willing to fight, and bodies jammed the corridors, with equipment, parcels, cases and baskets. With the air stale with closed doors, there was a great deal of bad temper. The stations and wayside halts were crowded with people waiting for transport east, or with local peasants on shaggy ponies for whom the arrival of a train was always a major event. It was obvious there was collusion between the railway staff and the Communists because the trains were always being halted and a truck detached on the excuse that it had a hot axle box and there was no one to repair it.

'It's a plot,' the British officer in command of the train snarled as they were held up for the fifth time.

'Waggons are worth a lot to profiteers,' Willie panted out. 'Try parking the train across a set of points and keeping it there. They'll soon change their minds.'

Sure enough, within minutes the axle box was pronounced repaired and they were on their way again.

There was incredible confusion at Irkutsk on the shores of Lake Baikal because Bolshevik forces were reported to have arrived in the vicinity. Soldiers and civilians alike were panicking to get to the eastern side of the lake, yet the track was jammed with rolling stock, none of it moving. Everybody was heading towards Vladivostok on the down line and only troops were moving on the up line. It was a nerve-wracking time, but Willie considered that his nationality would help him avoid trouble.

There had been a sudden rise in temperature by the time he arrived in Omsk. The front was disintegrating, but nearly two hundred of the White Army's guns were still on the wrong side of the River Irtysh and there was panic buying and hiring of boats and barges. The only bridge, which carried the railway, was impassable for horses, which meant that every gun would have to be loaded on to lorries if the retreat started. By this time, the Bolsheviks were less than forty miles away and it was being openly admitted that the town would fall within a fortnight. The foreign military missions had all left and the British railway mission, an officer and seven men, were the only foreign military personnel left in the city.

Even as Willie ate his evening meal the bottom started to drop out of the thermometer and he woke to find the place white with frost, and Kolchak's men struggling to get their guns across the river. Under the leaden sky and falling snow he could hear volleys of firing and thought the Bolsheviks had arrived, but he was informed that it was only political prisoners being shot.

'What's happening?' he demanded.

The officer of the British railway mission paused long enough in stuffing equipment aboard the train to answer him. 'I don't know who the hell you are,' he said, 'but you sound English and if you are I'd advise you to clear out. That bugger Kolchak's already heading for Irkutsk so there'll be no resistance when the Reds arrive and they'll have a field day collecting the booty and rounding up the prisoners.'

'Is Kolchak's advance finished?' Willie asked.

'If you ask me,' the officer said, 'it never started. And, just to make sure, the advance from Estonia and Archangel's also been flung back and Denikin in the south's been pushed out of Orel. The Whites are in reverse on every front, so the Reds up here have nothing to distract them.'

Willie reached Irkutsk an hour or two behind Kolchak. It was clear there was a doubtful loyalty among the railway staff and considerable partisan activity along the track. Conditions, which had dropped from indifferent to appalling within days, were rapidly becoming catastrophic and were aggravated by the snow and the bitterly cold weather which had set in. Heading westwards, he had kept his ears open and had learned that, although Kolchak had around fifty million pounds in gold with him, he was claiming it was purely to fight the Bolsheviks and hadn't troubled to pay the railway workers or build up coal stocks along the line, so that there was no co-operation and virtually no fuel for the engines.

Before leaving Irkutsk, Willie wired a message to Nadya Alexsandrovna to be passed southwards to George Kee in Shanghai and thence to Mallinson in London, '*Situation collapsing. Advise complete withdrawal,*' then he packed a kitbag he found with army biscuit, tea and tinned meat, and began to head eastwards. Whenever a breakdown caused a tailback of trains, instead of alighting and searching for food, he humped his load and set off along the track on foot to the first train in the line ahead he could force his way aboard, so that with every halt he advanced his position in the procession. There was no longer any westbound traffic at all and both tracks were monopolised by the exodus towards the east. News had arrived of a massacre in Omsk and, as the enormous traffic jam increased, Willie turned up his collar and plodded head-down into the wind.

In the intense cold, any engine running out of coal froze at once so that its boiler burst, and pumps at watering stations were put out of action by the frost. Soldiers muffled to the eyes formed chains to fill the boiler with snow and, with the stoves in the battered coaches consuming vast quantities of wood and constantly running short, the passengers always faced the danger of death from the cold. Food was scarce and the sanitary arrangements were non-existent.

The road ran beside the track and, along it, on a ribbon of trampled snow, flowed a stream of humanity on sledges on horseback or on foot, skeleton regiments reduced to a few sabres, batteries dragging dismantled guns on sledges, groups of men without officers, parties of officers without men. Among the debris of the army, competing with them for shelter, fodder, food and fuel, was a straggling column of civilians whose trains had foundered, peasants driving a few skinny cattle, children, lunatics, deserters. When the trains were stationary, the passengers eyed the pedestrians with envy. When the train was moving it was the other way round. Neither group pitied the other.

At the stations refugees waited in vain for trains whose numbers were steadily being reduced by breakdowns and hold-ups, and the stationmasters' offices were always the scene of constant shouted arguments. Bribes and threats were used and the railway telegraph, already inadequate to deal with the official business of the railway, was clogged by appeals. Lurid posters, depicting Bolshevik atrocities and designed to stimulate recruiting, were having the opposite effect and lowering morale.

All the way there were thousands of abandoned horses. Those still in harness had to be stopped every few hundred yards to clear their nostrils, which had become clogged with the ice formed from their breath. With Kolchak's White roubles worthless now, it was impossible to buy shelter, so that stables were cramped with human beings, while the horses had to spend the night outside. Great numbers of them had collapsed and the villages were full of them, all as tame as pet dogs, walking into cafés or wandering through the snow. Droves of them stood out stark and black against the white of the snow-covered hills. When they fell, their meat and hides were removed immediately and the remainder of the bloody carcass left in the snow.

With the overcrowding, typhus was rampant among the struggling horde. Because of the inadequate medical service, the unhygienic condition of the native huts and station rooms where they spent the nights and the insanitary habits of the peasants, the trains became infested, the lice, the carriers of the disease, swarming in the woodwork, the tattered uniforms of the soldiers, the peasants' sheepskins and the speculators' furs. Within no time, a new panic had started and, terrified of contracting the disease, any train known to be carrying typhus was hurried through without time to stop for supplies or help, and whole truckloads of people, boycotted by their fellow-travellers, perished. No one knew how many had been killed by the disease and how many by the cold as they grew too weak to feed the stoves. At every station the frozen corpses were stripped and piled on top of each other like logs because there were no coffins and no one had any time to build any.

The magnificent Trans-Siberian Railway, completed only twenty years before, had become a long, narrow stage on which thousands of tragedies were being acted. The snail's pace of its trains in the lethal cold spread the drama over hundreds of miles of desolate countryside in which there were no redeeming features. Misery, squalor and cowardice had brought about the chaos and only the crows, perched in enormous numbers on the trees along the track, their feathers fluffed against the frost, found any pleasure in the shuffling, jolting throng.

The whole campaign had descended into disaster. Willie arrived at Chita ahead of the British Consul-General and the British High Commissioner, whose trains had been anchored to the rails by great stalactites of discoloured ice hanging from lavatories and kitchens so that they had to be freed by men with axes, and it was Willie who brought the news to British Military Headquarters that Kolchak had been betrayed by the Czechs and taken prisoner. When his train had reached Polovina, the half-way point between Moscow and Vladivostok, the Russian leader had been able to continue only with difficulty. At Krasnoyarsk his men had thrown down their weapons and indulged in a vast *sauve qui petit*, fighting for places on the trains and prepared to kill to keep them, and at Glaskov he and his retinue had been turned over to the Bolsheviks by the Czechs. Tearing off their epaulettes as they had jumped out of windows in a bid for freedom, a few of his staff had escaped, but Kolchak had been placed in gaol and there was little chance of him ever emerging alive.

His mistress and some of his staff had also been imprisoned and the first thing that entered Willie's mind was that Nadya Alexsandrovna's husband, Zychov, had been among them. But at a town called Mysovaya he saw him on the station platform. It was crowded with people all struggling to get on to a train, starving men, women and children with pale frozen faces, fighting to get into carriages from which they were constantly pushed by other starving frozen people who had arrived before them and were afraid that their presence would hold up the train.

For a few seconds, among the tumult, he saw Zychov's head and shoulders above the shoving crowd. He looked well dressed and well fed with a fur cap over his eyes, and Willie couldn't believe what he saw. But he knew it was true and that somehow, inevitably, Zychov had been one of the few from Kolchak's train who had managed to escape.

For a moment, he thought of pushing through the throng and shooting him. Nobody would have noticed in the uproar because at every station there was always fighting and there were always a few dead left on the platform, but he felt too weak to attempt it and the next minute a concerted rush for the train ended in a confusion of flailing fists, screams and wails as people were trampled underfoot, and he was swept aside. When he recovered his balance, Zychov had vanished and the train was just beginning to move out, people who had failed to gain a place holding out their hands to relatives they knew they would never see again.

As the railway ground to a halt, Willie found a place on a loaded sledge. But he got no sleep because every time he dozed off he fell from the sledge and had to pick himself up and run after it and climb back, only to fall asleep and roll off again two hours later. Bearded, sick, exhausted, his face haunted, he struggled into Vladivostok. It was freezingly cold with a fierce high wind piercing the clothes of the starving scarecrows around him. Ships in the bay were covered with ice and the gale swept through the pitiful shelters of the refugees. Stumbling from British Mission headquarters, he stopped a cab, but the driver took one look at him and refused to accept him. Vladivostok was a sick, terrified city and all control of the White forces had been lost. All that anybody talked of now was escape.

For days he had struggled eastwards, still clinging with frozen fingers to his dwindling kitbag of food. Several times some starving man had tried to steal it from him, only to find himself staring into the muzzle of the huge revolver which had appeared from under Willie's coat. He had survived because he had been ruthless, determined above all else to reach safety, walking when necessary, plodding with one heavy foot in front of the other through the snow, picking up abandoned clothing, riding on a train when one was moving, catching and riding any skinny horse he could find until it dropped.

Indifferent, horrifyingly tired, he headed towards the Alexsandr Hotel. Suddenly it was difficult to place one foot in front of the other and, surrounded by the chaos of a destroyed army, he felt rotten in body and sick at heart. Brassard met him with a smile of delight which changed at once to one of alarm as he stumbled to a chair and flung himself down. Drifting in and out of sleep, he realised something was wrong. Surely he had dreamt it all. Nadya Alexsandrovna would know what to do.

'Mademoiselle Kourganova,' he mumbled to the anxious Brassard. 'Get her.'

After what seemed weeks, he heard someone saying they were taking him to a hospital and he couldn't understand why. He'd had headaches before and all he wanted was tea. Where the hell was the tea?

Then – who was this creature in front of him that was emerging from the mists. Was it Abigail? No, it was a man, and beyond him he could see Brassard wringing his hands. He hurt all over, not pain but a wish to pull the blanket over his head and die. Someone mentioned hospital again and he heard the word 'tyf' and he suspected he was probably dying.

He had been bitten by an infected louse from one of the overcrowded coaches he had ridden in or from one of the articles of abandoned clothing he'd been obliged to wear. He realised his head was shaved, his eyes bloodshot, the lashes gummed up, his lips cracked and sore, and that he could talk only in a whisper. He was almost deaf, half-blind and, staring at his bandaged wrists, he saw that he must have lost a great deal of weight. Brassard, looking terrified, was near him as he opened his eyes.

'Where am I?' he demanded weakly.

'At the home of Miss Kourganova,' Brassard said. 'And if I'd known what I know now I'd never have left London.'

'Am I ill?'

Brassard sniffed. 'She says you're recovering. You had a fever. Up to 105. Your tongue was coated with a yellow fur and your teeth were loose. Then spots started to appear. I was terrified I'd get it because you were delirious and I had to tie you to the bed because you got out and smashed the windows with your hands.'

'How long have I been here?'

'Ten days. The hotel sent you to the hospital, but I was worried you'd die there and told Miss Kourganova. She insisted on removing you. She nursed you devotedly.'

'Where is she now?'

'Buying food. You can eat now, it seems. You look dreadful!'

'How long before we can go home?'

'They say another week before you'll be fit to move. But you're over it now.' Brassard's face changed and a sly smile crossed his smooth features. 'William, old chap, I shall be eternally grateful for bringing me here. I've picked up enough to make a fortune. I've got crates of stuff.'

'I hope you enjoy it.'

Despite the encouragement, Willie found his lips were so swollen he could swallow only one drop of water at a time. Some time later a man in a black frock coat came to see him and introduced himself as being on the Consulate staff. 'I have a message for you,' he announced. 'From Sir Arthur Mallinson, at the Foreign Office. It says "Thank you. Message enabled us to pull out ahead of disaster." '

'That all?'

'That's all.'

'I hope he's satisfied.'

When Nadya appeared, her face was strained with anxiety. Seeing him awake, she knelt by the bed. Brassard stood behind her nervously and Willie gestured to him to make himself scarce.

'William,' Nadya whispered. 'You're going to be all right.'

'They say I can go aboard ship in a week or so.'

'You'll have to be carried.'

He clutched her hand. 'Come with me, Nadya.'

She said nothing and he went on trying to persuade her. 'I can help you set up afresh. Somewhere like Hong Kong. Or India. There are other Russians there. Or Constantinople. The place is full of them, setting themselves up in business.'

'*Some* of them.'

'Some of them,' he agreed, because there were some who hadn't the intelligence or the drive to start again.

The question he dreaded formed on his lips. 'Did *he* turn up again, Nadya?' he asked. 'Your husband.'

'No. I think he must be dead. He was with Kolchak when he was captured, I was told.'

'Yes, he was. But he's not dead. I saw him in Mysovaya long after we passed Glaskov.'

'How did he look?' The concern in her voice was unexpected.

'For God's sake, Nadya, surely you don't care?'

'No, no, I don't,' she said, but suddenly he wasn't sure, uncertain how great was the hold Zychov had on her. Women were strange creatures, sometimes unable to throw off a love for a man who had treated them appallingly. He felt she had to be given some security.

'Come with me, Nadya,' he said again. 'You'll be all right. I can back you.'

'I don't need backing,' she said quietly. 'I have money, and I've been sending money to the Bank of China in Shanghai, just in case.'

'Then come.'

She shook her head and kissed his hand. 'No. I'm Russian. And I'm safe. My family was driven into exile here. I shall be all right.'

'You might not be.'

She held his hands in hers. 'William,' she said earnestly, 'I can't give up everything. Too much is at stake. I have a good business built on a solid foundation.'

'Businesses can be transferred.'

'William – ' her words were still soft but they were firm in a gentle reminder ' – you are married and, I think, to a good woman. She doesn't deserve that.'

He was silent, knowing she was right. Abigail was a good, unselfish woman and he could never have Nadya near her.

'We could be friends,' he suggested weakly.

'I don't think so, William. We have been lovers.'

'Abigail doesn't know.'

'I suspect she does, William. Women have an instinct. They know these things. You can inflict no more punishment on her. Let her simply be happy to have you back, to know that her husband has survived typhus and Kolchak's disaster. Was it terrible, William?'

'There's no word to describe it.'

'I think you were brave. Your consul tells me they were very pleased with your message.'

'They didn't get their gold back. That's gone forever.' He held her hand silently for a while, then he said simply, 'Nadya, I love you.'

'You love your wife.'

'Yes, I do. Isn't it possible to love two women?'

She sighed and managed a wry smile. 'It's something novelists make much of,' she said. 'But it's very impractical.'

six

It was a haggard, subdued and thoughtful Willie whom Abigail met from the ship. He was gaunt and grey-faced, his head shaved, his lips still cracked, his face drawn in lines of strain, tiredness and illness. Seeing the grey that was appearing in his hair, it dawned on her for the first time that he was no longer young and neither was she, that they now had children almost as old as they had been when they'd first met.

'Willie,' she cried, her arms round him, tears in the eyes of both of them. 'What have they done to you? I thought it was some sort of diplomatic mission they sent you on.'

'It was,' Willie agreed slowly. 'But it turned out to be more than just that.'

He told her a little of the facts, of the journey from Omsk to Vladivostok, leaving out the horrors. By this time the exodus from Vladivostok was in full swing and with him on the ship south had been wild-eyed Russian aristocrats, suddenly aware that their titles no longer counted for a thing and that they were penniless and had no idea how to earn a living. With them were their wives and children, all scared and wondering what the future held, and dozens of their soldiers who by espousing the

White Army's crusade had given up all hope of ever returning to Russia.

Brassard was all officiousness, making it sound as though Willie's life had been saved entirely by himself. Willie let him go on because he'd made him swear not to mention Nadya Alexsandrovna or the fact that he had recovered in her house by the sea, as if he had spent all his time after his return to Vladivostok in a British military hospital. From what Brassard said, it seemed that Willie owed his lift to Brassard's initiative, that he had been rescued against all odds and cared for by no one else but Brassard. Willie was terrified he would talk too much and was glad to see him disappear to England.

The whole business of intervention had failed ignominiously. The last Allied troops had sailed from Archangel in September, and from Vladivostok in November. The remnants of the South Russian armies had been evacuated the following year. Wherever they had left, the vacuum had been filled at once by the advancing Red troops and, to the surprise of the politicians and soldiers who had advocated the intervention on the grounds that nobody wanted the Reds, they had been received with cheers. The tears in the eyes of the departing British soldiers were not of compassion for a martyred country but because quarantine regulations prevented them taking with them the hordes of dogs they had adopted, whose howls of distress as they were abandoned on the quayside had been too much.

The commanders had departed and Kolchak was dead, betrayed by the Czechs he had tried to incorporate into his army. He had been taken to Irkutsk, where he had been shot and his body pushed through a hole in the ice over the frozen River Ushakovka. Mallinson's bullion had never been recovered.

There were sheepish looks and red faces among those who had insisted the Russians did not want Communism, and a certain amount of nervousness in Shanghai as a source of trade disappeared. With the complete conquest of Russia by the Red Army, all news had ceased and it was no longer possible to enter her boundaries. Russia was building a wall round herself, determined to keep out the influence of the hated Allies until she had completed the revision of her political system.

Willie brooded on the complete absence of news. He had spent the last days with Nadya quietly and she had been with him as he had been carried aboard the ship to return. She had seen him to his cabin, provided him with a few titbits she had salvaged from her dwindling store of luxuries, and kissed him gently on the forehead.

'Is that all?' he had asked.

'Yes, William. You're going back to your wife. It's up to you to forget me.'

But it was impossible. Beautiful, intelligent, gentle Nadya couldn't be shut out of the mind as easily as that. Yet there was too much to do to dwell on the past. The Spanish 'flu epidemic that was ravaging a world weakened and impoverished by the war and was reputed to be killing people like flies in Germany and Russia had now reached Shanghai and everybody seemed to be standing in for someone who was sick or dead.

They heard that Henry Moberley, Emmeline Wishart's husband, had been one of the victims, but he had recovered and was now said to be drinking himself to death, while Emmeline had taken up with a new chief clerk, who was running Wishart's for her.

Yip Hsao-Li, all smiles and twinkling patent leather shoes, was still dancing, and the Chinese politicians were still watching to see what the Russians would do, delighted that, in contrast to the other powers, they had freely abandoned the privileges extorted from China by the Tsarist regime. The voluntary repudiation of this humiliating insult to China's sovereignty did not pass unnoticed and the Russians didn't fail to take advantage of the fact by getting in touch with Marxist students in China and offering help in the formation of a Chinese Communist party. Within months the party was holding its first general meeting and soon afterwards allied itself to Sun Yat-Sen's nationalist Kuomintang Party, which was pledged to give China back to the Chinese.

By this time, the homeless Russians were being absorbed into Shanghai society. The very first of them had arrived in style with their clothing, furniture and personal treasures. Their money had been safely transferred long before and all they had left behind them were the things they could not carry. They had brought their motor cars, their favourite horses, their pianos, their servants, but this stream had dried up quickly as the revolution had advanced and those who had followed had brought only their treasures, and what money they could carry, because what was in the banks had gone for ever as the Russian rouble lost its value. Then two dimly-lit steamers, the *Okhotsk* and the *Mongugai*, had swung into the East China Sea carrying the remnants of the Far Eastern White army, together with the band of an officers' mess which played as they passed liners and grey warships and reached Shanghai, to mark the end of the voyage from Vladivostok.

They remained in the river for months. But many of the men aboard sneaked ashore and sold their weapons. The warlords were always eager for weapons and the soldiers could raise 500 Chinese dollars for a Mauser pistol and fifty rounds of ammunition. There were enough gangsters in Shanghai to push the prices up even further, and the arms were often carried ashore by the women who were aboard. The Russians also brought church ikons, silver candelabra and sackfuls of Russian coins, most of which found their way eventually through Abigail's hands. For the most part, they didn't stay long in Shanghai because the members of the old aristocracy considered it beneath them to hobnob with what they called 'shopkeepers' and others in trade. Those with money took apartments in the French Concession because the restaurants there were better and they could entertain in their old style, while the women, unlike the British women who always assessed your income, preferred to assess what you were capable of after the lights had been turned down. It was a place alive with touts, pimps, white slavers, thieves and pickpockets, and the Russians lived by selling their jewels one by one.

Those who decided to remain in Shanghai drifted together and an area called Little Moscow grew up along the Avenue Joffre. As the Russians increased in numbers, forced to beg, to sell newspapers, even to try rickshaw pulling to keep body and soul together, their women, with their high-boned faces, were prepared to sell their bodies as well as their skills as hostesses, and the Europeans suffered tremendous loss of face as a result.

Because they had to make a living somehow, one of the Russians hit on the idea of introducing cabarets to the city. Starting in slum tenements round the Nanking Road, they knocked down walls to make bigger rooms, draped them with coloured streamers and cut the lighting to nothing, and immediately, with Chinese owners and Russian entrepreneurs, the city found it had a night life. Filipino bands played for dancing because the Chinese could never make sense of Western music and it was said the clubs were so small that if you were thrown out of one you landed in the one next door. But the hungry Russian girls, wearing cheap tinselled dresses lent to them by the club owners, were prepared to dance for drinks at fifty cents a time and commission, and there were so many fights the area was known as The Trenches. But, though the clubs lowered the moral tone of a city where it had never been high, the night life shifted relentlessly from staid hotel ballrooms to clubs with names like the Alhambra, the Winter Garden, the Carlton, where you bought dance tickets to acquire a partner and watched floor shows of Cossacks and Salomes in spangles. Willie found his daughter, Polly, was frequenting them with her friends and Yip Hsao-Li was in his element.

'They're terrible places,' Abigail said. 'The women are no better than they ought to be!'

'They think the same of English women,' Willie grinned. 'They say they're flat-chested, flat-footed from playing hockey, and worn out with the hunting and golf.' He dodged as Abigail threw a magazine at him. 'There's one thing. At least we've learned to eat zakouska and caviar washed down with vodka.'

Even reduced to penury, the Russians were a colourful lot. A few were dukes and counts and barons, and a great many more claimed to be and were not. But they had style. Shanghai was a city where optimism and opportunity were always present and, with almost every other detective on the force having a record and willing to look the other way for a consideration, it was a perfect place to make a living for people who weren't too concerned with how they did it, and the cry of 'Maskee', Shanghai's very own special word that linked the polyglot tongues and was the very symbol of optimism – Don't worry – was nothing but 'Nichevo', its Russian equivalent, though the Chinese 'Maskee' was accompanied by a grin while the Russian 'Nichevo' suggested gloomy foreboding.

The better-class Russians were superb riders and superb actors, liars and boasters. The lesser found it harder to find a niche in Shanghai society and, moving on to other cities where groups of refugees had established themselves, had dispersed to Harbin, Constantinople, Rome, Paris and London.

A few of them opened restaurants or merely accepted jobs managing them, while their women became hostesses or worse. Among the new restaurants was one called the Balalaika, which, they heard, had the backing of Yip Hsao-Li. Yip was always around, always obvious, still never doing any work. He didn't use the Stock Exchange and, since he didn't appear to touch opium or girls, it was difficult to tell where his wealth came from and, though the Balalaika didn't seem the sort of thing he normally went in for, he had gone into partnership with one of the Russians. With Yip's contacts and the Russian's knowledge of how a good restaurant should be conducted, they had turned it into an excellent rendezvous for Shanghai society, and finally Willie decided to try it.

Certainly the food was excellent, shashli on flaming swords, and blinis with caviare, all served to the sound of balalaika music in a sumptuous Russian décor. Abigail, who didn't normally like dining in town, thoroughly enjoyed herself, and Willie was egging her on to have champagne when a tall figure appeared from the back of the restaurant and crossed the floor to the door where a new group of diners had just appeared. He was kissing the hands of the women and showing them to their table, a superb *maître d'hôtel* in a perfectly cut evening suit, the blue ribbon of a Tsarist decoration at his throat.

Throwing down his napkin, Willie stood up so abruptly he jerked the table and the wine glasses toppled over, flooding the table top and staining the cloth.

'Willie!'

'Come on,' he said, his face grim. 'We're leaving!'

'Willie, why? I'm enjoying myself.'

He gestured with a trembling hand at the tall figure by the door. 'Do you know who that is?' he asked.

'Who?'

'Look again. It's that bugger, Zychov, who left us behind at Shantu! This place must belong to him.'

Abigail's eyes turned to the group by the door. 'It doesn't look like him.'

'It's twenty years ago. But it's him all right. I saw him in Port Arthur. I'll never forget the sod. I also saw him in Mysovaya with Kolchak's lot. Bolting for safety, as he always did.'

She didn't argue any further. Quietly she picked up her cape and they headed for the exit. As they passed the group at the door, the tall figure straightened and turned. For a moment Zychov's eyes rested on Willie, then he bent in a short bow, the smile on his face ironic.

They never went there again.

Edward arrived soon afterwards to join the Yangtze gunboat squadron. The Yangtze gunboats were the Royal Navy's hair shirt and everybody had to have a go at them at some time or other during their career. They were painted white with yellow funnels and carried two or three officers, six or seven petty officers and leading seamen and seventeen able seamen. In addition, there was an official Chinese complement of five, which included the chief steward and a wardroom cook, but they all had their makee learns who worked for food and board.

The life was not hard and they used a Chinese pilot for the gorges of the upper river, but sometimes bandits, Communists or disbanded soldiers removed the buoys and beacons and waited to loot the first steamer that ran aground. Occasionally they had to put down a riot or rescue a missionary or two, and facing a Chinese mob was a daunting experience, though Edward claimed that if you could make them laugh you could get away with it.

Because of the time he had been away, he noticed immediately the difference from the time when he had lived in Shanghai as a boy, seeing with greater clarity what the city's European residents were missing: 'There's hatred,' he told Willie. 'It wasn't here when I left. Then, everybody thought it had disappeared with the Boxers. But it's still here, Father, and to me it seems more powerful than ever.'

'We're not afraid of the Chinese, Edward,' Willie pointed out.

'Then you ought to be, Father. There are millions of them and only hundreds of you. They've only to notice that if they all pull together they could chase you out with ease. The whole set-up could collapse about your ears.'

It was difficult to accept what Edward said, because life in Shanghai, even in the concession ports upriver, was still easy, with the Europeans well protected from the raucous life of the Chinese by their money, their Sikh policemen, their patrolling gunboats, their parks, their splendid houses, their banks and their businesses. But, thinking about it clearly, it was obvious that things *were* different. The Russian concessions along the Yangtze had gone and there was something now the Chinese had never seen before, white men – Russians – begging in their streets, and white women prostituting themselves for money.

There was still a civil war going on in China, but no one took much notice of it any more because it didn't seem to interfere with business, and after all, it had been going on ever since 1911, when the Manchus had departed. Mostly it consisted only of ragged soldiers marching about the country, killing, raping, looting anything, but careful always to leave the Europeans alone.

The political situation couldn't be explained, because you couldn't explain chaos. Occasionally, they attempted for some visitor from Europe, but there was no outlining the tortuous moves of the generals whose only real ambition – certainly not to protect or defend their country – was to amass a fortune without being assassinated or captured.

A ghost of a movement was clanking its chains in Peking, but no one took any notice of it because in Canton in the south another government passed bills and made laws without reference to the one in the north. Both had appointed generals to run their provinces and left them to raise their own armies, but the only regular form of income for both was the Customs Service run by the

British. And that money went to pay off the indemnities caused by the Boxer Rising, so that in the end nobody was any better off, while the generals supplemented their meagre salaries by raising taxes, which they pocketed themselves, and, holding out promises of high pay and no fighting, recruited an army of discontented coolies, starving labourers and criminals. When pay fell into arrears and the general ran short of money, a little harrying of the countryside was indulged in and, if things became too difficult, just as the army was on the point of mutiny the general slipped away to safety with his fortune, while is men, who still had their weapons, became nothing more than uniformed bandits.

There were few battles, usually when some general had had too much samshui at dinner or when someone became over-ambitious. Normally emissaries met opposing emissaries and, after a few hours' bargaining to discover which general had the biggest following and the most guns, one army retired, leaving the city it had ruled to its successor. The new troops marched in, merchants were milked dry, a few people were beheaded, a few struggling women were dragged away and the new regime established itself. Cities were always changing hands, but it made no difference. Every general was the same as the one he succeeded and the foreign powers stayed clear of the mess unless their nationals found themselves in danger, when a gunboat would appear, a few shots would be fired, a party of sailors, gaitered and festooned with bandoliers of ammunition, would be landed, and the uproar subsided.

On top of all this were all of China's natural sorrows – famine, droughts, epidemics and floods. But still the long-suffering peasants, illiterate, superstitious, uneducated, using crude ploughs and the flails their father had used, went on working at their tiny plots, hoarding human excrement which they ladled on their plants in the spring, eating the produce of the soil and returning to it their bodily waste, raising their families, celebrating when there was something to celebrate, and always remaining on the verge of starvation.

This, however, was also not the problem of the Europeans who, believing that all the Chinese were idle and worthless, indulged in vast vulgarity while ignoring the exquisite jade, embroideries and porcelain China had to offer. For most of them Abigail felt only contempt.

'The Chinese were wearing satin,' she pointed out, 'when the British were still wearing woad and when there was no one in America except Indians.'

From the sale of the things she had acquired, she was now a wealthy woman in her own right, because her antiques business had always been kept separate from Willie's trading and shipping enterprises, and she had picked up a new fortune from the Russian refugees who were still managing to find their way to Shanghai with the treasures they hoped would finance their new way of life. There were minute gold and jewelled models by Fabergé, enamel, gold and agate miniatures of antique furniture, minute Weisweiler writing tables, models of John Bull or the Tsar, and animals and birds of all kinds. Aware of how much depended on what she gave, she always offered good prices, but she still made enormous profits when the articles were shown by Brassard or appeared in New York, Paris and Rome. Noticing her bank balance, it worried Willie at times that she would suddenly decide she had had enough and walk out on him.

The thought left him shivering because life without her seemed impossible. Yet, though she never hinted that she knew, he was certain she was well aware of what had happened between him and Nadya Alexsandrovna.

The thought of Nadya brought a new unhappiness at the memory of what he had left her to face. On their last night together she had clung to him, her eyes wet with tears, but had continued to assert that she could have no place in his life in Shanghai.

'That's another life,' she had insisted. 'It's a world away from mine.'

After she had left him aboard the ship, the worry had continued to torment him. The Red Army had been near Vladivostok by that time and there were hundreds of Russians lining the dockside begging to be taken aboard ships. Those who could afford it had paid their passage. Those who couldn't were offering their few treasures in exchange for a ticket, and aristocratic girls were willing to marry rough sailors for a passage to safety.

The ship had not sailed at once and every day he had scanned the quayside in the hope that Nadya would appear asking to accompany him, that some message would come on board, begging his help. But nothing did, and in the end he had fished out one of his cards and sent it to her. 'If you need me, here I am,' he wrote, and, putting it in an envelope, had addressed it to the office of A N Kourganov and got Brassard to give it to one of the officers to post on one of his last visits to the shipping office ashore. He had never heard from her since, had no knowledge whether the card had arrived. He was aware of missing her dreadfully yet when he looked at Abigail he was relieved that an uncertain and dishonest period of his life was over.

The end of the war had brought a boom in business and with ex-enemy ships still to be picked up for a song, the Sarth Line had expanded enormously. Willie made no attempt to compete with the big lines and never grew too ambitious, restricting his activities to trade through the China Seas, to Java, the Philippines, India and the Dutch East Indies.

Slowly it dawned on him he had become a rich man and that Sarth's had taken their place among the great names, so that Gerald Honeyford was suddenly pleased to acknowledge him.

Governed by its own municipal council, with its own police, its own Customs authorities, its own volunteer force, Shanghai continued to grow, with plate-glass windows in its shops and skyscrapers built after the fashion of America which it liked to ape. Near the British Consulate on the bund was the Shanghai Club, with what was claimed to be the longest bar in the world. The taipans, the owners and managers of the big hongs, stood at one end, the minor executives at the other. Not sure where he fitted, Willie always chose the middle.

Despite the fact that business was good, it involved harder work, however, because, as Edward had noticed, there was a scarcely veiled hostility towards the Europeans from the Chinese these days. Once, it had only been directed toward the Japanese, whose ruthlessness and greed had snatched so much Chinese territory, but now the hatred included all foreigners, and a new name had suddenly appeared in the south – a young general called Chiang K'Ai-Shek, a disciple of Sun Yat-Sen, who had become the head of the army of the Canton governments and was preaching fervent nationalism.

No one took much notice, because no one could ever imagine China becoming sufficiently co-ordinated to become a threat. After all, the country still had two governments and neither had an efficient army, though Russian instructors, made available by Moscow, were doing their best to give some semblance of efficiency to Chiang's troops.

But things were changing and, tired of being pestered by the warlords, a group of Chinese businessmen responded by forming their own volunteer defence corps of mercenaries.

They included Chinese, Czechs, Russians, British, French and Germans, and the Shanghai Banking Corporation, aware that it could help its investments and the investments of its customers, encouraged them.

'It won't work,' Willie told Gerald Honeyford. 'You're wasting your money.'

Honeyford blustered and jeered at Willie's doubts, but Willie proved to be right. Chiang K'Ai-Shek was too quick for the volunteers and, seizing a consignment of weapons for them, he ordered cadets from the military academy he had established at Whampoa to disperse the defence corps. The rapidity with which they did so indicated how small a threat it had been.

Edward was now well established in his duties aboard the gunboat *Ant*, which spent most of its time swinging at anchor at the China Merchants' Wharf. Occasionally the ship, shaped like a flat iron with twin propellers in tunnels and three huge rudders to make it easy to steer in shallow water, moved upriver, resplendent in its blinding paint and scrubbed woodwork. She carried two six-inch guns dating from 1898 and of a type never seen outside a museum or a gunnery school, and the ritual before it left was always to slip down to the APC wharves below the harbour to refuel and then spend the night at Woosung, where the officers obtained cartridges for shooting the snipe they expected to meet on the lakes on the journey upstream.

Edward loved the life, ecstatic about the distant ranges of mountains and the vast surging Yangtze and its fleets of junks, tugs and river steamers with their tiers of crowded decks.

'It's when you anchor at sunset,' he said. 'The breeze drops, the heat hangs over you like a blanket, and you lounge on deck, dripping with sweat, too hot even to make conversation. But then the sun goes down and the twilight comes and the landscape disappears into a sort of mysterious purple.'

His sister Polly eyed him adoringly, the elder brother who was serving his country in uniform. Alongside her was a young American boy, Elliott Wissermann, whose father ran Wissermann's in Shanghai and at Yangpo. He had a heavy crush on Polly and, as she watched her adored elder brother, never taking her eyes off him, Wissermann never took his eyes off Polly. Willie caught Abigail's eye and she gave him a quiet pleased smile. Things were working out well for them.

Later that evening, Thomas brought home a Chinese friend of his, a handsome young man called Chou with a shock of black hair and heavy eyebrows. He came from the province of Kiangsu, and spoke good French, English and German because, after schooling at Tientsin, he had studied in those countries after leaving the Nankai University.

These days Thomas looked almost more Chinese than the Chinese themselves, thin and tall with a long nose that made him look vaguely Manchu. He had studied at the university, jeered at Willie's beliefs and Edward's stiff naval patriotism, and was currently escorting a small Chinese girl called Chan Fan-Su, whose name when she appeared at the house with him was usually inverted to Fan-Su Chan or Fanny for ease.

Chou's father had been a minor mandarin, but he could see no sense in the present system of government, and while in Tientsin had put out a news-sheet outlining his beliefs. He admitted being involved in the mass boycott of Japanese goods in Shanghai three years before when a strike in support of the students had brought the city to a standstill.

'There can be no answer for China,' he insisted, 'except the sort of unity the Communists can give. If necessary we must use force to achieve it.'

To an old Shanghailander like Willie, this was blasphemy and he had seen enough of Communism in Russia to loathe the thought of it. But he thrust aside his prejudices and tried to be reasonable. He was talking to an educated young man whom he recognised as holding the future of China, and he tried hard to see a point of view he couldn't really accept at any price.

'I thought the Chinese were taught to look on soldiers as being in the same category as robbers,' he said.

Chou smiled. 'That is why our army was a thing of laughter,' he admitted. 'It was never the ambition of a Chinese to be a military leader. We were proud to produce intellectuals, literature, art treasures and merchants. Nowadays, however, it is different. We are learning that to have pride we must first be masters of our own souls and for that we *need* soldiers.'

'What about the Kuomintang? Won't Chiang's party get in the way?'

Chou's smile widened. 'We shall ally ourselves with them, because we can use their organisation to advance our cause.'

'Won't it be harmful to your Party's independence?'

'Last year,' Chou pointed out quietly, 'the strike we organised among the workers of the Peking–Hankow railway was ruthlessly stamped out by the warlord in control there. It seemed convincing evidence to us of the need to find allies. We believe in China for the Chinese. It will take time – too much of China belongs to other nations – but it will come. If I were you I would consider making your plans ahead.'

'He had a bloody nerve,' Willie said indignantly as they prepared for bed.

To his surprise, Abigail was unruffled. 'He's right, of course,' she said.

She was occupied with packing for one of her occasional trips to San Francisco and there were suitcases and trunks in the corner of the bedroom. From time to time she crossed the Pacific on business and, since the end of the war, her trips had become more frequent because the Russian revolution had brought into her hands almost more treasures than she could handle.

'Europe can't hold the reins in China for ever,' she went on. 'Whether they like it or not, the Chinese are being dragged into the twentieth century. We're teaching them how to manufacture things, how to run things, and there's bound to come a time when they'll know they can do without us.'

'And then what?' Willie was standing with his shirt in his hands, staring at her.

'And then we shall have to leave.'

'How will we know?'

Abigail smiled. 'I think it will become fairly clear,' she said.

Worried a little, thoughtful and concerned, Willie asked a few questions at the Shanghai Club. Honeyford laughed at his fears.

'Rubbish,' he said. 'The Chinks haven't the know-how to run their country.'

'They're learning,' Willie said.

'It would take generations.'

Suddenly Willie wondered if it would.

The following day, he saw his wife aboard a Glen Line ship. Polly was going with her because Abigail had always felt, in that shrewd way she had that she had never inherited from her narrow background in America, that Shanghai was too loud, too noisy, to be the only city in the world for her daughter to know. Because of the war, neither Thomas nor Polly had been to school in England and they had grown up knowing only the background of what was one of the brashest cities in the world and the people who lived in it – many of them uncertain of their background, insecure and loud-voiced. But Polly had accompanied her often to India to pick up antiques, and then on to Egypt and to Rome and Paris, and this time it was her intention to show her the west coast of America and take the trans-continental train to New York. It might be good policy, she felt secretly, if Elliott Wissermann were interested in her.

They drank champagne in the cabin and Willie beamed as the load of flowers he had ordered arrived. Standing on the quay as the ship departed, he waved cheerfully. He hated seeing Abigail disappear. She had been alongside him for over twenty years and he hated it when she went on one of her trips or when he himself had to leave her for the Dutch East Indies, Singapore, India, South Africa, or any other country where he did business.

Her disappearance left him feeling bereft and, calling in the Club, he recovered a little among the noisy crowd taking pre-lunch drinks. Henry Moberley was there as usual, but he was subdued these days. Though Wishart's were struggling on, it only required a crisis – and crises could arrive in China at any moment – for its slender resources to be swallowed up and the firm to disappear. Willie hadn't seen Emmeline for a long time, but he knew she was still around because Abigail occasionally brought news of her and her name occasionally appeared in the business papers.

Returning to his office, he sat at his desk, staring into space. What Abigail had said had struck home. She was shrewd and able and a good businesswoman and if she had seen the light perhaps he was foolish not to do the same.

As he brooded, George Kee appeared to inform him that the *Lady Roberts* had put in an appearance with a cargo of Indian coal. None of the British wanted Indian coal, but the Chinese manufacturers, trying to do things on the cheap, always welcomed it.

'Sometimes,' Willie said, 'I forget we've still got that old tub. I'm surprised she hasn't sunk. What does she cost us, George?'

'Probably more than she's worth, sir.'

'Perhaps we ought to get rid of her. Perhaps one of the Chinese merchants will buy her. That's where all old ships seem to end up. Let's think about it.'

As Kee turned away, Willie called him back and told him to sit down.

'George,' he said soberly. 'Have you got any money?'

'A little sir.' Kee smiled. 'I've put some away.'

'Where?'

'The bank, sir.' Kee frowned, puzzled. 'Are you suggesting I invest some of it with you?'

Willie shook his head. 'No, George, I'm not. I'm wondering in fact, if *I* ought to invest with me. Do you ever hear rumours about the city? Among the Chinese, I mean. Do they want to take us over?'

Kee laughed. 'A lot of them would like to, sir. The students talk a lot about it. But most of them are Communists and see their party or the Kuomintang as the only way for China ever to run her own affairs.'

'If they did, and you had your money in a Shanghai bank, George, wouldn't there be a chance of you losing it all?'

Kee frowned. 'I suppose there would.'

'George, I seem to sense a different atmosphere lately. My son, Edward, noticed it more than me because he's not been here for many years. It's like not noticing your own children growing because you see them everyday, while other people's, whom you see only occasionally, seem to shoot up. George, I'm going to transfer some of my funds abroad.'

'Are you suggesting, sir, that I transfer my small capital abroad also.'

'I think perhaps you should, George.'

Kee left Willie still sitting at his desk, staring through the window at the roofs of the business houses along the bund. He could see the Glen Line building, Butterfield and Swire's, Jardine Matheson's, the Yangtze Insurance

Building, the Yokohama Specie Bank, the Bank of China, and the tower of the Cathay Hotel. There were a lot of banks, he thought suddenly. Had Thomas' friend, Chou, been giving him a warning? Were things not quite as solid as some people seemed to think. There was always instability in China and the students were always calling strikes and intimidating people into joining them. Was he wise to keep all his eggs in one basket?

Perhaps he ought to think more about his business, he decided. Perhaps he was too old now for wandering. He'd been doing it ever since his early twenties – Russia, Japan, India, Korea, Malaya, French Indo-China, Burma. Back and forth across the China Seas, his business had taken him everywhere and he had enjoyed travelling, being part of a ship, smelling the hot engine oil and feeling the ship's heart beating as it came alive and curtseyed through the waves. The smell of the Eastern ports – Tjilitjap, Bali, Batavia, Samarang, Cheribon, Deli in Sumatra, Macassar, Soerabaya, Malacca and Rangoon – was like wine to him. It was the smell you caught everywhere east of Suez – foetid streets, teeming populations, temples, joss sticks, tropical sun on rotting vegetation, palm oil and patchouli, sandalwood and copra, dried fish and all the thousand and one abominations that made up the whole.

He knew what a tropical night at sea was like – dark, not the unfriendly dark of northern climates but a warm encircling shadow under the pervading monotone of the ship's screw. He knew what it meant to keep a calendar to mark off the days to the end of a voyage, he knew the pornographic wit of the forecastle, the smell of unwashed clothes, of tobacco and cockroaches, and newly greased oilskins. He had even done his stint in the engine room, and been aboard the *Sivrihisar* when she had almost sunk, the boilers amok, scalding ash everywhere, and a ladder coming down in a shower of nuts and bolts.

He had never passed on to Abigail his love of the sea because he was afraid she might demand that he stop risking his neck and stay at home. But being a shipowner to Willie didn't mean sitting in an office. That could be left to George Kee. It meant getting out and looking round, searching for cargoes, seeing the deep dark river of Samarang; the purple trees and dark branches of Calcutta; Honolulu, where you could smell the flowers miles out at sea; Samoa, Papeete, Chittagong and Haiphong, Saigon and all the other ports of the China seas.

Surely, he thought, it was finished now. The war was over and a period of peace had returned. Even in his own family life some stability had arrived. His marriage had survived the difficulties of the war and his own peccadilloes. He should sit back now and enjoy approaching middle age.

He was to be unlucky. The next day's post brought a letter marked 'Personal' that was dated five months back. It had been posted in Tientsin and seemed to have travelled via Harbin, Tsingtao, Peking and Hong Kong. He stared at the envelope for a long time, wondering who had sent it, then, reaching for a small silver dagger he used for opening letters, he slit the envelope. There was nothing inside except a pasteboard card which he recognised as his own. His name was printed on it with, underneath, in his own scrawl, the words '*If you need me, here I am.*' There was nothing else save a scrawled message. '*I need you, Nadya.*'

seven

'George! George! Come here!'

Willie's shout brought Kee running into his office.

'Sir?'

'When did this come?'

Kee eyed the envelope Willie held up. 'Today, sir.'

'Has it been held up in the office?'

'No, sir. Today's post.'

'It's been a bloody long time in transit, George. The postmark's Tientsin and it seems to have been posted five months ago.' Willie stared from the window. The warm weather had vanished and sleet from an overcast sky was tapping at the window.

'I'm going to Vladivostok, George,' he said and Kee gave him a surprised look. Willie had never told him anything of what had happened in Vladivostok, but Kee was a shrewd man and he had his suspicions. His employer was good-looking, strong, dark and intelligent and Kee had heard of more than one woman who was interested in him.

'It's late in the year, sir. I'd have imagined you'd had enough of Russian winters on your last trip.'

Willie looked round from the drawer he had opened. As he straightened up, Kee saw he was holding the big

Russian revolver he took everywhere with him and guessed that something desperate was afoot.

'I did George.' Willie shivered. 'Enough to last a lifetime. But I've had an appeal for help and I've got to go.' He paused, feeling a faint hint of betrayal. 'George,' he went on, 'this is between you and me. Understand? My wife mustn't know.'

'I understand, sir.'

'If anyone asks – *anyone*, understand, and that includes my wife, George – I'm going to Tsingtao. Got it?'

'I've got it, sir.'

'Right. *Lady Roberts*. What Chinese crew does she have?'

'They're all Chinese, sir. Except Captain Roper, whom you know.'

'I want Roper sent on leave. Reassure him his job's safe. Then I want you to find me a Chinese captain who knows the coast and the route. Understand?'

'Yes, sir.'

'Then see Yang and Co., and arrange to have the *Lady Roberts*' holds filled with cheap coal.'

Kee nodded, asking no questions as Willie went on.

'As soon as she's loaded, have her anchor well away from Yang's and have her name painted out and replaced with a new one – a Chinese one.'

'Very good, sir. How about *Simbang*? *Simbang* was the ship set on fire and sunk by pirates earlier in the year in the Yellow Sea. Registered at Tientsin.'

'That'll do to stop questions being asked. She can have the same owners.'

'I'll arrange that, sir, and see the necessary papers are prepared.'

'She'll need a Chinese flag, George. She'll be carrying the coal to Vladivostok.'

'Have we got a customer?'

'No. We might not even find one, in which case we'll bring the coal back. But we'll need an excuse for going there.'

'Vladivostok's an open port, sir. It still has a pronounced international character.'

'For everyone except the British, the Americans, the French and the Japanese, who sent troops up there to fight against the Reds. That's why the *Lady Roberts* will become the *Simbang* and why I shall be on the ship's register as the second mate. Name of William Kee, of your address, George. You've acquired a brother.'

Kee smiled. 'So I have, sir. But it occurs to me that my brother, having been educated in England, doesn't understand Chinese as he ought and it might be a good idea if I were to accompany him in case of difficulties.'

Willie stared at the young man with his handsome Chinese features and English smile. 'Thanks, George,' he said. 'I think you might be right at that.'

It was fortunate that Abigail had disappeared from the scene for a matter of two months – three months if things turned out as she wished and Polly was happy away from the side of young Wissermann. It was her intention to visit the Wissermann relations in San Francisco and anything could happen.

But Abigail's absence gave Willie time. A week to Vladivostok, a day there to accomplish all he needed to do, a week back. It gave him ample scope to settle again into his routine so that nothing would seem to have happened by the time she returned.

It wasn't hard for him to pass as a mixed-blood Chinese. There were thousands like Kee, with a Chinese mother or father, who spoke both English and Chinese and possessed the attributes and instincts of both nations. He and Kee could almost have been brothers because they were of much the same size and both possessed black hair and swarthy complexions. Kee's passport was in perfect order and any doubts about the one he produced for Willie could be explained by the fact that his 'brother' had gone to sea as a boy and had never had a settled home in any city or port.

Kee had found a master, a Chinese first mate called John Yeh. 'He's good,' he said, 'and he has all the necessary sea time and experience. He'll do it without question, especially if we make his fourth stripe permanent.'

'Tell him if we pull it off, he's got a job for life.'

Yeh was a burly, blank-faced young man who took over the ship without requiring explanations, moved Roper's belongings ashore, ordered the repainting Willie had demanded, and made a point of laying in half a dozen Chinese merchant marine flags.

There was a snowstorm blowing and it was cold enough to sting the nostrils as they made their way into Vladivostok. The sea was ice-blue under the leaden sky and the dock area seemed bleak and almost deserted. There were huge piles of timber stacked ready to be loaded aboard ship, and mountains of coal. Carts waited, their horses drowsing in the harness, but there appeared to be no fishing craft and very little in the way of shipping, while the dockside cranes were motionless, like great gallows hanging out over the water.

Leaving Kee on board, Willie went ashore alone. Fading posters edged in black were on all the fences and telegraph poles, announcing that the local soviet of workers and soldiers had replaced all former administrative and other authorities. Finding a telephone in a bar near the docks, he tried to contact A N Kourganov's, but the telephone system seemed to be operating only fitfully and he couldn't get through. The snow was still falling as he left the bar, eyed all the time by the occupants, hard-faced men in fur caps and greasy coats.

The harbourmaster's office seemed to be empty and with no sign of staff. An old woman, wearing a garment cut apparently from a worn carpet, lived in the basement. On the wall behind her she had pinned a row of epaulettes, emblems of the now-dead Tsarist army. The Refugee Control Office, which had existed during Willie's last visit, had vanished as if the refugee problem had ceased to exist with the closing of the frontiers.

There seemed a great shortage of transport. Trams were still running, but they were few and far between and, after trying to board three of them and being turned away because they were too crowded, Willie gave up trying and set off walking. It didn't surprise him to pass a body in the street stripped to its underclothes, its feet, hands and face blue.

The office of A N Kourganov was still functioning, but it looked shabby and the staff seemed lethargic and indifferent. When Willie entered for Nadya they informed him that she hadn't been in for some time. The man who answered his questions said he was the staff representative for the office and that he was in charge.

'Who does the business then?'

'I do.'

'What about Mademoiselle Kourganova?'

'She is still titular head of the firm, but she is no longer very active.'

'I see. Then to whom do I apply to do business?'

'What do you have?'

'Coal. Indian coal.'

The man sneered. 'We have better coal in Russia. Indian coal is a product of Imperial Britain and it is soft and of no use for railways or shipping.'

'It's very cheap, and I think there would be a very good bargain for whoever handles it.'

At the hint of a bribe, the man eyed Willie shrewdly. 'I'll need to think about it,' he said. 'But there are problems. I have to get in touch with the Ministry and that takes time.'

'Do you mean there's no one with initiative who can produce money to buy coal cheaply which he can sell at a great profit?'

The shrewd look came again. 'It might be possible.'

There was a discussion and an exchange of addresses. The man seemed satisfied with Willie's credentials and promised to go along to the ship and check the cargo. The greed in his face was clear.

Leaving the office, Willie ate a meal in a shabby restaurant where most of the diners seemed to be officials. The street outside was full of beggars, but no one took the slightest notice of them.

The Marizliyevskaya, where Nadya Alexsandrovna lived, seemed to have changed its character. The big houses had filled up with refugees and people from the working-class districts, whole families crowding into single rooms. As he reached Nadya's house the door was opened by a bearded man in a greasy leather jacket.

'V I Kursin,' he introduced himself. 'I'm the man on duty.'

'What does that mean?'

'Every able-bodied man has to take his turn. I lock the doors and open up, and when the Cheka want to know a thing, they come and ask me. I'm in charge.'

Willie had heard of the Cheka because reports had found their way south to Shanghai. It was nothing else but a secret police and existed to fight counter-revolution and sabotage. Its policy of terror was considered necessary for the survival of the new republic and it had the power of censorship, security, arrest and even execution.

'Does the Cheka often come here?' he asked.

'It's been known.'

The house seemed to be teeming with men, women and children, all of them starved-looking and dirty, and when Willie asked for Nadya, Kursin gestured.

'She's upstairs,' he said. 'She's nobody now. Why do you want to see her? You're not Russian.'

'No. I'm from Shanghai.'

'Then you're Chinese?'

'You could say that.'

'You don't look Chinese. But some Russians don't look Russian. We admire the way the Chinese are trying to get rid of the Imperialists. What do you want with her?'

'I'm here to do business. I've always traded with A N Kourganov's.'

'She doesn't run the firm now. The party are keeping a watch on it.'

It was as Willie had thought. Nadya had been dispossessed.

She answered the door warily, opening it gradually until she saw Willie's face. He saw her eyes light up, but she was wary because Kursin was standing by Willie's side.

'I'm from Yang and Co., Shanghai,' Willie said slowly. 'I've come to do business, but I've been told you're no longer running A N Kourganov's.'

'That's right.' She was fighting to keep the delight from her face. 'A N Kourganov is now under new management. Perhaps you'd like to come in and take a glass of tea, and I'll direct you to the new owners.'

Willie smiled at Kursin who scowled back at him and shuffled off. Slipping inside Nadya's room, Willie slammed the door and she flung herself into his arms and clung weakly to him. Eventually, she stirred and touched his face with her fingertips as if to convince herself he was real.

Then she recovered herself. 'Tea,' she said. 'We'd better have tea in case he comes back. Sometimes he does, though nowadays I never have visitors.'

She made the tea as he waited and he saw that she was paler and thinner and that she'd cut her lush reddish-brown hair. She looked ill, too, and she told him that she'd had 'flu.

'I thought I was going to die,' she admitted, 'but one of the women from the other rooms took pity on me. Even under the revolution there's still room for compassion.'

'Nadya, what happened?'

'They took over all the houses when the Bolsheviki arrived here,' she said. 'They insisted that the poor had as much right to a roof over their heads as anyone – which I suppose is true. But they pay no rent because everything belongs to everyone and nothing to anyone in particular.' She drew a deep shuddering breath, as if trying to control her emotions. 'Things have changed. There wasn't a lot when you left, but there was a little laughter. Even that's gone now.'

The room had the iron coldness of a refrigerator and he stared about him at the few items of furniture she had crammed in there.

'I thought you were going to be all right under the revolution.'

She gave him a sad smile. 'Oh, they're not accusing me of deviation,' she said. 'Nothing like that. Just of having money. I didn't allow for the fact that commissars might well have ambition. The commissar here is a man called Chelynin. He was my chief clerk and he fancied A N Kourganov's. He knew the firm was profitable so he simply took over. When I protested, he reported me to the local soviet for exporting goods against the orders of the Supreme Soviet. It didn't need much more for me to be denounced as a traitor to the cause. I was lucky not to be imprisoned. As it is, I have no rights, no property, no opinions, nothing. I had to send to you for help. It went against the grain to intrude again into your life, but I had no alternative.'

'Where's this Chelynin now?'

'Harbin. We had timber there. He's gone to claim it.'

'When will he be back?'

She shrugged. 'I don't know. He's been gone some time. It could be any day.'

He took her hand. It was ice-cold. 'Look, Nadya, I've got a ship here. I can get you away.'

'If they let you go. They search every ship that leaves port for Tsarist refugees.'

'We'll get over that. How soon can you be ready?'

She gave a little laugh. It was brittle and faintly hysterical. 'I can leave now,' she said. 'But they'll not let me take anything.'

'Have you no money?'

'A little. I transferred it to Hong Kong while I could. But the rouble had already lost its value, so I haven't as much as I expected.'

'Anything else? Anything of value we can take with us?'

She smiled. 'I remembered the trade we did. There are some small things of value I was going to send to your wife. When the Bolsheviki came everything stopped, though. Even the post, because they thought people were sending money out. The letter I sent I had to give to a ship's captain whom I had to bribe. I thought it hadn't reached you.'

'It nearly didn't. Have you much?'

She managed a wry smile. 'A surprising amount.' She gestured at a group of shabby suitcases in the corner of the room. 'It's all in there. Kursin thinks it's curtains and clothes.'

'Can you hide it about you? My overcoat has deep pockets. What about you.

'I have a coat. Not a fur. People daren't wear furs these days or you're accused of being a bourzhuki.'

'I'll bring George Kee. As businessmen, we can carry attaché cases. We'll get as much out as we can. As for now, I'd better not stay in case someone becomes suspicious.'

As he rose to go, she rose with him and he put his arms round her and kissed her. She looked up at him.

'What about your wife?' she asked. 'Does she know you're here?'

'Abigail's in America,' he said shortly.

She paused. 'How is it between you?' she asked.

'As it should be. I'll come back tomorrow with George Kee, with the ship's manifest and God knows what else to flourish in the face of our friend downstairs. Just be ready, that's all. But nothing except what you can carry.'

As she unlocked and opened the door, he pushed his cap on his head. 'It's no good, Mademoiselle Kourganova,' he said loudly. 'I can't do business with you.'

She was staring at him with a worried expression and he noticed Kursin waiting on the landing. On the stairs were other residents, all watching and listening.

'I can't do business with Monsieur Chelynin either without your signature on the papers,' he went on loudly. 'I shall need your signature to indicate that you no longer carry on business as A N Kourganov, then I can take it to Comrade Chelynin and get his signature and we can go ahead from there. I'll bring my chief clerk with me tomorrow so I hope you're not thinking of disappearing.'

He made his voice harsh and domineering, then turned to Kursin. 'Just see that no one talks to her,' he said, offering a Shanghai dollar. 'Not even you. I want her here when I come, not on a train to Moscow or somewhere.'

Kursin touched his cap. 'She'll be here, Tovarich. Have no fear.'

Returning to the *Lady Roberts*, Willie noticed that a string of railway waggons had been moved alongside and that a hoist had been rigged.

'I think we've sold the coal,' Kee said as he climbed the gangplank. 'A gentleman who said he represented someone called Chelynin appeared. He offered cash.'

'Roubles?'

'American dollars. I snatched his hand off.'

Willie grinned. 'It seems somebody can still do business in Russia.'

'There's just one thing,' Kee went on. 'We had one of their officials prowling around. He noticed we'd painted over the name of the ship and wanted to know why. I told him that Yang's had changed her name because they'd bought her from a British firm that had gone bust. Yours. He thoroughly approved of British firms being taken over by Chinese.'

Willie grinned. 'Well done, George. What's your overcoat like? Large pockets?'

Kee grinned. 'Big enough to get your hands well down.'

'Let's have Captain Yeh in.'

Yeh had served on British ships all his life and was willing to help. He had ideas, too, and dressed in his heavy overcoat and cap and wearing a leather belt and the bolstered revolver all captains working Chinese waters carried against pirates, he looked like a policeman. Removing the badge from his cap, he gestured with it to Willie. 'I can go one better,' he said. 'I can have a star made in the engine room and paint it red with the paint we use for the port side reflector.'

The unloading of the coal was finished by evening, too late to move the ship, and an official in a black leather coat and astrakhan cap exchanged documents and informed them they would be inspected before the weekend. Yeh took the ship from the quayside the following morning and anchored her offshore in the bay. There were several other ships there, all loaded and waiting for Russian officialdom to provide the necessary papers so they could leave.

During the afternoon, leaving the ship under the command of the engineer with instructions to have steam up, they were rowed ashore, three tall bulky men in heavy overcoats, carrying leather attaché cases, Yeh more like a policeman than ever now that he had attached a red metal star to his cap.

They found a droshky and headed for the Marizliyevskaya. A group of young people were throwing snowballs at each other and laughing, and it seemed a symbol that all was not evil in Russia. Kursin met them at the door, smiling broadly. 'She's still here, Comrade. She didn't get away.'

Despite the equality everybody preached, he wasn't against accepting another tip, and the three of them marched up the stairs and hammered on Nadya's door.

Not waiting for an answer, Willie pushed the door open. He saw that Nadya had lit two wax candles in front of an ikon to the Mother of God and was kneeling before it. As she rose to her feet, he started shouting at once.

'I'm not satisfied with these documents, Mademoiselle,' he roared. 'I think there are some deficiencies and more than a little falsehood. I've brought the police.'

As Kee slammed the door in the face of Kursin, he turned back to Nadya, who was staring at Yeh with an alarmed expression on her features.

'Captain Yeh,' Willie introduced. 'And George Kee, my manager. Are you ready?'

She swayed, almost fainting with relief. 'I really thought they were the police,' she said. 'Yes, I'm ready.'

Willie jerked a hand at Yeh. 'Tell that gadget outside to find us transport, Captain,' he said.

Yeh opened the door and began to jabber at Kursin, who touched his cap and scuttled off, but not before getting a good view of Willie flourishing a handful of documents in Nadya's face. As the door slammed again the act was terminated at once and small objects wrapped in handkerchiefs or tissue paper began to disappear into pockets.

'There's still a suitcase,' she said when their pockets were full.

'We'll take it with us.'

A scratching at the door told them that Kursin was back. 'Transport's outside, Comrade Captain,' he announced.

'Right,' Willie said, hoisting up the suitcase. 'I'm going to take this with me as evidence, Mademoiselle. And I'm going to insist you accompany me to the Comrade Captain's headquarters. We need to talk a little more.'

The crowd in the corridor and on the staircase fell back before them as they marched down to the hall, Willie leading, Nadya between Yeh and George Kee.

It was already dark with the darkness of a northern winter and there had been more snow during the night so that the place had an arctic look about it, the buildings black against the whiteness. A group of men in fur caps and heavy dark coats crossed with cartridge belts watched them from the street corner where they stood round a fire built on the pavement, but there was no attempt to stop them as they pushed Nadya roughly into a cab.

Reaching the main road, they joined a string of country carts and droshkies in a suburb that had been wrecked when the Red Army had arrived. There was a stark atmosphere of neglect among the houses, with broken windows hung with sacking or old blankets, even occasional stone chimneys smoke-blackened in the middle of the heap of ruins. In some they could see sabre-slashed drapings and broken furniture full of bullet holes.

Leaving the cab near the docks, they began to move among the narrow streets towards the water's edge. Occasionally soldiers moved past them, but Yeh's bulk and the red star on his cap was sufficient to prevent questions being asked. They passed boarded shop windows and found themselves pushing among carts, perambulators and barrows. But the looting had long since finished and there was only apathy now.

As they left the crowds behind they stopped in a street that was full of burned-out houses and Yeh held up his hand.

'I will find a boat,' he said. 'Wait here.'

They waited against the wall in one of the ruined corner properties while Yeh vanished. Just ahead of them they could see the glint of water and light flurries of snow against a leaden sky.

Yeh seemed to be away a long time and Willie shivered, uncertain whether it was with fear or the cold. Nadya stood close to him, and he could smell her perfume and the subtle fragrance she always seemed to carry with her. Kee's face looked grey and strained with anxiety. In the darkness they were worried they wouldn't find the *Lady Roberts*.

'Dobry vecher!'

The words made them swing round guiltily. At first they thought that the big figure in the dark clothes with the red star on his cap was Yeh, but it was a policeman, a flat-faced man with Mongol eyes. He wore a fur cap and stood with his feet apart, his thumbs hooked in his belt, and he was smiling.

Willie recognised him at once.

eight

'What are you doing here?'

The words were barked at them and Willie answered as calmly as he could. 'Looking for transport.'

'Where to?'

'The ship, *Simbang*. Registered at Tientsin. Chinese owned. We've unloaded coal.'

Willie's mind was working fast. If there were one person he didn't wish to see now, it was this particular policeman. He made as if to move away but a revolver appeared and he found himself looking down the muzzle.

'Stop! Halt! Nobody moves when Sergeant Mozhevsky tells them to stop.'

Willie held his breath. The poisonous Mozhevsky wouldn't fail to use his authority to stop what they were up to, he knew. He had clearly transferred his allegiance to the Bolsheviks as he had suggested he might.

'I have the authority to question everybody,' he was saying. 'The Cheka is fighting counter-revolution and sabotage. It's considered necessary for the survival of the country. They are right behind me.'

He moved closer, his eyes suspicious. Peering at Nadya, he grinned. 'Dobry vecher, baryshnia,' he said. 'Good evening, young lady.' He gestured at the suitcase. 'What's in that?' he demanded.

'Just clothes,' Willie said. 'The young lady's clothes. She's been spending the night with me and we're taking her back to her parents' house.'

'By sea?'

'They live down the coast.'

'Only a fool would travel by boat in weather like this, Tovarich. A fool – or a criminal. Open the case.'

Willie studied the policeman, wondering if he could silence him without being shot. He noticed that Mozhevsky's thumb was on the safety catch of the revolver and Mozhevsky looked so alert he couldn't imagine getting away with anything. He wondered if he might offer a bribe. Perhaps if he opened the case, the policeman might be persuaded to go away with part of its contents. On the other hand, he might want the lot, and if it came to a scuffle, they were all so heavily laden with valuables it would be impossible to handle him.

'I think you are a thief,' Mozhevsky said, pointing the revolver at Willie's head. 'You,' he said to Kee. 'Against the wall with your hands above your head. Take the baryshnia with you. This is the one I suspect as the ringleader.'

'Now, comrade,' he grinned. 'I think I know you. Policemen have good memories. Which is why I'm a sergeant now. I've met you before, haven't I? I remember you from when you were working with the Imperialist British against the Supreme Soviet.' He glanced at Nadya. 'And this, I suspect, knowing you, is some bourzhuki criminal you're about to smuggle out of the country.' The revolver lifted. 'Perhaps a bullet through the head will settle things, eh?'

He stepped forward, but as he did so there was a movement behind him, like a shadow appearing from deeper shadows. A gloved hand was slapped over the policeman's face so that he couldn't shout and as his head was jerked back, there was the flash of a sailor's knife and a red slit appeared across his throat with a horrifying gush of blood.

'Oh, Christ,' Willie said, and Nadya turned away, her face in her hands.

Kee was standing petrified against the wall, his hands still in the air. Willie swallowed and forced himself to recover.

'Put 'em down, George,' he said.

Yeh hadn't spoken. He wiped the knife, bent over the policeman who was still making gurgling noises at his feet and, taking the revolver from his hand, hit him on the head with it so that he became limp and silent. Stuffing the revolver into his pocket, he took Mozhevsky's feet and indicated that Willie should take his shoulders. Between them they carried him into one of the sour-smelling, burnt-out houses and dumped him there among the scraps of paper fluttering in the breeze, the old cans and bottles and the stink of human excrement.

Straightening up, Yeh gestured to them to follow. He had a rowing boat tied up alongside the quay, a man waiting at the oars. Scrambling down the green slime-covered steps, they fell into it and Yeh pushed off.

It was dark now and the overcast sky was growing darker by the minute. They had not gone more than a hundred yards from the quayside when it dawned on Willie that they were lost. The man on the oars kept turning his head and Yeh was peering out to sea, frowning. They could see the riding lights of ships in the bay but, with the darkness, the outlines of the vessels had disappeared and there was nothing to indicate which was the *Lady Roberts*.

It started to snow. Willie could feel the flakes on his face and he reached out and touched Nadya's hand. The cold seemed to strike up from the water and the wind had got up a little, to fling chilling wisps of spray over the bow. In no time they were all half-frozen and Yeh was muttering curses to himself in an undertone.

Willie's mind was clamped in an agony of anxiety. If they were found wandering around the harbour the following morning, one of the harbour boats operated by the Cheka would want to know why they had been out at night. And then they'd find the body of Mozhevsky and that would be the end of that. He glanced at Nadya, but it was impossible to see anything more of her face than a white blur. Perhaps the Cheka couldn't touch him or Kee or Yeh, because they weren't Russian nationals, but he dreaded to think what would happen to Nadya. The fear that the new Communist paradise would be overturned by subversion made them merciless. He was feeling weak with fear for her when suddenly Yeh thrust out an arm. 'There,' he said. 'That's the *El Malek Fouad*. She's an Egyptian ship and she was right behind us.'

The old man on the oars was half-collapsing with exhaustion and cold now and Willie and Yeh took his place, grabbing an oar each. In no time they came up under the overhanging stern of the *Lady Roberts* and for the first time since he'd owned her Willie regarded her with warmth. As the oars clattered in the rowlocks, a shout came from the deck and a torch shone on the ship's ladder rigged over the side. They manoeuvred alongside with some difficulty because the tide was pushing the boat away from the ship, but they made it at last and Kee grasped the ladder with a frozen hand.

Shipping his oar, Willie made fast the bow line and helped Nadya to the ladder. She was petrified with cold and could barely stand, but he managed to get her to the deck, followed by Kee and Yeh and the old boatman.

In the ship's ancient saloon, rum was produced and Willie sat Nadya on a bench and held the glass to her white lips.

As she swallowed the spirit, she began to cough and splutter but it seemed to bring her round. Then the cook appeared with a pot of soup. Though it was foul and smelled of cabbage, it was hot and brought colour back to their cheeks.

'We should be leaving,' Yeh said. 'We don't want to be here when that policeman's found and questions are asked.'

They remembered the old boatman, whom they could hardly take with them, but he had ignored the soup and gone for the rum and he was in a happy state of indifference and told them that if they put him in his boat with a bottle of what he'd been drinking, he'd survive without trouble.

They filled a bottle from the rum cask and handed him a jar of the soup and half a loaf to take with him, then Willie gave him his overcoat to put over the ragged garment he was wearing. As he shoved money in his hand, the old man left happily and headed for the ladder.

'I shall be all right, Gospodin Captain,' he said cheerfully. 'I'll fill myself with the booze and drift with the tide until daylight then make for the shore.'

As he vanished astern into the darkness, the winch started to clatter and the ship began to head for the open sea.

Yeh gave up his cabin for Nadya. She was shivering, her fingers icy, and Willie undressed her quickly and lifted her to the bunk. She looked at him with enormous eyes, touching his cheek with her fingertips.

'Don't go, my William,' she begged. 'Stay with me.'

Clutching her in the dark, he heard her whispering. 'Sometimes, when it was very bad,' she was saying, 'I went to the church. I found the words of the final prayer after the Dies Irae and the Agnus Dei very comforting. I sang them to myself.' Her voice changed and he realised she was chanting the Latin words. 'Pax aeterna dona eis, Domine, et lux aeterna luceat ei...'

For a long time after that she said nothing, clutching him with tensed fingers as though afraid he would slip away and she would lose him. 'It was the dark chasm of death that frightened me,' she whispered eventually. 'But if death meant dwelling in eternal light I decided I could reconcile myself to dying. It was the thought also that one day I'd meet you again that helped.'

The journey across the sea of Japan was uneventful, but, as they passed the Tsushima Islands and continued south-west past the Cheju Straits, leaving Shanghai on their starboard bow, a small twinge of guilt struck Willie. Thank God, he thought, that Abigail was in America.

He was committed now and he persuaded himself that he was only rescuing someone who was in danger of disappearing into one of the Cheka's concentration camps. He knew it wasn't merely that, though, because he had spent the nights in the big captain's bunk that Yeh used. Yeh had said nothing, merely moving his belongings into the mate's cabin, while the mate disappeared into the bosun's cabin and the bosun moved in with the ship's carpenter.

Hong Kong came up at last, Victoria Peak lifting out of the mist, then the deeply indented shores of the mainland and finally the white buildings of the harbour and the uneven tops of the new office blocks and the distant roofs of the hill properties.

Like Shanghai's waterfront, the harbour was jammed with sampans, tall Foochow junks gliding with unerring skill through the other vessels. A P & O liner lay alongside the main quay, preparing to leave, her decks brightened by the colourful clothes of her passengers. Passing her on the way to Macao was a squat ferry edging slowly into the stream.

Simbang, née *Lady Roberts,* lay out of the mainstream of shipping and they went ashore by sampan accompanied by George Kee, who was to negotiate a cargo and then travel back with the ship to Shanghai. A cool monsoon wind was blowing, keeping the temperature away from the humidity with which the port was plagued, yet the sun was brilliant, making the water glitter with diamond points and the white buildings ashore glow as if under a searchlight. They found a taxi at once and Willie pushed Nadya into it with her suitcase and a box containing the *objets d'art* they had brought away in their pockets.

They found a hotel, not the best but somewhere modest, because she preferred to be where it was quiet and where questions wouldn't be asked. It had a shabby Edwardian façade and a creaking lift with clashing grills and slowmoving fans in every room. It had been built for comfort, however, and the room they were given was light and airy and there was a balcony which gave a panoramic view of the rooftops of Wanchai and the tall buildings of Hong Kong and the Peak. Across the blue water of the harbour, covered with ships of every kind and nationality, was the waterfront of Kowloon with a view of the bare hills of the mainland.

Willie had always thought Hong Kong beautiful, with its mountains running down to the water and the green coves full of sand. It was a prosperous place, a useful outlet for Chinese produce and a useful channel for trade in gold and narcotics and, for that matter, for the agents the new Russia enjoyed passing out to the Western nations. Chinese from the mainland were always crossing the frontier, weeping with happiness as they arrived in the great Western centre, where they could earn better money in the sweat shops the Chinese and European tycoons had opened to produce cheap goods for Europe.

They spent the afternoon buying Hong Kong-made boxes, neat, attractive and leather-covered, and carefully placing in them what they'd brought from Vladivostok and wrapping them with tissue paper. They took a lot of trouble because they were to become Nadya's stock, her capital, what she was going to have to live on until she could get herself established.

For once, though, she would be unable to call on Abigail's expertise and would have to work on her own. She couldn't even pass anything on to Brassard because Abigail saw his accounts and would inevitably spot items which she herself had not sent. But Nadya had a shrewd judgement of beautiful things, too, because she had lived with them all her life and she decided she could handle her own affairs.

'There is enough to keep me for some time,' she said. 'But I must acquire a small premises with a room over it to live in, somewhere among Europeans because Europeans will be my customers. Then I shall spend time going round the shops and studying values until I know how much I must charge.'

There was a dreamlike quality about the few days Willie spent with her. They were registered at the hotel as Mr and Mrs Kourganov and nobody queried the fact that Willie always spoke English. They dined in the waterfront restaurants and wandered through the narrow streets, the bright yellow and red banners billowing over their heads, splashes of vivid colour alongside the Chinese characters painted on the shop walls. An occasional English matron staying at the hotel attempted to get them into conversation for no other reason, they knew well, than to satisfy her curiosity, but Willie had no wish to be recognised because shipping often took him to Hong Kong and it was amazing how news could flash along the China Coast by the bamboo grapevine.

At the end of the week, they had found a small place with a tiny flat above, between the Chinese quarter and the British shopping area, a small select-looking place which had once sold dresses, its décor and furnishings adequate until better could be provided. The walls and carpeting were pink and there were even pink curtains at the window. They found a Chinese carpenter who hurriedly knocked up a glass-topped showcase and installed a safe, and hired a Chinese girl as an assistant. A Chinese sign painter hoisted his steps into the window, and at the end of the day they stood back and stared delightedly at the words A N *Kourganov*, curving elegantly across the glass.

'You're in business again,' Willie said.

He had written her a cheque for a thousand pounds, but had not gone with her to deposit it in the bank in case he was recognised.

'It's a small gift to tide you over until you get going,' he explained.

'A loan,' Nadya insisted.

'I don't want repaying.'

'Which is all the more reason why I *must* repay. You have a wife.'

The reminder of Abigail was disturbing, and it kept coming back in a thousand and one ways. He had gone into the affair with his eyes open, however, and he knew there was no going into reverse.

'I shall have to go back to her,' he admitted.

'Do you wish to?'

He thought for a while. 'Yes,' he admitted. 'I do. I want to.'

'Then that is as it should be.'

'I'll come and see you again, though.'

'There is no need to. You've done enough for me.'

'I come to Hong Kong at least twice a year.'

'I shall always be pleased to see you. My house, small as it is now, will always be open to you.'

She didn't see him off when he boarded the coaster for Shanghai, and staring back at the flat façade of the water-front, the old feeling of guilt returned. Though he dearly wanted to see Abigail again, he was also afraid of what might happen when he did.

PART FOUR

1923–1939

one

Abigail returned soon after Willie reached Shanghai. She greeted him warmly.

'No,' he said in answer to her questions. 'Nothing much happened.'

Lying was becoming easy, but falsehood had always been part of business and he had been in business long enough now to accept that the truth was never the whole truth and nothing but the truth. There was usually a little to be discreetly hidden, a little more to say than need be said, otherwise business would never flourish.

Abigail's trip had been successful and Polly had confessed her fondness for young Elliott Wissermann and seemed ready to marry him as soon as he plucked up sufficient courage to ask her.

'He'll make a good husband,' Abigail confided. 'He'll be running his father's business at Yangpo before long and he seems to be getting on well with Edward, whose ship's stationed up there now. It all seems to be working out well.'

She paused and Willie glanced at her. 'Except for Tom,' he said.

His son Thomas worried him a little. Not because he was wild or difficult. Quite the contrary. He was a hard-working student who was doing well at the university. Very often, in fact, he brought home information from his friends there that helped his father in what was a growing climate of unrest in the Chinese quarter of the city. He seemed to know ahead of anyone else what was going to happen and usually he was right. The fact that he was a help to Willie was offset by the feeling that he was getting into the wrong company.

Abigail had thought about it, too, but her reaction was different. 'He's at the age when he feels deeply about things,' she said. 'Most people do when they're young. If they don't they have no heart.'

'And if they go on when they grow up,' Willie growled, 'they have no head.'

'He'll be all right. He only needs to settle down. He will before long. He's still crazy about Chan Fan-Su.'

Willie frowned. He saw nothing wrong in Tom's fondness for the Chinese girl. Mixed marriages might be frowned on by the wives of the taipans of the European community, but they often worked and he didn't give a damn, anyway, for the opinions of the British wives because he knew that a lot of their husbands, like Gerald Honeyford, for instance, supported Chinese girls, who gave them the opportunity to get away from the starchy atmosphere of the transplanted British suburb that their wives enjoyed.

He was reluctant to abandon his protest, nevertheless.

'He has some strange friends,' he said.

'Chinese, of course.'

'Of course.' Willie was trying to sound as if he'd been busy in Shanghai. 'Some of them very political Chinese, too. That chap, Chou, he brought home. I've heard he established a branch of the Chinese Communist Party in

Paris when he was there and now he's been appointed secretary of the Kwantung Province Branch of the Chinese Party in Canton and chairman of the political department of Chiang K'Ai-Shek's Whampoa academy.'

Abigail frowned. 'When the Communists and the Nationalists co-operate, Willie, it's not a good thing for us.'

'Nothing that Chinese politicians of any colour or creed do is a good thing for us,' he admitted.

Abigail's words, spoken so gravely so long before, had never left him, and the more he thought about them, the more he had come to the conclusion that she was right. Though he had never met a Shanghailander who was prepared to admit it, *they* were the foreigners, the white Chinese, yet to a large extent they were running the country.

'The one thing they want to see,' he agreed, 'is the back of us. Japs first, because they're the greediest, but in the end the rest of us will follow.'

It had been obvious for a long time that the Chinese were at last beginning to realise their own strength. The atmosphere had begun to change, subtly and probably not very obviously to many of the Europeans, but to Willie, with his ear closer to the ground through the crews of his ships, it seemed clear that the Chinese had finally decided it was time they took a hand in the running of their own country. Incidents – usually small and unimportant – had begun to multiply until not a day went by without some trivial but – to anyone who took the trouble to think about it – ominous occurrence being reported in the newspapers.

The tension seemed to increase with every week that passed and, driving to his office or to one of his ships, moored alongside with clattering winches and swinging derricks, Willie was increasingly conscious of it. It was as if the Chinese – almost as one man – had decided it was time for action, and coolie labour for the loading and unloading of ships was becoming more and more difficult to hire.

'The students are behind it, George,' he announced to Kee as they sat at his desk brooding over the new problem. 'There's going to be trouble.'

The truth of the remark was proved soon afterwards when a dispute at a Japanese-owned cotton mill in the Chinese area of Chapei ended in a flurry of fists and the killing of a workers' representative by the Japanese foreman.

The North China Daily News' headlines on the case were frightening, not so much to the European businesses but because of the implied threat to individuals. The workman had been a Communist and the streets were filled with angry Chinese posters demanding apologies, restitution, even the disappearance of the Japanese. In their house near the Bubbling Well Road they could hear the yells as the students swarmed on to the streets in protest.

Nobody was hurt, but a British car was overturned and its occupants manhandled.

'What do you expect, Father?' Thomas asked calmly. 'This is China and the Japanese behave as if it's *their* country.'

Willie listened to him with a grim face. It was going to be difficult for some time until the anger died down, he knew, because there were always strikes and protests. The place seemed to live on protests, and, sure enough, a few days later Thomas appeared with news that the students had called for a massive anti-Japanese demonstration.

'Not in the old town,' he explained. 'Here in the International Settlement. So *we* can see it, as well as the Chinese.'

'Are you going to be there?' Willie asked. 'You're still a student.'

Thomas gave a sheepish grin. 'They might not welcome me.'

'You can't get away from the colour of your skin, son,' Willie pointed out dryly. 'No matter how much you sympathise with them. Are you a Communist?'

'No, Father. Perhaps I'm a Socialist, but not a Communist. I'm in favour of equality, of course, because I have feelings and there's too much influence among the established classes, and far too much here from money. But I'd never be prepared to go as far as they've gone in Russia.'

'Perhaps *that's* not Communism, Tom. Perhaps that's just a dictatorship of power-hungry politicians, and you get those at all levels.'

On the day of the demonstration, Willie closed the office and sent everyone home for safety. By mid-morning the streets had filled with students, all shouting slogans and waving banners so that the traffic came to a standstill and all trade stopped. Watching from his office, Willie saw the police appear in a convoy of cars and spill out. As they began to lash out with clubs and drag screaming youngsters from the mob, his eyes narrowed and his mouth tightened into a grim line. Abigail's fears came back to him and he was glad he had begun to transfer capital to London.

As the students were jammed into cars, buses, vans and taxis – anything on wheels, it seemed – the mob's fury increased and before the afternoon was done the whole population of the old city appeared to be on the streets, odd ripples of the rioting swirling back and forth across the bund. From his office, Willie tried to monitor what was happening.

'They've surrounded the Louza police station.' George Kee, who was in touch with a contact on the newspaper, put down the telephone and turned to Willie. 'They've taken the arrested students there.' He managed a nervous smile. 'It seems to have got a little out of hand.'

During the early evening, they heard shots and, soon afterwards, Thomas arrived in the office. He was breathless and there was blood on his shirt.

'Father, can't you stop it?' he yelled.

'Stop what, son, for God's sake?'

'Some bloody fool ordered the police to fire on the crowd and they've killed a couple of hundred.'

'That many?'

'Well, I saw some bodies. About a dozen.'

'That's better, boy. But there's nothing I can do about it. I'm not a politician.'

The storm of fury that the killings started was not just local. *The North China News* announced that the Communists had formed an Action Committee and that there were to be demonstrations in Tientsin, Hangchow, Peking and a dozen other places, and that a Workers' General Union had been set up.

'Two hundred thousand members here, Ab,' Willie pointed out grimly. 'That's just about every worker in Shanghai. They're going to carry some punch. Things aren't ever going to be quite the same again.'

The punch was felt at once. As the Shanghai businessmen held panic meetings to condemn the killings and decide what could be done, the city came to a stop in the best organised strike they'd ever seen. Shops shut, street cars halted, even the rickshaw boys vanished from the streets. Students swarmed everywhere, many of them armed with sticks, intimidating anyone who dared try to defy the strike. News from the south indicated that even in Hong Kong the strikers had brought the place to a halt. The name Hong Kong meant Fragrant Harbour, but without coolies to attend to the menial tasks, the atmosphere was less fragrant than stinking. Some of the strikers had even moved up the Pearl River to Canton, to spread the movement there, certain of support because Canton was the seat of the southern government and the core of Chiang K'Ai-Shek's resistance movement against the 'foreign devils'.

Inevitably, there was an incident and it was obvious that the students had worked things so that there would be, driving the coolies to a frenzy of hatred with their slogans and demands for action, until the hard-pressed foreign troops had been forced to use their weapons for their own safety. Finally, the crowd demonstrating against the foreign concessions were fired on by British, French and Portuguese gunboats and two hundred people were killed or injured. In retaliation, the workers had simply organised a blockade of all goods from Hong Kong and established tribunals to beat up, even kill, any Chinese, of no matter what class, who tried to defy them.

'It seems to me,' Willie said grimly, 'that those changes we began to expect have already started happening.'

The effect of the troubles began to be felt immediately by foreign businesses. A few nervous operators pulled out to set up again in places like Singapore, Penang, Java and India, and as trading slowed, Willie heard that Wishart's were in trouble. The stories going round the Shanghai Club indicated that Henry Moberley, once apparently so secure in office as manager and husband to Emmeline, had disappeared and that Emmeline was thinking of marrying a man called Barnaby, who was her new manager. There had been rumours about Wishart's for some time and now the general belief was that they might not last long enough to enjoy whatever skill Emmeline's new husband might have. Their credit was still good, however, but only just, and people were beginning to look askance at them and trying to avoid doing business in case they found themselves landed with bad debts.

Emmeline herself had changed. She had lost weight and seemed to be all bones, angles and contours these days. Willie saw her occasionally, but she always looked straight through him as if he didn't exist. Then she disappeared and they learned that, for the sake of economy, she had given up her big house and moved away.

Chinese politics, for the most part beyond the Europeans in Shanghai, who weren't very interested, anyway, seemed to consist of assassinations and treachery. Since the death of Sun Yat-Sen, the two governments, one in Peking, one in Canton, seemed to draw further apart, and there was the beginning of a marked advancement to power of Chiang K'Ai-Shek, who suddenly started to wage a war of words on the warlords who had preyed on China since 1911. He was now the master of Canton and more than one warlord in the vicinity had decided that the old Chinese proverb, 'The soundest of the sixty-six principles of waging war is to run away', was a good one and had set off for a long holiday in Japan, Singapore or even the South of France.

Occasionally Willie heard from Nadya, but her letters were always addressed to his office, marked personal, and placed quietly on his desk by George Kee without comment. She had quickly established herself, as he knew she would, and every six months when the Sarth Shipping Line took him to Hong Kong, he called on her, discussed her business and stayed with her. There were no questions, no dispute about it. He simply arrived and that was that.

Abigail had noticed the absence of the antiquities and treasures from Russia and assumed that Nadya, who had put so many of them her way, had simply gone out of business with the revolution. Occasionally she asked Willie what had happened to her and he put on a show of not knowing. Then, in 1926, on a business trip to Hong Kong, she returned and announced that she had discovered where she was.

Willie had frozen with horror, but Abigail showed no resentment.

'No wonder I've had nothing for some time,' she said. 'Your Nadya Kourganova has set up in business on her own.'

Willie held his breath, wondering what she had discovered, but she went on cheerfully. 'I saw the name on the window and went in,' she said. 'Willie, she's beautiful.'

Willie pretended indifference, aware that Abigail was too shrewd to be deluded. But she still seemed unaffected.

'When the revolution came one of the commissars took over her business and she had to leave Russia. She had a stock of things for me, but decided to use them to start in business herself. I'm told down there that she's considered quite an expert.'

'You talked to her?' Willie hardly dared frame the words.

'Oh, yes. We had tea together and talked for a long time. She's charming.'

Willie's tenseness subsided. Thank God, he said under his breath. Obviously Nadya had been guarded in what she had said and had not implicated him in her escape from Russia so that Abigail was under the impression she had managed it on her own. Perhaps she would never know the truth. Perhaps she didn't want to. Perhaps, even, she was just too honest to suspect anyone of anything she wouldn't do herself. On the other hand – he eyed her warily – Abigail was no fool and, in her trips about the world, she had endured more than one pass at her from a man attracted by her good looks. Perhaps she did know, after all. He was in a quandary, lost in a morass of conflicting thoughts, so that he never quite knew whether to feel guilty or proud.

He must be one of the luckiest of men alive, he decided. He had two women and both of them considered that he – Willie Sarth, who was without doubt a liar and a cheat – was God's gift to womenkind. Neither of them made demands on him, both trusted him, and he knew he could trust both of them in return. He was, he thought, faintly bemused by the idea, like having two wives.

Young Wissermann had missed Polly while she was in the States and had finally plucked up courage to ask her to marry him. The ceremony was held in the Cathedral and the reception seemed to include everybody who was anybody in Shanghai. The Wissermanns had wanted it to be held at the Balalaika and had been startled at the vehemence of Willie's 'No'. The place had changed its location, expanded and was now considered among the best in Shanghai, because Yip Hsao-Li, probably wanting a place of his own where he could foxtrot, waltz and tango to his heart's desire, had put money into the business and expanded it into a place where tea dances and evening affairs were part of the programme. Despite the arguments, despite even Polly's pleading, Willie refused to consider it, refusing even to explain why. It almost caused a rift between him and the Wissermanns, but then the matter was dropped abruptly and he suspected that Abigail had explained something he had been unable to explain, because Yip's partner and manager, Zychov, was Nadya's husband.

Half a dozen nationalities were represented at the wedding, and Abigail, in pale blue, was tremulously pleased with the result. Among the hard-headed business types who had to be invited were a few of Thomas' student friends, including the luscious Chan Fan-Su and her family, Edward's navy associates in uniform, and a whole crowd of Americans who had arrived especially for the occasion from the west coast of America. Old Wissermann, a long, lean man with a pale face and grey hair, had settled what seemed to be an enormous sum of money on his son.

'Can't let 'em be short, hey?' he said.

To Willie, who had grown up knowing what being short meant, he seemed to be in danger of spoiling them.

'My boy's a lucky guy,' Wissermann went on. 'Still I guess your daughter hasn't done so badly either. We ought to see more of each other, William. We're in business in the same city but never see each other except at the Club. I'll have to put my wife on to your wife.'

Willie hoped he wouldn't, not because Wissermann wasn't a good and honest businessman, but because he did all the things that Willie chose not to do – play golf, go to church and attend all the edifying lectures and meetings that were held.

There seemed an enormous number of loud-voiced women with mouths that were vivid slashes of lipstick, all discussing Paris, where the honeymoon was to be spent.

'Why Paris?' Willie asked Abigail. 'What's wrong with China?'

After all, he thought, Hong Kong compared favourably with anywhere in the world, the Peak sparkling with light at night, the illuminations reflected in the black water where the unending ferries and native vessels plied backwards and forwards like shiny bugs.

'Or what's wrong with Penang?' he persisted. 'Or Macassar? Or Java. This part of the world has far more beautiful places than Europe.'

He had come to know them all – places that sang of adventure: Penang, rising precipitously from the water's edge crag on crag of naked rock jutting out from the green vegetation and surrounded by the deep blue of the Indian Ocean; Java, its creeks crowded with prahus waiting for the tide to work their way up to Soerabaya; Tananarive in Madagascar; Quantico; Macassar, the great emporium of the East, exporting sandalwood and beeswax from Flores and Timor, trepang from the Gulf of Carpentaria, oil of Cajuputi from Bouru, nutmegs, spices and pepper from the Spice Islands, mussoi bark from New Guinea; Zanzibar, where you could smell the cloves a mile offshore; Mombasa, where the skeletons back of Bagamoyo showed where the Arab slavers had murdered black men and women.

'They know the East,' Abigail pointed out gently to him. 'They want to go somewhere new. Everyone wants to go to Paris once in their lives.'

'I don't.'

'I did. And I've been. Leave it to them.'

When the newlyweds returned, they moved up to Yangpo, where young Wissermann had been manager of his father's interests. Wissermann had given his son a house there and Abigail, who'd been helping her daughter buy furniture, was going up on the three-decker, *Fan Ling*, to help them settle in. Willie saw them off, promising to join them within a month. Firecrackers were set off and paper serpentines were thrown from the ship until it began to pull away from the quay, and he watched it until it faded into the mist, then he turned abruptly and headed along the quay to step aboard the *Lady Roberts* bound for Hong Kong.

He had not forgotten the *Lady Roberts*. It was almost as if he felt gratitude to the old ship for the way she had brought Nadya out of Russia, but, in addition, he realised, despite their attitude of derision towards her, she had always been one of the Sarth Line's best earners. The function of a fleet of merchant ships was to close the physical gap of marine space in the economy between production and consumption, and of the tramp steamers that supplied the need most were owned by British companies carrying heavy and bulky commodities. With the British coalfields behind them, they had the advantage of always being able to obtain outward cargoes of coal so that they didn't have to go out in ballast. 'Coal out, grain home' was the cry.

Over the years, however, Willie had learned to compete with them and was careful to arrange his charters so that his ships moved around the East minimising ballast voyages and following the seasonal shifts in supply and demand, and tried to terminate the voyages where he could secure another cargo. His ships carried rubber, tea, coffee, tobacco, cotton, jute, palm oil, grain, Malayan tin, timber and iron ore for Japan. In the Eastern waters, where communities found it difficult to reach each other, ships were useful and he had taken care to develop his trade among the islands that needed seaborne cargoes to get rid of their flax, hemp, copra and vegetable oils, so that his vessels plied between the Chinese mainland, the Philippines, the Dutch East Indies, the Pacific Islands and Malaya, always with one eye on the Australian wheat season, because wheat always took ships southward in winter. The Dutch East Indies alone had 3,000 islands across an area covering 3,500 miles and a population of 100,000,000, and if ships didn't operate on schedule it could be difficult, even fatal, for the island populations.

The whole basis of shipping was exactitude, and he based his passenger schedules on the fact that businessmen needed to rely on them. For this reason, and with his growing attachment to the *Lady Roberts*, he had decided to fit her out as a cargo-passenger steamer.

She had always proved a bit of a surprise in that her engine had never let them down, so he had her cleaned from stem to stern, overhauled and re-equipped to carry a dozen first class passengers, a horde of deck passengers and a cargo, and had sat back to watch her become one of the Sarth Line's assets.

He climbed aboard her now, pleased with her appearance, enjoying the brass and the white paint. As he reached the deck, John Yeh, given the ship as a token of gratitude for his part in the Vladivostok adventure, came forward to greet him. He never smiled, never gave much away in the manner of words, but he was always loyal and accepted Willie, a fully qualified master now with a certificate and sufficient sea time behind him, as an equal.

Heading for the first class cabin which was always kept for him when he wished to travel, Willie reflected that the Sarth Line was still growing. It now consisted of ten ships, from 750 tons dead weight to the 2,500 tons of the *Apu Shani*, and the *Tahaf*, the latest additions, which he had bought from a firm running from Ceylon. He seemed to have a gift for knowing when someone was needing to get rid of some of his assets and, though the Sarth Line ships were all small and some of them shabby, they continued to make a steady profit. As he had often said, they would never be mail steamers, never Glen Line or P & O, but they were doing a steady trade and he had noticed that lately they were being trusted occasionally with specie or bank notes, something which had led to him having grilles fixed round the bridge and the entrance to the engine rooms, because pirates were still busy along the coast.

Nadya was waiting for him, more beautiful than ever. Her shop had acquired an air of graciousness and prosperity now and she was clearly happy at the way things had turned out. But the strained look in her eyes had returned and he knew something was wrong.

'My husband has found me,' she said.

Willie's eyes became cold and hard. 'What happened?'

'He turned up on the doorstep.'

'I hope you shot him.'

She managed a laugh. But it died quickly. Zychov had asked for money. As usual, he had spent more than he was worth and was short of capital.

'Why doesn't he ask for it from Yip?' Willie snapped. 'They're in business together. Was Yip here with him?'

'He said he was. He said they had come to attend to some affairs of theirs.'

Willie drew a deep breath. 'Nadya, did you give him anything?'

'Yes.'

'That doesn't make sense, Nadya. I didn't give you that money so you could pass it on to him.'

'I didn't pass on your money, William.' Her voice was suddenly cold. 'I passed on my own. Money I had earned here.'

Willie was taken aback by her anger. 'Nadya,' he said. 'Do you still love him?'

'No.'

'But you're still concerned for him?'

'He was my husband.'

'I'm your lover!'

Somehow, they managed to settle their quarrel, but it brought a little cold wind between them. She swore Zychov meant nothing to her, that the only man in her life was Willie, but, remembering Zychov, hating him as he had never hated anyone because he had once left him to die and was his rival for Nadya's affections, he wasn't sure if he could believe her.

But he was an easygoing man for the most part and, somehow, they managed to get back on an even keel and talk instead about her business. She was already doing well, she said. 'I can run it with one assistant,' she insisted, 'and that's enough for a middle-aged woman.'

'You're not middle-aged,' Willie protested.

'I'm no longer young and neither are you. I'm prepared to settle for calm.'

They made love that night and somehow, perhaps because there had been that period of anger, it was more passionate than ever and he reminded her of her words.

'With you,' she said, 'it's different. With you, it's always different.'

She talked freely about meeting Abigail so that he found it hard to understand that two women, both of whom claimed to love him, could be so naive. How could they accept each other, each knowing perfectly well that the other must constitute a challenge? It was one of the mysteries of the female mind he would never understand. He still found it hard to accept that he was a man with a wife and a mistress, because that situation had always seemed to him as a young man to be one which was reserved only for sophisticates, magnates of great wealth, Chinese taipans, the aristocracy and Frenchmen. He'd heard of this sort of thing happening before, where wives and mistresses accepted each other, each happy to concede the other had something to give, but he found it hard to believe that such a situation existed in his case. Abigail was never the woman to accept an intruder and Nadya had never seemed the person to accept another woman who might undermine her position. But it was a situation that did exist and he tried not to think about it too much.

Returning to Shanghai, he took the *Fan Ling* upstream. She looked top-heavy with her three tiers of decks and a black and red funnel blowing its siren at the tiny river craft. The Yangtze Kiang was known to the Chinese as the Ta Chiang, or Great River, and changed its name more than once over its three thousand miles as it ran from

Tibet into China; first the River of Golden Sand, then the Kinsha Kiang, then, as it deepened and boiled through its gorges to reach the sea, the Yangtze Kiang.

The channel was marked with buoys, the banks on either side dancing in a haze, then the banks rose and the scenery unfolded and the countryside came alive. Roofs peeped over the bund, some with green tiles, others of untidy rush matting. Water buffalo wallowed in cool mud under the trees, a train of pack ponies appeared, then a wheelbarrow loaded with a family of ten.

They overtook the crew of a junk bending double as they hauled on a thick rope of bamboo fibre with which they worked the vessel upstream. As it surged in the steamer's wash, it threw the panting men on their faces, then sank back, dragging them off their feet, so that a child sitting on the broad back of a buffalo burst into laughter at their antics. Fishermen working their nets from the end of long bamboo jetties looked up as the steamer passed. The river was always busy, the junks sailing in small convoys as a protection against warlord soldiers turned pirates. A motor vessel towing strings of other junks against the current was barely making headway, but the passengers were enjoying the trip and showing none of the impatience Europeans showed. At night the breeze dropped and the opposite bank became a low purple line across water that was beginning to reflect a yellow moon, and the lights on deck brought the ping of mosquitoes as they became the target for clouds of insects.

As the ship passed through a series of lakes, the edges of what seemed to be mats of floating weed twitched nervously as if under a flirt of breeze, then, as the ship approached, they broke up, followed by the beat of wings and the spatter of webbed feet on water, and the air echoed to harsh cries as clouds of duck whirred and creaked overhead.

A junk swung abruptly across the *Fan Ling*'s bow amid furious shouting from the ship's officers. The manoeuvre was to cut off the demons which the junk's crew believed they towed behind them. If their own bows were crossed, they too would collect demons, but now, having rid themselves of their unwelcome passengers, they let off fireworks and hammered gongs because Chinese demons were not very bright and, hating noise, could be put off trying to return.

Yangpo came up at last, a large city now, with the oil tanks clearly visible. A Japanese warship was anchored in midstream, close to an ocean-going cargo ship with a grey funnel. The buildings along the bund had grown taller, beyond them the smoke haze of the Chinese city. It always seemed strange to Willie to see ships eight hundred miles from the sea.

The heat shimmered on the dusty bund, the mountain behind hazy blue. Near the landing jetties where the clubs and brothels were situated, sailors in white shorts and black boots looked like small boys going to a party. The railway from Peking ran through and, as the ship came to a stop, a train arrived, heavily-built, grey and ugly, shooting steam into the air.

To Willie's surprise it was a rickshaw that met him, not Da Braga's automobile. The Portuguese shrugged.

'No petrol,' he said.

'Why not, Luis?'

'Something's in the wind. There was plenty of it and now there's none. Student trouble in the south, I think. It comes up in forty gallon drums, but the junks that carry them aren't sailing.'

There had been a few sporadic outbreaks of shouting along the bund and the matshed roof of the market place had been set on fire, but not much else. A new warlord was on the warpath, but nobody expected much in the way of trouble because all it meant, if he succeeded, was transferring the squeeze, and squeeze was always allowed for in the overheads. Otherwise there seemed to be very little military movement in the area. Occasional groups of the old warlord's soldiers appeared on the bund, shabby, ill-clothed and bullying, and sampans were sometimes stolen to ferry them across the river, but otherwise their general was still established north of the city, with his officers, cars and women, and was nervously counting his money.

'Chiang K'Ai-Shek's declared war on him,' Da Braga said bluntly, plonking the brandy bottle on the table. 'He's letting it be known that if a warlord isn't for him and the Kuomin-tang, then he's against them, and our boy's growing worried because at the moment Chiang's the only one with any real power. His agents are everywhere, dishing out propaganda and increasing his influence. But at the moment nothing's happened beyond a minor riot over a murdered coolie and a few Chinese beheaded. Mind you that's a bad sign. There are always riots and executions when a warlord considers he's in danger.'

'Will he bolt?' A change of warlord always meant small adjustments in business.

Da Braga shrugged. 'He has a tug waiting with steam up,' he said. 'And that usually indicates a midnight flit. The value of his banknotes has fallen, too, because he's already got all the ready cash in the area in his coffers. I reckon it's about time for him to turn up as a merchant in Hong Kong.'

'What do people think?'

'They're worried. His disappearance would mean an army on the loose, hungry and with no prospect of cash, no discipline and no scruples, but plenty of arms and ammunition. That means a crime wave, because, even if they don't use the arms themselves, they can always sell them for others to use.'

'Has it affected business?'

'There are less people in the streets and shops put up shutters occasionally. A few of the rich Chinese have hired junks and disappeared. A few more will go, I suppose, and not come back until the troubles are over.'

Willie stared from the window. He had been in China long enough now to develop a second sense and, with an instinctive nose for danger, he sensed an ominous feel about the situation. The generals were shrewd, brutal men, and foul play had been part of the Chinese political scene for a long time, but now the revolutionary tenets of Sun Yat-Sen, enhanced by the success of the revolution in Russia, were taking hold. The old trinity of landlord, loan shark and merchant that had been supported by the warlords was beginning to feel the pinch and there was a feeling in the air that the old confrontations could no longer be settled with the exchange of courtesies and a few suitcases full of dollars. A general could no longer govern the entire province with his captains and colonels because the slogans that emanated from the south were stronger than money, even stronger than weapons, and the jockeying for control had changed to a wave that was moving inexorably northwards from its beginnings near the coast.

The first thing Abigail did when he appeared at the house was to inform him that the servants had left.

He stared about him angrily, almost as if he expected to find them hiding in corners. 'Why?' he demanded.

'They didn't say,' she pointed out calmly. 'They just didn't turn up. Polly says the same thing happened to her.'

'Is it a strike?'

'It doesn't appear to be, but I gather other people have had the same trouble.'

It worried Willie because the departed servants had been with them a long time, and that night when they saw fireworks in the Chinese City instead of the usual night-time silence, somehow it seemed ominous.

'Sounds like trouble down there,' Willie said.

By daylight, the noise from the city seemed to be growing louder and Willie was just on the point of heading for his office when Da Braga appeared on a bicycle.

'There's been a battle,' he said. 'I've just heard. It was chiefly with words and silver bullets, but our boy's gone – pulled out and headed south. We've got a new warlord.'

'So that's what the fuss was about? What about petrol?'

'There'll be no petrol here now. Not for some time. The students have decided not.' Da Braga gave a sad smile. 'The Kuomintang supporters fight a different way from the old warlords. They use words as well as guns, and they've persuaded the students that the KMT's the party to support and that they must do all they can to make things difficult for its enemies. Our petrol's vanished into the gutters.'

Telephones and radios and the warships anchored off the bund gave them the rest of the news. The warlords of the north had begun to feel that Chiang was growing too big for his boots and had decided that together they were strong enough to oppose anyone and anything, even General Chiang. Nevertheless, the situation called for an immediate meeting of all owners and managers of businesses in Yangpo, and Elliott Wissermann arrived in a rickshaw to ask Willie to make sure he would attend. 'I reckon it's beginning to look nasty,' he said.

'I reckon it is,' Willie agreed. 'You should take Polly downstream to Shanghai. Or at least let Ab take her. If there's trouble, this will be no place for her.'

'I'm not leaving Elliott,' Polly insisted.

'And I can't leave Yangpo,' Wissermann said.

'Have you been in touch with your father?'

'He says that if the Whites stick together the Chinks won't dare do a thing. Not with the gunboats in the river. Dammit, sir, there's a cruiser and three gunboats just off the bund. They wouldn't try anything on with that lot on the doorstep.'

As Willie had half-expected, the meeting degenerated into a squabble. One half was for packing up and leaving, while the other half jeered at them as cowardly. In the end, nothing was decided and it was agreed to wait and see. Saying nothing, Willie sat with Da Braga and his brandy bottle in his office making plans.

'What can go, Luis?' he asked. 'I'm not risking your life or the lives of your family just to stay in business. I've got interests elsewhere and we can just shut up shop here if necessary until it's all over.'

It was decided that, while the trouble remained small and didn't concern the Europeans, they would carry on as before, but that they would arrange things so that everything could be closed down at the drop of a hat or the first Kuomintang shell to fall in the city. Abigail was in total agreement and was already crating up valuables from the house to be shipped downstream. She was worried about Polly, nevertheless, especially as she'd just heard that she was pregnant.

'Already?' Willie said.

Abigail gave him a little smile. 'I was pregnant *before* we got married,' she reminded him.

The city was in a turmoil. The effects of the old warlord's disappearance were everywhere. Discovering it had been abandoned, his army had sallied from its quarters in search of food, pay and loot and were now moving about the streets, disorganised, sullen and ready for trouble, and the mob, feeling the situation was the fault of the foreigners, had come out and were raging about foreign rule.

The cobbles were littered with the useless banknotes and fluttering pamphlets of the previous incumbent as governor, and the shop windows that hadn't been boarded up had been broken. Even now, however, the hatred was directed chiefly at the Japanese. There was a big placard, 'GO HOME JAPANESE' fluttering above a yelling crowd of shaven Chinese skulls that looked like pebbles on a beach. A Japanese merchant's car was overturned and went up in a puff of smoke and a flower of red flame, and the Japanese owner had to run for his life, pelted with stones, brickbats and filth. A few more shop windows were whacked by carrying poles into shining splinters of glass and Chinese rent collectors began to gather on the bund waiting to be taken off, while sampans in a tight mass circled the Japanese cruiser, the students yelling abuse until the crew began to rig hoses to drive them away.

That night fires were started and spread to the business quarter, so that the whole bund was lit up. Cries and shouts floated across the water, sparks whirled up, and dim black figures ran to and fro in terror. Some jumped into the river and escaped, but some were caught and flung into the flames.

The following day everything was quiet. There were no students on the streets, no soldiers in the city, no noise, no shouting, no threats, just a solitary dead Chinese, the breeze blowing the dust on to his staring terrified eyes and playing with the flap on his tunic. The silence seemed unbelievable and the rent collectors and the old warlord dependants began to make their way back to their homes, hoping they hadn't been too much damaged.

'You can unpack your treasures,' Willie advised his wife.

'Not likely,' Abigail said stoutly.

'It's over, Ab. As usual, it's come to a stop.'

'For the time being.'

They continued with their task for a while, then Abigail straightened up. 'Did you know Emmeline's up here?' she asked.

'I heard her business is due to go up for sale,' Willie said. 'I even thought of making an offer, but I doubt if she'd entertain it. What's she doing?'

'Saving money. It's cheaper here.'

'She picked a hell of a time to arrive.'

Abigail was silent for a moment. When she spoke again it was quietly and slowly. 'I shall go and see her,' she said.

Willie's head jerked round. 'What in God's name for?'

'She's on her own.'

'What about this chap she took up with? – the latest.'

'He's on his way back to England. He said he didn't come to China to get murdered.'

Willie grinned. 'She does manage to pick 'em, doesn't she? But what's that to do with you?'

'She might need help if anything happens.'

'And you're going to offer it?'

'Why not?'

It startled Willie. Abigail had never shown any interest in his old enemy, even though he had guessed that, in her shrewd way, she had some idea of what the enmity was based on, and he found it hard to comprehend now that she was prepared to put herself out to help. But then, Abigail had always been an understanding person, always willing to help a lame dog, always compassionate, idealistic and Godfearing. He couldn't resist tossing out a warning that was not entirely humorous.

'She'll probably throw something at you.'

'At *you*,' Abigail corrected him. 'I doubt if she will at me.'

'You seem sure.'

'Women know these things.'

'Sweet suffering J! After the things she tried to do to me, too!'

'Why, Willie?' Abigail's face was innocent of guile. 'Why should she hate you so much?'

Willie realised he had almost put his foot in it. 'Various things,' he said. 'Long ago. Before I met you. I worked for her father. I think she thought she might marry me.'

'You could never keep out of trouble, could you?'

He took her in his arms and kissed her, less to reassure her than to stop her asking questions. 'Ab,' he said, meaning every word, 'I'm the luckiest of men.'

But, as he released her, he felt the old inevitable twinge of guilt that he had never been frank about Nadya and was still, even now, not being honest with her.

t w o

The unrest continued to cause gloom among the foreign
investors and their managers and staff. A few sent their
wives and families downstream but for the most part they
did nothing. The plans he had made with Da Braga
completed, Willie fell to helping Abigail in labelling and
parcelling their belongings. Polly arrived occasionally,
chiefly to complain that she was feeling nauseous, but she
steadfastly refused to accompany them downstream.

'My place is here with my husband,' she insisted.

'We're best out of here,' Abigail insisted. 'I've heard
they've chopped a few more heads off and that the
students have all joined the Kuomintang.'

'An American gunboat's arrived,' Polly said defiantly.

True enough, American sailors were on the bund,
excited and curious. They had an ancient machine gun
and seemed to think they had nothing to worry about, but
soon afterwards, a car belonging to one of the American
businessmen knocked over a fruit stall so that it collapsed
in a welter of baskets and rolling fruit and the proprietor
began to screech abuse and hammer the car with his fists.
A coolie was almost too quick to join him, bringing down
his carrying pole to whack a dent in the bonnet before the
unlucky American could get the vehicle into gear and bolt,

his klaxon honking like a rising duck in a panic. Within minutes a mob had gathered round the overturned fruit stall, arguing and yelling at the owner, then, as the American sailors fired a few rounds over their heads, they hitched up their blue cotton pants and moved off to set fire to a wooden warehouse.

'Jeeze,' one of the Americans said. 'Is it always like this?'

'Not always,' Willie said. 'Just from time to time.'

That evening, the vanished warlord's soldiers began to straggle out of the town, a horde of undisciplined men holding umbrellas and parasols, even wearing boaters to protect their heads against the sun. As they slogged by, their rifles slung anyhow, their equipment missing, their officers jogged past on shaggy ponies, followed by the ragtag and bobtail of the army, the wives and children and camp followers. Their artillery, a single Maxim, a .75 and two or three battered Russian guns, rattled behind them with the ox-carts containing the luggage and equipment.

'That's an army?' the American sailor said.

'Shall we say they're soldiers,' Willie corrected him.

'They couldn't fight their way out of Mom's apple pie.'

'That's only because they've got nothing to fight for and never have had,' Willie said. 'Give 'em that something, and you'll find they're different.'

'What would that something be, sir, you reckon?'

'Nationality, unity and a little pride in themselves.'

'They'll never get it. The Slopeheads aren't like that.'

Willie shrugged. 'I suspect it won't be long before they are,' he said.

The gloom that had already appeared in Yangpo had taken a good hold on Shanghai by the time Abigail and

Willie returned. The place was constantly being brought to a stop these days by demonstrations as the workers showed their loyalty to Chiang K'Ai-Shek's growing Kuomintang party. The mood had even spread to the immediate hinterland, where Kuomintang agents were producing a frenzy of excitement.

Chiang was promising now to clear up the mess in the north. He had decided that the agreement the warlords had made to stick together was not worth the paper it was written on – if it *was* written on paper – and he clearly thought that now was the time, while the European powers were preoccupied with the strikes and riots, to make his move.

It was the long-cherished but still unfulfilled dream of Sun Yat-Sen that one day the Revolution, armed and united, would march from its base in Canton and move inexorably northwards to rid the country of the warlords and their masters, the wealthy merchants, moneylenders and rent collectors, and, above all, of the foreign devils who had battened like leeches on to China and drained her of her prosperity.

'There's one thing,' Kee pointed out as they sat in Willie's office discussing the possibilities that the move might provoke, 'if he doesn't have the support of the Chinese merchants and the men who control the money in Shanghai, he certainly has the support of the peasants.'

'And the women, George,' Willie said. 'They're flocking to join him. In any capacity, even as soldiers.'

It wasn't hard to see why. In the pointless and savage little civil war that had been tearing China apart for two decades, women had always been regarded as mere chattels who could be dragged off, raped or simply butchered and left in the gutter. The newspapers were always full of harrowing details whenever a town was taken over.

But, curiously, the trouble which had started the unexpected alarm died down just as suddenly as it had come.

'The only bloody fighting they're doing is being done with words,' Willie said, puzzled because it was something that was entirely new. The warlords had often negotiated but had always managed to retire full of wealth. Nowadays they were being *defeated*, and often only with words – pamphlets, posters and columns in the press.

'It's the Communists,' Kee said. 'They've learned the meaning of propaganda.'

'Which means,' Willie said, 'that if Chiang moves he'll be taking a big chance that Japan or one of the Western powers might be persuaded to intervene to prop up the warlords against him.'

The possibilities were endless and always fascinating.

'Allying himself to the Communists was a mistake,' he went on. 'The northern warlords are presenting him as a raging Bolshevik and that's enough to put people like Gerald Honeyford off him any time.'

'Do you think he's bitten off more than he can chew?'

Willie grinned. 'I'll bet Honeyford and his pals are taking heart that the alliance of the warlords will be enough to destroy him. After all, George, he's not very old or experienced. I bet they're hoping it'll all go wrong and that the students will decide they've backed the wrong man. Then, with the unrest dying down, the Chinese will slip back into the old ways, and Honeyford and his pals will go on making money from them as they always have.'

Chiang had still not left when June came and a meeting of Shanghai businessmen called by the Chamber of Commerce was advised that, even if he did move, it was unlikely that he would get very far. The US Consul-General felt that the opposition to him was too great, while the British Consul-General, who had always considered his post in Shanghai was in its way as important as the embassy in its backwater in Peking, outlined his views at a meeting of the British Residents' Association at the Country Club. 'We are under no threat,' he said. 'Most of the fears are founded on rumour and pure imagination, and I would advise people to continue with their jobs as before.'

With things quiet again and Abigail in Japan on the trail of Japanese netsuke and into antiquities, it seemed a good time for Willie to make one of his biennial trips to Hong Kong. The fog and low cloud which were common in the spring would be over and the south-west monsoons would have set in, and Da Braga could be relied on to look after his affairs in Yangpo. He and Willie had worked together for a long time now, first merely as friends, then as partners in the Yangpo concern, and Da Braga was never likely to let him down. All it required in the event of trouble was to organise a few coolies and everything could be saved, because they had been running their stock down for some time, just in case.

Despite her insistence on staying in Yangpo with her husband, Polly had finally agreed to move down to her parents-in-law in Shanghai until after the baby was born. It wouldn't be difficult for Elliott Wissermann to get down to see her from time to time and with his parents, her own parents, and all her friends and their families, there would be plenty of people to help her pass the time.

Abigail was expecting her before the month was out and was intending to get back from Japan in time to greet her.

'I've got business in Hong Kong, George,' Willie told Kee. 'I shall be going on the *Apu Shani* and coming back on the *Lady Roberts*. I'll be away for a week or so.'

Kee's expression was blank. 'I'll look after your interests,' he said.

'Good boy, George.' Willie slapped his shoulder. He was always a little more noisy, a little more friendly, when he was going to Hong Kong. He was aware of it, and put it down to guilt, but there was nothing he could do about it. He always promised himself that next time he'd be different, but he never was and he decided he was a pretty poor deceiver.

'I shall want to know if Chiang moves,' he said. 'That's important and it'll be urgent. If he moves north he'll pass through Yangpo and I want to be there when he does. I'm not having his bloody soldiers looting my property. Where's my son's ship, by the way?'

'Just downriver, sir. At Hankow.'

'Good. It would be nice to have him handy. Don't forget, George. I want to know. At once.'

Not that he expected anything. Chiang, he felt, talked more than he acted and the alliance of the northern warlords ought to be more than a match for him, because he would be a long way from his base in Canton, while they would be on home ground.

The *Apu Shani* looked more like a battleship than a passenger carrier, with wire mesh and barbed wire round the wheelhouse and engine room hatch, and a machine gun mounted on the wing bridge. With the unsettled state of the country and the uncertainty of the future, piracy in the China Seas had suddenly increased, with armed launches coming out from among the islands that dotted the coast. Only the week before the coaster *Shang Shu* had been attacked and set on fire, and the navy were still searching for the pirates' lair, while the police were making heavy enquiries in and around Shanghai and Hong Kong.

As the ship was about to leave, a big American car drew up and Yip Hsao-Li stepped out. A servant handed him an attaché case and he turned to head for the gangway. Then another man stepped from the car and Willie saw it was Zychov.

Zychov! For God's sake, Zychov!

For a moment he was tempted to get hold of the captain – his own captain – and have Zychov thrown off the ship. But then he paused. He knew Zychov was a coward, a man whose interest lay only in himself, and Shantu was twenty-seven years ago now and nobody remembered it. And was it really for that he hated Zychov? Zychov had been very young like himself at the time, and young people panicked easily in danger. Or was it more truthfully because he was afraid of his connection with Nadya, because he was afraid he might reclaim her?

As he calmed down, he began to wonder if his hatred over the years had been justified. There were a lot of men he disliked, but he had learned to cope with the problem. No man in business could afford to have enemies, any more than an officer in one of the armed services could. It was his job, as it was theirs, to deal with the situation.

In the end he decided not to bother, but, nevertheless, the thought of Zychov going to Hong Kong spoiled the trip. Was he going to see Nadya? Was he after more money? Was he trying to come between them? Willie rejected that idea at once. Zychov couldn't possibly have learned of Willie's interest and, as Willie well knew, Yip always had business in Hong Kong. Recently, he had hit hard times and the story was going the rounds that it was because he traded with the Japanese. Even the Balalaika had been affected. The Japanese officers liked to use it and the management was finding it hard to find chefs, waiters, hostesses, bouncers and hat check girls because the students were putting on pressure.

Feeling he couldn't bear the idea of meeting Zychov on deck, Willie sent the steward for a bottle of whisky and arranged to take all his meals in the big first class cabin that had been reserved for him.

The foredeck was lined with small fawn-coloured humpbacked bullocks due for the slaughterhouses of Hong Kong, and stacks of pigs in crates of split bamboo, all quietened with a dose of opium. There was a mist over the sea and the sun looked like a burst pomegranate, tinting the waves pink, and a fat Chinese was fanning himself in the heat. As they left, a typhoon warning was received, indicating heavy weather moving from the Philippines towards Swatow. At least, he thought, fingering the big revolver that went everywhere with him, it would keep the pirates quiet.

Islands and headlands faded past like ghosts, the sea melting into the sky, and the first dawn was one of emerald, sapphire, jade and hyacinth. The first class fans churned the stale air even as the wind came like the whimper of some lost wild animal, eerie and faint. The sea was growing lumpy and the ship began to surge, the decks wet with spray. There was a clamminess about everything and leaking in the caulking of the deckheads began to show as stains on the roof of Willie's cabin.

The weather grew wilder, a high wind sending bucketfuls of flying fish across the deck to the delight of the Chinese crew, but the following morning it was unexpectedly calm again and the temperature had risen, though the Chinese were laying out the scraps of maggoty pigskin which they used as medicine against seasickness. The deadlights remained down and the captain gestured at the horizon, where black clouds were spreading across the sky, and before the day was out the ship was driving her bows down into the sea so that the whole forward end disappeared in foam and spindrift and Willie was reminded uncomfortably that that was exactly what the Blue Anchor liner, *Waratah*, was supposed to have done in 1909 when she had disappeared without trace. The wind by this time was like a living thing, solid, muscled, flattening the skin on the face and pushing the eyeballs back, and the ship was reeling in a waste of tortured grey water veined with driven foam.

They arrived in Hong Kong with the saloon wrecked and the chairs torn loose and careering about with the apparently lifeless bodies of the steward and the pantry boy. One passenger was dead, two hands had gone overboard and there were bruises and scalds in the stokehold, to say nothing of the loss of all the cattle and pigs.

With streets awash, Willie struggled to his hotel, the hall of which was besieged by drenched people sheltering from the wind. As the ship had docked, there had been an uncanny silence as the eye of the typhoon passed over, but then the rain had slashed down again, driven by the screaming gale which slashed down doors and forced its way through locked windows. Bending palm trees looked like umbrellas blown inside out and a huge and ancient deodar outside the hotel collapsed with a crash.

Staring at it bitterly, impatient to reach Nadya's flat, Willie was obliged to watch as the bund disappeared under two feet of water, which swirled into department stores and cut off the hotel as it rushed into its front entrance and out at the back. For safety's sake, he had never written to announce his impending appearance, but with electrical supplies cut, it was impossible to telephone and he had to sit in the bar, terrified she might vanish to India or Malaya, where she was now beginning to do business, before he could get in touch with her. Reports came in of water washing away the homes of the poor on the hillsides, of whole slopes sliding down, carrying buildings, people, vehicles and animals with them, trapping men, women and children in the wreckage. Police, fire brigades and troops had long since been called out for rescue work.

Two days later, two whole days of being unable to telephone, or even to check that Nadya was safe, he learned it would be possible to reach her. Leaving the usual message about where he could be contacted if anything turned up from his Shanghai office, he had the hotel call a cab and set off with the wheels awash.

He found Nadya with her assistant and a Chinese youth she had hired drying out her carpets. The humid air of the typhoon was still with them and Nadya's face was shining with perspiration. It was impossible not to be impressed with the energy with which they all worked, and he couldn't resist taking off his jacket and piling in, too. She didn't say much, merely smiled, grateful for his help, and directed him to moving a glass-topped counter so they could lift the saturated carpet.

459

'Where's your stock? Were you looted?'

'No. I put it away. It's in the safe.'

They got the carpet up and hanging in the small space at the back of the shop where she kept the boxes and the old furniture, and they were walking on bare boards.

'It's a disaster,' Willie decided.

She shook her head. 'Not as bad as I've seen. We can recover because we're allowed to recover. There was no recovering in Russia.'

The rain was still falling, the street outside a grey river pock-marked by the heavy falling drops, so they locked up and the assistant and the Chinese youth disappeared, cowering under a black umbrella, the boy with his cotton trousers rolled up over his calves. The rooms upstairs were dry, though everywhere seemed to have soaked up the moisture because even the air was wet, but Nadya made tea for them and they sat together drinking it, both in damp sweat-stained clothes, their faces streaked with dirt, their bodies aching with the work they'd done, talking desultorily without the energy to make much of the conversation.

'Have you lost much?' Willie asked.

'Nothing. But the carpet's ruined, of course. I shall have to buy a new one.'

'I'll pay for it.'

'No.'

'I insist. It won't cost much.'

She bent over him and kissed his forehead. As he tried to grab her she slipped away, went to the desk and produced a cheque. It was dated some time back, but it was for a thousand pounds.

'What's this for?'

'It's what I owe you.'

'You owe me nothing.'

'This is what I borrowed to start here.'

'It wasn't a loan. It was a gift.'

'No, William.' She eyed him sadly, a wing of hair hanging over her face as she tucked the cheque into his breast pocket and kissed him again. 'It was not a gift. I can't accept gifts of that magnitude. I am not a kept woman. I am Nadya Alexsandrovna Kourganova, and I was born a baroness. I have enough pride left not to live on someone else's generosity.'

She was in a strange mood, and what was troubling her kept him at a distance. After dark the rain stopped and as the street cleared they called a cab and managed to find a restaurant where they could eat. The curious mood persisted and she seemed deep in thought most of the time.

'Is something wrong?' Willie's words were sharp and brittle. In his mind was the thought that Zychov had reappeared.

'No,' she said.

'Business good?'

'Excellent.'

'Then what's troubling you?'

She managed to hedge and change the subject but, when the cab dropped them at her door, she told the driver to move away a little and wait.

'Why does he have to wait?' Willie demanded.

'He'll, be needed.'

'We're not going anywhere.'

She had slipped inside the door and half closed it behind her in front of him, barring the way. The action surprised and annoyed him.

'Don't I come in?'

'I need to think.'

'What about? I've always stayed here.'

'I've got to think about it.'

'There's someone else?'

'No. No one else.'

'I find it hard to believe that nobody's noticed you.'

'Oh, I've been noticed.' She gave a little laugh. 'But not by anyone who matters. They often try, but I put them off. You are the only one, William.'

'Then why can't I come in? Has that bastard, Zychov turned up again?'

'No. He's not been here.'

He didn't know whether to believe her or not and started wondering if he had somehow managed to contact her while Willie had been marooned in his hotel.

'He's here, I know. He was on the *Apu Shani*. I saw him come aboard with Yip.'

Again she denied that she'd seen Zychov.

'Then what's it all about?'

She was silent for a moment then she looked at him straight in the eyes. 'Not very long ago I met your wife, William. She's far too good a woman for me to double-cross her.'

The words staggered him. 'We've already double-crossed her,' he said, beginning to grow angry.

'Then it's time we stopped.'

'She doesn't know.' He wasn't sure of this fact, but he felt he needed some sort of lever.

'Are you sure?'

'Did she say something?'

'No. And I don't think she would. You have a good woman, William. I think you should return to her.'

He stared at her suspiciously. 'There is someone else.'

'No, there's no one.'

'You really mean it?' He still couldn't believe it, any more than he could understand her motives.

'Yes.'

For a moment he couldn't take it in, then suddenly anger took hold of him. 'My God,' he said. 'After all I did for you!'

'What did you do for me, William?' She was curiously lacking in emotion. 'You got me out of Russia. But thousands of people were snatched from the clutches of the Cheka, usually by people who didn't know them and never met them again. I was only one of thousands who were rescued and you were only one of the thousands who did the rescuing.'

'We were lovers!' He'd made the plea before and somehow this time it sounded stale.

She seemed to think the same. 'And am I supposed to feel in your debt for that, William?' She was still not angry, just unbelievably, shockingly, reasonable. 'I provided you with trade. I made money. You made money. Surely we don't have to remain forever in debt.'

'You needed me then. And not just for business. Don't you need me now?'

'I'm older, William. The storm goes out of the emotions. And I think of your wife. I have thought constantly of her. She doesn't deserve it. Though I still want to be your friend.'

'It's not a friend I want!'

While the taxi waited down the road, they continued to argue, but she remained adamant, and in the end talked him into a reluctant acceptance. Angry, frustrated, he finally decided that it was doubtless only temporary and that eventually there would be a letter on his desk, apologising and begging him to return. As he left, she kissed him gently.

'This is how it must be,' she said.

As he kissed her back, not with passion but, he thought bitterly, as a friend, he saw a taxi had halted across the road. From the window Yip Hsao-Li was watching them with interest.

'Good evening, Mr Sarth,' he said smoothly, his wide smiling mouth full of gold teeth. 'I must tell your wife I saw you. I am looking for porcelain again and need to visit her. She'll be most interested.'

He waved cheerfully and the taxi moved off.

'Who's that?' Nadya asked.

'Yip,' Willie rapped. 'Partner to your husband, and just as big a bloody twister.'

Without another word, he turned up his coat collar and stalked angrily to his taxi. 'Cathay Hotel,' he snapped.

At the hotel, he strode to the bar. It was late and, because of the weather, the place was empty. The barman was just considering closing when Willie arrived.

'Whisky-polly,' he snapped. 'Double.'

When it arrived he sat glaring at it, his feelings towards Nadya bitter. Again and again, he thought 'After all I did,' but when he considered it, he was reminded again and again that most of the giving had been on her part and his rescue of her from Vladivostok was no more than many other men had done for many other women – even whole families – who, as often as not, were total strangers.

Then, staring at his glass he remembered Yip Hsao-Li's veiled threat to tell Abigail what he had been up to in Hong Kong. The fact that he'd been up to nothing because he hadn't been allowed to get up to anything wouldn't mean a thing. Whatever Abigail had thought previously, she could hardly ignore the information, because Willie had never told her of his visits to Nadya and that alone was sufficient to show his guilt. He knew she occasionally met Yip when he was after porcelain and he had no doubt that Yip would carry out his promise. He was noted as a gossip, and a vicious one, too, and he had no liking for Willie, who had more than once refused to do business with him. Christ, he thought, just let Yip start talking, and that would really put the cat among the bloody pigeons!

As he emptied his glass, he suddenly wondered if Yip was intending blackmail. Was that how he made his money? There was plenty of opportunity for it in Shanghai because half the taipans who played golf and went to church so earnestly on Sunday had some little Chinese girl discreetly tucked away in a flat, unknown to their wives. It would certainly account for the money Yip had, because a profession of that sort needed no more than a few well-paid spies.

Then he began to be resentful against Abigail, feeling his dilemma was of her doing, that somehow she had known all the time about Nadya, had pleaded with her to give him up. But this wasn't in character, he knew. If Abigail had felt she'd lost his love, she would have been frank about it, questioned him and, if still unsatisfied, would have walked out on him. She wasn't lacking in courage or forthrightness and she wasn't short of money. But he still wasn't certain she knew what had been going on, because she had always maintained a blank expression that was either naivety or cleverness – he had no idea which. The resentment grew but, with his fourth large whisky and Apollinaris, he rejected the idea altogether. Abigail wasn't that sort and, come to that, he had to admit, neither was Nadya. They had met. There was no doubt about that, and it was clear Nadya had been so impressed with Abigail she had accepted that it was her duty to forget Willie.

'You ever been in love?' Willie asked the barman.

The barman shrugged. 'Once or twice.'

'Ever with two women at the same time?'

'I've never been that lucky, sir.'

Willie stared at his glass again. His mood changed and he began to experience a drunken sense of pride in Abigail. Her honesty was enough to make anyone quail before it. He had, many times. It had clearly made Nadya doubtful. But then Nadya must have the same sort of pride, the same sort of honesty. Until she had met Abigail, she had been worried, but, meeting her, she had felt she should have no part of Willie's life. The unbelievable had happened. His mistress had backed off because she admired his wife.

'One thing,' Willie said, pushing his glass towards the barman for a refill. 'If you ever do fall in love with two women at once, make sure one of them's dishonest.'

Ignoring the refilled glass, he rose to his feet and, watched by the puzzled barman, who had no idea what he was getting at, steered a careful course between the tables towards the door. He was singing – a trace defiantly.

'I'm a flying fish sailor. Just home from Hong Kong...'

He went to his room, convinced he would never sleep that night because there was too much on his mind, but in fact, he rolled on to the bed without undressing and, after the whisky, fell sound asleep. He never normally drank much and he sank into a bottomless pit in which all his worries vanished and he began to snore.

During the night the wind dropped and the cloud cleared, but it seemed there was thunder in the air. Thunder? He opened one eye and saw the sun was out. It didn't look like thunder, but it sure as hell sounded like thunder.

He began to lift his head and immediately felt as if his brains were slopping about inside. He put his hand to his temple, which seemed in danger of dropping off, and was about to turn over in the hope of sleeping off some of the hangover when it dawned on him that the thunder he heard came not from outside but from inside. He sat bolt upright with a jerk that made him yelp, convinced that a riot had started and that demonstrators had got into the hotel. Then he realised that someone was hammering on the door.

Groaning and cursing alternately, he went to the door and unlocked it. The undermanager of the hotel was outside, all smooth face, black coat and striped trousers.

'Forgive me, sir. There's a message for you. It came early this morning on the telegraph. I telephoned the premises   of A N Kourganov as you've always instructed, but I was told you weren't there. I was puzzled because you always stay there – in spite of having a room here.'

'Give me the telegram,' Willie said.

The undermanager went on talking, 'I couldn't think where you were – '

'Telegram.'

The envelope was handed over and, as Willie struggled to open it, the undermanager's explanation went on. 'Then the barman said you were in the hotel and had been in all night. So – ' he gestured ' – you must forgive me, for disturbing you, but you insist on having all telegrams delivered at once and that one is marked "Personal. Most urgent." '

'It is?'

Dully Willie turned the envelope over to confirm the fact, then, suddenly alarmed, wrenched at the paper so hard it tore the contents as well as the envelope.

It was from George Kee and it was alarming '*Suggest immediate return,*' it said. '*Chiang on move north. Trouble Yangpo. Da Braga badly hurt.*'

three

'Jesus Christ on a tightrope!'

Willie groaned, passed a hand over his face and turned to the under-manager. 'Book me a berth on the first ship going north,' he said. 'Send some black coffee up – immediately – and then ask one of the maids to come here and pack for me. Have my bill ready for when I come downstairs.'

They had all the information at the docks when he arrived, because Canton, where Chiang had been based, was just up the Pearl River, and, by Chinese standards, not far away. The news had been brought down overnight by steamer and the place was agog with excitement.

Chiang had left the city the previous day gathering about him more than fifty thousand troops, formed into three columns, one of them heading for Wuhan, the triple city of Wuchang, Hankow and Hanyang astride the Yangtze and not far from Yangpo. The warlords, distrusting, argumentative and jealous of each other, all of them suspicious of their neighbours, had failed to implement their alliance as, it seemed, Chiang had known they would, because his agents were swarming across the countryside, passing information.

And, as Willie knew, the Kuomintang troops were different from those of the warlords. They were smart in green uniforms and, instead of teapots, parasols and umbrellas, carried the banners of the Kuomintang, red squares with a blue quarter containing a white sun insignia. They were young too, mostly of student age, and they didn't wander or loot, and they didn't murder unless ordered to. Their discipline was tight and it was obvious why they were popular. Instead of rape, arson and death they were bringing what looked very much like hope to the peasants.

For a moment, he wondered if it would be worthwhile going up to Canton to find out what was really happening. He knew its high walls and crooked streets well. He had an agent there to organise the produce of Kwangtung province in the shape of tea, silk and cassia, but, since the troubles in South China, he had kept clear of the place and left it to him. When the Merchants' Volunteer Corps had been crushed, a lot of damage had been done to European prestige and it was never an easy place for foreign devils, because it was the centre of the new nationalistic spirit of China.

In the end he decided not to go and, instead, called at the newspaper office, where they had always been willing to keep him abreast of any news he'd missed. It seemed that the speed of Chiang's advance was surprising everybody. The ground ahead of him had been very well prepared by the skilful propaganda of the Communists, supplemented by Kuomintang agents who moved ahead of the army. The resistance everybody had expected was already showing signs of crumbling and, while the peasants were flocking to the KMT arm, in the north the warlords were impeded by riots, strikes and missing supplies.

When he returned to the hotel the undermanager had found him a first class cabin on the MacDonald Line coaster *Tien Quan*.

'She's well guarded,' he said, 'because I understand she's carrying silver for the Shanghai banks from Canton. The merchants are alarmed by Chiang's moves and decided they preferred their money further north, where it'll be safer.'

Willie nodded dully, the thought crossing his mind that if the manager knew what the *Tien Quan*'s cargo contained so would a few other people.

Still suffering from a hangover, he sat on deck, waiting for the ship to leave and letting the fresh air get to his brain as he tried to work out his plans. There seemed nothing to worry about. Abigail must still be in Japan, and Polly, despite her insistence on staying with her husband, had said she would move down to Shanghai for the sake of the baby.

His mind returned to Nadya and from Nadya to Zychov, and finally from Zychov to Yip Hsao-Li. What did that bastard do? What did they both do? How did they live in the style they did? Now that Nadya had rejected him, would she turn again to Zychov? The thought of Zychov, opportunist, boastful, overbearing, cowardly, holding Nadya in his arms made him squirm.

As the hangover wore off, so did his gloom. There had to be no regrets, he decided briskly. He'd start again, get back to Ab and try to make up to her with something. But what? Gifts were pointless when she wasn't aware that anything had happened? Or was she? Or was it simply his own guilt that was bothering him? In any case – he swung back again to Yip and his threat – perhaps there'd be no chance to start again. Yip had seen him. If he told Ab where he'd seen him and what he was doing, Ab might not *want* to start again – ever.

Christ, he thought, what a mess!

The deck had filled up now with coolies returning north from jobs as houseboys or labourers, their yellow skins tight over skeletal bodies laced with stringy sinew, each with his roll of matting and his camphorwood box containing the earnings he would fritter away gambling. The ship's compradore was talking to a clerk in a suit of cheap drill and a felt hat. The compradore looked nervous, as well he might because, holding the keys to the ship's safe, he was always the first man to be sought out by the pirates if there were an attack.

Just as the ship was due to leave, a car screamed to a stop by the gangplank and a man ran aboard and climbed to the bridge. He was met by the captain and there was a hurried discussion before the man hurried back down the gangplank. The winches stopped and the deck crew sat down, waiting. There were only one or two first class passengers, all of whom had been carefully searched for hidden weapons. The coastal ship's captains had been caught too often to take chances.

The bar was opened and the captain appeared to announce that there were a few last-minute passengers, then a car rolled to a stop by the gangway and a woman was helped aboard.

Mincing and slender, an elaborate headdress hiding her face, her hands concealed in voluminous sleeves, she was led to a cabin in the first class area of the ship.

'Wind-up,' the captain explained. 'On the *Chung Chih* when she was attacked last year. Name of Ching Chei-Lin.

Wife of a Canton merchant. She's got her servants with her. Says she's going to visit her sister.' He laughed. 'It's my belief she's keeping an eye on Ching's silver.'

A large crate, seated and secured with metal strips, was carried aboard and deposited on the foredeck. 'Porcelain,' the captain said. 'Sealed for safety. There's one thing; it can't be carrying weapons. It would take too long to open.'

Moments later, another car appeared and from it an enormous number of people appeared, first an old man and two old women who handed out boxes and bags, then a group of Chinese girls. Like the woman who had arrived just ahead of them, they wore silk trousers and tunics brilliant with the patterns of flowers and birds, and studded with filigree buttons, their hair held in place by gold-headed pins. They squatted down near the crate round a small stove, waited on by the old man and the old women. Their faces were heavily painted with a great deal of white and red and, with cigarettes in their mouths, waving fans, gesturing and giggling, they looked like a group of sing-song girls.

'Dancing troupe,' the captain said. 'Probably some mandarin's concubines or the contents of a knocking shop. Probably the woman who arrived first's the Madame.'

A last search of the ship was made by a white police officer, who announced he had found no weapons, and the captain nodded. As the ropes were cast off the *Tien Quan* began to move. The weather was warm and still humid and there was an air of nervousness about the ship. Everybody had heard of Chiang's move and most of the first class passengers were businessmen returning in a hurry to Shanghai to keep an eye on their affairs up the

Yangtze. Willie kept himself apart, one part of his mind on Kee's telegram, another on Nadya's decision, a third on the fact that Yip had seen her kissing him. Whatever Abigail might have thought of Nadya in the past she would soon change her mind if she knew her husband was in the habit of visiting her and kissing her goodbye.

As they left the coast behind, the sea filled with junks. Close behind was a black-funnelled ship, followed by a small French vessel burning atrocious coal, that was picking its way through the coastal traffic. The heat was enough to make everyone fall asleep after lunch, all except for the girls on the foredeck, who went on with their chattering and giggling. Sunset flooded the sky with crimson and the sea was the blue of a peacock's throat. In the glare, the whole ship seemed to glow, the upper works the colour of coral, the black hull purple in the extraordinary light. As it changed to dusk, the sea, which had been full of crimson diamonds, changed to the colour of pewter.

The ship's guards, Sikh soldiers who had taken their pensions, dozed outside the first class area, their rifles alongside them. The moon rose and the dancing girls remained on deck, still smoking cigarettes and chattering in low-pitched voices with the two old women. Willie watched them for a long time before retiring, his mind in a turmoil. Why the bloody hell had Yip happened to see him with Nadya? What the hell was he doing in Hong Kong, anyway? Why had Nadya let him down? Why the hell couldn't a man love two women without being unfaithful? And why, above all, had Chiang chosen this moment in time to start his bloody march north against the warlords?

His mind was still seething as he headed for his cabin. By this time, two of the dancing girls were performing for the rest of the passengers, who were chirruping with delight as they moved their feet in small intricate steps. The older woman who had come aboard first joined them, moving with them, in a small scene that looked like one of the Chinese prints Abigail sold. Except – Willie frowned – except that somehow it seemed wrong. At the back of his mind something stirred, nagging at his consciousness, but he shrugged it off, his thoughts once more preoccupied with his problems.

Though it was not yet fully daylight, the Chinese deck passengers were already astir when Willie went on deck the next morning, some of them already heading for the galley with their bowls for their morning rice, one or two of them setting up little stoves and cooking themselves. The captain and the chief engineer were talking by the bridge ladder.

Sniffing the air, he decided it hadn't changed much and was an improvement on the typhoon that had accompanied him south. As he turned into the alleyway to go to his cabin to shave and dress, he noticed the ship was wallowing in an oily, lifting sea. A junk with its brown bat-wing sail was heading towards them, almost as if it intended to ram them, and it crossed his mind to wonder what it was up to. The foredeck was still littered with sleeping shapes, as if it were the aftermath of a battle, and in the doorway to the engine room two naked sweating firemen gulped air into their lungs.

Then, from the corner of his eye he saw the woman in first class who had come aboard the ship at the last moment fish something from one of her wide silk sleeves and toss it to the old man who had accompanied the dancing girls and almost immediately heard a shot. Wheeling round, he saw the Sikh guard at the open end of the alleyway staggering backwards, clutching his stomach. Standing over him, holding a smoking revolver, was the old man, straight now, his back no longer bent. Beyond him, he saw the dancing girls struggling with the crate and realised that the metal strips that had sealed it had been cut during the night and that they had already almost got the lid off.

Still unseen, for a second Willie stared, wondering what was happening, before it suddenly dawned on him. The object he'd seen tossed to the old man had been a revolver and without doubt the crate on the foredeck contained more. Even as he watched, he saw the lid fall to the deck and one of the dancing girls reach inside among the wood-wool that packed it. Christ on a tightrope, he thought, it was the piracy job he'd been fearing for years on his own ships! And that junk that was bearing down on them to starboard was full of bloodthirsty sods with guns, hopped up with opium, who were about to board them and slit their throats.

Diving into his cabin, he snatched up the big Russian revolver he had carried on his journeys ever since his youth. More shots rang out and he swung the door open again to find himself staring at the old man who, he saw now that he was at close quarters, was not an old man at all, but a young man skilfully made up. He was still glancing over his shoulder at the squirming Sikh as Willie shot him in the back.

There was a tremendous amount of shouting and screaming going on, on deck, and a lot of wild shooting, and nobody noticed his single shot. Still clutching the revolver, he picked up the groaning Sikh's rifle and headed for the deck, banging a warning on cabin doors as he passed. As he emerged, he saw the captain and the engineer lying in a huddle at the top of the bridge ladder and two of the 'dancing girls', their wigs discarded, the white paint still on their faces, climbing up to them to take control of the ship.

The woman who had come aboard at the last minute was now on the foredeck, pointing, and as she turned, with a shock he saw it was Yip Hsao-Li in woman's clothing. For a second, he couldn't grasp the meaning of it, then the facts hammered themselves into his brain. Of course! The dancing steps the night before should have told him! He realised now what had worried him as he had watched the dancing girls. Somehow Yip's love of dancing had nudged its way into his mind and, because of his problems, he had failed to recognise the warning.

Yip – and probably that bastard, Zychov! – had been the brains behind all the piracy swoops of the last few years, with Yip probably responsible for a long time even before that. The first revolvers, the ones it was always necessary to hide against the search, had been inside Yip's flowing female garments. With the first shots, more weapons had come from the sealed crate, and following that, it was easy.

The 'dancing girls' were now armed with the weapons of the captain, the engineer and the dead Sikh guards. Among them also were a few of the deck passengers, clearly also part of the gang, passing up cans of kerosene from the foredeck. The junk to port was still bearing down swiftly on the stopped ship, and Willie knew they were intending to sink the *Tien Quan* with dynamite, by setting fire to her or by opening the seacocks. They would then vanish aboard the junk and get away quite cleanly, because there would be no trace of the ship beyond a little floating wreckage and perhaps a body or two, and it would be assumed she had been lost in one of the squalls for which the South China Sea was notorious.

The phoney girls and the infiltrated passengers from the foredeck were gathered round Yip while the rest of the passengers, screaming women, children and shouting men, were herded into the bows. Two men headed for the captain's cabin and Willie guessed that, sent for the silver that had been taken on board, they were seeking the compradore who had doubtless tucked himself away in some previously arranged hiding place. Yip's contacts in Canton must have warned him of Chiang's unexpected advance north and the movement of the silver, and the plot to attack the ship had been hatched quickly, with Yip joining at the last minute dressed as a woman. No wonder he and Zychov were so close. Zychov had been a naval officer and knew everything there was to know about ships. He'd probably even led a few raids himself, because, not very long before, one of the Pirate gangs had been found to have been led by a rogue officer from the German Imperial Navy, left rootless and futureless by the mutiny in the High Seas Fleet in 1918.

By this time, the pirates had dragged the wounded mate and the wireless operator forward. Yip was performing what seemed to be a small dance of triumph, stepping daintily as Willie had seen him more than once in one of the Shanghai hotels, and, as he nodded, one of the 'dancing girls' raised his revolver. It was too much for Willie and he lifted the Sikh's rifle. He had always been a good shot and he dropped the man with the revolver without effort.

As the other pirates swung round to see where the shot had come from, he saw Yip halt in the middle of his little dance and his eyes widen as he recognised Willie.

The second shot took Yip in the throat. He disappeared backwards as his stumbling feet caught in a ringbolt, and ended up flat on his back with his feet supported on a coil of rope. Incongruously, Willie noticed, as they stuck out from the voluminous robes he'd worn, that they were encased in his patent leather dancing pumps. At least he thought, he wouldn't be using them again.

Without their leader, the other pirates were confused and began to head for the ship's side. As they did so, the two men who had been sent to look for the compradore reappeared, carrying the box of silver. Reaching the top of the ladder, they stared about them, wondering what was happening and Willie shot one of them with the revolver. The box dropped at the feet of the second one as his partner rolled down the ladder with flying arms and legs.

'Quick!' The mate, his face covered with blood, had dived for the shelter of one of the winches. 'The machine gun!'

The gun on the bridge was pointing up in the air and Willie scrambled up the ladder, expecting a bullet in the back every inch of the way. As he swung the weapon, the pirates yelled and began to jump overboard, but, when he pulled the trigger, there was nothing but a heavy 'clunk'.

'How the bloody hell do you work this thing?' he screamed in fury.

The mate had struggled up beside him. 'It needs loading,' he croaked and, elbowing Willie out of the way he shoved the end of the belt into the breech, yanked at the cocking handle and swung the weapon towards the approaching junk. The clack-clack as it fired sounded deafening.

'Up!' Willie yelled. 'Up a bit!'

The mate raised the muzzle and fired again, and immediately they saw men running along the junk's deck. The slatted sail shifted and the bow swung away from the *Tien Quan*. His face contorted with pain and fury, the mate gave the vessel a few more bursts, then swung the gun round and began to aim at the men swimming in the water alongside.

'Murdering bastards!' he was snarling over and over again like a litany. 'Murdering bastards! Murdering bloody bastards!'

With the captain, the chief engineer and the compradore dead and the mate and the wireless operator wounded, the engine wrecked, and Willie struggling half-naked in the engine room in an attempt to get the electricity working, the *Tien Quan* wallowed for three days in the oily, lifting water before the destroyer which was finally called to her rescue appeared. It had taken all of twenty-four hours before the wounded wireless operator had been able to repair his damaged set and send out an SOS, and another forty-eight before help arrived, and they were taken in tow.

They had taken several prisoners from among the deck passengers, and had captured two of the 'dancing girls', their hands tied behind their backs, the paint still on their faces as evidence of the plot. The bodies of the dead were lying in a row in the lazarette, Yip at the head of them, still in his women's clothing, and there were several more, victims of the mate's machine gun action, floating in the sea.

When they arrived at the naval base, there were representatives of *The North China Daily News* and other papers and agencies to meet them. Somehow, they had got hold of Willie's name, which was well known to them, and reporters tried to waylay him for an interview. But he wasn't interested, and, thrusting them savagely aside, he headed for his office. As the cab roared down the bund, he saw the sign of the Balalaika and, shouting at the driver to turn off towards it, dragged at the old revolver. A message had already been radioed ashore to question Zychov, but the fury that was still in Willie drove him to make a confrontation on his own.

He was too late. A policeman was waiting inside, but Zychov had vanished, it was said to Yip's friends in the Chinese town, and the restaurant was closed. Scrambling back into the taxi, Willie continued to the office of the Sarth Line. Kee was waiting for him with a ticket for the *Fan Ling*, which was due to leave for Yangpo.

'Everything's ready, sir,' he said. 'All you have to do is board her. You have two hours.'

'What happened, George?'

'It's hard to say at the moment, sir. The students beat up Mr Da Braga when he stopped them setting fire to our godown.'

'Is it bad?'

'I think so, sir. I'm waiting to hear from Mrs Sarth. She promised to get in touch.'

'Mrs Sarth?' Willie had snatched the ticket and was already heading for the door when he stopped and turned. 'What does she know about it?'

'She went up two days ago, sir.'

'She's in Japan.'

'She returned, sir.'

'How the hell did she hear? Did you tell her?'

'I wired her as I did you, sir. Naturally.'

It was obvious that Abigail had set off home at once and, with the hold-up Willie had suffered, had arrived ahead of him.

'She should he there now, sir,' Kee said.

'By God, she should,' Willie snapped. 'And by God, so should I!'

There was no time to go home, so he headed for the nearest shop and bought clean shirts, collars and socks before hurrying back to the bund. At the end of two hours, he was on his way north.

His mind was in a turmoil. The irony of it, he kept thinking. The bloody irony! There was no need now to fear Abigail learning of his association with Nadya. Yip was dead. Willie's shot had been accurate, and he wondered if he'd been so careful because Yip was the organiser of the pirates or because he could tell Abigail what Willie was up to in Hong Kong. Not that it mattered, he realised. It had all been over between himself and Nadya anyway. It was all a bit bloody odd, he thought.

China was living up to its reputation.

The first thing they saw as the *Fan Ling* turned the bend in the river was the Hong Kong and Shanghai Bank building, but behind it somewhere something was on fire and a pillar of black smoke was lifting up to the sky. Three gunboats were anchored in midstream, near them two of the big multidecked passenger ships, to which a constant stream of boats was moving. The air was electric, like the sultry atmosphere before a thunderstorm.

As he tried to go ashore, Willie was stopped by a naval petty officer armed with a revolver.

'Sorry, sir. Nobody allowed to land.'

'I have to land. I have business here and my wife's there somewhere.'

The petty officer fetched an officer, who reluctantly gave Willie permission. His route carried him past his office and godown. It hadn't been destroyed but it was charred where an attempt had been made to set it on fire. The windows were broken and he could see Da Braga's car lying on its side, wrecked. There were no rickshaws so he half-ran, half-trotted to his house. The first person he saw was one of Da Braga's sons, a strapping youth who was holding a pistol.

'Mister Sarth. I'm glad you've come.'

'What's been happening?'

'The crowd's come out for Chiang.'

Inside, Willie bumped at once into Polly.

'Poll,' he snapped. 'You ought to be in Shanghai.'

'I was,' she said. 'But when this started, I felt I ought to be with Elliott. He's sitting in his office with a loaded revolver in case they come again.'

'Again?'

'They tried to break in but were driven out. He's still there.'

'Where's your mother?'

'Upstairs with Luis.'

He ran up the stairs, almost bumping into Abigail as she appeared from the spare bedroom.

'Ab!'

'Willie!'

'For Christ's sake, you ought not to be here!'

483

'When I got back from Japan I found Polly had come up to be with Elliott, so I came to take her home. I found Luis half-dead.'

Da Braga was recovering a little now, but he had a broken shoulder blade where he had been whacked with a heavy carrying pole, bruises on his head and body where he had been beaten and kicked before he could be rescued, and his left leg, struck several times with a crowbar, had been shattered.

'The doctor says it's bad,' Abigail whispered.

'Oh, Christ! Poor old Luis.'

His face twisted with pain, Da Braga was able to explain what had happened. For the most part, the bitterness of the Chinese was being expended on those of their own nationality who traded with or worked for the Europeans, but muddy sandals were trampling over cherished patterns of life and strikes had closed down foreign-owned shipping lines and factories. Communist agents had worked on the crowd's anti-European feeling and it had started with the rickshaw coolies asking twice as much for their fares, while the students had held a parade with a forest of flags and placards that demanded the end of foreign interference in Chinese affairs.

Da Braga gave the news in neat sentences, as he always had. There had been executions on the bund and heads attached to poles. Criminals, making the most of the situation, had demanded more squeeze from businessmen and shopkeepers, at first only against the Japanese, whom the Chinese had always loathed, but finally against all non-Chinese.

The warlords had been beaten, Da Braga said, and their soldiers, ragged, jaded, often bootless, had tramped through the city. Their horses had been nothing but skin and bone and their guns battered and dusty. No one had moved as they had passed through, but the minute they had disappeared the students had come on to the streets again to take advantage of the situation with their shouts of 'Go home, foreign devils!'

The city was brooding and silent again now, with a few aimless groups of students still about, but no one was kidding himself that it was over. The long-awaited Kuomintang advance northwards was well under way now. Changsha had fallen and the Kuomintang troops had reached the border of Hupeh. The warlords had failed entirely to co-operate and the Chiang flags, red with the blue quarter containing the white sun insignia, were appearing everywhere.

four

For years the warlords had trailed disease and terror across China and at last, whether you approved of Chiang or not, there was a chance of them vanishing for ever. The three Chiang columns were going from strength to strength, their numbers increasing every day instead of decreasing, as they should, as they left garrisons behind. The Communist agents had destroyed loyalties and beliefs ahead of them, and one warlord after another was toppling.

It was quite clear the Kuomintang was emerging as the most powerful party in China and, as its troops advanced, the people were rising solidly behind them. A vast revolutionary fervour was tearing China apart. There was no longer any disguising the fact that she was going through the first throes of a full-scale rising in which there was little mercy or discrimination, as the peasants, striking out with ferocious brutality, saw a chance to end the era of murder, looting and rape, and at the same time rid themselves of the hated foreign devils.

A naval surgeon, fetched by Da Braga's son, appeared to examine Da Braga's leg. Watched by Da Braga's weeping wife, he studied the pulped limb from which fragments of bloodied bone protruded, then straightened up and turned to Willie.

'It'll have to come off,' he said. 'It's a mess and we can't put it together again. And in that case, he can't stay here. There's talk of evacuating everybody and he ought to go before it gets too difficult. Will his family agree?'

There was no alternative and, doped and unaware of what was happening, Da Braga was carried to the landing stage, where he was placed aboard a launch and taken with his wife out to the sick bay of the *Fan Ling*, where the naval surgeon removed the mangled limb.

The surgeon had news from the other treaty ports. 'There are forty-two warships off Hankow,' he said. 'It started when KMT supporters broke into the race club and picked flowers.' He frowned. 'Why? Why bother with bloody flowers?'

It wasn't really so silly. In any other country it might have been, but from KMT supporters it was calculated defiance, an indication that the holy of holies of the Europeans was no longer inviolable.

'We landed a party of Marines,' the surgeon went on, 'but they couldn't get in the city gate because of Chinese soldiers. Then the sergeant had a bright idea and sent them in three at a time in taxis and they weren't stopped.'

He seemed to think the whole thing rather funny, but to Willie the incongruities he was describing were really the first hostile moves of two wrestlers. Bismarck had said that China was a sleeping giant, but now she was a waking giant, touching fingertips with the giants of the West before the struggle really started. There had been agitation for higher wages for years, and waves of anti-foreign feeling, the coolies for the most part not knowing what they were rioting for, though the students who led them were always happy to have them killed or maimed to get across this idea of theirs the coolies didn't fully understand. Many of the students were the children of rich families who had deliberately chosen to work as coolies to organise their revolution. Sometimes, when they had been caught by one of the warlords, they had been killed or tortured, and one of the girls, to Willie's certain knowledge, had been disembowelled and her intestines wrapped round her neck while she was still alive.

'There's barbed wire everywhere,' the naval man went on cheerfully, 'and the taipans are all gloomy because they can't go visiting any more. Oh, well, so long as no woman's touched it'll be all right. Decapitate a missionary or two or boil a merchant in oil, and no one will worry, but violate a white woman and the whole of the British Empire will rise in wrath.'

There was a parade along the bund that afternoon, with paper lanterns and strings of popping firecrackers. It ended inevitably in an uproar when a Chinese merchant who had done business with the Europeans had the misfortune to get in the way and was left for dead in an untidy flattened heap. Feelings were fanned to flames by the agitators and, in a sudden spontaneous combustion, stalls were overturned in the market, rush-mat booths pushed over, and ducks, pigs and chickens released because the stallholders had been selling to foreigners.

But the Europeans were still powerful, still had gunboats and were backed by armed forces which were more efficient even than Chiang's troops so, as it became clear that all-out war was impossible, the agitators began using more subtle methods. As the Europeans made ready their belongings for transportation downriver they discovered it was impossible to find porters, and when Willie tried to get a rickshaw to take him to the waterfront to find others, he was informed that the rickshaw coolies were refusing to carry Europeans. Strike pickets were already about the town, some wearing crude uniforms and carrying the heavy staves with which they had already beaten to death more than one foreign-employed Chinese. Even the coolies had set up a militia force – ragged groups of men carrying ancient two-handed swords and old muskets and wearing red armbands that reminded Willie uncomfortably of the Boxers.

That night the rioting exploded again with the violence of a bomb. For two days the wind from the mountains had been cold, but now it was hot and humid again, enough to stir ragged tempers to a fury. Some European – they never found out who – slapped a coolie. The coolie hadn't objected to what was normal enough treatment, but the incident had been seen by one of the agitators, and before anyone knew what had happened the coolie's attacker had been chopped to pieces and two thousand men and boys, brought to fever pitch by propaganda, were rampaging through the city, brandishing carrying poles and whacking out shop windows in showers of glass.

The first godown to go was Wishart's. There was very little in it, but, as the flames began to catch and they streamed past it through the streets, burning cars, beating up Chinese and wrecking European property, Emmeline appeared, terrified, to tell them all her servants had disappeared. It was Abigail who broke the news to her that her godown had gone up in flames.

'It wasn't insured,' she said bitterly. 'My insurance company refused to cover anything up here.'

They could hear the drums and the gongs and the sporadic shooting and, slipping into town, dressed in a Chinese tunic and black trousers, as he had years before in his attempt to rescue Russell Gummer, Willie managed to contact the officer in command of the shore party from one of the British gunboats.

'I'm afraid it's the end,' the officer told him. 'We've just heard on the wireless that Hankow's gone. The Chinese have occupied the British concession and the British government are going to accept the fact that it's impossible to maintain such places so deep in a hostile country. There's talk that they'll let Kiukiang go, too. They'll have to. And if they do, everybody else will let their concessions go as well. The navy's sending up more passenger vessels and I'd advise you to leave. We're expecting two more gunboats tonight.'

It was obvious that this time it was different. There had been uproars and riots before, but, while the others had been only skin-deep, this one, Willie sensed, came from deep down in the Chinese soul. The wounds this one would administer were going to be more than just scars on the flesh. They'd be mortal. This time the Chinese were not just protesting, they were lashing out.

He carried out the plans he had made with Da Braga, altering them considerably when he realised they would have to carry everything they wished to salvage themselves. There were no cars because there was no petrol, and no rickshaws or porters because they daren't move in face of the hatred for the Europeans.

Towards midnight, there was a hammering on the door and, going to open it, Willie found himself staring into the face of his son. Behind him was a burly chief petty officer. Both of them were armed.

Willie snatched them inside and for a while there was a noisy excited reunion.

'*Ant* arrived early this evening,' Edward said. 'I think it's the end, Father.'

Abigail shrugged. 'It won't ruin us,' she said.

Willie produced drinks for everybody and Edward raised his glass. 'It's funny, isn't it? All my life I assumed Yangpo was as British as India or South Africa. Now it's going to be Chinese again. I came to tell you we'll be escorting families to the river from eight tomorrow morning. Be ready.'

'Thank God there are no small children.'

'I've been in touch with Elliott already,' Edward went on. 'He'll be along with Poll as soon as it's light to join you all, and then I think you'd better set off.'

It was strange for Willie not to be giving the orders but to be receiving them from his own son. Edward was tall and good-looking and was now a full lieutenant and spoke with the authority that seemed inbred in all naval officers.

When he left with his petty officer, Willie and Abigail made a last round of the house. Again and again they picked up something they had treasured for years, meaning to take it with them, then discarded it – even a favourite red Peking rug Abigail had had since their marriage – knowing that they wouldn't be able to carry it. It was in the early hours before everybody settled down, sleeping in beds, on chairs, on settees, on the floor, a house full of people, including Da Braga's sons, neighbours from deeper in the concession, a group of French people who wished to be nearer the river – and Emmeline. Her face was gaunt and grim and she spent most of the evening opening and shutting her suitcase to make sure she had everything. She had not grown older gracefully and was embittered by the loss of everything she possessed.

As they lay together in bed in the darkness, Abigail's hand sought Willie's.

'Things are turning out differently from what we expected, aren't they?' she said.

He tried to sound confident. 'We'll get over it,' he insisted. 'We're not finished yet.'

Turning to her, he kissed her gently, still uneasily aware of guilt. 'I love you, Ab,' he said, meaning every word of it.

'I know.'

Their lovemaking was gentle and tender but was marked by more passion than for a long time. Afterwards, as they lay quietly alongside each other, their skin filmed with perspiration, Willie's anger against what he considered Nadya's ingratitude, even treachery, caught him again. With it came another wave of guilt, so that, before he knew what was happening, almost against his will, he found himself confessing everything to his wife.

'I think it was because I was lonely,' he explained. 'I was missing you and she was like you. It wasn't planned. It was never planned. It just happened. At first, it was just business between us. And then there was this thing about her being stuck in Russia and in danger from the Cheka. I had to get her out, Ab. That's how it occurred.'

Even now, he wasn't being entirely honest because the affair had started long before Nadya had been in any danger, and he had to push the truth behind him into the shadows. 'I wish it had never happened,' he said.

For a long time, Abigail said nothing, lying quietly alongside him. She made no attempt to withdraw her hand from his and for a time even seemed indifferent to what he was trying to tell her. Hardly daring to breathe, he was about to force her to say something when she spoke.

'I knew, Willie,' she said. 'I knew all the time.'

He felt faintly shocked, staggered that she had been aware of what he had been up to yet had never complained, never tried to stop him, even faintly indignant that she had made no attempt to hang on to him or save him from his own stupidity.

'You knew?' he said. 'How?'

'Most women know these things. It's a sort of instinct.'

'Why didn't you stop me?' His humiliation burst out of him. 'Oh, Lor', Ab, why? What a rat I've been!'

She reached for him and pulled him to her. 'No, Willie. No. You're never that kind of man. It was something you were caught up in. These things happen. They can come to anyone.'

'How can you forgive me?'

'You're my husband,' Abigail whispered. 'And I was taught to forgive.'

Her generosity made him feel worse, especially since he was aware that if Nadya crooked her little finger at him, he'd still probably go hurrying to her side. It was puzzling. He loved Abigail. Of that he was sure. He loved her for her honesty, her decency, her loyalty, the truth in her. But he also loved – or had loved – Nadya, too, though for an entirely different reason.

Unaware that he had made a sound, he gave a low groan of despair as he tried to find the answer. Assuming he was suffering from remorse and guilt, Abigail enfolded him in her arms.

'It's over, Willie,' she said. 'Just go on loving me. Forget everything else. We must always be together now.'

The morning was cool and as the first light arrived the naval patrols appeared. The town looked old and grey and they could still hear the mob, but there were landing parties along the bund from the gunboats, each consisting of a few sailors under the command of a sub-lieutenant or a midshipman. Wearing fixed grins to show they weren't afraid, they stood immovable wherever the mob collected, targets for filth and brickbats and abuse, their rifles held in front of them, not threatening but also not budging.

Facing them there seemed to be half the population of China, screaming abuse and waving carrying poles, sticks and pick handles looted from the burning godowns. 'Out, King George,' they were yelling. 'Shoot, white pigs! Shoot!'

The front of the crowd seemed to be all young girls, their faces contorted with hatred, their hands wrenching at their blouses to expose their yellow bodies.

'Shoot! Shoot! Kill us, English!'

'Jesus – ' the words came from a sailor whose uniform was covered with human ordure – 'just look at them knockers, Dusty! Pity we ain't better friends.'

The line of rifles lifted and the bluejackets gritted their teeth, immovable under the showers of dung, decaying vegetable matter and dead cats and rats. The pagoda that dominated the bund, its roof shining under the morning dew, lifted above them as the party made their way to the water's edge. Someone had tried to set it on fire and smoke was still coming from its door. The shouting they'd heard all night had quietened now, but they could still hear the occasional crackle of sporadic shooting. Idols and dragon symbols were flourished at them as they stumbled along, part of a large group, escorted by sailors. The faces that stared at them were ugly with hatred and coolies with snot-smeared faces were making messy sacrifices with chickens and goats as they passed. The British, American, French and Japanese flags had all disappeared, all torn down, set on fire or daubed with filth, and one group of students was occupied with making a bonfire of portraits of President Coolidge and King George V.

The streets were full of smoke and wet ashes. Chinese wearing European dresses over their rags were running from looted shops and two coolies were smashing a heavy cast-iron grating edgewise down on to the nose of an abandoned car. Defiant-looking militiamen hung about on street corners, and a bunch of students shouted their fury from behind the placards they carried – DAM   EYE , KING GEORGE; GO HOME, POISO ER OF CHI A. The Chinese, Willie reflected, never managed to get their English letters correct.

Around them telegraph wires hung in loops above pavements strewn with broken glass, broken stones, torn paper and blowing chaff. Near the landing stage, another motor car burned fiercely, sending up a column of black smoke. For the Europeans it was a new and frightening feeling to have the bitterness and hatred directed towards *them*. They had always been indifferent to the strong feelings growing in China and regarded the rise of nationalism as nothing to do with them. Now the hatred was like living through the era of the Boxers all over again. As they passed the end of one of the streets, they saw a militiaman struggling with a girl. Her tunic hung in tatters round her waist as she was dragged away between the houses, a harsh dry scream coming from her throat.

Further along the bund, more militiamen were hurling stones at people who had traded with the Europeans. Godowns were nothing but heaps of smoking timbers and scorched bricks stinking of roasted grain. A feeling of horror hung over the doomed town and the enormous crowds spread like an ugly fungus along the river's edge, everybody shouting and throwing things at the gunboats. Most of what was thrown splashed harmlessly in the water, but the gunboats' crews had rigged hoses with which they kept at bay the sampans that circled them full of yelling students with banners. The market was a burned-out ruin, the breeze slapping the broken roofs in a soft clapping. Shattered earthenware, water jars, pots and rice bowls were trampled into the dirt and the metal workers' booths were empty in a debris of sheet metal and rusty chains.

Just ahead of them as they stumbled along was an English doctor who had run a small hospital in a weird ornamental building near the bund surrounded by willows and smelling of ether. He had given years of his life to it, but now he had abandoned it without a backward glance. Occasionally they passed cars standing outside European houses being loaded with possessions, but there were no drivers and the Europeans were having to do the loading and driving themselves.

The news that the British government was about to give up their concessions had brought the whole city out to cheer at the humiliated foreigners. Not a single coolie had come forward to offer his rickshaw, and the Sikh policemen just weren't enough to keep order. Every white man carried his own luggage, every white woman carried her own small children. There were no servants, no amahs, nothing, as they moved to the river, losing face with every step, humbled in front of the Chinese, the women fighting back the tears, their children wailing with terror, some of the men bloodstained where they had been hit by a flung brickbat.

'We shall be back,' Wissermann said.

'Not on your life, lad,' Willie said grimly. 'For the first time they've realised there are enough of them to chuck us out neck and crop.'

Chiang and his Communist propagandists had shown the Chinese that, simply by joining hands and marching together, they could tear up treaties, and guns and flags meant nothing.

Edward was waiting for them by a little wooden jetty the navy had taken over and the sailors began to stuff people into the boats which kept appearing, handing children into them one after the other, passing them to tense, dry-eyed mothers, trying to make them comfortable, trying to give confidence with smiles and jokes. As they packed the terrified people aboard, more arrived. By this time, an enormous crowd of refugees had assembled by the little landing stage. Not far away a warehouse was burning, the roar of the flames deafening, the smoke depositing little smuts of soot over the gathering people so that they grew dirtier by the minute. Further along, the water's edge contained corpses and there were two men floating in the shallows who had been shot.

The Sarths' party waited at the back of the group they were with, trailing behind because Emmeline was unable to manage the huge suitcases she had insisted on bringing with her.

'Please keep up, Ma'am,' a bearded petty officer begged. 'It's all we can do to keep an eye on all of you.'

Emmeline refused to be hurried and the petty officer tried again. 'Do you need all that luggage, Ma'am?' he asked. 'We was told that there was to be nothing but hand luggage and not much of that.'

Emmeline gave him a look of sheer hatred and, in the end, shouldering his rifle, the petty officer attempted to take one of the cases from her. She snatched it back at once, as if getting her possessions to the boats herself were a matter of pride, and for a moment or two there was a silent tug of war until the petty officer gave up.

They reached the jetty at last and joined the queue. Emmeline flung down her suitcases and, squatting down, began to open one of them and move things around inside it. Standing with his hand on his revolver, Willie watched his son push Polly on board the waiting boat, then Da Braga's sons, and he was just about to follow with Abigail, when she broke free.

'Emmeline needs help.'

It was Willie's feeling that Emmeline had thrust aside all offers of help, but Abigail refused to listen and turned back. Edward didn't hesitate. Filling the remaining seats in the boat with other people, he ordered it away and it began to move into the river towards the passenger steamer waiting in midstream with its gangway down.

It seemed to take a long time before the next boat arrived and the crowd pressed forward, screaming abuse. Seeing the big revolver in Willie's belt, one of the Chinese girls stripped off her blouse and then her trousers and stood stark naked in front of him, thrusting her belly forward, her yellow skin shining in the sun.

'Kill me English bandit,' she screamed. 'Kill me, so our people will avenge me.'

The boat finally grated alongside the jetty and even then Abigail found it hard to persuade Emmeline to budge. Finally, all three of them moved forward and Edward motioned them aboard, smiling a fixed smile, his eyes everywhere at once. Packed in like sardines so they couldn't move, with Abigail huddled next to Emmeline holding a single leather bag containing the few treasures she had considered worth removing, they waited for the rest of the boat to be filled.

Abigail had her head close to Emmeline's and for a moment they looked like sisters discussing what to wear at a dance. Emmeline was scowling, but Abigail's face was calm, as it always was, compassionate and full of gentleness.

'It's going to work out all right,' Willie heard her say. 'This will all die down before long and, even if it doesn't, you still have your properties in Shanghai.'

'They're worthless!' The words were spat out with all Emmeline's familiar bitterness.

Abigail was still murmuring encouragement as Willie turned away, standing on the jetty with Edward, staring about him, his hand on his revolver, his eyes alert for movement. As the boat finally filled, Edward touched his arm.

'All right, Father,' he said. 'Get aboard.'

Willie nodded, not arguing. 'Good luck, son,' he said.

As the boat pushed off, there was an unexpected burst of loose firing from a machine gun hidden among the buildings. A few bullets hit the water alongside the boat and he saw Edward duck, bent double, and remain like that, his head down, one hand on the ground. Horror-stricken, Willie thought he'd been hit, but then he saw him rise and straighten up with his men, and the shooting died as suddenly as it had come. The boat was crowded and he saw Abigail up in the bow, her arm around Emmeline, talking earnestly to her. Staring back over the stern, he could still see his son's tall figure backgrounded by the lifting smoke from the burning warehouse.

There was no shooting as the boat drew away from the jetty and made its way into midstream, but then a single shot came. Several heads bobbed automatically, but Willie didn't see where the bullet struck. Then, as they approached the waiting steamer he became aware of some sort of disturbance at the other end of the boat. As he turned to see what it was, he heard a wail and recognised the voice at once as Emmeline's.

Sweet suffering J, he thought savagely, what in hell was she up to now? Then, through all the bobbing, turning heads, he saw she was trying to stand up and that there was blood on the bosom of her dress.

'Where are you hit, Ma'am?' the petty officer in charge of the boat yelled and she let out another wail.

'Not me,' she yelled. 'It's not me! It's her!'

And then Willie saw that Abigail's head had drooped. Her figure, still held upright by the people crowded round her, was sagging, and the whole front of her clothing was red and glistening in the watery sunshine.

'Just a stray bullet,' Willie spoke bewilderedly. 'And they're such rotten shots! They probably weren't even shooting at *us*. Just one in the whole boat. How it missed everybody else I don't know.'

He sighed. He had often thought of the irony of things but this was the irony to beat everything. He'd been terrified of Yip telling Abigail of his association with Nadya, but that had been removed when Willie's bullet had hit him in the throat; and now, it seemed there had never been any need at all to be afraid because now Abigail was gone, too.

five

He was still finding it hard to accept, especially after holding Abigail in his arms so short a time before she had died. He had met her twenty-seven years before and he had literally grown to maturity with her. They had made a fortune together. Abigail's extra years giving him steadiness and strength, his own drive pushing her into using her undoubted but hidden talents. She had calmed him when he was afire with eagerness, held him back when he was being too precipitate, and he had jockeyed her into seeing a fine future for them which, with her training and her background of humility at the Mission, she had not been able to visualise.

In recent years, however, though they had by no means drifted apart, somehow they had gone their separate ways, each pursuing their own methods of making money. Had they forgotten each other in their anxiety to become wealthy? He didn't think so. It was simply that they had become too absorbed in what they were doing, so that they had failed to notice each other as much as they had, failed to be aware that they were each managing to live long periods without the other close at hand. He suspected that they'd never even considered the financial aspect of what they were doing – simply that they had become too involved, Abigail with her antiquities, Willie with his ships. The truth, of course – and he had to admit it to himself – was that the fault really lay with him, and that Abigail would have abandoned everything for him if he'd wanted it that way. Perhaps, even, her activities in buying and selling had been a refuge for her. He had had an itching foot and had found settling down to a staid married life too difficult when the width of the sea, the width of the world, continued to call to him.

Yet, despite all this – despite Nadya – they had always needed each other, both mentally and physically, had always been glad to see each other again, eager for each other's arms. And though there had been many occasions when he had been alone in the house when Abigail had been away, it had always been different from now. Though Abigail had sometimes not been there, there had always been the feeling that her presence was about him. Now, because he had seen her die, it was no longer like that. There was no longer the sense that, despite the silence in the house, she was only in the next room, in the next town, the next province, the next country. The silence now was the silence of death. There was nothing beyond it and it left him empty and bewildered.

'I don't understand it,' he said.

Nadya listened quietly as he spoke. He had been able to think of nowhere else to turn but to her and she had responded at once to his telegram and turned up at the house near the Bubbling Well Road, quiet, dignified, gentle. With the funeral over, the family were still at home and eyeing her with suspicion.

There was a marked hostility in Polly's manner, but Edward and Thomas were merely curious. Both of them, despite their different characters and environments, had always got on well with their father, despite the occasional disagreements that arose. As children, they had regarded him as a sort of modern-day pirate – indeed, the first thing Edward remembered of him, with his crisp dark hair, strong black eyebrows and fierce eyes was how much, even then, he had resembled the gasconading heroes of their boyhood stories. He hadn't changed much even now. His hair still hadn't turned grey and the deepening lines on his face served only to add to the illusion. Now, the presence of this woman, beautiful in anybody's view with her huge eyes and reddish-brown hair, enhanced the feeling, because they had always been aware of his occasional never-explained jaunts when he disappeared into the blue, either for himself or for the lanky British Foreign Office official who had turned up from time to time. Was she part of it? Where had he found her?

'Who *is* that?' Edward asked when Willie returned from seeing her to the *Lady Roberts* to be taken back to Hong Kong, and he told them everything in the need to purge his soul.

'Do you love her?'

'Yes.'

'What about Mother?'

'Curiously enough, I loved her too.'

'Both of them?'

'Is it impossible? Nadya and your mother had met and there was a mutual respect between them. I think Nadya understood that I still needed your mother. I suspect your mother guessed about Nadya and she understood, too.'

Neither Edward nor Tom seemed to mind. Only Polly was unable to reconcile herself to the fact that her father had had a mistress.

'I don't know how you could have done it,' she said bitterly.

'But I did.'

'What about Mother? I suppose you tired of her and this one was younger?'

'I never tired of your mother and she was exactly the same age.'

'It didn't stop you giving her the things you ought to have been giving Mother.'

'I gave her nothing. I never supported her or paid for anything because she wouldn't let me. Until the revolution in Russia she was far wealthier than I was. Perhaps your mother was wealthier, too, come to that.'

'Well, I shall never accept her. She'll never come into my house.'

'Dammit,' Willie snapped. 'She hasn't asked to!'

Polly's eyes flashed. 'It's a good job, because I'd have refused if she had. And I'd be just as pleased if you didn't, too.'

It meant virtual estrangement, but, Willie supposed, it was a price he had to pay. You never got anything for nothing in life and this, he supposed, was payment for his deceit. He tried hard to understand Polly's attitude. She was a wife and would soon be a mother, and under those circumstances, he supposed, women probably thought differently.

Slowly the extremes of unexpressed grief and rage began to moderate with the passing days, as Willie began to realise he was not the only one who had been injured or bereaved. But though the pain went, the guilt remained, and with it came the strange idea that Nadya was somehow to blame. For a while he shunned her, writing no letters, making no attempt to go to Hong

Kong. But, apart from her and Abigail, on the whole he'd not been interested in women and he began to find he knew no others and that he needed her.

Again and again he found himself thinking of Emmeline. All his life she had plagued him in one way or another and now she had deprived him of the one person he had always leaned on, because, but for her stubbornness, Abigail would have been safely aboard a ship before the shooting had started. He could never forgive her for what had happened. For that matter, he couldn't forgive Zychov. Somehow he felt that, because Zychov was involved with Yip and because Yip's attempt on the *Tien Quan* had delayed him reaching Shanghai in time to stop Abigail going to Yangpo, he was to blame, too. He knew in his heart of hearts it wasn't so, because nothing in the world would have stopped Abigail going upriver to look after her pregnant daughter, but, somehow, it eased his conscience to think that way.

But he was determined not to be sorry for himself. There were too many in Shanghai at that moment bewailing the loss of their possessions at the treaty ports up the Yangtze, among them old Honeyford, whose overconfidence had led him to invest too heavily. Willie had never been a moaner and had always regarded himself as a survivor and now he felt he could see the writing on the wall and the need to readjust.

The hatred of the Chinese was still directed chiefly at the Japanese, but it was obvious the Nationalist movement was going to affect all foreigners and foreign-owned businesses in the future, particularly British and American interests. Eventually they were all going to be thrown out and, though Shanghai didn't believe her turn was near just yet, the city waited with baited breath for the arrival of the Nationalist armies. So far the European casualties had remained few, but the strikes kept occurring and banners were paraded and slogans chanted. Agitators whispered in the teashops, along the wharves and among the godowns, and orators ranted on every street corner. The malice was always there, with the bitter feeling that Shanghai was not China at all but belonged to the Europeans who ran it.

The tension remained marked, like a coiled spring, with more trouble clearly brewing. Troopships arrived from India and British battalions clanked through the town to the relieved cheers of the British population and the muttered resentment of the Chinese. A Punjabi battalion followed, brawny men, heavily bearded and with dark gleaming eyes, and immediately the strikes grew worse. One day it was the dock labourers, next day the rickshaw men, the following day the taxi drivers or the tramway workers. Even the prostitutes went on strike. The actions were clearly well organised so that the city could never function efficiently.

Many of the gunboats lost their Chinese cooks and dhobi boys and their makee-learns. Idle labourers from the docks hung about the street corners in threatening crowds, staring bitterly as the troops began to man the essential services. Houses were broken into and bodies of loyal Chinese left in doorways. Even the missionaries found they could no longer exist, because whenever one of their Chinese patients died they were accused of poisoning them.

There were riots in the Nanking Road and the Shanghai Volunteer Force, raised among the foreigners, even the White Russians, was called out. Outside the International Settlement, the city was run by a group of ex-warlords, who had held control for two years, and the Shanghai Municipal Council had kept well out of the way, anxious to avoid trouble. But, with the city bowed down under a massive crime wave brought on by the strikes, when the warlord in charge decided to put an end to it with a series of public executions, the authorities nervously decided he had better have his head with a couple of dozen men from the city jail.

'They're nothing but the victims of capitalist persecution,' Thomas said bitterly. 'What a lot of cowards you all are, Father.'

Willie gave a grim smile. 'You should get your facts right, son,' he said. 'There isn't one of these men who isn't a murderer. Three of them at least were from the *Tien Quan* and they'd happily have sunk the ship and left everybody on board to drown. And, as it happens, I have nothing to do with it. I've never been part of the city authority and I don't ever want to be.'

It shut Thomas up but it didn't stop the executions.

Twenty-five thousand gaping spectators lined the pavements as the condemned men passed through the streets, even those of the International Settlement and the French Concession, followed by cars, carriages, carts, bicycles, small boys and dogs by the dozen. The condemned men had been crammed into open-sided buses specially hired for the occasion and still carrying the advertisements of the Grand Garage Français, the Oriental Luggage Factory and a few others, their guards and executioners in Model T Fords. To make an occasion of it, two film units had their cameras set up on the execution ground and the condemned men, each one secured by wrists and ankles and with a placard proclaiming his misdeeds strapped to his back, were forced to kneel six at a time to be shot at point blank range with rifles which scattered fragments of skull and warm brains over the spectators.

'It was barbaric,' Thomas insisted.

'But you went to see it,' Willie pointed out.

'To protest.'

'And did you protest, lad? Or hadn't you the courage? I don't see you in prison.'

Thomas dissolved into muttered objections, but it was true that the executions had not caused any rioting. Rather they had stopped it. But Willie was by no means convinced of the efficacy of the example, and the municipal authorities were as shocked by the barbarity of the killings as the students.

Somehow, somewhere in the future, Willie suspected, Shanghai was going to receive a terrible shock. The place was full of people who had come to assume it was their home, that this corner of China was European. Determined not to dwell on his loss, however, determined not to show his unhappiness over the death of his wife, he involved himself more deeply in his business. He had often been told by associates that he was too involved, but, just then, he *wished* to be involved. He saw his business as one of being involved. He couldn't afford not to be involved because – he had to admit – being involved was business, and business was money.

Then one night Thomas turned up with two of his Chinese friends. One of them was Chou, the young man he had brought before, bearded now and tired-looking, the other a plump, bespectacled man, slightly older. As he stood with Thomas by the dresser mixing drinks, Willie spoke quietly.

'Aren't you getting too involved with the Communists, Tom?' he asked.

'I'm not involved, Father,' Thomas said. 'Just friendly.'

'The Nationalists could consider you're involved and they'll be here soon.'

As they drank, Willie questioned Chou about Chinese aims. The young man was polite but not in the slightest inclined to deviate from his views.

'Why?' Willie asked.

Chou shrugged. 'Why not?' he asked. 'China has a lot of sorrows, not all of them of her own making. She doesn't even rule over her own land. Shanghai doesn't belong to us. It seems to belong to the council and all of them are Europeans.'

Willie had to agree. 'Who's your leader?' he asked. 'Chiang?'

'At the moment.'

'And after Chiang! You?'

'No.' Chou smiled. 'Not me. But there are others.'

By this time, Shanghai was so crowded with foreign troops it was difficult to move for them. There were eight British battalions, Italians, French, Japanese and Americans. Though there was no unified command, the French had agreed to act with the British in the event of trouble.

The retreating Chinese northern army passed alongside the cordon that had been formed round the International Settlement. The soldiers were jaded and often bootless, their clothes hanging off them in rags. Their horses were skeletal, their guns old, battered and dusty. As they vanished, it was clear that Chiang's Nationalist troops would be close behind and, watching the reports, reading the newspapers, Willie wondered again and again what he should do. He had been busy transferring his capital to British-owned Hong Kong for some time, because he was well aware that if the Nationalists decided to wreak their vengeance on all those nations who had humiliated them his business would inevitably be hit.

Then he hit on the idea of making his firm non-British. 'Da Braga,' he said. 'By God, Da Braga!'

Stumping around on crutches, determined to be mobile, Da Braga had set up his home in a house to the north of the Bubbling Well Road with his plump wife and sons. There had been no suggestion that he should return upriver and he now had a room alongside Willie's in Sarth's office block on the bund. Since his interests had always been in Yangpo, he was having to learn the business afresh. Sitting down at the other side of his desk, Willie offered him a cigar and in return Da Braga placed a brandy bottle on the tab as usual. 'Luis,' he said. 'How much was your interest in Sarth's in Yangpo?'

Da Braga leaned back in his chair and studied Willie with his dark spaniel's eyes. 'You know very well what it was. One half.'

Willie smiled. 'How would you like to be part of Sarth's, Shanghai?'

Da Braga smiled. 'Of course I would. I've lost something but, thanks to your suggestion that we move everything downriver, not all by a long way.'

'I'm thinking of changing the name of the firm.'

Da Braga smiled. 'I wondered how long it would take you to think of that,' he said.

Willie smiled back. 'How about making it Da Braga-Kee?'

'George Kee?'

'Why not? He has a little money put by. He's invested well and he'd love to have his name on the list of directors.'

'It sounds sense. What's behind it? What I suspect?'

Willie grinned. 'I imagine so, Luis. Da Braga-Kee's would be a different firm – Chinese and Portuguese. Nothing to do with me.'

'Except that your money would be behind it and you'd expect a share of the profits.'

'It wouldn't be a British firm, Luis. That's the important thing.'

'You're thinking of when the Nationalists come, of course?'

'Further than that, Luis. I suspect the Nationalists will leave us alone. But if the Communists get into power, *they* won't. I saw Communism in action in Russia. They'll want to take over, and everything belonging to the British, the Americans, the French, the Japanese will disappear. I'd bet on that. Because they have no concessions in China, the Portuguese might be acceptable. So would George Kee, so long as we're careful that we don't trade with any of the concessionaires. How do you feel about trading with the Chinese and only with the Chinese?'

'If it means that I'm not kicked out of China, I'm very much in favour.'

'The price needn't be known. I'm looking elsewhere for profits.'

'For instance?'

'South, Luis. Malaya. Indo-China. Dutch Indies. Why not Australia? You know the joke: It's there but nobody's ever seen it. Why not us? New Zealand? The Philippines?'

'Profits will fall.'

'Security will rise. What do you say?'

Da Braga studied Willie for some time, his dark eyes shining. 'I think you're going to have to put up with a few sneers from your British business associates.'

Willie shrugged. 'They've always sneered at me. It won't be very different.'

'Then, yes, Willie. I will come in, especially if George Kee will too.'

Willie grinned back at him. 'Fine,' he said. 'Let's have him in and pop the question.'

Shanghai waited, the foreigners with some unease, the Chinese working class with their never-ending patience. They had never changed, their sinewy backs bent, their properties destroyed by typhoons or floods, their families wiped out by drought or famine, their very lives crumbled by all the plagues and wars that passed over them, always on the verge of starvation but always surviving to rebuild and start again. They had suffered centuries of domination by the Manchus and their predecessors, centuries of cruelty that had bred in them a humility that had never changed until now, when they seemed to he waiting with bated breath for something which they felt would give them not only freedom but hope.

As Da Braga-Kee and Co. began to take shape and Willie gave more and more of his attention to the Sarth Shipping Line, the Nationalists arrived outside the city. They were a very different kettle of fish from the northern armies. They were without the habitual kow-tow the Chinese had always given to Europeans, and as they stopped with their sun banners near the British lines, they looked confident, fit and well equipped. Watching them, Willie tried to decide what they were after. There had been no incidents because the city was an armed camp, with infantry and even artillery stationed on the high buildings and armoured cars making regular patrols along the outlying roads where the foreigners had their homes. On the only occasion the Nationalists had attempted to enter the Settlement, they had been firmly turned back by grim-faced British soldiers determined not to give an inch, and the municipal council had arranged for armed sentries to guard foreign properties beyond the settlement boundaries.

The change brought about by their arrival was clear at once, but not quite in the way they'd expected. It was the night life of the city that changed. The Cantonese troops had been on the march for a long time through a succession of empty spaces, and they were looking for excitement, and, with the owners of the nightclubs largely opportunistic young Chinese who were totally in sympathy with them, they were soon crowding the foreigners off what they had always considered their own dance floors. And, being Chinese, they wanted Chinese girls to dance with, so that the White Russians and French began to disappear. More girls were rushed up from the south to supply the demand and sing-song girls hurriedly changed to taxi-dancers as everybody opted for the new drug, jazz. The only concession that was made was to import musicians from Manila because the Chinese still seemed totally unable to master waltzes, fox trots and tangos, and a Chinese singer trying to handle *Shepherd of the Hills* sounded like a cat with its head caught in the railings. Driven from their playgrounds, the Europeans fell back on those establishments that operated a colour bar and used only Russian and Eurasian hostesses. Yip Hsao-Li, Willie felt, would have loved it.

'The bloody country's being won for the Chinese in the nightclubs,' he laughed.

But there was another side to it, too, because the gangsters, friends of the late Yip Hsao-Li, also moved in and, with a rash of new night spots, began to take over. There was no shortage of experts in criminality and no shortage of weapons. As the warlords had disappeared, their soldiers had sold their weapons to buy food and there were now so many firearms in Shanghai it was no longer worth smuggling them in, and any small operator not prepared to pay for protection had his club closed – either by his own sudden demise, a riot, or by having a box of snakes let loose on the dance floor while the dancers were smooching in the half-light to a waltz.

They hadn't heard of Zychov for some time, but Thomas had heard he'd been seen at the headquarters of Chiang K'Ai-Shek, who was still waiting in the wings to make a triumphal entry into the city. Not for him the scuffling and exchange of shots, and he remained out of sight until the Nationalists were properly masters of the Chinese quarter and a revolutionary administration was in being to welcome him as a liberator.

Willie was upriver at a place called Wanchu near Sinkiang when he arrived. A steamer, the *Po-Li*, which had run aground, contained a cargo of rice he was very much in need of and, with the new firm taking shape, money was short and he was eager to get his hands on the rice for which he already had a customer prepared to pay cash on delivery.

When he reached the Sarth launch to take him along to the *Po-Li* however, his coxswain warned him to wait.

'Best, Mastah,' he said.

'Why? What's wrong?'

The coxswain gestured at the gunboat lying out in the river flying the Kuomintang flag. 'General Chiang go aboard gunboat, to go to Shanghai. All told to wait.'

Looking up, Willie saw a big launch at the next jetty, its coxswain standing nervously on the quay, his deckhand busily polishing the brasswork.

'How long's the bugger going to be?'

'No savvee, Mastah. But no boats move. Orders, mastah.'

For an hour Willie waited frustratedly, then, just as he was about to get in the launch and order it away in a fury, several large American Packards arrived. They contained senior officers of the Kuomintang and, as they climbed out, he recognised among them Chiang K'Ai-Shek himself, small, thin, impassive faced, and looking incredibly young in a neat high-collared uniform with breeches, lace-up boots and a Sam Browne belt.

'Dogleg himself,' he muttered.

He had no love for Chiang K'Ai-Shek. Thanks to him, Willie and Da Braga had suffered a considerable loss, because their property in Yangpo had been valuable, and he couldn't imagine anybody buying it or paying rent for it now. And above all there was Abigail.

He stared with narrowed eyes as a dozen officers climbed into the waiting launch. There was a great deal of saluting then the Nationalist coxswain bent over the engine. It fired once then promptly died, but after a few struggles, started again. Willie leaned over and shouted.

'There's no water coming through,' he yelled.

The coxswain looked up in alarm and moved aft, nervously pushing through the waiting officers. Returning to the engine, he switched off and removed the engine cover. A lot of shrill chatter broke out among the uniformed men, then one of them slashed at the cringing coxswain with his stick and a second climbed back to the quay and strode to where Willie was waiting.

'We are commandeering your launch,' he announced in English.

'Oh, no, you're not!' Willie snapped back.

'General Chiang wishes to go to the gunboat out there.'

'Then let him take a sampan.'

The officer gave Willie a sour look. By this time, Chiang, still surrounded by his officers, had arrived on the jetty alongside Willie's launch.

'You're not having this launch,' Willie told him bluntly. 'It's mine. I need it. Business is waiting.'

Chiang's eyebrows rose. 'You speak our language,' he observed.

'Have done for years.'

'We need your launch.'

Willie glared. 'Your troops have just ruined my business in Yangpo. And your supporters killed my wife. Why should I back off?'

'Because,' the officer who had first spoken said, 'it isn't fitting for a general of the Kuomintang Army of Liberation to travel by sampan. We are Chinese soldiers winning back China for the Chinese people.'

'And a lot of affection you'll win if you just take over things. You're not having my launch.'

One of the men alongside Chiang unclipped the flap of his revolver holster, but Chiang laid a hand on his arm and turned to Willie.

'What do you say,' he asked, 'if we arrange to pay you for the use of the launch? Would that satisfy you?'

It was an unexpected offer and Willie saw that Chiang was actually smiling. So far, though he'd seen dozens of photographs of the KMT leader, he'd never seen one of him smiling. It was impossible to refuse.

'Very well,' he said. 'Payment on the dot when we arrive.'

Chiang smiled again and started to climb into the launch. The other officers followed and Willie gestured to his coxswain to start the engine. Casting off the lines, they began to chug out into midstream. Alongside the gunboat, Chiang smiled, thanked Willie, and climbed aboard for his trip downriver in the direction of Shanghai. Willie smiled back, but his smile died as the other officers climbed after the general.

'Hey,' he yelled at the English-speaking officer. 'Who pays me?'

The officer ignored him and vanished after Chiang into the wardroom of the gunboat. Willie was about to climb after him, but the Chinese sailor on gangway duty pointed a rifle at him and flicked off the safety catch.

'I hope the bastard's right leg drops off,' Willie said sourly to the grinning coxswain as he pushed off and turned the boat back to the *Po-Li*.

Despite the arrival of Chiang close to the city, there were only occasional clashes, one to the north of the settlement, another at Chapei, but the Nationalist leaders seemed to be well in control and trouble seemed chiefly to be stirred up by Communists in an attempt to embroil Chiang with the Western powers. Willie had heard that Thomas' friend, Chou, was busy among the workers and certainly the timing of the strikes seemed to indicate the touch of a man with brains and organising ability. But still nothing of great gravity occurred beyond an occasional murder – never regarded as serious in Shanghai where violence always existed in the shadows – and the sporadic sniping by Communist gunmen. The European leadership was torn two ways, because one group of advisers was all for setting about the Chinese in the good old Victorian gunboat way, while the other, terrified of losing lives and property, advocated care and a softly-softly approach.

Even when several foreigners were killed as the Nationalists entered Nanking and foreign gunboats shelled the city in retaliation, still the Nationalists held their hand. By now, however, Shanghai was living in a state of virtual siege.

'Bloody Chinks,' Honeyford snarled from behind a whisky and Apollinaris at the Long Bar of the Club as he swung on Willie. 'It's people like you, Sarth, that cause the trouble, pandering to 'em, treating 'em as if they knew what they were talking about.'

Willie said nothing, but he didn't hesitate to take it out on his son, whom he regarded in much the same way as Honeyford regarded him.

Thomas was unrepentant. 'If the Europeans in China had ever been strong enough to hold their position,' he said, 'it would have been different. But they never were and the Chinese are just beginning to realise it.'

Certainly the vast undisciplined anarchy of strikes, protests and riots had jelled at last into a great campaign of detestation for the Western powers who had preyed on the country for a hundred years. The whole of South China was on the march, each uprising starting another in a chain reaction, and millions of pounds' worth of property upriver was being abandoned without even a thought to its value.

The Chinese had seen the Westerners humbled, struggling to safety between shouting, spitting mobs, and it was an earth-shaking experience. For generations, the Chinese had accepted their inferiority without question, but now, with the subtle propaganda of the Communists backing the blunter success of the Nationalist armies, they had become a nation – simply by joining hands and marching together. It seemed obvious to Willie – despite his own indignant complaints and the defiance of people like old Honeyford – that the days of the treaty powers were numbered and it was going to be even more difficult in the future with the growing dissent between the Communists and the Kuomintang, which he could already see adding to the problems.

His first trip to Australia produced immediate results. Tough, uncompromising and ignored for years, the Australians were more than willing to do business. They always had grain to sell and were anxious to buy Hong Kong produce. Another ship, the *Fuku Maru* was bought in Japan and the Sarth Line merged with a small Australian line consisting of two small ships, the *Keverne* and the *Dunnose Grange*. They were both old but they were enough to send Willie hurriedly to Hong Kong to drum up cargoes. Nadya allowed him to stay with her, but it wasn't the same and he decided that next time he'd stay at a hotel. It brought back too many memories of Abigail and all the old sorrows, all the old guilt. But the pain, the resentment, the bitterness, were wearing off now and he had come to the conclusion that a man in his right mind could overcome any disaster if he set his mind to it.

He arrived back in Shanghai to find that the trouble he had expected was already brewing. The Communists were stirring up trouble again and the blame was being put on the Nationalists. British aircraft arrived to make reconnaissance flights over the areas where fighting was taking place and the railway lines to Hankow and Nanking were cut, but it was like trying to plug a leak as hundreds of other breaks appeared. Another demonstration in the Chapei area resulted in native police stations being attacked, the police murdered and their armouries seized. Dozens of large fires were burning at once and rumour had it that the Communists were itching to rush the International Settlement in the confusion they had caused. At his headquarters outside the city, however, Chiang informed the newspapers that he had no intention of causing trouble and gave a laconic interview to the press, posed with them for pictures, and offered tea and cakes.

Two days later, gunfire seemed to be coming from a different quarter and the presence of armoured cars and Indian soldiers on the streets was noticeable. The firing continued, but no one knew very much beyond the fact that there was trouble again in the Chinese City. Shots could he heard all the way from Chapei and Hongkew, sometimes single shots, sometimes ragged fusillades. At the Club it was believed it was the Communist attempt to wrench control from the Europeans at last, but then they heard it was something else entirely.

Thomas knew exactly what.

'It's the gangs attacking the Communists,' he said.

Da Braga looked startled. 'Why, for God's sake?'

'An arrangement made by Chiang,' Thomas said dryly. 'He wants them cleared out before he takes possession, but he also wants to keep his hands clean. So he's come to an agreement with Yip Hsao-Li's friends. If they do his dirty work for him, he'll allow them to operate.'

As more information came in, Thomas' estimate proved correct. The headquarters of the Workers' General Union had been surrounded and most of those active in the movement had been shot out of hand. Gunmen belonging to the secret societies were now raiding the lodgings of known Communists and carrying them off for execution, while a Communist-led crowd which tried to demonstrate outside Chiang's headquarters was dispersed with a great deal of bloodshed. Within a few hours all anti-Chiang opposition had been wiped out in a series of bloody reprisals which did little harm to Westerners and left Chiang basking in their good wishes. As they learned the whole story of how Chiang's private army of gunmen had put the Communists to flight in one of the grimmest, bloodiest no-quarter fights ever, they learned that the same thing had also started at Canton.

As the firing died down, the radio station announced that the disturbances in the Chinese suburbs were now under control. Only an occasional shot like a fire cracker came over the night air and, staring from the window towards the lights of the river, Willie was miles away, thinking of Abigail, when he heard the door open.

It was Thomas and he looked young, pale and scared.

'Hello, Tom,' Willie said. 'I hope you haven't been trying to interfere in what's going on.'

'No, Father,' Thomas said. 'Not me. Not this time.'

'How's Fanny?'

'She's fine.'

'You ought to bring her here more often. It becomes lonely with Polly in the States, Edward down in Hong Kong and your mother –'

He stopped and, making an effort to smile, looked up. 'What brings you here anywhere, anyway?'

'Father,' Thomas said, 'I need a little help.'

Willie's eyes narrowed. 'What have you been up to?'

'Nothing, Father. I've not been up to anything.'

'What is it then?'

'Have you one of your ships due to move out? To Hong Kong? Or north?'

Willie's eyes narrowed. 'Go on, boy.'

'I have a couple of Chinese friends the police are looking for.'

'Communists?'

'You could call them that. You've met them.'

'Chou?'

'Yes.'

'What's in your mind, son?'

'You're in the shipping business and I was approached to see if you'd do him a favour.'

'Who by?'

'Another friend of mine. An Englishman.'

'Is *he* a Communist?'

'No, sir. He's not. Just a man with a little compassion. You probably know him, but I won't mention his name then you're not involved.'

'It sounds as if I'm going to be very much involved,' Willie snapped. 'What's Chou been up to?'

'Nothing more than he was always up to. He was working for the Chinese Communist Party. Chiang's gangsters were well organised.'

'By Chiang?'

'No. But they've been organised. I heard someone picked up a lot of money to get them organised. Some Russian, they say.'

Willie turned quickly. 'Chap called Zychov?'

'I think that was the name. Chou was arrested but managed to escape. He has to leave before they find him again.'

Willie stared at the lights in the river again. The request didn't present a great problem. Many coastal steamers took human freight if the money was right and the right man was approached. There was always deck space for another individual among the crowded passengers and he was more than willing to thwart Zychov and Yip's gangster friends.

'The *Lady Roberts* is due out,' he said slowly. 'Cargo and passengers. It won't be a comfortable trip.'

'I don't think he'll quibble, Father.'

'Where is he now?'

'Outside.'

'You'd better bring him in. Don't let the servants see him, though.'

As Thomas disappeared, Willie reached for the telephone. By the time his son returned, it had been arranged. The men with him looked thin and tired but they smiled at Willie.

'I'm grateful, Mr Sarth,' Chou said.

Willie nodded. 'I'll get things organised. You'd better try to find some food for your friends, Tom. They look as though they need some.'

When he returned, the Chinese had finished eating.

'Ready?'

'Of course.'

They went to the door where the car was waiting. Pushing the Chinese down behind the front seat, Thomas tossed a blanket over them, then climbed in alongside his father.

They were stopped once by a policeman. Behind him, Willie saw two Nationalist soldiers and a man in a dark suit and white spats looking like a Chicago gangster.

'What's the trouble?' he asked.

'Looking for troublemakers, Mr Sarth,' the policeman said. 'Have you had any trouble near your house?'

'Nothing at all.'

'Where are you going?'

'One of my ships, the *Lady Roberts*, is due to leave in an hour. I have to see the captain.'

The car was waved on and twenty minutes later they had arrived alongside the *Lady Roberts*. Her square bow looked blunt and ugly. Many times Willie had decided she'd have to go, but when it came to the pinch, he'd always backed away from the decision. The *Lady Roberts* had been his first maritime acquisition and he realised he was more sentimental about her than he had imagined.

A ship was loading in the river, clusters of lights flaring over the junks and barges alongside, but there was no one about to see them go aboard. Yeh met them as they headed up the gangway and the two Chinese were spirited out of sight without a word. As Willie stood by the car in the shadows watching the ship, Thomas took his hand. 'Thank you, Father. They asked me to tell you that one day perhaps they might be able to help you.'

'Just don't involve me in politics again, boy. The one thing I want to be at the moment is uninvolved.'

'That's what I thought, Father,' Thomas smiled. 'That's why I'm saying goodbye for a while.'

'Goodbye? Where the hell are you going?'

'With my friends. I remembered your advice about the Nationalists. A man was making enquiries about me at Fan-Su's. Fortunately I wasn't there and she said I was at the university. She knew I wasn't and she got a message to me.'

'Is Fanny a Communist?'

'Let's say that, like me, she sympathises with China. Keep an eye on her, Father.'

'Where do you expect to end up?'

Thomas smiled. 'Wherever my friends end up.'

Giving his father a hug, he turned and ran lightly up the gangway. Almost at once the winches began to clatter and within ten minutes the *Lady Roberts* was on the move. Willie stared after her as she moved away into the shadows in midstream.

The world, he decided, was in a bloody mess.

six

It was the unexpected retirement after a heart attack of Julian Brassard that took Willie to London again.

Brassard was looking old and feeble when Willie called on him at his house in Esher. He was sitting in front of the fire with a blanket round his legs, looking pale and white and close to death.

'They say I'll get over it,' he said, 'but it seemed to me it was time I sold the business. Since you had a large hand in building it up I felt you ought to be the first to know.'

Willie shrugged. There hadn't been a lot of business with Brassard's since Abigail's death. He had tried for a time to keep up an interest in the antiques she had bought and sold but he had made a few bad mistakes and had finally come to the conclusion that he really knew little about them and, without Abigail, couldn't carry it on. Polly had said she thought she'd like to try and, indeed, she had learned a little about it, but her interest wasn't really in it and there was talk now of Wissermann's pulling out of China.

'Nothing seems worth while these days,' Brassard mourned. 'What with this idiot, Hitler, in Germany, shouting the odds and sucking up to Mussolini. He's after another war. You mark my words.'

Seeing no future in Abigail's business, in the end Willie had turned everything over to Nadya in Hong Kong and, with the big cruise liners now calling in more often, she was finding she had no need to send things to London or the States and could sell them to the wealthy passengers coming ashore for the day.

There was a conference and shipping business to be done in London but not very much. Markets had run wild in America and it was affecting things too much and, with too little money chasing too few investments, there were too few jobs and no expansion, and the irony of it was that, with falling prices, people with money found they were actually better off. Shipping was on its beam ends however. The Japanese merchant fleet was expanding rapidly and snatching business, so that it became a struggle to maintain profitability with the adverse trading. There were a dozen things that touched it – unrest in India, Yangtze floods, the depression in Europe, all of them having their effect on exports and imports, and, for lack of cargoes, vessels were being laid up in all the rivers and creeks round England, gathering weeds, one caretaker looking after half a dozen ships.

'To hold a ship for years is murder,' Willie growled. 'Ships are for sailing, not for collecting all the stinking mud from a river bed.'

With capital short, once again it had crossed his mind that he might find a buyer for the *Lady Roberts*, which was surely reaching the end of her long life, but, with captains unable to find berths and going to sea as mates, mates as bosuns, and bosuns as ordinary hands, no one was interested, so he allowed sentiment to take over, forgot his plans and decided to leave her to operate in Far Eastern waters.

It was a sorry period of volatile trade and ephemeral solutions, and Hitler, as Brassard had prophesied, seemed to offer nothing but hostility. A demagogue with a spellbinding oratory and a propaganda machine that might well, Willie felt, have been copied from the Chinese Communists, he was getting away with murder, while the League of Nations, designed for no other reason than to stop aggression, seemed hopelessly inadequate.

After the brilliant colours of the Far East, with the Depression absorbing all the spirit of the people, and the streets full of unemployed, Europe was overpoweringly grey. In China Chiang K'Ai-Shek was firmly in the saddle now. There was still fighting, but he was clearly running the show these days and had even discarded his wife and family to marry a daughter of the Soong family, which seemed to have made a speciality of producing girls who were femmes fatales. For one of them Sun Yat-Sen had also repudiated his wife. A second had married the scion of a famous banking house, and now Chiang had married the American-educated third, for whom he had also abandoned his religion and become a baptised Christian.

His methods were also often American, and he was surrounded by a cohort of smart young generals who knew exactly where they were going. Chiang had quarrelled with his older supporters and many of the new men had been students not long before, and they were clever and educated enough to see a bright future for China, even if they had to indulge in a little treachery on the side to achieve it. Prominent among them was Zychov, wearing the uniform of a military and naval adviser, always close to Chiang in the photographs that appeared in the newspapers, as if he were making sure of the protection of the most powerful man in the country.

Chiang's assault on the Communists had totally alienated them from him and he had quarrelled with the Russians sent by Moscow to back him, but Zychov, who had been in the ranks of those who had opposed Lenin and the Red Army during the Russian Civil War, was more than acceptable and, according to Thomas, who always seemed to learn from his Leftist friends exactly what was going on behind the scenes, was doing very well out of it, too.

Despite Chiang's hold on the country, however, politically it was in a mess. It was impossible to assess the chaos that was China. 'How do you?' Willie asked. 'When there are three – sometimes four – governments, all claiming to be in control.'

Since Chiang was causing little trouble to the Europeans, he was being backed by Gerald Honeyford and his friends of the pro-Chiang China Friendship Group as the man most likely to bring China out of the anarchy into which it had sunk and, above all, as the man to look after their personal interests. With their encouragement he was even being supported now by London and Washington as the only man with whom the Western powers could deal.

Perhaps it was Shanghai's acceptance of Chiang that turned Willie against the place. He considered Chiang dangerous and distrusted him, if only for his protection of Zychov. He was also too much in the hands of people like Gerald Honeyford and Yip's friends, though Willie had heard that the secret societies who had removed his Communist opponents considered they had had a raw deal because money promised to them for their efforts had not materialised. Suddenly there were too many complications and he was glad he had diversified his business. With the loss of Abigail, Shanghai seemed suddenly to hold little for him.

He had watched it grow from the beginning of the century, revelling in the enormous strides forward it had taken, enjoying its prosperity, its building programmes, even its bold self-confidence, feeling that somehow it reflected his own life. But now, unexpectedly, he saw that, as it had grown, it had acquired a pompous and purse-proud arrogance. Great banks towered above streets where the Chinese were still – even now – little more than beasts of burden, a contrast as vivid as that between the painted and polished warships and the shabby Chinese junks and sampans that clustered, noisy and impotent, around them.

Despite its race clubs and the great artistes who appeared in its theatres, the place was really still only an outpost and had nothing but its money and its fear of losing it. It was now four cities, all so close you merely crossed the street to move from one to another, and he knew that everyone – police, Customs and government officials, reformers, preachers, even diplomats – dirtied their fingers occasionally in their attempts to take advantage of the get-rich-quick atmosphere. It was not only the centre of European evangelism, it was also a centre of the opium trade and, as Willie had personally discovered, of piracy. It was big and brash and filled with a collection of the world's shrewdest men. In Hong Kong it was said that Shanghailanders were always easy to spot because they had too much money and too-loud voices. But it was an exciting place, it had to be admitted – one of the wickedest cities in the world, where two civilisations met, where morality was irrelevant, where the atmosphere was exactly right for making money – and he had always enjoyed it, but now, abruptly, he wondered if he still did. Cowering behind its barricades against the growing threat of Chinese nationalism, it exhibited human nature without dignity or generosity. The evacuation of the upriver concessions had infuriated the old China hands and, though the impossibility of hanging on to them in the growing tide of nationalism had been clear, they had still selfishly expected their countries' soldiers and sailors to risk their lives to help them to do so.

It was Emmeline's remarriage more than anything else that seemed to highlight the place's determination to hang on to its ill-gotten gains. To Willie's surprise, she had not disappeared to England after the incident at Yangpo. Wishart's had vanished, bought up by one of the big trading houses, but she had remained in Shanghai living on her capital, which was said to be dwindling rapidly because she hadn't drawn in her horns a great deal. He saw her occasionally, driving about in a chauffeured car, large and gaunt now but somehow still attractive, then he heard she had married old Honeyford, whose wife had died the previous year. At first he was surprised, then, as the thing sank in, he gave a great shout of laughter.

'Honeyford!' he yelled. 'God's great green footstool, Honeyford!'

Honeyford's first wife had been a drab little woman who was noted throughout Shanghai as never having said anything original in her life, and the idea of the old man having to cope with the determined and forthright Emmeline was just unimaginable. With his dull wife and his little Chinese mistress, Gerald Honeyford, he had always considered, had never seemed to have both oars in the water, but now, with Emmeline behind him, it looked very much as if he were going to be totally adrift.

'Good God,' he said to Da Braga. 'There's no end to that woman. She's like one of those Kelly dolls. Knock her down and up she comes again. It'll be God help Honeyford, because she won't sit back and talk in clichés like his first wife. She'll want a hand in the business and he's old enough to be pushed out if she's clever.'

Sure enough, almost immediately, they heard that Emmeline had installed herself in an office alongside Honeyford's at Mason and Marchant's and was beginning to take work off his hands. It seemed to highlight Shanghai's frenetic pace; its indifference, its lack of finesse or concern for decency, for what was going on around it, in the need to go on making money; its apparent blindness to what was happening and what was clearly going to happen in the future. To Willie it was as if he had suddenly started seeing the place through a magnifying glass and finding he didn't like it very much. More and more he used his ships to move about the Far Eastern waters. He enjoyed the forthright bluntness of the Australians and New Zealanders, the cleanliness of the Dutch in their clusters of islands, the soft French atmosphere of their Indo-Chinese possessions and Singapore's languid self-assurance. But Singapore was still a foreign city, whereas Hong Kong was the China he loved. You could stroll for no more than a minute from its centre and you wouldn't see a European face among a teeming, jostling populace in an atmosphere tingling with activity, excitement, movement and confusion.

Following his plans to develop his business, he sold two old ships, opened a small office in Sydney to handle the cargoes he was carrying across the Pacific, and arranged for agents in Auckland, New Zealand, Singapore, Soerabaya in the Dutch East Indies, and Saigon in French Indo-China. Agents were important. Hamburg-Amerika had over three thousand in the United States alone.

Often he thought of Abigail, but the pain had finally gone and he found his thoughts turning again to Nadya. Occasionally he heard of her but hadn't seen her for two years now. Without Abigail his life was empty and, with his children now adult, he was more alone than ever. Edward was back in England, unmarried but a lieutenant-commander and executive officer in a cruiser. Thomas, back from his self-imposed exile, was a lecturer at the university and married to Fan-Su, still a dreamy man of ideals, entirely different from his brisker elder brother, whose career came before everything, even marriage. Polly was in Singapore now, because Wissermann's had not changed their minds about pulling out of China and had transferred all their Far East business to the British colony. She had a growing family of three and, with his father dead, her husband, Elliott, was running the firm.

Almost without conscious effort, Willie found his way back to Hong Kong. He told himself it was because he had business there and because the *Lady Roberts* was due to sail south and he felt like being aboard. But he knew it was more than that. He needed to see Nadya. Once she had meant a great deal to him. But so had Abigail. He was still at a loss to explain how it had happened that he could have loved them both. But he had. He had.

He hadn't heard anything from Nadya for some time, but he knew she was still in business. She had expanded her properties and was now running a large antique store in the centre of the city. There were always plenty of buyers among the wealthy taipans, and always cruise ships and visitors from Australia, on business or pleasure, on the look-out for things to beautify their homes.

The warm air that lay over Hong Kong's anchorage as the *Lady Roberts* arrived seemed to indicate a storm. The air was still and reminded him of the time when he had arrived in a typhoon just before he had received the brush-off from Nadya, just before the attempt had been made to take over the *Tien Quan* and he had shot Yip, just before – he drew a deep breath – just before he had gone to Yangpo to return with the body of his wife.

The hard brassy sun held the white buildings in a shimmering haze and even the narrow streets, crammed with surging humanity, crouched in a stifling pressure of heat. He attended to business but his mind wasn't on it and eventually he headed for the new premises of A N Kourganov. It was a shop with a frontage far wider than normal for Hong Kong and it seemed to be crammed with exquisite furniture. The interior had been decorated with all Nadya's taste and, he noticed, she seemed these days to be concentrating on pictures. He could only assume that the fashion had changed or the flow of saleable jewellery and *objets d'art* had dried up and, like himself, she had diversified.

The girl who came forward looked like the same one who had been with her when she had first moved to Hong Kong, but he couldn't be certain and she showed no sign of recognition.

'Mademoiselle Kourganova hasn't been in today,' she said.

'Away, is she?'

'No, she's at home.'

'Anything wrong? Is she ill?'

'I don't think – ' the girl stopped. 'I remember you, sir,' she went on, finally acknowledging that she knew Willie. 'And I'm a little worried. She telephoned yesterday to say she wouldn't be in and I haven't seen her since and no one answers the telephone.'

Willie frowned. 'Let's have her address,' he snapped.

The address was on the Peak, the Mayfair of Hong Kong, a district of good-sized bungalows set around with flame trees. They were crowded closely together because Hong Kong was always short of space, but clearly Nadya had moved into a good area. As the cab drew near, Willie was fidgeting restlessly on the rear seat. As it climbed, another cab passed, heading down the hill. In the back was a tall figure wearing a white tropical suit and a straw hat whom Willie recognised at once.

'Zychov, by Christ,' he said aloud.

'Sir?' The cab driver slowed and turned his head.

'Nothing, nothing! Hurry, please!'

All the old hatred came back, all the old feeling of treachery and betrayal that dated back to Shantu. Since the *Tien Quan* incident nothing had been seen of Zychov. He had vanished into thin air after Yip had been killed because he knew the police were looking for him and so, it seemed, were the Communists after the disaster to the Party when Chiang had set the Shanghai gangsters on them. They had established themselves now in Kiangsi Province under the leadership of a man called Mao, whose face appeared occasionally in the Chinese newspapers, with that of his second-in-command, Thomas' friend whom they had spirited away from Shanghai in the *Lady Roberts*. He called himself Chou En-Lai and he was now one of the major figures in the

Communist hierarchy which, according to Thomas, would never allow themselves to forget the treacherous attack on them in Shanghai or Zychov who had engineered it with Kuomintang money.

Paying the driver quickly, Willie hurried to the house. No one answered the door but it was unlocked and he pushed inside. A radio was playing somewhere and, as he entered the hall, it stopped abruptly and he heard a step on the stairs. Looking up, he saw Nadya at the top, staring down at him.

'William! What are you doing here?'

She was pale and looked ill and he could see she had been weeping. He moved up the stairs to her and she put out her hand at once, almost as though she had been waiting for him.

'Nadya! There's something wrong!'

She look her head, but the movement was too vehement. 'No,' she said. 'No. It's all right.'

'Are you in trouble? Is it money?' Willie studied her narrowly. 'Why have you been crying, Nadya?'

'I haven't been crying.'

'Yes, you have. I've seen you before when you've been crying. Was it because of Zychov?'

'How did you know about that?'

'His cab passed mine. I recognised him at once. I'd recognise that twister anywhere. I've had his face stamped on my heart ever since he deserted me at Shantu. If he lived to be a hundred I'd still recognise him. What's he want?'

She sighed. 'Money,' she said.

They moved downstairs and she led the way across the veranda to sit in the shade of one of the flame trees and stare over the harbour where they could see shipping moving like beetles across the water.

'Have you given him money before?' Willie asked.

'Yes.'

'Much?'

'Not much. Enough.'

'That was a mistake. That's why he came back. Did you give him some today?'

'I was just going to the bank to arrange for it.'

'Don't. When is he coming to collect?'

'This afternoon.'

'Leave this to me. Just telephone for a cab.'

Returning to the *Lady Roberts*, Willie went to the big cabin and dug from his luggage the old revolver he always carried. It seemed to look bigger than ever. Stuffing it in his belt, he returned to the cab and directed the driver up the hill. Nadya was waiting quietly, sitting still, her hands on her lap. She managed a faint smile.

'You were always very decisive, William,' she said.

'Let's have a drink.'

'Better still, let me provide you with a meal.'

'I'd rather have a drink. I might get drunk enough to shoot our little friend when he turns up.'

Two hours after the sun had passed its height, they heard a cab toiling up the hill. It stopped by the house and Willie saw Zychov climb out. The old panache was still there, he noticed, as he saw him pay the driver.

Stepping out of sight behind the stairs as the doorbell rang, he gestured. 'Let him in,' he said.

Zychov entered cheerfully, taking Nadya's hand and kissing it with a flourish. Willie watched him through the curtains, his stomach twisting with hatred. Zychov was still handsome but he'd grown fatter as if he drank too much.

'You have the money?' Zychov asked.

'No.'

Zychov smiled, a wide curling smile, full of teeth but equally full of menace. 'That's very foolish,' he said. 'I could arrange for you to have quite a lot of trouble.'

'I don't believe you.' Nadya answered quietly, but her voice trembled as she spoke.

Zychov's smile came again. 'There are people in Shanghai who I know would be more than willing to come down to Hong Kong. Your premises – both this house and your shop – are very vulnerable. Especially as you don't have a man about the house.'

'That's where you're wrong,' Willie said. 'She has.'

Zychov whirled as Willie stepped out. Lifting the big revolver, he pointed it so that Zychov was looking directly down the muzzle.

'Remember this?' he asked. 'Know where I got it? Just outside Shantu. From the body of your sergeant. He was murdered by the Boxers after you bolted.' He gestured with the weapon. 'So get out. Before I blow your bloody head off.'

Zychov's jaw had dropped, but he recovered rapidly. 'You wouldn't dare,' he said. 'I have friends in Shanghai.'

'Not many, I think. And there are people in Shanghai *I* know – Communists – who would like to meet you. They'd like to know where you are. I have friends, too. Probably more than you these days. And they're powerful. More powerful I suspect than yours ever were.' Willie was bluffing because he had never toyed with the Shanghai underworld. He knew others had – and sometimes burned their fingers, too – but he had always avoided dealing with the secret societies or the gangs, or even dealing with the things they handled.

Zychov's smile had died. He was obviously uncertain about the threat and was assuming that, because he had contacts with the underworld himself, Willie had, too. The fact that he would be unable to find them – and Willie knew he'd try – would make him all the more uneasy. He was watching Willie closely, and the smile returned, uncertain at first but eventually with confidence.

'Why have you returned?' he asked. 'I thought it was all finished between you and my wife.'

'She isn't your wife and it never finished. Now get out and don't come back! If I hear of any more interference or demands for money I'll deal with you so well you'll wet yourself without fail every year on the anniversary.'

Zychov shrugged and swung away. The movement put Willie off his guard. As Zychov passed him, Nadya screamed a warning and, turning, Willie found himself moving into Zychov's swinging arm. Knocked off balance, as he staggered Zychov reached down, and picking up a bronze statuette from a low table alongside him, swung it at his head. The blow missed and struck his shoulder.

Furious, as much at his own carelessness as at Zychov's blow, Willie stepped back and, as Zychov blundered forward, aimed with his left hand at Zychov's head. The blow caught him on the cheek bone and sent him staggering sideways into a standard lamp which went down with a crash. As he recovered, Willie lashed downwards with all his strength with the heavy revolver. It caught Zychov across the forearm.

The heavy statuette spun out of his hand to crash against the wall and, as Zychov screamed in pain, Willie swung again. The barrel of the weapon opened a slit in Zychov's cheek and, as he stumbled sideways, the gun crunched against his nose and he went backwards like a felled tree through the door and down the steps. Staggering to his feet, his nose crushed, the slit on his cheek pouring blood over his tropical suit, his right arm hanging as if it were broken, he turned away to the waiting taxi.

Hardly able to speak with rage, Willie felt his arm grasped.

'No,' Nadya begged. 'No!'

As the taxi drew away, Willie stared after it, his chest heaving. 'You shouldn't have stopped me,' he grated. 'If he ever turns up again, I'll kill him.' He put his arm round her. 'I'm going to arrange for someone to watch this house and if he ever comes near it again, I'll have him beaten within an inch of his life.'

'Can you do that, Willie?' Nadya asked.

Willie's fury was subsiding and the trembling rage had died away. He took the whisky she offered and downed it in a couple of gulps.

'No,' he admitted. 'I don't have any connections with the secret societies. But I do know a policeman or two and I can get them to keep an eye on you. He won't bother you again. You'll be safe.' He paused. 'There's another way of doing it, of course. You could marry me.'

She stared at him, her eyes huge. 'No, William,' she whispered.

'Why not? Don't tell me he's saying you're still married to him.'

'No. That's all finished. I saw to that. I have the papers now.'

Willie took her hands. 'Nadya, why did you give him money?'

'Because he was once my husband.'

'That's a reason?'

'He was part of my life.'

'So was I,' he reminded her.

'You still are, William.'

Hope leapt in his heart. 'Then why *not* marry me?'

'Give me time.'

'How much time do you need? We're growing older every day. For God's sake, Nadya, how long do you want?'

She sighed. 'I saw the look on the faces of your children when I appeared in Shanghai. I know what they thought of me.'

'They didn't think that, Nadya.'

'Your daughter did. I couldn't face it.'

Willie watched her gloomily as she moved away. She was quite different in looks from Abigail, but there was the same decency, the same honesty about her. He'd met other men who had married more than once, one of them four times and every one of his wives had looked exactly like the one before her.

'Like a set of barmaids,' Da Braga had commented. 'I don't know why he bothers to change them.'

But it seemed normal enough. If a man liked one type of woman it was not unreasonable that he should go on choosing that type. And there was a lot of Abigail about Nadya. They had slipped once – something which, he supposed, was his fault – but the inherent decency in her had led her to end it all when she had met Abigail, and had seen the disaster she could bring on her.

He pressed his case. 'My daughter's based in Singapore now,' he pointed out. 'My elder son's in England. There's only one member of the family apart from me still in Shanghai. Married to me, you'd be safe.'

She touched his cheek with her fingertips, gently, affectionately, but there was no budging her.

'Perhaps if I were married to you,' she said, '*you* would be in danger. You'd have an unforgiving man for an enemy.'

Willie snorted his contempt. 'I've never been short of enemies,' he said. 'And you know what they say: Why bother with enemies when you have friends? I've hundreds of them in Shanghai who'd happily see me dead if they thought they could get their hands on my business.'

As he had promised, Willie called on the Hong Kong
police and persuaded them to keep an eye on Nadya's
home and business premises. Back in Shanghai, he also
made a point of checking what had happened to Zychov.

His guess that the Communists were looking for him
had been right. He had returned to Shanghai and was at
Chiang's headquarters enjoying the protection of the man
who was now the acknowledged leader of the
Kuomintang and grateful for what Zychov had done in
Shanghai, because he was still, as everyone knew, set on
his extirpation of the Communists.

Zychov remained a threat, inevitably, but even while
he was a threat, he was a threat which was well under
control. And in any case Emmeline, using Mason and
Marchant's as if they were a bludgeon, remained an equal
threat as she undercut with her prices all that Da Braga-
Kee's could offer. Though Da Braga and Kee ran the firm,
inevitably Willie was touched by the warfare.

It didn't seem possible that anyone could harbour an
enmity as long as Emmeline had, unaffected,
undiminished even, by the fact that Willie and his family,
and in particular, Abigail, had rushed to her assistance in
Yangpo. The bitterness he felt that she had been the cause

of Abigail's death had never left Willie, but while Emmeline, like Zychov, remained a threat, also like Zychov at that moment she was not a dangerous threat. Da Braga-Kee's were sound and Mason and Marchant's weren't strong enough to do them much damage. Minor vendettas such as Emmeline was conducting had been around for a long time, as they always were in business, but for the most part businessmen didn't waste money on such things, and he had a feeling that eventually she'd grow tired of it and back away.

The Sarth Line's business picked up again as Willie concentrated on the China Seas and the Western Pacific. There were twelve ships now, the *Lady Roberts* still among them, ancient, ugly, but somehow still plodding her way resourcefully across the ocean. Willie's cargoes went regularly to Mindanao, Batavia, Japan, the Aleutians, and as far south as Port Moresby, Sydney and Auckland. Whenever he could manage it, he was with them, enjoying the poinsettia, palms and flame trees of Haiphong, the hot shimmering islands outside Keppel Harbour in Singapore, even San Francisco, dominated by the dark crown of Nob Hill with its little strings of beaded lights; once as far south and west as Cape Town and Table Mountain with its snow-white cloth. But with Da Braga-Kee's his foothold in China, and offices in Hong Kong and Singapore to look after his interests in the China Seas, he was never far away.

His ships had never attracted a lot of attention because they were none of them new, and sometimes he suspected that only string and the prayers of the ships' engineers kept them going. But there was a limit even to the ingenuity of Scottish-born chief engineers, and not long after his trip to Hong Kong he learned that the *Dunnose*

Grange, almost as old as the *Lady Roberts*, had come to a stop because a shaft bearing for the ancient engine had finally given up the ghost and she had arrived in Hong Kong at dead slow speed with a hose pipe playing on the faulty part.

Either because he employed good engineers or because he had had a great deal of luck, his ships had been remarkably resilient, but now it seemed as if they had seen the last of the *Dunnose Grange*. Though they tried Singapore and Shanghai for a spare, there didn't appear to be one that would fit the ship's old engine in the whole of the Far East and she was now immobilised and, instead of earning money, was costing it in wages and harbour dues.

'We'll sell her,' Willie suggested.

Da Braga laughed. 'Who to? Who's going to buy her?'

The comment set Willie thinking. The *Dunnose Grange* had value as scrap, but she had more as a working ship that could earn a profit. Checking her papers, he found she had been built at South Shields in 1902, one of a small flotilla, all with similar names. *Rufford Grange*, *Wimley Grange*, *Ladywell Grange* and *Ortton Grange*.

'The man who built 'em must have had an itch to be part of the landed gentry,' he observed.

Having discovered the *Dunnose Grange*'s sister ships, he set out to find if any of them were still on the move and it was George Kee who learned that the *Ladywell Grange* was in Sydney harbour, having long since sailed her last voyage. She had carried copra and Aussie tin and rice from Rangoon, but her engine had finally given up the ghost and she was now used simply as a depository for the city's rubbish. When she was full she was to get towed out to sea and scuttled.

'There might be a spare part on her,' Willie said. 'Normally they have the spare shaft bearing bolted to the bulkhead in the engine room. If there is one, all we need is a block and tackle to hoist it out.'

A telegram to Sydney enabled them to find the present owners of the *Ladywell Grange*. They turned out to be the city council and a second telegram requesting to know if there was a spare shaft bearing aboard her brought the answer '*Yes. The last in the world* of *its type.*'

'I'm going down there,' Willie announced.

As usual, he was caught by the blunt straightforwardness of the Australians. They were a people devoid of sham, even sometimes of politeness, but they knew where they were going. For a small sum, he was given permission to remove the shaft bearing for use on the *Dunnose Grange*.

Hiring a launch and a marine engineer called MacFee, he headed away from the shipyard to where the *Ladywell Grange* was anchored near the ferry to Kirribilli and Cremorne. The stern of the launch was full of wire strops, ropes, a Weston purchase and, for MacFee and his assistant, a crate of beer.

The old ship towered above them as they went alongside, her stern dark and high, her smoke stack like a great cigarette, a single rusty propeller half out of the water.

'*Ladywell Grange*,' MacFee said. 'Registered in South Shields. She's been here ever since Pontius was a river pilot.'

There were two men on board keeping up enough steam to work the winches which hauled the city's rubbish aboard and dumped it into the holds, and they helped make the launch fast so that Willie and MacFee and his assistants could climb aboard. A rope went down for the crate of beer and the blocks, tackles and wire strops. MacFee had brought two or three car batteries and in no time he had strung up a cluster of lights to work by, then they got the engine room hatch off and rigged up the purchase. It didn't take as long as they expected and after a while the chain of the purchase was hanging taut and vertical and they began to hoist the bearing to the deck. MacFee's face was damp with sweat and streaked with dirt and eventually, with the sort of swearing that would have turned milk sour, the result of fooling about with two and a half hundredweight of dead metal, they had the bearing in the launch. Putting the hatch back, they climbed down to the launch with all their equipment to finish off the beer, pleased to be out of the *Ladywell Grange* because she was full of feverish-eyed rats. They had seemed to be in every corner, living on the rubbish and the scraps of copra and breeding like mad.

They dumped the spare part in the back of a lorry and deposited it in a shed in MacFee's yard, then retired to the nearest bar to celebrate. In his hotel room that night, Willie was reading the paper when he came across an item which made him sit bolt upright.

Two Americans were about to fly to Shanghai with medical equipment needed by the Kuomintang army. The thought of the *Dunnose Grange* lying at Hong Kong collecting weeds and debts brought him to his feet and heading for the telephone. Ten minutes later, he was heading in a taxi for the airfield.

The Americans, brash youngsters in plus fours, bow ties and boaters, were the sort of men who had been opening up the airways of the world for some time now. Their names were Biggit and Simpson and they had an old

Ford Tri-Motor which they had bought originally without engines or instruments, all of which they had fitted themselves.

'Sure,' Biggit said. 'We'll carry your spare part. We fly from here to Brisbane; Brisbane to Darwin; Darwin to Soerabaya; Soerabaya to Singapore; Singapore to Hong Kong; Hong Kong to Shanghai. Those are refuelling stops. Easy stages all the way. No trouble at all. We know this ship like we know our own hands. We built everything except the shell and before we got her she was part of an expedition to Alaska that folded. You want to come as well? We could take two passengers. Helps to pay for the trip –'

Willie had never been inside an aeroplane before, let alone flown in one and he wasn't very certain. But aeroplanes were the coming thing and the British had used them to watch the troubles in Shanghai. It occurred to him if he let the part go without him, it might get misplaced or lost and, after all the trouble he'd taken to acquire it, that would be a pity.

'How safe is it?' he asked.

'Couldn't be safer,' Biggit laughed. 'We've got every kind of safety equipment on board you can think of. Radio-direction finding gear, even an inflatable dinghy because we're flying over a lot of sea. Byrd had one when he flew the Atlantic.'

Willie didn't know much about flying, but he'd heard of Byrd and knew that the Atlantic and the Pacific had been flown non-stop and that the world's skies seemed to be packed with both men and women in aeroplanes, all trying to break records between one place and another.

'I'll come with you,' he said.

Two days later, the second passenger turned up, a British businessman called Crittenden who had flown as a passenger in England and, wanting to get to Canton in a hurry, couldn't resist the temptation of a trip.

The flight from Sydney was smooth and easy enough to quell any fears Willie had felt. With the spare shaft bearing lashed down in the middle of the aircraft where it couldn't affect performance, the machine lurched into the sky. Despite the extra weight it seemed not to be affected and the refuelling stops fell behind them without trouble one after the other and they landed at Singapore well ahead of time. If this was flying, Willie felt, there was nothing to it and he began to see himself using aeroplanes more and more. The flight would mean that the *Dunnose Grange* would be under way two months before she would have been had the part been delivered by coastal steamer progressing through the islands, dropping cargoes here, picking up cargoes there.

It was hot at Singapore with a humid heat that made them sweat. All four of them helped with the refuelling, Biggit not trusting the local mechanics.

'We got a lot of sea in front of us,' he pointed out.

Taxiing the big machine on to the runway, he revved the engines for a final test, received the green light and proceeded to the take-off. The machine was half-way down the runway building up speed when a tyre blew. As the plane swung right, heading for one of the airfield sheds, Biggit throttled back and jammed the rudder to the left in an attempt to swing the tail into a ground loop. They came to a screeching halt that flung up dust and grit in a shower, and shot things off tables with a clatter of falling objects.

It meant spending another night in Singapore, but Biggit and Simpson were confident the machine had not been damaged. They had spent until darkness checking everything about it, and were quite satisfied they could take off again the following morning. To Willie it was a disturbing reminder that flying wasn't quite as simple as it had seemed. At first light they climbed into the aircraft again, and were quickly airborne. They had been flying about six hours when Willie, waking from a doze on the floor of the cabin near his spare part, became aware of some sort of trouble forward, where the two Americans sat. Biggit was leaning to his left to peer downwards, his eyes narrow, his face taut and concerned. As he did it again and again, Willie noticed that the movement took place every time a dark spot appeared on the surface of the sea beneath them. It always turned out to be a cloud, and he realised that what Biggit was looking for was an island and it dawned on him they were lost.

'Sweet suffering J,' he muttered to himself.

There was nothing beneath them to indicate where they were, but, judging by the absence of islands, it seemed to Willie that they were somewhere in the middle of the South China Sea midway between Borneo or the Philippines and Indo-China.

'What are they looking for?' Crittenden asked.

Willie studied the chart he'd bought to follow the route and came to the conclusion that what Biggit was seeking was one of the Paracel Islands close to Hainan and directly south of Hong Kong.

'I guess we ought to get some bearings, Sam,' Biggit said to Simpson. 'Try calling Hong Kong.'

By this time, staring nervously at the sea, Willie was seeing one island after another, all of which turned out to be nothing but shadows. The distance seemed endless. His charts showed islands ahead of them and he assumed they were bound to hit one sooner or later. Then all they had to do was get down. But – the thought occurred to him with a start – the island didn't have an airfield, that in itself was going to be a problem. Flying suddenly seemed very different.

An hour later, when they still had seen nothing, he knew they were in grave danger. Simpson and Biggit were arguing quietly but furiously and he heard Simpson suggest that his octant might have been damaged when it fell from the navigator's table after the flawed take-off at Singapore. If that were true, even Willie could see, every reading he had made would have been wrong. They could be hundreds of miles off course.

By this time, Biggit had cut one engine and the remaining two were running on the leanest mixture possible and he was making no pretence that all was well.

'Send out an SOS,' he said. 'Somebody will pick it up.'

But nobody did and that, Willie realised, meant that if they came down in the sea nobody would know where they were.

At Biggit's suggestion, they started lightening the aeroplane. Out went the small cot where Willie had been resting, with the blankets, Willie's coat, suitcase and briefcase. As he watched them spinning down out of sight it occurred to him that it might have been better to rely on a ship after all, because, if they had to land on the sea, the aeroplane would sink and that would be the end of the shaft bearing he'd acquired at so much trouble and expense. They couldn't even throw it out to lighten the machine because it was too heavy to move, and Willie made sure of a position well to one side in case the crash tore its fastenings loose and sent its two and a half hundredweight of dead metal skating forward.

They placed the few rations they carried on one side with water and a flask of coffee, and started preparing the life raft for ditching. Noticing that Biggit was slipping his shoes off, Willie did the same, then he noticed Crittenden had removed his jacket and trousers, too.

'For swimming,' he said sheepishly.

Willie decided that if he were going to die he was going to die with his trousers on and remained fully clothed.

Time was running short. The sea was coming closer and he saw that a long swell was running. Biggit was bringing the machine down parallel to the lifting sweeps of water, hoping to land in a trough, when one of the engines fluttered and died. The other engine cut almost immediately afterwards and they were in a sudden aching silence. No one spoke.

As they hit the sea, a heavy piece of equipment in the tail of the machine broke loose and smashed forward, sending chunks of aeroplane flying in all directions. There was another violent crash and then the sea water poured in. They had already loosened the door and, as it was torn off, they began to scramble out.

'Look slippy,' Biggit roared. 'She won't float long.'

Not likely, Willie thought, not with the solid weight of the shaft bearing carrying her down.

The aeroplane had settled by the nose under the weight of the engines, but they were able to climb on to the wing. For a moment, they thought Crittenden was missing but he appeared in the water alongside. The raft was afloat, the rope held firmly by Willie, who didn't fancy swimming all the way to Hong Kong without help.

There was blood in the sea and Willie saw that Crittenden had cut his arm to the bone on a ragged piece of metal. The swells were around ten feet high and, as they scrambled into the lifting dinghy, it dawned on them they had left their few rations behind, together with the water and the coffee.

'We ought to go back and fetch them,' Willie said.

'Don't be goddam silly,' Biggit said. 'She's going to sink any moment.'

In fact, the machine stayed afloat for almost ten minutes before the tail lifted and remained there for a second before sliding out of sight, taking with it the spare shaft bearing for the *Dunnose Grange*, according to MacFee the last one in the world. The result would be the end of the *Dunnose Grange* as a working ship so that, like the *Ladywell Grange*, she would probably end her days as a rubbish dump before being scuttled out at sea. Curiously the only thing that crossed Willie's mind as the tail fin slid out of sight was 'Thank God it's not the *Lady Roberts*.'

The raft was sloshing with water and Willie started to bail with his hat. Crittenden was in a lot of pain with his arm, but they managed to wriggle around until they all had a space inside the inflated sides of the raft. There were a pair of paddles, but they were broken and they could see no alternative but to throw them away.

As they drifted away from the spot where the aeroplane had disappeared, Willie noticed a long shadow in the water and then a triangular fin broke the surface.

'Oh, Jesus,' Simpson said. 'Sharks! That's all we want.'

Riding up and down in the steep swells brought seasickness, and to Crittenden, who was a poor sailor, it was miserable. Sunburn was also a problem and out of the four of them only Willie was fully clothed, even to his hat which, though sodden with the sea, still managed to shade his face.

As night came, a mist settled in a low sheet over the water as the moon rose, a mere glow through the silver of the mist, and it became wretchedly cold because they were all wet through. This, Willie thought, isn't what I expected and it looks as though I'm going to die. But then he thought, someone would be sure to look for them because their time of arrival had been radioed ahead. Crittenden was already moaning and muttering in a half-sleep and it occurred to Willie that it was going to be a case of fighting for survival. Anybody who gave up trying was going to die.

During the night they felt a bump against the thin rubber bottom of the raft and Crittenden woke immediately. 'Sharks,' he said.

The bumps continued all night as they huddled together, painfully cold. The sun was well up next morning before it broke through and dispersed the mist and by that time they were all practically rigid with the chill. The wind had subsided a little and the sea had quietened down, so that the raft was motionless. But as the sun rose higher it began to burn. Using his hat, Willie sloshed water over himself and the others to cool them down. Crittenden was in the worst condition and his bare legs began to grow pink and look sore while his torn arm continued to ooze blood.

As the salt water dried in a white crust over everything, they began to discuss their position, but they couldn't agree where they were. The long day passed, leaving them weak from the sunshine and glad when it disappeared, only to start wishing it were back when the cold started to make them shiver. Though Biggit and Simpson had been careful to load the plane with every kind of device, the only one of any use was the raft; all the others had gone down with the machine.

Bodily functions became an agony until finally, hungry and thirsty, they stopped altogether. The dead calm continued and, during the night, the mist disappeared so that the next morning when the sun rose, almost at once it became torture, burning the skin red, then blistering it to leave it raw and bleeding. Willie was still better off than anyone with his hat and his suit, but Crittenden was in torment. They shared the hat and Willie's jacket, but being unable to change positions made things much worse and the slightest movement of the raft was enough to make their wet skin raw as they chafed against each other.

The day seemed endless and was followed by another and then another. Unable to keep the raft bailed, they began to get fresh sores from the salt water. And, as they blistered and burned and ached with thirst, all around them were miles of cool water. During the day they could see each other, talk and discuss their predicament, though curiously nobody blamed Biggit or Simpson. The nights were much worse because then they were alone with their thoughts, unable to see anything.

Willie began to see things, beautiful and sinister things. Once it was Ab and another time it was Nadya. Then somehow he began to think that Zychov or Emmeline Wishart was responsible for his predicament. Crittenden began to babble about drinks – long, cool drinks such as they served at the Shanghai Club – and Willie began to think of his mistakes, the things he had not done, the things he had done and ought not to have done. They tried to catch a seagull and failed dismally, but then, as the bird flew off, it occurred to Willie that birds like that didn't live miles out over the ocean.

'We can't be all that far from shore,' he said.

The others were too weak by this time to be concerned with his optimism, but he refused to give way, certain he'd be rescued. There was no reason why he should be so sure, he knew, but he continued to hope, knowing that if he gave up he was old enough to die.

Suddenly it started to rain. Willie was the first to smell it, then the heavens opened and they revelled in the falling water as it washed away the encrusted salt. They had nothing to collect it in except Willie's hat, so they took it in turns to drink from it and then they filled it and held it carefully. By the time the squall vanished they had all drunk as much as they could hold and Willie's hat held another pint or so.

The next night, however, Crittenden died. It seemed to happen when no one was looking and Biggit looked up and said, 'I think he's dead.'

He had been terribly burned by the sun and, though they had tried to shelter him with Willie's jacket, they'd been able to do very little for him. At first they didn't know quite what to do because none of them wanted to pronounce him dead with finality. But by the next dawn it was obvious Crittenden was feeling nothing any more. He was cold and they could find no heart beat. Even then, they hesitated to get rid of the body, until eventually they realised their chances would be better without it taking up room in the raft and they rolled him over the side. For a long time the body floated alongside until finally with a sudden jerk from below that brought it abruptly upright, it disappeared from sight

The sharks which had torn Crittenden down were still with them. During the next night they must have drifted across a shoal of smaller fish and as the sharks ravaged the school, the fish began to jump. Three of them landed in the raft and they pulled them to pieces and ate them raw.

It helped, but not much, and the next day they seemed hardly able to move. Biggit was lying with closed eyes, Simpson leaning against him. Willie watched them with a haggard stare, wondering why his ears were humming. Then it dawned on him that what he heard wasn't a sound inside his head but came from a searching plane. He woke the other two and they waved and shouted as if they could be heard, but the machine passed clean over them and disappeared. As it vanished, they sank back and Willie found he was having to blink back bitter tears.

But two hours later another plane flew over them. Once again the crew seemed not to see them, but towards the evening just before it began to grow dark, they saw a spot on the horizon that grew larger and continued to grow until they saw it was a ship and that it was heading for them.

'Holy Jesus Christ and all his shining angels,' Willie breathed. 'I think we're saved!'

For the first time since they had ditched he allowed himself to relax.

When he awoke he was in a hospital bed staring at the mosquito net above him. At first he thought he was dead after all and that the mosquito netting was the mistiness that came from being in Heaven. He couldn't hear any heavenly music, however, and as his head turned quickly in alarm, wondering why not, he found himself staring hazily at someone who was sitting alongside the bed.

'Where's this?' he asked.

'The hospital.'

'Not Heaven?'

'No, William darling, Hong Kong.'

The words and the way they were spoken brought him back to earth. His vision cleared and he wondered if it had been impaired by the ordeal in the raft.

'Am I safe?' he asked.

'Yes, you're quite safe.'

'I think in future,' he said slowly, 'I'll stick to shipping.' His vision cleared as he blinked and he saw he was looking at Nadya.

'Is it really you, Nadya Alexsandrovna,' he asked.

'Yes, it is. I thought that this time you'd gone for good. It was in all the papers. Your name. Everything. They said you couldn't possibly be still alive.'

'Takes more than that to kill me.' Willie's cracked lips opened in a grin that hurt his mouth. 'I'm back from the dead. So why don't you marry me, while you can?'

She smiled. 'I think,' she said, 'that since you've already used up eight of your nine lives, I'd better, before it's too late.'

eight

Willie was flattered when his family turned up – first Thomas from Shanghai with Fan-Su, then Edward and Polly, arriving together. Edward's ship had been in Singapore, and, the first to hear of the rescue, he had telegraphed his brother then picked up Polly and taken a ship north. Willie hadn't thought he meant that much to them and he was surprised to find they seemed to be pleased to see him alive, so he tried on them his news about Nadya and, to his delight, his sons were even enthusiastic.

'I think,' he said to Nadya, 'that they're frightened of having to look after me when I'm an old man.'

Since the whole family was there, they decided to marry at once and the whole business was carried out at the hospital, with the clergyman and the family clustered round the bed. Only Polly was unable to accept it. She tried to explain and he tried to understand. She had always been close to Abigail and he realised he must wait for time to have its effect.

As soon as he was on his feet again, he began to think of closing the house in Shanghai and moving down to Hong Kong. It would mean allowing George Kee and Da Braga to take over completely the operations in Shanghai, and he tried on them the idea of buying him out completely. They were all for it because they knew they were getting everything far more cheaply than they would otherwise and the thing went through without a hitch.

By this time, the authority of Chiang's Nanking government was undisputed from the Yangtze to the Amur. But the southern half of China was still far from pacified and the Communists there were still masters of a sizeable slice of territory, while beyond them were the Kwangsi warlords, as active as ever and always ready to encourage troublemakers. Another split was the signal for the exodus of more politicians to Canton and the bewildered country found it had yet another brand-new government, quite separate from Chiang's. It made little difference, however, because that autumn the first shots were fired in a war between China and Japan.

Never fools even if they were oppressed, the Chinese had retaliated to the Japanese seizure of the Manchurian ports of Dairen and Port Arthur by diverting traffic to other harbours, and the resentful Japanese were beginning to be restive again. Willie was far from being a political animal but he seemed to see much further ahead than many people in Shanghai, most of whom were still chiefly concerned only with making money and unable to believe that their way of life could ever come to an end. Grimly he started shifting his capital again.

Though Japan was busy with the subjugation of Manchuria, she was nevertheless finding it hard to digest the enormous areas of China she had acquired and her writ ran in effect no further than the towns in which her troops were garrisoned, so that she was having to fall back on terrorised Chinese puppet administrators. There was a great deal of talk at the Council in Shanghai and more at the League of Nations, but, while their recommendations were received by the Japanese with politeness and appropriate ceremony, they had little effect on the situation.

By this time, the Sarth Line offices and agencies in Hong Kong, Singapore, Mindanao, Sydney and Auckland were going concerns and the Sarth Line ships continued to waddle their unobtrusive way round the Far Eastern waters. Like Shanghai itself, Chinese politics left Willie untouched and he preferred to spend his time keeping an eye on what Emmeline Wishart was doing with Mason and Marchant's, never his friends and always eager to undercut Da Braga-Kee's.

'She'll bankrupt 'em,' he suggested to Da Braga. 'As she bankrupted Wishart's.'

Zychov seemed to have disappeared again and they learned he was engaged somewhere in the west, remodelling part of Chiang's army. Then George Kee said that the Balalaika had reopened and that Zychov had been seen there and Willie knew at once he was back, safe under the protection of Chiang K'Ai-Shek.

He still had no proof that Zychov had been involved with Yip in the attempted sacking of the *Tien Quan*. All Yip's papers had disappeared in a mysterious fire in his office soon after his death and it was Willie's belief that it had been started by Zychov. But with their disappearance he could never be accused of involvement – even if he *were* involved.

His reappearance in Shanghai put Willie on his guard and then Da Braga announced that he'd seen Zychov in Mason and Marchant's and the old enmities suddenly took on an entirely new look. Somehow, Willie knew,

Zychov had heard of Emmeline's hatred, and Emmeline had heard of Zychov's and, like filings to a magnet, they had come together.

Occasionally Thomas appeared with news of what was happening politically. The Japanese aggressiveness and the struggle against the Communists had enhanced the importance of Chiang K'Ai-Shek as Commander-in-Chief of the Nanking-Canton armies and he was fully occupied now with attempts to halt Japanese forward movements and with opposing the Communists. Chou, Thomas' old friend, was now part of the main political committee of the Communist Party, having survived a number of political storms and contrived a niche for himself, and he was devoting himself these days to the organisation of the urban proletariat.

'Which means what?' Willie asked.

Thomas shrugged. 'I suppose,' he said, 'that when the revolution comes – as I suppose eventually it will – they'll be ready.'

'What are their plans for Shanghai?'

Thomas smiled. 'The same as their plans for the rest of China. They want it back. *They* don't consider it an international city. They consider it part of China.'

'What will they do with it when they get it?'

Thomas laughed. 'Ruin it, I suspect,' he said. 'They don't have the know-how to use it.'

'So what will happen to it?'

'I expect it will be badly run-down within ten years, but ten years after that they'll have acquired the know-how they lack and eventually it'll take its proper place in the world again.'

'What will you do then, boy?'

Thomas smiled. 'I've always sympathised with the Chinese, and I've never seen eye to eye with the money-makers here. Chou knows my position. I'll be all right.'

Willie frowned. 'Don't be too bloody sure, lad,' he advised.

The next few years were as happy for Willie as his years with Abigail had been. His feet still itched and he was always restlessly on the move. Occasionally he was in Singapore, but he never called on his daughter. She hadn't kept in touch and he accepted that she preferred it that way, and that, anyway, she was probably too busy as the wife of the head of Wissermann's Far East Trading, Incorporated. His own business was developing well in the Dutch East Indies and Australia, where he had taken over a bankrupt shipping company consisting of two elderly freighters, and he was regularly aboard one of his ships, sometimes accompanied by Nadya, *en route* to one of the outlying islands – Bali, Fiji, Papeete, Samoa. The unease over the future that was obvious in Shanghai was reflected in the South Pacific.

'What the hell's goin' on up there?' MacFee, the Australian marine engineer who had helped salvage the shaft bearing from the *Ladywell Grange* for him, was indignant. 'Why don't someone clobber those Jap bastards?'

There wasn't really any answer. The whole of the Far East had been kept in a turmoil by Japanese aggressiveness for years and Willie could only put it down to the fact that the loss of the best men in the British Empire in the monstrous hecatombs in France between 1914 and 1918 had led to the years of fumbling politics, because exactly the same was now happening again in Europe. Few of the men in charge in London had served in the trenches and those who had were not prepared to risk it again. With the most intelligent, forthright and courageous vanished on the Somme and at Passchendaele, the men who were left had not the courage to make a stand.

As Brassard had suggested, it seemed to Willie that the world was shaping up for another confrontation and more than once he suggested to Da Braga and George Kee that they should sell.

'It isn't just Mason and Marchant's who're angling for the firm now,' George Kee said. 'It's Zychov from the Balalaika.'

'Same thing,' Willie said shortly.

'What does he know about the business?'

'He doesn't have to know anything,' Willie said. 'He's the front man. I'd advise getting the highest price you can and get out.'

'Out of Shanghai?' Kee seemed startled.

'I got out.'

The Japanese appetite for territory increased with every bite she took out of China, but Chiang, his attention concentrated on his political enemies, the Communists, rather than the national enemies, Japan, remained imperturbable, showing his friendship towards the Japanese by savagely suppressing anti-Japanese demonstrations.

'It deludes nobody,' Da Braga said. 'He's thinking of himself, not of China.'

The hostility towards Japan brought about a national solidarity of a sort, but, after the massacre of their supporters in Shanghai, the Communists were now openly hostile to the regime, which meant that one half of

China was always in open disagreement with the other, and it brought little peace to the European businessmen.

'There will be trouble with Japan,' Da Braga said. 'And Soviet Russia won't object. She denounces imperialism with one hand but with the other shows a marked disposition to profit from the rights acquired by the Tsars.'

Willie had always regarded Da Braga as a calm man well able to work out the path of coming events. More than once when Willie had wished to rush into some project, Da Braga's wiser counsels had held him back.

'There's constant tension in the north,' the Portuguese was saying. 'Because Japan's always watching for an opportunity to increase her boundaries. Things will happen soon because it's like sitting on a powder keg with the fuse lit.'

His prophecy proved correct. The killing of a Japanese officer by the Chinese gave them the impetus, and the exploding of a bomb on the railway outside Mukden – said to have been planted by the Japanese themselves – gave them the signal. More tracts of land passed into their possession, and there was another bout of nervous worrying by the Europeans because, despite the fact that the fighting was all taking place in the north, Shanghai didn't come out of the business unscathed. The city was rocked by demonstrations, strikes and an intensification of the boycott on Japanese goods. Then, when a Buddhist friar was killed in a brawl, a Japanese naval flotilla, which included an aircraft carrier, appeared off the Shanghai waterfront. The Mayor of Shanghai virtually had to go down on his knees to apologise and promise indemnities and the punishment of the culprits.

On business near Frenchtown the following day, Willie saw a crowd of Japanese women and children boarding ships. He noticed the ships were new and fast and he guessed there must be a good reason for the exodus. Heading for George Kee's office, it took him no more than a few minutes to discover they were bound for Nagasaki.

'Nagasaki?' he said slowly. 'There must be something in the wind, George.'

'I think there is,' Kee said. 'The boundaries of the International settlement are being manned. Each nation to be responsible for its own sector.'

'Why?'

'The Japanese, I hear.'

'What are they up to?'

'The trouble between them and China. They've been authorised to push their troops outside the settlement to occupy a portion of Chinese-administered territory.'

'Who's given them the authority?'

'A committee representing all the powers with interests in Shanghai.'

'Did they inform the Chinese?'

'I haven't heard so.'

'They must be barmy, George. The Chinese will think a war's started. They'll resist.'

Willie was dead right and fighting started almost immediately, and when, as a major property holder and businessman, he was asked to join the protest that was to be sent to the Chinese, his reaction was one of disgust. Old Honeyford, who had been sent to see him, received a blast of anger that rocked him back on his heels.

'No,' Willie snapped. 'No! And no again!'

'But it's been decided that the Japanese *should* go outside the boundaries!'

'Who decided? The Chinese? Good God,' Willie snarled in fury, 'the bloody arrogance! It's their country, not ours!'

Honeyford looked indignant, as though Willie had failed to grasp something which should have been quite clear.

'For Heaven's sake, man,' he said angrily. 'The Japanese will be protecting British nationals. That's important.'

Willie stared at him contemptuously. 'I'm sick to God's green death of you lot posturing about the sanctity of British lives,' he snorted. 'The only thing you're thinking about is your own bloody interests and nothing else!'

Honeyford's face went red. 'The Japanese are our allies!'

'Don't be bloody silly!' Willie's rage made Honeyford back away. 'The only people the Japanese are concerned with are the Japanese! Japan's looking after Japan – not you!'

Willie's anger remained with him all day. It was clear the decision to allow Japanese troops to push beyond the perimeter of the settlement had infuriated the Chinese. Posters appeared on walls and there were protest meetings, the students as usual well to the fore to proclaim China's national identity. If the taipans weren't clear on the subject, they were.

The Japanese menace was spreading. It had been with them, Willie decided, ever since the turn of the century, when Shaiba had been spying on the Russians in Peking. Even that bloody half-wit, Kaiser Wilhelm, had spotted it as early as 1914 with his warnings to the world of what he called the Yellow Peril. But, because of fear, greed, envy and the demands of national interests, nobody had ever done anything about it, and now, here it was, fully grown, the ugly little lizard become a dragon.

He was still brooding over the stupidity of people like Honeyford when a message arrived that the old *Kum Kum Kiuw* had appeared in the Whangpoo from the Philippines with sugar and molasses, and he decided to get rid of his bad temper by going down to meet her. He liked to keep in touch with his captains and their crews and the company launch took him upstream. Being small and unimportant, the Sarth vessels usually dropped anchor near Nantao, where Chinese-owned vessels lay, and the *Kum Kum Kiuw* was lying among a whole cloud of small vessels surrounded by barges, lighters, sampans and junks.

Climbing on board, he nodded to the mate, pulled the leg of the old Chinese bosun who had been with the company since its formation, and headed for the captain's cabin. He was sitting in an armchair discussing the ship's next move over a Jossman gin when there was a shout from on deck. As his head jerked round, the shout came again, this time full of alarm.

Bursting on deck with the captain, he saw one of the Chinese crewmen staring at the sky and, following the pointing finger, he saw a line of small black dots beyond Pootung change to the shape of aeroplanes as they swung in the sky to run in over the city.

'Who the hell are they?' he said.

Then, as the aircraft banked, the sun caught the insignia on their wingtips and he saw the solid red circle the Japanese used on their machines, the red blob the Americans had started calling a meatball.

'What the hell are they up to?' he snapped.

The machines came low over the buildings, their engines howling, heading for Chapei. As they crossed the river he saw black blobs detach themselves and begin to fall towards the Chinese quarter of the city.

'Bombs!' he roared. 'For Christ's sake, they're dropping bombs!'

For a moment, he stood on deck with the captain of the *Kum Kum Kiuw* and his crew, bewildered by what was happening but not afraid, then a second wave of aircraft followed the first, clearly aiming at the shipping in the river.

The Japanese pilots knew exactly where the Chinese-owned ships were lying and it dawned on Willie that they were too close to the *Kum Kum Kiuw* for the old ship's safety.

'Get this bloody thing moving!' he roared.

The Chinese bosun ran for the winch, followed by the mate, and the clank of the anchor cable being hauled in began to fill their ears.

By this time, columns of smoke were lifting over the building to the north and they could hear what sounded like a solid cry of protest coming from every Chinese in the city. It was compounded of honking horns, the bells of fire engines and ambulances, screams and wails, and the shouts of frightened or injured people – as if everybody ashore was giving tongue.

A neighbouring ship, the Chinese freighter *Ting Fee*, had been hit and was sinking and not far away a three-decked ferry was on fire. A junk, her masts removed by blast, was drifting past on the tide, her slatted sail draped over her side, her decks covered with dead men. The anchor cable of the *Kum Kum Kiuw* was upright and the hook had just come out of the mud of the river bottom so that she was actually beginning to make way when she was hit.

The bomb struck her amidships, blowing out the side of the vessel. Metal fragments began to clang down and stokers came tumbling up the ladder from below, staggering through the smoke and dust followed by clouds of white vapour and showers of soot from the funnel. The noise of escaping steam hurt the ears and the ship, which had already started to list to port, began to slow down and drift towards the blazing ferry. By a miracle they scraped past the ferry's stern, the rails screeching, metal on metal, as they were buckled by the ferry's overhang, then, with the last of the steam in the boilers, the old ship was driven into shallow water where she settled on the bottom until only her upper works were visible.

By this time the Japanese aeroplanes had disappeared, but there were several damaged ships in the river, more than one sinking on her anchor, and the whole sky was filled with black smoke from burning buildings. Soaked to the skin and blackened by the smuts from the funnel, his suit saturated and smeared with oil, Willie struggled ashore, spluttering with fury, to find a cab and head into Shanghai.

He found the representatives of the Western powers in a panic. Having set the thing in motion, they had lost their nerve as the bombing opened to them a brutal view of the future, and they were already struggling to bring about an armistice.

'Whoever expected the bloody Chinks to start fighting?' old Honeyford complained.

'Why shouldn't they?' Willie snarled. 'If someone set his dogs on you, wouldn't you try to kick them off?'

'They never have before.'

'Jesus Christ and all his shining angels, you lot never learn! Didn't the idea of finding out first what might happen ever enter anyone's head? Didn't a single bloody soul think it necessary to tell the Chinese what was happening to their own territory? It just shows how the International Settlement thinks. I suppose you thought there was more to be made from the Japanese than the other side, so it would be all right.'

The moves to halt the fighting were already too late and, with the bit between their teeth, the Japanese refused to listen. People had climbed to rooftops to watch the battle and the Chinese, endeavouring to retaliate by bombing Japanese shipping, hit the Palace Hotel instead, killed hundreds in the packed Chinese quarter, and turned Tibet Road into a litter of human limbs and torsos. Only when they had inflicted what they considered an undeniable defeat did the Japanese consent to a cease-fire.

The Kuomintang had resisted the invasion in the Old City and had sunk freighters in an attempt to block the river, but the Japanese had been relying on aircraft and their bombers had devastated Nantao and Hongkew and, when the Chinese fighters had lifted up against them, they had been shot out of the sky.

When it was all over, the Europeans, considering it none of their business, drove out to the scene to look at the trenches dug by the Chinese, the spilled cartridges, the discarded rifles, the artillery still with the dead horses in the traces, the belts of machine-gun ammunition, even the dead soldiers in the ditches, in the canals, among the reeds. Occupied with his rage over the loss of his ship, to Willie their behaviour seemed obscene.

Several other Western-owned ships besides the *Kum Kum Kiuw* had been sunk and Honeyford tried to win people round to his view with the prospect of compensation.

'It will be paid,' he reassured claimants. 'The Japanese government has said so.'

'Not to the bloody Chinese, I'll bet,' Willie snapped.

'Of course not! A state of hostilities between them and the Japanese has arrived.'

'That doesn't mean a damn thing! To Japan this war with China's only a step forward. The final bloody reckoning will be with all the rest of us with land in the Pacific and the China Seas.'

Honeyford's protest that he was talking through his hat was indignant, but Willie knew he was right. The fighting spread and continued on and off until the American and British governments finally brought about peace. The European powers were falling over themselves to placate the Japanese, who did nothing to help and, with odd bursts of fighting, continued to spread their influence.

Chinese nationalism brought constant friction and the League of Nations seemed powerless. It was obvious to Willie that the Japanese had not withdrawn and he was well aware that the Europeans in the East could never profit from what was happening. For the Chinese, though the enemy was Japan, there was also no love for the foreign settlements, of which the most important was always Shanghai. Despite a population of a million Chinese against a mere forty thousand Europeans, the Chinese still had little say in its administration and the Municipal Council was still elected by foreigners, while foreign investors complacently supported Chiang in his efforts to eliminate Communism. They had failed in Russia but they were determined not to fail in China.

Willie watched the manoeuvrings with some disgust. 'Chiang's chief concern's money,' he told Nadya, 'and China's administered chiefly for the benefit of himself and his relations.'

He was in Singapore when the new war between China and Japan started. The first shots were fired in Peking in an incident which appeared to be very obscure and was more than likely due to Japanese provocation, and it was obvious even from across the China Sea that the Japanese had a crushing superiority both in equipment and training. Within weeks they were in Peking and Tientsin, and within a few more in Shensi, and Chiang began to move his government to distant Chungking out of their reach.

Almost immediately, Willie's agents passed the news that Zychov had gone with them. Willie had never forgotten Shantu or Port Arthur, never forgotten the fact that he ought to have finished Zychov for good somehow in Hong Kong. While he was alive there was always a threat to Nadya and his new marriage. Again and again, he had made plans to face him, but they had all come to nothing and now he began to wonder if it were worth going to Chungking.

But the war was in the way, even if hundreds of miles to the north, and it didn't seem worth it. But then he heard that Chiang, cut off from the coast, was planning to bring in the supplies he needed from Burma.

'By lorries,' Willie pointed out as he and Kee sat round Da Braga's brandy bottle discussing what it could mean.

'It's not possible,' Kee said. 'There isn't a single road over the border that would take the heavy lorries they would need.'

Willie gestured. 'I've heard they're going to build one.'

'Who are?'

'The Chinese. My son, Tom, heard. Through the students.'

'But what with? They haven't the tools. No tractors, no bulldozers, no diggers. What are they going to use?'

'People,' Willie said. 'They've never been short of those. If I go to Chungking and fix it, are we prepared to back it up?'

'Who's supplying the lorries?'

'America and Britain.'

'Tom's heard all this?' Da Braga asked.

'Tom hears a hell of a lot.'

'So what do we get out of it, if the Americans and the British are supplying the lorries?'

'Tyres. Spares. Servicing. To run fleets of lorries you have to have a back-up system and there'll never be enough British or American "experts" to cover the thing.'

'It'll mean going to Chungking.'

'What's wrong with that?'

Da Braga tapped his artificial leg. 'I can't go,' he said.

Willie leaned forward. 'I can, Luis.'

Da Braga grinned. He could see Willie was itching to be off. As long as he'd known him, he'd always been restless, ready to disappear over the horizon at the drop of a hat.

'It'll be difficult,' he said. 'It's around fifteen hundred miles.'

'I've checked. It can be done. By rail, steamer and junk. What's more, I've just found an Australian who can use

Chinese silk, wax candles, varnish and lithographic inks. That would pay for the trip even if the other part didn't come off.'

Da Braga studied Willie shrewdly. 'Is this lorry project the only reason?' he asked.

Willie's face hardened. 'No,' he admitted. 'Zychov's up there, too. I've been making enquiries for a long time. I might bump into him.'

Da Braga smiled. 'Rather you than me, Willie,' he said.

Willie wasn't in the slightest put off by the pessimism of Da Braga and Kee. Getting to difficult places had always been a challenge to him and he arrived in the west on a small, powerful flat-bottomed steamer with the Stars and Stripes painted on her sides. Her passengers included a group of three business men out to make money from China's new crisis, who practised golf strokes on the after deck for half an hour every day at the same time. Leaving the steamer, they took a train along a battered railway line that was constantly being bombed by the Japanese and just as constantly repaired with amazing speed by Chinese coolies.

Chungking was a sleepy town above the Yangtze at the junction where the Chialing River joined the main stream and, after five centuries, its boundary wall was still virtually intact. Once the place had been remote and self-sufficient because Szechwan province had always been regarded as backward. But now it was impossible to find a room in a hotel, so Willie unearthed an American he knew called Putnam who had been doing business with him from Chungking for years and was prepared to loan him a sofa for the nights.

'It's kinda crowded,' Putnam said. 'Chiang's government personnel are pouring in. Offices are migrating *en masse*, by bus, car, truck, rickshaw, barrow, boat and on foot. And, following the goddam officials and politicians come their families, and after the families the shopkeepers seeking their trade. Behind the shopkeepers come the pedlars, and finally behind the pedlars the prostitutes and the beggars.'

'How about Russians?'

'There aren't any Russians here,' Putnam said. 'Chiang quarrelled with them years ago.'

'Not with this one, I heard. Name of Zychov.'

Putnam frowned. 'The only Russian I know of is somewhere in the south with one of Chiang's generals. The general's a crook – but then, so are more than a few of Chiang's boys – and since this Russian guy's his sidekick, he's probably one as well. Did you want to meet him?'

Willie wasn't sure what his plans were. He had brought the old Russian revolver with him in the faint hope that he might blow Zychov's head off down a dark alley, but he wasn't sure now that he could do such a thing in cold blood. There were always Chinese, of course, who would do anything for a price, but he wasn't sure he was capable even of that and he decided to leave it and see what happened, especially as Zychov seemed out of reach, anyway.

Chungking was totally unlike a seat of government. New buildings had spread like fungus. Since there was no steel, bamboo was used. Since there were no nails, bamboo was split and interlaced for walls and then coated with mud and roofed with thatch. On every new building there was a sign. *Nanking Hat Shop. Shanghai Garage. Hankow Dry Cleaners. Huschow Coffee Store.* Every province was represented and, because they didn't like

Szechwanese cooking, the newcomers had brought their own.

'You can get Fukienese fish food, Hunanese chicken, Peking duck,' Putnam grinned. 'If you ask your way in Mandarin, ten to one you'll be answered by a Cantonese who speaks it worse than you do. Everything's written down because the Szechwanese messengers can't understand what's said and even the street names are a mess. The government's renamed them all, but to the rickshaw boys the Road of the Republic's still the Cliff of the Kindly Buddha, and the Road of the People's Prosperity's the Slope of all the Stars.'

It was obvious that the refugees from the more developed areas of the coastal plains disliked Chungking and regarded the Szechwanese as second-grade people, with their dirty headcloths and whining voices and their suspicion of motor cars. The Szechwanese, who still cured their ills with recipes of husk, herbs and children's urine, just as firmly regarded the downriver people as interlopers who were here to be swindled. They disapproved of boys and girls eating together in restaurants and of the lipstick and waved hair the newcomers' women brought with them.

Hated most of all was the weather. Winter was a time of fogs and rains that made everything cold and damp, while the summer sun brought a humid heat that dripped perspiration and encouraged swarms of insects – orange ones in the drinking water, huge brown ones on the walls, and always the mosquitoes. Putnam insisted they worked in threes – two to lift the mosquito net and the third to zoom in for the kill.

Meat spoiled, there was never enough water, and dysentery was spreading. The noises you heard about the city were the ancient sounds of China – pigs, babies, hens, gossiping women, yelling men. Always there was the sing-song chant of coolies, the rhythmic clack-clack of a cotton salesman beating on a block of wood as he walked, the cries of the notion dealer, the chant of the night soil collector, the clinking of the brassware man, with his cats' bells, knives, toothpicks and earcleaners dangling from a pole, the violin strumming of vibrating strings in the shops that made cotton quilts.

'Watch for the Jap bombers,' Putnam advised. 'They haven't been for a while, but the winter fogs have finished now so they'll be along before the month's out.'

It wasn't difficult for Willie to arrange for the consignment of silk and wax and, while he was at it, tea, rice, hides and wool which he knew Da Braga-Kee's could sell, and the Chinese were all in favour of accepting help in the shape of tyres, spares and servicing. They had been promised munitions from Russia and they *were* planning to bring what they needed over the Burma border. The rumours Tom had heard were sound and the road had been planned to run between Lashio, at the end of the Burmese railway from Rangoon, and Chungking, and thousands upon thousands of Chinese peasants were being pushed into the area with nothing but the ancient tools their forefathers had used for centuries, and baskets to carry away the spoil.

It didn't take long to find a Chinese entrepreneur to work with. He looked pretty shifty to Willie and as if he were probably lining his pockets from the Chinese people's misery, gut there was no one else and he knew he would have to accept that the Chinese would doubtless syphon off some of the money involved for himself. But the profits were sound and, with everything in writing,

Willie was all set to vanish again the following day when Putnam appeared in a hurry.

'Your buddy, Zychov,' he said. 'He's here in Chungking.'

'Doing what?'

'Sent his general to report. If you want him, you'd better get cracking. I hear questions are being asked and we've got proof that money's missing. There are also strong rumours they've been selling Chinese rice to the Japanese.'

'Does Chiang know?'

'Probably. But it isn't Chiang who's interested, because I reckon he's syphoning off government money, too. No, it'll be one of the lesser lights who's doing it, and is worrying his share's dwindling. Anyway, what's so goddam important about this guy, Zychov? What are you goin' to do when you see him?'

Willie still hadn't made up his mind. He was certain at least that he could never destroy Zychov in cold blood, but Putnam's knowledge that the Chinese general he worked with was corrupt gave him a weapon he thought he might use at some time.

It was difficult to obtain a rickshaw and Putnam decided that something must be happening. 'They always disappear when something's in the wind,' he said. 'We'd better walk.'

It was late evening and the lights of the city had just come on when Putnam noticed that passers-by were beginning to hurry and that on gallows-like poles on the surrounding high hills large yellow paper lanterns had been lit.

'Oh, bejesus,' he said. 'It's an air raid!'

Willie was still brooding on how he should tackle his problem. Zychov was a slippery customer and he realised he had no plan to deal with him. An outright accusation might work, however. If Putnam had proof of corruption, it might force someone to look into it.

His mind was full of pictures of Zychov languishing in prison when he noticed that the people around him were beginning to move faster, the rickshaw boys heading away from the centre of the city, the barrow men pushing their heavy vehicles into alleys and yards and removing a wheel so they couldn't be stolen, before following the rickshaw coolies. Then the siren went again and they saw the large paper lanterns had been replaced by two red ones.

'Close now,' Putnam said. 'We'd better get off the road.'

The noise of the teeming streets had changed now to a panicky sound and then, as they headed for the caves dug in the cliffs for air raid shelters, they saw the red lights had also disappeared, and the chatter of the crowd changed to shouts and everybody started to run. Babies were crying and women were wailing. A few peasants were hurrying by with chickens, mattresses, tea-kettles, here and there the corpse of a relative; sometimes in a rickshaw, sometimes in a car or even a sedan chair, all heading for the fields outside the city.

Willie and Putnam had reached the shelter of a ditch when the planes arrived and they waited with a crowd of Chinese who were clutching their children to them, their eyes lifted upwards. The planes came in wingtip to wingtip and the light jade-coloured evening sky that tinted the silvery crescents of the paddy fields along the slopes was spotted with the antiaircraft shells bursting in pink puffs of smoke, all of them short or off-target because the gun barrels were worn out.

The wailing had stopped now and throughout the din of the bombs Putnam went on talking, shouting his observations in Willie's ear as they ducked and flinched at the explosions. 'The Slopeheads all accept they can be killed any sunny day,' he yelled. 'So they keep their office files ready stacked for whipping into a dugout. If the sun's going to shine, people set off early so they can be close to a shelter. They save their longer errands for a cloudy day.' He smiled. 'There's one thing the bombing's done, though. It's made the Szechwanese and the Cantonese and all the other "eses" realise they aren't as different from each other as they thought. They've discovered they're all the same people and the youngsters have even started to marry each other.'

The raid was a bad one and went on a long time. When the all clear went – represented by a long green paper windsock on the hillside – Chungking seemed to be on fire from one end to the other. Shop fronts were smashed and there were acres of burned-out devastation where the bamboo and mud squalour of the new housing had vanished. The incendiaries had chewed out a series of old slums, and ancient temples had caught fire, so that they could hear the timbers whistling and cracking and the popping of the bamboo joints as they burned.

It was obvious they were not going to see Zychov and, sure enough, when they asked the next day they learned he had left. They had worked most of the night with the Chinese, dragging out corpses and carrying away the injured until, with daylight, covered with dirt and ash, they had stumbled back to Putnam's flat and fallen into chairs.

'Not as bad as the first time,' Putnam pointed out grimly. 'Then, they didn't know what to expect and they packed the main street so goddam tight they couldn't move, and men, women and kids were roasted where they stood.'

'Does Chiang ever try to drive the Japs back?' Willie asked.

Putnam grimaced. 'Old Dogleg has too many shifty people round him,' he said. 'He thinks Japan can't be defeated, but he thinks the good old USA will finally have to take sides with him, so it's his job to look after the Communists.' He shrugged. 'I guess he's right, too. China's so big, the Japanese can never capture all of it, and all he's got to do is retreat a bit more when necessary and keep out of the way.' He handed Willie a drink. 'He'll get all he wants,' he added, 'when we finally slap the Japs down.' He paused. 'As we're bound to eventually,' he added.

PART FIVE

1939–1945

one

'Eventually' proved to be much sooner than anyone expected. Despite the new war in China, in the East business did not come to a halt and if care were taken to choose a route between battle zones, it was always possible to travel between the occupied and free zones. The Chinese post office even maintained its service between the two areas so that you could send mail from Chungking to Shanghai and vice versa, even send Japanese goods for sale to Chiang's new capital, where they were immediately snapped up by the luxury-deprived inhabitants.

Among them were the products of the Shanghai factories. As often as not the factories consisted of no more than two or three rooms crammed with machinery and operatives, many of them small boys, bought outright from their parents for twenty dollars, who worked up to fourteen hours a day, their only wages food and a sleeping place in a loft. In accumulator factories many of them showed the blue line in the gums which indicated lead poisoning, in the steamy silk winding mills the girls' hands were white with a fungoid growth, while in the dusty air of the cotton mills tuberculosis was almost a certainty. If the young workers slackened the overseers plunged their elbows into hot water.

But Shanghai had been developed in an atmosphere of a bar-room brawl on a charter that included no thou-shalt-nots, and tolerance had always been the watchword. Seeing his business associates gambling on the Stock Exchange, making money from fitting in with the plans of the aggressive Japanese, Willie was glad he had got rid of his interests in the city and was concentrating solely on shipping. His Chinese crews, he felt, were always better than they would have been trying to make a living as farmers or fishermen, and few of them seemed to want to leave his employ. He knew how they lived because he had shared their forecastles, long, narrow places with two tiers of bunks where the lean yellow torsos shone in the dim light as they played their endless games of mahjongg. He'd helped with coaling, working among the coolies, indifferent to the jeers of white men who thought he was belittling himself, and he knew the failings of the Chinese sailors, of the money they owed to the crimps and the secret societies, the way they gambled away their earnings for two years ahead. Once, when seven bells had been sounded and there had been no reply from the old seaman on look-out on the forecastle, he had gone down to see why not and found the old man had hanged himself by hitching the old-fashioned pigtail he still wore over a stanchion because he was so heavily in debt he could see no other way out.

There were shipping lines and manufacturers who operated differently, however, and some of his associates were making money indecently quickly. Mason and Marchant's, in particular, under the direction of Emmeline, her hand freed by the unexpected death of old

Honeyford, had increased their holdings in the sweat shops ashore and were more than happy to co-operate with the little yellow men from across the East China Sea, who more and more were coming to be regarded as 'the enemy'.

Indignant at the resistance of the Chinese, the Japanese had taken a high moral stand, interpreting in their propaganda the objections to their attacks as rebellion against lawful Chinese authority which, out of the goodness of their hearts, they were supporting. But, as they had subjected Chungking to increasingly massive air attacks, America had, as Willie had heard, retaliated by granting Chiang an enormous loan while Britain had sent the trucks to transport the much-needed supplies along the freshly opened road from Burma, constructed by the bare hands of thousands of ant-like peasants.

While recognising the Chungking regime and in favour of Chinese resistance, the coastal settlements were careful, nevertheless, to exercise a measure of censorship to avoid provoking the Japanese who surrounded them and, occupied as they were with their own problems and the everlasting chaos in China, the busy Shanghailanders barely noticed what was happening in Europe. They were largely unaware of, even indifferent to, the increasing brutality of the Nazis in Germany, and failed to see the drift towards a conflict. The British Prime Minister's mission to Munich in 1938 – 'a kow-tow to Hitler', it was called in Shanghai – came as a tremendous shock. In the East, a long way from European tensions, it seemed impossible that Britain, which had won the war of 1914–1918, should be going down on one knee before the dictator of a humbled nation who, it was easy to see –

especially from Shanghai – was clearly bluffing and was as mad as a hatter, anyway.

The efforts to contain Hitler seemed pathetic when seen at a distance. Even the Anglo-French military delegation which had gone to Russia to try to stave off any pact between that country and Germany seemed totally ineffectual.

'One monocle and at least two hyphenated names,' Willie growled to his wife. 'No wonder the Russians don't like 'em. They're still the men who made the revolution, and they're the same political breed exactly as the Germans. They're never going to see eye to eye with 'em.'

Nevertheless, despite increasing tension, nobody believed it would come to hostilities. But it did and Chamberlain's announcement of the fact to the country was lugubrious and far from likely to stir up any patriotic feeling.

'He sounds as if he's an undertaker whose hearse's just lost a wheel,' Willie said.

Immediately, a few young men disappeared westwards to join the forces as they had in 1914, but most people remained firmly where they were, because memories of the last affair were still clear in the mind and, while it was known that European wars left the Far East untouched apart from an occasional sinking and a little loss of business, in Europe they meant disaster, mutilation and death.

Besides, there was always the excitement of making money, of jockeying for power and prestige. The big firms remained untouched as they had for a hundred years, but the smaller ones, both foreign and Chinese, continued to change hands as someone guessed wrong or grew too ambitious. Old Honeyford, Emmeline's latest husband, had disappeared from the scene just as Chamberlain had returned from Munich – 'In disgust, I expect,' Da Braga said – while the Balalaika closed once more and George Kee discovered that Zychov, still under Chiang's protection, was working with the old man's widow.

'He wants Da Braga-Kee's,' he said. 'He's acting for her.'

'I'm not sure which one to pity most,' Willie observed. 'I wouldn't trust Zychov as far as I could throw him, but there's a fair amount of venom in Emmeline.'

From the beginning, the conflict in Europe seemed to follow the same pattern as the earlier one, with the opposing armies facing each other in France, though this time with none of the hideous slaughter of the first war. The Germans seemed to be matchlessly efficient, however, while the British bumbled through with their usual sporting amateurism and, inevitably, the first casualty at sea had been a British ship, the Donaldson liner *Athenia*, sunk without warning in the first hours of the conflict.

'First blood to the Germans,' Willie said.

Within days of the war starting, Polly wrote from Singapore to say how relieved she was that Wissermann's had moved there from the mainland of China, where the tensions were increasing every day. Thomas suggested that he ought to go to England to join up but was persuaded by Willie not to, and instead, considering that by this time he was more Chinese than European, decided he would remain where he was in case trouble flared up in the Far East. The only member of the family likely to be involved in any danger seemed to be Edward, who was now a senior commander, but since he was at the Admiralty, he also seemed unlikely to be involved with shot and shell.

For the Sarth Line the pattern repeated itself. The German pocket battleship *Graf Spee*, which everybody thought was in the South Atlantic, turned up in the Indian Ocean, where, among other victims, she sank Willie's latest acquisition, a small freighter called the *Gentiana*. She was a reasonably new ship, built in Hong Kong and bought to replace the ageing *Sivrihisar*, and he was proud of her; but she went down nevertheless under a scuttling party from the German battleship, while the elderly *Lady Roberts*, under Captain Yeh, steamed gaily past only fifty miles away to the east on her way from Bombay to East London.

It was infuriating to lose his best ship while his oldest acquisition escaped scot free, but, having made sure the crew of the *Gentiana* were safe and that the ship was properly covered by insurance, Willie nevertheless felt a sneaking sort of pride that the *Lady Roberts* had got away with it again. She was old now, ancient in fact, and he had once again been thinking of getting rid of her, but had held on to her from sheer sentiment. Now, with the war, she was important again and with the Germans using U-boats which were likely to be just as much of a threat as in the earlier war, every ship, every scrap of tonnage, every vessel that could carry a cargo, was of value. The *Lady Roberts* had been saved by the bell.

Everyone knew what war meant, because they had been experiencing it for years in China, but when the disaster in Europe came it was unbelievable. After six months of nothing happening beyond a few sinkings, a few aircraft shot down, a few men killed in patrol skirmishing (while a war between Russia and Finland had provided the only real casualties and when it seemed that the war in China against the Japanese was the only genuine war available), the bubble burst as the Germans unleashed their onslaught in France.

At first it was hard to understand what was happening and the news that the British had been flung out of the Continent of Europe and that France had been defeated was hard to accept. The horizon seemed to be growing darker. Britain wasn't beaten but she was reeling and it seemed immediately to Willie that her possessions overseas could hardly expect any help when she was fighting for her life at home. And then, in a diplomatic coup equal to the one he had pulled off with Russia to enable him to attack Poland, Hitler produced another – a pact between Germany, Italy and Japan in which each undertook to go to the aid of either of the others in the event of an attack by any state not yet at war. It was obvious Japan was afraid of finding herself at war with Russia, America and Britain all at once, and the net result was an open invitation for aggression in the Far East and, since Shanghai was too far away to be helped, the garrison was largely evacuated and the military hospital shut down. The feeling was that it could never hold out because it was virtually surrounded and even in parts, already actually occupied by the Japanese, and that the troops could probably he more sensibly used elsewhere.

Britain was being outmanoeuvred all along the line and Willie could only assume that the politicians back home were still as much out of touch with events as they had been at the time of Munich. Once again he began to look at his holdings and contemplate shifting them, because the British government had clearly begun to regard Hong Kong, the base of the British China Squadron, as an indefensible outpost like Shanghai and were concentrating on Singapore.

Still stumping round on his artificial leg, Da Braga had been thinking of the situation, too, and was equally uneasy. He wished to operate in a more compact way and had been trying for some time to get rid of Da Braga-Kee subsidiaries; there had been a court case involving Mason and Marchant's in which an unfair conspiracy to block shareholders from accepting a share-all cash tender offer from another British company had surfaced and Da Braga was nervous of the future. He wanted to go public, to offer shares on the Shanghai stock market. George Kee was none too keen and they were constantly at loggerheads.

'Why not sell and get out?' Willie asked. 'Like it or not, the war's coming here.'

'If it comes, it'll come to Hong Kong,' Da Braga pointed out. 'The Japanese are at Amoy and Bias Bay, only thirty miles away.'

'I haven't failed to notice it, Luis.'

Da Braga shrugged. 'So where do you go from Hong Kong? The Japanese army virtually surrounds that place, too.'

'They're also so placed they can seize airfields in Indo-China any time they like for an attack on Malaya – which is nearer to Japan itself, anyway.' Willie gave a wry smile. 'And now the Navy's had to withdraw ships from these waters for home defence, I don't give us much longer before the bomb bursts out here. I'm going to get out of China, Luis.'

He was still curious about Mason and Marchant's activities, however, and placing a block of his shares on the market, he waited for them to be snapped up. Emmeline didn't move and the shares went elsewhere.

'Zychov,' Da Braga said.

'Anybody else interested?'

'Satorelli-Wint's were bidding.'

'Keep 'em at it, Luis. Then let's go while the going's good. You could be a rich man. George, too. Go back to Goa, or Portugal even.'

Da Braga gave him a sad smile. 'You think I could? I've been in China most of my life.'

'China won't be the same when the war's over. Britain will have to sell her possessions to pay for it as she did last time and she'll be too weak to resist Chinese pressures.'

Da Braga considered thoughtfully. 'You may be right, Willie,' he said. 'But don't forget I'm Portuguese and, with Portugal not in the war, I could stay here and look after your interests.'

It was a point Willie hadn't considered and George Kee's view was roughly the same as Da Braga's. 'I'm more Chinese than European,' he pointed out. 'I'm already operating under Japanese control in many areas, anyway. Why don't we start up a new firm and continue to work together? We always have. Then you'll still have a foothold here to build on when the fighting stops.'

The rest of the Da Braga-Kee shares went on the market. Satorelli-Wint's were still interested because Da Braga-Kee's had plenty of good will, but they were outbid again and Zychov ended as the new owner. It didn't mean a thing, of course. The money had come not from a restaurant owner with no experience but from a woman who was manipulating Mason and Marchant's, something that became obvious at once when their plate went up on the wall in place of Da Braga-Kee's.

'I hope she enjoys it,' Willie said.

The new firm, Shanghai Traders, was set up. George Kee wanted to put his name into the title because he was proud of what he had achieved, but Willie advised against it.

'Play it quiet, George,' he suggested. 'You're Chinese. Stay that way.'

Willie's share in the new firm was carefully hidden. The money was moved about between different banks in Hong Kong and Shanghai until it would have been hard to find where it had originated, and his name was kept out of all correspondence. Though there was still no sign of aggression from Japan and movement was still possible about the sea, there was a continuing sense of tension. When business took Willie to Tokyo, he made a point of looking up Shaiba, by this time a highly respected retired senior admiral.

'What's Japan after, Yuhitsu?' he asked bluntly.

Shaiba sighed. 'Japan is following her destiny,' he said.

'I thought she'd followed it. I thought she'd reached it.'

Shaiba's sigh came again. 'There are people who consider there is further to go.'

He would say no more and the subject was dropped. It left Willie worried and thoughtful.

1940 brought new disasters. With Britain under constant bombardment from the air, in Greece, Crete and North Africa she was thrown on the defensive, and it seemed clear to Willie that Japan was looking for an opportunity to snatch what it could from the spoils. Italy had already capitalised on Hitler's victories and, with Britain reeling and France out of the fight, their possessions were up for grabs.

The news that Hitler had gone into Russia came like a thunderclap. At first it seemed just another giant step of conquest, but Willie's naval friends saw it differently. To them it meant that Hitler was fighting on two fronts, and they were quick to point out what had happened to Napoleon's Grand Army in 1812. It made Willie hold his breath. Now, surely, Hitler had made a mistake. He had never expected to see Britain beaten, but after the disasters of the previous year it had seemed the war might go on for ever. Now, victory seemed not only certain but nearer.

On the other hand, it was also possible to see it as a spur to the Japanese. If Hitler were to be beaten, it made sense to grab what was going while it was still there. It was common knowledge that Japan was on a war footing and had bases from which she could launch attacks. Diplomatic moves were going on with the Americans, but they showed few signs of succeeding and Elliott Wissermann had it that Japan's oil reserves were diminishing daily and that the time to find a solution to the differences between Japan and the United States was rapidly running out.

Willie made his decision as he made all his decisions. He thought it through then made up his mind firmly.

'We're moving from Hong Kong,' he told Nadya.

'But I like Hong Kong,' she said. 'I've grown to love it.'

However unwillingly though, she accepted his point and agreed to move when he decided. That other people were thinking the same way became obvious as he was constantly asked his advice – to go or stay?

'Go,' he said bluntly. 'And don't waste time.'

Both soldiers and civilians came to ask whether they should send away their wives and children. 'It'll mean that things will be difficult for them,' they pointed out.

'They'd be more difficult in Hong Kong if the Japanese come. Go while it's easy to do so.'

'Will you go?'

Willie paused. He had already explored Singapore and Penang as possible bases. Malaya produced half the world's tin and there were always huge stocks of rubber to be carried, to say nothing of sugar, timber and other products. He had long considered either base as adequate as Shanghai or Hong Kong.

'I'm already making arrangements,' he said.

There was still no sign of any Japanese movement against British or Dutch possessions in the Far East, but nobody was deluded that it wasn't coming, and Willie made no attempt to make their stay in Singapore a permanent one. Watching the newspapers, keeping in touch with his friends in the Navy, he began now to transfer his headquarters in Singapore further on to Sydney, where his shipping office already provided a base. Surely to God, he thought, the Japanese would never reach Australia.

In July, his Hong Kong office was contacted by one of the Governor's aides. Would Mr Sarth care to call to discuss a few things?

The Governor was a brisk man and made no bones about what was in his mind. Could Mr Sarth provide ships?

'Of course,' Willie said. 'For what reason?'

The Governor was quite open. 'The Foreign Office in London considers the evacuation of useless mouths from the colony to be a sign of weakness,' he said. 'Why, I can't imagine, because in France before Dunkirk it was considered good sense.' The Governor allowed himself a small smile, as if the ways of the politicians in London were beyond him. 'And it doesn't seem to have been considered odd at Shanghai. True, Shanghai was our most isolated garrison. But here we have to look after ourselves, and there can be no more than two battalions to spare to come to our aid. So there you are, Mr Sarth, since the decision has been given to me I'm going to go ahead and evacuate everybody I can. I prefer to take no chances with women and children. They have no idea in London what it's like out here.'

Willie smiled. 'Did they ever have?'

Two of his ships, the *Cenerentola* and the *Carpathian Prince*, were soon engaged in transporting women and children to South Africa and India. A lot of them were Chinese who had worked with the British and knew that in the event of a Japanese attack they would be on the black list for liquidation. A few were unable to pay their fares and Willie shrugged.

'Pack 'em in,' he told his captains. 'They can pay later.'

The evacuation marked one more step on the downward path. Evacuation might not be a sign of weakness but it was certainly a sign of nervousness. When Willie returned to Singapore he found Nadya had moved into a large rented house on the Bukit Timah road. She was delighted with the place. Singapore was beautiful, a city with green everywhere, with sports rounds, golf courses, parks and gardens, and a glimpse of the sea at every corner. Lying as it did for four miles along the coast, you could always catch a glimpse of a passenger liner, a junk, even a battered Sarth Line freighter, while Singapore River, stretching through the city, was alive with sampans.

It was an exciting polyglot place with a tropical smell all of its own – of drains, swamplands, dried fish and spices – which once caught was never forgotten. You could buy anything you needed there from the latest fashions to the newest book from Kelly and Walsh's store. Women could get a facial at the chemist's in Raffles Place or meet friends in Robinson's restaurant, yet the dripping jungle was still only just outside the city and at night the air was stiff with the sound of bullfrogs. You could pick orchids close to the house Nadya had rented or watch the monkeys near the tennis courts of the Tanglin Club, and nobody carried money because everything was paid for simply by signing a chit. There was only one drawback. Polly had still made no move to contact them and Nadya's only attempt to contact Polly had come to nothing.

'Leave it,' Willie said. 'She'll come round eventually. In any case, we're not staying here. You've got to learn to talk Australian.'

Nadya's face changed. 'But I don't want to go to Australia,' she said. 'I don't like Australians.'

'Too forthright,' Willie agreed cheerfully. 'They'll tell you your stuff's decadent and that you're charging too much. But that's just the way they talk. They're not stupid and they'll do business. They're doing business with me without trouble.'

'William.' He could see she was angry with him. 'I've given up my home in St Petersburg, in Vladivostok, and now in Hong Kong. I'm not moving again.'

'Yes, you are,' he said. 'Otherwise, I'll be coming to fetch you out as I did in Vladivostok.'

She looked quickly at him. 'Will it come to that?'

'I'm sure it will.'

'Have you warned Polly?' Nadya was still unable to reject her stepdaughter, despite her stepdaughter's refusal to accept her.

'Polly's all right,' Willie pointed out. 'Elliott's American. That makes Polly and the children American and, since America's not involved, she's nothing to worry about and we can concentrate on our own affairs.'

Once again they began to pack their belongings and arrange to have what furniture they wished to take with them crated up and placed aboard the *Cenerentola*, bound for Sydney. Eventually Willie accompanied his wife on board the liner *Orontes* and kissed her goodbye. Her eyes were on his face as though she were afraid she might never see it again.

'When will you come, William?'

'When Singapore's been evacuated.'

'Will they evacuate it?'

He smiled. 'Of course they will. They did Hong Kong. Singapore's no safer.'

two

Feelings in Singapore remained very much mixed. Nobody believed that the war could touch them but they welcomed the possibility of help all the same. There had been talk of an aircraft carrier arriving to assist the air defence if it came to that, but, while the idea was welcomed in the bars and clubs, Willie's naval contact, a commander called Ruffard, who had been at school with Edward, considered the Admiralty and the politicians in London were talking through their collective hat.

'It's just a sop to the Australian government, who've blackmailed 'em into it,' he said. 'But Japan won't be deterred by the presence of one carrier. She could easily detach four of her modern ships to deal with her. She's got plenty.'

Nevertheless, in October Willie heard that the additional naval strength was to become a fact. The brand new *Prince of Wales*, at that moment in Cape Town, would be arriving shortly, and the battle cruiser *Repulse*, which was in Ceylon, was to join her to form a Far East squadron. Unfortunately, the aircraft carrier *Indomitable*, which was also to have joined, had been damaged in an accidental grounding, was not available, and was quietly forgotten.

Which, Ruffard observed, left the *Prince of Wales* and the *Repulse* entirely without air cover.

'Charming,' he commented.

The news of the impending arrival of the big warships made Willie wonder where Edward was. His last letter had indicated that he was still at the Admiralty but was expecting his fourth stripe and a return to sea duties, with the hope of a cruiser or a flotilla of new destroyers. It seemed to bring the war nearer and Thomas seemed to think the same. On Willie's next visit to Shanghai, his son was waiting for him.

'I'm going north, Father,' he said. 'The Chinese are still resisting and if it comes to a war between us and the Japanese I'd be legitimately involved anyway.'

'Chungking?' Willie asked.

'No, Father. Not Chiang. I don't trust him. His government's decaying. There are too many offices available for purchase and too much venality and incompetence. It's the old warlord system again run by officials instead of soldiers. I don't trust Chiang. He's not fighting for China, he's fighting for his political future, and any man who can breach the Yellow River to stop the Japanese and drown around a million of his own countrymen in doing so doesn't need my help.'

Willie had heard of the incident. Propaganda had made a lot of Chiang's 'sacrifice', but few details had emerged.

'I'm joining Mao Tse-Tung,' Thomas went on.

'You'll get nowhere with the Communists, lad,' Willie warned.

'I'm not wanting to get anywhere, Father, and the Communists are at least fighting the Japanese. I just want you to look after Fanny and the boys.'

An anxious Fan-Su and the two boys, both sloe-eyed and black-haired like their mother, were placed aboard the *Cenerentola* bound for Sydney, and a cable was sent to Nadya asking her to find them a home. Willie was glad to see them safe.

'They're best out of here,' he told Da Braga. 'The bright days for Far East businessmen are over. Once the last of the treaty port system's disbanded, it'll never exist again.'

The Japanese had already more than once blockaded the foreign concessions on one pretext or another and, though it was still possible to move out, even through the Japanese lines, it was only at the cost of exhausting waits and humiliating searches. The Japanese were virtually in control.

'What's even worse,' Willie growled, 'are the smiles of the Chinese. They've no cause to love the Japanese – and it's my guess they'll have even less before long – but they know they're putting down the mighty – us – who've lorded it over the East for so long.'

He visited Abigail's grave and stood at its foot for a while. Dear loyal Ab. He could only remember her with the deepest affection. She had been a splendid wife, backing him up in everything he did, supporting his wilder dreams, forgiving him his trespasses, giving all and asking nothing.

Later he called on Da Braga and George Kee. Outside the shops in the Old City, even in parts of the International Settlement, were pictures of Chiang exhorting the Chinese to greater effort. The Japanese simply ignored them and they were a little pointless, anyway, with the Japanese everywhere in the city and allowing German supply ships to refuel in the river –

swollen from lighters owned by Americans. Most of the Europeans and Americans had gone, though, their homes closed, their wives and children returned to their homelands, to India or South Africa, the few husbands still remaining hanging on to watch the businesses they owned or represented, living in hotels or on their own in their echoing houses.

Chinese refugees from the fighting were trying to crowd into the city bullied by the Japanese with their long swords and wooden revolver holsters, slapped, beaten, their possessions kicked and scattered, the few British troops still there powerless to do much beyond put in an appearance. The Japanese were still tolerating the British and the Americans, but, in fact, they were rarely seen. The *Shanghai Times*, trying to sit on both sides of the fence, was being sympathetic to them while not being unsympathetic to the Chinese. Japanese civilians were everywhere in their frock coats, striped trousers and spectacles, sometimes with Germans or Italians in uniform, and there were said to be German submarines in the estuary.

It looked grim, and the blockhouses containing British soldiers didn't convince Willie, any more than the defiant magazines and the Pathé and Movietone news in the cinemas that the place was safe. So much so, he even sent a warning to Emmeline. After all, she was British and a woman and he had once been her lover. He had no affection for her at all these days, but the appearance of the city was sufficient to make him feel forgiving.

'Tell Emmeline to get out,' he asked Da Braga.

It got them nowhere. Da Braga showed him the reply. 'Tell Mr Sarth to go to hell.'

'She thinks we're after Mason and Marchant's,' Da Braga said.

When Willie returned to Singapore, there was still no sign of any general evacuation. Singapore looked and smelled the same as it always had, with its vivid tropical colours, the laundry hanging from bamboo poles, the fish in the native quarters drying on the pavements, each portion the target of a million noisy flies.

The fact that London didn't believe in everlasting peace was obvious from the troopships that kept arriving and the long columns of khaki-clad men who clambered aboard the waiting lorries in the docks to drive through the bedlam of straying chickens, rickshaws, natives and fast traffic to their camps.

Willie watched them with Commander Ruffard from the bund.

'Think the build-up helps?' he asked.

Ruffard was a cynic. 'It doesn't seem to the people here to presage turmoil and war,' he smiled. 'It merely adds an interesting ingredient to their existence.'

The soldiers themselves seemed totally unworried and even arrived in a holiday mood. After being penned up in the United Kingdom with its rationing and black-outs. Singapore was a paradise. They were young and for the most part untrained, and when Willie gave them lifts in his car, their naivety startled him.

'It'll all right,' he was told. 'The Nips are only little and they're frightened of the dark. Besides, everybody knows they have bad eyesight. That's why they're such rotten pilots.'

'Who told you that?' Willie asked.

'Everybody knows it. They've collected all their old kettles and kitchen utensils to turn 'em into aeroplanes, and their guns go back to 1900.'

The first acts of the new arrivals were to start inter-regimental battles, English against Scots, Scots against Australians, and they were totally ignored by the residents, who seemed even worse than the Shanghailanders in their indifference to what was happening. Since they spent all their time delivering snubs to the troops, the troops inevitably turned to the natives, who disliked the European residents as much as they did. Working about the camps, they questioned the new arrivals enthusiastically about their training and weapons, and proudly counted them as they paraded. Considering the posters, THE ENEMY IS LISTENING, that were displayed, it seemed to Willie that somebody had got things a little wrong and that the natives, some of them probably even Japanese, were doubtless passing on the information they picked up. Though sentries were warned of Fifth Columnists and told to shoot if they saw an eyelash moving, the natives were quite unconcerned and continued to smile and walk past them without fear. No one was shot.

Half-expecting to be asked to co-operate in an evacuation of women and children, Willie was surprised to find there was no sign of an attempt to remove the useless mouths. The Sarth Line had placed ships at the disposal of the authorities, but they were sailing practically empty. In fact, the authorities seemed to be against evacuation. The British women and children in Malaya were many times more numerous than those in Hong Kong, but, while it had been agreed that anyone who wished could leave voluntarily, with no discrimination of race or creed, no compulsory order was made, and remarkably few people were choosing to go.

Once again, Willie found people coming to him for his advice, which was always the same as it had been in Hong Kong – 'Go while you can.' There even seemed no sense in *not* evacuating the Chinese and Indians because they didn't wish to travel to Britain, Australia, South Africa or India, which required large ocean-going ships. Most of them wanted only to reach the Netherlands East Indies, but, though there were plenty of suitable craft for such short coastal trips, they were not made available, and nobody took any positive steps to organise an evacuation.

From time to time Willie's thoughts dwelt on Polly. He had not contacted her even now and he often wondered if she had ever regretted her decision never to have anything to do with Nadya. Was it simply because she couldn't lose face? Face was important in the East and Polly had lived there long enough to have absorbed the idea behind it. In the end, he decided to chance it and drove out to her home. She met him with a suspicious look in her eyes, a grim determination not to give way, but then her expression crumpled and she ran forward and flung her arms round him, and he could hear her weeping.

'Oh, Pa,' she said. 'It's been so bloody long.'

'Come off it, Poll,' he said. 'Some people go a whole lifetime without seeing their parents or their children. Especially out here.'

'Yes, I guess so.' He noticed her accent was becoming American, but that was natural enough because she'd been married to young Wissermann a long time now.

'How's Elliott?' he asked.

'Bit worried about the situation.'

'He's not the only one. Where is he?'

'He's in the States. He wants to transfer all Wissermann Far East operations to Hawaii or even San Francisco, but it's not long since they were transferred from Shanghai and he's afraid the shareholders won't stand for it. He's gone to try to convince them.'

Willie knew the way his son-in-law was thinking. The Japanese would inevitably want to move towards the British, Dutch and French areas of influence and, with France and Holland flat on their backs and Britain fighting for her life, the time was surely ripe.

Polly sighed. 'He thinks nobody will believe there can be hostilities between Japan and the United States, and the shareholders won't agree to a gap in trading and a loss of profits. I must admit, with talks going on with the Japanese in Washington, it doesn't make much sense.'

'It doesn't have to, Polly.'

She gave him a worried look. 'What's going to happen, Pa? Will there be fighting here?'

Willie shrugged. 'Japan's only just to the north, Poll, and that's the best place in the world for an attack. And they've been building ships like hell's delight for years. I know that for a fact. Everybody operating a tuppenny-halfpenny freighter knows it. They're ready, even if we aren't.'

'Won't we be all right. We're Americans now.'

'A bomb can't read passports, Poll.'

'But the British would never let Singapore go, Pa, would they? It's the naval base for the Far East.'

'Poll, I'm not trying to frighten you –' Willie paused ' – yes, by God, I am! I'm trying to frighten you like hell! Have you seen what we've got here to stop them? Out-of-date aircraft. A few old ships. Guns facing the wrong way.'

'How can they be? They'd have to come from the sea.'

'Suppose they come down the peninsula and in by the back door? You should be packing, Poll, and preparing to go to the States.'

'I can't, Pa. I've got to wait for Elliott to come back. I've got to be at his side.'

'Poll, you said that in Yangpo and you had to run for your life. At least, send the kids away. Elliott's mother would take them and they'd be a lot safer in San Francisco.'

He had obviously made her think and she frowned. 'I'll talk to Elliott about it when he gets back, Pa,' she said.

'Talk hard.'

'It'll soon be Christmas, Pa. Why don't you come round? It never seems the same having Christmas without Santa Claus, a big turkey and lots of booze, but that seems silly here. In this climate, we'd all fall asleep with our heads on our plates.' She paused. 'But what about – ?'

He could see she was uncertain, after all she'd said about Nadya. She probably found it hard to take it all back and wasn't sure how to deal with it. He made it easy.

'Nadya's in Sydney,' he said. 'And I'm going to join her for Christmas.'

The two great ships which had been expected appeared at the beginning of December. Half Singapore turned out to watch them arrive. Despite Commander Ruffard's pessimism, to Willie their sheer size seemed enough to frighten off any enemy. As they headed for their berths a squadron of Brewster Buffaloes howled overhead, snub-nosed heavyshouldered machines which, so rumour had it, looked a great deal better than they were.

He stood for a long time, watching the two ships, the activity on their decks and the small boats which had turned out to give them a welcome. Their presence worried him, despite their size, because danger was implicit in their arrival and he decided that, while he was glad he was going to Sydney, he ought perhaps to telegraph Elliott Wissermann in San Francisco and warn him of the situation. He was even tempted to stay on longer than he'd intended, but he decided Nadya might be worried and came to the conclusion that he should stick to his arrangements. But, as he arrived at his suite at the hotel, the telephone went. It was Polly.

'Pa,' she screamed. 'You must come round at once! Teddy's here. He's in the *Prince of Wales!*'

Shaving and scrambling into his clothes, Willie called one of the little yellow Ford taxis that plied round the city. With the Wissermann children overexcited at the prospect of seeing something of a war, something which to them was no more dangerous than a Western film, the gathering turned into a riot. But it was a riot with its more sombre moments because for the adults the future remained dark, and Edward, arriving with Ruffard, had none of the incurable optimism of those who had lived out their lives in the Far East. He didn't believe the arrival of the two great ships substantially altered the situation.

'Big ships,' he said firmly, 'have something in common with cavalry and dodos. They're out of date.'

Standing in the sunshine with a drink in his hand, to Willie it didn't seem possible, and Edward went on bluntly.

'In 1914–18,' he said, 'the cavalry had to transport about three times their own weight in fodder for their horses, far more than was transported in the way of ammunition for fighting. Big ships are the same. They're so valuable, both in monetary terms and in terms of prestige, to protect them they have to have a fleet of destroyers which would be of far better use protecting convoys.'

It was decided that they should all be together for lunch at Poll's on the Sunday and that they should make a day of it, starting with breakfast. The excitement of meeting again had died a little by this time and they were all a bit subdued now. The weather was as magnificent as it always was as they gathered in the garden and the servants brought out the coffee and rolls. Edward, however, seemed to have his thoughts elsewhere. The negotiations between the Americans and the Japanese in Washington were still deadlocked and Ruffard had heard of mysterious radio messages that seemed to indicate a movement of the Japanese fleet not westwards towards China and Malaya as they had expected but eastwards towards Honolulu.

Edward didn't like the situation at all, in fact, but he held his tongue when Polly or the children were near and only began to discuss the situation when he was alone in the garden with his father. Newly out from England, where they had been closer to the war for a long time, he and his friends hadn't been slow to notice the things that were wrong in Singapore, and took a poor view of the quality of the British troops garrisoning the place. The tropical climate had brought softness and they had grown too accustomed to the easy living conditions.

'Back home,' he insisted, 'they're living like Spartans, preparing for what's to come. The Admiral went to see the army the other day and I was part of his staff, and one of the things that was brought up was the fact that nobody's considered using the Chinese and Malays. Why not? They've as much to lose as we have.'

'The trouble with this war,' he went on, 'is that communications have developed too much and that allows Whitehall too big a say in what's to be done and we have to face the fact that at the moment Malaya's not a very important issue at the War Office. But you also can't run a war from the other side of the world, Father, and here they're letting 'em, and taking far too much for granted. Including the oldest and most unforgivable mistake of all – underestimating the enemy. The Japs might still surprise America by deciding they're strong enough to declare war.'

Willie frowned. 'There's one other thing that everybody seems to have overlooked, too,' he pointed out quietly. 'You'll remember I was in Port Arthur in 1905 when the Japanese attacked without warning. Why do people think they've changed?'

As he finished asking, he turned and saw that Polly had appeared at his side. The look in her eyes was one of doubt.

'Surely they'd never try anything, Pa,' she said. 'When we came back from the States the last time we stopped at Honolulu, and the harbour was full of battleships. Enormous ones. The whole Pacific Fleet, Elliott said. Surely the Japanese wouldn't attempt anything with that lot waiting to snap them up.'

As the telephone rang, she stopped dead, excused herself and disappeared. After a while she returned.

'It's for you, Teddy,' she announced. 'They said it was urgent.'

Edward disappeared. A few moments later he, too, reappeared. His face was grim and Willie knew at once that something momentous had occurred.

'I have to get back to the ship,' he said. 'We're going to sea.'

'Has something happened?' Polly asked.

Edward kissed her gently, his face grave. 'Yes, it has, Poll, old love,' he said. 'The war's started. The Japanese have attacked that Pacific Fleet at Pearl Harbour you were talking about. The Americans seem to have guessed wrong and they've lost eighteen ships, some of them big ones, around three hundred aircraft, and God knows how many people. Pearl's a ruin and the Pacific Fleet's destroyed.'

three

The Sarth Line passenger-freighter *Cenerentola*, about to leave Singapore for Port Morseby in New Guinea, was promptly ordered to stay where she was, and the *Lady Roberts*, heading south from Rangoon, was signalled to get a move on, while the *Man of Harlech*, heading north from Batavia in the Dutch East Indies, was expected within forty-eight hours. A fourth ship, the *Sunga Kavalan*, carrying trucks and steam rollers for the building of airstrips in the north and due to pick up a cargo of tin from Kuala Lumpur, was in Penang somewhere and out of touch.

The destruction of the American Pacific Fleet had abruptly stirred things up, and for the first time there appeared to be signs of life about Singapore. The streets were suddenly full of military police and steel helmets appeared in large numbers. Trucks galloped everywhere at full speed and the dance halls became silent and the cafés and bars deserted because every soldier in the place was heading back to camp. Those who couldn't obtain transport were commandeering cabs, rickshaws and passing cars to get them to where they ought to be.

With Robert Edward unreachable, Willie had to fall back for information on his friend Ruffard.

'There's a Japanese fleet at sea,' Ruffard said. 'And we know troop transports are near the tip of Indo-China steaming westwards. I'd advise you to start organising your affairs.'

It wasn't Willie's own affairs that worried him. The shipping office where the business of the Sarth Line was conducted was normally well in control, but suddenly it was being besieged by people seeking passages. No official order for evacuation had been given, but, though many people still felt that it was safe to stay, a lot had started to use their own initiative. It didn't take long to fill up the few places on the *Cenerentola* and she was fuelled, turned round, and left the following day, passing the *Man of Harlech* coming in as she headed southwards for the Indian Ocean.

'This is bloody silly,' Willie said. 'Here I am worrying about everybody else's family and neglecting my own.'

When he spoke to Polly on the telephone, she was anxious but calm. 'Elliott telephoned,' she said. 'He says he's been told it'll be all right.'

'Poll, it *won't* be all right!' Willie snapped. 'It'll be all wrong, and you tell Elliott that from me. People are getting out and you should be planning to get out, too. The Japanese are coming.'

'They'll never reach Singapore, Pa.'

Willie's thoughts churned. The fighting units in Singapore which should have been going through an intensive preparation for war months before had been doing nothing and as far as he could see, the total lack of preparation was compounded by unimaginative leadership, both civil and military. 'Poll, listen,' he said. 'Malaya – and especially Singapore – is living in a fool's paradise. They do bugger-all here but drink, dance and sign chits. The policy's "Don't worry. It may never happen." They should be forgetting red tape and files and starting to act.'

It was true enough. The Europeans in Singapore seemed even worse than the people of Shanghai, who at least were hard-headed business people. With their eyes on their money, they were too concerned with their possessions to be indolent. In Singapore the festive mood still prevailed and people set more store in dressing for dinner than preparing to meet the Japanese.

He tried to tell his daughter what he knew. 'The Japanese,' he said sharply, 'are desperate for rubber and oil. And both those things are here in this part of the world. Pack your bags, Poll. There are berths going begging on ships that are leaving. You could be away in twenty-four hours. This evacuation thing's all cockeyed and I'm going to be busy as hell with getting my ships and the people on board to safety, so you'll have to cope with your own. But get on with it, Poll. For God's sake, get on with it!'

Though Poll remained uncertain, Willie was swamped by telephone calls from others asking once again if he thought it best to leave.

'Of course it's best to leave,' he said angrily. 'Now! I have two ships coming in and there'll be places for anyone who wants them.'

On his way back to the hotel, he called at the Air Raid Precautions Headquarters to find out how shipping would be affected. But nobody knew anything about it and he found the place practically deserted.

'Nobody's told us anything about that,' he was informed. 'We were told we weren't likely to be affected just yet.'

'Why not?'

'Surely it can't happen to us!'

'*It's happened*,' Willie snarled. 'At Pearl Harbour!'

Returning to his hotel in a fury, he learned it had already started to happen in his own neck of the woods.

'Hong Kong's been attacked,' he was told at once. 'And they've gone for the Americans in Guam. The little bastards are also landing in Siam just north of the border with Malaya and they're putting men ashore at Kota Bharu just to the south. The airfield's expected to fall at any time, they say.'

'Who says?'

His informant looked startled. 'Everybody says.'

Instead of going to bed as he'd intended, Willie headed for the bar. While before Europe starved or burned or cowered, Singapore seemed determined to enjoy its luxurious life, and it was full of men, planters on leave from upcountry wondering whether they should return and remittance men in white ducks, busy with gin slings brought by silent waiters moving deftly among the rattan. They were drinking steadily, some of them half-drunk.

'Hello, Sarth,' one shouted to Willie. 'Happy now that war you've been going on about's finally come?'

Willie didn't answer and the speaker went on. 'Some people get the wind up easily,' he said pointedly, his red face shining with sweat. 'Woman asked my wife this morning if she was leaving. My wife gave her the beady eye. Good with the beady eye, my wife. Voice like ice. "Surely *you're* not," she said. That shut her up. You going, Sarth, or do you think you can drum up enough of the old necessary to see it out?'

'You,' Willie snapped, 'are a bloody fool!'

The red face grew redder. 'Come off it, Sarth! Isn't it showing a tiny bit of the old yellow to bolt as soon as things start moving? Good God, the nearest Jap airfields are six hundred miles away in Indo-China.'

'And that, I suppose,' Willie retorted, 'is why no one's ordered a black-out or dug any trenches.'

The other man laughed. 'Trenches would only fill with water and breed mosquitoes.'

Willie glared. 'God help you,' he said. 'This place belongs to yesterday and we're already into tomorrow!'

He downed his whisky and had just put his glass down when he was called to the telephone to be informed that the *Man of Harlech* had signalled her estimated time of arrival. He acknowledged the message and, deciding that being tired would help no one, headed for his room to get some sleep.

He was still angry and frustrated. The threat to Singapore was clearly regarded as remote, and the lazy fans, the music every evening, the spells of drenching rain that brought humid heat, drained everyone of energy. Huge stocks of rubber were still piled on the wharves, but there was nobody to load them because there was a dispute going on and there were no labourers. Yet labourers could always be found to cut the grass outside the Supreme Court.

It was already into the early hours of the new day, but he had an uneasy feeling that the next twenty-four hours would bring news of disasters and, taking his revolver from his baggage, he placed it alongside him near the bed. It was still the same gun he had acquired as long ago as 1900 and it was a huge weapon, double-action, self-cocking and with a glossy blue finish. He had rarely used it, but it was big enough to frighten most people when they saw it. Perhaps, he thought, it might frighten a Japanese.

He fell on his bed fully clothed and had just dropped off to sleep when he woke to feel the hotel shuddering to the roar of aircraft engines. Leaping to his feet, awake at once, he headed downstairs and on to the street. The lights in Orchard Road were still blazing as were those of military headquarters at Fort Canning. Cars were also moving about with their headlights on and, as the anti-aircraft guns stuttered into action, along the waterfront a crowd of Malays and Chinese stood gaping skywards as if expecting a fireworks display.

'Christ on a tightrope!' he said aloud.

As he spoke, half a dozen aircraft howled overhead and he heard the scream of a bomb. As the crowd started to scatter, yelling with alarm, he began to run.

The bombs fell in the thickly populated Chinese quarter, and almost immediately he heard fire engines arriving, followed by ambulances and police cars. He stopped the first taxi he saw and demanded that they be followed.

'No, tuan.' The Malay at the wheel refused point blank.

'There are people dying.'

'No, tuan.'

Willie dragged at the revolver in the waistband of his trousers and, finding himself staring down the enormous barrel, the driver changed his mind at once. 'Yes, tuan,' he said. 'I take you.'

It was the same shock Willie had experienced previously in Shanghai, in Chungking, in Port Arthur – and having seen it before he was able to cope with it. Some people couldn't, and he saw a white man sitting on the pavement holding his head in his hands and weeping. Willie gave him a kick.

'Get up,' he snapped. 'You can do better than that!'

To his surprise, the man rose and followed him into the smoke.

Because of the early hour, there had not been many people about the streets, but dozens in the Chinese quarter had been sliced to pieces by the daisy-cutter bombs the Japanese had dropped, and the bloody remains lay on the pavements, in the gutters, in doorways, at alley-ends. As they started to seek out the still living, a few British planes lumbered overhead in pursuit of the long-departed Japanese.

Willie was there all day and only headed back to the hotel at the end of the afternoon. As he arrived, he noticed that the two great battleships had gone and uttered a silent prayer that his son would be safe.

Singapore remained breathless – especially when it read in the papers of the disaster at Pearl Harbor. As Willie had expected, Shanghai had gone at once. With the Japanese virtually in control of the place already, it had been taken over rather than conquered. More men were also being pushed ashore from Japanese ships in the north and, despite the damage that was being done to them, were having little difficulty in reaching their objectives. Visiting naval headquarters to try to find out if anything had been heard of the *Sunga Kavalan*, he found Ruffard was Duty Commander. He was on the telephone and a great deal of activity was going on round him. Guessing he had stumbled into a crisis, Willie was about to back out when he was called back.

'Mr Sarth! Hang on!'

He waited until Ruffard put the telephone down. Rising and offering a cigarette, he faced Willie squarely.

'Mr Sarth, we've just had bad news. I'd prefer you kept it to yourself until it's made official – as it's bound to be before long because it's something we're not going to be able to hide – but under the circumstances I think you ought to know. Because of Edward.'

Willie's eyes narrowed. 'Spit it out,' he said gruffly.

'They've sunk the *Prince of Wales* and the *Repulse*.'

It was more than Willie had expected. The minor crisis he had been waiting for had turned out to be a major one. 'How?' he asked bleakly.

'Bombs. Aircraft.'

'Both of them?'

'Both.'

'What about Edward? Have you heard anything?'

'Not yet. But we've heard the loss of life's not been great. We're optimistic.'

At the hotel, Willie found Ruffard's warning to keep the matter quiet was pointless because the men in the bar already knew.

'They've sunk the *Prince of Wales*,' he was told. '*Repulse* as well.'

There was no point in denying it. 'Yes,' he agreed. 'Bombs. Dropped by myopic airmen from aeroplanes made from tin kettles and old saucepans.'

It seemed to Willie that Singapore was in its death throes already, but reinforcements were still arriving, complete with trucks and equipment.

For God's sake, he thought wildly, surely they could be better used elsewhere! Untrained, untried troops, unaccustomed to the situation, were offering to walk straight into a prisoner of war camp. He hadn't a scrap of faith in Singapore's ability to defend itself, despite all the talk of 'Don't worry. It'll be all right.' The whole atmosphere was one of indifference, sloth and rampant bureaucracy, and that, he felt, would never win battles.

Ruffard provided him with the information that the *Sunga Kavalan* was at Port Weld and in trouble because the coal she was expecting to pick up there had not turned up. The captain was an Englishman and Willie had often suspected him of being self-important, lethargic and too busy feathering his own nest to put the concerns of the Sarth Line first. It seemed to be time to go up-country and stir him up a little.

By a stroke of luck he was able to scrounge a lift in an RAF transport plane with a wing commander called Woodburn whom he knew. Since the *Sunga Kavalan* was likely to be needed, nobody argued about his presence on board.

But while they were in the air, they heard that Penang had been evacuated and the machine landed at a small air strip near Taiping, where Willie was able to acquire a Morris car from a man who was due to leave for the south by train. Port Weld had just been attacked by a wave of Japanese bombers and was on fire, two ships burning and aground, but, to his surprise, the *Sunga Kavalan* had found her coal and had already left, so that he had to review his opinion of her captain.

Wing Commander Woodburn turned up. The transport aircraft had returned south and he was hoping to make his way back by car. 'The retreat's already started,' he said. 'The boys at Kota Bharu were done for by rumours that the Japanese were behind them. Fifth

Columnists, I suppose. You'd better push off. It's going to be unhealthy up here before long.'

The retirement from Kota Bharu had already become a helter skelter panic and was reducing the army of the defenders to a near rabble. As they had discovered Penang had gone, its Asian population bitter because some panicking official had ordered a secret evacuation of European women and children, leaving the local people to face the Japanese alone. Three steam ferries operated by the Navy were now trying to get them away.

The RAF field at Port Butterworth had been flattened, George Town had gone up in flames, and the exodus of Europeans had started. Carrying everything they possessed in pillow cases because there had been time to collect nothing else, people were joining the moving horde heading south, deafened all the way by the roar of passing vehicles and terrified of the possibility of stray Japanese.

Woodburn was still around, trying to round up RAF personnel and put them in trucks or on trains. He was furiously angry.

'The bloody Japs always catch us on the ground,' he said. 'Time and time again they arrive just as we're getting ready to take off. It's as if some bastard's signalling to them.'

It was more than possible, Willie knew, because the Malays resented the Chinese who had settled in their country and blamed the British for allowing it to happen, and nobody had ever troubled to weed out the Japanese barmen, barbers and masseurs who existed in every town and city in the peninsula.

The roads were crowded with refugees. With all that was happening, Singapore in the south seemed a symbol of stability in an environment that was racing towards chaos. Simply getting there had become an objective that gave some semblance of sense to the anarchy around them. A tropical downpour reduced everybody to a common misery and the lights of vehicles, thrusting through the streaming rain that shone like golden stair rods, showed a throng of bewildered humanity concerned only with keeping going. At Taiping the tide of casualties had already become a flood and, as Willie rattled through Ipoh's deserted streets, there were distinct signs of a burgeoning collapse.

In Kuala Lumpur he was able to telephone to Singapore and learn that the *Sunga Kavalan* had turned up, and there seemed to be no further need to hang around. But the disaster, gathering momentum, was beginning to catch him up so that he left Kuala Lumpur only just ahead of the Japanese arrival, by this time with two wounded RAF men in the back of the car. Woodburn appeared as he left and demanded a lift because everything else was already on the road. He was bitter.

'Some bastard *was* signalling the sods,' he snarled. 'And we found him.'

They had hoped to catch a train at Seremban, but the Japanese bombers had smashed it and Willie found himself spending Christmas hiding from the bombs in an irrigation ditch.

'Sweet Suffering J,' he said bitterly to Woodburn. 'I started my adult life in a siege. Surely to God I'm not going to end it in one.'

It was in Seremban that they heard on the railway tele-graph system that Borneo had gone and Hong Kong had surrendered. The Japanese had got at the booze and there had been fearful atrocities, but it seemed the place had put up a stout defence, which to Willie didn't seem likely in Malaya.

He finally reached a badly bombed Singapore railway station to find fires burning and bodies everywhere. The last stages of the journey had been made on a train driven by two British soldiers because the Eurasian driver had bolted into the jungle. It seemed to Willie that he had shown a great deal of common sense.

four

There was one consolation in the panic and defeat. Edward was safe. Commander Ruffard passed on the news. He was looking strained and exhausted now and was struggling to complete the evacuation of naval personnel.

'The loss of life wasn't too bad,' he said. 'Two thousand three hundred were picked up by destroyers out of two thousand nine hundred. They were brought here.'

'Where's Edward now?'

'Gone to India already. Senior officers like him are going to be needed. The rest have gone to other ships or put on coastal ferries.'

'It was kind of you to let me know,' Willie said. 'What about you?'

Ruffard shrugged. 'I shall be going, too. I think we're in a mess here and probably all of us will go in the end. There are wounded everywhere. Restaurants, halls, schoolrooms, the Cathedral, maternity hospitals, large houses. The Australians are blaming us for betraying them and our lot are saying the Australians lack discipline. Christ knows what the truth is, but it seems nobody expected to have to fight in the jungle or the mangrove swamps and nobody trained for it. The buggers set off north hung all over with the paraphernalia of a European war. I saw 'em go.'

Heading for his hotel in the purple evening light, Willie saw dancing was still going on, people in evening dress standing on the veranda with their drinks as if nothing had happened. After what he'd seen in the north he couldn't believe his eyes.

The *Straits Times* had been left for him. It was still advertising houses to let and was making a great deal of the arrival from England of a consignment of pure silk stockings. Alongside the personal ads requesting the whereabouts of relatives lost in the north, it seemed a hideous mockery.

During the night there was another air raid, directed this time at Keppel Harbour, that left dockyard oil tanks blazing in a huge cloud of dense black smoke, and he rose the next day to hear that a big battle on the west coast had destroyed an Indian brigade. As he went downstairs he learned that, with the news of one defeat after another, the final signal that the Malays had lost faith in the Europeans had been given. A man who had been out to do some early shopping was complaining loudly to the manager. 'The bastards refused to accept a chit,' he was saying. 'They've all started insisting on cash. All of them. The buggers have obviously got together.'

The bombers came again during the day and that evening Willie was surprised when the telephone in his rooms went and the voice he heard was his daughter's.

'Poll! What the hell are you doing here still?'

'Pa! Never mind me. Are you all right? For God's sake, I've been trying to find you for days. Where have you been?'

'I've been looking at the mess in the north,' Willie said grimly. 'At close quarters. It's worse than anybody here seems to realise. You should be away. Where's Elliott?'

'Pa, that's what I've been trying to find out. I'm scared. I can't get in touch with him. He cabled from Washington to say he was returning, but I've heard nothing since. I've tried his office and neither have they, so I tried Washington and then San Francisco, and they say he's left. He should have arrived already but he's disappeared. Pa, you don't think – ?'

'That he's bolted with another woman? Not likely. Not Elliott. He's not the type. All the same, you ought to be thinking of leaving.'

'Pa, how can I, when I don't know where Elliott is? He might turn up and find me gone. It'd be like running away.'

In the hope of forcing her hand, Willie went to the office of the Colonial Secretary to try to persuade someone to make the evacuation compulsory. He was shunted down different corridors by people clearly concerned only to protect senior officials. The man who met him wore a white drill suit, collar and tie and, in his cool, shaded room, looked as if he'd just come out of a bandbox. A tray of tea stood on the desk alongside him. Hot, angry and tired, Willie hated him.

The man in the white suit listened to his demands politely but shook his head. 'I've heard nothing official,' he said.

'Why the hell do you need something official?' Willie snorted. 'Does no one round here have the guts to make a decision off his own bat? They've just bombed the docks again. Or hasn't that fact reached your bloody files yet?'

The man in the white suit looked down his nose at him. 'People are free to go any time if they wish,' he said.

'It shouldn't be up to them to decide,' Willie snapped. 'How the hell do women with kids assess the prospects or know what the dangers are? Not telling them to go is a bloody perverted kindness. It's cruel to them, and the men who have to stay behind would find it a relief to know their families are safe. I'll provide places in my ships – '

'Mr Sarth!' The man in the white suit raised his voice. 'It probably won't come to that.'

'It's come to it already, God damn it! I've just come from the north. The Japs are closing in for a siege. They'll soon be in a position to deal with anything we try in order to get away.'

It made no impact whatsoever. The man in the white suit drained his teacup complacently. 'We can't apply pressure if it's not policy,' he said.

The behaviour of such men seemed incredible as the news grew worse. The Japanese had been swift to exploit their success at Pearl Harbor and had overwhelmed the American garrison of Guam, and invaded Wake and the Philippines. In Malaya, the British remained firmly on the retreat, and, while in the Philippines the Americans were buckling down to a hard defence, in Malaya things were only deteriorating. The best soldiers of all ranks had been retained at home to defend the United Kingdom and in Malaya there seemed only a soft residue. Morale was poor and, faced with disaster, the European residents were lost. They had felt that wherever the war went it would not arrive in Singapore and the first two untouched years had confirmed the belief. Like the official at the Colonial Secretary's office, nobody was prepared to assume any other responsibility beyond producing tin and rubber and coping with the climate.

The Sarth Line shipping office reported liners still sailing half-empty, but then, that night, they picked up on the radio Winston Churchill's warning to the House of Commons of the possibility of bad news from the East. It seemed to have more power even than falling bombs and the telephone went early the next morning.

'They've made four troopships available, Mr Sarth,' the clerk at the shipping office informed Willie. 'They've finally set up the apparatus for evacuation.'

'Who's handling it?'

'P & O are making the bookings.'

'Bookings? What are they organising? Cruises? Why don't they just pack the damn things and send them away?'

Setting off to see what could be done, Willie found the P & O officials operating from Agency House, a large bungalow outside the city centre. They had set up two tables, one for those who wished to go to Colombo, one for those who wished to go to Britain, but the two lines of waiting people had blended into one monstrous slow-moving queue of which the end was quite out of sight. Those cool women the Malays were so used to seeing were becoming hysterical and some were half-fainting in the pitiless heat as they clutched their children and begged for a place on a ship. Along the road, scores of cars, some marked by bomb splinters, had been left anyhow, some with their wheels in the ditch. The police were fighting to unravel the queue, but, even as Willie arrived, the first Japanese planes of the day appeared and there was a rush for the monsoon drains. When the planes vanished, the exhausted women clambered out and, as they fought to find their places, the police had to start all over again.

When Willie reached the table a fierce argument was going on with a half-hysterical woman who had lost her passport.

'For God's sake,' he snapped. 'Give her the bloody booking!'

The clerk looked shocked. 'We can't let people go without papers or their nationality and marital status being known.'

'What bloody difference does it make? If she's not here who's going to worry?'

In the middle of it all, it was discovered that the woman, who had gone to enormous lengths to obtain money from the bank to pay her fare, could have had it paid for by the government.

Determined by this time to see her aboard, Willie drove her to the docks with her children only to find another vast queue had formed to pass through the gate to the quayside, where a lone Malay clerk with a pencil and ledger was slowly inscribing in excellent copper plate every passenger's name.

'What in God's name for?' Willie demanded.

The Malay looked up. 'So we shall know who's aboard, sir.'

Snatching up the ledger, Willie tossed it aside and, while the clerk was retrieving it, waved the queue through. The clerk fetched a white official, who was almost dancing with rage.

'As a shipowner, Mr Sarth,' he yelled, 'you know this is something you can't do!'

'I've done it,' Willie said bluntly.

The whole business had become ridiculous, anyway, because, as the number of useless mouths was reduced, a complete reversal of the evacuation was taking place with thousands of up-country Asians from Johore starting to flood on to Singapore Island to double the normal population. Dormitories had been prepared in Raffles College and in schools, but many of the women who were arriving had neither clothes nor the means of providing food for their babies, some of them even without any knowledge of where their husbands were.

As the last of the big ships sailed, the monsoon rains, which had made everything damp and mildewed, began to abate. Heading back into the city, Willie found a stream of motor transport, guns, bren carriers, ambulances and cars were arriving from the end of the Johore Causeway. As the procession thinned and eventually dwindled to nothing, the infantry began to appear, their boots crunch-crunching in the roadway. Despite the clear defeat, placid communiqués were still being issued to insist they had been withdrawn to protect the naval base, but when Willie went to the base to demand wire hawsers for the *Sunga Kavalan*, which had been obliged to abandon hers in Port Weld, he found it empty. Millions of pounds' worth of equipment had been left behind – shirts, gas masks, lockers, steel plate, a great crane, a floating dry dock, ships' boilers, coils of chain cable, wire, rope, cord, the shabby hulls of three small ships. It even looked as if the occupants had fled at the last minute because there were still meals on the tables. He helped himself to the wire he required and returned to the city as the last of the defeated, bewildered, leaderless and demoralised troops stumbled into Singapore itself. Even as they arrived, there was a shattering explosion when the Causeway went up in a cloud of black smoke and flying fragments of masonry. By this time the city was in hopeless confusion, the hospitals filled with wounded and the Japanese planes sailing unheeded over the roofs. Because of the nature of the place and the type of society it contained, it couldn't change its habits even in extremity, and while some died or gazed at appalling wounds, others – even now – were still eating, drinking and dancing.

When he saw her, Polly was haggard with worry. 'I can't go, Pa,' she insisted. 'What'll Elliott think? He said he'd come back here. I've got to hear from him.'

In the last three days when it had finally dawned on everybody that all the talk about 'It might not happen' was just rubbish and it was not only going to happen, it was already happening, the numbers of those wanting to leave suddenly multiplied. For two months evacuation had remained a trickle, but now it was an unmanageable torrent, quite impossible to deal with and a serious risk to those who left. The thought that occurred to Willie was that throughout the years he'd always thought well in advance and managed to get away ahead of invading troops. This time he hadn't.

Already the Sarth Line office had had reports of ships being bombed or shelled and sunk, with the women and children passengers killed outright, drowned, captured, or starving to death on islands they had managed to reach by lifeboats. Those who were left alive were going to undergo a long and unpleasant internment.

Brave words on the radio couldn't hide the fact that the Japanese had reached the Johore shore and that to the crash of bombs was now added the whine and crump of shells. Determined to get Polly and her children away, he hired one of the little yellow taxis and arrived at her house to find her, to his surprise, surrounded by suitcases.

'I've heard from Elliott,' she said. 'Or at least not from him. From his mother. He was on his way to San Francisco by car when there was an accident. He's got a broken leg and a fractured skull and been unconscious for days. He's going to be okay, though, and I've got a message to take the first ship to America.'

'It's a bit late for that now,' Willie said bluntly. 'You'll have to go wherever you can. However, I'll see to it. Just be ready. I'll come and fetch you.'

Greatly relieved, he headed in the dark for his office. For the moment Singapore was quiet. Having created a panic, the Japanese bombers now seemed curiously indifferent and were operating further north, and aimless and exhausted soldiers had begun to wander the streets, getting drunk whenever they saw the opportunity.

There was a great deal of noise from the guns, however, and the news that the Japanese had landed on the north shore of Singapore Island seemed to bring the place to its senses, so that, as he returned, he noticed that the dancing had finally stopped. Vast palls of smoke from demolished oil tanks and stores were mingling with the funeral plumes from blazing warehouses and the air was full of the fumes of alcohol. When Hong Kong had fallen, alcohol had fuelled Japanese lusts and it had been decided not to take chances, and thousands of bottles of spirit were being thrown at cellar walls in a desperate bid to get rid of them.

Occupied with telephone and radio, Willie was struggling to raise ships. There were hundreds of people now wanting to leave and eventually he picked up news that one of his vessels was due to arrive. Inevitably, it was the *Lady Roberts*, these days, in the extremity of the disaster, called a sloop and with the letters HMS before her name.

The raids started again. At the office of the Dunlop Rubber Company, he just had time to dive into a ditch as the bombs came down. There was a tremendous roar that hurt his ears and he saw a lamp post go down and a body flying through the air. A lorry was hurled through a plate glass window and cars were set on fire. A man with the bleeding stump of an arm was pointing at a petrol tanker parked near a set of apartments and yelling for someone to move it. As he flopped to the ground, unconscious, a Malay climbed into the high cab and, crashing in the gear, drove the vehicle away in a series of jerks.

Scrambling to his feet, Willie slapped the man's shoulder. 'Well done,' he said. 'You've probably saved all those buildings.'

The Malay gave him a cold look. 'We shall be here when you've gone,' he said. 'We shall need them.'

When the din stopped, there seemed to be bodies everywhere in the grotesque attitudes of death. The place reeked of burning flesh, cordite and smoke, yet, even now, the indifference to disaster was unbelievable and an air raid warden was stamping up and down in a fury because the picks and shovels he needed for rescue work were locked up and the storekeeper had gone to the cinema.

The indifference even seemed to affect the children. As the chaos was cleared and they started playing again, one of them fell over a body, sat up staring at his red hands, sniffed them, wiped them on his shirt went on with the game. A group of elderly women were knitting in the doorway of a shelter and an old Chinese threw cupfuls of water on to the flames of a burning house in an attempt to help. As they laid the bodies on the pavement they were serving tiffin at a hotel just round the corner.

As the city began to shrink, the days seemed more beautiful than ever with no humidity and the sea like burnished steel. At night the sky was laced with stars and lit by a huge moon, but across it were the writhing black plumes from fires, and in the air was always the stink of burning rubber, tar and rope, and the smell of decaying bodies trapped under the rubble of bombed buildings. Gas, water, electricity, drainage, were all gone and, to prevent looting, the big stores were giving away their stock. Singapore, the impregnable fortress, had become a curse and the British administration, which had been regarded with such pride for so long, was now exposed as a sham. The languid habits which the British had so complacently regarded as permanent had been swept away overnight and all the reserves of pride had been used up. It looked very much as if the Empire were dying. Its life and soul abroad had always been based on prestige and the final indication that the end was in sight was a Sikh soldier exchanging his uniform in the street for a suit of civilian clothes.

A message giving the estimated time of arrival of the *Lady Roberts* was telephoned through to Willie's suite at his hotel, from where he was now conducting all his affairs. He had closed down the shipping office and told his employees to think only of themselves. He was in the docks when the ship arrived. The sight of her blunt ugly nose and the gun on her 1917 mounting lifted his heart. Damn the old bugger, he thought. She seemed to have been linked to his life forever. Ill-shaped, ill-behaved in a bad sea, here she was again, always on hand when she was wanted.

By now, with her cockroaches and bushy-tailed rats, she was practically all that was left in Singapore. Because his car had been destroyed, Willie managed to bribe a cab driver he knew to get his vehicle out and they headed for Polly's house. Packing everybody in, they set out for the docks. Even now the curious indifference of Singapore to disaster was clear. In Raffles Place, Indian street traders were still doing business, and people in drill suits or sarongs were calmly shopping. Kelly and Walsh's were still selling books and soldiers were still buying souvenirs to take home.

Keppel Road was a tangle of potholes, craters, twisted telephone wires and smashed trees, and a large crowd was outside the closed gates of the docks. The police and the army had given up trying to control the traffic; cars were left anyhow, in the way of lorries trying to head into town, and the place was an indescribable scrum of women and children with luggage, a sweaty mass of humanity without a single porter to help.

In addition to the *Lady Roberts*, there were three other ships still in the harbour, but the launches that carried out would-be passengers were being turned away because the ships were already crammed with people. The separations were heart-rending, wives from husbands, children from fathers, girls from the men to whom they'd just become engaged. The roads were littered with wounded soldiers who had run out of energy and now sprawled among the women sitting on their luggage, their eyes wet as they waited their turn.

One of the soldiers, driven beyond normality by strain and exhaustion, suddenly started shouting that they were all done for and, as his friends dragged him away, the faces round them stiffened in blank shock. Further along the quay, brand new cars were being pushed into the sea, and employees of the Hong Kong and Shanghai Bank – Honkers and Shankers to everybody who used it – were dumping long coffin-like crates into the harbour. Occasional shells fell among the wharves so that everybody ducked, cowered and ran for shelter. Except for a line of Australian nurses, straight and calm in their white uniforms, who didn't even bother to look up.

Women already on board the *Lady Roberts*, the only ship still alongside, were screaming; their husbands, not allowed up the gangplank, were frantically waving papers. Most didn't have passes or berths, and there were Chinese who had worked for the British complaining they had been refused permits to leave, although it had been repeatedly announced that all were to be treated alike.

As they left the taxi on the edge of the crowd, the sky filled with an iron roaring and they had to cower in a ditch as half a dozen Japanese bombers came over, flying low, dropping bombs and strafing the docks with their machine guns. A woman clutching her child and a suitcase was about to head for shelter when her husband shouted to her not to move. 'We'll lose our places,' he said. As the machines disappeared over the buildings, Willie saw that one of them had been hit. It was only the second he'd seen damaged during the whole of the fighting. It came low across the water and as it passed overhead he saw it was on fire. Flames were pouring out from underneath the engine and it was trailing a thin plume of smoke. It was low enough to see the pilot struggling with the controls or trying to open the cockpit hatch so he could parachute to safety. As it passed them, it swung to the right and the sky blossomed with a huge ball of flame from which other smaller balls of flame were ejected haphazardly like misdirected rockets. They could still see the pilot in the middle of it, still fighting; then, just as the machine dropped behind the houses, they saw him fall clear. His body struck one of the buildings, bounced off and vanished from sight as the machine also disappeared and they saw the smoke from a vast funeral pyre lift up to darken the sky.

'Oh, God, Pa!' Polly was holding her children to her, trying to hide their eyes in her breast, but they were struggling to free themselves so they could see.

Even the death of the Japanese pilot wasn't enough to stir the crowded people from their wretchedness and terror and, while once they might have raised a cheer, this time they hardly bothered to look up.

Then Willie saw that the woman holding the child and the suitcase had dropped the suitcase and was standing clutching the child and staring at the body of her husband lying at her feet. 'Oh, God,' she sobbed, then one of the officials grabbed her arm and told her to get a move on. For a second, Willie saw the agony in her eyes as she stared at her dead husband then, realising she could do nothing and that it was her duty to save the child, she swallowed and pushed forward with the others.

'Oh, Pa,' Polly sobbed.

The *Lady Roberts* was already crammed with people as they boarded her – in the cabins, in the saloon, on the decks. In case it proved impossible to shed her moorings, the order was given to cast off so that the ship could stand out from the quay. There was a wail as she prepared to move and, as she called goodbye to her soldier husband on the dockside, a woman threatened to jump overboard with her child. At the last moment, Willie pressed the husband into service as a ship's clerk and he was allowed to accompany her.

There were now hundreds of passengers aboard a ship with the normal accommodation of a dozen. With twilight, the jade sky turned pink from the fires that were consuming rubber, timber and fuel, the flames roaring across Keppel Road. Singapore lay under a pall of heavy black smoke that hung over the business section, the European homes and the shattered native quarter alike. It hid the dying sun and made the air stink of charred wood. Aircraft were burning on Kallang airfield and tanks were on fire on the oil islands a few miles away.

It was clearly going to be impossible to leave in daylight because the Japanese were sinking everything that appeared, and they had heard that a Dutch ship, the *Konige*, had been set on fire, while the Japanese tentacles were already reaching out towards Java. Death seemed to hover over the dark dying city, occasional shells screaming over to burst among the blackened buildings, and beyond Fort Canning and Mount Faber you could still hear the rattle of musketry and machine-gun fire. The streets, once so clean and tidy, were littered with rubble and blackened scraps of burnt paper. Here and there, leaning against a wall or lying in a gutter, was a hastily covered body.

There was no longer any point in asking people for tickets or permits to leave. All that could be done was cram aboard everybody who appeared in launches, among them a few weary soldiers, their eyes dull with fatigue, who had fought their way back down the Malayan peninsula and over the Johore Causeway to the illusive safety of the island; stretchers containing wounded, escorted by a few European or Eurasian nurses, their faces tired and strained; children with amahs; women with babies; Chinese, Malays, Indians, the light from the flames catching the angles and curves of their faces. The foremost thing in the minds of every one of them as they stumbled to the deck was the wish to reach safety. A lot of the women were weeping, but the children were staring about them wide-eyed, unable to understand what was happening, and over the roar of flames and the rattle of musketry there was a constant wailing sound, as if the whole population of the city were giving way to despair.

The ship was treated to a final air raid as it steamed past a burning Blue Funnel liner, and the crazy pattern of colour in which the city died was reflected in the water. One of the Australian nursing sisters began singing 'Waltzing Matilda' and the rest took it up. Gradually a few other people joined in defiantly, until half the ship was singing. The buoy intended to mark the minefield outside the harbour had disappeared and, with his skin crawling, Willie watched Yeh as he conned the ship to sea. The sky was red with flames stabbed through occasionally by bursts of shellfire. Even the sea seemed to be ablaze. It was Friday the Thirteenth.

five

There were far too many people aboard the *Lady Roberts* and, because there had been no time in the confusion to attend to stores, far from enough food, but the Australian nursing sisters organised a rationing and feeding system so that no one went hungry. Huddled on deck, sitting with their heads together, at first the passengers tended to keep to themselves, but the indefatigable Australian women refused to let anyone sink into misery. Sing-songs started in the saloon, Willie played the piano as badly as usual. Card games were started, names were collected to make lists.

Almost at once, however, they began to hear of other ships which had left just ahead of them and run smack into Japanese vessels rendezvousing in the Bangka Strait for the assault on Palembang. The *Man of Harlech* had disappeared in a vast pyre of flames. The *Vyner Brooke* had been sunk. The *Mata Hari* had been boarded and captured. The *Giang Bee* had been bombed and set on fire. Bangka Strait had become known as Dive Bomb Alley.

The *Lady Roberts* was lucky. Slipping through the Karimata Strait, they headed into the Java Sea away from the land and, beginning to feel safer all the time, the games on deck began to spread and there was even a little tomfoolery as one of the passengers celebrated her twenty-first birthday.

They were beginning to think they had got beyond the range of the Japanese planes when they picked up a boatful of survivors from one of the flotilla of forty ships which had left ahead of them. Only a small number survived by dodging among the islands and Willie began to think that, by leaving late, they were going to be better off and that the Japanese had given up the search. But then, just to the north of Samarang, they were spotted. The aeroplanes came in with steady ferocity as the ship began to twist and turn in an attempt to escape. At least a dozen bombs exploded close by with no damage, to set up wails of terror from the deck passengers as gigantic geysers of water lifted alongside the ship then dropped back to drench them. They thought they had escaped, then the last plane to appear above them dropped its stick almost casually, the final bomb striking the forward hatch. The blast made matchwood of half the lifeboats, killed the first mate and turned the deck into a shambles.

The ship shuddered and lurched and Willie, scrambling to his feet from the floor of the saloon and bursting through the door, saw everybody flat on deck, bodies everywhere, so that the ship looked like a giant sardine tin. There was a hiss of escaping steam, and stokers came hurtling out from below, staggering through the smoke. The noise was incredible.

As someone shut off the steam and the screams of the ship died, the air became blessedly free from the screeching din, but now all the other sounds were audible – the people screaming with pain or fear, the siren going.

As they tried to comfort the wounded, the aeroplane came back, its machine guns stuttering, and more people were hit. A plume of smoke was coming between the decks and as the order was given to swing out the remaining lifeboats, Willie could only assume that the ship was lost, and the fact that it was the *Lady Roberts*, his first and his oldest ship, wrenched at his heart. As he went below to collect Poll and her children, there was surprisingly little panic. It was almost as if the women had seen so much horror in the last few weeks they were immune to shock.

The ship had stopped and the boats were lowered. Finding soldiers and seamen stuffing their pockets with cigarettes from the saloon bar, Willie waved the big revolver at them and told them to load food instead. Bulkheads were riddled, the deck was a carpet of splintered wood, glass and fragments of metal, festooned with fallen rigging and stained with blood. At a cry of 'Fire in the bunker', a chain of buckets was organised, but it spread to a pile of planks and was only accessible from a hole above. By the time it was damped down the wind had dropped and the heat was terrific.

As he returned to the deck, Willie saw that Yeh had cancelled the order to fill the boats and, instead, the crew were assembling hoses. In no time, as the pumps started, the deck was awash, the water sweeping paper, deck chairs and fragments of clothing towards the scuppers. A man had jumped overboard in panic and was now alongside the stopped ship yelling that he couldn't swim. One of the soldiers jumped in after him to support him, but was immediately grabbed round the neck in a frantic embrace.

The fire was extinguished by evening and, gasping in the heat, blackened by smoke, the firefighters stared at each other, surprised to find that the old *Lady Roberts*, though now with a bad list, showed no signs of sinking. The chief engineer was sent back below and eventually they heard the slow chunk-chunk as the engine was set in motion again. Slowly, the old ship began to make way through the water, this time with Willie on the bridge with Yeh in place of the dead mate.

The saloon was cleared of people and the Australian nurses began to attend to the wounded, who were carried to the makeshift sick bay. When daylight came the next morning. Willie was surprised to find they were still afloat and moving. The dead were sewn into canvas by the ship's carpenter and weighted with lumps of coal from the bunkers before being dropped overboard to the haunting words of an exhausted-looking military padre with one arm in a sling.

It seemed unbelievable that the ship could survive, but she crept along the north coast of Java, for some reason unnoticed by the Japanese fleet heading for the conquest of the Dutch East Indies. Islands came up and disappeared astern as the *Lady Roberts*, her list not getting any better but also not getting any worse, trudged her way east and south. As they passed Flores, they ran into a screaming gale which Willie felt sure, would be the end of them, but they passed Timor, where they had to bury two more passengers with the ship still heaving on the dying sea. The one-armed padre read the burial service and the two bodies hardly made a splash.

After that, the *Lady Roberts* almost sailed herself to Sydney. At Darwin, where they stopped to pick up coal and supplies, Willie learned that out of an allied naval force of five cruisers and nine destroyers that had been hastily scraped together from the British, American and Dutch navies, all at the limit of their endurance, only four destroyers had survived a battle with the Japanese, and their sacrifice had managed to delay the invasion of Java by no more than twenty-four hours.

A P & O liner out from Brisbane took their passengers, but Willie insisted on staying with the *Lady Roberts*.

'Whatever happens,' he said, 'I'll never sell the old lady now.'

With plenty of room, Polly decided to stay with him and the two children were happy enough to have the full attention of the crew. A few repairs were made, then they set off again across the Gulf of Carpentaria. There were Australian naval ships near the Cape York Peninsula which saw them safely heading south along the Great Barrier Reef before they left them to finish the voyage alone to Sydney.

A liner coming up towards Brisbane as they approached North Head and North Point edged closer to take a better look at the listing ship with the wreckage still on her deck, the smashed rails, the bent and buckled ventilators, and the shattered skylights and windows. Dover Heights was a mass of glowing lights as they turned in, and they could see the ferries from Cremorne and Manley. With Australian thoughts on their losses at Singapore, and with the Japanese on the move in Burma and near enough to their coast to threaten Darwin, there were no crowds to greet them as they were tugged alongside. A car was waiting on the docks, however, and as soon as the gangway went down, Nadya and Tom's wife, Fan-Su, began to struggle up it. Willie was waiting on deck with Polly and the two children and immediately Nadya held out her arms and enveloped them all.

'Thank God you are safe,' she said and Polly promptly burst into guilty tears and started accusing herself of a lack of understanding and sympathy.

Nadya placed a finger over her lips. 'Don't say any more. It's over. It's done. I have heard from your husband. He's all right. That's all that matters – you, your husband and your children, William's grandchildren.'

Tense with all the strain, Polly burst into tears again. '*Your* grandchildren, too,' she said, sweeping aside half her objections in one magnanimous gesture. 'I want you to call them yours.'

To his surprise, Willie found he was still in business. Only the *Man of Harlech* had been lost and, with losses to Australian-based lines from the depredations of the Japanese navy, there was room for his ships in Australian ports and along Australian trade routes. What was even better, they learned that Edward was safely in England and even heard from Thomas in North China. How he had got the letter out, whom he had bribed, they had no idea, but there it was, announcing that he was with the Communists opposing the Japanese.

Willie was bitter at the fact that, instead of fighting the Japanese, Chiang's Nationalist troops were blockading areas held by the Communists and that the Communist New Fourth Army in the south of Anwhei Province had even been attacked and dispersed with heavy casualties.

But China was a long way away, as was England, and Australia was a land without fighting, without rationing, without black-outs, and for the first time in months they felt safe. As the year progressed even the news improved.

After a setback in North Africa, British troops had got the German Afrika Korps on the run, the Americans had landed at the other end of Africa, in Russia the Germans were being forced to retreat, while at long last the Americans, gathering their strength after the first setbacks, were starting to hit out, and had halted the Japanese advance in two big battles in the Coral Sea and at Midway.

Willie was still working, going daily to his office in Sydney, determined to maintain profitability despite the adverse trading caused by the war. The danger of invasion had changed Australian attitudes and it brought occasional jarring meetings with people who considered Australia let down by London, but on the whole it didn't really affect relations, and his ships began to ply between Australia and New Zealand and in the safe areas of the Pacific.

He had heard nothing of Da Braga or George Kee, but assumed that Da Braga, being a Portuguese, and Kee, being an adaptable Chinese, were keeping the business above water in occupied Shanghai. He was beginning to wonder if he shouldn't retire, because Edward had said he wouldn't mind leaving the Navy after the war and taking over the reins. As it happened, however, quite unexpectedly he found himself in hit-and-run tactics against the scattered Japanese garrisons to the north.

The old Japanese fishing boat he had bought years before, the *Fuku Maru*, always known to her crew as the *Fuck You, Mary*, had a speed of nine knots and with a cruising range of eight thousand miles had been claimed by the Navy. Filled with explosives, limpet mines and foll boats, towing miniature submarines and carrying a group of vengeful commandos determined to get a little of their own back for Singapore, the Australians fell on the Japanese outposts. It had been intended to place a naval officer in command but, with everybody already occupied, Willie unexpectedly found himself in the uniform of a lieutenant in the Australian Naval Reserve and in command. It took Edward only a week to learn about it and send a signal insisting that, as senior officer, he would expect a salute the next time they met.

Both Nadya and Polly insisted Willie was too old to put on uniform, but he found he rather fancied the idea. They carried out one or two raids, the old *Fuku Maru*, her Japanese name exchanged for the more hostile *Cobra*, transporting the raiders to a point from which they could make their attacks, then waiting until they returned before transporting them back to their base, in and out of uninhabited islands, sheltering when they had to close under the shore among the overhanging foliage.

Though he was over-age for war, it seemed it was to become Willie's wartime career when a letter arrived asking him if he would call at Government House. As he headed for the Governor's office his arm was touched and it was indicated that he should head down a corridor towards another part of the building. As he entered the room indicated, he was surprised to find a figure rising that he knew. It was Mallinson, whom he'd last seen in Shanghai before the war.

'Mallinson,' he said. 'Arthur Mallinson.'

'Farmagh now,' Mallinson said. 'Lord Farmagh. They gave me a title to keep me quiet.'

Willie smiled. 'What in God's name are you doing here? Aren't you retired yet?'

'Retired in 1937, but you know what it's like. With everybody under forty in the Forces, if you can still stand upright – sometimes even if you can't – you have some value.'

Willie's eyes narrowed. 'Is that why I'm here?'

' 'Fraid so.'

'I already have a job. They gave it to me because I was the only one available.'

'Temporary, Willie. That's all. We've found a replacement and you're free.'

'To do what?'

Mallinson smiled. 'Hear you've heard from your son in China,' he said.

'How the hell did you know that?'

'We have our means. What does he have to say about Chiang?'

'Nothing flattering. He says that instead of going for the Japanese, he's busy destroying the Communists.'

'That's what we've heard. Suspect that if it's true he's gone a little too far. Heard the Communists have started to boycott the meetings of the Political Council, in fact, and one might be justified in thinking that the united front against Japan's come to an end. It's even suggested that all the money being sent to Chiang in the form of aid against the Japanese is being used to remove his political rivals and make his own future secure. What's more, while the Communists *are* fighting the Japanese, he's trying to stop them. Of course – ' Mallinson offered a cigarette ' – he knows perfectly well that now the United States are in the war, all he has to do is retire and let the Americans do the job for him.'

'Go on.'

'There are Chiang generals in the south who we think are selling him to the Japanese.'

'Zychov,' Willie said at once.

'What's that?'

'Nothing.' Willie changed step quickly. 'I shouldn't be surprised if you're right.'

'What we want to know is, are they, and if they are, does Chiang care? What do you think?'

'Yes to question number one. No to question number two.'

Mallinson smiled. 'A lot of money's gone to them,' he explained. 'We're wanting to know what he's doing with it, if it was a mistake, and if it could be put to better use.'

'And where do I come into it?'

'London's worried. Like the Americans, we're concerned that our supplies are not being used for the purpose for which they were sent.'

'Aren't you getting the truth out of Chungking?'

'There's a great deal of publicity showing Winston, Roosevelt, Stalin and Chiang together, as if they were all equal. But that's nonsense, and the Americans are in a turmoil because people in Washington think, since the Communists fight, that the sun shines out of their backsides. But another lot in Chungking, who depend on Chiang for favours, say the opposite. Winston doesn't trust what he hears and he wants to know. How genuine is Chiang? How genuine are the Communists?'

'For God's sake!' Willie said. 'And you want *me* to find out? That would mean going to Chungking.'

'You've been before. There are all sorts of missions there. American. British. French. Military missions. Air Force and naval missions. Trade and economic missions. You're an obvious choice for a trade delegation. Chiang couldn't possibly object. Besides, I gather you've met him.'

'I didn't like him.'

'You don't have to. But you do have to be acceptable.'

'How do I get there? With Japan in control of the coast.'

'Since the loss of the Burma Road, the Americans fly everything in from Assam.'

Willie remembered with alarm his trip from Australia to Shanghai . 'The last time I flew any distance,' he said, 'I spent seven days sitting in a raft in the China Sea.'

Mallinson smiled. 'If anything happens this time, they'll send a mountaineer. You'll be going over the Himalayas.'

'Good God! Do you know how old I am?'

'To the month. I also know that for an ageing man you're remarkably fit, very active and surprisingly resourceful. I've heard a bit about what happened at Singapore. Nasty business, that, but you seemed to come out of it with roses growing on you as usual.'

'You want me, in effect, to become a spy?'

'You've been a spy before, Willie.'

Willie was about to protest when he realised the truth in Mallinson's statement. 'You need an expert,' he said.

'You are an expert.'

'There are other experts. Younger than me.'

Mallinson gave his dry, crooked smile. 'Unfortunately, at the moment they're all in Japanese prison camps.'

'What do I get out of it?'

'Willie, people are giving their services to the nation free. Of course, we can arrange for a small bauble afterwards to hang round your neck – something for the grandchildren to play with.'

'I was hoping to spend some time with my wife and with those grandchildren you're talking about. I hardly ever see them. Besides, I have a shipping line to run.'

'But aren't doing, preferring instead to Errol Flynn it round the islands. It's quite clear that William Sarth has the sort of managers who can be trusted to run things for him until he returns.'

'*If* I return.'

When you find out what we want, you'll be flown out the same way you were flown in.'

'Suppose it doesn't work out that way?'

Mallinson pulled a face. 'I can't think of anyone more suited to sort it out,' he said.

When Willie informed Nadya and his family what was in the wind, their immediate reaction was the same as his.

'This is a young man's job.'

Willie grinned. 'That's what I said. He said they needed an old man.'

'But China's overrun by the Japanese.'

'There are large tracts where it isn't. They're only in control in the areas where they have garrisons. China's too big for anything else.'

That night, Nadya held him to her, certain in her mind that once he'd gone she'd never see him again. Like Abigail before her, she had got to know him well and was aware that he couldn't resist taking a risk. He had been taking them all his life and they had become second nature to him. She kissed him gently, sadly, feeling somehow he was slipping away from her. 'How long will it take?'

He put his arms round her, feeling the warmth of her body against his. He guessed what was in her mind, but he could no more resist Mallinson's offer than he could have flown to the moon. Now that he had agreed to go, he was growing more and more interested. He had lived most of his life in China, it had absorbed his attention for over forty years, and the thought of returning pleased him. He tried to calculate.

'Week or two to get there. Month or two to find out what they want to know. Week or two to return to India. That's about all. It shouldn't take long.'

He didn't know how wrong he was.

s i x

Chungking hadn't changed much and, though the bombing seemed to have stopped, the scars remained.

The Liberator that carried Willie there left Assam in the atmosphere of a steam bath, and the idea of flying in an unsuitable aircraft in an area of storms, unmarked peaks, icing, overloading, accidents and unpredictable winds didn't leave him overjoyed. As it happened, however, the weather was clear and they landed safely at Yunnan, from where they travelled by road and river to Chungking.

Putnam was still there, by this time pushed into uniform and acting as adviser to the American general in command. He greeted Willie rapturously, particularly when Willie produced a bottle of Scotch whisky.

'It's a load of crap,' he said as they shared it. 'All this hero-worship of old Dogleg. There's plenty of courage but it's being shockingly wasted. Most people here are interested not in the war but in finding the money to pay for what they need. There's no problem about buying things. Fur coats, electric razors, silk stockings, army boots, guns, petrol, diamonds – it's all available. All you need is the dough. Prices have risen two hundred and fifty times in two years. The war's been left a long way behind.

And just to help matters we've got typhus because of the rats. You see 'em dead in the streets and nobody bothers to collect 'em. The alleys stink.'

'What about the Russians? Are they here?'

Putnam gave him a quick look. 'One or two trade missions. That sort of thing. Only other guy I know of is in the south somewhere with one of Chiang's generals. Some White Russian admiral or something, acting as adviser.'

It was Zychov. Willie was certain it was Zychov. There weren't many Russians because Chiang didn't like them, but Zychov was a White Russian, which always made him acceptable, and it would be like him to advance himself in rank.

'I think I'll probably get to meet him somehow,' he said.

Putnam stared at Willie with narrowed eyes. 'It's the same guy you were looking for before, isn't it?' he asked.

'Yes. Same man.'

Putnam frowned. 'What's he done to you? What makes him so all-fired important?'

Under the influx of enormous numbers of refugees, Chungking was expanding rapidly, and the new buildings going up in the bombed areas of the city were spreading like fungus, though, as Putnam had suggested, the place seemed to have lapsed into lethargy and indifference. Because Chiang was doing so little for China most people had given up doing anything for him and merely tried to cope with the corruption. The British called him Old Dogleg, the Americans Chancre Jack, and it seemed to be the policy to avoid him whenever possible.

Basically, however, Chungking hadn't changed much and the streets looked as though nobody had attempted to clear away the refuse since Willie's last visit before the war. As Putnam had said, the rats could be counted day and night in their hundreds, rummaging around in the bombed buildings for buried bodies among the debris and running as nonchalantly as cats between your legs.

For Willie accommodation was provided on the top floor of a block of offices which the British had taken over. Part of it was used for working, the remainder for living quarters. The bottom floors were occupied by Chinese government departments and the entrance was full of the children of the staff, and their washing.

'Things are a bit overcrowded,' a young Foreign Office official called McAleavy explained. 'They sleep in the basement and even seem to like it because it's warm in winter.'

Eating had grown more difficult since Willie had last been there and food for the Europeans all had to be flown over the Hump. Water was also scarce and every drop had to be carried from the river by coolies and boiled, so that a bath in a few inches was a luxury.

It wasn't difficult to discover that Mallinson's interpretation of the situation had been correct. Chiang was well aware that so long as he kept his armies in being the Japanese could never conquer the vast territories of China and he was only waiting for the Americans to win the war so that he could claim his rewards at the peace conference. McAleavy was in no doubt about his object.

'It's to keep the Communists pinned down in the north,' he said. He was a tall, grave young man with horn-rimmed spectacles and not a lot of humour.

'Vast areas of the country are still in Chinese hands,' he explained. 'Simply because the Japanese garrisons daren't move far. Chiang's never been happier, in fact. Pearl Harbor made sure the Japanese would be beaten eventually, and, now they're flying things over the Hump, even the loss of the Burma Road doesn't matter all that much. It's a pity a lot of it's squandered by Chiang's favourites and their women. Even the petrol that comes in is used for joy-riding.'

To keep his armies in the field, Chiang was making more and more use of conscription and it was an ordinary sight to see squads of soldiers chained together for deportation to the fighting areas. Conscription was as corrupt as everything else, however, and no one with money had to fight. In the meantime, people wore their dirty clothes for weeks, the telephone system was nothing but snarled coils of wire in the streets, there was no electricity for days on end, the sewage piled up and stank, and every disease imaginable flourished.

'You could say the war's sapped the virtue of the regime,' McAleavy observed in his solemn way. 'And for your information, I've discovered that a growing number of people are looking longingly towards the north where Mao Tse-Tung's running a much more efficient show. We all know the Communists are too rigid to go in for corruption, of course, but by contrast, the Nationalist areas are a morass and Chiang's always threatening that China's on the point of collapse, because the more he says it the more Washington gives him.'

'Is he fighting the Communists?' Willie asked.

'Of course he is. The New Fourth Army attack was sheer treachery. They were set up.'

'Set up?'

'There was a hell of a lot of toing and froing going on and a lot of talk of the Communists joining Chiang's people in a big attack on the Japs. They were actually coming out when they were trapped, and there were a lot of casualties. Whether Chiang knew or not I don't know. You never do. But I heard some staff officer of his was behind it all. He was a Pole – or he said he was, but it turned out he was a Russian – and the Commies are furious because they know him from the past or something.'

'Yes,' Willie agreed. 'They do. And this Russian? Where is he now?'

'In the south, I heard.'

'I guessed he might be.'

'*How* did you guess?'

'It's a man I wanted to meet before, a man I've always wanted to meet.'

McAleavy's eyes widened and he stared at Willie for a while, wondering what powerful hatred drove him on. He saw he wasn't going to get an explanation and went on. 'Chou En-Lai was actually here in Chungking at the time, trying to work out a solution to their differences. Whatever Washington might think of Chiang, the Americans here loathe him. But they're building airstrips for his bombers. Whole villages are being torn down.'

'Will they bomb Japan?'

McAleavy shrugged. 'If the Japanese don't mount a major campaign to overrun them first. They're well aware of them.'

Willie considered. 'This general in the south who does so little,' he said. 'I think we ought to go and see him, don't you?'

McAleavy had obviously never expected to go far from his office. 'Me too?' he bleated.

Willie smiled. 'At my age, Mr McAleavy, I need someone to pick me up if I fall down.'

The group to take a look at the southern front included, in addition to Willie and McAleavy, two American army officers, one of them Putnam, and a Chinese-American doctor who was going up to the front to make a report on the hospitals.

'Dr Sim,' Putnam said. 'That's the name I've got.'

It was necessary first to meet Chiang and be introduced as part of a British trade delegation. The Generalissimo was rigidly calm, his tunic spotless and bare of decorations, though he seemed to be having trouble with his false teeth. He greeted Willie in a high voice but without the slightest hint of recognition.

'The Generalissimo speaks only Chinese,' Putnam said, 'and I guess he's pretty silent in that. He doesn't give much away.'

Not even the price of a launch, Willie thought, remembering Chiang's entry into Shanghai.

Madame Chiang was small, beautifully dressed and spoke English with an accent acquired in America. McAleavy whispered in Willie's ear. 'Don't be misled,' he said. 'The charm doesn't stop her signing death warrants if necessary. She gives him all the support she can. It's probably becoming necessary these days because a lot of his generals have gone over to the Japanese.'

The Generalissimo was surrounded by officials and a group of intellectuals whose attitude to the war was clear. 'It's a coolie's war, of course,' one of them told Willie. 'If the Japanese kill a few there are plenty more and China can't afford to lose her small educated class.'

The other American officer who was to join Willie on his visit to the front was a blond ex-fighter pilot who could get pleasure from anything so long as there were girls and drink available. Dr Sim was the surprise because she turned out to be a woman. Although of Chinese descent, she was pure American.

'University of California,' she said coolly. 'My parents left China in 1900 and settled in San Francisco. I was actually christened Su-Lin – Sim Su-Lin, but that translates very well into American as Sue-Lynn Sim. It even sounds Scottish.'

She was unmarried and in her middle thirties, tall, pale-skinned with high cheekbones that gave the impression that her eyes were more slanted than the actually were. Her chin was stubborn for all its roundness, her nose small and wide-nostrilled, and she wore her long hair in a soft curve round the top of her head, black as polished lacquer over a face that was a neat oval on a long slender neck. She had decided that, in her travail, China needed her more than the United States and had returned to work there, but there was still enough of America in-her for her uniform to have been more neatly tailored than most so that it didn't fail to show her figure.

She had a case full of supplies provided by the Americans, mostly things like iodine, aspirin and bandages, because her job was chiefly to report on what was needed.

She was well aware that there was far from enough. 'China,' she said sharply as if she had spent her time on the statistics, 'has one doctor to every forty-five thousand people and some of them are really only pharmacists. The supplies come in the same ratio.'

It wasn't hard to discover where the so-called Russian admiral advising Chiang's general was, and this time Willie determined to do something about him, if only bribe someone to see he was captured by the Japanese. It was an easy solution that would remove him from the scene without Willie being involved. It was cowardly, but he knew he could never shoot Zychov himself or even pay someone else to shoot him. It must be that he was growing too bloody old, he thought, and the hot blood that would once have countenanced the act without a murmur had cooled.

They travelled south in a train packed with soldiers in a mixture of flat cars, box cars and old coaches, whose driver carried with him a bale of straw which, if he were attacked by Japanese aircraft, he laid under the engine then climbed on to it to read a book until the raid was over. The roofs were packed with more men, bracing themselves against the vibration and the curves. Occasionally by the track there were the bodies of those who had been unsuccessful, but nobody even looked at them because dead human beings were nothing new in China. At every station people tried to climb aboard, but were beaten off by the soldiers already in residence.

As they moved further south, they came across men wearing scraps of Japanese uniform performing curious exercises near the stations which seemed more allied to ballet than war.

'New recruits,' Willie explained to Dr Sim. 'After the last war, Chiang hired Prussian officers to train his men. All they learned was the goose step – '

Every few hours the train stopped at a station, where peasants offered scraggy boiled chickens, waffles of bean flour, vermicelli, sugar cane and hard-boiled eggs. One had a green cart pulled by a green-painted horse. 'Camouflage, Mastah,' he explained. 'Against Japanese aeroplanes. I also changed white shirt for black one, so they don't see me either.'

Leaving the train north of Kweilin, they headed south on shaggy ponies whose trot was hard on the spine, and spent the night at a drab little town where the proprietor of the Flowering Peace Hotel wore a long gown, patent shoes and a European bowler hat. They were welcomed by a crowd of people with umbrellas and a lot of bleary-nosed children like dolls, dressed in padded jackets and holding a banner with one word, WELCOM, on it. Apparently they turned out whenever Europeans appeared. During the evening they drank Chinese gin with the mayor while the mahjongg players kept up a perpetual chatter and women wandered in and out selling bread and fruit. In the bedroom the mosquitoes almost drove them mad and they couldn't put the light out until Willie unscrewed the bulb. Even then it was impossible to sleep for the noise outside.

The following day they managed to find an old Dodge in which they were driven further south past troops moving up in a bitter wind, curling in long columns along every ditch and bank. There wasn't a single vehicle among them and almost no pack animals, so that everything apart from light weapons was carried in the old way by coolies. There was no artillery and the rifles were old, the yellow-brown uniforms threadbare. The soldiers were small, wiry and thin, and wore old First World War German helmets. They all carried grenades and long cloth bags like socks full of their rations of dry rice. Their feet were swollen and broken and, as they trudged past in the rising grey dust, their faces were expressionless and blank.

A separate stream of humanity moved with the soldiers, peasants carrying their household goods – sometimes even aged relatives – on their shoulders. Among them were men and women hefting large pieces of metal.

'Machinery,' Putnam explained. 'Everything's being moved further inland. They did it from Nanking, from Shanghai, from Hankow. They once moved a whole power station piece by piece.'

The Chinese trudged past them, like a lot of ants, carrying boxes, girders, bricks, rolls of wire.

'They're doing it because of the last Japanese advance,' Dr Sim said proudly.

'Or because of the next one,' Willie observed. 'I reckon these people know something's going to happen even if Chiang doesn't.'

By the river, huge crates were being placed aboard a log raft for transport to safer areas – iron frames, coal, tables, chairs, sewing machines, an enormous steam roller, even cattle. More were moving along the bank on trains of mules, pack ponies and camels. The din was tremendous with shouting men, screaming women, wailing children, bleating goats, and always the clink-clank of metal.

At Jangjao there was a small hospital filled with exhausted Chinese boys in brown uniforms shivering against the cold. It was a one-storey building of stucco totally devoid of beds or mattresses but full of patients lying on straw, three to a blanket. Many of them were raving or in a coma and the smell of gas-gangrene made the stomach heave. None of them had been washed and there were no anaesthetics, while the instruments were so blunt as to be virtually unusable.

There were no bandages or lint and many of the men had treated their wounds themselves in the way they'd seen in their villages, stuffing them with straw, strips of uniform, leaves or the intestines of freshly killed chickens. They all seemed to be suffering from disease and to Willie it looked like typhus.

The general had made no arrangements whatsoever for their removal or even for their comfort, and the picture of Zychov, as he had imagined him at Port Arthur, rose again in Willie's mind, with his feet up on the table and doubtless with a girl and a bottle nearby.

Dr Sim was furious and her eyes were bitter as she said goodbye. 'This is where I leave you,' she said. 'There's plenty for me to do here, and saving lives is more important than writing a report.'

They were all sorry to see her leave the party because she was graceful, attractive and intelligent, and possessed a plentiful supply of American generosity of spirit. Putnam and the other officer disappeared later in the day, heading eastwards on some mission of their own near the front. By this time it was becoming quite clear that the army in this sector was nothing but a skeleton outfit padded with the names of dead men for whom the general was still drawing wages which disappeared into his own pocket. They had his name by this time and the names of his staff, and Willie hadn't the slightest doubt they were all busily filling their pockets, too. Certainly little had been done for the well-being of the Chinese soldiers and, what was worse, it was clear that the information being passed back to Chiang in Chungking was only what he wished to hear. Towns which had been reported captured were still firmly in the hands of the Japanese, while there was a big trade in the smuggling of Chinese goods across the lines. Willie hadn't the slightest doubt that Zychov was among those who were running it.

The following day they ran into a car full of Chinese officers who greeted them with smiles and agreed to conduct them to headquarters.

'The General will be pleased to answer all questions,' the colonel in command said. 'We will take you there tomorrow.'

To be on hand when Zychov appeared, Willie and McAleavy put up at an inn, where they were given a room with two cots and a charcoal brazier. It was cold and comfortless and McAleavy's long face grew more gloomy. The further they moved from civilisation and the gloomier he became, the more exhilarated Willie began to feel. This, he felt, was what life – his life, anyway – had always been about.

There was a lot of coming and going at the inn, and a certain amount of irritation among the Chinese which Willie put down to the approaching cold weather. The wind had become bitter suddenly and people kept appearing in furs, while a few soldiers wore quilted coats, though their sandals were thin against the hard earth. When they woke the following morning, it was icy and there was a mist lying like a blanket over the river, where a ruined pagoda, its sides scarred by fire, stuck out above it like an immense phallic symbol floating above the vapour.

A column of Chinese troops went past, long files of small blank-faced men without discipline or fixed pace. Their shuffling feet lifted the cold dry earth in clouds of dust so that they looked like a serpentine of vapour, their officer riding ahead on a bony horse, their rear brought up by the usual coolies carrying ammunition boxes and a single soot-blackened cauldron which was the company kitchen. Finally came a few pack guns on mules and a cart carrying sacks of rice.

As they ate a breakfast of chicken and warm beer, Willie, more attuned to China than McAleavy, noticed an atmosphere or excitement and apprehension and began to grow suspicious. It didn't take him long to find out what it was all about. Everybody from the proprietor of the hotel downwards knew what was happening and were preparing to disappear. Aware all the time of the airfields that were being built, the Japanese had struck. Their attack had been aimed at the worst defended sector and round them Chiang's army was already in retreat. Its defences had consisted only of a few old French 75s with no more than two hundred shells between them, a few light mortars with only a handful of bombs each, and only two thousand rifles between fourteen thousand men.

They waited all morning for the General's aides to appear until, about midday, a car arrived in the village at full speed, carrying what appeared to be several high-ranking officers. One of them was Zychov. He was wearing the green uniform of a Kuomintang officer and there were red tabs at his throat. He looked clean and well fed and it was as much the thought of the suffering, neglected and sacrificed young Chinese boys as his own hatred for him that drove Willie into the road. But the car didn't stop and, in a fury, Willie dragged at the old Russian revolver he always carried. Quite forgetting his qualms about removing Zychov in cold blood, he fired several shots after the speeding vehicle. None of them hit anything and McAleavy came up behind him as he stood panting and red-faced with rage.

'Bastard, bastard, bastard,' he was repeating in a low voice.

McAleavy looked shocked. 'You can't do that sort of thing, Mr Sarth,' he said. 'We're supposed to be His Majesty's official representatives. You'll have us chucked out.' He made a weak attempt at a joke. 'Perhaps even shot. You might have hit one of them.'

Willie turned and glared at him. 'I wish to Christ I had,' he snarled.

McAleavy's long face looked startled. 'Someone in there you don't like or something?'

'By God, there is! I ought to have shot him years ago.'

McAleavy didn't ask any more questions, but it was obvious he considered Willie a very odd type to send on a diplomatic mission. McAleavy was the sort of man who, properly brought up and involved for years in the cool corridors of foreign diplomacy, had probably never lost his temper in his life. But he was astute enough to realise that Willie had, and kept out of his way.

An hour later, another car which they recognised as the one they were waiting for came into sight. Running into the road again, Willie refused to budge until it stopped. The Chinese, their faces devoid this time of smiles, made no attempt to climb out and one of the colonels spoke from his seat.

'The General has already appeared in the village,' he said. 'He was just ahead of us.'

'He wasn't intending to talk to us,' Willie snapped. 'He was bolting. With his bloody adviser.'

'The General would not bolt. Neither the General nor any of his staff would bolt. We fight with spirit.'

'It seems to be all you've got. Where are you going?'

'We are going to bring up reinforcements.'

'All of you?'

The colonel gave Willie a cold look and waved a hand, and the car started with a jerk and spinning wheels that threw grit in his face. Making no attempt to halt the passing troops, the officers shot away at full speed, heading northeast.

'You ask me,' Willie said to McAleavy, 'that's the last we'll see of the General or his staff.'

McAleavy looked shocked. 'You mean they've abandoned their army?'

'It's not a new thing with Chiang generals.'

By the afternoon, as more Chinese troops came through, they were able to discover what had happened. The Japanese offensive, made up of troops which had been moved south from Manchuria, had burst against the front like a thunderclap and was roaring across South China at full speed. Already one airfield had fallen and another was about to. The Japanese had started with probing attacks and the Chinese, suddenly bereft of senior officers, were struggling at regimental level to strengthen their positions near the Yangtze, mere clusters of frightened youths facing artillery with rusting machine guns and old rifles.

Back at the village where they had spent the night, they found soldiers pulling down doors to make fires and seizing what animals, chickens and vegetables they could. A man who protested as his pig was driven away was shot without argument and left sprawled in the roadway, his wife weeping over his body. At the inn, their luggage had been rifled and an exhausted officer was asleep in their room so that they had to spend the night in an attic papered with sheets from the *Illustrated London News*, showing pictures of the British Grand Fleet in 1909 and portraits of Edward VII and Queen Alexandra.

The following morning, the trickle of wounded through the village had become a flood, men struggling desperately towards the rear on their own two feet because there was no transport, limping, dragging themselves along by clutching trees, leaning on sticks. Their eyes were empty, they were surrounded by a smell of decay, and there was hardly a stretcher between the lot of them.

Towards midday news came in that the Japanese were across the route to the rear and the limping men began to swing westwards in the hope of bypassing them. There seemed no alternative but to follow and, packing the rear of the car with wounded, they set off, devoid of everything but what they wore. They soon realised they were in trouble because they began to see dead Chinese soldiers spreadeagled on the ground. There were shell holes alongside the road and houses were scorched by fire. A few soldiers carrying the coffin of an officer on yellow ropes moved near the river, where more bodies were floating, caught in the barbed wire which had been erected in the shallows.

They stopped to eat what little food they possessed in the courtyard of a shattered house. Soldiers were preparing to defend the place and were setting up an old Hotchkiss machine gun and making loopholes for their rifles. A dead officer lay in one corner.

Unable to move further west, they turned north, but during the afternoon they ran out of petrol and as it was impossible to buy more, they left the car and began to walk.

'I think we're in rather a mess,' Willie observed.

McAleavy's long face lit up for the first time since Willie had met him. 'We'll cope,' he said cheerfully. 'I think I've never been more satisfied with myself. Not that it's very pleasant, of course,' he explained lamely, 'but I've never done much except sit in an office and this at least enables me to prove that there's more to me than that.'

Willie said nothing, hoping he wouldn't have to change his mind.

The Chinese army was already disintegrating. Rice dumps were being looted and soldiers were staggering off with leaking sacks across their shoulders, less concerned with the battle than with filling their empty bellies. They managed to find another inn for the night, but it was already crowded and food was short. The next morning the countryside was white with frost.

In the distance across a hillside they could see black snakes winding down into the valley and it dawned on them it was the Japanese. The were trying to encircle the Chinese with two great arms of a pincer movement.

'It's time we got out of here,' Willie said.

He had managed to buy a couple of shaggy ponies and, as they set off, the sun was like a fiery ball in the winter sky. At the next town, soldiers had been raiding the shops and started setting fire to stores. As they trotted in, a tremendous explosion shook the earth. Roofs twisted back in the blast, and gold, white and scarlet flames leapt into the sky topped by black oily smoke. A shed full of ammunition caught fire and tracer bullets started popping and whizzing upwards in red and white arcs.

People caught by the explosion lay against wrecked walls, stripped of their clothes, their flesh pitted with gravel and sand. A few were still alive, their faces smeared with blood, their mouths gaping, their fingers opening and shutting, but the refugees continued to plod by without a look in their direction. Crowds gathering at the railway station had lit fires to warm themselves as they waited. Most of them were hungry and a horse that had fallen was being fought over, its carcass stripped into red slivers of meat.

The hopelessness of the situation was as wearing as the cold that penetrated clothing and even buildings. The Japanese were slicing through the Chinese as if they didn't exist. Hungry, sick, untrained, badly equipped, their transport non-existent, as the Chinese boys tried to seize peasant ox-carts they were attacked by furious villagers armed with forks who disarmed them, first in ones and twos, then in groups and whole companies, until there was nothing left to face the advancing Japanese.

The Japanese were sweeping through South China like a wind by the time Willie and McAleavy came to a halt. Their long pilgrimage had ended back at the town of Jangjao, where they had left Dr Sim, and they promptly headed for the hospital to persuade her to move on with them. There was little hope in Willie's mind that they would succeed.

She looked tired but determined and very angry. The supplies she had brought were virtually exhausted and others which she had arranged for had disappeared.

'I expect,' she snapped, 'that they never got any further than Chungking, where they were used to cure Chiang's women of headaches.'

'The Japanese are coming,' Willie said. 'Oughtn't you to be thinking of getting out of here?'

She stared at him as though he had suggested something obscene. 'The people who come here,' she said, 'are dying on their feet of malaria, dysentery and hunger. Half of them have scabies and the other half the itch. There's no washing because there's no soap, there's beri-beri, leg ulcers, tuberculosis, typhus, influenza and worms. The only thing missing is venereal disease and that's because they can't afford to go with a prostitute. And there are no cures, because all the medicines, all the kaolin, quinine tablets and penicillin we handed over have been sold. And you talk of bolting.'

They were still arguing when the Japanese bombers arrived. They came without warning, swooping over the hill so they couldn't be heard until the last second. As they dived for shelter the world turned into a roaring, falling, confused chaos. Shouts turned to screams as chunks of flying masonry ricocheted among the fleeing people and houses slid sideways in a torrent of timber, tiles and dust. Almost the last bomb that dropped hit the corner of the hospital, bringing down the whole of one side in a pile of splintered debris.

When Willie came round, he was lying on his face with a weight across his back, but already he could hear voices nearby and the debris was quickly removed. He was bruised and shocked, but he dusted himself down and looked round for McAleavy. Dead, dying, wounded and bomb-shocked lay everywhere and the street was littered with masonry and half-buried bodies. People still trapped were screaming for help and groups of shocked survivors were limping away. There was no sign of McAleavy and Willie was just about to start dragging at stones and timber when he saw him lying across the road, so covered with dust he had merged into the grey background. His spectacles were still on his nose but one lens was broken and his leg lay at a strange angle. Willie saw at once that he was dead.

Turning away, brushing the dust and splinters from his clothes, he became aware of Chinese soldiers running past. Then an officer on a horse galloped up and shouted at him. The soldiers scattered and in a daze it dawned on Willie that the Japanese were almost on top of them.

The work of rescue stopped immediately. As people started to run, patients began to emerge from the wreckage of the hospital, limping, shuffling, crawling, trailing bloody bandages, determined to get away before the Japanese put in an appearance. Coming to life with a start, Willie began to push between them, barging his way through the crowd into the hospital where he had last seen Dr Sim.

He found her half-buried by rubble, her clothes, her hair, her face grey with dust. She was unconscious and he dragged the rubble aside and pulled her clear. There was a cut on her head, and her hair at the back was clotted with blood in which the dust had congealed in a grey drying scab. He managed to get her on to her feet, still only half-conscious, and dragged her outside. Weakly she tried to insist on returning to her patients.

'No,' Willie snapped. 'No!'

The two ponies Willie and McAleavy had ridden seemed to have disappeared. Then he saw one of them standing nearby, its neck and chest streaming blood. It was badly wounded but he found a heavy stick, pushed Dr Sim into the saddle and, climbing up behind her, kicked the pony into life. It seemed to weave from side to side, but he lashed cruelly at it until it broke into a trot and then into a gallop.

Dr Sim was still struggling to free herself, but he clung on to her, beating the failing animal mercilessly. After only a few hundred yards, however, it faltered and came to a stop. Even as he climbed down to drag it forward, it crashed to the ground, snatching the reins from his hand and sending Sue-Lynn flying.

She seemed to be unhurt. There was a clump of trees about half a mile away and, ignoring her protests, he dragged her towards them. As they reached them, he turned. A few people were still moving away from the hospital, shadowed by a column of black smoke that coiled slowly into the sky. Then he saw the Japanese soldiers, advancing in a steady line on each side of the road.

'I must go back.' Dr Sim came to life with a jerk and pulled herself free.

As she started to walk unsteadily down the hill past the carcass of the dead pony, he ran after her and, as he grabbed her, they fell to the ground together. She sat up abruptly.

'Let me go!'

Without arguing he slapped her face so hard that a long dark wing of hair was flung across her cheek as she jerked sideways. She stared at him, shocked, then, as her eyes filled with tears, he clutched her to him and allowed her to sob against his chest.

seven

From the shelter of the trees they saw the Japanese reach the village and listened to the sound of murder. Shots were fired and shouts came from the burning hospital. Then they saw one of the Chinese nurses run out, her black hair flying. She was half-naked and a Japanese soldier ran after her and grabbed her wrist to drag her away. As she struggled he turned and punched her hard in the face before dragging her out of sight. A moment later a shuddering scream came to them and, clutching Sue-Lynn Sim to him, Willie covered her ears with his hands.

The murder and rape went on all afternoon, nerve-shattering sounds reaching them on the hill, so that the only thing in Willie's mind was the memory of a similar butchery near Shantu forty-four years before when he was also clutching a woman to him and trying to hide the horrors from her. This, he thought, is like the re-run of an old film, a return full circle to where it had all begun.

As it grew dark, he pulled Dr Sim to her feet. 'We've got to get away from here,' he said. 'Before they find us.'

She didn't argue. She had nothing but what she stood up in and, no longer of much use to anyone as a doctor, she nodded silently and followed him through the trees.

They were well away from the Japanese column by daylight and by evening had reached the little town of Shi-Lo. Because of the cold, there were fires, built from the timbers of ruined houses, burning in the streets and a few Chinese soldiers trying to keep warm. There were no lights and no civilians about because of the curfew, but Willie was able to bribe someone to give them shelter.

The following day they moved on, forced north again by the presence of Japanese troops moving across the south, and continued for the next four days until they considered there was enough distance between them and the Japanese to be safe, before calling a halt at a town called Yusiao. Food was scarce because starving units of the retreating Chinese army had passed through, but a few market stalls had been erected and a few tough-looking vegetables, sweets and rice cakes were available, all watched over by sharp-eyed men and women.

They managed to find a stone-built restaurant with a sign of peeling red and gold characters outside a carved entrance marked by bullets and shell splinters. It was a grimy place thick with cobwebs, the bare crooked wooden tables littered with greasy bowls and chopsticks among the scattered grains of rice and chicken bones. The place smelled of joss sticks and the paraffin in the hissing lamps, and outside beggars and dogs crouched waiting for a dropped morsel of food, but they managed to buy tea and a hot meal of beans drowned in flavourless stock. The wind was whacking a cane roofing mat against a wall outside with a dreary monotonous slap-slapping. After they had eaten, they learned of a small house where the owner had once been a civil servant but who now, because there was no longer any order and no job to bring in any money, was willing to let them a room. He laid two blankets and cushions on the bare floor and, ill at ease, Willie ushered Sue-Lynn Sim inside.

She stared at him with black expressionless eyes. Since leaving Jangjao she had been silent and troubled, not speaking much. The change in her worried Willie.

'We may have to be here a long time,' he warned. 'The winter's just starting. We'll move on as soon as possible.'

She seemed indifferent. 'I expect we shall manage,' she said.

The next day the snow came and there was no hope of moving. When a few scattered wounded appeared, victims of the war or Japanese bombing, Sue-Lynn found she couldn't resist the need to help them. They had no medical supplies, but she found cotton wool, and bandages were made from torn-up linen. Then Willie unearthed a bottle of potassium permanganate in one of the shops which they could use as an antiseptic. His knowledge of medicine was restricted to the first aid he had learned as a stretcher bearer at Peking forty-four years before, but, with Sue-Lynn's directions, he was able to be of help. Establishing a small hospital in a school-room, very soon she had people coming every morning to the little surgery she held there.

They slept on the floor in the same room, separated only by a makeshift screen made from a worn shawl, an old flattened carton and a cut-down reed basket, all strung together with cord. It was possible to hear each other moving, dressing and undressing, sleeping and waking, Willie sometimes roused in the darkness by Sue-Lynn's whimpering nightmares. But neither went into the other's half of the room, both always remaining rigidly correct, always careful to keep a distance between them in a curiously unnatural sort of 'marriage' that seemed to work. Sue-Lynn tried her hand at cooking, at which she was not very good, so Willie took it over to allow her to give all her attention to her patients. He noticed she was eyeing him strangely but she said little, though he noticed the sharpness had gone out of her voice.

The hospital and the long winter kept them in Yusiao. Always there seemed to be a heavy wet snow on the ground and a weak white snow-light in the dark alleys of the town. Dressed in blue Chinese clothes and an old fur coat he had managed to obtain, on his head Willie wore a padded cap which looked no better for the boiling he had given it to kill the lice. Pulled down over his eyes, it enabled him to pass for a Chinese. Sue-Lynn wore a quilted coat and a fur hat they had managed to buy.

Many people in the area were starving because of the disruption caused by the war. Bombed and shelled, the hundreds of people who came in from the surrounding countryside found little comfort. The buildings of Yusiao were largely empty shells devoid of roofs and the people who occupied them looked like ghosts. The whole town stank of urine and human excrement as the grey-faced people shivered in the bitter wind from the north. Occasionally they found a body by the roadside, starved or dead from exposure.

As the town became a tomb peopled by ghosts, finding it impossible to do anything to relieve the misery, they could only shut their minds to it. There were dozens of hungry children, their tear-stained faces smudgy and lost, small shrunken shapes with slits for eyes, their hair falling out with hunger, their skin chapped and raw, their voices only an unhappy whining. The villages around were just as bad, with terrifying silences and deserted streets. Fields had been stripped and the peasants were searching the heaps of refuse for rejected scraps of food. Occasionally bodies, buried in shallow graves, were exposed by hungry dogs, and Willie heard of parents killing their children rather than see them starve.

Mallinson's little reconnaissance had not come off. There had been no messages to him but now it didn't seem to matter, because it didn't take a very clever man to see what was happening. Perhaps all the tomfoolery of elevating Chiang's China to the rank of a Great Power would now be dropped. The Japanese had supplied the answers.

It was obvious that the war had bogged down to a stalemate. The Chinese had burned whole villages and towns and destroyed every road, bridge, railway line and ferry. The blockade had been useless for a long time because the Chinese had been obtaining cloth, rubber, tyres, medicines and petrol from corrupt Japanese commanders, in the same way that the Japanese had long since been obtaining tungsten, tin and other things, even rice, from the Chinese. The campaigns of both sides had become nothing but foraging expeditions and the unexpected Japanese attack had upset all calculations.

But that had run out of steam now and the country had lapsed back into its inertia and indifference. Occasionally they saw aeroplanes passing overhead, too high to be interested in their immediate area, and they were able to identify them as American.

'The Japanese must be retreating,' Willie said. 'We've never seen those boys before, and they're beginning to come more often.'

Sometimes they heard scraps of news and at night they talked of what everybody seemed to know – that the

Communist-controlled areas in North China were being expanded at the expense of Chiang's Nationalists.

'There are upwards of a hundred million people under their control now,' Sue-Lynn pointed out. 'I saw a pamphlet. Even in the south they have twenty-seven thousand men under arms against the Japanese.'

As the winter ended, they saw the American aeroplanes more often, always heading for some distant target, and began to learn a little about the outside world. The Allies had landed on the continent of Europe and were advancing eastwards, while the Russians were heading westwards to meet them over the mauled remains of the German armies. Japan's great leap forward had been halted and they, too, were now in retreat. Their navy, according to the rumours that filtered northwards from the coast or the titbits shouted by disillusioned Japanese along the fighting line, was shattered and the Americans were advancing towards Tokyo island by island.

There seemed to be corpses everywhere. The Japanese were hungry now. As the Americans began to attack their supply lines, their huge armies, unable to feed themselves, were beginning to fall back to the coast, so nervous of American bombing, they hid at any noise that sounded like an aeroplane. They left their sick and dying behind them and bodies were being found in tanks, lorries, cars, even ships, hundreds of them, Japanese boys hardly out of school. There was cholera everywhere and in one of the houses into which they stumbled by mistake, there seemed to be dozens of bodies in all stages of death and decomposition, red, white, green and blue, bloated and shrivelled, eyes staring, fingers clawing, hands raised in what seemed to be an attitude of prayer.

'I think it's actually coming to an end,' Willie said. 'I think we're beginning to win.'

'What will happen when it does?' Sue-Lynn asked.

'I should think a lot of people will turn up who were thought to be dead. Me, for instance. And you.'

She looked at him with a sombre face. 'William,' she said, 'I think I owe you an apology.'

He was startled by the admission because she had always kept herself aloof, even faintly suspicious of him. 'What for?'

She frowned, as if finding the admission difficult. 'I had one of the women here from the hospital at Jangjao,' she said. 'She was raped twenty-four times. It went on all day. Then, when they'd finished with them, the Japanese bayoneted them. She managed to escape.' She paused. 'That would have happened to me but for you.'

Willie gestured that she should forget about it, but she insisted on going on. 'It was you who brought me here,' she said, watching him carefully so that he was conscious of being faintly embarrassed under her gaze. 'You've been brave and resourceful, as well as very kind and understanding.'

Willie shrugged. 'I'm not brave. I've never been brave.'

She remained distant as she continued to go to the little hospital every day. There wasn't much she could do, but she boiled water and bathed away encrusted dirt and blood that was making wounds septic. Sometimes she was bitter at her inability to do more and depressed at the condition of her patients. She was uncertain. She had arrived in China full of idealism and hope, certain she could help. Now, confronted with the country as she had been, she was no longer sure she was right. There was so much to do, so much to put right.

He could tell how her thoughts were moving and knew that sometimes she found it all a little too much. Despite China's intellectual past, despite the giant strides she had made, most of the country was still barely out of the Middle Ages and the steps she was taking to drag herself into the present century involved ruthlessness, cruelty and often treachery, and they appalled Sue-Lynn. They were not what she had expected, weren't even touched by the idealism she had brought from America. There was idealism enough, but it was a different idealism from hers and somehow it shut her out.

Yet she persisted in trying to belong, to believe that her background made her at one with the Chinese. When something happened that showed they disagreed, however, when some villager she had attempted to treat simply ignored her and returned to the safer village antidotes and cures they had always known, she became cast down and morose so that Willie had to jerk her out of the mood. Despite her eagerness to share the sorrows of China, she had grown up in an American city and missed the conveniences of civilisation. Willie had learned to live anywhere and he had long since developed his psychology of survival. To survive, you had to *try* to survive.

Often she looked angry, bewildered and desperate, as if something she'd believed in had vanished, and she lost weight so that her cheeks lost the roundness they'd had when he'd first seen her. But, if anything, it made her more beautiful, even in the hideous blue suit she'd acquired that chafed at the soft skin at her throat and made marks on her wrists and ankles.

Occasionally, by the warm hearth of the charcoal stove, they talked of their past lives. But never of Zychov, who always remained a canker in Willie's heart, smouldering, gnawing, making him go hot with rage when he thought about him. She had long since guessed there was something which troubled him, but she didn't ask questions. Instead she concentrated on her own background. She had always wanted to he a doctor and had been a brilliant student. But always she had felt that her destiny was not in America where she had been born and brought up, but in suffering China, which she had never seen. 'What do you do?' she asked. 'You've never told me.'

'I sail ships.'

'You're a sailor?'

'An owner.'

'Then you must he wealthy.'

'I suppose so.'

'But you gave it all up to come here, to help China?'

He managed a little laugh. 'I think I was conscripted,' he said.

Eventually they began to realise they hadn't seen a Japanese soldier for some time. They had left Yusiao some time before because the Japanese were believed to be in the countryside around, but as they started their foraging expeditions for food and news, it suddenly occurred to them that perhaps they had been withdrawn.

There were still hungry people about, shuffling by in a soundless hush that was broken only by the scrape of feet or the squeak of wheels. They walked mechanically, concentrating on putting one foot in front of the other, bodies bent, heads wobbling weakly, fathers dragging carts, mothers pulling at ropes, all but the smallest children carrying huge loads. But there were also a few hardy characters who had survived the winter to sow wheat, protecting their crops with clubs, knowing that if they were stolen they, too, would starve.

It was some time before they learned the war was over. They had seen no aerial activity for some time and slowly it began to dawn on them that the Japanese had gone, that in their area hostilities had ceased. Then they began to hear rumours of a terrible new weapon the Americans had introduced, and that the Japanese, unable to face it, had surrendered. It seemed unlikely, because surrender was against all the Japanese military code of ethics, but the rumours persisted and finally a man on an old stumbling horse came into the village where they were sheltering to tell them it was fact, that the Japanese had lost the war.

The surrender caught everyone by surprise, not only themselves but the Chinese around them. They had all expected the Japanese to make a last desperate stand, but it hadn't happened. It was hard to believe, but finally they were convinced and Sue-Lynn turned to Willie and, quietly putting her arms round him, held him to her. For a while they clung to each other, leaning on each other, too full of emotion to say anything.

'Thank God,' Sue-Lynn said eventually. 'Thank God.'

A few days later they learned the war had been finished for weeks and that the Americans were bringing in food for starving people and even talking of looking among the Japanese for the men who had committed the atrocities that had made the struggle so bitter.

With the opening up of the country and the freedom to pass on information, they discovered that the Communists had refused point-blank to work with Chiang. It didn't seem to worry Sue-Lynn, who had grown thoroughly disillusioned with the Kuomintang. Although Chiang appeared to have won several intoxicating victories against the crumbling Japanese forces, there were stories of strong discontent which had accumulated during the war years.

'The civil war will start again,' Sue-Lynn said calmly. 'And that can only end with the destruction of Chiang.'

'Is that what you want?' Willie asked.

'It'll be what China wants.'

'And you? What will your part be in it? I suppose you've decided you've got a part.'

She looked at him quickly as if she thought he was offering criticism, then the bewildered expression returned to her face. It seemed to come more often these days.

'I don't know,' she admitted wearily. 'I expect they'd welcome a helping hand.'

Willie's experience suggested otherwise. 'Will they?' he asked, and as she turned her head away quickly, he saw that her eyes were suddenly moist.

With the end of the war, it was important to return to civilisation and, as they considered ways and means, it seemed easier to make for the coast rather than head north for distant Chungking.

'We're bound to be able to get word to the Navy or something,' Willie suggested. 'God knows, we might even bump into one of my ships.'

But because of the delay in hearing of the Japanese defeat, too much time had elapsed and it was once more too close to winter to attempt to move out of the mountains. Already the fogs and the rain had started and the mists came every morning, creeping along the valleys like ghostly serpents. The roads were already deep in mud that clung to the ankles as you walked, and when the cold

687

came it would set hard in a black frozen coral that would make walking impossible.

'We have to wait until the weather changes,' Willie said. 'So we might as well make ourselves comfortable.'

There was still some left of the money Mallinson had provided and, for a few coins, they rented a small two-roomed house at the end of a village on the lower slopes of the hills. It contained practically nothing, but Willie managed to construct sufficient furniture for them to live. They scrubbed the place out and though it could hardly be called comfortable, as least it was bearable after Willie had stopped up the hole under the door and started a fire.

The state of the surrounding countryside was still chaotic. China had slipped back into the dark ages that had existed before the rise of the Kuomintang. A few British and Americans who had escaped being rounded up in places like Shanghai and the coastal ports where they had happened to be working had tried to reach Chungking but they heard they had been betrayed and handed over to the Japanese by villagers terrified of reprisals, and now, roamed by starving people, bandits and deserters from the renegade Chinese regiments employed by the Japanese, the countryside was as dangerous as it had been before the war.

From time to time, groups of men appeared, ragged, tired and ill, and once again, with nothing to offer but her knowledge, Sue-Lynn started a small surgery of sorts. They could offer nothing in the way of medicine, but the advice they gave was welcomed and there was a steady stream of sick to see them. Many of them had been mutilated by the war and there were legless, armless and blind. But slowly, around them, people were trying to start their lives again and one day they saw one of the peasants trying to hack at the earth with an old-fashioned mattock.

There was typhus in the village and, terrified of it after suffering from it in Russia, Willie immediately began to think of moving on. But then he noticed that Sue-Lynn was listless and low in spirit and the following day he saw she was shuddering and swaying on her feet. Without arguing, he hurried her back to the house and pushed her into bed. By this time she was sweating, her face bloodless, and by evening her body was covered with red blotches so that he knew her condition was serious.

By the following morning she was unable to think coherently and had no idea who he was. Remembering all he could from what he had seen in Russia, he tried to look after her. Managing to find disinfectant, he worked through the whole of the house, but by this time she was delirious, her eyes bloodshot, the lashes gummed up, her lips cracked and sore. He bathed her body, kept her warm and tried to push weak soup into her.

Having once suffered from the disease himself, he was terrified he would also catch it and they would both die, but he seemed to have become immune. Sue-Lynn was feeble and often in a sort of wakeful stupor, staring at him with contracted pupils and an obviously diminished capacity for perception. He had no means of judging her temperature but eventually, as she began to perspire freely and all the distressing symptoms of the disease began to abate, he judged she was past the crisis.

Finally she opened her eyes and stared at him through half-closed lids. 'What happened to me?' she asked.

'Tyf,' he said, trembling with relief that she was going to survive.

'Did you nurse me?'

'As best I could. I had it myself in Russia in 1920.'

'Am I going to be all right?'

'You know that better than I do, but I think so.'

Her hand lifted instinctively to her hair. Then it fell weakly to her side. 'What happened to my hair?'

'I had to cut it off. It'll grow again.'

He was staring down at her, his face concerned. It was a good face, she felt now, after too many months of suspicion, a strong face, with a straight, narrow nose, crisp hair streaked with grey, fine eyes and lines that were strong, grim even, but still full of humour and occasionally, as now, gentleness. Suddenly she was overwhelmed with shame at her indifference to him in the past and she reached out weakly to touch his hand. 'Oh, William,' she said, and he saw tears streaming down her cheeks.

For a long time she was silent, then she looked at him, her eyes moist and gentle. The relationship between them had grown warmer over the months they had spent together. She had treated his hand when a splinter had made it septic, and now he had nursed her through typhus. But he was also aware of a change in himself. She had started to do catastrophic things to him. The constant proximity, watching her wash, bathe, living closely with her, and now nursing her from the edge of death, had been more disturbing than he enjoyed and, with a shock, he realised that, in her calmness, her compassion and her sense of duty, like Nadya, she too was a copy of Abigail.

'Don't be a bloody fool,' he kept telling himself. 'She's years younger than you.'

'The winter's almost over, Sue-Lynn,' he said quietly. 'It'll soon be spring. Then we'll go south.'

But it was a long time before she was able to stand on her feet and, with his help, take a few hesitant steps.

'Soon,' she said.

But the warmer weather had come before she was strong enough to face the journey south.

'We'll be all right,' Willie encouraged.

There was a strange inner glow coming from her face these days, a glow he hadn't seen before, a glow that came from serenity and a curious mature calm, as though all her strong feelings had been ironed out. Humbly, he touched her cheek, oddly grateful for the warmth of her expression.

'We'll make for the Pearl River,' he said shortly. 'Perhaps we can persuade a junkmaster to take us down to Macao or somewhere like that.'

Two days later they set off south. Every road in China seemed to be edged with ruins and full of people trying to find their way back to homes they had quitted years before, Their journey was slow because their shoes were shrunken and stiff with mud and Sue-Lynn still hadn't the strength to walk long distances. Mallinson's money was almost gone and Willie was hoarding what was left so he would have enough to bribe the junkmaster when he found him. Sue-Lynn was in total agreement and insisted there was no other way to travel. But she tired quickly and, grudgingly, Willie paid a man with an ox and a cart to carry them, and for two days they rolled to the jolt and jerk of the clumsy vehicle, their ears filled with the squeak of the wheels.

'Squeaks are cheaper in China than oil,' Willie pointed out.

Even the ox-cart was slow, but within three weeks and with Sue-Lynn growing stronger with every day, they were staring at the Pearl River in the evening light wondering how they were going to use it. There was a small river port where junks collected and at a village a few miles further on called Yai-Ten they found a junkmaster due to head downstream who agreed to take them to Canton.

'Tomorrow,' he said. 'Come tomorrow. Bring food.' He grinned, showing a set of teeth like discoloured gravestones. 'Bring money also.'

They agreed on a price and, because it was raining, they went in search of somewhere to sleep. There was still a little money left so they decided to use the last of it to stay the night at an inn. They were given a room with a charcoal brazier and a single large bed. Willie was about to protest when Sue-Lynn shook her head and spoke stiffly, defiantly almost.

'It doesn't matter,' she said. 'After all this time, it doesn't matter.'

After they'd eaten, they began to worry that the junkmaster might have taken their money and gone without them, so they walked to the port in the drizzling rain to make sure. The junkmaster knew what they'd been thinking and grinned at them.

'You think I go, Mastah?'

Slightly shamefaced, they began to retrace their steps to the inn, but the rain began to fall more heavily until in the end it became a downpour and they were soaked. They fell into the inn and went to their room to dry off by the brazier. As Willie stoked up the charcoal, the rain hissed and spattered outside. Sue-Lynn dragged off her clothes and, flinging more charcoal on to the brazier, Willie turned to her. She was shivering and her teeth were chattering but she insisted on helping him to pull off his wet clothes.

They had only a square of cotton to dry themselves and he insisted on drying her first, rubbing at her skin until she began to protest.

'Warm now?'

'Yes, I'm warm.'

Heated by his exertions, he passed her one of the blankets to put round herself and started to dry himself as she hung her clothes in steamy bundles near the brazier.

'Let me dry you.' She turned to him, staring at him over the top of the square of cotton, then she stopped dead, wide-eyed and silent. As she lowered the cotton cloth, he reached for it and took it from her, and unexpectedly she took a step forward, then, catching at his hands, she pulled him to her, mouthing little sad longing sounds, her body relaxed against his and shaken by a dreadful paroxysm of sobbing. Her arms went round him and she was clinging to him as if she had lost all courage and he was her last refuge. The contact made him giddy and, as they sank to the bed, their mouths searching eagerly for each other, he gave up the struggle with his conscience.

When Willie woke, she was lying in the crook of his arm, her cropped head against his shoulder, her face peaceful and purged of all uncertainty. His thoughts were confused.

Why had she done it, he wondered. Was it gratitude because he had nursed her, or because she needed to feel needed? Or was it simply because she needed love and Willie was still a strong man whose muscles had not sagged and whose hair showed very little grey; because she was lost and lonely and because his was the only white face she had seen for months?

Last fling, old lad, he thought to himself. After this, the old wheelchair and crutches.

She moved slightly and he found she was looking at him, her eyes soft, then she turned on her side, her face in the curve of his neck, her lips moving against his skin.

'I'll never forget you,' she whispered. 'Never.'

'Rubbish. I'm an old man.'

'You're not old.'

'Not a day over ninety.'

'Don't be silly.'

Willie didn't answer because he knew he *was* silly. Love happened like a whirlwind. It changed you and changed the world around you into a kind of heaven. He gestured weakly. 'I shall miss you, Sue-Lynn,' he said. 'I think I've been in love with you for ages. It would be impossible not to be after all this time.'

For a while she remained motionless, then she gave a sudden shudder that shook her whole frame and her hand clutched his. As he drew her to him, her eyes were full of tears. She moved her head in a little troubled gesture and tried to explain her feelings.

'I didn't think it possible for anyone to love me,' she said.

'I don't believe it.'

'No, it's true. I never allowed them to. I was too conscious of what I was, of the need to help China. There've been other men, of course, but they didn't love me. They merely wanted me.' As she tilted her head to rest her cheek against his, his hand moved round the back of it so that his fingers were in the softness of the hair at the nape of her neck.

'Forget it,' he said. 'We'll be away from here soon and you'll find someone. There must be hundreds who would want you, given the chance.'

In silence, they packed up their few belongings, wondering as they did so how they had managed to live through the winter with so little. The junkmaster was growing fidgety as they climbed aboard. He watched them gravely for a while, then he grinned and produced a meal of chop suey and rice wine.

There was no cabin to sleep in but there was a corner on deck where they could sit. Eventually the crew appeared and the coolies began to march up the gangplank with sacks of rice and bales of hides, singing in the high-pitched, two-noted tune that accompanied all working coolies in the Far East, a sad resigned song like the humming of insects, rising and falling, the two notes never ceasing as the men jogged back and forth with their loads.

Dragging a few sacks forward, Willie made a corner for them out of the wind, and they sat and watched as the occasional steamer slipped past, its siren giving off a deep booming note, then the junk cast off and moved into midstream. The next thirty-six hours were spent dozing in the shelter of the rice sacks, Willie with his arm round Sue-Lynn, the fitful sun warming their bodies as they talked.

'I seem to fall in love a lot,' Willie admitted. 'But I do my best to stay married. I've been married twice.'

She seemed surprised and he explained. 'My first wife was killed,' he said. 'Eighteen years ago. I'd known my second wife some time and married her some years later.' He didn't explain the relationship they'd had because he felt she'd disapprove. 'I have three children, all grown up, and five grandchildren, two of them like you, more Chinese than anything else.'

As he spoke, he wondered what had happened to them all. They had been cut off from civilisation for months now, totally unable to send a message. Doubtless by this time in Chungking he was considered dead, caught up in the unexpected Japanese attack, and a message must have been sent off to his family to that effect. He wondered what Nadya had thought when she received it.

He found he still loved her, despite falling in love again with Sue-Lynn. It was something he had managed to do before and it didn't surprise him, just left him wondering how it was possible. The fact that it was, however, was quite unalterable and he tried to accept it.

'What will you do now?' he asked. 'Go back to the States?'

She shook her head. 'No. I shall go north.'

'To join the Communists?'

'They're honest.'

'That's only because they've not been in power yet and haven't learned to be corrupt.'

'They may be different from Chiang and I must take my chance.'

He thought of the strict morality of the Communists he'd met, their self-righteous rigidity of thought, the narrowness of their behaviour.

'It would be a terrible waste,' he said.

At Canton they went ashore, to find the Royal Navy was back. The Duty Officer refused to believe their story and insisted on them seeing a more senior officer. Even he was sceptical until Willie talked of Edward, whom he knew, then he began to take an interest in what they had to say and Willie managed to get in touch with the consul who loaned him enough money to cable home.

Soon afterwards they were taken downriver to Hong Kong, where the Royal Navy were in command once more. By a miracle, the *Lady Roberts* had just arrived from Australia with one of the first batches of returning people since the war had ended. Yeh was on the bridge, talking to a Chinese compradore and arranging for a cargo of cotton to be taken aboard, and he couldn't believe his eyes as Willie walked up the gangplank.

But, as usual, his expression was as fixed as if it were nailed to his face. 'I expect you want to get home in double-quick time,' he said. 'Do I forget the cotton?'

'No, you don't,' Willie said. 'We're still concerned with profitability and our financial position was strong and broadly based when I last heard of it. Let's keep it that way.'

That evening, Willie found a waterside restaurant remembered from before the war and he and Sue-Lynn ate and drank enough to he happy. As they left, they stood on the bund watching the lights, neither of them able to say the words they knew had to be said. Eventually, Willie signed.

'It's time I went,' he pointed out.

'Yes,' she agreed. 'I must go, too.'

'What will you do?'

'I'll catch a train to Hankow or somewhere like that, then go up into Shensi.'

'To become a Communist?'

'To try to help China.'

'I shall never forget you, Sue-Lynn.'

She smiled. 'And I'll never forget the old man who took such care of me.'

They didn't say much more. They kissed quietly, a farewell kiss without passion, then Willie turned and walked up the gangway to the deck of the *Lady Roberts*. At the top he turned and stared back. Sue-Lynn was walking to where a few rickshaw coolies were smoking. He saw one of them rise to his feet and speak to her, then he turned and picked up the shafts. Sue-Lynn climbed aboard and the rickshaw moved off. She never looked back and Willie stared after her until she disappeared into the shadows.

PART SIX

1945–1949

one

With the end of the war, the whole Far Eastern world was upside down. Stateless people still filled every port, airport and station, trying to find their way back to families who thought they were dead, Japan was still reeling from the atom bombs, China was in turmoil again, and there were problems for the British in India, for the French in Indo-China, and for the Dutch in the East Indies. Nothing was working properly. Telegraph, telephone and postal communications had been smashed or disconnected, and in the chaotic conditions still existing Willie's cable had not reached Australia. And, just to make matters worse, while the *Lady Roberts*' ancient engine pounded as stolidly south as it ever did, her radio gave trouble and it was impossible to send a message ahead.

Puzzled to find there was no one to meet him as the ship docked, Willie didn't wait to telephone but caught a taxi to his home. Nadya was in the garden when he arrived and he noticed she looked pale and there were grey streaks in her hair that made him realise just how old he himself had become. She didn't notice him at first as he appeared in the drive, then he saw her frown, look up, pause and look up again. This time her expression changed to one of blank astonishment. A moment later she was running to meet him.

'William! William! We thought you were dead!'

'It takes more than a war to kill me,' he said, his arms round her.

Her hand went to his face as if to make sure it was real. 'I can't believe it. What happened? Why did you never write?'

'Where I was, there was no post.'

'Oh, William, we must tell Polly. She's still here.'

Polly arrived like a tornado with the family and for ten minutes it was impossible to say anything coherent as they hugged him and flung questions at him. Nadya watched with sad eyes.

'You look tired, William,' she said. 'Tired and old.'

The comment reminded him of Sue-Lynn and he brushed it aside with a smile. 'Just hungry chiefly,' he said. 'It was always cold and I was always half-starved.'

'Elliott went into the navy when he recovered,' Polly said. 'Desk job, of course. But he's here. He's here in Sydney waiting to be discharged.'

'Then you'd better get him round tonight and we'll celebrate.'

The party was riotous. Willie played the piano – as badly as usual – and the neighbours all appeared to add their good wishes and congratulations. But behind all the noise and laughter, Willie couldn't help thinking of Sue-Lynn, rigid in what she considered her duty, her face bleak and expressionless, heading north towards Hankow to join the Communists. He knew he would never see her again and somehow it made the future a little greyer.

By the beginning of the following year, Willie was beginning to feel the urge to visit Shanghai again. It had been his background for so long he needed to find out what had happened. It was no longer the centre of his business because he had transferred the head office of the Sarth Line from one end of their main shipping route to the other and branched out anew from there, but he had spent so much of his life in Shanghai he couldn't ever ignore it.

Secretly, he also half-hoped he might pick up news of Zychov. It was something that he hardly dared admit to himself. He had never forgotten him and held him responsible for so much that had happened, the long months he had had to spend in virtual poverty in the mountains, Sue-Lynn's typhus, all the starvation and misery he'd seen, something which now perhaps took precedence over all the other hatreds.

Polly's husband, Elliott, anxious to see if anything could be salvaged from Wissermann's holdings in Shanghai, arranged to go with him.

Outwardly the place hadn't changed much, and, curiously, exactly the same sort of people as those who had run it before it fell to the Japanese were back in control, though now there were Chinese representatives on the Council. The same atmosphere prevailed, a slightly hysterical atmosphere of apprehension now, though, because those who had emerged from the Japanese prison camps to regain their places in Shanghai society had discovered something they had not been aware of while they had been incarcerated. A change of great significance had taken place, because Britain, America and France has signed a treaty abrogating their extra-territorial rights, so that the International Settlement, which had given protection to the foreign devils for so long, had come to an end at last. Chiang's troops were totally in control and the men who had trooped out of the concentration camps had found themselves aliens in what they had always thought of as their own city.

Only the belief that China would need Western expertise more than ever and would be unable to do without them sustained them in the loss, but the old happy-go-lucky community where sixty-three different races had managed to live and do business together, the wickedest, the most exciting city in the world, where two civilisations met and morality had been irrelevant, had gone for good.

Willie's first call was to see his son, Tom. Fan-Su had returned long since and he had just reappeared from the north, after spending most of the war as an interpreter and intelligence officer with the Communists. He looked older and a little tired, but he was lean and handsome, intelligent in a way that the more forthright Edward was not, a scholar, an academic with a job now as a lecturer at the university and hoping before long to be running his own department.

He talked of his time with the Communists with enthusiasm, certain that they, not Chiang, were the hope of China.

'Ever meet a Dr Sim?' Willie asked innocently. 'An American.'

'I met a few Americans, but not many,' Tom said. 'They weren't very popular, because the States supported Chiang. What was he like?'

'It wasn't a he,' Willie said. 'It was a she.'

Thomas looked at his father. 'No,' he said quietly. 'I never did. Did you know her?'

'I worked with her for a long time. She decided to join the Communists.'

'God help her,' Thomas said. 'She'll be frozen out in no time.' He paused. 'If nothing else happens first. They're a pretty unforgiving lot. They've learned to be.'

It left Willie with a chill round his heart, and he tried to change the subject. 'Did they convert you?' he asked.

Thomas smiled. 'No, Father, they didn't. Quite the contrary. They'll make something of China in the end but I shan't like the way they'll go about it. They're quite ruthless in their determination to make her a nation and, while you can't argue with that, a lot of people are going to be hurt in the shaping of it.'

'Wouldn't you be wiser to move? A man with your qualifications could get a job at any university in the world.'

'I signed a contract. I have three years to do. After that, we'll see.'

'You could join my business,' Willie pointed out. 'Edward's thinking of doing so. He'd be useful with his knowledge of ships and you'd be useful with your knowledge of the East. We could make Sarth's important between us.'

Da Braga was still in Shanghai, stiffening a little with age, his limp more pronounced, but still running Shanghai Traders with George Kee. Throughout the Japanese occupation, with Kee keeping well out of sight, he had handled the firm so that it had not suffered too much. Though British and American concerns had been taken over, business ventures run by neutrals had been left untouched and Da Braga had always claimed to be a Portuguese. Though the Japanese had seized the title deeds of British properties, Shanghai Traders had been left with enough to build a future and had already started making money again.

As he always did, Da Braga fished out a bottle and they sat at the desk with George Kee and Elliott, swopping stories.

Mason and Marchant's seemed to have vanished off the face of the earth and Emmeline had disappeared with them.

'Nobody has any further news of her after she went into a Japanese concentration camp in 1942,' Da Braga said. 'I heard Zychov was with Chiang's troops.'

'Still?'

'He turned up here when the war ended but he left again in a hurry.'

'You know he organised the gangs in 1927 to get rid of the Communists for Chiang. But you'll remember he welshed on the money he was to have paid them, and Yip's friends would like to meet him. I gather he's a senior officer now.'

'Yes,' Willie said. 'He is. And filling his bloody pockets as usual.'

Business, Da Braga said, was not easy. Shanghai was exhausted after four years of Japanese 'co-prosperity' and he was faintly depressed by its condition but not without hope. No useful constructive work had been done and many plants had been closed down for lack of raw material or fuel. With the exception of a few profiteers and speculators, the standard of living had declined and British investments had deteriorated, been liquidated, shut down or robbed.

'But there was no Japanese bombing,' he said cheerfully. 'And none from the Allies until the last months of the war. Even then only carefully selected targets. None of the major factories, wharfs warehouses or railway stations were badly damaged. We'll get going again.'

Business up-country was a different kettle of fish, however.

'Partisan warfare's raging again,' he pointed out. 'North of the Yangtze, Chiang's control is shaky and his hold on the railways is feeble. He's already retreating on his bases at the coast. This place's just waiting to see what's going to happen. The Communists aren't so inclined as he is to give assistance or provide passes to us.'

As the Communist hold increased, Chiang, it seemed, was beginning to realise he dared not push far into Manchuria because the soldiers he was facing now were equipped with Japanese weapons the Russians had made available after the surrender.

'And even better weapons of American manufacture which they captured from the Nationalists,' Da Braga pointed out. 'Everything favours them now. There's no longer any pretence of reforms. What's happening is a full-scale revolution. And it promises rewards for the poorest.' Da Braga gave a grim smile. 'Among them revenge.'

'And are the peasants responding?' Willie asked.

Da Braga smiled again. 'Of course. And now there are men who know how to use them. The Communist Chinese People's Liberation Army is already gaining new recruits, a lot of them Nationalist deserters. It numbers as many as the Nationalists now.' Da Braga took a sip of brandy and sloshed more into Willie's glass. 'What's more, they're all totally committed. A lot of Chiang's old comrades have begun to see the writing on the wall and they're finding pretexts to disappear.'

Leaving Da Braga closeted with Kee, Willie took his bag to the hotel where he was staying with Elliott Wissermann and set out to explore his old haunts. It had been a very confused period after the Japanese had left, with hundreds of former internees in the city suffering from beri-beri, malaria, dysentery and heart trouble cause by malnutrition. Thousands of desperate Chinese peasants, many dying of cholera but often armed with knives and hoes, had tried to get into the shelter of the city with the starving soldiers and bandits who had been living in the devastated countryside around. They had been prevented by Kuomintang troops wearing American uniforms and riding in American tanks.

The damage that had been done was very obvious, but most public services were functioning normally now and the trams were running again, their connector rods hissing and throwing off sparks as they always had from the overhead line. The smell of cooking fish and bean curds was strong along the waterfront where the city of sampans and ferry boats were moored, while the Bubbling Well Road seemed to have its normal complement of nightclubs, gambling dens, bar girls, gangsters, shoe shine boys, typists and beggars, and the neon signs were on again among the Coca-Cola adverts. There were now also huge screens set up portraying the heroic resistance to the enemy, and the industrious Chinese, always willing to make a living from other people's leavings, had long been at work among the wreckage of vehicles, ships and aeroplanes left by the Japanese, which they were busy reducing to their component parts for sale as spares.

The Nantao and Hongkew districts, devastated by the Japanese aircraft in 1937, had never been rebuilt and the shabby streets of Chapei had become a wilderness of deserted, decaying tenements, tin-roofed cotton mills, factories, godowns, depots, and lopsided hoardings carrying advertisements for articles that were no longer available. The open drains were blocked by refuse and beggars lived in shanties made from packing cases and tarred paper, while huge rats inhabited the streets, moving about without any sign of fear.

The most noticeable thing was the adulation of Chiang. The Kuomintang had managed to reoccupy the city and there were huge pictures of him everywhere, with the cinemas showing newsreels glorifying his deeds. Though the Americans were also featured, even sometimes the RAF, there was no mention, he noticed, of the Communists who had struggled so hard in the fight against the Japanese. When the war had ended, the Nationalist armies had closed round the city, determined to fill the vacuum left by the retreating enemy, aiming to gain control of their weapons before the Communists arrived. Chinese renegade troops and the warlord militias who had sided with the Japanese had switched sides yet again and their aim had been to keep the foreign businessmen out of the city. None of the airborne food supplies that had been dropped by the Americans had gone to the Communists, and those of them who had continued to oppose the Japanese to the very end among the ruined warehouses of Pootung had been wiped out like the Japanese they had been fighting. The Communists' role in the victory had been written out of the script.

Faintly saddened and depressed, Willie went to look at his old home, but it was empty, not damaged but stinking of human excrement and devoid of furniture, all of which, he learned, had been taken by the Japanese. The city that had once meant so much to him was now a sad place struggling to regain its position, and the only consolation came when he got down to business with Da Braga and George Kee and found that his assets hadn't diminished a great deal. Under the circumstances, it seemed not only safer but a fair reward to the other two to withdraw and leave everything to them, and an arrangement was drawn up to everybody's satisfaction.

Elliott was under no delusions about his position and was planning by this time to forget the East and take Polly back to the States to start up afresh in California. 'America gave too much support to Chiang,' he said. 'If the Commies gain control, we can expect short shrift.'

'The British here,' Willie pointed out dryly, 'take the opposite view and feel they're under no immediate threat. As far as I can make out, they're not even considering the possibility of a Nationalist defeat.'

'The British are going to have a big surprise,' Da Braga smiled.

'All the same,' Kee said, 'China will *have* to do business with Europe somehow. She can't live without the West and it's unthinkable that Europe will let her shut them out.'

Willie wasn't so sure.

As 1949 arrived, Willie was again in Shanghai cleaning up the last of his affairs. The winter had been cold, with the temperatures below freezing, but there seemed to be a tentative thaw in attitudes towards the Communists. Realising how shaky Chiang's hold was becoming, people were trying to do business with them.

Da Braga shrugged it off. 'A waste of time,' he said. 'The Communists just aren't interested, and the Nationalists are watching for any approaches to them.'

The Royal Navy was very much in evidence again with several of its ships, keeping a watchful eye on things now that the Communists were poised in force on the banks of the Yangtze. Nobody was really worried, however, because Mao Tse-Tung's was a land army and shipping remained under the control of Chiang, so that the Shanghai taipans continued to feel their future would be secure.

Willie remained unconvinced. 'If I were you,' he suggested to George Kee, 'I'd get out. There's a place for you in Australia if you want it.'

Kee smiled. 'I'll stay here,' he decided. 'I'm not afraid and, like them, I'm Chinese and quite prepared to work with them in any way they wish.'

Despite the general belief that the Communists would never gain control, it seemed they intended to have a good try, and it was felt that if they attacked it would be across the river between Nanking and Shanghai. Willie, however, assumed that the Nationalists, as usual, were being told what they wanted to hear.

'Inland Chinese aren't sailors,' he was told at the Club.

'The Yangtze runs through the whole of China,' he said. 'There must be a few of them who know what they're about.'

His opinion was met with smiles. 'The river's a mile wide south of Nanking where they're concentrating. It'll need more than a few inland sailors to get across there, and soldiers don't know the local currents and shoals.'

In the belief that soldiers could be trained and that there were peasants and fishermen who knew the river, he couldn't resist taking a ferry upstream to have a look. The northern bank of the river was peopled by men and women who, to the peasants of the far north, lived in what was a life of luxury because there were fish and every inch of the marshy land along the banks was cultivated.

The captain of the new *Fan Ling II* had noticed other things, too. 'There are bamboo groves behind the swamps,' he said. 'And there are trees shielding the villages. Men can hide there.'

It wasn't hard to see that from every creek, every hidden inlet along the hundreds of miles of river a motley flotilla of river boats was moving south. They ranged from junks and sampans to narrow fishing boats and even rafts, and along the bank there was intense activity as everything that had been damaged by the retreating Nationalists was hurriedly repaired. Soldiers were even being given swimming lessons.

It was quite clear something was about to happen because even from the deck of the *Fan Ling* it was possible to see with the aid of binoculars that there were dozens of boats hidden among the reeds and in the creeks. Stripped to the waist, soldiers were breaking down the dams that contained them and digging channels to connect them to the river. Behind them, women carried away the soil in wicker baskets, and the villagers were making strange-shaped waterwheels.

'Paddle wheels actually,' the steamer captain said. 'They attach them to sampans and then even soldiers can make them go forward.'

At the other side of the river the Nationalist armies waited, with their trenches, artillery emplacements, blockhouses and machine-gun positions. Nationalist gunboats were patrolling the river and, as Willie knew, their air force could be over the area in minutes.

Three weeks later he had occasion to go upriver again. One of his ships, the *Gemelta*, was lying off the bund at Shanghai, waiting for a cargo of rice that had somehow got stuck just beyond Sin Kiang and he had to get it free. This time he noticed that the Communist guns were clearly visible and that triumphal arches had been built, all with red pennants fluttering from them. Even from the river he could see huge portraits of Mao Tse-Tung surrounded by more red banners, and could hear martial music from on shore.

He freed the rice and saw it on its way and, convinced by this time that the Communists were finally about to get rid of Chiang's corrupt regime for ever, he returned to Shanghai, determined to persuade Da Braga and Kee to move. Neither would agree.

'My children grew up here,' Kee pointed out. 'They'd be alien anywhere else.'

'Better alien than dead,' Willie said. 'The Communists are about ready to move. It'll be too late when they arrive.'

Returning from the *Gemelta* by launch, he passed the naval moorings near Holt's Wharf. One of the Royal Navy's frigates, her code number, F116, painted on her side in large letters, was just preparing to leave for a tour of duty upstream. The weather was mild, almost like an English summer day as the ship cast off her moorings. Veils of mist hung over the surface of the water, the frigate's bows pushing them aside as she began to move.

For a while Willie watched as the ship slipped slowly past, then he gestured to the coxswain and the launch headed for the bund and Da Braga's office.

'*Amethyst*'s just left,' he said.

'She'll be all right,' Da Braga decided.

'They've cut it bloody fine all the same, Luis. The Communists have made it clear they're intending to cross in a full-scale offensive at any time. I reckon she's got only a few hours to get past before they start.'

During the afternoon one of the clerks bringing in coffee to them informed them that news had arrived that the Communists were about to start crossing the river.

Willie looked up quickly. 'Where's the ship?'

'*Amethyst*, sir? She's anchored at Kiang Yin.'

Da Braga gestured. 'The Chinese navy doesn't allow passage by night. There are always warships at Kiang Yin these days, Chinese as well as British.'

At lunchtime the following day, Willie headed for the Club for a drink. The first words he heard were 'Christ, first the bloody Japs, now the Chinks!'

'What's happened?' he asked.

The bastards have shelled the *Amethyst*. Near Low Island. There've been casualties.'

Willie swallowed his drink quickly, cancelled his lunch, and headed for the *News* office. Details of the incident had already begun to arrive.

'It was an unprovoked attack,' he was told. '*Amethyst* was about her business.'

'A bit ill-conceived at the moment,' Willie said dryly. 'Why wasn't she sent a week earlier?'

The newspaperman had heard that the Communists had started firing because the warship's wash had smashed up their newly-built rafts. 'More than likely they assumed that any ship moving along the river just now must be Nationalist,' he said.

Willie's contacts told him a different story: The Nationalist naval units had been expected to defect.

'Which means,' Willie said, 'that if the Communists thought the *Amethyst* was a Nationalist ship they'd assume she was doing a classic Chiang double-cross. No wonder they fired on her.'

It didn't take long to learn that nobody had thought it necessary to notify the Communists of the ship's movements. By this time the newspaper office was noisy with telephones and shouts for messengers, and by midnight it was clear the incident had been deliberate, but that the British government had done nothing in the way of a protest beyond a request for a cease fire.

'Request a cease fire?' Willie said to Kee. 'Is that all? "Stop your war of liberation, please, old chap, so the bloody navy can move." George, I have a suspicion things are never going to be quite the same again out here. More than ever, I think you should leave.'

By the following morning they learned the truth. The *Amethyst* had been hit several times, her captain mortally wounded and two gun turrets silenced. Eight men had been killed outright and thirty wounded and, with her steering disabled, making it impossible to manoeuvre, the ship was now aground. Attempts by the cruiser *London* to reach her had been thwarted. With fifteen men killed and twenty wounded, the *London* had had to turn back and the *Amethyst* was now virtually helpless. With wounded still on board and seventeen bodies waiting to be buried, the Communists were expected to complete their crossing of the river at any moment.

Thomas seemed to know more about the incident than anyone. 'There are sixty-six ratings and Chinese employees on Rose Island,' he informed Willie. 'They had to swim and they're barefoot or in underclothing. They're at a farm and they're being looked after, but there are still about seventy-six unwounded still on board. They've lost their doctor, but the RAF's managed to get one to them, and they're trying to get a new skipper there, though so far he's not been able to make contact. They expect the wounded to be put on a train to Shanghai very soon.'

Willie didn't ask where he'd got his information, knowing it must have come from some of his old Communist friends waiting in Shanghai for the take-over.

'Didn't anyone think it necessary to inform the Communists she was about to pass through their line of fire?' he snorted.

The omission was significant and it seemed that old habits died hard. 'I don't think we've started to understand the quality of this new lot,' he said. 'It makes you wonder, in fact, if we're attuned to the twentieth century.'

t w o

The first wounded from the *Amethyst* arrived the following day, dirty, ragged, unshaven and shocked, many of them barefooted and all looking thoroughly dejected.

What dismayed the British in Shanghai about the affair was the timid reaction of the government in London. But, as Da Braga said to Willie, 'It looks as if Mao means business and, with what's at stake here, nobody feels it's a good idea to quarrel with the next government of China.'

Communist newspapers in the city crowed their delight at what they termed a victory and all the British authorities could say in reply was 'We have the situation under control.' The non-Communist newspapers were deliberately silent and unaccusing.

Chiang's reaction was predictably excuses and the declaration of martial law in the city, so that trigger-happy Nationalist soldiers no longer waved to passing European cars. They stopped them and insisted on examining them.

They were just trying to digest this when George Kee appeared in the office with the newspapers and a letter he had received.

'They've decreed that all firms and individuals with holdings in gold, silver and US dollars have to hand them over at once,' he roared.

Willie's reaction was one of relief that he had long since transferred most of his holdings. Then he saw that Kee was still spluttering with rage.

'What have you got, George?' he asked.

'A little,' Kee growled. 'And I'm keeping it. It's Chiang's advisers who are behind it. It's obvious what's happening. He's pocketing it to transfer overseas against the time when he has to bolt.'

The consternation at the Club was noisy. For the first time the Europeans were really beginning to understand that they were no longer lording it over a British possession but were living in a country ruled by a government indifferent to their wishes.

The edict was being applied by one of Chiang's sons in person with a severity that horrified. George Kee brought in a list of Chinese financiers and merchants who had been put to death for trying to dodge the law.

'They were friends of mine,' he said, shocked. 'And there are dozens of others I know who see the only alternative is to give up their life savings.'

'For worthless banknotes,' Willie growled.

Chiang was clearly growing nervous and soon afterwards, in a panic move to protect the crumbling Nationalist façade, suspected Communists were dragged out and shot, and photographs of the executions filled the newspapers. Da Braga was beginning to look nervous, but when Willie once again suggested that he and Kee should take advantage of the Sarth Shipping Line and transfer their homes lock stock and barrel to Australia, their reply remained as before. It appeared to be madness, but it didn't seem so strange when the evacuation of Europeans was advised by the European authorities and there was an almost total lack of response.

'China's home,' Da Braga said.

Remembering the chaos in Singapore and determined to do anything he could to start things moving, Willie offered berths at half-price on Sarth ships to anyone who wanted them. Only a few people took them and when the time came to sail half of those backed down. He could only put it down to the fact that the recent Communist take-overs of Peking, Nanking and Tientsin had been accomplished without blood-shed. He knew how people were thinking. Why, they were saying to themselves, should they help to destroy Shanghai, the greatest prize of all, when they knew perfectly well that the Nationalists would never fight for the place?

A few people left. The Europeans were tolerantly treated, but rich Chinese trying to smuggle out valuables had their tickets torn up by Nationalist officers and their passages cancelled. A few British businessmen, known to be involved on behalf of their governments or firms with attempting to contact the Communists, found it expedient to leave. Journalists believed to be antagonistic to what they considered a corrupt regime were arrested and imprisoned without trial and, though they were later released, they emerged shaken by the experience and far from unwilling to go. Even shipping was in a straitjacket with Chiang obviously about to disappear from the political scene, his navy – one or two old destroyers, a few gunboats and launches – had retreated downstream, determined to prevent supplies reaching the Communist forces. The blockade had been in force for some time at Tientsin and Amoy and other ports already controlled by the Communists, but Willie's ships had continued to slip through, occasionally aided and abetted by officers of the Royal Navy who placed their ships between the Kuomintang ships and the merchant vessels endeavouring to do business with beleaguered British businessmen.

There was always a sharp watch kept along the Shanghai wharves, but it still wasn't hard to use the old trick that had so often bamboozled the Customs officials in the past. Changing places and berths at the Upper Section Wharves, small ships could still appear to change their identity and, with a little money in the right pockets, *Gemelta* changed hers with that of an Indian-registered ship and was able to make her way downriver.

As she left, her place was taken two days later by the *Lady Roberts*, due to pick up a cargo that Willie knew now would never appear. As she moved to her berth, he went on board and was surprised to find John Yeh in command. Yeh had run the ship for years after the Vladivostok adventure, but the *Lady Roberts* was old and he had graduated after the war to a newer ship.

'I thought you might be glad of someone who knew his way around,' he said, his face as expressionless as always. 'Nationalist warships are at the entrance to the river and turning ships back. *Gemelta* only just got through. The blockade's going to make it difficult to leave, but I've been in and out of this river all my life – even as a smuggler in the old days. I know every trick of the tide. There's just one snag. We need coal.'

A visit to the Kuomintang headquarters confirmed Yeh's fears. No ship was to be allowed to depart from the Yangtze.

'The British Navy has been involved in too many incidents,' the Nationalist officer in command informed

Willie. 'We have therefore had no option, since British warships are waiting outside the Yangtze to aid British merchantmen, but to make sure they stay on this side of the rivermouth. No ship will leave without permission.'

'And how do I get this permission?' Willie asked.

The Nationalist officer smiled. 'It will be very difficult,' he admitted.

It didn't take long to find out that what he'd said was correct, and within days the blockade began to pose a problem. The city had always depended on its maritime trade, but now it was impossible to bring in the raw materials it needed for its factories – coal, oil, spare parts for machinery – just as it was impossible to take out finished products. The *Lady Roberts* had brought in a varied cargo of machinery and was due to take away every imaginable thing that was available, from silk to ham, and vegetables to processed duck. With the blockade, the goods were already starting to rot in the warehouses.

Still London made no protest over the attack on the *Amethyst* and, as the Communists drew nearer the city and people began to realise there might be danger after all, the demands for berths at Sarth's, Butterfield and Swire's and Glen Lines suddenly increased, and Da Braga, who had never considered himself a brave man, finally decided to sell out to George Kee.

'Goa,' he said, slapping the brandy bottle on the desk. 'Where I came from. My children are grown and there's only my wife and me now.'

'Why not Australia, Luis?' Willie tried. 'You're far from being a poor man and there's more for you in Australia than in India since independence. Besides, old son – ' he grinned ' – we've known each other a long time now and it wouldn't be the same without you around.'

Da Braga's eyes filled with tears. 'I'm a sentimental man,' he admitted. 'I didn't wish to be in the way but I, too, would like to go on meeting you. We've had many a drink to celebrate success or to console us in disaster and I would like it to continue. I'll be ready when you call me.'

In May, with nothing further heard of the *Amethyst*, Nationalist troops, demoralised by defeat, began to pour into the city, carrying pots, pans, vegetables, even firewood, filling the cinemas and tying up the streetcars for hours as they demanded free rides. Since the war they had suffered from a dreadful reputation, because most of them now were simple young peasants plucked unwillingly from their villages to fill the gaps in Chiang's armies and abominably treated, with wretched pay and worse rations, and they had always stolen, begged and looted to stay alive. Now they saw no difference between Shanghai and a village in the country, and when refused anything, didn't hesitate to use their weapons.

Others, many in rags, some on crutches, their arms in slings, their heads bandaged, fought their way on to trains leaving the city and crowded the jetties for southbound ships. By a strange turn of events, the European businessmen began to pray for the arrival of the Communist Liberation Army with its well-known discipline.

Shanghai was already beginning to look like a battle-ground, with showcases and shop windows boarded up against looters, the latest Paris creations seen only behind closed doors. Sandbags were going up and ditches were being dug in parks and private gardens and, while the Nationalist communiqué's gave stirring stories of victory after victory, the only result that could be seen was an increased anxiety among the Nationalist soldiers. Even the night life had come to a halt as ballrooms and nightclubs were commandeered as barracks. When the hostesses complained, half a dozen of them were whisked away for an indefinite stay in jail and the protests died at once.

With the arrival of the retreating Nationalists, it was obvious that the battle for Shanghai could not now be far off. Still nothing had been heard of the *Amethyst*, and Willie learned that the Communists, eager to claim a propaganda victory, were refusing to grant her safe passage unless the British admitted responsibility for the incident.

Still haunting the Nationalist commander's headquarters for permission for the *Lady Roberts* to leave, he learned from George Kee that the post office was still accepting parcels and letters but that they were being held up by the blockade. Making enquiries, he found that this was true. Occasionally a ship was given permission to leave with mail, but at the moment there was nothing suitable in the river, while mountains of mailbags waited to be removed. Knowing he hadn't seen a mail steamer in the river for some time, he made a suggestion.

'Suppose I can get permission for my ship to leave,' he said, 'would you allow me to take the mail out for you?'

'Of course,' the Chinese official told him. 'We're putting it on any ship that's allowed to go.'

'Where would I get permission?'

'From the Kuomintang?'

Willie had already tried that and been refused, but he accepted that the situation required some guile.

'Would the word of the Generalissimo himself be good enough?' he asked.

Worried by the imminent fall of Shanghai, Chiang had moved the seat of his government to Canton, but it was still possible to reach the southern capital by a roundabout route. The railway went to Nanking and Wuhu and permission to travel by rail through the interior was still possible. After Wuhu, it would mean going by river to Hankow, from where you could take another train to Canton.

For safety, Willie informed Da Braga and George Kee what he was about to do and was on the point of leaving when Edward arrived. He was in civilian clothes but as buoyant as ever.

'Fancy a rear-admiral on the staff of Sarth's, Father?' he asked.

'Who?'

'Me. I've just had a step up in rank, but I'm due to retire soon and at the moment I'm working out my time at the Admiralty. Because nobody else could be spared and they need someone here with a bit of punch, they flew me in. I'm getting married.'

Willie stared at his son. 'Left it a bit late, haven't you?' he said.

Edward smiled, that superior smile all naval officers seemed to acquire. 'Oh, there's life in the old dog yet. You'll approve. Good family. Pretty face. Bags of brains. Wren officer. She's my secretary at the Admiralty. Name of Wyatt. Philippa Wyatt. Knows of you, because she's some sort of relation to that chap who did business with you in London. Brassard, wasn't it? That's how we sort of got together.'

Willie studied his son. Edward was good-looking, tall and strong with greying hair. 'Pity you didn't get on with it earlier,' he said.

Edward shrugged. He admired his father and was quite willing to accept criticism from him. 'The war got in the way a bit,' he admitted. 'I'm thinking of bringing her out here to meet the family. The RAF would fly her out.'

'I don't recommend it,' Willie said grimly. 'I don't recommend bringing anybody out here just now. Things are a bit too dicey. Anyway, why are you in mufti? I'd have enjoyed swanking round the place – such as it is now – with an admiral in uniform.'

Edward smiled again. 'Well,' he admitted, 'things are a bit difficult, as you've just said. As you probably know, the Navy's moved down to Woosung for safety, but they need someone senior here to keep an eye on things. Uniforms are out, though, and my passport – specially prepared – indicates that I'm part of the Consulate staff. Guessing you'd know more about what's going on than anybody, I thought I'd call and see you before I report.'

Willie rounded on him angrily. 'What are those bloody fools in London up to?' he demanded. 'Aren't they aware that around ninety men are stuck up the river in the *Amethyst*? Why the hell don't they apologise and get them out?'

'It wasn't the Navy's fault, Father,' Edward snapped back with all the self-righteousness of a senior naval officer whose service is demeaned.

'I didn't mean the Navy, dammit! I mean the bloody politicians. I suppose they're sitting on their backsides in the House of Commons, enjoying the sound of their own voices and totally indifferent to the fact that British subjects are prisoners.'

Edward smiled. 'Oh, *that* lot,' he said. 'We needn't expect anything from *them*. If *Amethyst*'s coming out, she'll have to do it on her own. On the other hand, from what I can see, the whole bloody business has become stalemated. Where *is Amethyst*? I expect you know.'

'She moved downriver but she's still held. Chap called Kerans, one of your people – commander, I think – has taken over up there, but the Communists won't be backing down. They acknowledge no authority but their own. They aren't Chiang, Eddie, kow-towing to foreign powers. They even refuse to speak anything but Chinese, which makes it a bit difficult for some of the British because, of course, half the silly buggers out here have never learned any more Chinese than they need to ask for a drink. There's nothing you can do, old son. Gunboat diplomacy's come to an end.'

Edward digested the news with a wry expression. 'Perhaps I'd better simply go and get drunk at Tom's then.'

'I think it's a good idea. I'd join you, in fact, except that I'm busy just now.'

Edward grinned. 'I thought you looked as though you were up to something.'

The journey south was wearying and it occurred to Willie that once upon a time he would have taken it in his stride. I'm growing old, he decided. Too old for this lark, anyway. It's time I retired and let other people run the show.

The train to Wuhu was crowded, the compartments stuffed with luggage. The steamer up the Yangtze was no better, and the train from Hankow to Canton was worst of all. Dozens of people were fleeing south, either because they had worked in some small way for Chiang and feared reprisals when the Communists arrived, or because they had decided it would be better to set up a new life in the British colony of Hong Kong. It was impossible to sleep, and by the time Willie arrived in Canton he was feeling twice his age.

Chiang's personal headquarters were in a large house outside the city. Taking a cab there, Willie spent half an hour arguing with the guard commander at the gate before a more senior officer was called and he was allowed into an anteroom to plead his case.

'The Generalissimo won't see you,' he was told. 'He's a busy man.'

'I thought the Generalissimo liked to remember old comrades of the fighting.'

'The Generalissimo never forgets his old friends.'

'Then tell him I'm one. Tell him I was with him in Chungking and that I spent a year behind the Japanese lines on his behalf.'

It wasn't entirely true because Mallinson's project had been less for Chiang than against him, but that had been the excuse given at the time.

The officer agreed to put Willie's case and after another half-hour's wait, he reappeared and beckoned Willie to follow him. Chiang looked older, but as small, neat and slim as ever in his immaculate uniform, his pate shaved now to hide the grey hairs. As Willie appeared, he nodded unsmilingly and a tray was offered containing a cup of coffee.

'What is your request?' one of the aides asked in English.

Willie answered in Chinese so that Chiang could understand. 'I wish to move my ship, the *Lady Roberts*, from Shanghai to Australia,' he pointed out.

'There is a blockade in force.'

'Ships are being allowed to leave provided they're carrying mail. At the moment, there are mountains of it waiting to go but no ship. Mine is available. Besides, the Generalissimo owes me a favour.'

Several sets of eyes switched to Chiang, who put down his cup before speaking.

'What is this favour I owe?' he asked.

'Twenty-two years ago I loaned you my launch,' Willie said. 'Your own wouldn't work and I was hesitant to lend you mine until you told me it would be paid for. Perhaps the Generalissimo doesn't remember, but I do. It was never paid for and when I protested I found myself looking down the muzzle of a rifle held by one of the Generalissimo's sailors.'

Chiang stared at Willie impassively and totally without expression for a long time. Come on, you bugger, Willie was muttering under his breath. Say something for a change.

Eventually Chiang spoke to the English-speaking aide, then turned abruptly and left the room. Willie stared after him, his heart sinking, but the aide stepped forward.

'The Generalissimo remembers the incident,' he said. 'He very much regrets that you were never paid for your trouble and he asks if you will feel recompensed if he gives you a permit for your ship to leave. It will last for two months, which should be long enough. After that it will have to be renewed.'

Willie could have kissed him and very nearly did.

The journey north was easier because few people seemed eager to go to what was rapidly becoming Communist China. It was tiring, nevertheless, but Willie was buoyed up now by the sheet of paper in his pocket.

He arrived in Shanghai just as the Communists started their move towards the city. He had telegraphed ahead and Thomas met him at the station with his car.

'They're on their way, Father,' he announced. 'They've not only crossed at Kiang Yin, they've also crossed near Nanking, and I don't think Chiang's going to stop them. They learned too much from the Japanese during the war. They'll decide to be here by a certain date and you can bet your last Hong Kong dollar they'll make it.'

'Thanks for the tip, son.'

'There's just one other thing, Father. It seems the *Amethyst*'s now behind the Communist lines.'

The first clap of gunfire came the day the Country Club opened its grass courts for the season and served strawberries and cream for dinner. The occasion was well attended, everybody formally dressed for the affair, so that Willie was forcibly reminded of the dancing at the Raffles Hotel during the last days of Singapore.

There wasn't a single British warship at Shanghai now, and by this time the oil depots six miles away were ablaze. Everybody knew that if Mao gained control of Pootung his guns could fire across the river against the magnificent blocks of the bund, and a few more of those still left in the city made arrangements to be evacuated by air.

When the Nationalists mounted a colossal victory parade, Willie hooted with laughter. 'Pure propaganda,' he said. 'The buggers are preparing for the end.'

As the Communists pounded away at the suburbs, the streets were decked with flags and military bands blared out. A traditional dragon writhed through the streets and children sang patriotic songs. The battle lasted for two days, but the Europeans were affected by little more than stray bullets, and were able to watch a lot of the fighting from their office windows high in the blocks on the bund. Through the whole period Willie slept in Kee's office at Shanghai Traders. Fires were still burning furiously at Woosung and the approaches to the docks looked like a Chinese Dunkirk with a two-mile-long column of tanks, artillery, ammunition wagons and trucks, all abandoned and set on fire.

Then he learned that the Mayor, the Chief of Police and the garrison commander had disappeared, but not before helping themselves to what remained of the municipal funds, and, at the end of four days of skirmishing and sporadic firing, it was all over.

'The whole bloody thing was prearranged,' Willie growled at Kee. 'They, put up just enough resistance to let them get clear. They haven't lost the art of fighting their battles with silver bullets.'

Now the Nationalists had gone, the streets began to fill with different soldiers and different trucks. The newcomers, often tall raw-boned men from the north with none of the old signs of deference to the Europeans, were armed with modern weapons and handled their tommy guns with confidence. Anti-Communist graffiti and posters were hastily scraped off shop windows and walls and the bunting and banners and photographs of Chiang which had been put up under orders a few days before were hurriedly removed. Almost immediately, the city returned to normality and coolies began to pull down the pill box they had erected near the Shanghai Traders' office and repair the streets and gardens. Within twenty-four hours the first vandals had been arrested, the rickshaw coolies had become suddenly strangely polite to each other, the police had become courteous, and it had become impossible to offer either a bribe or a tip. European shops, restaurants, offices and hotels remained untouched, however, and it was only too easy to feel nothing had changed. Even the Balalaika was open again, still frequented by Europeans, and when the police, now under Communist control, came to see Willie, informing him that they had received information that he had been in contact with Chiang K'Ai-Shek, it dawned on him that Zychov was back, too. He must have seen Willie at Chiang's headquarters and, never forgetting the old feud, had taken the precaution of silencing his enemy ahead by informing the Communists of his visit.

Willie managed to convince the police officer that the visit had been for nothing more than business and because with China in its present state of chaos, there had been no one else to approach until the Communists could take over. He made no mention of the permission he had received to take away his ship.

The policeman wasn't entirely reassured but he had had dealings with Willie in the past and knew him well, so that he did no more than give him a warning. But the incident led Willie to make enquiries and Kee soon found out that the re-emergence of the Balalaika was due entirely to Zychov, who was back in charge, though these days, Kee pointed out, he was always surrounded by bodyguards. Willie could only admire the man's nerve.

'He's taking a chance,' he said. 'Yip's friends haven't forgotten him, I bet.'

'I heard he intended to leave with the Nationalists,' Kee explained. 'But he was occupied with getting his personal possessions to the coast and the Nationalists were too concerned with their own skins and he left it too late.'

Zychov's chances of leaving were now nil, so he was doing his best to make what he could of the new regime, confident that as a Russian – and the Russians had always backed the Chinese Communists – he was safe. For a long time that night Willie considered making arrangements to pay a visit to an old if not revered acquaintance of his in Chapei, a colleague of the late lamented Yip Hsao-Li. But in the end he couldn't bring himself to embark on the sort of treachery he knew Zychov would have countenanced without turning a hair and he let the matter slide.

It was clear the long and painful civil war that had torn China apart for generations was coming to an end at last, but no move to recognise the new regime was made in London. As the Communist newspapers renewed their crowing against the 'capitalist and imperialist brigands', it became clear that the *Amethyst*, still immured upriver, was merely a pawn in the struggle to retain British interests in China. She had dropped entirely out of the headlines by this time and the plight of the naval men marooned at Kiang Yin was forgotten; and, as the press became occupied with the problem of not offending the new regime, Willie began to lose patience. The Europeans didn't give a damn about the *Amethyst*, he realised, so long as they were allowed to continue to make money. The only hope for the ship now was that something would come out of the talks that had been started upriver by her new commanding officer and the local Communist leader. The crux of them, it appeared, was that the Navy had to admit to being guilty of infringing Chinese sovereignty, accept the blame for the incident and guarantee compensation for damage and loss of life. Since the Navy showed no sign of doing so, it looked like being a long siege.

three

There had been no chance of the *Lady Roberts* leaving until the battle for Shanghai was over and, with the Communists suspicious of everyone, it seemed a good idea to wait a few days more until they had settled in.

Their victory parade used the same trucks and buses which not long before had trundled Nationalist supporters through the streets. The same people shouted slogans, waved flags, raised clenched fists, all trying to show how Communist they had always been. Everybody who had admired Chiang for years was now busy admiring Mao Tse-Tung.

The transfer of power had taken place without trouble. Though there were long delays, it was possible to send cables and make telephone calls, and food was beginning to come into the city again. Executions still took place on the racecourse, but this time the victims were Nationalist sympathisers who had worked against the Communists and foreigners weren't invited to watch. The obligatory photographs of Mao appeared, and for a moment the Europeans were left in peace, though European apartment blocks had been taken over as barracks for Mao's young peasant soldiers who spent their time riding up and down in the lifts and using the lavatory bowls to wash their rice.

Because of the absence of hostility, the Europeans were quickly recovering their former self-assurance and optimism and, because there had been no expulsions, and bribes were no longer *de rigueur* and 'squeeze' had disappeared, they were even beginning to believe things might be better in the end. Though they considered it a little cynical to do business with the people who had shot up British naval vessels, the tremendous amount of capital involved somehow made it possible.

'After all,' Willie was told, 'if they don't do business with us, they'll do it with the Russians.'

The new regime had certainly made a difference. The black market had disappeared abruptly after a few operators had been taken away. Unfortunately, servants had also disappeared. The Communists had issued no orders; they had simply made it difficult for anyone to be employed by foreigners, and slowly, inexorably, Shanghai began to come to a stop. The night life had terminated abruptly under the rigid Communist idea of morality, and their commissars, without the experience to administer a vast city, were careful to do nothing without asking for a decision from higher authority.

Gradually Willie began to notice the difference. New taxes were imposed on the houses of foreigners and the tax inspectors thought nothing of appearing during private parties to make checks and slap on extra tolls on the spot. The servants at the Club became hostile and, well indoctrinated by the Communists, began to hint that the imperialist aggressors should hand over the furniture and effects, while people found their godowns filled with refugees or even with their employees' wives and children. Then, in retaliation for the American government freezing all Chinese accounts, the Communists retaliated by taking over all American businesses, plus a few others for good measure, and once again it seemed imperative to persuade George Kee to leave.

His mind full of his problems, all working at once and all interrelated, Willie decided to see Kee the following day, but, even as he woke, the telephone went. It was Kee's wife, and she was in tears.

'They've got George,' she wailed.

'Who have?'

'The Communists.'

'Hold tight. I'll see to it at once. It can't be important.'

But it was, and his attempt to bring about Kee's freedom was met with a blank stare from the officer in charge of the jail.

'That will not be possible,' he insisted. 'He is to be accused of co-operating with the Kuomintang bandits.'

'Rubbish,' Willie snorted. 'George Kee's a loyal Chinese who's never done anything for Chiang. He's also a good businessman of the sort your new China's going to need. You'd be silly to despatch George Kee and you might even find yourself in trouble.'

The angle of approach seemed to strike the right note and the Chinese officer agreed to consider Kee's case carefully.

'You must return in a week's time,' he said. 'In the meantime, he must remain in prison.'

'Can I see him?'

'Of course. We are not barbarians.'

Kee looked drawn and worried. Standing up as Willie entered his cell, he gave a wry smile. 'It seems you were probably right,' he observed.

'What's happened to Shanghai Traders, George?'

'It's been taken over.'

736

'Everything?'

'Everything. God knows, I've never been pro-Chiang and I have certainly believed in China for the Chinese, but they claim I've forfeited the right to trade.'

'Can the decision be changed?'

Kee gave a sad smile. 'It might. But will it ever be really possible after this? It'll happen again – and again – until everything comes to a stop.'

Willie slapped his shoulder. 'Keep your chin up, George,' he said. 'I'll sort it out. I'll get you out of here. I've made 'em think a bit already.' He paused. 'If I do, will you come with us?'

Kee smiled. 'Perhaps I should have taken your advice when it was first offered.'

'Right, then. I'll get your family aboard the *Lady Roberts* with as many of your possessions as possible. Just keep smiling –'

As he left the jail, Willie was frowning and preoccupied. Kee's imprisonment had given him a new problem. Da Braga was already aboard the *Lady Roberts*. Which left only his own son, Tom.

Not for a minute could he believe that Tom would be immune to Communist attacks. No matter what he'd done for them during the war, no matter how he had sympathised with them, he couldn't imagine them allowing him to remain, because their whole concept of China for the Chinese was obviously that foreigners should hold no positions of trust or importance. It might take time because the Communists, with their curiously moral codes, would not throw him out but would simply make it so difficult he would choose to go of his own accord. And go he would. In time. As part of their great scheme to tear out, root and branch, all foreign influence

JOHN HARRIS

or interference with their affairs. Eventually, they would
doubtless realise they needed foreigners – at least in small
numbers – and foreign know-how, but for the moment,
their idea was to show the world that, contrary to the
beliefs held for a hundred years, China knew how to
handle her own business.

Somehow, however, he felt his son would not be easy
to persuade. He had many friends among the Chinese
because he had been among the first to sympathise with
them in their struggle, and he would find it hard to accept
that they would turn against him. Age and experience told
Willie otherwise and he knew he must try.

He had permission to move his ship and Kee and Da
Braga had agreed to go. With Tom and his family aboard,
too, it would have cleared his decks for a new start in
Australia for them all.

He had just decided to see his son the following day
when the telephone rang. It was Fan-Su begging him to
come at once because Tom wished to see him.

'Sweet Suffering J,' he thought. 'What now?'

He could tell from Fan-Su's voice that she was upset and
he set off at once. He found her in tears and Tom, his face
sombre, packing a small bag with clothing.

'What the hell are you up to?' Willie demanded.

'I'm going up to Chinkiang, Father.'

'Why?'

'Because I've been asked. Everybody knows I was with
the Communist army during the war and it's been
suggested by the Navy that I might be able to help.'

'Will you?'

Tom shrugged. 'Discussions are still going on up there.
They've been going on for weeks, as you know, but things

738

are desperate now. The ship's short of vegetables, they no longer have sufficient fuel to run the ventilation, it's growing hot, and one or two of the men are beginning to fall ill. I might be able to do something.'

Willie wasn't taken in by his son's casual tones. He knew him too well. Tom wasn't like Edward, who was extrovert, outgoing and enjoying the flair the Navy gave him. Tom had been quiet, introvert, studious and concerned.

'Where do I come into it?' he asked. 'I'm sure I do or you wouldn't have asked me to see you.'

'No. That's correct.' Thomas lowered his voice. 'I think Father, that we have to accept that the Communists are determined that the Chinese are going to run China and that they'll stop at nothing to make sure they do. But they'll probably listen to me because I fought with them and know them. On the other hand, I know what you're going to say, that they'll never forget I'm a foreign devil – like you, a Chinese White.' He smiled. 'That's true, of course. They might well prove difficult.'

'So?'

'So I want you to look after Fan-Su and the boys. You did once before. I'd like you to do it again.'

'Of course I will. When do you leave?'

'At once. By train. After that, I don't know.'

It seemed a good idea to Willie to get Fan-Su and her family with the others aboard the *Lady Roberts* and he drove them to the docks, where he hired a tug to take them and everything they possessed which could be moved out to the ship. When he told Yeh that the sailing orders were cancelled for the time being, Yeh shrugged, his face as expressionless as ever.

'You're taking a chance,' was all he said. 'We should leave while we can. There's a typhoon moving this way from the Philippines.'

'I know, John,' Willie agreed. 'But I've got to wait. If we're getting out everybody who wants to go, we might as well include my own son.'

Yeh nodded and handed him a radio message which had just arrived for him. It had come by a roundabout route and contained several errors of transmission. But its message was clear. Nadya was begging him to return while it was still safe. But now, with Tom upriver somewhere, he knew it wasn't possible.

As the weather grew hotter there was still no hard news of the *Amethyst* and the newspapers had completely lost interest, while Tom seemed to have disappeared behind a blank wall. Kept in touch with what was happening by Edward, Willie continued with his negotiations on behalf of George Kee. He was still in prison, but another visit to the jail brought the information that he would be allowed to go free, provided he undertook not to leave Shanghai. Signing the necessary document, he left with Willie, who drove him home.

'Your family's aboard the *Lady Roberts*, George,' Willie informed him quietly. 'I shall want you aboard, too, as soon as Tom returns. So stay put. Nowhere but your home. Have a bag packed with everything you'll need and keep it light. It might happen any time and it's got to be quick. I want Tom away as soon as he reappears.'

Time was running out. The two months Willie had been given to get the *Lady Roberts* away was almost up and he was having to think of ways of extending the permit.

With Chiang on the point of leaving the mainland of China, the commander of the Kuomintang Navy had been changed. New orders had been issued and the new man was reported to have expressed very forcibly his dislike of the way the British merchant ships, assisted by the Royal Navy, constantly tried to break the blockade. To Willie's certain knowledge, his own ships had been guilty on more than one occasion, and he knew that Yeh had often slipped into Tientsin, Nanking and other places along the coast to pick up or deliver a cargo.

Then he heard that Chou En-Lai, second only now in importance to Mao in the hierarchy of the Chinese Communist Party, had turned up in Shanghai as if to keep an eye on things. As became a man educated at the Sorbonne, he had quietly taken up residence in an apartment in Frenchtown. Though he disliked the Russians and favoured the West, he was still a Communist and had clearly arrived to make sure that Shanghai became Chinese. Already the Communists were refusing to acknowledge the existence of the British Consulate and were returning all letters from there marked 'Address unknown.' Their refusal to speak anything but Chinese to British businessmen was all part of the policy of making the Westerners lose face, of showing them that, with Chiang about to leave, China was now a nation dependent on nobody but herself, and he was worried that in their blank-faced attitude to foreigners, they might refuse to recognise British ownership of the *Lady Roberts* and counter the Nationalist permission for her to leave with a refusal of their own.

He worried over it for a long time, then he realised that in Da Braga, already aboard the *Lady Roberts*, he had the very man he needed. Taking a cab to where the ship was berthed near the old French Concession, he bearded the Portuguese in his cabin.

'Luis,' he said, 'You've just become a ship-owner.'

Da Braga looked alarmed. 'I know nothing about the sea,' he said.

'You don't have to. But, as a national of a neutral country that's never had any interests in China, you've become the owner of the *Lady Roberts*.' Willie smiled. 'Not for good, of course. I want her back eventually. I find I've grown attached to the old lady. But I don't want the Communists to seize her and non-British ownership will help. I have the papers here, Luis. All you have to do is sign them.' He paused. 'There's just one snag.'

Da Braga frowned. 'I guessed there would be.'

'You'll need to see the commander of the Kuomintang squadron lying offshore. The permit to leave's running out and you'll need, as the owner, to negotiate a new one.'

A tug was chartered for the journey downriver and a telegraphist from the post office was hired to do the signalling. Heading down the Whangpoo, between the thronging junks and sampans, it seemed to Willie that Shanghai was starting to die already. There were few ships in the river now, where once it had been full of them, and it was clear that foreign businesses were shrivelling.

There was a mist over the water as they turned into the Yangtze and came in sight of Chiang's small squadron. It consisted of gunboats and large motor launches, with one small destroyer lying in the background. A light started to flash and the tug captain stopped engines.

'Get the telegraphist.'

An Aldis light flashed back. 'We have message from Generalissimo Chiang for commander-in-chief.'

There was a long silence then a message came back. 'Send.'

'Documents to be handed over. Request permission to come aboard.'

There was another long delay then the light flashed again. 'Proceed to port side of flagship and anchor.'

Telegraphs clanging, the tug got under way again and, swinging round to face upstream, dropped anchor near the destroyer. They were about to put a boat in the water when a launch left the destroyer's side. As it came alongside, Willie and Da Braga dropped into it.

Nothing was said as they returned to the gangway of the destroyer. At the top they were met by an officer who led the way through an iron door and down a short corridor.

The Chiang commander-in-chief, a small man wearing a captain's stripes, rose to meet them. 'State your request,' he said.

Da Braga, never a bold man, swallowed quickly. 'My ship,' he said, 'the *Lady Roberts*, has permission from Generalissimo Chiang to proceed to sea.'

The captain blinked, but his expression didn't change as he held out his hand. Da Braga handed over the letter Chiang had given Willie, and the captain scanned it before looking up again.

'According to this, the ship is British-owned.'

'It was,' Da Braga agreed. 'Australian, in fact. But it has recently been sold to my company, Shanghai Traders.'

They were taking a risk because Da Braga had given up his interest in Shanghai Traders, and Shanghai Traders was finished, anyway, but they could only hope that the captain wasn't interested in financial affairs and didn't know. The necessary documents, worked over during the

743

past forty-eight hours at full speed by Willie and a shipping lawyer were handed over. The captain studied them and passed them back.

'When do you intend to leave?'

Da Braga hummed and hahed and talked of a cargo of hides for Canton, but claimed he was unable to specify dates because, due to the situation ashore, the cargo had still not arrived. He wished, however, to leave as soon as possible after it did.

The captain managed a thin smile. 'I should warn you,' he said, 'that things have changed a great deal since this permit was issued. The Generalissimo is contemplating establishing himself in Taiwan, from where he will continue to conduct operations against the Communist usurpers. My orders are to see that no raw materials reach them via the Yangtze and that no finished products leave. Nevertheless, you have your permit and it will not be rescinded. However – ' he paused significantly ' – I must tell you that I cannot accept it if you delay too long. You have until July 31st and no longer.'

four

___

As Willie stepped ashore from the tug, Edward met him with news of the *Amethyst*.

'She's in trouble,' he said. 'Short of food and fuel and alive with rats. They're still arguing and we know Tom's in Chinkiang working at it, but so far they're not getting very far.'

'Keep me in touch with everything that happens,' Willie said. 'Everything. It's over two months now. Something's got to give soon.'

With the Communist grip on Shanghai growing tighter, the weather became hot, sultry and trying, the air breathless, heavy and still. Nerves were frayed, because people trying to live with the financial difficulties being imposed by the new regime on top of the long hot summer were on edge and there were sudden explosions of temper at the Club. It was rapidly becoming obvious that anyone who couldn't learn to live under the rules imposed by the new government would have to get out.

Waking up in his hotel, Willie was aware of a desolate silence. There was no sound of cars moving, none of the sounds of Shanghai's normal life. It was uncanny and the darkness seemed to smother everything. Not a tree moved, not a leaf rustled. Shanghai was in utter stillness.

Staring at the ceiling, he lay motionless for a moment, then he sat up recognising it for what it was. There had been typhoon warnings for days and this he knew was the sign of its arrival.

Even as he scrambled out of bed, the rain came. It arrived with a roar, driven by the sudden howl of the wind. Doors slammed and he could hear voices as other residents of the hotel rose to close windows and secure shutters. Within minutes the rain was pounding down in a tremendous downpour and the wind was screaming round the building like a demented giant. Dressing, he went downstairs to find porters struggling with doors blown in by the force of the sudden gale and busy with mops and brushes getting rid of the water which had forced its way inside. Outside, palms were bending like bows and there was a crash as a tree keeled over and smashed to the ground.

The rain was lashing down in torrents, roaring against the beaten foliage, filling the monsoon ditches and scattering petals across the road. The sky, apparently resting on the roofs of the buildings, was filled with an eerie light. A man ran across the forecourt of the hotel, his clothes plastered to his body, then, as the wind caught him, he was forced into a gallop until he fetched up hard against a swaying tree, bounced off and continued his dash for shelter.

A fresh gale of wind arrived like the explosion of a bomb, filling the air with spray from the waterfront, while whipped foliage scattered fronds across the road. By daylight the bund was under water, which swirled knee-deep in Wing On's famous department store in Nanking Road. The hotel had already been cut off for hours, the water rushing past its entrance and across the road into the Whangpoo. People were crouching over every telephone in the place, trying to find out what was happening, but the electricity had failed and none were working. From his window Willie could see the Yangtze, a mass of swirling currents, the mat of sampans rising and falling in the waves. Several had been driven ashore and, as he watched, he saw men struggling to pull a drowned body from the water. A junk that had dragged its anchor had smashed into another vessel; and a second, whose anchor chain had snapped, was drifting broadside-on in the wind.

Going downstairs, he found Edward asking for him. He looked elated.

'What's happened?' Willie demanded. 'Something has, I can tell.'

'*Amethyst*'s broken out,' Edward said. 'When the storm was forecast, Kerans knew it was time to leave. The Communists had threatened to blow him out of the water if he tried so he decided there was nothing to lose, and the typhoon fixed it. With the Yangtze in flood and everybody concerned with battening down, it was his chance. He changed his silhouette, slipped his cable and followed a Chinese merchantman so he wouldn't be noticed.'

'Where is she now?'

'At three o'clock she was forty miles away. At five-thirty she signalled *Rodney*, asking them to cover her at Woosung. She's been under fire but she's made it and we've just heard she's rejoined the fleet. It was quite a night.'

'Thank God,' Willie said fervently. 'What about Tom?'

Edward was suddenly at a loss. 'If he's not on board I don't know. I've been assuming he's with her.'

Willie frowned. 'Don't be so sure, lad,' he said. 'China isn't England and he might not be.'

The typhoon was fading and the wind dying as the Communist newspapers bellowed the news – repeating the howls for vengeance and increasing their demands for compensation. The *Kiang Ling Liberation*, a Chinese merchantman that the *Amethyst* had followed, had been fired on by mistake and sunk by Chinese shore batteries and the Chinese were claiming it was the *Amethyst*'s guns that had done the work.

It was generally felt that the prestige the Communists had gained with the capture of the frigate had been lost and there were a few extra drinks in clubs, offices and homes. The escape was a great fillip for the thinned British colony and put heart into them, though Willie was certain it would not improve their conditions. The old tolerant attitudes of the Chinese had already gone and this, he felt sure, would only exacerbate the difficulties.

When he left the hotel, he found the police already making spot checks on people, concentrating chiefly on foreigners and holding them up long enough to make it difficult to carry on business. That night a curfew, announced on the radio in English and Chinese, was imposed. Soldiers immediately began to move about the streets putting up posters to the effect among the vast Communist propaganda sheets that had been daubed on the walls. No cars were to be allowed to move after 9 p.m. and offenders were to be arrested at once.

And suddenly there was a flurry of unexpected disappearances – journalists who had criticised the Communists, businessmen who had dealt with the Nationalists, lawyers who had prosecuted Communists during the troubles of the twenties, people who had businesses or premises the Communists needed – and Zychov. Suddenly the Balalaika closed and Willie heard that Zychov had been arrested.

The news left him unmoved, even with a feeling that justice had finally been done, yet somehow, knowing how ruthless the Communists could be, he was curiously concerned, as he might have been for any European thrown into a Communist prison. Even so, the message that came from the police stating that Zychov wished to see him startled him.

He appeared at the prison in a mood of uncertainty overlaid with a feeling that at last Zychov was going to grovel before him and ask him to bring about his release. The police, who knew him well, still managed to treat him with some respect – far more than most Europeans were receiving these days – but Zychov was as arrogant as ever.

'Ah,' he said. 'My good friend, Mr Sarth.'

'I'm no friend of yours,' Willie snapped. 'What do you want?'

Zychov eyed him. He was still handsome, though his hair had become grey and he had grown thicker round the middle. But he was still straight-backed and his eye still had the old imperious look in it.

'I need help,' he said bluntly, though there was nothing about the statement that was humble or in the nature of an appeal.

Willie studied him warily. 'So?'

Zychov gestured. 'As a fellow-European – and one, I have to admit, who still has some influence in this place – I am expecting you to do what you can to get me out of this hole.'

For a moment there was a look of dread behind the arrogance in his eyes, as if he were well aware of what might be in store for him. It lasted no more than a fraction of a second, but Willie knew that, despite the show he was putting on, Zychov was afraid.

'Do you think you have any right to ask me for help?' he said.

Zychov shrugged. 'You stole my wife. Isn't that enough?'

'You'd abandoned her long before I even met her.'

'Well –' Zychov shrugged ' – that's a matter of opinion, I think.'

The discussion descended into an arid argument in which Willie was aware of no feeling whatsoever. He owed Zychov nothing and if Zychov was in trouble it was his own fault. But then, as he turned away, convinced that Zychov was condemning himself by his own self-importance, the Russian suddenly caught at his sleeve.

'Wait!' he said and his voice had changed. 'Sarth, I need your help! God knows, I suppose there have been things in my life I ought to be ashamed of and I have no claim for sympathy over my wife. There have been too many others both during my marriage and since it collapsed. But I'm a European, Sarth, and I'm in a mess. I need someone on my side.'

It was entirely unexpected, but Willie wasn't convinced even now.

'You've hardly worked at getting anyone,' he said.

'No. To that I admit.' There was another touch of the old arrogance but it collapsed again quickly. 'They'll kill me, Sarth. There probably won't even be a trial.'

Willie thought it unlikely. Whatever their faults, the Chinese Communists had a rigid attitude to legality.

Zychov saw his hesitation and suddenly he grasped Willie's hand in both of his. 'For the love of God, Sarth,' he begged, 'get me out of here!'

Whether it was his sudden descent into pleading, the sudden break in the stiff-necked arrogance, or whether it was simply the sight of a frightened man in danger of losing his life, something threw a switch in Willie's mind. He had nothing for which he could thank Zychov and a great deal for which he could blame him. More than once his life had been in danger because of this man who stood in front of him, but the thought of a life sentence in a Shanghai jail stirred something in him. He was wary, however.

'Why the hell should I do anything for you?' he demanded.

'Because we've known each other a long time. Almost fifty years.'

'We've never been friends, damn it!' Willie exploded. 'Quite the contrary. Haven't you any better friends than me to do your dirty work?'

Zychov's shoulders sagged and Willie was aware of a small feeling of triumph. All his hatred seemed to evaporate as Zychov's courage collapsed.

'No,' Zychov said. 'Perhaps I've never deserved any.'

It wasn't an appeal for help this time, and Willie knew it wasn't intended to be. It was a simple statement of fact as though Zychov had finally been forced to come face to face with his own evil. Somehow, it was this very thing that, if it didn't melt Willie's resolve, made him feel he had to do something. He was a fool, he decided, and softer-hearted than he'd realised. After wanting to destroy Zychov for years, he found he hadn't the courage he'd thought he had.

'What happens if I manage it?' he said. 'I don't want you here.'

Zychov's hands dropped to his side, but his smile reappeared and Willie knew that the victory was somehow still with his old enemy. 'You have ships, Sarth.'

Willie's temper blazed. The last person he wished to know about the *Lady Roberts* and what he had planned was Zychov. 'No,' he snapped. 'By God, no! I've said I'll try to get you out of this place but after that you're on your own! Don't come to me for any more!'

'Very well.' The gleam had died from Zychov's eyes and his face was expressionless. 'I'll leave. But I can't go back to Russia, can I?' His shrug came again. 'Perhaps the United States? They're notoriously warm-hearted towards the homeless. And I'm not without money. I've salted a little away in Australia and Switzerland. I could go there.'

'What certainty have I that you'll go?'

'Only my promise.'

'Your bloody promises were always worthless!'

Zychov sighed and his defences crumbled again. 'No promise from a man in danger of death is worth much,' he said. 'A man with his head in a noose will promise anything, I know, but I also know that these people trust you far more than they do me, and that you could destroy me any time you wish. I'll go.'

'All right,' Willie said. 'I'll see someone.'

He had no expectation of success but, to his surprise, the police chief was not unwilling to listen. He proffered arguments against Willie's suggestion that Zychov should be set loose, but they seemed strangely half-hearted, almost as if he weren't giving Willie's words his full attention. He even promised to take the matter to Chou En-Lai who, as Willie new, was still in the city, and three days later Willie heard that Zychov had been allowed to go.

Despite the police chief's indifference, it still surprised Willie. The Communists had many good reasons for holding Zychov, many reasons for wishing to see him dead, and he couldn't work out why getting him free had been so easy. Calling at the jail, the news was confirmed for him, but again the police chief was vague. He was all smiles, too, as if he had been relieved of some great responsibility, and it puzzled Willie. The Communists weren't in the habit of forgiving.

'I saw Comrade Chou,' the policeman said. 'We discussed it. We went into some detail and in the end he left it to me. I decided we need have no fear of our friend Zychov worrying us again. So he was freed.'

Somehow, it seemed too glib, too simple, and it left Willie feeling uneasy. At a time when things were being made deliberately difficult for Europeans, it didn't make sense that Zychov's release had been engineered with so little trouble.

'Has he left the city?' he asked.

'Not yet. I gather he has many enemies and to avoid them he has gone into hiding for the time being.'

Within hours, Willie was deciding he had been a damn fool. Zychov had never been a man he could trust, never a man with much feeling of gratitude. At that moment, he was probably plotting Willie's downfall with the police. There was too much at stake and Willie was nervous and by this time kicking himself for being too soft.

Then, however, a few days later, halting his car at a set of traffic lights, he saw a large limousine draw up alongside him and a window roll down. The driver was one of Yip Hsao-Li's old associates. The Communists were busy purging the city of them, but there were still a few powerful enough to survive. Willie had known this one for years, but there had never been an enmity between them because he had never been involved. He was being greeted with wide smiles.

'I see our friend Count Zychov has vanished, Mr Sarth.'

'You've noticed?'

'How could we fail to?'

'Do you know where he's gone?'

'We have heard rumours.' There was a wide smile. 'I would advise you to be careful, Mr Sarth. I understand he has not forgotten you and he's not the man to take kindly to a little help.'

It was in character and Zychov, malicious as ever, was still bent on destroying Willie, it seemed. Willie was about to offer thanks for the warning when the lights changed, there were more smiles and the limousine drew ahead. Willie followed, frowning, faintly bemused, already on his guard, and wondering how Yip's friends knew of his connection with the missing man.

There was still no sign of Thomas and it was Edward who brought the news of his whereabouts.

'The Communists have him,' he said. 'He was still arguing with them when *Amethyst* escaped so they promptly arrested him.'

Willie's face flushed with anger. 'So that he pays for the fact that the Navy's being its usual arrogant self?'

'For God's sake, Father!'

Willie waved his son to silence. 'It's all right, boy. I'm not blaming you. Or the Navy. I'm just worried. I know the Navy couldn't tell everybody they were going to break out.'

'Even the ship's company didn't know until it happened.'

'All the same, it's the usual answer to problems, isn't it? Small people hurt so that countries don't lose face.'

It was the death of Zychov that made Willie realise the urgency of the task he had set himself. The news appeared in one of the Communist papers. He had been found dead in one of the streets of Chapei and the paragraph called him a 'capitalist-imperialist traitor swine, tool of the Chiang regime and lackey of the American brigands'. It suggests that the Communists had removed him, but Willie knew better. Zychov was none of the important things he'd been called – just a coward and a petty swindler with one eye to the main chance, who'd finally guessed wrong. It didn't take long to dawn on Willie what had happened. It wasn't the Communists who had removed him from the scene; it was the vengeful remains of the gangs he'd persuaded to remove the Communists for Chiang in 1927. They'd never been paid for their grisly work and they'd never forgotten. Using Chiang's own methods, the Communists, who believed less in chopping off heads than in reshaping them, had preferred to leave the matter to Zychov's enemies, and had simply made it impossible for him to leave the city. Before he could do any harm and knowing he was likely to be arrested again at any time for a variety of crimes, he had been obliged to flee into the Old City and the gangs had found out where he was hiding and he'd been tortured and shot. The gangs had claimed their pay at last.

Willie heard the news with a frown, not because of any compassion for Zychov, who had undoubtedly been responsible for the deaths of many men – women and children, too, he thought, remembering Shantu – but because it reminded him that the Communists were also looking for revenge. At the moment, they were still avoiding open hostility, despite their extra taxes, their spot checks, their curfew. They were still being rigidly correct, but there had been isolated incidents and he knew he couldn't ever be sure. The Chinese had a lot of hurts and humiliations to remember.

Edward brought more news of his brother. He was in prison now in Chinkiang and would remain there as a hostage until the British apologised for the *Amethyst*, not only for infringing Chinese territory, but also for the sinking of the *Kiang Ling Liberation* and half a dozen other crimes which, dressed up though they were in the florid language of political hatred, still meant the same thing.

'They're holding him until compensation is paid and guilt admitted.' Edward flushed. 'It won't be given, of course.'

Willie frowned. 'I didn't expect it would,' he said. He drew a deep breath. 'I think there's something I've got to do.'

Edward looked quickly at him, knowing his father was far from being a man who would accept what was happening without a struggle. 'What do you intend, Father?'

'I need help. And I don't know anyone else I can turn to but you. Can you arrange to be free?'

'Of course.'

'Right. Well, first, I want to make sure that when the *Lady Roberts* clears the river there'll be a British destroyer or something on hand to see her safely to Hong Kong.'

756

'I can arrange that.'

'We might even need a tow. We're short of coal.'

'The Navy's towed most things.'

'You'll be coming with us, I suppose. At least, that far. The other thing I want is someone to collect George Kee before the curfew starts and have him on board the *Lady Roberts*. He'll be ready. I don't know when it will be exactly, but it'll happen. It's got to.'

'I'm here to help, Father. What are you going to do?'

Willie sighed. 'I'm going to do something I've never done before. I'm going to beg. What's more, I'm going to beg to a Chinese. I've treated them well, I think, and never regarded them as inferiors, unlike some I've known. But I've also never begged for favours. This time I've got to.'

Frenchtown hadn't changed. With its flat façades of apartment blocks, its spacious parks and wide avenues, it offered a more elegant existence than the neighbouring Chinese areas, which clung to the foreign cities like cancerous growths. From outside, the block of luxury flats looked a little shabbier than it had but Willie had no doubt that inside it was still comfortable enough.

The soldier on guard at the door refused to let him pass. But he was young and uneducated and Willie's glib tongue persuaded him eventually to call his sergeant. The sergeant was even more adamant, but when Willie told him whom he wanted to see, he agreed to call an officer. The hostility seemed to increase with rank, but in the end Willie was shown to a lift and escorted up in it by the sergeant.

He was met as the lift stopped by an officer, who indicated that he should follow him. As the door opened, Willie saw Shanghai-made pseudo-French furniture and a large balcony with rattan chairs, with, beyond, a magnificent view of the waterfront. No one offered him a drink and he had to wait a long time without being offered a seat. He guessed it was deliberate.

Eventually the door opened and the man he had come to see appeared. Chou En-Lai had changed. He had thickened and the beard he had worn when Willie had last seen him had disappeared. Despite the frigidly simple single-breasted high-collared tunic he wore, however, he still managed to look like a cultivated man. He approached Willie, whose heart sank as he saw no smile on the severe, black-browed countenance, no sign of recognition.

He motioned Willie to a corner and Willie began to talk quietly, stressing Britain's wish to be neutral in the affairs of China.

'Is this,' Chou asked when he had finished, 'why your ship fired on an unarmed Chinese merchantman?'

'I understand it wasn't the British ship which fired on the *Kian Ling Liberation* but the guns on shore.'

'Chinese guns would never fire on a Chinese ship.'

'Perhaps they were trying to hit the *Amethyst*.'

'It is not a good thing for Sino-British relations. I hope you haven't been sent to plead the British case.'

'No.' Willie took a deep breath. 'I've come to ask your help.'

Chou frowned. 'I don't think many British would admit to that.'

'I'm not "many" British,' Willie said. 'Perhaps you remember me?'

'I have not forgotten that I escaped from the Nationalists in 1927 in one of your ships. What can I do for you?'

'I've come to plead for my son. You knew him well in 1927.'

Chou frowned again. 'I remember 1927 very well. It was a year of great treachery. I was in great danger that night. Where is your son now?'

'He's at Chinkiang.'

The heavy eyebrows lifted. 'What is he doing there?'

'He was involved in the negotiations for the freeing of the *Amethyst*.'

Chou stared coldly at Willie. 'What a pity your navy wasn't more patient and didn't allow them to finish.'

'Navies, like armies, are sometimes laws unto themselves.'

Chou nodded. 'It is very difficult. Chinkiang is not under my jurisdiction and I have nothing to do with the army. My work is entirely different. There would have to be many conditions and everything would have to be on a basis of equality. The days when China kow-towed to foreigners are over. China has too much to remember.'

'I've never expected any Chinese to kow-tow to me.' As Chou continued to hesitate, Willie burst out, 'Do you wish me to go on my knees? I'm not too proud to do that for you.'

For the first time a hint of compassion appeared on the stern face. 'I don't think that will be necessary, Mr Sarth,' Chou said. 'I am not a Russian, and my father, who was a mandarin, taught me the elements of good manners. When we met all those years ago, I knew at once I was safe. I will arrange for your son to be released. Good day.'

five

There was one more thing to do. Despite the fact that Chou had agreed to arrange Thomas' freedom, it would not be beyond the Communists to refuse to allow him to move beyond Shanghai. It had happened before.

The *Lady Roberts* once more had to be their salvation and Willie headed along the bund of the old French Concession to the Upper Section Wharves, where he found a sampan handled by a one-eyed old crone and a boy of twelve and had himself taken out to midstream and put aboard the Panamanian freighter *Kubu*, of much the same tonnage and silhouette as the *Lady Roberts*, which was lying at her berth alongside not far away. He had done business with the captain of the *Kubu* before and an exchange of money settled the plan that had been forming in Willie's mind.

Hurrying back ashore, he found a taxi and headed along the bund of the French Concession to where the *Lady Roberts* was moored close to the old walled city. Yeh was half expecting him and listened to his proposals gravely. Willie watched him anxiously. He had known him a long time now and Yeh had never shown any friendliness towards him. On the other hand he had never failed to give him total loyalty. But was he this time asking too much of him?

'If we pull this off, John,' he pointed out, 'it means you're finished here.'

Yeh shrugged. 'A sailor's home's his ship,' he said.

'You'll never be able to come back.'

'There are plenty of other ports, and my family's safe in Hong Kong.'

'So you'll do, it?'

As always, Yeh's expression seemed to be frozen to his face. All he did was nod.

The following day Willie made a request at the harbourmaster's office for permission for the *Lady Roberts* to move to the coaling wharf to take on coal. The official who received him smiled.

'Of course,' he said. 'Why not? But galley coal only, no bunker coal, because your ship will not be given permission to leave.'

'I have a permit.'

The slant eyes widened. 'Let me see it.'

Willie hesitated, knowing the permit had come from Chiang and, because of the delays, was out of date, anyway. He decided to brazen it out. The Chinese stared at the permit and passed it back. For a moment Willie thought he'd not noticed the date or the signature, but then he smiled.

'It's a Chiang permit,' he pointed out. 'And it has expired.'

'It has?' Willie feigned innocence and stared at the paper. 'So it has. Oh, well, it won't matter, will it, because the Nationalists no longer count, do they?'

'No, they don't.' The Chinese gave him a beaming smile. 'But, as it happens, for once it does matter. For once we are entirely in agreement with the Nationalists. We also do not wish you – or anyone else either – to leave. But for an entirely different reason. *They* don't want you to arrive or leave because they don't want us to profit by receiving goods brought in by foreign firms, or by goods taken out in foreign ships. *We* don't want *them* to profit by a propaganda victory, which, of course, we should be presenting to them if we allowed you to leave and you were then stopped by the Nationalist-bandit warships. So –' again the wide smile ' – I'm afraid, Mr Sarth, that you're here until we say you can go. I'm afraid it will be a long wait.'

The way of thinking seemed convoluted almost to the point of Willie being unable to understand it, but it was political and backboned with propaganda, and he could see what they were getting at. He made one last effort.

'We're carrying mails,' he pointed out.

The big smile came again. 'I think a few people are going to have to wait for their letters.'

At about the time Willie was arguing about his move, a request was received at the same office for the *Kubu* to leave her anchorage temporarily because her anchor cables had fouled. As the *Lady Roberts* departed through the mist to the coaling wharf, the watching clerk in the harbourmaster's office made a note of the fact. As she returned, with her galley bunkers full to overflowing and more coal stacked on her deck, the *Kubu* left her anchorage and was lying in midstream as she approached. As the light began to fade, the two ships lay close alongside each other for a while, then there was a mournful boom of a ship's siren and one of them headed through the damp grey veils to the berth on the Upper

Section Wharf, while the other took up her position in midstream. Watching from the window of their office, the harbourmaster's clerks were pleased to note everything returning to normal before it grew too dark to see.

As the daylight vanished, Willie was waiting at the northern station. He was on edge because the Communist refusal of a permit to leave had been unexpected and meant that he would be taking a dangerous chance. In addition, the train was late and it was beginning to approach curfew time when all motor vehicles had to be off the streets, and his plans didn't allow for delay. Thomas' family were aboard the *Lady Roberts*, with Da Braga and his wife and George Kee's family. The Nationalist permit for the ship to leave was now days out of date and, with the Kuomintang government beyond reach, he knew he would never get it renewed, so that the chances of being stopped had doubled. It was now or never, he knew, and he had spent the day quietly moving round the city. George Kee had been warned to ready. All they needed now was Tom Sarth.

When he was beginning to give up hope the train appeared, an hour late. There was just over an hour to go to curfew time as Thomas appeared through the milling crowds of passengers, tired, dirty and unshaven.

'Hello, Father,' he said. 'I get the impression that you pulled a few strings.'

'Here and there, son. Are you ready?'

'I ought to collect a few things.'

'There's no time to collect anything. Fanny and the boys are aboard the *Lady Roberts*, together with everything they considered necessary. Edward's waiting with the car. We have to collect George Kee and we haven't a minute to lose.'

Kee was ready. As soon as he saw the car arrive, he appeared at the door. He carried no bag of any sort.

'Everything I need is in my pockets,' he said.

As the car drove quickly along the bund through the increasing darkness, Thomas stared through the window. 'Where are we going?'

'Upper Section Wharves.'

'If that's where you've got the *Lady Roberts*, Father, you can forget her. You'll never get her away. I heard at Chinkiang that she's being watched. They don't trust you.'

'Don't let it worry you, son. We're working an old sleight-of-hand trick.'

The car roared along the dark dirty waterfront to a point that lay in the shadow of the high warehouses. At the bottom of a set of stone steps a sampan waited in the mist and they were aboard and in the dark midstream within seconds. The *Lady Roberts* loomed up, a black shadow in the dark.

Fan-Su was waiting on deck, her eyes full of tears and, as Thomas put his arm round her, he put his hand out to Willie.

'Thank you, Father,' he said.

'You know the saying,' Willie pointed out. 'Family first. First, second and all the way.'

Yeh had not been idle. The *Lady Roberts* had never been a ship with a lot of white paint, but what there was had been blackened and grease had been smeared over the brasswork. Not a sound had to break the quietness of the night and he had decided they would have to abandon the anchor, because the rattling of the chain cable through the hawse hole would alert the harbour officials at once. He had arranged to knock the pin out of one of the shackles that joined the lengths of chain, to allow the parted cable to drop into the water. To silence it he had had the inboard length of what they were to lose bound with canvas and greased.

'There is a proverb,' he said gravely as Willie joined him on the bridge. ' "Keep your plans as impenetrable as the night." '

He had been on the bridge for some time to accustom his eyes to the dark, look-outs had been posted, and everybody was in position, the forecastle party ready to slip the cable, every man working quickly and in silence.

The evening was hot and still, a sheet of mist over the river, the moon making the water sparkle with silver lights. Yeh had decided not to use the engine room telegraph, which would be heard for miles in the stillness, and passed his orders to the engine room by messenger. 'Slow ahead.'

As the ship began to move ahead, he spoke to the helmsman – 'Midships.' The bosun on the forecastle raised his arm as the ship's bow came directly over the anchor.

'Up and down,' he said.

'Slip.'

With the cable vertical, there was hardly a splash as it dropped away.

'Hard a starboard. Half ahead.'

In a matter of a minute, the *Lady Roberts* was moving downriver. With the tide making, she was already facing in the right direction and as she moved ahead slowly and steadily not a light showing, they saw a blurred shape through the grey veil nearby that they recognised as the *Kubu*, which had quietly slipped her moorings in the *Lady*

Roberts' berth and returned, as arranged, to take up her position in midstream again.

'This ought to puzzle them a bit tomorrow,' Willie observed.

As the *Lady Roberts* faced into the stream, they felt the subtle vibration as the engines increased revolutions to Yeh's quiet orders. Willie was watching the shore, his eyes narrow, but nothing happened. There were no cars screaming to a halt, no shouts, no shots.

'I think we've made it,' he said.

They progressed slowly down river. The Whangpoo was empty of moving craft as they edged slowly between anchored vessels towards the Yangtze. Most of the ships were silent, with no sign of their crews, only their deck and anchor lights visible. A ghostly junk slid past astern of them, its bat's-wing sail black against the sky. The moon was just beginning to lift over the horizon and they could see the low hills inland. There was only one more trick to play but they had thought it out carefully.

Edward was talking quietly to Yeh, his eyes on the entrance to the river, watching for Chiang's navy.

'I radioed from the Consulate for a destroyer to meet us,' he said. 'They'll be waiting outside.'

A Nationalist gunboat was near the southern shore of the river where the deep channel lay and Yeh stared at it for a long time.

'We'll have to go by the north side,' he said. 'You had better warn everybody that the deck cabins don't keep out bullets and that if we're attacked they must go below and screw down the deadlights over the portholes.'

By the time first light appeared and the harbour officials were trying to work out how the *Lady Roberts* had managed to get away, the ship was heading past

Woosung, pushing through water that was as calm as a mill pond. Behind them the main channel glistened, calm and deserted. The northern waters contained several shoals and sandbanks, as Willie well knew, and there was one dangerous sandbar over which the waves sometimes broke at low tide.

Yeh looked worried and Willie saw Edward glance at the chart. 'We're a bit behind schedule,' he said. 'The tide's turned. It's beginning to run out.'

A seaman was sent to the bows to cast the lead and, as he took up his position, there was a sudden soft jar and the ship slowed.

'We're over the sandbar,' Yeh said.

As he moved to the wing bridge to stare at the water alongside, Edward spoke. 'I also think we've been spotted,' he said calmly.

Swinging round, Willie saw that the Nationalist gunboat had left her station and was racing towards them.

'Give her all she's got,' he ordered.

'She's got it all,' Yeh rapped back. 'It was never much.'

They struggled ahead, the engine pounding, the ship shuddering with the vibration so that a pencil on the chart table danced along its surface until it fell over the edge to the deck. They were barely moving now and the gunboat was drawing closer. Staring at it, Willie felt his heart sinking.

'Sweet suffering J,' he said softly.

There was a long silence as they watched the approaching gunboat, then Edward, who had been staring in the opposite direction, spoke again. 'Perhaps we won't need Him Father,' he said. 'We have friends.'

Following his gesturing hand with his eyes, Willie saw a destroyer appearing through the mist and racing to place itself between the *Lady Roberts* and the gunboat. At its masthead was the White Ensign.

'Done it,' he said.

At that moment, the *Lady Roberts* slowly and inexorably came to a stop. They were aground.

The clang of the telegraph came as Yeh ordered the engine astern. Stirred yellow mud bubbled up round the ship as the telegraph clanged again and the wheel was swung to probe for deeper water. Once again they felt the soft jar as they touched bottom, and, as they tried to struggle forward, there was a flash and a puff of smoke from the gunboat. The shell exploded ahead of them, but it was off target, and the British destroyer, swinging round in a great arc, leaning with the turn, fired a shot in return. It was considerably closer to the Nationalist ship than the Nationalist's shot had been to the *Lady Roberts* and they saw the gunboat's silhouette begin to grow shorter.

'She's turning away,' Edward said.

As the gunboat swung, showing her stern, the *Lady Roberts* gave a great shudder, seemed to shake herself, then slithered across the mud into deeper water.

'I think, Father,' Edward said, 'that, thanks to the Royal Navy, you've probably made it.'

As he spoke, Yeh grinned and it occurred to Willie that he'd never seen him smile before.

'All you have to do now, Father,' Edward pointed out, 'is get to Hong Kong, where you can sort out your affairs, play piano at the party, and head for Australia.'

They were well beyond the mouth of the river now and in open waters opposite Chusan Island. Ahead of them at the other end of a towing hawser the destroyer laboured under their weight. They had used up their bunker fuel and all the galley coal they had acquired – plus the excess they had taken on – but a collier, alerted by radio, was on its way north to refuel them. They would have to do the bunkering themselves with their own derricks, but at least they could consider themselves safe.

Willie was still too full of emotion to speak. Out there, ahead of him, were the seas where he had made his life. The Yellow Sea. The East China Sea, where he'd fought off pirates. The South China Sea, where he had almost lost his life in an aircraft dinghy. The Sea of Japan, which he'd crossed half-dead from typhus on his return from Vladivostok in 1919. The Java Sea where by a hair's breadth they had missed the Japanese fleet as it had massacred the last small ship survivors from Singapore. The Timor, the Arafura, the Coral Sea, and down to Sydney, where they were now bound.

He drew a deep breath. He could still smell China, that strong mixture of odours that pervaded all its cities, villages, paddy fields and roads. He hadn't noticed it for years and had thought he'd smelled it so often it had disappeared from his consciousness. But tonight it was stronger than he'd ever noticed it – probably, he thought, because he knew he would never smell it again.

He'd seen some changes: the Empress Tzu-Hsi. Yuan ShiK'Ai. The warlords, every wicked one of them. The Kuomintang. And now the Communists. Surely they had come at last to the end of the road. There had been a war in China ever since he'd arrived there, but at last China was in charge of China again. There could surely be no more permutations of power and he could only wish them well.

And he'd lived through it all! He'd seen the old mediaeval superstition-riddled, barbaric China fade away; seen girls abandon the flat, pressed hairstyle for disastrously dyed permanent waves; seen them marry foreigners; seen them discard the tortured lily feet, satin trousers and cork-soled slippers, and adopt the cheongsam, three-inch heels and nylons, and then abandon them again for the Communists' stark boiler suits and caps; seen them elbow the foreigners off the dance floors; seen them crooning into microphones to American jazz until political dogma had killed it all dead.

It was over. After fifty years, he was finished in China. He had finally dragged up the last of his roots and those of his family and their dependants and planted them elsewhere. He had a new life to look forward to now. Not for all that long, he supposed, because he'd already lived more of his life than he still had left to live. But he wasn't afraid. He'd had a ball.

The Boxers. The massacre at Shantung. His heart gave a little jump as he thought of Abigail and the women in his life. Four of them. Emmeline – treacherous, spiteful, vengeful, voracious, hating Emmeline, who had died in a Japanese concentration camp. Dear Ab. Old Honest Eyes, whose loyalty and good sense had made him what he was, who had trusted him when he sometimes didn't deserve to be trusted. Port Arthur and his introduction to the faithful *Lady Roberts*. Yangpo, Vladivostok and Nadya, who'd taken the place of Abigail, his wife now, good, decent, beautiful Nadya. He wasn't sure he deserved the love he'd received. Especially when he thought guiltily of poor lost Sue-Lynn Sim, who had disappeared into the darkness of

God alone knew what future, and left him saddened at the memory of her.

America. Japan. Australia. India. Indo-China. The East Indies, now no longer Dutch. He'd covered a lot of ground, risked his life here and there, made a lot of money, and come a long way from the offices of Wainwright and Halliday in the City of London. He came back to the present with a shiver. It was all lost life, lost love, lost youth, disappeared downwind years ago, all dead and done with. It had been tender at times and terrifying at others, not only when he'd been shot at, or almost died but also when funds had run out and he'd thought he was going bust. But he'd made it and could leave something for his children to build on.

He remembered how Abigail had once quoted Ecclesiastes to him soon after they'd first met, and he recalled the words now. For everything there was a season, a time for every purpose under the heaven. A time to be born. A time to die. A time to kill and a time to heal. A time to weep and a time for laughter. A time for war and a time for peace.

A time also to slow down. A time to stay at home. A time to let his children take over. If they didn't manage it, it was their fault and not of his doing. If Sarth's weren't Cunard, Cathay-American, the Glen Line, P & O or any of the big outfits, at least their ships had come to be respected. They kept to their timetables and their promises and delivered their goods. And – he smiled – though she was hardly the flagship, the old *Lady Roberts* was still incredibly ploughing on. He patted the rail, looking about him at the old ship as her battered hull wallowed through the waves.

A thought occurred to him and he called to Yeh. 'John, let's have a red at the masthead. For the first time, and probably the last time, a Sarth ship's carrying mails.'

As Yeh waved acknowledgement, Willie became aware of Edward alongside him and turned, in sentimental mood.

'This ship,' he said quietly, 'has been involved in more incidents than the Royal Navy ever dreamed of.'

Edward laughed. 'What'll you do with her now, Father? Sell her at last?'

Willie gave him a startled look and he tried to explain. 'Dammit, she's donkey's years old! She's full of cockroaches and rats and doesn't manage more than eight knots with the wind and tide up her backside. You *must* be running her at a loss.'

'I am,' Willie agreed. 'But the *Lady Roberts* goes on until she finally gives up the ghost. And then I think I'll have her mounted in concrete and set up on the front lawn as a monument to British shipbuilders and to what she's done – and might still do – for Willie Sarth.'

Edward laughed again. 'Surely to God, Father,' he said, 'you've finished now. You're not young any more.'

Willie nodded his agreement. 'I'm old, son,' he admitted. 'Damned old.'

'Then *haven't* you finished?'

Willie smiled. On the foredeck his other son, Thomas, was standing with his family. Nearby were George Kee and Da Braga with their families. He had brought the whole lot out, he thought, pleased with himself. He'd repaid loyalty with safety. There was nothing more to do except go home to his wife. Yet he had the feeling that even now it wasn't finished.

John Harris

The Old Trade of Killing

Harris' exciting adventure is set against the backdrop of the Western Desert and scene of the Eighth Army battles. The men who fought together in the Second World War return twenty years later in search of treasure. But twenty years can change a man. Young ideals have been replaced by greed. Comradeship has vanished along with innocence. And treachery and murder make for a breathtaking read.

The Sea Shall Not Have Them

This is John Harris' classic war novel of espionage in the most extreme of situations. An essential flight from France leaves the crew of RAF *Hudson* missing, and somewhere in the North Sea four men cling to a dinghy, praying for rescue before exposure kills them or the enemy finds them. One man is critically injured; another (a rocket expert) is carrying a briefcase stuffed with vital secrets. As time begins to run out each man yearns to evade capture. This story charts the daring and courage of these men, and the men who rescued them, in a breathtaking mission with the most awesome of consequences.

JOHN HARRIS

TAKE OR DESTROY!

Lieutenant-Colonel George Hockold must destroy Rommel's vast fuel reserves stored at the port of Qaba if the Eighth Army is to succeed in the Alamein offensive. Time is desperately running out, resources are scant and the commando unit Hockold must lead is a ragtag band of misfits scraped from the dregs of the British Army. They must attack Qaba. The orders? Take or destroy.

'One of the finest war novels of the year'
– *Evening News*

THE UNFORGIVING WIND

Charting the disastrous expedition of Commander Adams, this novel follows the misfortunes of his men across the Arctic after his sudden death. Whatever can go wrong does go wrong as transport, instruments, health and sanity begin to fail. The team seems irretrievably lost in the dark Arctic winter, frightened and half-starving even when it finds a base. Only one man can rescue them, the truculent Tom Fife who must respond to the faint radio signals coming from the Arctic shores. A powerful and disturbing novel, this story aims to take your breath away.